Countries in which English is the / an official language

**NAME** Indep

mmonwealth states

**Name** Dependent territories of Commonwealth states (in brackets)

# Orange Line 5

für Klasse 9

Das Lehrbuch versteht sich als Gesamtangebot. Welche Texte und Aufgaben verpflichtend sind, wird durch die schulinternen Curricula festgelegt.

1. Auflage ISBN 978-3-12-548075-9 (fester Einband) 1 7 6 | 24 23
1. Auflage ISBN 978-3-12-548275-3 (flexibler Einband) 1 7 6 | 24 23

Alle Drucke dieser Auflage sind unverändert und können im Unterricht nebeneinander verwendet werden.
Die letzte Zahl bezeichnet das Jahr des Druckes.


**Herausgeber:** Dr. Frank Haß, Kirchberg
**Autorinnen und Autoren:** Chris Caridia, London sowie
Geraldine Greenhalgh, Hamilton; Wolfgang Hamm, Marktredwitz; Melanie Ku, Hanau; Sheila McBride, Leinfelden-Echterdingen
**Beratung:** Brunhilde Biek, Leonberg; Wilma Brings, Bedburg; Amanda Chisnell, Lollar; Ulf Degen, Braunschweig; Tanja Frank, Ulm; Sandra Haberland, Recklinghausen; Wolfgang Hamm, Marktredwitz; Ulrike Heringhaus, Altheim; Michael Herrmann, Ludwigsfelde; Christa Kathmann-Fuhrmann, Bonn; Dr. Margitta Kuty, Greifswald-Eldna; Michael Meisenzahl, Karlstadt; Beatrix Pierce, Eppingen; Annegret Preker-Franke, Bielefeld; Dr. Hubert Schwandt, Parchen; Christian Straukamp, Nordhorn; Ines van Hove, Oldenburg; Dieter Vilimek, Helmstadt-Bargen

**Redaktion:** André Schmitt; Joanne Popp; Regina Kleinhenz, Stuttgart; Birgit Piefke-Wagner, Korntal-Münchingen
**Herstellung:** Frauke Maier

**Umschlaggestaltung und Gestaltungskonzept:** know idea, Freiburg; Koma Amok, Stuttgart
**Umschlagfotos:** plainpicture GmbH & Co. KG (Jim Erickson), Hamburg; Corbis (Shaun Egan/JAI), Berlin;
**Illustrationen:** Marek Blaha, Offenbach; Kirill Chudinskiy, Köln; Christian Dekelver, Weinstadt sowie
Friederike Ablang, Berlin; Dorothea Ackroyd, Bielefeld; Martina Burghart-Vollhardt, Kamenz; Anke Fröhlich, Leipzig; Susann Hesselbarth, Leipzig; Fabian und Christian Jeremies, Münster; Hendrik Kranenberg, Drolshagen; Katja Leuschner, Halle/S.; Pawel Miedzinski, Kozieglowy/Polen; Lutz-Erich Müller, Leipzig; David Norman, Meerbusch; Liliane Oser, Hamburg; Katja Rau, Berglen; Silke Reimers, Mainz; Myrtia Rockstroh, Berlin; Dorina Teßmann, Berlin; Katja Wehner, Leipzig; Sylvia Wolf, Wiesbaden; Dorothee Wolters, Köln

**Satz:** Satzkiste GmbH, Stuttgart
**Reproduktion:** Schwabenrepro GmbH, Stuttgart
**Druck:** PASSAVIA Druckservice GmbH & Co. KG, Passau

Printed in Germany
ISBN 978-3-12-548075-9 (fester Einband)
ISBN 978-3-12-548275-3 (flexibler Einband)

9 783125 480759

9 783125 482753

# Orange Line 5

Herausgeber: Dr. Frank Haß

Ernst Klett Verlag
Stuttgart • Leipzig

# Inhalt





L = Listening S = Speaking R = Reading W = Writing V = Viewing I = Intercultural

L = Listening S = Speaking R = Reading W = Writing V = Viewing I = Intercultural

L = Listening S = Speaking R = Reading W = Writing V = Viewing I = Intercultural

免學費
前途好
$8,000
$15,000

# So lernst du mit Orange Line

## Way in

Hier steigst du in das neue Thema ein.
Dazu gibt es auch einen kurzen Film.

Im gelben Kasten siehst du, was du in der *Unit* lernst.

## Stations

In jeder *Unit* gibt es zwei *Stations*, in denen du viele neue Dinge lernst. Diese Symbole zeigen dir, wie schwer die Übung ist und ob es im Anhang eine leichtere Variante gibt:
◒ → ○ p. 95, ●

In der *Your turn*-Aufgabe kannst du zeigen, dass du alles verstanden hast, und deine eigenen Ideen einbringen.

## Reading corner

In der *Reading corner* gibt es verschiedene Geschichten und Sachtexte.

## Mediation / Film corner

Auf der linken Seite geht es darum, englische Informationen auf Deutsch weiterzugeben oder umgekehrt.

In der *Film corner* gibt es eine Dokumentation aus der jeweiligen Region.

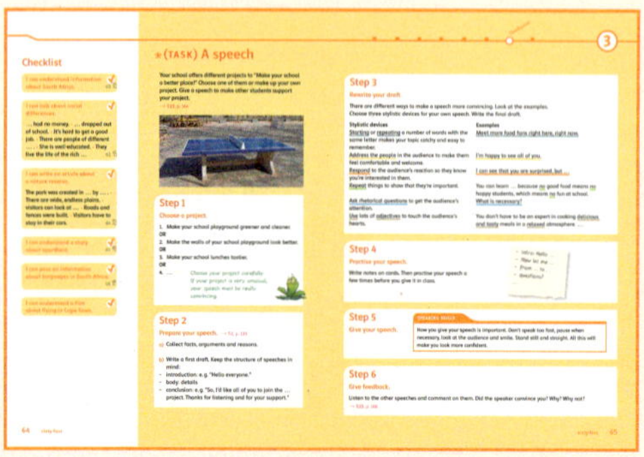


## Checkpoint

Auf dieser Seite kannst du überprüfen, ob du in der *Unit* alles verstanden hast.
In der *Checklist* sind alle Lernziele noch einmal aufgelistet.

Die Abschluss-Aufgabe (*task*) sollt ihr zu zweit oder in der Gruppe lösen.

## More about

Hier findest du interessante weiterführende Informationen zur Region der Unit.

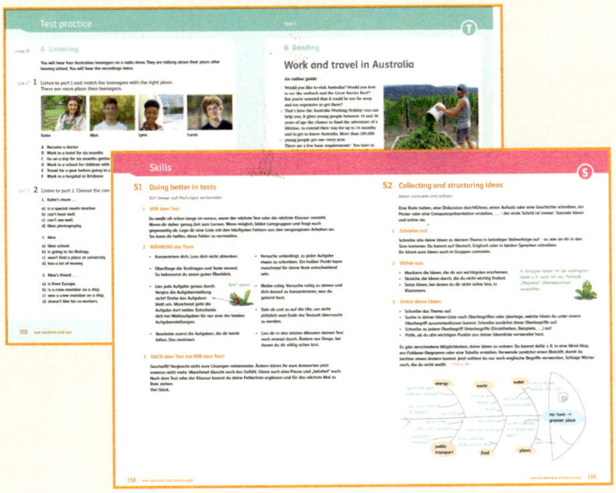

## Test practice

Hier findest du Musterprüfungen, mit denen du dich auf die Abschlussprüfungen vorbereiten kannst.

## Skills

Hier findest du zahlreiche Tipps und Strategien, die dir beim Lösen der Aufgaben im Buch und auch bei der Prüfungsvorbereitung helfen.

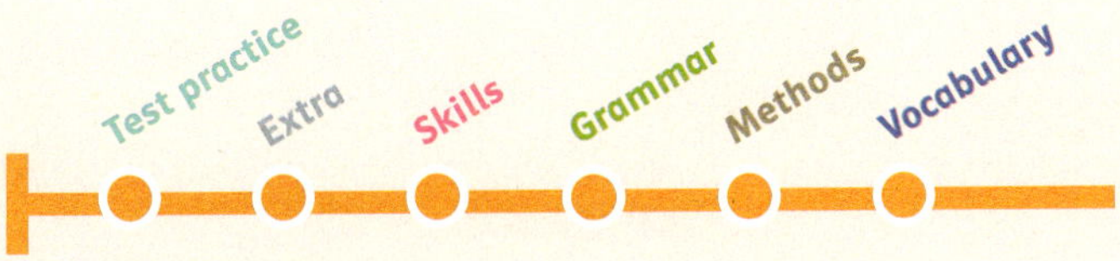


Außerdem gibt es noch weitere nützliche Seiten:

**Extra:** Hier erwarten dich weitere Lesetexte und vieles mehr.

**Grammar:** Hier findest du alle Regeln und Erklärungen zur Grammatik sowie weitere Übungen.

**Methods:** Manche Übungen könnt ihr auf eine bestimmte Art und Weise bearbeiten.
Wie es genau funktioniert, kannst du hier nachlesen.

**Vocabulary:** Im *Vocabulary* findest du alle neuen Wörter in der Reihenfolge, in der sie in der *Unit* auftauchen, und die wichtigsten Arbeitsanweisungen.
Im *Dictionary* sind die Wörter noch einmal alphabetisch aufgelistet: zuerst Englisch-Deutsch und dann Deutsch-Englisch.

Am Schluss des Buches findest du noch
- Sätze, die du im Unterricht sagen kannst, z. B. bei der Gruppenarbeit
- eine Liste mit den unregelmäßigen Verben.

| Symbol | Erklärung |
| --- | --- |
| ○ ◒ ● | leicht / mittel / schwer (Niveaudifferenzierung) |
| | individualisierende Aufgabe (natürliche Differenzierung) |
| → ○ p. 95 | Verweis auf leichtere Parallelübung auf der *Diff corner*-Seite |
| OR | Aufgabe zur Auswahl (Wahldifferenzierung) |
| | Entwicklung von Schlüsselkompetenzen |
| P | Hier entsteht ein Produkt für das Portfolio. |
| 4/1 | Verweis auf eine Übung im *Workbook* |
| → G6, p. 174 | Verweis auf den Grammatikanhang (*Grammar*) |
| → M | Verweis auf die Methodenseite (*Methods*) |
| → V | Verweis zum Wortfeld im Vokabular (*Vocabulary*) |
| → S | Verweis auf den Skills-Anhang *(Skills)* |
| | Partnerarbeit |
| | Gruppenarbeit |
| | Verweis auf die Lehrer-CD (Audio) |
| | Verweis auf die Lehrer-DVD (Film) |
| Find more online: | Code auf www.klett.de eingeben und Zusatzinformationen erhalten |

1,1

# Do you speak English?

## 1 ( SPEAKING ) Talk about the situations.

a) Take turns to describe the situations. Why do you think they are speaking English?

b) Think of other situations where people from different countries speak English.

**CULTURE**

English is often used by people from different countries who don't know each other's languages. Have you ever been in a situation where you didn't speak someone's language, and he or she didn't speak yours? How did you communicate?

1,2 **2** ( LISTENING ) **Listen to four dialogues.**

a) Match each dialogue with one of the scenes.

b) Which countries do the people come from? Take notes for each scene.

**3** ( SPEAKING ) **Discuss in a group.**

"Everybody needs English. It's the world's most important language." Do you agree? Say why or why not.

Find more online: i8ce82

In this unit you will ...
- find out about Australia.
- discuss respectful behaviour.
- write a job application.
- read a text about dangers to the environment.
- pass on information about signs.
- watch a film about Australia's underwater world.

1 1,3

# Unit 1
# Exploring Australia

Most Australians live in cities near the coast, like Sydney and Perth. Many people are very easy-going and love the beach, where they have parties and do sports like swimming and surfing. One of the country's most spectacular sights is the Great Barrier Reef near the coast of Queensland.

Australia is one of the largest countries on earth, and the only country that is also a continent. About 30 million years ago, it completely broke away from Antarctica. In this isolation, unusual animal species developed that only exist here, like the koala and the kangaroo.

## 1 What do you know about Australia? → S20, p. 161

Before you read the texts, look at the photos and make a mind map.

## 2 Read the texts and add more information about Australia to your mind map.

2/1

Australia is the country of many people's dreams. Today immigration control in Australia is very strict, though. But there are still jobs available for skilled workers, like carpenters and nurses who want to move to Australia.

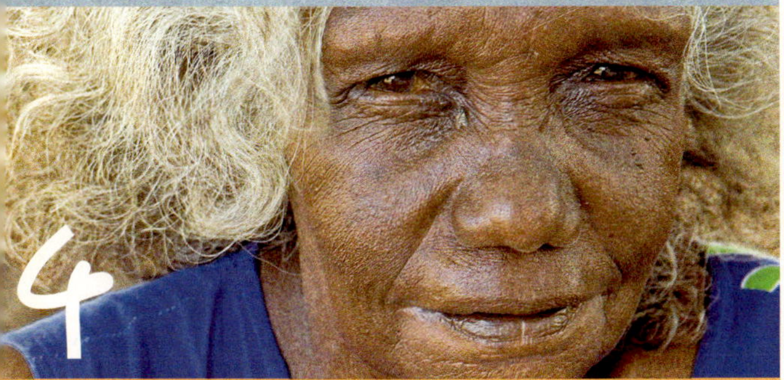


Aboriginal people have been in Australia for over 50,000 years. In the 18th century the first British settlers arrived. They and the diseases they brought killed thousands of Aboriginal people. Since then they have struggled for their rights.

Few people live in the huge area in the centre of Australia known as the 'outback'. The distances are too great to have hospitals or schools here. Instead, there is the Royal Flying Doctor Service, and children attend classes at the School of the Air.

**3** ( LISTENING ) **Listen to Peter talking about the School of the Air.** → S5, p. 142

1,4

Complete the sentences.

1. The school covers an area that's … the size of Germany.
2. The students have a satellite dish and all the necessary … .
3. An online lesson can be up to … every day.
4. Peter can always … his teacher or … him once a week.
5. Three times a year all the students … together in town.
6. It's Peter's … at the School of the Air. He'll go to a boarding school next year.

satellite dish ['sætlaɪt ˌdɪʃ] – Satellitenschüssel
necessary ['nesəsri] – notwendig
term [tɜːm] – Semester
in addition [ˌɪn‿ə'dɪʃn] – zusätzlich; außerdem
boarding school ['bɔːdɪŋ ˌskuːl] – Internat

I can understand information about Australia. ✔

# Just a rock?

## 1 (SPEAKING) Look at the photos. Why shouldn't people climb this mountain?

## 2 (READING) Read the text.

1,5
3/1

Koa: What a beautiful sight! You can see the early morning sun on Uluru in the distance. It's stunning! I always enjoy it whenever I'm here. I'm Koa. I'm 17 and I'm from Titjikala, which is a small village four hours south of Alice Springs. My family is from an Aboriginal tribe that has lived in this area for generations.

I want to do a course at the university in Alice Springs next year to become an officially recognised tour guide. Then I'll be able to show tourists around Uluru. I just had to send in my application. I'm so excited.

Our culture and traditions might seem difficult to understand for other people. Our legends say that a long time ago the earth was flat and grey. Then giant creatures came and created the mountains, rocks and rivers that we still see today. We call that time the 'Dreamtime'. Because of this belief, each part of the landscape has a special meaning for us. Places like Uluru are sacred to us, and we believe that those places and the people who visit them need to be protected. That's why there are special rules for visitors to Uluru. Some tourists follow them, but others are really disrespectful and ignorant. They throw their rubbish on the ground and don't walk on the paths. Others ignore the fact that Uluru can be a dangerous place because of the weather. Some have already died or have been hurt. I remember days when there were very strong winds. Tourists weren't allowed to go up, but the guides were able to keep them happy by offering 'survival' trips through the desert instead. They could learn how to look for water or how to make a fire.

Tourists shouldn't go up Uluru. We Aboriginal people don't want them to as we find it really offensive. If you ask me, I think it's great that visitors aren't allowed to climb the rock. Of course, people won't be able to make as much money from tourists. But you needn't go up Uluru to enjoy the landscape. There are a number of walks around Uluru, painting workshops, helicopter flights and even camel tours!

I think if people are interested enough to visit, they should accept our beliefs. I hope that I can help people to find out who we are and what we believe in when I work as a tour guide.

**CULTURE**

Uluru has belonged to the Aboriginal people since 1985. In 2017 the decision was taken to ban tourists from climbing the rock. What other places do you know where visitors have to follow certain rules?

## 3 Complete the sentences.

1. Koa wants to become a tour guide at Uluru because … .
2. Aboriginal people believe that giant creatures created … .
3. Some tourists are disrespectful. For example, they … .
4. The Aboriginal people find it offensive that … .
5. If tourists don't climb Uluru, there are … .
6. People who are really interested in Aboriginal culture should … .

## 4 Sort the words.

a) Copy the table and sort the words into the three groups. → ○ p. 86 → M Peer correction, p. 181

3/2

ignore ✓ | politeness | accept | rude | respect | tolerate | polite
rudeness | compromise | tolerant | acceptable | ignorant | respectful

| Verbs | Adjectives | Nouns |
|---|---|---|
| ignore | … | … |
| … | … | … |
| … | … | … |

– there isn't always a word for every group
– *-ness*, *-ion*, *-ance* are endings of nouns
– some words are the same as a verb and as a noun

b) Use a dictionary to find the missing nouns in the table from a) and complete the table. → V Respect, p. 186 → S4, p. 141

3/3

## 5 (SPEAKING) Talk about the cartoon. → S20, p. 161

a) Describe what you can see in the cartoon. Then discuss it with a partner. The words in Ex. 4 can help you. → ○ p. 86

4/4-5

b) Think of things the other two people in the cartoon could say (they could be funny, angry, confused, …).

"DON'T YOU REALIZE YOU'RE INSIDE A CHURCH?! TAKE OFF YOUR HAT!"

## Language → G1, p. 169

The guides can keep the tourists happy. The guides were able to / could keep them happy.
Tourists can't go up. Tourists weren't allowed to / couldn't go up.
I must send in my application. I had to send in my application.
They needn't climb Uluru. They didn't have to climb Uluru.

| | |
|---|---|
| The guides can keep the tourists happy. | The guides were able to / could keep them happy. |
| Tourists can't go up. | Tourists weren't allowed to / couldn't go up. |
| I must send in my application. | I had to send in my application. |
| They needn't climb Uluru. | They didn't have to climb Uluru. |

Compare the sentences in the simple present with the ones in the simple past.
How do the modal auxiliaries change?

## 6 ( SPEAKING ) What happened to the tourists?

a) Make sentences with modal auxiliaries. Use the simple past. → ○ p. 87

4/6

Sam

1. not be allowed to • swim — be able to • escape — have to • call

Anna

2. not be allowed to • drive fast — not be able to • see — not have to • go far

1. Sam wasn't allowed to swim in the river. He …

b) Look at these pictures from a tour of Australia. Explain what the signs said.

5/7

1. We weren't allowed to …

## 7 Choose the right form.

5/8

To become a tour guide, (1) Koa **will have to** • **will be allowed to** take part in a course. To complete the course, (2) he **will have to** • **will be allowed to** pass a test. During the course he (3) **will be allowed to** • **will be able to** learn about visitor safety. He (4) **won't be able to** • **won't have to** pass the test if he doesn't study for it. After he has passed the test, he (5) **will be allowed to** • **will have to** take tourists on survival tours. He (6) **will be able to** • **will be allowed to** avoid dangerous animals.

**GRAMMAR** → G1, p. 169

I'll be able to help you.
You won't be allowed to take photos.
We'll have to leave.

## 8 ( WRITING ) Complete Len's post from Sydney to his friend in Hong Kong.

a) Put the modal auxiliaries in the right tense. → ○ p. 87

5/9

On our trip last year we (1) were able to (can) spend three days in Sydney before we took the plane back to Hong Kong. Sydney Harbour Bridge was amazing! I (2) — (can) do the Bridge Climb with my dad, but my sister is only seven, so she (3) — (cannot) come. I (4) — (must) leave my phone at the bottom and I (5) — (cannot) take any photos.
We all loved Sydney so much. The whole family agreed that we (6) — (must) come again. But if we come back next year, we (7) — (cannot) climb the bridge – it's too expensive. Next time we'll just walk over the bridge. That won't cost anything. And we (8) — (can) take photos of the fantastic view from there too.

b) Fill in suitable modal auxiliaries in the right tense to complete Len's sentences.

1. When we did the Bridge Climb last Monday, we — wear special clothes.
2. And we — carry anything. They were very strict.
3. Before we started the guide said, "At the top it's fantastic. You — see for miles."
4. After the climb I — keep my Bridge Climb cap. They were OK with that!

## 9 ( YOUR TURN ) Respectful behaviour → S21, p. 162

a) Are the people in these situations behaving respectfully?

A Dave arrives half an hour late for a job interview. He just goes into the room, sits down and doesn't say anything. His girlfriend has just told him, "I've met another boy."

B An old lady gets on the bus. Tina stays in her seat. Tina is expecting a baby.

C Ellie's mum is talking to her. Ellie is looking at her phone all the time. Her mum tells Ellie to stop it and listen to her. Now Ellie can't answer an important text message.

- People have to …
- They should …
- They shouldn't be allowed to …
- There is no excuse for …
- People really needn't …

*You can find help for all skills on pages 138–167.*

b) Think of two more situations in which someone behaves disrespectfully.

c) Make up five rules for respectful behaviour to help deal with the five situations.

1. 'Always be on time. But if you're late, let the person who is waiting for you know when you'll arrive.'
2. …

d) Discuss your rules in class. → M Fishbowl, p. 180

I can discuss respectful behaviour. ✓

# A job in Melbourne

1,6
6/1

## 1 (READING) Read the job ad and the application.

**A**

**Receptionist, Waterfront Hotel** ☆☆☆☆

We are offering a job in one of the largest hotels in Melbourne, one of the most amazing cities in the country.

**Are you able to:**
- work in a team?
- deal with guests from different cultures?
- work efficiently and communicate well?
- work weekends and holidays?

**We require:**
- work experience in customer service.
- intermediate computer skills.
- a native speaker or a Certificate in Advanced English.

**We offer:**
- a good salary and on-the-job training.

Send your CV and letter of application to Dan Pitt: dan.pitt@thewaterfront.au

**B**

**Notes for my CV:**
Personal statement
Education
Skills
Work experience
Interests
References

**CULTURE**

English CVs don't have a photo of the candidate, but they often include a personal statement (p. 153).
What do German CVs look like?

**C** E-MAIL

Dear Mr Pitt,

I would like to apply for the job as receptionist at the Waterfront Hotel. I have one and a half years of work experience in this field. As a student in Cork (Republic of Ireland), I worked part time in a B & B for guests from all over the world, so I am easily able to deal with people from different countries. In my current temporary job in Australia I have six months of experience as a receptionist at the Flying Emu Lodge, where I check in guests and work as part of a small team. Now I am looking for more permanent work as part of a larger team.

In addition to my work experience I have strong skills in communication, customer service and administration. I also have good computer skills.

I think that I work more efficiently than most people my age because of my experience, and my skills qualify me for this job.

Please find my CV attached. I look forward to hearing from you.

Yours sincerely,

Amy Wynner

## 2 Make a checklist.

a) Compare Amy's application with the job ad. Does she address all the points? → p. 88

b) Which of the requirements would you meet? Would you apply? Say why (not).

| Job ad | Amy | You |
|---|---|---|
| Teamwork? | ✓ | |
| Guests from different cultures? | | |
| | | |

## 3 Name these jobs.

a) Match the pictures with the right job. → ◯ p. 89

6/2

carpenter | chef | hairdresser | electrician | nurse | travel agent

1 

2 

3 

4 

5 

6 

b) Match the sentence parts to make definitions. → V Jobs, p. 188

1. A preschool teacher …
2. A physiotherapist …
3. A plumber …
4. A mechanic …

A repairs or builds machines.
B repairs pipes in buildings.
C uses games, music and art in classes.
D works with patients who have injuries.

*Use an online dictionary to check your pronunciation.*

## 4 (SPEAKING) What do you think?

6/3

Which of these strengths are important for the jobs in Ex. 3? Talk to a partner.

pay attention to detail | punctual | reliable | good communication skills | self-motivated | work well in a team

A: I think a chef has to pay attention to detail because the food in a good restaurant must be perfect.
B: You're right. But in my opinion it's more important that a chef …

## 5 (LISTENING) Listen to the phone call and complete the notes. → S5, p. 142

1,7
7/4

HAIR HOUSE

Date: 12 Oct 2017 Time: 11:20
Taken by: *Sarah White*
Name: —
Reason(s) for calling:
*application for* — *qualifications:* —
*working hours:* — *transport:* —
*→ will send her* —

**LISTENING SKILLS**

At the beginning of a phone call, people usually say their names. Listen carefully at the start. Take notes while listening (for example name and message). Check and complete your notes the second time you hear the phone call.

**Language** → G2, p. 170

The Waterfront Hotel is larger than the Flying Emu Lodge. The job is more permanent.
Waterfront Hotel is one of the largest hotels in Melbourne.
Melbourne is one of the most amazing cities in the country.

How do you form comparatives and superlatives with a) short words and b) longer words?

## 6 (SPEAKING) Compare the working conditions.

a) Use the adjectives to compare the working conditions. → p. 89

7/5a)

large | long | high | experienced

| |  Helen, waitress |  Lisa, shop assistant |  Derek, electrician |
|---|---|---|---|
| Journey to work | 15 minutes | 45 minutes | 30 minutes |
| Team of ... | 4 people | 10 people | 2 people |
| Salary | A$ 30,000 | A$ 40,000 | A$ 45,000 |
| Worked for | 1 year | 2 years | 1 month |

A: Derek has a longer journey to work than Helen. Lisa has the longest journey to work.
B: ...

b) Complete the sentences using a comparative or a superlative.

7/5b)

1. I've never seen such a hard worker. → He's the hardest worker that I've ever seen.
2. I've never dealt with such a difficult customer. → No one is ___.
3. I've never known a receptionist who is so patient with hotel guests. → She's ___.
4. Helen is the fastest and most efficient waitress in the restaurant. → No one is ___.

## 7 How did Greg get the job as an adventure guide? Put in the right form of the adverbs.

8/6

1. I prepared more carefully than the last time I applied for a job. The interview went well. (carefully)
2. The five people who performed ___ in the interviews were taken to an island for a test. (successfully)
3. I swam ___ than the others in the swimming race. (strongly)
4. I only finished in second place in the boat race. A woman from Sydney sailed ___ than me. (fast)
5. Of all the people, I worked ___ in a team. (well)
6. I worked ___ than the other four people to build our island camp. (hard)

**GRAMMAR** → G2, p. 170

efficiently –
more efficiently –
(the) most efficiently

fast – faster – (the) fastest

well – better – (the) best

## 8 Compare the people who applied for a travel agent's job in Perth.

a) Look at the interviewer's table and complete the sentences. → ○ p. 90

8/7

| | Oliver | Emily | Jack |
|---|---|---|---|
| Computer skills | *** | ** | * |
| Reliable | ** | * | *** |
| Communication skills | * | ** | *** |
| Speaks Chinese fluently | * | ** | *** |
| Experienced | *** | * | ** |
| Works efficiently | *** | * | ** |

1. Emily's computer skills are better than Jack's, but Oliver has the best computer skills.
2. Jack is probably the most —, but — is — than Emily.
3. Emily has — communication skills than Oliver, but Jack …
4. Emily speaks Chinese — than —, but …
5. Jack is — than Emily, but …
6. Oliver works the —, but …

b) Complete Jack's answers to these interview questions. He always thinks he's the best!

8/8

1. Do you work efficiently? – Of course, I work the most efficiently of all the people I know.
2. Can you give a presentation? – No question about it. I can … you have ever seen.
3. Are you always punctual? – People say that I'm … person they know.
4. Do you think you are qualified for the job? – I'm … of all the candidates.
5. Can you learn new skills fast? – Sure. I can … than anybody else.

## 9 (YOUR TURN) An application and a CV

→ V Jobs and qualities, p. 192
→ S10, p. 148 → S13–14, p. 152–153

Write an application and a CV for one of the jobs:

9/9
11/1
11/2

bike courier | shop assistant | waiter / waitress | mechanic

1. Find out on the internet: What are the requirements for each of these jobs?
2. Make a list: What are your strengths and weaknesses?
3. Choose one of the jobs.
4. Write your application for the job.

I am interested in …
I have experience as …
In addition to my experience …
I am able to …
My … make me an excellent …
I look forward to …
…

I can write a job application. ✓

# Great Barrier Reef in danger

## 1 ( SPEAKING ) What wonderful or spectacular places in the world do you know?

## 2 ( READING ) Read the online article. → S7, p. 144

1,8

INTERNET

The Great Barrier Reef is one of the greatest wonders on earth. This amazing underwater world, with its thousands of individual reefs and hundreds of islands, stretches for 2,300 kilometres. That's about the distance from London to Sicily. The area it covers is larger than the United Kingdom, and you can even see it from the moon! This ecosystem is home to more than 350 types of coral and hundreds of species of fish and birds. It's such a special place that every year animals migrate there from thousands of kilometres away. Visitors come here to see whales from Antarctica and turtles from the Pacific Ocean. But the future of this paradise is uncertain. The state of the reef has slowly become worse since European settlers arrived. Old photos, some of which go back 100 years, show that most of the coral has disappeared.

**Climate change and coral bleaching**

The greatest threats to the reef today are climate change and the increase in water temperatures. These result in what is called 'coral bleaching'. Coral bleaching was completely unknown until the 1980s. It happens when coral are under a lot of stress because of changing conditions. When the water gets warmer, it kills the algae on the coral and the coral loses its beautiful colours. The death of the algae, in turn, causes the death of creatures that need them for food. Whole areas of the reef have become ghost towns.

**Tourists**

The two million tourists who go fishing, diving and snorkelling on the reef every year bring in a lot of money and provide many jobs. Unfortunately, they are also responsible for a lot of damage to the reef environment. Snorkelling platforms for tourists, for example, attract sea birds. For the birds, the platforms are places where they can rest, which they do in great numbers. Their waste is washed into the sea and it pollutes the water.

## 3 Find the information in the text.

1. How long is the Great Barrier Reef?
2. When was coral bleaching first noticed?
3. How many tourists visit the reef every year?
4. What kind of ships is the reef a destination for?
5. What is the land opposite the coast used for?
6. What is the most difficult problem to solve?

## 4 Complete the sentences.

What were the effects of the following things?

1. As a result of climate change ... .
2. The millions of tourists cause ... .
3. Because of the 2010 oil spill ... .
4. When chemicals are washed into the rivers ... .

READING SKILLS

You can understand new words without a dictionary if you look carefully at the context. For example, you may not know the word 'bleaching', but in the sentence it says 'the coral loses its beautiful colours', so you know that the general meaning is 'to lose colour'.

INTERNET

**Ships and oil spills**

A lot of ocean traffic passes through the waters of the Great Barrier Reef. It is a popular destination for cruise ships and sightseeing boats. The worst accident so far happened in 2010, when a Chinese ship sailed outside the official lane and hit the reef. Three kilometres of coral were damaged, and there was a big oil spill. It will take many years for the reef to recover.

**Farming**

Much of the land on the coast opposite the Great Barrier Reef is used for farming. In the tropical rainy season the rain washes chemicals from farming, like pesticides, into the rivers, and the rivers carry them into the sea. The chemicals pollute the sea and do damage to the plants and animals of the reef.

**What can the government do to stop the decline?**

Saving the reef costs money, so the Australian government pays for programmes to protect it. It has spent millions of dollars on trying to save the Great Barrier Reef and it has also made stricter laws to control shipping. However, climate change has to be solved globally together with other countries, which probably makes it the most difficult problem of all.
The governments of the world have struggled for a long time to agree on what action to take to stop climate change or at least limit its effects. But if no solution is found, scientists are afraid that the reef may be extinct by 2030. Do we care enough about our earth to protect one of its greatest wonders?

## 5 Choose one of these tasks.

a) Give a presentation about other threats to the Great Barrier Reef (crown-of-thorns starfish, overfishing, …).

12/1
13/2-4

Find information and photos on the internet and take notes. → S3, p. 140
Speak from your notes. Don't read the text itself.
Speak for 3–4 minutes. → S22, p. 164

OR

b) Make a collage for a 'Save the Great Barrier Reef' campaign.

Choose one of the problems mentioned in the text and find photos on the internet. Present your collage in class.
→ M Gallery walk, p. 181 → S3, p. 140

I can understand a text about dangers to the environment.

# Safety signs in Australia

1

2

3

4

5

## 1 Beantworte die Fragen. → S 24, p. 167

14/1-2

1. Wovor warnt dieses Schild?
2. Welche drei Dinge darf man hier nicht tun?
3. Was sollte man tun, wenn man dieses Schild sieht?
4. Worauf sollte man auf dieser Straße achten?
5. Wie sollte man sich vor Sonnenbrand schützen?

## 2 Explain these signs in English.

1

2

3

I can pass on information about signs.

# Amazing creatures

## 1 Talk about Australia's wildlife. → M Think-pair-share, p. 183

What Australian animals do you know? What do you know about them? Make a mind map.

**CULTURE**

Australia is home to some of the most dangerous animals in the world, like deadly spiders. But most Australians know how to avoid the danger. They shake their shoes before putting them on and don't leave clothes or towels on the floor.
What animal(s) are you most afraid of?

## 2 (VIEWING) Watch the film. → S6, p. 143

2

a) Match the facts with the photos from the film. There are more facts than you need.

whale shark

saltwater crocodile

dolphin

manta ray

1. The best place to see this animal is Kakadu National Park.
2. This animal can't swim very well.
3. This animal lives in close family groups.
4. You can see this animal from May to November.
5. This animal is the world's most dangerous fish.
6. This animal can be up to 15 metres long.

b) Watch the film from 00:23 to 04:01 and take notes about the structure of the main part.

How do the clips about each animal begin? Why do the clips begin this way?

**VIEWING SKILLS**

Most documentaries have a clear structure. There's usually an introduction, a middle and a final part that sums up the most important information.

## 3 (SPEAKING) Talk about the animals in the film.

Have you seen any of these animals in real life? Where? Which one would you like to see the most? Say why.

I can understand a film about Australia's underwater world.

## Checklist

I can understand information about Australia. 15

I can discuss respectful behaviour.

If you ask me … . • … we find it offensive . • … others are disrespectful. • People should / shouldn't … • You will be able to … . 15

I can write a job application.

Dear … • I would like to apply for … . • I have experience in … . • I am looking for … . • I have good … skills. • Please find my CV attached. • Yours sincerely, 16

I can understand a text about dangers to the environment. 16

I can pass on information about signs. 17

I can understand a film about Australia's underwater world.

# (TASK) A job interview

Imagine you applied for the job of a 'wombat cuddler'. Now you have been invited for a job interview. Prepare and act the interview with a partner. → S21, p. 162

**CULTURE**

When Tourism Tasmania offered this job on the internet as a joke, it went viral in Australia. There were more than 13,000 applicants. What's the funniest job you've ever heard of in Germany?

## Step 1

### What's important when you're invited for a job interview? → S2, p. 139

Make a mind map. Discuss it in class.

## Step 2

### Prepare for the role of the interviewer.

Work in groups of four. What is important for you to know? Compare your questions with the other groups. Here are some sample questions:

- Why should we hire you?
- Have you ever worked with animals before?
- …

## Step 3

### Agree on the six most important questions.

Work with a partner. Choose six questions from Step 2 that are most important to you. Write them on cards.

## Step 4

### Prepare for the role of the interviewee.

a) Each of you thinks of your answers to the questions. Make notes.

b) Think about how to begin and end the interview.

**SPEAKING SKILLS**

It's very important to keep in mind who you are talking to. Always be polite and smile. Call the interviewer Mr, Mrs or Ms X. Don't just say "Hello!"

## Step 5

### Practise the interview with your partner.

Take turns. First you're the interviewee, and then you're the interviewer.

**SPEAKING SKILLS**

When you don't know the answer to a question, don't make things up. Be honest and either say that you don't know the answer or ask the other person to repeat the question.

## Step 6

### Act one version of your interview in front of the class.

## Step 7

### Give feedback. → S23, p. 166

What was good about the interview? What could be better next time? Would the person get the job?
→ M Tip top, p. 183

*When you're invited to an interview, always be on time and wear smart clothes. Be prepared to answer questions on the job and the company. And don't forget to switch off your phone!*

1,9-14

# Animals down under → S7, p. 144

## 1. Australia's most famous animal

A large kangaroo (or 'roo') can be up to two metres tall and weigh 90 kilos. When it moves, it hops. Kangaroos have been known to travel at speeds of 70 kilometres an hour. If a kangaroo feels it is in danger, it stamps its feet on the ground. In a fight it kicks and boxes. Kangaroos carry their babies in pouches, sometimes for over a year.

## 2. The largest bird

The emu is Australia's largest bird. It can't fly, but it can travel great distances and go for days without food or water.
According to an Aboriginal myth, the emu's egg was the origin of the sun. In the beginning, there were only the moon and the stars. One day the emu got in a big fight and one of her eggs was thrown into the sky. It broke on a pile of wood and caught fire. The light was so bright that it almost blinded the people on earth because they had lived in the dark until then. When the Creator saw how good it was, He decided to light the fire every day.

## 3. The most destructive import

Rabbits are not native to Australia, but they have been a major problem for 150 years. They destroy plants, especially those that cattle need for food. From the 24 rabbits which were imported in 1859 the population grew to millions in just a few years. Many methods have been tried to control their numbers, including building fences. These have helped, but there are still too many. The farmers' battle with the rabbits never ends.

## 4. The deadliest creatures

Although they are only responsible for about five deaths a year, Australia is home to the most poisonous, dangerous and scariest creatures on earth. The huge saltwater crocodile, for example, hunts in the sea or in rivers. Its bite is stronger than a shark bite, and it eats anything that moves.

## 5. The strangest creature

The platypus is not scary – it's just strange. The first time one was brought to Britain, people said it was a joke. They thought somebody had put two animals together. The platypus has a tail like a beaver, fur like an otter, feet like a duck and it lays eggs. It looks soft and cuddly, but it's not: there's a poisonous sting on its back feet!

## 6. The funniest, loudest bird

The kookaburra has an amazingly loud call which sounds like human laughter. It has been called the "bushman's alarm clock". The bird – which eats meat and sometimes even steals from barbecues – often appears as a film or TV character, and it is celebrated in a number of popular songs.

**1** **What did you find interesting about the texts? Talk about them with a partner.**

**2** **Research another Australian animal on the internet. Take notes and give a short presentation to the class.** → S3, p. 140 → S22, p. 164

to hop – *hüpfen*; to stamp – *stampfen*; pouch – *Beutel*; myth – *Mythos*; rabbit – *Kaninchen*; cattle – *(Rind-)Vieh*; fence – *Zaun*; poisonous – *giftig*; bite – *Biss*; beaver – *Biber*; duck – *Ente*; soft – *weich*; sting – *Stachel*; laughter – *Gelächter*

Find more online:
i8ce82

In this unit you will ...
- find out about the Caribbean.
- write a fictional story.
- talk about standards and values.
- read a pirate story.
- pass on information about tourist attractions.
- watch a film about the weather in the Caribbean.

3 1,15

# Unit 2
# Colourful Caribbean

The Caribbean consists of thousands of islands. Some have large populations; others are very small and not inhabited. The sandy beaches, tropical climate and warm seas attract a lot of tourists. But in the autumn months, powerful hurricanes threaten the area.

Although there are jobs in the tourist industry, many people in the Caribbean are unemployed. Some have to emigrate to do job training or find work in another country. Most of them go to work in the United States, Canada, the United Kingdom or France and send money back home.

## 1 (SPEAKING) Talk about the photos.

Describe the photos. 26/1-2
You can use these phrases:
→ S20, p. 161

- In the foreground ... .
- In the middle ... .
- In the background ... .
- On the left ... .
- On the right ... .

## 2 Read the texts and name ...

1. three reasons why tourists visit the Caribbean.
2. the reason why people leave the islands.
3. four countries where most people have their roots.
4. three different Caribbean music styles.
5. the reason why the pirates often attacked Spanish ships.

Most Caribbean islands were once British, Spanish, French or Dutch colonies, and there are still big differences in population groups today. For example, most people in Cuba have Spanish roots. However, nearly all of the people in Jamaica are descendants of slaves who were brought from Africa and had to work in awful conditions.

A number of amazing styles of music come from the Caribbean, like reggae, calypso and salsa. Every island seems to have its own style, and all of them have a rhythm that makes you want to get up and dance.

In the 16th and 17th centuries pirates made the Caribbean Sea a highly dangerous place to be. At first Britain encouraged them to attack the ships of their Spanish rivals. But later they lost control over the pirates, who began to attack all ships in the Caribbean.

## 3 (LISTENING) Listen to the interview about Bob Marley and reggae music. → S5, p. 142

1,16

Right or wrong?

1. Greg worked for Bob Marley in the 1980s.
2. Bob Marley made reggae famous around the world.
3. You can hear the influence of African music in reggae.
4. When Greg met Bob Marley, he was already an international star.
5. Marley had a clear idea about how musicians should play his songs.
6. Hip hop and soul music took some musical ideas from reggae.

role model ['rəʊl ˌmɒdl] – Vorbild
return [rɪ'tɜːn] – Rückkehr
full-time job [ˌfʊltaɪm 'dʒɒb] – Vollzeitstelle
goal [gəʊl] – Ziel

I can understand information about the Caribbean. ✓

# Caribbean dreams

1 ( SPEAKING ) Which of the photos do you find the most appealing? Say why.

27/1

2 ( READING ) Read the brochure.

1,17

## Beautiful Caribbean

Island hopping is a great way to experience the Caribbean. The islands of the Bahamas are simply perfect for it – and you don't need your own boat. Use one island as the place to start and then take trips by ferry to the islands that are nearby. Or take flights to the more distant ones.

Some of the finest beaches in the world can be found in the Caribbean, with its white sands and warm, blue seas. Their beauty will take your breath away, and there's no better place to learn the art of doing nothing than Jamaica's Seven Mile Beach.

Lots of tropical reefs and clear waters make the Caribbean a paradise for divers. Discover the beautiful sea life and watch the dolphins and turtles swim by. Don't worry if you've never tried it before – there are lots of diving schools which offer courses for beginners. And hiring the equipment is easy and cheap. Shipwrecks are popular with experienced divers who are looking for a real adventure. The RMS Rhone, which sank in 1867, is a fascinating destination off the coast of the British Virgin Islands.

Are you a 'party animal'? Some Caribbean islands are famous for their big parties. If you love colour, costumes and the carnival festival, then Trinidad is the place for you. People here really know how to party. Their fantastic carnival takes place every year on the Monday and Tuesday before Ash Wednesday. There you can listen to the sound of steelpans playing calypso rhythms. And don't forget to try the local food at the carnival. The seafood they sell there is especially fresh and delicious.

Nature here is more than just beaches. Visitors who like hiking can find lots of interesting places in the Caribbean too. Some islands have volcanoes, and these are the best ones to explore on foot. On the island of Dominica, the most famous tour takes you to an extraordinary lake with very hot water.

Do you want to stay in a special place? Then choose one of the beautiful old hotels in the centre of Havana, Cuba, which go back to colonial times. But of course there are all types of accommodation in the Caribbean from luxury resorts to hostels.

## 3 Work with the text.

a) Match the headings with the texts on page 30.

A. Accommodation B. Diving C. Festivals D. Hiking E. Island hopping F. The beaches

b) What would be your main reason to visit the Caribbean? Say why.

## 4 Practise holiday words.

27/2

a) Sort the words into the table. → ○ p. 90

hostel ✓ | sunshine | departure | hurricane | luxury resort | thunder and lightning | delay | holiday flat | boarding | passport

| Accommodation | Travelling | Climate and weather |
|---|---|---|
| hostel | | |

b) Explain the meaning of these words. Then add them to the table. → V Holiday words, p. 194

couch surfing | check-in | breeze | guest house

## 1,18 5 (LISTENING) Listen to the airport announcements. → S5, p. 142

27/3
28/4

a) Answer the questions from passengers at the airport in Kingston, Jamaica. → ○ p. 91

1. Excuse me, but I didn't catch that. Which gate does the New York flight leave from?
2. Are you flying to London too? When can I begin boarding with my two small children?
3. We're looking for Gate 3. We're very late. Do you know when the gate closes?
4. Excuse me, but we're waiting for a flight from the Bahamas. Did she say how late it is?
5. Did you understand that? When does the flight to Miami leave?

*Read one of the sentences below before each announcement.*

**Language tip** → G 11, p. 179
The plane **leaves** at 2:15 p.m.

b) Listen again and find out one more detail from each announcement.

1. flight number
2. boarding for all other passengers
3. destination
4. reason for late arrival
5. gate number

**LISTENING SKILLS**

When you listen to airport announcements, listen for the important information – arrival and departure times, flight numbers, gate numbers, … .
They are usually repeated, so you don't need to understand everything the first time.

## Language → G3, p. 171

There are lots of diving schools which offer courses for beginners.
The seafood which they sell here is delicious.
It's popular with divers who are looking for an adventure.
Take a ferry to the islands that are nearby.

What kind of sentences are these? How do you form them? When do you use them?

## 6 (SPEAKING) What did they say about their holiday photos? Use who or which.

28/5

1. ferry • took us • to Jamaica

2. hotel • we stayed in

3. instructor • showed us • reef

4. most beautiful place • we visited

5. people • we met • on beach

6. girls • played • steelpans • in carnival band

1. This is the ferry which took us to Jamaica.

## 7 Rewrite the sentences.

a) Which sentences can you say without who or which? → ○ p. 91

29/6a)

1. The receptionist **who** told us to visit the island was a really nice guy.
2. This is a photo of the plane **which** we flew in.
3. Look at the dolphins **which** we saw in the distance.
4. The carnival **which** we watched takes place every year.
5. We met a dancer there **who** taught us a few moves.
6. The ferry **which** took us back was very slow.

**GRAMMAR** → G3, p. 171

That's the plane (which) we took.
That's the guy who danced at the carnival.

b) Complete the sentences with who or which where necessary.

29/6b)

1. This is the volcano ___ I told you about.
2. The man ___ sold me this T-shirt gave me too much change.
3. The fish ___ we ate there was the best we've ever had.
4. The old lady ___ we met in Trinidad still writes us postcards.

## 8 (WRITING) Rewrite Steve's story about his holidays.

a) Join the sentences to make relative clauses for the underlined words. → ○ p. 91

29/7

One day (1) I did a diving course in the Bahamas. The diving course was the most exciting part of my trip.
Before we started, (2) the instructor told us the safety rules. The instructor was a funny guy.
(3) He told some jokes. The jokes helped us to feel a bit more relaxed. He led us down to the beach.
(4) Then we had to get into a boat. The boat didn't look very safe. But we arrived at our destination without any problems.
Suddenly (5) I saw a turtle in the water. The turtle was huge.
Soon (6) we arrived at a shipwreck. It had sunk in a storm 100 years before.
I swam towards it. What I saw next took my breath away …

1. The diving course which I did in the Bahamas was the most exciting part of the trip.

Start with the underlined words.

b) Go through your sentences from a) again. Leave out who and which where possible.

## 9 (YOUR TURN) A Caribbean story → S18, p. 158

a) Plan a story that takes place in the Caribbean.

30/8

One of these sentences MUST be in your story. Choose A, B or C.
A "I took the equipment which I had borrowed from a friend and went into the water."
B "At that moment Rosie thought she would never come back home again."
C "They became scared when the hurricane they had noticed in the distance began to get closer."

Now decide:
- Who is telling the story? (narrator)
- Where and when did it happen? (setting)
- Who is in the story? (characters)
- What happened? (plot)

Look at pages 30–31 to find ideas for the setting, activities for your plot and useful vocabulary.

**WRITING SKILLS**

Adjectives make a story more interesting. Use them to describe people or places more precisely:
The **tiny** island had **dense**, **tropical** forest and **white**, **sandy** beaches. (places)
We were a **happy**, **friendly** group of tourists. (people)
They found some **old** toys and a **broken** computer. (objects)

b) Write your story. It should be 120–150 words long.

Use adjectives and complex sentences to make it sound interesting.

c) Give each other feedback. → M Writers' conference, p. 183 → S23, p. 166

I can write a fictional story. ✓

# Young Caribbeans

**1** (READING) Read Tara's blog.

1,19
32/1

BLOG

## Growing up in paradise

17/02/2017

by Tara Clarke

This is me, Tara. At the moment I'm finishing my last year at high school.

At eight o'clock last night I was doing my homework when I heard the noise of a gun in our street. 'That's Kingston for you,' I thought. I've got to say that I'll be really happy to get out of here. You see, I'm going to leave Jamaica soon because I'm one of the lucky few who were accepted for a nursing course in Toronto, Canada. Isn't that exciting?

I know, I know: Tourists think Jamaica is the perfect paradise. Sunny beaches, delicious food, happy people – that's all most people see. But the easy life they imagine doesn't exist for most of us here. My part of town is a very poor area. Violence breaks out regularly between street gangs; there are shootings almost every day, and drugs are sold nearly everywhere. It really is a constant struggle for everyone who lives here.

However, I also have some positive things here that help me to keep strong – like my family. In a family you help each other. The way I see it, there are special bonds between family members. My parents will be part of my life forever. They'll always give me advice, even though I'm an adult now. And everyone else is involved too, including all my uncles and aunts. For example, when I was a child, my aunt Serena took care of me while my mum was working. But, of course, family can also be complicated. Jamaican families can be very big. Traditionally, they expect you to get a job, find a partner, marry and start a family. I'm not sure that's what I want in life.

And then there are the friendships I have in our community. Like many Jamaicans I go to church, and religion is very important to me. My church offers many free-time activities for disadvantaged teenagers, and I often take part in these as a counsellor. I think my faith helps me to be a strong and confident person.

So now I'm wondering what living in Canada will be like, so far away from my family, my friends and my community. I'll let you know as soon as I find out.

*Mi soon farwud, bless up.* (I'll be back soon, have a nice day.)

**Comments:**

**Layla:** 18/02/2017 at 6:09 a.m.

I think education is a privilege here, not a right. My family couldn't afford to send all of us to high school. The fees were too high.

**Danielle:** 18/02/2017 at 12:15 p.m.

I know what you're talking about. Life in a family can be difficult. My brother came out as gay. What a shock to our family! Like most families here they are really conservative and have old-fashioned values.

**Frankie:** 18/02/2017 at 9:15 p.m.

I'll probably leave Jamaica next year too. On the one hand, I want to stay in Jamaica because I'm proud of it. On the other hand, I need a well-paid job.

## 2 Work with the text.

a) Answer the questions. → ○ p. 92

1. Who is Tara?
2. Why does she want to leave Jamaica?
3. What does Tara say about family life in Jamaica?
4. Why is the church important to Tara?
5. What problems do Layla, Danielle and Frankie write about?

**CULTURE**

The last sentence of Tara's blog is written in Jamaican 'creole', which is a mixture of English and African languages.
What words or phrases from other languages do you use when you speak to family and friends?

b) Read another comment on Tara's blog. Answer the questions.

**Comments:**
**Aman:** 19/02/2017 at 0:22 a.m.
I can't understand what some of you are talking about. I don't think Jamaica is such a bad country. You say that families here are conservative. What's wrong with that? You say that your family will always be there. Isn't that a good thing?
You should be happy to have them.

1. Does Aman agree with the other comments? Find evidence in the text.
2. What is Aman's opinion of Jamaican families?

## 3 (SPEAKING) Talk about values.

a) What do you think is more important? Give one reason. → ○ p. 93 → M Think-pair-share, p. 183

32/2-3

1. friendship or family?
2. wealth or health?
3. happiness or success?
4. love or independence?
5. respect or power?
6. fitting in or standing out?

1. Family is more important to me because my family will always be there.

b) Say what these words mean *to you*. → V Standards and values, p. 195

commitment | honesty | responsibility | tolerance | solidarity

To me commitment means not giving up when things become difficult.

## 4 (SONG) Three little birds

1,20

Listen to the song. Is its message happy or sad? What words or phrases give you the information?

Don't worry about a thing,
'Cause every little thing gonna be all right.
Singin' don't worry about a thing,
'Cause every little thing gonna be all right.
Rise up this mornin'
Smiled with the risin' sun,
Three little birds pitch by my doorstep,
Singin' sweet songs, of melodies pure and true
Sayin', this is my message to you-ou-ou.

## Language detectives → G4, p. 172

At the moment I'm finishing my last year at school.
At eight o'clock last night I was doing my homework when I heard the sound of a gun.

What's the difference between the two tenses? In what way are they the same?

## 5 (SPEAKING) What's happening in Kingston at the moment? → S20, p. 161

a) Describe the picture with a partner. Take turns. → ○ p. 94

33/4 It's Sunday morning in Kingston, Jamaica ...

get up | sell | walk to | wait for | feed | ask for

A: A woman and three children are walking to church.
B: ...

b) What else is happening? Make more sentences. Add details.

A young man is ...

## 6 Complete Tara's sentences.

while → past progressive
when → simple past

33/5
1. While I was writing my blog last night, my mum phoned. (write)
2. When she called, my brother — dinner in the kitchen. (cook)
3. While I — my text, my mum told me about her day. She was on the bus home. (check)
4. While we —, my little sister came into the room. (talk)
5. I — with my sister when my brother said that dinner was ready. (play)
6. Mum came home while we —. (eat)

## 7 (WRITING) Write sentences about problems in Jamaica.

a) Write these notes from a report about problems in Jamaica as sentences. → ○ p. 94

33/6 At the time the report was written there were a lot of problems.

1. more than a million people • live • in poverty
   More than a million people were living in poverty.
2. poverty • grow • fast
3. shootings • happen • almost every day
4. more people • use • drugs • every year
5. but many young people • take part in • church activities • too
6. and many teenagers • look after • younger • brothers and sisters • to help their parents
7. some parents • struggle • to feed • their children
8. many people under 30 • think about • leaving • the island

b) What did people say when they were interviewed for the report? Complete the sentences.

34/7
1. "My brother — drugs one day last month when the police — him." (sell, arrest)
2. "Somebody — a man here last week while he — home." (shoot, walk)
3. "I — to the radio when my sister —. She said that she wanted to leave Jamaica." (listen, phone)
4. "When they were little, my two cousins often — at our flat while my aunt —." (stay, work)

## 8 (YOUR TURN) Values → M 1-minute-presentation, p. 183 → S22, p. 164

a) Choose one of the statements:

34/8
35/1-2

"Money is more important than love."
"Children should follow the family values of their parents."

b) Do you agree with the statement? Why (not)?
Make notes.

c) Give your opinion in a short talk.

The statement says … .
It may be true that … .
In my opinion, … . Let me explain … .
On the one hand, … . On the other hand, … .

However, I think, … . In the past … .
Nowadays … .
Still, you have to / mustn't … .
Although many people agree that …,
it could be that … .

I can talk about standards and values. ✓

# Eliza's voyage

**1** What usually happens in pirate stories?

**2** ( READING ) **Make groups of four.** → M Reciprocal teaching, p. 182 → S7, p. 144

**Read Part 1 of the adventure story and do the tasks. Each student does one of the tasks.**

A Find the meaning of the difficult words or phrases. List the most useful ones.
B Make notes and summarise the part of the story. → S11, p. 150
C Write four questions about the text.
D What happens next? Write down your ideas.

**Talk about your results in the group.**

**Then do the same with the other parts of the story. Change roles each time.**

1,21

## Part 1: A new life

My name is Eliza Austin. I was born in Brighton, which lies on the southern coast of England. I grew up there in a happy family with two older brothers. We played together a lot, and I was always proud of being as strong and tough as the boys. We had many adventures, and I was never the one who became scared first. But the good times were over much too soon. When I was 25, we lost both our parents in a terrible fire. After that I couldn't stand living in England any more, and so I decided to look for a position abroad. And I was lucky: Lord Winton offered me a job as governess to his children on his sugar plantation on Barbados.

In April 1730 I left England to start my new life in the Caribbean. Our ship was the Lady Margaret and we sailed from Bristol. I had heard stories about terrifying storms on the Atlantic Ocean, but our journey across the sea was quiet and peaceful.

Five weeks later our long voyage was almost over, and our ship was waiting near a small island. It was then that the pirates chose to attack. In the early hours of the morning I was woken by terrible shouts and the sound of cannons and guns. I looked through the porthole and I saw the pirate ship sailing under the flag of the brutal Captain Blackheart.

We all knew about the pirate attacks that often took place in the Caribbean at that time.

However, I knew what I could do. I had brought some men's clothes with me. Perhaps they would save my life – well, my training as a governess surely wouldn't. So I quickly put the men's clothes on.

1,22

## Part 2: The first pirate

Suddenly the door flew open and a girl ran in screaming. She was so scared! Her eyes were huge and her face was so white that she looked like a ghost. It took me a moment until I recognised who it was: Carol, a young girl who was hoping to find work in Barbados too. Just like me, Carol was travelling alone, and I had been happy to find someone to talk to. And so we had slowly become friends during the long voyage.

Carol had grown up in the country in Wales. She came from a family of poor farmers, with too many children to support. Her parents didn't have the money to send her to school either. But that had never stopped Carol from having big dreams. When she heard that there were jobs in Barbados, she didn't waste much time. Although she didn't know anyone there, she took the ship as soon as she could pay for the ticket. Carol impressed me, and I promised to help her if I could.

**INFO**

Even today there are still pirates. They attack cargo ships on major sea routes around the world to rob or to hijack them. For example, they are a threat off the coast of East Africa, in the Indian Ocean and also near the Panama Canal, which connects the Pacific Ocean with the Gulf of Mexico and the Caribbean.

Now a pirate was following Carol into the cabin. When he turned around and noticed me, he had an evil look on his face.
"You'll come with us, man," he shouted to me, "I'm sure our captain will be happy to meet you two." I can't explain it, but suddenly I was very angry and not at all afraid for myself. All I wanted to do was protect Carol. I picked up a glass that was on the table and threw water in the pirate's ugly face. Then I pushed him as hard as I could, and he hit his head against the table as he fell to the floor.
But before I could run, the door opened a second time, and another pirate walked in. Oh, the horror! It could only be Blackheart!

1,23

## Part 3: A terrible punishment

He looked awful – a tall man with black hair, black eyes and yellow teeth. Blackheart's clothes were all black too. He was holding a sword and a dagger.
I expected him to kill me right away, but he just seemed amused by the scene. As if he wanted his prisoners to resist in order to show that *nobody* could beat Blackheart.
"This one will walk the plank," he said with a horrible smile to the pirate on the floor, who was slowly getting up again. He pointed at me.
"Everyone knows that I only love two things," he continued. "One is gold, and the other is when men try to fight me. Then I can think of special punishments for them. I'll enjoy watching the sharks eat you later, boy. Arrh!"
Of course I kept my mouth shut. I didn't answer him because I was too afraid that my voice would give me away.
'They are not going to like it if they find out that I've tried to fool them,' I thought.
So Blackheart's men took Carol and me away and put us in a cabin with the other prisoners. We had no food or water for hours.
There was no hope left, and I expected to die there and then. So I said to Carol, "If you should survive all of this, please write to my brothers about what happened here."
Until then she had been brave, but that was when she started to cry.
Finally, they came and took me to the deck and led me to the plank.
I was terrified, but I didn't want to show it in front of Blackheart and his crew. I looked down. I could see the sharks. They were swimming in circles. They were waiting for me!

1,24

## Part 4: Ship ahoy!

The sun was high in the sky as I slowly put my left foot on the end of the plank.
Suddenly there was a shout.
"Ship ahoy!"
We all looked up. No one had noticed the ship that had come from behind the island and was now sailing fast towards us. I was just able to read the name of the ship, HMS Revenge, and recognise the Royal Navy flag.
I had heard about the HMS Revenge. It hunted pirates in the Caribbean, and I knew that many pirates were afraid of it. A cannon fired and the shot landed in the sea close to our ship. Blackheart showed no reaction, but the crew was obviously terrified.
The pirate who was leading me stopped, white with shock. While he was just standing there, I looked around and suddenly I knew how I could get away. I had seen …

### 3 (WRITING) Rewrite this beginning of a summary and correct the five mistakes in it.

The story 'Eliza's voyage' by Eliza Austin takes place early in the 19th century.
It is about a pirate attack.
A ship called the Lady Margaret is sailing to Barbados, when one night it is attacked by pirates.
Carol puts on men's clothes. In a fight she kills one of the pirates. Then Blackbeard, the captain of the pirates, comes in. So Eliza and Carol have to walk the plank.
Before this happens, the pirates fire a cannon at the HMS Revenge. …

### 4 Choose one of these tasks.

36/1
37/2-3

a) Write a character profile.

1. Choose one of the characters in the story (Eliza, Carol or Blackheart).
2. Make notes about the character.
3. Compare your notes with a partner who chose the same character.
4. Write your profile of the character.

OR

b) Write an ending to the story.
Use the past tenses. → S19, p. 160

**WRITING SKILLS**

When you write an ending for a story, make sure you keep in mind what has happened in the story so far.
This way …
- you can pick up information from before.
- you can make up new things and not create contradictions.
- your characters will act in ways that fit the story.

I can understand a pirate story. ✓

# The swimming pigs of the Bahamas

**STUDY SKILLS**

From English to German: Only give the general meaning and tell the most important facts.
From German to English: Make short and simple sentences. Paraphrase words you don't know.

## 1 Play Daniel's part in the dialogue. → S24, p. 167

38/1-2

A German family is in the Bahamas. They're interested in a day trip, but they aren't sure what to do. Their son, Daniel, speaks English the best, so he's the one who helps them out at the tourist information office.

Clayton: Hello and welcome. My name is Clayton. How can I help you?
Daniel: *Begrüße Clayton und sage, dass eure Familie einen Ausflug machen möchte. Ihr wisst aber nicht, was man hier unternehmen kann.*
Clayton: You can go snorkelling with tropical fish and sea turtles or watch sharks. If you want to enjoy the beautiful islands, a boat trip would be a perfect option.
Daniel: Clayton sagt, dass …
Mum: Was sollte man sich unbedingt ansehen?
Daniel: My mum wants to know … .
Clayton: There are swimming pigs on one of the Exuma islands.
Mum: Was war das mit den Schweinen?
Daniel: My mum understood 'pigs'. She'd like to know … .
Clayton: There are a number of pigs living on the island. They run around freely and swim in the sea. They are very friendly. It's a once-in-a-lifetime experience for the whole family.
Daniel: Clayton sagt, dass …
Dad: Das ist ja interessant. Warum gibt es die Tiere dort?
Daniel: My dad wants to know … .
Clayton: It's not clear how they came to the island. It's possible that sailors dropped them off.
Daniel: Clayton sagt, dass … .
Mum: Also, ich würde gerne so einen Ausflug machen.
Daniel: …
Clayton: Awesome. Have a look …

## 2 Which fun activities can you do in your area? Make suggestions for an English-speaking visitor.

I can pass on information about tourist attractions. ✓

# A trip to Grenada

## 1 Talk about the weather in the Caribbean.

Look at the photo. What do you know about the weather and the seasons in the Caribbean?

## 2 ( VIEWING ) Watch the film. → S6, p. 143

4

a) Watch the film until 01:47. Right or wrong? Correct the wrong sentences.

1. Grenada has very cold winters.
2. In Grenada it's dry from December to May.
3. When it rains, it usually rains for less than an hour.
4. Andy is prepared for the wet weather.

b) Watch the film from 01:48 to the end. Choose the right answer.

1. Grenada is a very **green** • **rich** • **large island**.
2. Many houses in Grenada are built **in sandy areas** • **on flat land** • **on the side of hills**.
3. Janet is the name of **a news reporter** • **a hurricane** • **a fishing boat**.
4. At the end of the film we see a tropical **storm** • **beach** • **meal**.

**CULTURE**

The weather has always had a big influence on how people in different parts of the world live – their houses, the clothes they wear, their work and their free-time activities. How does the weather at different times of the year influence how you and your family live?

## 3 ( WRITING ) Write Andy's e-mail.

a) Compare the weather in the Caribbean with the weather in Europe.

b) Write Andy's e-mail to his family in England, in which he complains about the weather while filming the documentary.

**VIEWING SKILLS**

In many documentaries a narrator makes comments. In this film there's also a man from the UK called Andy. He shows us how a European experiences the weather in Grenada so we can see the island through his eyes and get a better idea of how it feels to be there.

I can understand a film about the weather in the Caribbean. ✓

## Checklist

I can understand information about the Caribbean. ✓ 39

I can write a fictional story. ✓

... with white sands and warm, blue seas .... • ... took my breath away .... • I got scared when ... • At that moment ... 39

I can talk about standards and values. ✓

... is important to me because .... • Traditionally, they expect you to .... • I'm proud of .... • Many people agree that ... 40

I can understand a pirate story. ✓ 40

I can pass on information about tourist attractions. ✓ 41

I can understand a film about the weather in the Caribbean. ✓

# ❀ (TASK) A short essay

One of your parents got a job offer in the Caribbean. Would you like to go and live there with them? Write a short argumentative essay.
→ S17, p. 156

## Step 1

### Find arguments and reasons.

Collect two to three pros and cons.
Find a reason for each of them.
Example: As a fan of the outdoors I think I would like living there *(argument)* because the landscape is fantastic, and there is clear water and great tropical rainforests *(reason)*.

## Step 2

### Prepare your essay.

a) Put the pros and cons in a table.

| Pros (yes) | Cons (no) |
|---|---|
| ... | ... |

b) Number your arguments. The weakest one comes first, the strongest one last.

## Step 3

### Decide on a structure.

There are different ways to structure the arguments of your essay. Choose one for your text. → S17, p. 156

## Step 4

### Write a draft.

**Introduction**
Introduce the topic in two or three sentences.
Make readers curious and tell them what you'll be discussing.

**Body**
Structure your arguments in the way that you chose.
Write in paragraphs and connect the paragraphs.

**Conclusion**
Sum up your opinion and the most important points.
Answer the question: Would you like to go there or not?
Don't add any new arguments.

| | |
|---|---|
| **The Caribbean – music, pirates, happy people**<br>Many people say that … | *title + introduction* |
| First, I have to say that …<br>Second, the people who live there are so friendly. … | *pros* |
| However, there are also lots of problems. …<br>Furthermore, … / In my opinion … | *cons* |
| In conclusion, … / Finally, … / To sum up, I can say that … | *conclusion* |

## Step 5

### Write your final version.

Check your spelling, your grammar and the content.
→ S10, p. 148

## Step 6

### Read two other students' essays.

Give feedback. Did the essays of the other students convince you? Is the structure OK?
What's good about the essays and what could be better next time?
→ S23, p. 166

1,25-29

# The Caribbean world → S7, p. 144

## 1. The islands and their inhabitants

There are nearly 40 million people in the Caribbean region. But about 75 % of them live in three large countries: Cuba, the Dominican Republic (where they speak Spanish) and Haiti (where they speak French). Jamaica is the largest English-speaking island. On some islands there is an Indian population because the British brought in labour from India. In Trinidad, for example, more than a third of the population have an Indian background. The name 'Caribbean' comes from the Carib people, who were living on the islands when the Europeans arrived. The Europeans believed that they were cannibals, and they used this as an excuse to kill them. A study has found that 60 % of the population of Puerto Rico have native ancestors.

## 2. Religions

Christianity is by far the most popular religion in the Caribbean, but most people probably know the two smaller Caribbean religious groups which have African roots. **Rastafarianism** developed in Jamaica in the 1930s. It rejects material things and allows the use of marijuana in its rituals. However, only about 5 % of the population in Jamaica practise it. **Voodoo** was brought to Haiti in the 18th century. It was popular among slaves who were forced to become Christians. Its African rituals include Catholic elements.

## 3. Rum, lime and the Royal Navy

The Caribbean produces coffee, bananas and sugar. When sugar production exploded in the 18th century, rum was a by-product. Planters needed to sell it, and they found a market in the Royal Navy. For 300 years, until 1970, rum was the official daily drink for all sailors.
Until the 19th century sailors were often ill because they didn't have enough vitamin C in their food. Then it was discovered that sailors stayed healthy if they drank lemon or lime juice every day. Limes for the whole Royal Navy were bought in the British Caribbean islands and mixed with the daily ration of rum.

## 4. Jamaican athletes

Jamaica has some of the world's best athletes, especially in sprinting. Olympic champion Usain Bolt is just one example.
Jamaica won six gold medals during the 2016 Olympics in Rio de Janeiro. For a population of under three million, that is quite amazing. Sprinting is wildly popular on the island. While in other countries most young kids with a talent for sport choose football or basketball, in Jamaica a lot of them take up running.

## 5. Caribbean cruises

The Caribbean is the most popular cruise destination in the world. New cruise ships can carry 6,000 passengers and have amazing facilities, such as state-of-the-art fitness centres with rock climbing walls, theatres with Broadway shows, water parks and ice rinks. Cruise companies also own private 'fantasy islands', which only passengers can visit. They spend a day on land, but with all the luxury of a cruise ship.

**1** **Agree on one interesting fact in each of the five texts. Make notes and tell the class. Try not to read your notes.**

**2** **Write a newspaper report about a competition in which the Jamaican Olympic team won the gold medal.** → S16, p. 155

labour – *Arbeitskraft*; cannibal – *Kannibale, Kannibalin*; study – *Untersuchung, Studie*; ancestor – *Vorfahre, Vorfahrin*; practise – *ausüben*; Royal Navy – *Kriegsmarine des Vereinigten Königreichs*; facilities – *Einrichtungen*; state-of-the-art – *hochmodern*

Find more online: i8ce82

In this unit you will ...
- find out about South Africa.
- talk about social differences.
- write an article about a nature reserve.
- read a story about apartheid.
- pass on information about languages in South Africa.
- watch a film about living in Cape Town.

5 2,1

# Unit 3
# Around South Africa

South Africa has three capital cities: Pretoria, Cape Town and Bloemfontein. The main one is Pretoria, where the president has his seat. The population of the country is 80% African and 20% European, mixed race or Indian. South Africa has large amounts of gold and diamonds.

Many people dream of going on safari once in their lives and seeing Africa's wild animals like elephants, lions and rhinos. South Africa has lots of national parks and nature reserves. The Kruger National Park, with its amazing scenery and wildlife, is the largest and oldest.

## 1 Work with the photos. → S20, p. 161

50/1

a) What first impression do the photos give you of South Africa?

It looks like South Africa is ....
South Africa seems to have ....

b) Write a heading for each photo.

## 2 Read the texts and correct the sentences.

1. The president has a seat in one of the two capitals.
2. The Kruger National Park is the only South African park or nature reserve.
3. The three most popular sports in South Africa are football, cricket and volleyball.
4. Apartheid was introduced when South Africa was a British colony.
5. Today rich people in South Africa live in townships.

3

Most South Africans love all kinds of sport, especially football, cricket and rugby. Newspapers and other media are full of reports about the games and the background stories of their teams and players.

4

People lived in South Africa long before the first European settlers, the Dutch, arrived. Then the country became a British colony. Later, after independence, the government introduced 'apartheid'. This system strictly separated black and white people. Apartheid was abolished in 1994.

5

In 1994 President Nelson Mandela promised to build a new 'rainbow nation' for all the people of South Africa. But even today many rich people still live in gated communities with high security, while poor people live in townships. These often have no electricity or clean water.

## 3 (LISTENING) Listen to a guided tour at a museum. → S5, p. 142

2,2

a) Look at the historical events. Listen and put them in the right order.

A The Union of South Africa was created.
B There were democratic elections for the first time.
C There were a lot of problems between the different tribes in the south of Africa.
D It became a British colony, and the Dutch moved to a new territory.
E The Dutch settled in Cape Town.
F The apartheid system started.

b) When did each event happen? Listen again and take notes.

territory ['terɪtri] – Gebiet
war [wɔː] – Krieg
peace [piːs] – Frieden
constitution [kɒnstɪ'tjuːʃn] – Verfassung
democratic ['demə'krætɪk] – demokratisch
election [ɪ'lekʃn] – Wahl

I can understand information about South Africa.

2,3-7

# After the accident

**1** (SPEAKING) **Why do road accidents often happen?**

**2** (READING) **Read the texts.**

**A** INTERNET

Daily News | NEWS | SPORTS | LIFESTYLE

### Accident near central Durban

*10 Jan* – There was an accident between a bus with students from the private Redhill School and a car at around 1 p.m. yesterday. The driver of the bus died and a student, Piet Jansen (16), went to hospital with face injuries.

The driver of the car, Kagiso Sekibo (40) from Cape Town, suffered back injuries, but her daughter, Cebile (17), wasn't hurt.

The reason for the crash is not clear yet. But a young worker from the Umlazi township, who had seen the accident, was taken to the police station for questioning.

**C**

DURBAN POLICE

Police officer: Why were you at that street corner?

Lefa (16): Officer, I don't understand why you're asking me that. The bus to work picks me up there. I stand on that corner every day. I swear I didn't do anything. I just saw the car driving out of control towards the bus. That's it.

Police officer: Answer the questions about your personal background that I asked you earlier, please. We'll decide how to go on when you have answered them.

Lefa: OK, I grew up in a township. My dad left two years ago, and my mum had no money. Either I could go to school hungry or I could go to work. So I dropped out of school like most of my friends. You know, being poor and black, it's hard to get a good job, especially if you live in a township.

Police officer: Thank you. You'll have to stay here for further questioning.

Lefa: Officer, please! I work in construction. I'm paid by the day. If I don't show up in an hour, I'll lose my job!

**B** E-MAIL

Dear Sir or Madam,

I read your report about the bus accident in Durban yesterday.
We really need to talk about this problem! Why are there so many crazy drivers on South Africa's roads? Don't those drivers think about the consequences for themselves and for others? The number of deaths and accidents every day is terrifying. I feel so sorry for the victims. I think bad drivers should pay for the accidents they cause!

Yours faithfully,
Tinus Botha

**D** E-MAIL

Hi Dawn,
Mum said you called. I feel a bit better now, but I often have flashbacks at night. They frighten the hell out of me. I always see the car coming closer and closer. Since the accident I haven't been sleeping well, so I'm going to see a doctor about it. Having good health insurance makes things a lot easier.
Our school rugby team was on the bus. We had just left school for a game ten minutes before. Now the doctor won't allow me to play for two months. Grr! ☹ You know how I love rugby. It's a nightmare. But I can still go on my trip to the UK in March. Dad just told me.
After I talked to Dad, I had a thought: we all live in this gated community for whites only, with high walls and guards. But then someone stupid ruins your career in one second. It's so unfair.
See you,
Piet

**E** CEBILE'S DIARY

15th January

*I can't forget that horrible accident. My body still hurts. And I can't forget those pictures of people bleeding and crying. I don't think Mama can either.*
*I know she struggles with the situation. She thinks it was her fault. And that's why she feels guilty. She probably wasn't concentrating. A few hours before the accident happened, she had heard some bad news. She had lost her job. Looking at Mama, I'm proud of her. She is well-educated. Not many black South Africans were able to go to a white state school. She got a place just after apartheid ended.*
*And now I go to the same state school as Mama did. My dream is to become a journalist. We don't really live the life of the rich (we're middle class, I'd say), but we've got everything we need.*
*Except good health insurance. I wish we had that. Mama needs some treatment.*

**Language tip** → G 5, p. 173
I saw the car **driving** towards the bus.
**Being** poor and black, it's hard to get a job.

## 3 Work with the texts.

51/1-2 52/3 **a)** Answer the questions.

1. Where and when did the accident happen?
2. Who was involved in it?
3. What was Lefa's role in the accident?
4. How does Piet feel after the accident?
5. Why is Cebile worried about her mum?
6. What is Tinus Botha's opinion of the South African traffic situation?

**b)** Find out the information from the texts for each person. Make a table. → M Jigsaw, p. 181

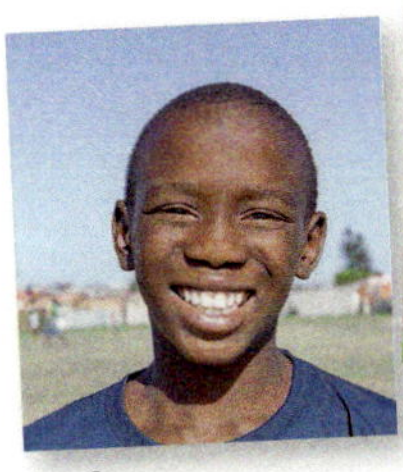
Lefa

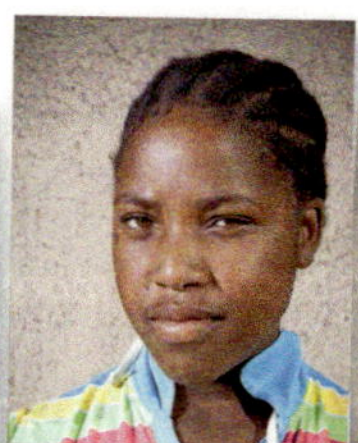
Cebile

Piet

a) Age?
b) Social status?
c) Black or white?
d) Lives in?
e) School?
f) Health insurance?
g) Plans for the future?

## 4 Work with words to describe social differences.

52/4
52/5a)

a) Make pairs of opposites with the adjectives. → ○ p. 95

privileged · equal · underprivileged · fair
poor · rich · unequal · unfair

52/5b)

b) Choose the right word. → V Social differences, p. 200

1. There still is strong **equality** • **inequality** in South Africa today.
2. In South African townships a lot of people live in **poverty** • **wealth**.
3. The government should do more against ~~**fairness**~~ • **unfairness** in society.
4. Nelson Mandela fought for **justice** • ~~**injustice**~~ in his country.

## 53/6 5 ( WRITING ) Write about social differences.

a) What statements can you make about South African society with the information from Ex. 3b)? Write about 60 words. → ○ p. 95

In South African society there are different … .
There are people of different … .
Some people are … . Others are … .
On the one hand, … . On the other hand, … .
…

*Make general statements here. Think about what types of South African people the three people represent.*

b) Comment on the statement 'The streets are a poor kid's game console'.
Write 60 – 100 words.

## 6 Find out about South African desserts. → S3, p. 140

Check the internet. Which dessert would you prefer to eat? Why?

A

Amagwinya

B

Melktert

**CULTURE**

Melktert is a popular South African dessert which came with the Dutch settlers. But traditional dishes from the townships, like Amagwinya, are also becoming more and more popular in all parts of South African society.

**Language** → G6, p. 174

We had just left school ten minutes before.
A few hours before the accident happened, Kagiso had lost her job.

What tense is this? Does it describe events before or after the accident?

## 7 Say what the people had done or hadn't done before the accident happened.

a) Put in the verbs. Use the past perfect. → ○ p. 95

53/7-8

1. Before the driver picked up the students, he had cleaned (clean) the bus.
2. He — (listen) to the news on the radio before he went to pick up the rugby players.
3. Piet and his friends — (have) lunch before they left the school building.
4. Piet — (send) his dad a message just before the bus arrived.
5. Lefa — (be) at the corner for a few minutes when he saw the accident.
6. His bus to work — (not arrive) when the car hit the bus.
7. Kagiso — (not tell) her daughter about the bad news yet when the accident happened.

b) Read Cebile's to do list. What had she done or not done before the accident happened?

To do
- buy birthday present for Mum ✓
- ask Mrs W. for reference ✓
- apply for waitress job
- tidy up room ✓
- make birthday card

## 8 (YOUR TURN) Comparing photos → V Social differences, p. 205 → S20, p. 161

54/9

A

B

a) Decide who describes which photo. Make notes. Compare the photos.

b) What do you think: How did the person in each photo get to where they are? Discuss your ideas in class.

The lady in photo A probably had … before she …
Maybe the girl in picture B …

I can talk about social differences. ✓

# Exploring the wild

## 1 ( READING ) Read the interview with a ranger at Kruger National Park.

2,8

55/1

→ M Dramatic reading, p. 180

**Carlie:** This is Radio Cape Gold FM. It's four o'clock and you're listening to *Exploring the wild* with me, Carlie Keita. Our guest today is Tony Okonwo, a ranger at Kruger National Park. Welcome Tony. Nice to have you here.

**Tony:** Hi Carlie. Thanks for inviting me.

**Carlie:** Our listeners are very interested to hear what work is like in such a great park. Would you tell us about your job? What do you like about it?

**Tony:** Being a ranger in one of the most amazing parks in the world is fantastic. There are wide, endless plains and the land is quite flat, with only a few hills and no mountains. But most of all I've always been interested in our wildlife and I've always wanted people to learn more about how to protect it.

**Carlie:** Tony, what's special about the park?

**Tony:** Kruger National Park was South Africa's first national park. It was named after President Paul Kruger when it was created in 1926. And it has been a success ever since. Its goal is to protect and conserve the South African wildlife. Evidence of early human life has been found in the park too, like rock art. So visitors can also look back at the history of mankind.

**Carlie:** How did tourism in the park develop?

**Tony:** The value of tourism wasn't really recognised before 1926. In the next year the first three tourist cars came in. After that roads and visitor centres were built, fences were put up and guides were hired to show tourists around.

**Carlie:** There were problems too, right? Weren't animals hunted before the park was founded?

**Tony:** Yes, they were. A lot of elephants were killed for their ivory. Even today we face lots of challenges. But many rules regulate what's happening in the park. Visitors have to stay in their cars for their own safety, for example.

**Carlie:** Most people come to see the 'Big Five': the elephant, the lion, the leopard, the rhino and the buffalo. Where does that name come from?

**Tony:** The name was first introduced by big game hunters. It was difficult for them to hunt these large animals. And once an animal was hurt, it could attack the hunters. We rangers also think that these five animals are the most dangerous ones. Therefore, we treat them with the respect and the caution they deserve. So, a lot is done to save and protect the wildlife of the park. We do our best to take action against poaching too.

**Carlie:** Poaching will be part of our next edition. Tony will join us again then. Time's up. Thanks a lot, Tony. He is going to be in our chatroom where you can ask him questions. We'll leave you with that. Now over to James and the news.

## 2 Work with the text.

a) Take notes about these four aspects of the national park. → ○ p. 96

1. landscapes  2. history  3. tourism  4. animals

b) What are the pros and cons of letting tourists into a protected area?

## 3 Describe the landscapes. → S20, p. 161

a) Describe the photos with the help of these words. → ○ p. 97

55/2
56/3

coast | desert | forest | mountain range | plain | marsh

Photo 1 shows .... In it you can see....

b) Match the words with their definitions. → V Landscapes, p. 201

1. A pond is ...
2. A source is ...
3. A hill is...
4. A valley is ...

A where a river starts.
B the opposite of a mountain.
C a small mountain.
D a small lake.

## 4 ( WRITING ) Use these words to rewrite the sentences.

56/4

conserve | recycle | reduce | regulate | save | survive

1. There are strict laws which **control** what is going on in the national parks.
2. A ranger's job is to **stop the killing of** the wildlife in national parks.
3. For example, they must **protect and look after** the plants and animals in the parks.
4. Baby elephants can't **live** without their mothers.
5. The rangers want to **have less** rubbish in camps.
6. They collect the rubbish so that they can **use** it **again**.

## 5 ( LISTENING ) Listen to a South African radio news programme. → S5, p. 142

2,9

Listen to four news stories. Copy and complete the table.

| Category | Who? | What? | Where? |
|---|---|---|---|
| 1. local news | people without homes | | |
| 2. local news | rangers | | |
| 3. sport | Lood de Jager | | |
| 4. weather | x | | |

**LISTENING SKILLS**

News reports on the radio, on TV or on the internet are a good way to practise listening. You usually hear the same categories of news stories in the same order. Listen for pauses between each news story. This will help you to follow better.

## Language → G7, p. 175

The park was named after Paul Kruger.
Fences were put up and guides were hired.
The name was introduced by hunters.

When do you use the passive? How is it formed?

## 6 Make sentences about a school safari trip.

a) Put in the verbs in the passive. → ○ p. 97

56/5

find | like | take (2x) | put | organize ✓ | answer

1. Our trip was organized by Mr Wessels, the Biology teacher.
2. The students — on a tour of the park. The guide was a ranger, Tony Okonwo.
3. The tour was very interesting. All the students' questions — .
4. One student left his hat at the picnic place. It — again later.
5. Lots of photos of the animals — in the park.
6. Some of them — online the next day.
7. One photo — by more than a hundred people.

b) Write more sentences about the trip (one for each picture).

1 

2 

3 

4 

share | buy | leave | collect

## 7 Make the questions that tourists ask a ranger and give short answers.

57/6

1. park • close • all last winter? (✗)
2. animals • bring • to park? (✗)
3. the nature reserve • plan • an architect? (✗)
4. lions • bring • here to live? (✗)
5. those leopards • feed • local people? (✓)
6. dinner • cook • in the camp? (✓)
7. corn • grow here • before it was a national park? (✗)

1. Was the park closed all last winter?
   – No, it wasn't.

**GRAMMAR** → G7, p. 175

Were you born in this region?
– No, I wasn't.

Was the Kruger National Park created in 1926?
– Yes, it was.

## 8 ( WRITING ) Rewrite sentences from an interview about the park. → M Peer correction, p. 181

a) Rewrite the answers to make passive sentences. Start with the underlined words. → ○ p. 98

57/7a)

1. Q: When did people discover gold in South Africa?
   A: They discovered gold there in the 1860s.
2. Q: Why did the hunters kill elephants?
   A: Hunters killed elephants for their ivory.
3. Q: Did they only kill elephants?
   A: No, they didn't. They also shot lions and other big cats.
4. Q: When did they create the park?
   A: They created the national park in 1926.
5. Q: Are there roads in the park?
   A: Yes, there are. People built hundreds of kilometres of new roads.
6. Q: What else is special about the park?
   A: They also found beautiful rock art in the caves of the park.

1. Q: When did people discover gold in South Africa?
   A: Gold was discovered there in the 1860s.

b) Rewrite these sentences. Use by to say who did it.

57/7b)

1. Tourists from all over the world visited the park last year.
2. South African workers built the new roads in the park.
3. A ranger found the rock art in the caves in 1911.
4. Rangers like Tony Okonwo repaired the gates in the park last year.

Rock art from South Africa

## 9 ( YOUR TURN ) A magazine article → V Nature, p. 205 → S10, p. 148

a) Write an article about the Kruger National Park for a travel magazine. Use the information on p. 54 and your notes from Ex. 2 → M Writers' conference, p. 183

58/8
59/1-2

**WRITING SKILLS**

When you write an article for a magazine, think about your readers' perspective. Make your article informative but also appealing for them – in content, writing and layout.

- Then check your draft: Are the spelling and the grammar correct? Ask another student to check them too.
- Next, find and add a spectacular photo. Write a caption for your photo.
- Finally, think of a catchy headline for your article.

b) Make a wall newspaper in class. Decide which article you would send to the magazine and why. → M Gallery walk, p. 181 → S23, p. 166

I can write an article about a nature reserve. ✓

# The Playground by Beverley Naidoo, 1999

**1** How do you feel when you go to a new place for the first time? Think of different situations.

**2** (READING) Read the short story. → M Dramatic reading, p. 180 → S7, p. 144

2,10

*The short story 'The Playground' by Beverley Naidoo is about Rosa, an eleven-year-old girl from the townships. Rosa has attended a black school so far. Now that apartheid is over, schools must open their doors to all children, but some white parents and teachers still want to resist. At the beginning of the story Rosa looks through the fence at a white school which she is going to attend soon.*

Through the fence she saw the playground was alive with skipping, running, shouting. A few children sat quietly on benches under the trees. The well-kept grass stretched from the main road as far as a line of trees in the distance. They were the same tall grey trees that Rosa saw as she crossed the rough dry land which separated the township where she and Mama lived from what she had always known as 'the white people's town'.

It was lunch break at Oranje Primary School. Inside the orange brick building with its shiny windows, children had classes in the morning and in the afternoon. Not like her school. *Her* school in the township had so many pupils they had to take turns to use the classrooms! When she and her classmates finished lessons at 12, the afternoon children were just arriving. There was no playground to speak of, just a piece of dry ground and a few cactus plants.

*Rosa's mother works for a white family with Dutch roots. Rosa remembers what happened at their house a few years ago.*

Mama had worked for them for years and Rosa had known Hennie since they were babies. At the age of three they had played together. Mama used to take her every weekday. While Mama cooked, cleaned, washed and ironed, Rosa and Hennie had run around the garden, built castles in the sandpit, made houses at the end of the long garden where the plants grew wild.

Their playing together had come to a sudden end one day when Hennie's father came home early. The two of them were running under the sprinkler. They were shouting and making funny faces. He walked across the lawn very fast. Like a storm he swept Hennie up with one arm and began to hit him on the bottom. Hennie stopped laughing and began to cry.

"What do you think you're doing? Running around like a savage?"

Hennie's mother and Mama had come running from the house.

"Is this how you're letting him grow? It's time he learnt to be a real boy – and to know he's a *white* boy!"

Mama had taken Rosa silently by the hand and led her away. She heard Hennie's mother say, "They were just playing, Willem. Just children's games. Look how you've scared them."

After that, Mama left Rosa with their neighbour, Mrs Moloi, every day.

*Rosa doesn't see Hennie often over the next few years. But she hears that he goes to Oranje Primary School and has become a very good rugby player.* 2,11

*Rosa experiences the end of apartheid.*

**INFO**

Nelson Mandela (1918 – 2013) fought apartheid for much of his life. In 1962 he was sent to prison on Robben Island near Cape Town, where he spent the next 27 years. After years of protests at home and abroad, the government finally released him from prison.
He became South Africa's first black president in 1994. He led the change from white rule to the multiracial society of today. Many people in South Africa call him 'the father of the nation'.

A spirit of joy was like an unexpected rainbow for the next few days over all the township. Neighbours and friends crowded their tiny living room. Rosa sat on Mama's lap and she watched a tall, grey-haired man with a warm, serious but smiling face who waved at them from their small TV. All around Rosa people were crying and laughing. They couldn't believe it. It was a day they had almost thought would never come. Nelson Mandela, the man the white government had put in prison for life, was walking free from his prison! He was coming to help them. They prayed for him to take away the heavy grey clouds which white people's government put over their lives.

*For the first time there are democratic elections and black South Africans can also vote.*

Only a few months earlier, for the first time in her life, Mama had stood in the same long queue as Hennie's parents and the other white townsfolk, and waited to vote for the new government. A 'rainbow government', Mama told Rosa. A government that would make sure her daughter could go to a school with enough classrooms, teachers, desks, books and playing fields for everyone. The school that white parents had kept just for their own children would have to become a 'rainbow school', Mama had laughed.

*Mama wants Rosa to go to the white school.*

One evening, they passed the boy who sold newspapers to people in cars that were waiting at the traffic lights. She read the headlines WHITE PARENTS TO PROTEST. Mama stopped to buy a copy.
"Do you know that President Mandela wants every child to be in school?" Mama asked as she paid. "When will your mother send you to school?"
"My mother is dead," the boy said seriously. "If I go to school, I won't have money for food."

*Mama takes Rosa to Oranje Primary School on the first day. Outside white people are protesting.* 2,12

New Year arrived and soon after it was the day that Rosa had begun to be afraid of. When she walked down the road for the first time in her new uniform, she felt like everyone was staring at her and Mama.
"Don't let anyone take who you are away from you, my child," she said firmly.
Mama squeezed her hand more tightly as they reached the protesters. Rosa didn't look at the faces and the signs, but she had to listen to the ugly screams. "NEVER! WHITE AND BLACK DON'T MIX! NO BLACKS HERE!"

## READING SKILLS

When you read a longer story, it may be difficult to remember important aspects about the plot, the characters and their relationship to each other.
You can take short breaks, re-read some paragraphs and take notes about the plot or make a sociogram of the characters like this:

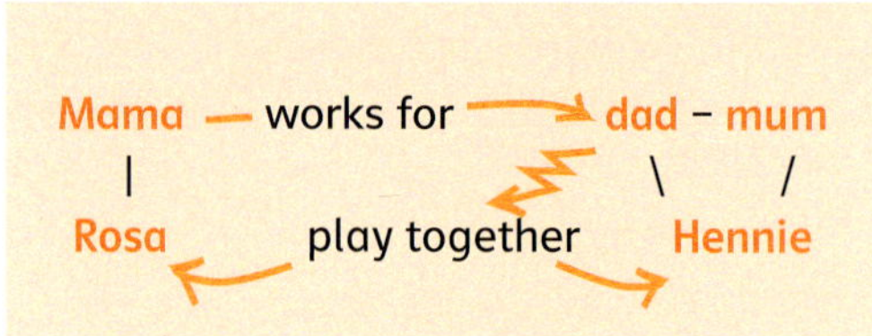


A man was arguing with the headteacher. "If you let this one in, we'll take all our children away! I'm warning you!" He tried to stop Rosa and Mama going up the stairs into the school.

"If I don't let her in, the government will close the school! Don't you understand? We have no choice!" the headteacher said angrily.

2,13 *Mama and Rosa aren't stopped by the protesters and they enter the school. The headteacher takes Rosa to her classroom. There is one girl in the class, Marie, who seems friendly. The break starts, and another girl tells Rosa that the headteacher wants to see her. But it's a trick. She takes Rosa to a dark, quiet part of the school, where there is a small group of unfriendly children.*

"You!" the leader said. "Come here!"

"My name is Rosa."

"Anyone seen a rose this colour?" he joked to the others. "Do you think we can pick her?"

"Leave Rosa alone!"

She knew that voice! She turned around. Hennie was walking fast towards them. His angry eyes were so like his father's! Even his voice had the same fierceness.

"Hennie, we're only playing," said the girl who had brought Rosa there.

Hennie didn't listen to her. The atmosphere in the group seemed suddenly flat and empty, like a balloon with no air. Hennie turned to Rosa.

"The playground is over there. I'll show you."

Before they were gone, Rosa heard one of the boys complaining loudly.

"Just because he's older and good at rugby, he thinks he's the boss."

Hennie took no notice.

"I saw you and your mother come to school this morning … with all those people." He paused awkwardly. "You were very brave."

"Somebody has to be first," she said. "Thank you, … Hennie." She paused a moment before she said his name.

His face went a little red, then he disappeared into a group of boys chasing a rugby ball. Rosa looked at the playground. She took no notice of the stares. Her eyes travelled past the children who were skipping, running and shouting, to the fence. In the distance, she saw the newspaper boy. He was moving between cars at the red light. On the way home she would ask him if something was in the newspaper. If the protesters came again, she would have to learn to deal with them alone. Mama couldn't come with her every morning and be late for work.

But that was tomorrow. Rosa gave her head a little shake. One step at a time, as Mama would say. Her eyes reached the benches under some trees. A girl was looking in her direction. It was Marie. Was she smiling? Rosa took a deep breath and began to cross the playground.

## 3 Work with the text.

a) Answer the questions.

1. How was Rosa's school different to Oranje Primary School?
2. Why did Rosa and Hennie stop playing together?
3. Why did people cry when they saw Mandela on TV?
4. What did Mama do for the first time?
5. Why did white parents protest?
6. Why do the group respect Hennie?

b) Explain the quotes and the background to them.

1 "It's time he learnt to be a real boy." *(ll. 48 – 49)*
2. "… was walking free from his prison." *(ll. 71 – 72)*
3. "Mama had stood in the same long queue as Hennie's parents." *(ll. 79 – 80)*
4. "If I don't let her in, the government will close the school." *(ll. 119 – 120)*
5. "You were very brave." *(l. 151)*

## 4 Do you think it was a good idea to send Rosa to Oranje Primary School? Discuss with a partner.

## 5 Choose one of these tasks.

60/1
61/2-4

a) Turn one scene from the story into a film with toy figures.

1. Choose one scene from the story: ll. 28 – 56 or ll. 103 – 121 or ll. 129 – 154
2. Decide …
   - how many and what type of figures you need.
   - what they say. Write the sentences.
   - how they move. → S19, p. 160
3. Act the scene: Move the figures with your fingers and say their sentences. Film it with your phone.
4. Show the film in class. Which film does your class like best? Why? → M Tip top, p. 183
→ S23, p. 166

OR

b) Make a poster about Nelson Mandela.

Mandela has appeared in many books, films, TV programmes, songs etc.

1. Research one of them. → S3, p. 140
2. Write a paragraph about how it describes Mandela.
3. Add a picture (for example the book cover or a picture from a film) or some lines from a song.
   Present your poster.
   → M Gallery walk, p. 181

I can understand a story about apartheid. ✓

# One voice, eleven languages

**A** Language isn't only the way we communicate with one another. Language also expresses who we are and where we come from. In a country like South Africa, where there are now eleven official languages, this can be a very complex topic.

Before 1994 in the days of apartheid, only English and Afrikaans were the official languages. But when Nelson Mandela became president, more African languages were officially recognised under the same status. There are also a number of unofficial ones.

English is the most commonly spoken language in public life (business, politics and media) but not the most spoken language in South African homes. Most South Africans are multilingual, so they speak more than one language.

**B** **South Africa Home Language (%)**

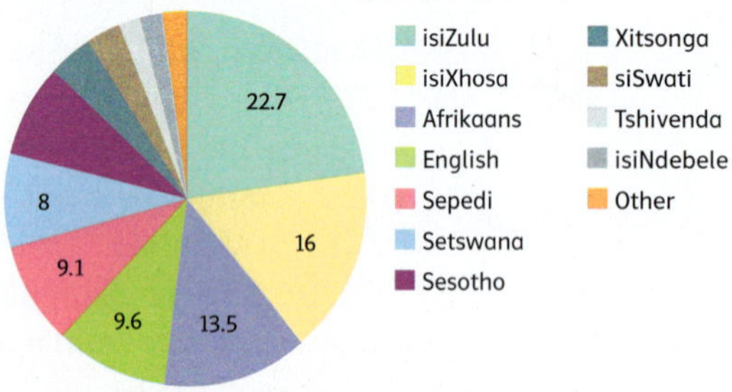


*Source: Statistics South Africa, 2011*

**C**

Since 1994 the national anthem has included five of the most important languages in South Africa – Xhosa, Zulu, Sesotho, Afrikaans and English.

## 1 Beantworte die Fragen. → S24, p. 167

62/1-2

1. Was sind die drei Hauptaussagen des Textes?
2. Welche Bedeutung hat das Englische in Südafrika? → S9, p. 147
3. Was ist das Besondere an der südafrikanischen Nationalhymne?

**CULTURE**

An official language is a language with a special status within a country. It's the language used by the government or courts but not necessarily by the people in everyday life. What's the situation like in Germany?

## 2 Which languages are spoken in your town? When and where are they used?

I can pass on information about languages in South Africa. ✓

# Different faces of Cape Town

## 1 Talk about where you live.

a) What do you like about the city, town or village where you live?

b) What would you show a visitor? Why?

## 2 (VIEWING) Watch the film. → S6, p. 143

6

a) Which of these topics does the film deal with?

the baboon problem | Robben Island | an old part of Cape Town | the port of Cape Town | Cape Town Stadium | local industry | sports activities

b) Watch the film again from 01:26 to 02:09 and listen carefully. Why are the baboons seen as a problem? Take notes. Compare your results with a partner.

c) Watch the film from 02:09 to the end.
What are the puppets made of?
What are they used for?

## 3 (SPEAKING) Talk about the film.

a) Watch the film until 01:26, but this time without sound. What impression of life in Cape Town do you get?

b) Does this impression fit with what you already know about life in South Africa? Discuss.

**CULTURE**

The architecture in a city can tell you a lot about its history. In Cape Town, for example, the colourful houses of 'Bo-Kaap' were built by people who moved there from Malaysia. There are also white 'Cape Dutch' buildings that go back to the times when South Africa was a colony.
What old buildings or areas are there where you live? What can they tell you about the history of the place?

**VIEWING SKILLS**

At the beginning the documentary shows the faces of a number of different people who look straight at the camera. The film doesn't give any information about these people, but it uses these images to give an impression of the city.

I can understand a film about living in Cape Town. ✓

## Checklist

I can understand information about South Africa. 63

I can talk about social differences.

… had no money. • … dropped out of school. • It's hard to get a good job. • There are people of different … . • She is well-educated. • They live the life of the rich … 63

I can write an article about a nature reserve.

The park was created in … by … . • There are wide, endless plains. • visitors can look at … • Roads and fences were built. • Visitors have to stay in their cars. 64

I can understand a story about apartheid. 65

I can pass on information about languages in South Africa. 65

I can understand a film about living in Cape Town.

# (TASK) A speech

Your school offers different projects to "Make your school a better place!" Choose one of them or make up your own project. Give a speech to make other students support your project.

→ S22, p. 164

## Step 1

### Choose a project.

1. Make your school playground greener and cleaner.

**OR**

2. Make the walls of your school playground look better.

**OR**

3. Make your school lunches tastier.

**OR**

4. …

*Choose your project carefully. If your project is very unusual, your speech must be really convincing.*

## Step 2

### Prepare your speech. → S2, p. 139

a) Collect facts, arguments and reasons.

b) Write a first draft. Keep the structure of speeches in mind:
- introduction: e.g. "Hello everyone."
- body: details
- conclusion: e.g. "So, I'd like all of you to join the … project. Thanks for listening and for your support."

## Step 3

### Rewrite your draft.

There are different ways to make a speech more convincing. Look at the examples. Choose three stylistic devices for your own speech. Write the final draft.

| **Stylistic devices** | **Examples** |
|---|---|
| Starting or repeating a number of words with the same letter makes your topic catchy and easy to remember. | Meet more food fans right here, right now. |
| Address the people in the audience to make them feel comfortable and welcome. | I'm happy to see all of you. |
| Respond to the audience's reaction so they know you're interested in them. | I can see that you are surprised, but … |
| Repeat things to show that they're important. | You can learn … because no good food means no happy students, which means no fun at school. |
| Ask rhetorical questions to get the audience's attention. | What is necessary? |
| Use lots of adjectives to touch the audience's hearts. | You don't have to be an expert in cooking delicious and tasty meals in a relaxed atmosphere. … |

## Step 4

### Practise your speech.

Write notes on cards. Then practise your speech a few times before you give it in class.

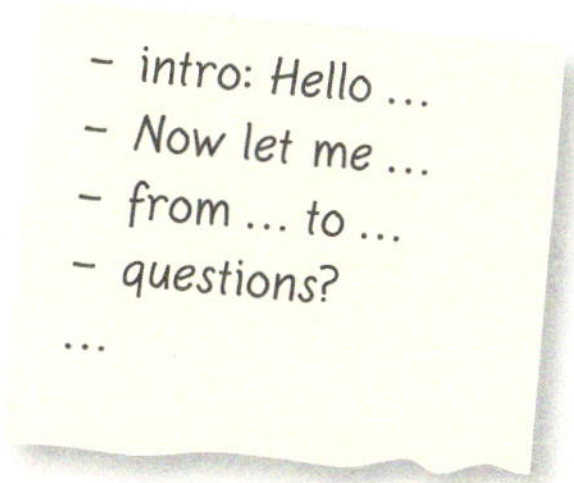


## Step 5

### Give your speech.

**SPEAKING SKILLS**

How you give your speech is important. Don't speak too fast, pause when necessary, look at the audience and smile. Stand still and straight. All this will make you look more confident.

## Step 6

### Give feedback.

Listen to the other speeches and comment on them. Did the speaker convince you? Why? Why not?

→ S23, p. 166

2,14

# A sports crazy nation → S7, p. 144

Nelson Mandela at the Rugby World Cup in 1995

Football fans at the World Cup in 2010

Today it may seem difficult to believe, but under the apartheid system sport in South Africa was segregated. Teams with both black and white players weren't allowed. In the 1970s and 80s there were protests because of this all around the world, and South Africa was banned from international sport, including the Olympic Games. This only changed in 1994 when the government decided to hold democratic elections.

Today things are different. Everyone loves sport, and sports organisations have tried hard to break down racial barriers. In cricket and rugby, for example, there is a 'quota system'. This means that teams must always include a percentage of black players. However, there's a lot of discussion about this because white players might be disadvantaged now or black players might only be chosen because of the colour of their skin.

The 'big three' most popular sports are rugby, football and cricket. **Rugby** was always seen as a white man's game in South Africa. The Springboks – that's the nickname of the national team – are amazingly good at rugby, and it is not at all easy to beat them. The only other team that their proud supporters really respect are the New Zealand All Blacks. But in 1995, just after the end of apartheid, the Springboks beat the All Blacks, who were the favourites, and won the Rugby World Cup. The whole country celebrated when President Mandela put on a jersey with Springbok colours – the colours of a white man's sport – to present the cup. This was a really proud moment for the new South Africa, which was on its way to becoming a more equal society. Five years after that match Mandela said, "Sport has the power to change the world. It has the power to inspire, it has the power to unite people in a way that little else does."

**Football** is without question one of the most popular sports in South Africa with a huge number of supporters in the black community, especially among young people. In 2010 South Africa hosted the World Cup – it was the first time the competition was hosted by an African country. Although South Africa didn't do well in the competition, there was a great atmosphere in the stadiums and the cities. Many will remember the loud noise of the vuvuzelas – whether they liked it or not.

**Cricket** was introduced by the British in the 19th century and it has a long history in South Africa. Many people don't know that although top-class cricket has always been more popular with white people, it has also been played by black people for many years in towns and villages. Today there are a number of successful young black players who are role models for the next generation.

But don't think that sport in South Africa is just about the 'big three'. People also follow many other sports. Here are a few.

**Swimming** is another sport where the country has been successful in big international competitions. Three of its ten Olympic medals in 2016 were for swimming. The world's largest open-water swim, the Midmar Mile, takes place in a lake near the city of Durban every February. Thousands of competitors of all ages and from all over the world take part.

**Horse racing** is another popular sport. The Durban July race, which was first held in 1897, is Africa's greatest horse race with about 50,000 spectators every year. Check out the fashion events before the race. These have become as popular as the race itself. All over South Africa you can find horse riding trails. If you are experienced and you feel brave, you can even ride among wild animals in national parks.

**Cycle races** attract many people who want to experience the country's most spectacular scenery very closely. With more than 35,000 cyclists, the Cape Town Cycle Tour is one of the largest cycle events in the world. The race begins in Cape Town and the 109-km route takes cyclists on a beautiful coastal road around the Cape Peninsula.

Whatever sport you like – you will find it in South Africa!

A cricket game in South Africa

The Cape Town Cycle Tour

## 1 What did you find most interesting? Talk about it with a partner.

## 2 What role does sport play in South African society? Give quotes from the text and explain them. → S7, p. 144

segregated – *nach Rassen getrennt*; to break down racial barriers – *Rassenschranken aufbrechen*; percentage – *Prozentsatz*; skin – *Haut*; to beat – *schlagen, besiegen*; supporter – *Anhänger, Anhängerin*; jersey – *Trikot*; to unite – *vereinen*; to host – *ausrichten*; vuvuzela – *Vuvuzela (Plastikhorn)*; role model – *Vorbild*; open-water (swim) – *Freiwasser(schwimmen)*

Find more online:
i8ce82

In this unit you will ...
- find out about Hong Kong.
- write an online comment.
- talk about how to make a place more eco-friendly.
- read a text about the media.
- pass on information about cyberbullying.
- watch a film about living in Hong Kong.

7 2,15

# Unit 4
# Living in Hong Kong

Hong Kong is one of the biggest cities in Asia and it has more skyscrapers than any other city in the world. Hong Kong is part of China today, but for many years it was a British colony. That's why both Chinese and English are spoken there.

Hong Kong is a great place for shoppers, and its luxurious malls attract many foreign visitors. But there are also exciting night markets, where one can bargain for specialist clothes, electronic goods and souvenirs. Many stalls sell delicious seafood and noodles, and some night markets also have fortune tellers and street singers.

## 1 (SPEAKING) Talk about the photos.
→ S20, p. 161

Look at the photos and talk about these questions with a partner.

1. Which photos could be from cities that you already know? Which cities?
2. Which things in the photos haven't you seen in any other city?
3. What could the pros and cons of living in Hong Kong be?

## 2 Read the texts and choose the right answer.
74/1

1. Hong Kong is now
   a British colony • a Chinese city • part of the UK.
2. People can get a good price at
   restaurants • shopping malls • night markets.
3. Hong Kong is trying hard to reduce
   car numbers • air pollution • recycling.
4. Hong Kong is an important place for
   movies • music • the computer industry.
5. The city has been part of China for more than
   50 years • 20 years • 100 years.

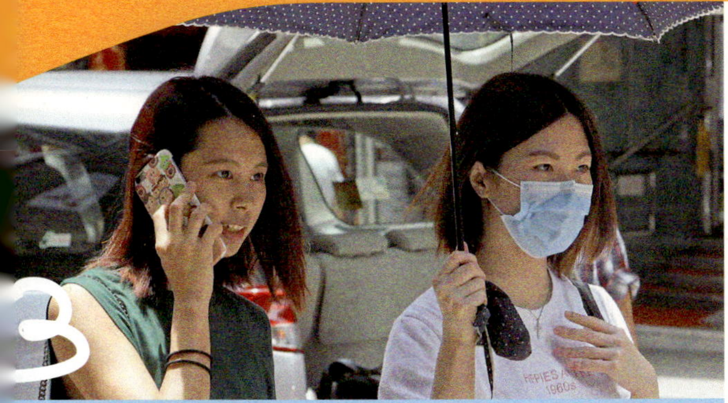

3

Like many large cities Hong Kong has a lot of problems with pollution. There is often thick smog, which can cause serious health problems. The city's population also creates too much waste. But Hong Kong is making a big effort to reduce smog and to recycle more.

4

Hong Kong has a busy media scene. There is a large film industry and a lot of martial arts films are made there. Although many people use special Chinese social media sites, the US ones are more popular. There are also many newspapers in Chinese and some in English.

5

Hong Kong became a Chinese city in 1997, but it is still a fascinating mixture of east and west. Cars drive on the left, for example, and many of the streets have English and Chinese names. And the 100-year-old British tram line is still used today.

## 3 (LISTENING) Listen to the survey about life in Hong Kong. → S5, p. 142

2,16

Copy the table. Listen and take notes.

| | From | Points (1–10) | + | – |
|---|---|---|---|---|
| 1. Emily | USA | | | |
| 2. Christian | | | | |
| 3. Yong Guang | | | | pressure at school |
| 4. Alison | | | network of mums | |

pressure [ˈpreʃə] – Druck
network [ˈnetˌwɜːk] – Netzwerk
scale [skeɪl] – Skala; Maßstab
hurry [ˈhʌri] – Eile
to relax [rɪˈlæks] – sich entspannen

I can understand information about Hong Kong. ✓

# Sneakerheads

**1** (SPEAKING) **Talk about things that you or other people collect.**

I collect .... I know people who collect ...

**2** (READING) **Read the online teen magazine article.**

2,17

75/1

INTERNET

**Everyone wants them** by Cindy Chan

Sneakers Street in the heart of a busy Hong Kong shopping district is where Hong Kong's fashionable youth goes to buy their latest sports shoes. Are you trying to get that one super-rare special pair? Then Sneakers Street is where you should look. There is a stunning number of shoes to browse through with rows and rows of sneakers. And sneakerheads want them all.

For those who don't know, 'sneakerheads' are people who collect sports shoes. You can see them stand in line for hours or even camp overnight in front of a shop just to buy a particular pair of shoes.

Kenneth Lee (32) is one of those sneakerheads – and also a shop assistant in a Sneakers Street shop. I wanted to find out more about this scene, so I met up with him there and asked him a couple of questions.

Kenneth told me, "Sneakerheads are just a group of people who have the same interest." He claimed that he didn't really look for new sneakers all the time. But he added that he walked by the shop windows of Sneakers Street almost every day. He said, "When I see a new pair that I like, I just go crazy. I feel that I've got to have it right away."

Sneaker culture started in New York in the 1960s. It only became big in Hong Kong in the 1980s, when hip hop stars and basketball players made sneakers status symbols.

Back then Michael Jordan became the most famous basketball player in the world and then he started his own line of shoes.

"Everyone wanted them," Kenneth explained. "They were a must-have."

He told me that as a kid he had nagged his parents for ages and had saved all his pocket money for months to buy his first pair.

"As a grown-up, I work and make money, so I sometimes buy ten pairs a month."

So I asked him how many pairs he had. He looked at his smartphone, where he keeps a record of everything he buys and sells. He had 297 pairs. He said his girlfriend often complained that there was no more space in their flat.

I wanted to know if he really wore all those shoes. He said that he did. When he buys a brand-new pair, he always takes a photo and he wears them at least once. Then they go back in the original box.

His younger customers are different. Kenneth told me that sneaker culture had changed a lot in the last few years. He said, "Many kids today don't care if the shoes are beautiful; they don't want to wear them anyway."

Kenneth explained to me that they only bought the shoes to resell them at five times the original price.

"It's just different, I guess. For them the fun part is the trading. For me it's owning the shoes."

## 3 (SPEAKING) Talk about the article.

a) What did you find the most interesting about the article?

b) What do you think of Kenneth's hobby? Which questions would you ask him?

## 4 Work with the text.

a) Finish the sentences. → ○ p. 98

1. Sneakers Street is popular because …
2. A 'sneakerhead' is somebody who …
3. Kenneth Lee is …
4. The two groups which made sneaker culture big in the 1980s were …
5. To be able to afford his first pair, Kenneth …
6. He keeps a record of …
7. Today many younger sneakerheads …

b) Describe how sneaker culture has changed over time.

## 5 Work with verbs for buying and selling. → S4, p. 141

a) Write definitions for the verbs. Use a dictionary. → ○ p. 99

75/2

to save | to browse | to resell | to swap | to collect | to be able to afford

'To save' means to spend less money than the original price.

b) Explain the verbs in your own words. → V Buying and selling, p. 207

75/3

1. I will try to **bargain** for a better price.
2. Get a free toothbrush with every toothpaste you **purchase**.
3. You can **return** most things that you order online.
4. Do you **stock** this brand?

## 6 (SPEAKING) Talk about two events.

76/4

a) Each partner looks at a different ad, A or B. Tell your partner about the event. What is it? What can you do there?

**A**

**'Help the poor' market**

(Sat, 5 March 10–4)

- second-hand clothes
- 100s of stalls for browsing
- special 'Swap it' stall
- cheap new clothes

→ All the money collected will be donated. ←

Please contact: Trish Wong

**B**

**To all you sneakerheads**

The latest sports shoes are out now! Visit our store near Kowloon Park. We'll present the shoe on Sat, 5 March at 11 a.m. You can win a very special pair of shoes.

Come browse and get a surprise!

Get a 20 % discount on last year's shoes.
Buy your ticket at the store.

b) Which event would you like to go to? Do you agree?

### Language detectives → G8, p. 176

Kenneth: "I walk by the shops every day." → Kenneth said (that) he walked by the shops every day.
Kenneth: "I don't know." → Kenneth replied (that) he didn't know.
Cindy: "Do you wear all the shoes?" → Cindy asked if he wore all the shoes.
Cindy: "How many pairs do you own?" → Cindy asked him how many pairs he owned.

Which tenses are the verbs in? How do they change?

## 7 Make sentences in reported speech.

76/5 Complete the sentences with these verbs in the correct tense.

own | fly | wear ✓ | write | not be | order | not keep

1. Kenneth claimed that on some days he wore four different pairs.
2. He told me he also — for a sneakerhead magazine.
3. He explained that a customer from Japan — 30 pairs of shoes every month.
4. He added that the customer often also — to Hong Kong.
5. He said his friend Jen — hundreds of sneakers.
6. He also said that Jen — a record of her sneakers.
7. Kenneth said his girlfriend — happy about all the shoes in their flat.

## 8 (SPEAKING) Do a survey about shopping habits and report the results.

a) Do a survey in your group. → ○ p. 100

77/6 Ask the people in your group these questions. Then report your results to the class.

| Do you … | |
|---|---|
| … ever buy sneakers? | II |
| … own more than five pairs of shoes? | |
| … spend most of your money on clothes? | |
| … usually look for clothes online? | |
| … prefer to browse in shops? | |
| … have a favourite shop? | |
| … prefer shopping alone or with friends? | |

"We asked our classmates if they ever bought sneakers. Two of them said (that) they often … ."

b) Make up five more questions and short answers of your own.

## 9 ( WRITING ) Report how these people reacted to the article.

a) Rewrite the sentences as reported speech. → ○ p. 100

77/7

1. Jeff: "I enjoyed the article. I've already read a lot about Hong Kong."
2. Rob: "Sneakerheads were already around in the 1960s."
3. Linda and Derek: "We have often ordered sneakers online."
4. Steven: "I've never bought shoes for more than $100."
5. Marc and Julie: "That was interesting. We didn't know anything about that scene."
6. Neil: "I've always worked hard for my money and I've never wasted it on stuff like that."
7. Fran: "I've only been to Sneakers Street once. It was much too busy for me."
8. Kate: "Have sneakerheads really changed that much? I'm not sure."

**GRAMMAR** → G9, p. 177

"I moved to Hong Kong in 2010."
→ He said (that) he had moved …

"I've lived in the city for a long time."
→ He said (that) he had lived in the city …

1. Jeff said (that) he had enjoyed the article. He added (that) he had already read a lot about Hong Kong.

b) Choose four statements from the text on page 70 that are in direct speech. Rewrite them as reported speech.

## 10 ( YOUR TURN ) An online comment → M Peer correction, p. 181 → S10, p. 148

77/8

Write a comment for an online forum. What do you think about the article on page 70? Write 120 words.
Include:
- what you found interesting,
- what you disagree with and
- any questions you have.

I thought that was a very interesting …
You wrote that … But most people …
I agree / disagree with …
You said that … But I would never …
I don't understand why …
I can see why …
One thing I'd like to know …
Could you suggest where …

**WRITING SKILLS**

When you comment on an online article or blog, always give reasons to support your opinion. Don't just write that something is 'wonderful' or 'interesting' or write 'You're wrong'. If you disagree, say why and include new information. Make your point clearly.

I can write an online comment.

# For a cleaner Hong Kong

2,18 78/1 **1** ( READING ) **Read the dialogue.** → M Dramatic reading, p. 180

*Rachel Ho is the host of the TV programme* Hong Kong Conversations. *Tonight she is talking to Peter Lai, an engineer and expert on renewable energy.*

**Rachel:** The Hong Kong skyline is one of the city's biggest sights. You see photos of it everywhere in brochures. But we don't get that stunning view of the city's skyscrapers very often any more because of the terrible air pollution. On bad days we can't see the skyscrapers at all because of the smog! The traffic, the ships from all over the world and our coal power plants are causing the heavy pollution of our air. My guest this evening is an expert on future technology and the environment, Peter Lai. He is going to tell us about several options for dealing with this problem. Hello Peter, thanks for being here.

**Peter:** Thanks for having me.

**Rachel:** Air pollution has become such a big problem in this city that more and more people are wearing masks to protect themselves. So what can we do about it?

**Peter:** One answer to the problem is to save energy. If we use less energy, our power plants won't have to produce so much electricity. But in the long run, I think it'll be more important to increase the amount of clean energy. Of course, we're already taking small steps in this area with individual buildings.

**Rachel:** Can you explain that to our audience, please?

**Peter:** I'll give you an example. At present I'm advising a school here in Hong Kong. The headteacher wanted to talk to me about options to make the school more eco-friendly. One is to install solar panels there. I've also suggested motion sensors so that the lights only go on when rooms are actually used. The problem, as always, is money. I'm going to talk to the headteacher again in a few days to see what we can do.

**Rachel:** As you've talked about solar panels: Are there any new developments in that area that could be useful?

**Peter:** Yes, there are. Transparent solar cells. I think they're a great innovation. They can be used in windows and will convert light into electricity – and there are a lot of windows in Hong Kong's skyscrapers.

**Rachel:** Are there also any new ideas around to help reduce the pollution from traffic?

**Peter:** Sure. I think the city will also use new technologies to reduce exhaust fumes. I hope we'll have PRT pods quite soon. If you ask me, we won't take buses or trains in the future. Instead we'll travel around the city in something like ski lifts, ten metres above the ground. I believe we have a picture of what they'll look like. … Yes, there.

PRT – Personal Rapid Transit

Pods – the size of cars but without drivers – will pick up and drop off passengers. The traffic under them won't need to stop, so there will be fewer traffic jams. And they will help improve the quality of our air because they will use renewable energy.

Rachel: One last question: If you could change one thing in the city and money wasn't a problem, what would you do?

Peter: Well, my favourite idea is to cover all the roofs with grass and plants. They reduce $CO_2$ and absorb pollution. It would have a positive effect on the air quality and the climate in our city – and it would make Hong Kong a nicer and greener place too.

Rachel: Yes, just imagine the view of the city from the air, with all those green roofs! Thank you, Peter, for your time.
Tune in again next week, when I'm talking to a blogger who writes about eco-friendly inventions.

**Language tip** → G 11, p. 179

Next week I'm talking to a blogger.

**CULTURE**

Hong Kong gets its electricity mostly from fossil fuels: about half of the energy is generated with coal, and about 20 % comes from gas. Hong Kong has no nuclear power plants, but nuclear power is imported from mainland China. Renewable energy is at about 2 %. Where does your country get its energy from?

## 2 Which sentence describes best what the text is about (A, B or C)? Say why.

A The problem of air pollution and smog in Hong Kong is getting worse.
B New technology in Hong Kong – PRT pods and transparent solar cells are the future.
C How technology can help reduce pollution in Hong Kong in the future.

## 3 Right or wrong? Give evidence from the text. → M Bus stop, p. 180

1. On some days smog hides the skyscrapers.
2. Peter is advising a school on safety rules.
3. Solar cells in windows could be a way to use the skyscrapers to produce energy.
4. Pods will probably cause traffic jams.
5. Rachel wants to know Peter's favourite idea if money wasn't a problem.
6. Peter wants to build more parks.

## 4 What's the verb?

a) Find the verb in the text with the same meaning. → ○ p. 101

78/2a)

1. to be the reason for something
2. to use less of something
3. to create something
4. to make something more or bigger
5. to make something smaller
6. to make something better

b) Find the synonyms of these verbs in a). → V Verbs for effects, p. 208

78/2b)
79/3

decrease | raise | generate | conserve

## 5 ( SPEAKING ) Talk about a Hong Kong survey on green living. → S9, p. 147

a) Analyse the chart. Say what it tells you about young people's ideas for green living. → ○ p. 101

79/4-5

### What can we do to lead greener lives? (2017)

Answers from young people aged 12 – 25

| | |
|---|---|
| Have short showers, not baths | 40 % |
| Produce less food waste | 55 % |
| Don't throw plastic bottles away | 75 % |
| Don't use plastic cups and plates | 30 % |
| Wash clothes with cold water | 55 % |

reduce · save · increase · recycle · …

The chart shows …
40 % of the people think we can save water if we …
Most of them want to … the amount of …
… think we should / shouldn't …

b) Compare the bar chart from a) with this older chart from 2014.

### What can we do to lead greener lives? (2014)

Answers from young people aged 12 – 25

| | |
|---|---|
| Have short showers, not baths | 35 % |
| Produce less food waste | 55 % |
| Don't throw plastic bottles away | 80 % |
| Don't use plastic cups and plates | 25 % |
| Wash clothes with cold water | 60 % |

Since 2014 the number of people who think … has decreased.
More people thought we should conserve energy by …
…

**STUDY SKILLS**

Charts are a good way to present a lot of different information in a complex way.
To better find and understand the information …
- read the heading: it will give you the basic idea of what the chart is about.
- read all the labels for extra information about the chart.
- look at the numbers, colours and symbols. Find out what each of them can tell you.

## 6 ( LISTENING ) Listen to the radio report about a smog warning. → S5, p. 142

2,19

Listen and choose the right answer. More than one can be correct.

1. The announcement is from **Monday, 9th January** • **Monday, 9th July** • **Tuesday, 9th January.**
2. Pollution levels will be high **this afternoon** • **today and tomorrow** • **all week.**
3. In the morning the pollution level was already at **7** • **10** • **8.**
4. The government advised people to **stay inside** • **go outside** • **not to do outdoor activities.**
5. On Wednesday **the weather will change** • **rain will come** • **the smog will clear.**
6. Pollution increases **during the summer** • **in the autumn months** • **in the winter.**

## Language → G10, p. 178

The city will use new technology to reduce pollution.
We won't take buses or trains in the future.
I'll give you an example.
I'm going to talk to the headteacher in a few days.

Which tenses are these?
When do you use them?

## 7 Complete the sentences.

a) Will-future or going to-future? Put in the verb in the right tense. → ○ p. 101

80/6-7

Tom: Has your family made a decision about Hong Kong yet?
Ida: Yes, my dad —— (1. move) to Hong Kong next month and start a new job there.
Tom: That's cool. Hong Kong sounds like such a fascinating place.
Ida: Yes, I hope he —— (2. like) it.
Tom: Does he plan to stay there for a while?
Ida: Yes, he —— (3. live) there for the next two years.
Tom: Does he already have a place to live?
Ida: No, and I guess it —— (4. be) difficult to find a flat.
Tom: What do you think? —— (5. you, visit) him there?
Ida: Yes, sure. My mum and I —— (6. visit) him in the summer holidays.
Tom: I'd like to talk with him before he leaves. But I'm not sure I have his phone number.
Ida: Wait a second. I —— (7. give) it to you.

*Remember: You can use the going to-future to talk about plans.*

b) Prepare a short dialogue about your plans and hopes after you finish school.

80/8

A: What are you going to … ? – B: I don't know yet. Maybe I'll … What about you? …
A: I'm going to …

## 8 (YOUR TURN) An eco-friendly neighbourhood → V Environment, p. 212

→ S2, p. 139

Think of ideas to make your neighbourhood more eco-friendly. Present them in class.

81/1-2

1. Collect ideas: Make a list of things that you could do to make your neighbourhood more eco-friendly. → M Placemat, p. 182

   Here are some things to think about:
   - solar energy
   - lights
   - coffee shop cups
   - rain water
   - trees
   - local food
2. Discuss: What will the results of each idea be?
3. Agree on which of the ideas is the best.
4. Present your favourite idea to the class.

I can talk about how to make a place more eco-friendly. ✓

# Free media?

1 (SPEAKING) **Think about an event that has been in the news in the last month. Where did you find out about it first? Discuss it with a partner.**

2 (READING) **Read the comment.** → S7, p. 144

2,20

**The truth is out there ... somewhere** – by James Chow
Monday, 6th November 2017

Every day we are surrounded by a never-ending flood of information. Whether you read a newspaper, look at a magazine, listen to the radio or watch TV, there is so much information trying to tell you how the world works. It is like a huge puzzle. How do you know that what you read or hear is true, has not been changed or just invented? The fact is that what you read and see in the media influences the way you look at things.

In an open, democratic society the press and other media are free. This means that journalists and others can publish facts or give their opinion without being threatened or punished by the government. People who read their articles and reports are free to decide what they think. Without this freedom governments can abuse their power and oppress people.

The situation in Hong Kong is special. When Hong Kong was returned to China by the British in 1997, the Chinese government promised that there would still be freedom of the press and other media. So there are still lots of international newspapers. This is very different from the situation in the rest of China, where all information is strongly observed and censored.

In the last few years, however, China has slowly begun to increase its control over the news and the media in Hong Kong. Some publishers of books which are critical of the Chinese government have 'disappeared'. Some journalists have even been attacked on the streets of Hong Kong. Others have lost their jobs, and pro-China journalists have replaced them. These events have made journalists very worried, and now many are afraid to write what they believe to be true.

In China the flow of information on the internet is controlled too. China has been known to close internet sites that it sees as a threat to the

3 **Which of these issues does the text deal with?** → M Think-pair-share, p. 183

A The problem of finding reliable information
B The role of the press in a democracy
C On-the-job training of Hong Kong journalists
D Dangers to the freedom of the press in Hong Kong
E Germany's influence on Chinese media
F The amount of information that is available

4 **Find the examples in the text.**

Find the examples that the author mentions of …
- China's influence on the media in Hong Kong.
- limits to the freedom of speech and of the press in Germany.
- how to deal with huge amounts of information.

system or moral standards. Posts, links and letters are searched for blacklisted words; that means certain words or phrases the government does not allow (e.g. democracy, oppression and human rights). All this could threaten what Hong Kong is used to.

What's the situation like in other countries? Let's look at Germany. I asked a friend, "Do you think the media in Germany is free? Or is there some kind of control too?"

He said, "The freedom of speech and of the press are guaranteed, but there are limits. Glorifying violence or right-wing extremism are some examples. Social media companies check their sites too, and remove these posts."

At the moment, however, there are people here who claim that the media influence people's minds and aren't objective. For example, there is a danger that the media help to spread fear when they report about events like terrorist attacks. Other people believe that the huge flood of information is too much. The problem is that most of it is unfiltered and hard to control. Just think of all the posts on social media sites. Everybody can say things about everything and everybody without having to prove that they're right. So, how do you know the truth? Who do you believe? You have to think critically and you shouldn't take everything for granted. It's important to check different sources of information. I think that's a challenge we are confronted with these days.

To sum up, I can say that in a world where many people have access to all kinds of sources, we should be critical of the information that is presented to us. However, restrictions will not keep people from communicating with each other to find out what is really going on.

## 5 (SPEAKING) Talk about the cartoon.

a) Describe the cartoon. → S20, p. 161

b) How is the cartoon related to the text you read?

## 6 Choose one of these tasks.

82/1
83/2-3

a) Talk about how an event is presented in the news.

1. Choose an event from the news.
2. Look for the same event in two different kinds of media.
3. Compare the texts. Do they have the same information? Are there any differences?
→ S7, p. 144

OR

b) "The news on TV shows disasters, war and violence – people under the age of 18 shouldn't be allowed to watch it."

Write a short essay (150 words) about this statement from your point of view. What are the pros and cons? Give examples.
→ M Writers' conference, p. 183 → S17, p. 156

I can understand a text about the media. ✓

# Cyberbullying – real life stories

INTERNET

Hong Kong International Schools (German edition) 中 / ENG / D

## Cyber-Mobbing: ein weit verbreitetes Problem

LOGIN / REGISTER

1. Ein Teenager aus Wan Chai fand heraus, dass es eine Website gab, auf der Klassenkameraden schlimme Dinge über ihn gepostet hatten. Darin ging es um sein Gewicht und seinen möglichen Tod. Auch Fotos von ihm wurden dort ohne seine Zustimmung veröffentlicht. Die Eltern des Teenagers forderten ein Einschreiten seitens der Eltern der Klassenkameraden. Aber es passierte nichts.

2. Zwei Passagiere im Bus nach Kowloon stritten sich um einen Sitzplatz. Ein anderer Passagier filmte den Streit mit seinem Handy und stellte das Video online. Andere Internetnutzer fanden die Namen der beiden heraus und veröffentlichten sie. Die beiden Streithähne erhielten massive Kritik.

3. Als ein Pärchen aus Sha Tin sich trennte, veröffentlichten sie in einem Onlineforum beleidigende Kommentare über den jeweils anderen. Die Kommentare waren so bösartig, dass ihre Accounts offiziell gelöscht wurden.

4. Einem Teenager aus Tai Po gefiel eine Klassenkameradin sehr. Dieses Mädchen verbrachte viel Zeit mit ihm, wurde aber bald zu seiner ärgsten Feindin. Sie gab vor, ihn zu mögen, aber machte sich online über ihn lustig. Der Junge wechselte die Schule.

> Contact us > FAQ

Last updated: 26/02/2018

**1** Summarise the four examples in English. Write the main points. → S24, p. 167

84/1

**2** Collect ideas. What can you do if someone is being bullied?

**CULTURE**

In Hong Kong, like in many other countries, there isn't a law against cyberbullying.
Some people say a law would limit freedom of speech.
What rules about cyberbullying are there at your school?

I can pass on information about cyberbullying.

# A life in the sky

## 1 Talk about the photo.

a) What do you think living in one of these buildings would be like?

b) Why do you find skyscrapers like these in many cities? Give reasons.

## 2 ( VIEWING ) Watch the film.

8

a) Watch the film without sound. Answer the questions.
1. What colour is the T-shirt of the man with the glasses?
2. What's the speed limit (mph) on a street in Hong Kong?
3. Which floor do the woman and her daughter live on?
4. How many umbrellas are there next to the family's fridge?

b) Watch the film again with sound and finish the sentences.
1. Hong Kong was built on the side of a — .
2. You can live most of your life without walking on the — .
3. Jinjin Tong's family lives — metres up.
4. About — people live in each block.

c) Sum up the film in one sentence. → S6, p. 143

**CULTURE**

There are a number of unusual ways to get around in Hong Kong. You can use the 100-year-old tram line or take the cable car up to Victoria Peak, Hong Kong's most famous mountain. Or you can use a system of escalators to get from one building to the next without having to go outside. What's the easiest way to get from one place to another where you live?

**VIEWING SKILLS**

The film moves from one shot to the next very quickly. The camera also often tilts upwards when we see the skyscrapers. This shows what life is like in an exciting, modern city.

## 3 ( SPEAKING ) Talk about living in a big city.

a) Find two or three reasons for living in a city like Hong Kong. Your partner collects two or three reasons against it.

b) Would you like to live in a big city like Hong Kong? Why or why not? Discuss. → S21, p. 162

You can buy / learn / work / spend time (with) / enjoy / go to / meet / …

I don't think so. / No, that's …! / Really? But you would have to …

I can understand a film about living in Hong Kong. ✓

## Checklist

I can understand information about Hong Kong. 85

I can write an online comment.

That was interesting. • I've already read a lot about .... • I wanted to ask if .... • You wrote that .... • I agree / disagree. • I can see why .... 85

I can talk about how to make a place more eco-friendly.

... options to deal with this problem. • One answer is to .... • ... increase the amount of ... • .... reduce the pollution from ... • We can save water if we .... 86

I can understand a text about the media. 86

I can pass on information about cyberbullying. 87

I can understand a film about living in Hong Kong.

# (TASK) A slide show

You will give a presentation called 'Life in the future', using a special way of presenting. You're only allowed a certain number of slides and a limited time for talking. Present different aspects of the topic. Work with a partner.

## Step 1

### Follow these rules.

- 10 slides
- 1 photo or picture per slide
- No diagrams, no text on the slides
- 20 seconds per slide
- Total time of presentation: 3 min 20 sec

*This way of presenting things is fast-paced. You must be well-prepared. Notes are usually not allowed.*

## Step 2

### Read and answer the questions.

1. Read the 10 questions on the right.
2. Think about answers for each question. Make notes.
3. Which question would you like to talk about first? Which one last?
4. Decide who will present each aspect.

**Questions about our future**
- What will school be like?
- Where and how will we work?
- How will we travel?
- What will we eat?
- How will we live?
- How will we produce energy?
- What will we do in our free time?
- How will we communicate?
- What will we wear?
- Where and how will we go shopping?

## Step 3

### Prepare your presentation.

Find a photo or picture for each slide. Remember that the slides should not have any words on them.

**STUDY SKILLS**

Don't use photos or pictures that have lots of small details. Make sure the message is clear.

## Step 4

### Practise your speech. → M Read and look up, p. 182

Practise again and again. Start with one slide at a time. Then combine more slides until you feel comfortable and safe and know your presentation by heart.

*Use a stopwatch to watch the time and to see how much you can say in 20 seconds.*

**SPEAKING SKILLS**

Make notes for each slide. Use your notes the first time you practise, but try to use the notes less each time. Your goal is to do the presentation without notes.

## Step 5

### Give your presentation and give feedback to others.

Give your presentation. Listen to other presentations. Which one did you like best? Why?
→ M Tip top, p. 183 → S23, p. 166

2,21-25

# Where east meets west → S7, p. 144

## 1. History

Hong Kong's history is a very turbulent one. In the 15th century the Portuguese arrived and started trading with the Chinese. As usual the peace didn't last long. After some fights both sides stopped trading. At the end of the 17th century the British came and started doing business. Hong Kong became British after the Opium Wars in the middle of the 19th century. It then slowly grew to become a world centre for business and trade. In 1997 Hong Kong was returned to China but kept British law.

## 2. Languages

There are two official languages in Hong Kong, English and Chinese. About half the population can understand basic English. All the universities use English, and many schools teach some of their subjects in English.
Most people from Hong Kong speak Cantonese. Cantonese is different enough from the official Chinese language (Mandarin) to sound like a foreign language.

## 3. Architecture

Hong Kong is a world centre for modern architecture. The city is changing all the time. In the centre only a few historical buildings remain. Most of the old houses have been knocked down to make room for new buildings.
But from time to time you also come across traditional bamboo scaffolding around these modern skyscrapers. Bamboo is used because it is light and flexible, so it doesn't break in a storm.
The Hong Kong skyline is not only spectacular – it's also quite unusual (at least in the eyes of Westerners). Some of the skyscrapers have big, square 'holes' in them. Why the holes? The Chinese believe in 'feng shui', a system of laws which architects must follow when they design a building. It is believed that dragons live in the hills behind the city, and they need the holes to find their way to the sea to drink and wash.
Many buildings in Hong Kong don't have a fourth floor, or perhaps any floors with the number four in them. This is because four is an unlucky number in Cantonese culture. It sounds like the word for 'to die'. Of course in Western superstition, the unlucky number is 13. So some buildings in Hong Kong have neither a fourth floor nor a 13th floor.

## 4. Entertainment

The film industry is big in Hong Kong. The city became world famous for its kung fu films in the 1970s. Hong Kong films often borrow ideas from Chinese culture and most of the time they don't follow a particular genre. You may also find horror, comedy, romance, fight scenes and songs all in one film. Some Hong Kong actors, like Jackie Chan, and directors, like John Woo, have become internationally famous and even moved to Hollywood.

## 5. Festivals

A good time to visit Hong Kong is during the city's biggest and most colourful festival, the Chinese New Year. The celebration lasts 15 days. On the first day people clean their houses and then eat a big family meal. Instead of presents under a tree, children are given red envelopes ('lai see' in Cantonese) with money inside.
The festival ends with the Lantern Festival, where you can see thousands of lanterns in different colours and shapes.
But European festivals are also celebrated. Christmas, for example, is a public holiday in Hong Kong. There are Christmas trees, beautiful light decorations and Christmas songs everywhere.

**1** Make a table of the differences that can be found in Hong Kong.

| | East | West |
|---|---|---|
| Language | Chinese, Cantonese | … |
| Architecture | … | … |
| … | … | … |

**2** Research 'Cantopop' on the internet as another example where east meets west. Write a short info text about it like the ones above. → S3, p. 140

to remain – *bleiben*; to knock down – *niederreißen, abreißen*; scaffolding – *Gerüst*; light – *leicht*; square – *quadratisch*; dragon – *Drache*; superstition – *Aberglaube*; neither … nor – *weder … noch …*; entertainment – *Unterhaltung*; lantern – *Laterne*; shape – *Form*

Unit 1, p. 13

## 4 Sort the words.

Copy the table and sort the words into the three groups. → M Peer correction, p. 181

ignore ✓ | politeness | accept | rude ✓ | respect (2x) ✓ | tolerate | polite | rudeness | compromise (2x) | tolerant | acceptable | ignorant | respectful

| Verbs | Nouns | Adjectives |
| --- | --- | --- |
| ignore | … | … |
| … | respect | … |
| … | … | rude |
| … | … | … |

- *-ance, -ness, -ion* are the endings of nouns
- *-ise* can be the ending of nouns and verbs
- *-able, -ant, -ful* are the endings of adjectives
- some words are the same as a verb and as a noun

Unit 1, p. 13

## 5 (SPEAKING) Talk about the cartoon. → S20, p. 161

Describe what you can see in the cartoon. Then discuss it with a partner. The words in Ex. 4 can help you.

" DON'T YOU REALIZE YOU'RE INSIDE A CHURCH ? ! TAKE OFF YOUR HAT ! "

Who are the people in the cartoon?
Where are they?
What are they wearing?
What are they doing?
What do you think about their behaviour?
Do you like the cartoon? Why? / Why not?

You can start like this:
In this picture you can see a priest, … .

You can find help on how to describe a picture on page 161.

Unit 1, p.14

## 6 (SPEAKING) What happened to the tourists?

Make sentences with modal auxiliaries. Use the simple past.

1. Sam • not be allowed to • swim • in the river.

He • be able to • escape • the crocodile.

He • have to • call • the emergency service.

2. Anna • not be allowed to • drive fast • on the road.

She • not be able to • see • the kangaroo.

She • not have to • go far • to the hotel.

1. Sam wasn't allowed to swim in the river.

Unit 1, p.15

## 8 (WRITING) Complete Len's post from Sydney to his friend in Hong Kong.

Put the modal auxiliaries in the right tense.

On our trip last year we (1) were able to (be able to) spend three days in Sydney before we took the plane back to Hong Kong. Sydney Harbour Bridge was amazing! I (2) ___ (be able to) do the Bridge Climb with my dad, but my sister is only seven, so she (3) ___ (not be allowed to) come. I (4) ___ (have to) leave my phone at the bottom and I (5) ___ (not be allowed to) take any photos.
We all loved Sydney so much. The whole family agreed that we (6) ___ (have to) come again. But if we come back next year, we (7) ___ (not be able to) climb the bridge – it's too expensive. Next time we'll just walk over the bridge. That won't cost anything. And we (8) ___ (be able to) take photos of the fantastic view from there too.

## 2 Make a checklist.

1,6

**A**

### Receptionist, Waterfront Hotel ☆☆☆☆

We are offering a job in one of the largest hotels in Melbourne, one of the most amazing cities in the country.

**Are you able to:**

- work in a team,
- deal with guests from different cultures,
- organize efficiently and communicate well,
- work weekends and holidays?

We require:

- work experience in customer service.
- intermediate computer skills.
- a native speaker or a Certificate in Advanced English.

We offer:

- a good salary and on-the-job training.

Send your CV and letter of application to Dan Pitt: dan.pitt@thewaterfront.au

**B**

**Notes for my CV:**

Personal statement
Education
Skills
Work experience
Interests
References

**CULTURE**

English CVs don't have a photo of the candidate, but they often include a personal statement (p. 153). What do German CVs look like?

**C**

E-MAIL

Dear Mr Pitt,

I would like to apply for the job as receptionist at the Waterfront Hotel. I have one and a half years of work experience in this field. As a student in Cork (Republic of Ireland), I worked part time in a B & B for guests from all over the world, so I am easily able to deal with people from different countries. In my current temporary job in Australia I have six months of experience as a receptionist at the Flying Emu Lodge, where I check in guests and work as part of a small team. Now I am looking for more permanent work as part of a larger team.

In addition to my work experience I have strong skills in communication, customer service and administration. I also have good computer skills.

I think that I work more efficiently than most people my age because of my experience, and my skills qualify me for this job.

Please find my CV attached. I look forward to hearing from you.

Yours sincerely,

Amy Wynner

Compare Amy's application with the job ad. Does she address all the points?

| Job ad | Amy |
| --- | --- |
| Teamwork? | ✓ |
| Guests from different cultures? | ✓ |
| | |

Unit 1, p. 17

## ○ 3 Name these jobs.

Match the pictures with the right job.

carpenter | chef | hairdresser | electrician | nurse | travel agent

1

2

3

4

5

6

Unit 1, p. 18

## ○ 6 ( SPEAKING ) Compare the working conditions.

Use the adjectives to compare the working conditions.

large | long | high | experienced

| | Helen, waitress | Lisa, shop assistant | Derek, electrician |
|---|---|---|---|
| Journey to work | 15 minutes | 45 minutes | 30 minutes |
| Team of ... | 4 people | 10 people | 2 people |
| Salary | A$30,000 | A$40,000 | A$45,000 |
| Has worked for | 1 year | 2 years | 1 month |

A: Derek has a longer journey to work than Helen. Lisa has the longest journey to work.
B: Helen's team is — than Derek's. Lisa's team is — .
A: Lisa's salary is — than Helen's. Derek's salary is — .
B: Helen is more experienced than — . Derek is — .

Unit 1, p. 19

## ○ 8 Compare the people who applied for a travel agent's job in Perth.

Look at the interviewer's table and complete the sentences.

adjective needed
adverb needed

| | Oliver | Emily | Jack |
|---|---|---|---|
| Computer skills | *** | ** | * |
| Reliable | ** | * | *** |
| Communication skills | * | ** | *** |
| Speaks Chinese fluently | * | ** | *** |
| Experienced | *** | * | ** |
| Works efficiently | *** | * | ** |

1. Emily's computer skills are better than Jack's, but Oliver has the best computer skills.
2. Jack is probably the most —— , but —— is —— than Emily.
3. Emily has —— communication skills than Oliver, but Jack … .
4. Emily speaks Chinese —— than —— , but …
5. Jack is —— than Emily, but …
6. Oliver works the —— , but …

Unit 2, p. 31

## ○ 4 Practise holiday words.

Sort the words into the table.

hostel ✓ | sunshine | departure | hurricane | luxury resort | thunder and lightning | passport | delay | holiday flat | boarding

| Accommodation | Travelling | Climate and weather |
|---|---|---|
| hostel | | |
| | | |

Look up the words that you don't know in the dictionary on pages 216–304.

Unit 2, p. 31

Read one of the sentences below before each announcement.

## 5 ( LISTENING ) Listen to the airport announcements. → S5, p. 142

1,18

Choose the right answer.

1. Excuse me, but I didn't catch that. Which gate does the New York flight leave from?
   D7 • G1 • A1
2. Are you flying to London too? When can I begin boarding with my two small children?
   now • in ten minutes • in half an hour
3. We're looking for Gate 3. We're very late. Do you know when the gate closes?
   in about 5 minutes • in about 10 minutes • in about 45 minutes
4. Excuse me, but we're waiting for a flight from the Bahamas. Did she say how late it is?
   45 minutes • half an hour • one hour
5. Did you understand that? When does the flight to Miami leave?
   3:50 • 5:30 • 2:40

Unit 2, p. 32

## 7 Rewrite the sentences.

Which sentences can you say without who or which?

1. The receptionist **who told** us to visit the island was a really nice guy.
2. This is a photo of the plane **which we flew** in.
3. Look at the dolphins **which we saw** in the distance.
4. The carnival **which we watched** takes place every year.
5. We met a dancer there **who taught** us a few moves.
6. The ferry **which took** us back was very slow.

**GRAMMAR** → G3, p. 171

That's the plane (which) we took.

That's the guy who danced at the carnival.

Unit 2, p. 33

## 8 ( WRITING ) Rewrite Steve's story about his holidays.

Join the sentences to make relative clauses with who / which / that for the underlined words.

One day (1) I did a **diving course** in the Bahamas. The **diving course** was the most exciting part of my trip.
Before we started, (2) the **instructor** told us the safety rules. The **instructor** was a funny guy.
(3) He told some **jokes**. The **jokes** helped us to feel a bit more relaxed.
He led us down to the beach.
(4) Then we had to get into a **boat**. The **boat** didn't look very safe.
But we arrived at our destination without any problems.
Suddenly (5) I saw a **turtle** in the water. The **turtle** was huge.
Soon (6) we arrived at a **shipwreck**. **It** had sunk in a storm 100 years before.
I swam towards it. What I saw next took my breath away …

Start with the underlined words.

1. The diving course which I did in the Bahamas was the most exciting part of the trip.

## 2 Work with the text.

1,19

BLOG

# Growing up in paradise

17/02/2017

by Tara Clarke

This is me, Tara. At the moment I'm finishing my last year at high school.

At eight o'clock last night I was doing my homework when I heard the noise of a gun in our street. 'That's Kingston for you,' I thought. I've got to say that I'll be really happy to get out of here. You see, I'm going to leave Jamaica soon because I'm one of the lucky few who were accepted for a nursing course in Toronto, Canada. Isn't that exciting?

I know, I know: Tourists think Jamaica is the perfect paradise. Sunny beaches, delicious food, happy people – that's all most people see. But the easy life they imagine doesn't exist for most of us here. My part of town is a very poor area. Violence breaks out regularly between street gangs; there are shootings almost every day, and drugs are sold nearly everywhere. It really is a constant struggle for everyone who lives here.

However, I also have some positive things here that help me to keep strong – like my family. In a family you help each other. The way I see it, there are special bonds between family members. My parents will be part of my life forever. They'll always give me advice even though I'm an adult now. And everyone else is involved too, including all my uncles and aunts. For example, when I was a child, my aunt Serena took care of me while my mum was working. But, of course, family can also be complicated. Jamaican families can be very big. Traditionally, they expect you to get a job, find a partner, marry and start a family. I'm not sure that's what I want in life.

And then there are the friendships I have in our community. Like many Jamaicans I go to church, and religion is very important to me. My church offers many free-time activities for disadvantaged teenagers, and I often take part in these as a counsellor. I think my faith helps me to be a strong and confident person.

So now I'm wondering what living in Canada will be like, so far away from my family, my friends and my community. I'll let you know as soon as I find out.

*Mi soon farwud, bless up.* (I'll be back soon, have a nice day.)

**Comments:**

**Layla:** 18/02/2017 at 6:09 a.m.

I think education is a privilege here, not a right. My family couldn't afford to send all of us to high school. The fees were too high.

**Danielle:** 18/02/2017 at 12:15 p.m.

I know what you're talking about. Life in a family can be difficult. My brother came out as gay. What a shock to our family! Like most families here they are really conservative and have old-fashioned values.

**Frankie:** 18/02/2017 at 9:15 p.m.

I'll probably leave Jamaica next year too. On the one hand, I want to stay in Jamaica because I'm proud of it. On the other hand, I need a well-paid job.

Answer the questions.

1. Who is Tara?
2. Why does she want to leave Jamaica?
3. What does Tara say about family life in Jamaica?
4. Why is the church important to Tara?
5. What problems do Layla, Danielle and Frankie write about?

*Look at the underlined parts of the text to find the information. But when you give your answer, try to do it in your own words.*

Unit 2, p. 35

## 3 (SPEAKING) Talk about values.

What do you think is more important? Give one reason. → M Think-pair-share, p. 183

1. friendship or family?
2. wealth or health?
3. happiness or success?
4. love or independence?
5. respect or power?
6. fitting in or standing out?

1. Family is more important to me because my family will always be there.

In my opinion … is more important than … because … .
I believe that … is much more important because … .
To me … is more important because … .
I can't really say. I think both are important because … .
I don't think … and … are very different because … .
I don't think that either … or … are important because … .
I don't really care about … because … .

Unit 2, p. 36

## ○ 5 (SPEAKING) What's happening in Kingston at the moment? → S20, p. 161

Describe the picture with a partner. Take turns.

get up | sell | walk to | wait for | feed | ask

A: A woman and three children are walking to church.
B: A young man —— .
A: A woman —— her baby at the breakfast table.
B: A poor man —— people for money.
A: A young man —— something to another man at a street corner.
B: An old man and an old woman —— the bus.

Unit 2, p. 37

*I / he / she → was reading*
*we / you / they → were reading*

## ○ 7 (WRITING) Write sentences about problems in Jamaica.

Write these notes from a report about problems in Jamaica as sentences.

At the time the report was written …

1. more than a million people • live • in poverty
   more than **a million people** were living in poverty.
2. **poverty** • grow • fast
3. **shootings** • happen • almost every day
4. **more people** • use • drugs • every year
5. but **many young people** • take part in • church activities • too
6. and **many teenagers** • look after • younger • brothers and sisters • to help their parents
7. **some parents** • struggle • to feed • their children
8. **many people** under 30 • think about • leaving • the island

Unit 3, p. 52

## ○ 4 Work with words to describe social differences.

Make pairs of opposites with the adjectives.

privileged | equal | underprivileged | fair
poor | rich | unequal | unfair

*Some opposites are formed by adding a syllable like un-, in-, im-, under- at the beginning.*

Unit 3, p. 52

## ○ 5 (WRITING) Write about social differences.

What statements can you make about South African society with the information from Ex. 3b)? Write about 60 words.

In South African society there are different groups of people.
There are people of different … .
Some people are … . Others are … .
On the one hand, … . On the other hand, … .
…

*You can write about …*
- *social status: poor / middle class / rich*
- *colour: black / white*
- *live in: gated communities / townships*
- *school: private school / state school / often leave school early to earn money …*

Unit 3, p. 53

## ○ 7 Say what the people had done or hadn't done before the accident happened.

Put in the verbs. Use the past perfect.

1. Before the driver picked up the students, he had cleaned (clean) the bus.
2. He —— (listen) to the news on the radio before he went to pick up the rugby players.
3. Piet and his friends —— (have) lunch before they left the school building.
4. Piet —— (send) his dad a message just before the bus arrived.
5. Lefa —— (be) at the corner for a few minutes when he saw the accident.
6. His bus to work —— (not arrive) when the car hit the bus.
7. Kagiso —— (not tell) her daughter about the bad news yet when the accident happened.

*past perfect: had + past participle*
*You can find the past participle of irregular verbs on pages 213–215.*

Unit 3, p. 54

## 2 Work with the text.

2,9

Carlie: This is radio Cape Gold FM. It's four o'clock and you're listening to *Exploring the wild* with me, Carlie Keita. Our guest today is Tony Okonwo, a ranger at Kruger National Park. Welcome Tony. Nice to have you here.

Tony: Hi Carlie. Thanks for inviting me.

Carlie: Our listeners are very interested to hear what work is like in such a great park. Would you tell us about your job? What do you like about it?

Tony: Being a ranger in one of the most amazing parks in the world is fantastic. There are wide, endless plains and the land is quite flat, with only a few hills and no mountains. But most of all I've always been interested in our wildlife and I've always wanted people to learn more about how to protect it.

Carlie: Tony, what's special about the park?

Tony: Kruger National Park was South Africa's first national park. It was named after President Paul Kruger when it was created in 1926. And it has been a success ever since. Its goal is to protect and conserve the South African wildlife. Evidence of early human life has been found in the park too, like rock art. So visitors can also look back at the history of mankind.

Carlie: How did tourism in the park develop?

Tony: The value of tourism wasn't really recognised before 1926. In the next year the first three tourist cars came in. After that roads and visitor centres were built, fences were put up and guides were hired to show tourists around.

Carlie: There were problems too, right? Weren't animals hunted before the park was founded?

Tony: Yes, they were. A lot of elephants were killed for their ivory. Even today we face lots of challenges. But many rules regulate what's happening in the park. Visitors have to stay in their cars for their own safety, for example.

Carlie: Most people come to see the 'Big Five': the elephant, the lion, the leopard, the rhino and the buffalo. Where does that name come from?

Tony: The name was first introduced by big game hunters. It was difficult for them to hunt these large animals. And once an animal was hurt, it could attack the hunters. We rangers also think that these five animals are the most dangerous ones. Therefore, we treat them with the respect and the caution they deserve. So, a lot is done to save and protect the wildlife of the park. We do our best to take action against poaching too.

Carlie: Poaching will be part of our next edition. Tony will join us again then. Time's up. Thanks a lot, Tony. He's going to be in our chatroom where you can ask him questions. We'll leave you with that. Now over to James and the news.

Take notes about these four aspects of the national park.

1. landscapes
2. history
3. tourism
4. animals

Unit 3, p. 55

## ○ 3 Describe the landscapes. → S20, p. 161

Describe the photos with the help of these words.

1

**mountain range:**

rocks / snow / high

2

**coast:**

sea / rocks / beach

3

**forest:**

many trees / green / big area

4

**plain:**

flat / field / some trees

5

**marsh:**

wet land / plants in water / trees

6

**desert:**

sand / dry / heat

Photo 1 shows ... .
In the photo you can see ... .
There is ... . / There are ... .
It looks like ... .

Unit 3, p. 56

## ○ 6 Make sentences about a school safari trip.

Put in the verbs in the passive.

1. Our trip was organized (organize) by Mr Wessels, the Biology teacher.
2. The students — (take) on a tour of the park. The guide was a ranger, Tony Okonwo.
3. The tour was very interesting. All the students' questions — (answer).
4. One student left his hat at the picnic place. It — (find) again later.
5. Lots of photos of the animals — (take) in the park.
6. Some of them — (put) online the next day.
7. One photo — (like) by more than a hundred people.

## Unit 3, p. 57

### 8 ( WRITING ) Rewrite sentences from an interview about the park. → M Peer correction, p. 181

Rewrite the answers to make passive sentences. Start with the underlined words.

1. Q: When did people discover gold in South Africa?
   A: They discovered gold there in the 1860s.
2. Q: Why did the hunters kill elephants?
   A: Hunters killed elephants for their ivory.
3. Q: Did they only kill elephants?
   A: No, they didn't. They also shot lions and other big cats.
4. Q: When did they create the park?
   A: They created the national park in 1926.
5. Q: Are there roads in the park?
   A: Yes, there are. People built hundreds of kilometres of new roads.
6. Q: What else is special about the park?
   A: They also found beautiful rock art in the caves of the park.

1. Gold was discovered there in the 1860s.
2. Elephants were … .
3. Lions and other big cats were also … .
4. The national park was … .
5. Hundreds of kilometres of new roads were … .
6. Beautiful rock art was … .

Rock art from South Africa

## Unit 4, p. 71

### 4 Work with the text.

2,17

INTERNET

**Everyone wants them** by Cindy Chan

Sneakers Street in the heart of a busy Hong Kong shopping district is where Hong Kong's fashionable youth goes to buy their latest sports shoes. Are you trying to get that one super-rare special pair? Then Sneakers Street is where you should look. There is a stunning number of shoes to browse through with rows and rows of sneakers. And sneakerheads want them all. For those who don't know, 'sneakerheads' are people who collect sports shoes. You can see them stand in line for hours or even camp overnight in front of a shop just to buy a particular pair of shoes.

Kenneth Lee (32) is one of those sneakerheads – and also a shop assistant in a Sneakers Street shop. I wanted to find out more about this scene, so I met up with him there and asked him a couple of questions.

Kenneth told me, "Sneakerheads are just a group of people who have the same interest." He claimed that he didn't really look for new sneakers all the time. But he added that he walked by the shop windows of Sneakers Street almost every day. He said, "When I see a new pair that I like, I just go crazy. I feel that I've got to have it right away."

Sneaker culture started in New York in the 1960s. It only became big in Hong Kong in

INTERNET

the 1980s, when hip hop stars and basketball players made sneakers status symbols.
Back then Michael Jordan became the most famous basketball player in the world and then he started his own line of shoes.

"Everyone wanted them," Kenneth explained. "They were a must-have."
He told me that as a kid he had nagged his parents for ages and had saved all his pocket money for months to buy his first pair.
"As a grown-up, I work and make money, so I sometimes buy ten pairs a month."

So I asked him how many pairs he had. He looked at his smartphone, where he keeps a record of everything he buys and sells. He had 297 pairs. He said his girlfriend often complained that there was no more space in their flat.
I wanted to know if he really wore all those shoes. He said that he did. When he buys a brand-new pair, he always takes a photo and he wears them at least once. Then they go back in the original box.
His younger customers are different. Kenneth told me that sneaker culture had changed a lot in the last few years. He said, "Many kids today don't care if the shoes are beautiful; they don't want to wear them anyway." Kenneth explained to me that they only bought the shoes to resell them at five times the original price.
"It's just different, I guess. For them the fun part is the trading. For me it's owning the shoes."

Match the sentence parts to find the answers.

1. Sneakers Street is popular because …
2. A 'sneakerhead' is somebody who …
3. Kenneth Lee is …
4. The two groups which made sneaker culture big in the 1980s were …
5. To be able to afford his first pair, Kenneth …
6. He keeps a record of …
7. Today many younger sneakerheads …

A hip hop stars and basketball players.
B everything he buys and sells.
C you can buy fashionable shoes there.
D only buy shoes to resell them.
E collects sports shoes.
F saved all his pocket money for months.
G a sneakerhead and a shop assistant.

Unit 4, p. 71

## ○ 5 Work with verbs for buying and selling. → S4, p. 141

Match the verbs with the definitions.

1. to save
2. to browse
3. to resell
4. to swap
5. to collect
6. to be able to afford

A to get and keep things of one type
B to buy something and then sell it again
C to walk around a shop and look at things
D to exchange one thing for another
E to have enough money to buy something
F to spend less money than the original price

Unit 4, p. 72

## ○ 8 (SPEAKING) Do a survey about shopping habits and report the results.

Do a survey in your group.

Ask the people in your group these questions.

| Do you … | | |
|---|---|---|
| … ever buy sneakers? | | |
| … own more than five pairs of shoes? | | |
| … spend most of your money on clothes? | | |
| … usually look for clothes online? | | |
| … prefer to browse in shops? | | |
| … have a favourite shop? | | |
| … prefer shopping alone or with friends? | | |

Then report your results to the class:
We asked our classmates if they ever bought sneakers / owned …

*(number)* students said (that) they … often / never / sometimes
— sneakers.
— more than five pairs of shoes.
— for clothes online.
— to browse in shops.
— a favourite shop.
— shopping alone / with friends.

Unit 4, p. 73

## ○ 9 (WRITING) Report how these people reacted to the article.

Rewrite the sentences as reported speech.

1. Jeff: "I enjoyed the article. I've already read a lot about Hong Kong."
2. Rob: "Sneakerheads were already around in the 1960s."
   Rob said (that) sneakerheads … .
3. Linda and Derek: "We have often ordered sneakers online."
   Linda and Derek said (that) they … .
4. Steven: "I've never bought shoes for more than $100."
   Steven said (that) he … .
5. Marc and Julie: "That was interesting. We didn't know anything about that scene."
   Marc and Julie said (that) the text … . They added (that) they … .
6. Neil: "I've always worked hard for my money and I've never wasted it on stuff like that."
   Neil said (that) he … .
7. Fran: "I've only been to Sneakers Street once. It was much too busy for me."
   Fran said (that) she … .
8. Kate: "Have sneakerheads really changed that much? I'm not sure."
   Kate asked if … . She added (that) she wasn't … .

1. Jeff said (that) he had enjoyed the article. He added (that) he had already read a lot about Hong Kong.

**GRAMMAR** → G9, p. 177

"I moved to Hong Kong in 2010."
→ He said (that) he had moved …

"I've lived in the city for a long time."
→ He said (that) he had lived in the city …

Unit 4, p. 75

## 4 What's the verb?

Find the verb in the text on pages 74–75 with the same meaning.

1. to be the reason for something *(lines 1–9)*
2. to use less of something *(lines 15–25)*
3. to create something *(lines 15–25)*
4. to make something more or bigger *(lines 15–25)*
5. to make something smaller *(lines 46–55)*
6. to make something better *(lines 56–61)*

Unit 4, p. 76

## 5 (SPEAKING) Talk about a Hong Kong survey on green living. → S9, p. 147

Analyse the chart. Say what it tells you about young people's ideas for green living.

**What can we do to lead greener lives? (2017)**

Answers from young people aged 12–25

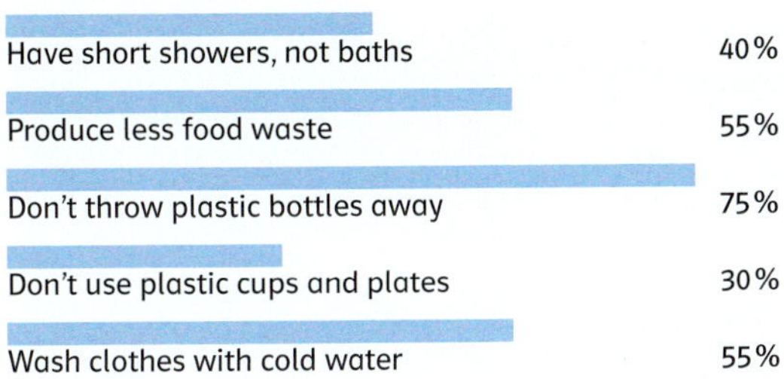


*First say what the chart is about.*
"The chart shows young people's ideas for …"

*Then find the information in the chart and present it in your own words.*
*These phrases can help you:*
"40% of the people think we can save water if we have … instead of … ."
"Most of them want to reduce the amount of …"
"… think we should recycle …"
"… say we shouldn't use …"
"… think we can save energy if we wash …"

reduce · save · increase · recycle · …

Unit 4, p. 77

## 7 Complete the sentences.

Remember:
You can use the going to-future to talk about plans.

Will-future or going to-future? Choose the right verb form.

Tom: Has your family made a decision about Hong Kong yet?
Ida: Yes, my dad **will move** • **is going to move** (1.) to Hong Kong next month and start a new job there.
Tom: That's cool. Hong Kong sounds like such a fascinating place.
Ida: Yes, I hope he **will like** • **is going to like** (2.) it.
Tom: Does he plan to stay there for a while?
Ida: Yes, he **will live** • **is going to live** (3.) there for the next two years.
Tom: Does he already have a place to live?
Ida: No, and I guess it **will be** • **is going to be** (4.) difficult to find a flat.
Tom: What do you think? **Will you visit** • **Are you going to visit** (5.) him there?
Ida: Yes, sure. My mum and I **will visit** • **are going to visit** (6.) him in the summer holidays.
Tom: I'd like to talk with him before he leaves. But I'm not sure I have his phone number.
Ida: Wait a second. I **will give** • **am going to give** (7.) it to you.

# Test practice

uc7j5b

## A Listening

You will hear four Australian teenagers on a radio show. They are talking about their plans after leaving school. You will hear the recordings twice.

2,26 **1 Listen to part 1 and match the teenagers with the right plans. There are more plans than teenagers.**

Katie

Max

Lynn

Lucas

A Become a doctor
B Work in a hotel for six months
C Go on a trip for six months getting work in different countries
D Work in a school for children with special needs
E Travel for a year before going to university
F Work in a hospital in Brisbane

2,27 **2 Listen to part 2. Choose the correct answer.**

1. Katie's mum …

a) is a special needs teacher.
b) can't hear well.
c) can't see well.
d) likes photography.

2. Max …

a) likes school.
b) is going to do Biology.
c) won't find a place at university.
d) has a lot of money.

3. Max's friend …

a) is from Europe.
b) is a crew member on a ship.
c) was a crew member on a ship.
d) doesn't like his co-workers.

4. Lynn …

a) doesn't like working with people.
b) isn't good at Maths.
c) became a doctor at an early age.
d) will need good grades.

5. Lucas …

a) is from Brisbane.
b) doesn't like hard work.
c) is going to work in a big hotel.
d) will help the breakfast staff.

6. When Lucas comes back, he will …

a) know what he wants to do.
b) have no money.
c) go surfing.
d) listen to the radio.

## B Reading

# Work and travel in Australia

**An online guide**

Would you like to visit Australia? Would you love to see the outback and the Great Barrier Reef? But you're worried that it could be too far away and too expensive to get there?

That's how the Australia Working Holiday visa can help you. It gives young people between 18 and 30 years of age the chance to fund the adventure of a lifetime, to extend their stay for up to 24 months and to get to know Australia. More than 200,000 young people get one every year.

There are a few basic requirements[1]. You have to apply for the working visa outside of Australia before you arrive and you need to show that you have enough money to live until you find a job.

Because the purpose[2] of the visa is mainly to support your extended holiday, you are not allowed to work at one job for more than six months.

What type of work can you expect to find? A lot of jobs are on farms or cattle stations. Many farms in the outback are 100 kilometres away from the nearest neighbour or supermarket, so finding workers can be a problem. Also, a lot of the work, such as sheep shearing[3] or fruit picking, is seasonal. Farm work is fun, and you don't need to have experience. But it's hard work and you'll get dirty.

They also need teachers in the outback who live with families on large stations and teach small groups of children. You should like kids and be flexible. Children often help on the station during busy times, so they have lessons in the evenings.

If you're not very interested in the outback, you can find factory jobs, office jobs or catering jobs (waiters, cooks etc.) in towns.

There are many organizations in Australia which support people when they first arrive. They welcome you at the airport, find you a place to stay for the first few nights and prepare orientation meetings about the job market, places to stay, travel and safety. If you wish, they'll support you during your whole trip.

But you won't just come to Australia to work. You'll do some exploring in between jobs, so it's often best to plan what you want to see. This will help you to choose a job location[4] that is best for your travel plans.

Linda (18): I took a job on a sheep station with 6,000 sheep – which is small for Australia. I worked as part of a team with an Italian girl and an English girl. I've never worked so hard in my life, and it really brought us together. I'm so thankful for those three months in the outback.

Sven (19): I worked at the kitchen of a top restaurant in Sydney. Later I worked as a cook on an organic farm[5]. Anyone coming to Australia should work *and* travel. I had some experiences I'll never forget.

1 requirement [rɪ'kwaɪəmənt] – *Voraussetzung*; 2 purpose ['pɜ:pəs] – *Zweck*; 3 sheep shearing ['ʃi:pˌʃɪərɪŋ] – *Schafschur*; 4 location [lə'keɪʃn] – *Standort*; 5 organic farm [ɔ:'gænɪk ˌfɑ:m] – *Biobauernhof*

## 1 True, false or not in the text?

1. You can stay in Australia for two years on a Working Holiday visa.
2. You can apply for the visa in Australia when you arrive.
3. It is easy to find work on farms and cattle stations.
4. There are a lot of organizations who can help you when you arrive.
5. Linda didn't have to work hard.
6. Sven likes organic food.

## 2 Answer the questions with 1–5 words / numbers.

1. How old do you have to be to get a Working Holiday visa?
2. How many young people take part in the programme every year?
3. How long can you work at one job?
4. Where do teachers live in the outback?
5. What kind of help can you get from work and travel organizations? Name three things.
6. In which city did Sven work first?

# C Language

### A, B, C or D? Fill in the gaps.

Young people in Britain often — (1) a so-called 'gap year' between school and college or university. Some go to foreign countries because they want to — (2) different cultures and learn another language. Others are fed up with exams and school rules. They want some free time before — (3) something new. Money is often a real problem, so a working holiday can give young people the chance to pay for their trip even if they have very little money. Australia and New Zealand are popular destinations: wide-open spaces, warm weather and beaches are very — (4) with kids who live in Northern Europe. At the same time — (5) are different types of jobs there for healthy young people who — (6) have a problem with long hours or getting their hands dirty.

| | A | B | C | D |
|---|---|---|---|---|
| 1. | takes | took | take | taken |
| 2. | exchange | experience | express | excite |
| 3. | starting | to start | started | start |
| 4. | famous | popular | appealing | unhappy |
| 5. | their | there | they're | they |
| 6. | do | does | don't | doesn't |

T

## D Writing

Choose one of the following tasks:

### 1 Write about your future plans.

You are in your last year at high school. Write a text about your plans after school for the school magazine.
Include the following information:

- Name
- Age
- Class
- What you like and dislike
- What you are good at / interested in
- Your plans (go to college, find a job, apply for …, travel, …)

Write 100 – 120 words.

Start like this: My name is … .

**OR**

### 2 Write an e-mail to apply for a job.

You joined the work and travel programme in Australia. You are looking for a new job.
Read the job ad and write an e-mail to apply for the job.
Include the following information:

- Name
- Age (18)
- You joined the work and travel programme
- What you are looking for
- What you are good at
- Why you are a good candidate for the job

Write 100 – 120 words.

Start like this: Dear Mrs …,
My name is … .
I'm 18 years old and I joined … .

INTERNET

**Workers needed at Milford Sheep Station**

Our station, with 7,000 sheep, is just two hours from Melbourne.
We are looking for full-time workers to help work with our sheep, including cleaning, feeding and shearing them.
Payment: A$15 an hour and two free meals a day.
There are cottages for accommodation.

If you are used to hard work and like working outside, this could be the perfect job for you! Interested? Please send an e-mail to Mrs Rachel Smith here.

# E Mediation

INTERNET

CALENDAR | NEWS | STUDENTS

## Class trip Year 9

This year all classes in Year 9 are going to the famous Osdown sheep station west of Sydney for their class trip. The station offers a large number of hands-on activities, such as a sheep-shearing competition, feeding the animals or making wool. There will also be a boomerang show. Visitors can ride on horses or watch the sheepdog at work.

**Important details about the trip:**
Date: Wednesday 16th October
Time: 8:00 – 4:00

**Don't forget:**
- Wear your school uniform.
- Meet in the classroom at 7:45.
- Bring water and a packed lunch.
- Switch off your phones.

Du recherchierst mit deinem Freund auf der Internetseite eurer australischen Partnerschule. Ihr stoßt auf ein Infoblatt zu einem geplanten Schulausflug. Dein Freund hat Probleme, den englischen Text zu verstehen. Fasse folgende Punkte auf Deutsch für ihn zusammen:
- Wo befindet sich die Farm?
- Welche Aktivitäten kann man dort machen?
- Wie lange dauert der Ausflug?
- Wann und wo treffen sich die Schüler?
- Was muss man mitbringen?

# F Speaking

**1** Introduce yourself (1 – 2 minutes).

- Name
- Age
- Where you're from
- Family
- School
- Hobbies / interests
- Holiday events
- Future plans
- ...

Start like this: My name is ...

## 2 Information gap activity

**a)** Partner A asks questions and partner B gives the answers.

Partner A:

- Name of camp?
- Where?
- When?
- Who?
- Activities?
- More information?

Partner B:

### Camp Wildwater

Still looking for a cool place for your class trip? Our campsite in the hills just three hours from Melbourne is the perfect adventure for you:

- Sleep outside
- Make a fire
- Explore the forest
- Learn how to canoe
- Go on the camera trail

Open from October to April.
For school groups (ages 14 to 18).

Interested?
Check our website
www.camp.victoria.au

**b)** Now change roles. Partner B asks questions and partner A gives the answers.

Partner B:

- Who?
- Where?
- What?
- Working hours?
- How much money?
- How to apply?

Partner A:

### Deep Water

*– Your fish restaurant in Brisbane –*

We are looking for friendly part-time staff to serve tables from 11:00 to 2:00 in the afternoon and help in the kitchen from 7:00 to 10:00 in the evening. We will pay you A$15 an hour and you will get a uniform and free meals. You should be able to start work next week.

Interested?
Please send an e-mail to:
info@deepwater.au

uc7j5b

## A Listening

You will hear an interview with Hetty Simpson.
She is talking about her job on a boat in the Caribbean.
You will hear the recordings twice.

2,28 **1 Listen to part 1. True or false?**

1. Hetty comes from Bristol.
2. She has worked on the boat for three years.
3. Her job is to keep the ship clean and the equipment in good condition.
4. She never works on Sundays.
5. When everything looks perfect, she can have a break.
6. She usually goes to bed at about ten o'clock.

2,29 **2 Listen to part 2. Answer the questions with 1 – 5 words / numbers.**

1. Where was Hetty when she got the idea for the job?
2. Why was it difficult for her to find the job?
3. How many people work on the boat?
4. For how long do the rich guests usually stay?
5. What does Hetty say about famous guests?
6. Hetty likes her job. What else does she say about it?

## B Reading

**1 What information do these signs give you? Choose A, B, C or D.**

**1**

To all passengers on the boat
NO SMOKING
NO ANIMALS
NO PUSHING

A Smoking is allowed.
B You aren't allowed to eat here.
C Smoking is forbidden.
D You can bring your dog.

**2**

Please do not leave your equipment in the office. There is a garage at the back.

A You can't hire equipment here.
B The school is closed.
C There is no office.
D The garage is for equipment.

**3**

2 FOR THE PRICE OF 1!

Buy one and get a second absolutely free

A You can get free fish and chips here.
B You pay for one and get two plates of food.
C The fish is fresh.
D Only the chips are free.

**4**

Tobago Independence Day
Parade at 8 a.m.
Fireworks at 8 p.m.
ALSO ON LOCAL TV

A You can watch the parade on TV.
B It's expensive.
C The parade is in the evening.
D You can only watch it on TV.

## 2 Match the people 1–5 with the holiday ads A–F on p.110. There are more ads than people.

1. 

Wendy (40) from Edinburgh has two children, Jason (11) and Mark (13). Wendy wants her children to learn to sail. But the boys are not interested; they both prefer to go swimming. It's important for Wendy that the boys have something to do at the end of the day in the hotel.

2. 

Margaret (41) and Bob (40) from Manchester have been married for ten years and they want to celebrate with a holiday they will always remember. Margaret loves nature and wildlife. Bob prefers the sea. He can't dive, but he would like to learn one day.

3. 

Steve (20) is a student from Perth. He loves travelling and he always needs to be busy. He hates just lying on the beach. Two years ago he went diving in the Great Barrier Reef. Last year he went windsurfing[1] in Portugal. He's looking for a different option now. He doesn't like cooking and he isn't interested in music.

4. 

Tobias (25) is a chef at a top restaurant in Cologne. But when he goes on holiday, he doesn't like to think about work. His hobby is music, and he plays the saxophone in a band. He doesn't like hiking.

5. 

Donna (44) is a sales manager[2] at a big company in New Orleans. She works very hard and has a lot of stress at work. When she is able to take a short holiday, she always stays in a very good hotel by the sea. She doesn't do very much there. She just likes to lie on the beach.

1 windsurfing ['wɪndsɜːfɪŋ] – *Windsurfen*; 2 sales manager ['seɪlz ˌmænɪdʒə] – *Verkäufer, Verkäuferin*

**A** **Blue Lagoon Hotel, St Lucia**

The best place to be on the island. This elegant five-star hotel used to be a sugar plantation. Guests have a personal butler to give them everything they need. All the beautiful rooms have a view of the sea. Relax in the amazing spa. If you get tired of lying on the beach, there is excellent snorkelling and diving in the bay.

---

**B** **Chocolate Bay Hotel, Martinique**

The stylish hotel is located in a rainforest on an old cocoa farm about ten kilometres from the town centre. The hotel specialises in cooking. Guests from all over the world come here for Chef Pierre's famous dessert cooking classes. They learn to cook Caribbean recipes with cocoa, bananas, pineapple, lime and rum.

---

**C** **Water Park, Bahamas**

We have non-stop water fun and tons of excitement for the kids! Go on a one-kilometre river ride with waves, tunnels and other surprises. There are five pools, a giant aquarium and activities such as swimming with dolphins and rock climbing. In the evenings there's a club for teenagers with video games, karaoke and dancing. And if you want to get away from it all, you can enjoy miles of sandy beaches and clear blue water.

---

**D** **Adventure Travel, Dominica**

Dominica is the Caribbean's nature island. There are mountains, rainforests, waterfalls and rare parrots – it's a hiker's paradise. We offer hiking holidays for small groups. Our guides will take you along the coast or on forest paths. Most days you will walk for four to five hours, and your bags are transported between hotels.

---

**E** **Study Tours, Cuba Music and Dance**

Havana is one of the best cities for music in the Americas. We will introduce you to Cuban music and dance. You will learn about our music with its rich mix of African and European styles. And you will have lessons in salsa, rumba and more. Enjoy Havana's clubs in the evenings. You will stay with local families.

---

**F** **Forest Inn, Tobago**

Tobago is home to many kinds of birds. The inn is located in the middle of a green forest, so don't be surprised to find birds at your breakfast table. There are bird watching paths everywhere on the hotel grounds. Not far from the Forest Inn you can also find some great places to dive. We have qualified instructors for beginners. So you can dive in the morning and go bird watching in the afternoon. There's something for everyone here.

## 3 True or false? Give evidence from the text. Write the lines.

1. The Blue Lagoon Hotel used to be a train station.
2. The hotel in Martinique is right in the centre of town.
3. At the Water Park you can go rock climbing.
4. Dominica isn't a very good place for hiking.
5. Study Tours offer hotel rooms in Havana.
6. Activities at the Forest Inn include bird watching.

T

## C Language

**1** Find the words in texts 1–5 on p.109 that mean the opposite.

1. it doesn't matter (1)
2. in the morning (1)
3. forget (2)
4. the same (3)

**2** Find the words in texts A–F on p.110 that mean the same.

1. very good (A)
2. permanent (C)
3. coming from this area (E)
4. near (F)

**3** Complete the sentences. Choose a), b), c) or d).

1. Many tourists from Europe and the USA choose a holiday in the Caribbean because of its — climate.
a) awful b) windy c) tropical d) colonial

2. When people think of the Caribbean they often imagine a beautiful, sunny island with a carnival atmosphere where all the — people are singing and dancing in the streets.
a) location b) local c) located d) locate

3. But not everybody who lives on a Caribbean island would — their home that way.
a) describe b) make c) move d) description

4. There are jobs in tourism, but there aren't a lot of other jobs on some of the islands, so many people are — .
a) experienced. b) happy. c) fascinating. d) unemployed.

5. Some of them emigrate to countries like Canada and England to find a job — .
a) ahead. b) apart. c) abroad. d) along.

6. Tourists should try to avoid booking their holiday in the autumn because that is the season for tropical storms when — become more and more of a problem.
a) dolphins b) hurricanes c) tourists d) climate

7. But the Caribbean is still an amazing place to visit, whether you are looking for a quiet time away from it all or whether you are an active type of person looking for — .
a) peace. b) adventure. c) status. d) accommodation.

## D Writing

Choose one of the following tasks:

### 1 Write a hotel review.

On your last holidays you stayed at the Hostel No. 1.
Write a review for checktrips345.com.

- Write where and when you stayed.
- Write what you liked and what you didn't like.
- Would you stay at the hostel again? Why/why not?

Write about 120 words.

**OR**

### 2 Comment on a statement.

"Beach parties should be banned on our island."
Comment on this statement and give your point of view.

Include the following aspects:
- reasons for your opinion and
- examples to support your arguments.

Write about 120 words.

T

## E Mediation

You and a friend are in a tourist office on Grenada in the Caribbean. A German tourist is trying to explain something in German. The woman at the desk doesn't speak German, so you offer to help.

Tourist: Guten Tag. Ich mache eine Rundreise in der Karibik. Ich suche eine Unterkunft für ein paar Tage.
Woman: I'm sorry. I don't understand.
You: *Biete deine Hilfe an. Erkläre, was der Besucher macht und was er möchte.*

Woman: Oh, I see. Do you want to stay in a hotel here in the city or along the coast?
You: *Gib wieder, was sie gefragt hat.*

Tourist: Ich möchte zwei Nächte hier bleiben und dann ein Auto mieten, um die Insel zu erkunden.
You: *Vermittle.*

Woman: All right. I will find a hotel for you first. And then I can arrange a car. What sort of room would you like?
You: *Gib wieder, was die Frau gesagt hat.*

Tourist: Danke. Ich möchte ein Einzelzimmer mit Meeresblick.
You: *Erkläre der Frau, was er gesagt hat.*

Woman: OK. I will show him some pictures of a room in a good hotel and show him where the hotel is on the map. Can you ask him if the room is OK, please?
You: *Erzähle ihm, was sie gesagt hat.*

Tourist: Ja! Es sieht sehr gut aus. Ich nehme es. Wie soll ich bezahlen – bar oder mit Karte?
You: *Vermittle.*

## F Speaking

Your class wants to go on a one-week class trip at the end of Year 9. Look at the holiday destinations and discuss the pros and cons of each with a partner. Agree on one destination. You have five minutes.

1

2

3

uc7j5b

# A Listening

You will listen to the recordings twice.

2,30 **1 Listen to text 1. Choose the right answer.**

You will hear a podcast with five travel and safety tips for South Africa.

1. The best way to cover long distances quickly is to go by — .
   a) train
   b) plane
   c) bus

2. If you want to enjoy nature and talk to local people, it's better to go by — .
   a) bike
   b) plane
   c) bus

3. In South Africa people drive — .
   a) on the left
   b) on the right
   c) wherever they want to

4. When you're in a crowd, pay attention to your personal — .
   a) things
   b) feet
   c) clothes

5. Malaria is a disease that is a problem — South Africa.
   a) all over
   b) anywhere in
   c) in some areas of

6. In the evenings you should wear — to protect yourself from mosquito bites.
   a) T-shirts and long trousers
   b) pullovers and long trousers
   c) T-shirts and shorts

2,31 **2 Listen to text 2. Which topic is NOT mentioned?**

You will hear five short announcements about different topics.

A

B

C

D

E

F

T

# B Reading

## An attack on the beach – a story.

Daniel was in Hout Bay on holiday. It had been a stressful time at school in Leipzig, and he was glad that his exams were all over. Now he could start planning his future. But he couldn't concentrate. Every time he closed his eyes, he only saw books and exam papers. He needed to clear his head before he could make any decisions. Then Daniel got a text message from his cousin Leo in Cape Town, which gave him an idea:
*Just off to the beach. Great surf. Bit boring. Friends all away. Come over!*

Cape Town. Of course! His cousin Leo lived there now. A couple of weeks in a foreign country would be the best medicine. And he could practise his English at the same time.
Daniel's parents had protested at first. "South Africa is too expensive. And I don't think you really want to practise your English!" said his dad. "You only liked the word 'beach' in Leo's text message."
"And it could be dangerous," his mum complained. "There's a lot of crime[1], especially in the townships." But Daniel told her, "Don't worry, Mum. I'm going to stay with Leo – not in a township."
He managed[2] to find a special offer for a flight to Cape Town, and a few days later he was on his way to South Africa. The flight was uneventful and his aunt picked him up at the airport.
Daniel felt at home right away. He loved the climate, and he got along really well with his cousin Leo. Leo lived with his parents in a small house about a ten-minute drive away from the beach.
'The perfect place to be,' thought Daniel.
One morning Leo borrowed his dad's car and he and Daniel went down to the beach with two surfboards. Daniel had been in South Africa for two weeks. He had texted his parents several times and told them they needn't worry.
*Hout Bay is a peaceful place. No crime, no worries!*

1 crime [kraɪm] – *Verbrechen*; 2 manage ['mænɪdʒ] – *schaffen, erreichen*

Now the boys were relaxing on the sand after surfing for an hour in the early morning. Daniel looked across the bay. Over to his right there were two other men with surfboards. The surfers seemed to be packing up their equipment. They would soon be on their way back to their car. As Daniel watched, two other young men ran up to them. Both of them were tall and athletic. One of them had shiny blond hair.

"Let's get some breakfast," Leo said, starting to get up. "I'm so hungry!"

"Wait!" whispered Daniel as he grabbed Leo's arm, pushing him back down onto the sand. Daniel looked towards where the surfers were standing. Leo turned his head slowly to find out what Daniel had noticed. Suddenly Leo saw the knife in the young man's hand. He turned back towards Daniel. Leo tried to find his mobile, but he had left it in the car. He took a deep breath. But his thoughts were racing. 'What happens if they come over to us? Will they hurt Daniel or me?' Leo now noticed how scared Daniel looked. "Stay cool, Daniel," he whispered. "What's happening?"

Daniel spoke slowly in a whisper. "The guy with the knife has grabbed one of the surfers around the neck[3] – he's threatening him. The man is looking for something in his pocket. Now he's holding out something in his hand. The second guy has just grabbed it."

"And the other surfer? What's he doing?" whispered Leo.

"He's giving something to the other guy. Now they're running off towards the road."

Leo turned slowly to see what had happened. The surfers were just standing there – shocked and helpless.

3 neck [nek] – *Hals, Nacken, Genick*

## 1 Answer the questions.

1. Why had Daniel's last few weeks at school been stressful?
2. What did Daniel's parents worry about?
3. Why did Daniel choose to go to South Africa?
4. What was South Africa like for Daniel in the first couple of weeks?
5. How did Daniel and Leo feel when they saw the two men on the beach?
6. What did the men do to the surfers?

## 2 Find the sentences in the text which mean the same. Write down the line number(s).

1. The last few weeks at school hadn't been easy for Daniel.
2. Daniel got a plane ticket which wasn't too expensive.
3. His dad said, "I don't think you're going to improve your English there."
4. Daniel liked the place from the start.
5. Two other men hurried towards the surfers.
6. "Just one moment," said Daniel in a quiet voice.

## C Language

### 1 Complete the sentences using words from the text.

1. Daniel couldn't make any —— about life after school because he couldn't concentrate.
2. At first his parents were against it, so they —— .
3. Daniel's dad thought that Daniel probably wouldn't learn English and that South Africa was too —— .
4. Leo was sometimes allowed to use his dad's car, so one morning he —— it to drive down to the beach.
5. The two surfers were packing up the surfboards and the rest of their —— .
6. Leo —— his head so that he could see what was happening.

### 2 Rewrite the underlined sentence parts using your own words.

1. Jane was <u>glad to</u> find a special offer for a hotel in Johannesburg.
2. The trip from London to Johannesburg <u>took her</u> more than 15 hours.
3. The flight was <u>uneventful</u>, and she arrived safely on Saturday morning.
4. <u>Her goal was to</u> see as much of the country as she could.
5. She thought South Africa was <u>amazing</u>, especially the wildlife.
6. After three weeks she <u>was on her way back</u> home.

## D Writing

Choose <u>one</u> of the following tasks.

### 1 Write a short essay.

Your family is making holiday plans and is thinking about going to South Africa. Discuss the pros and cons. Give examples and state your opinion.

Write about 120 words.

OR

### 2 Write an ending for the story.

The following questions can help you:

Did they ask other surfers for help?
Did they wait for the police to arrive?
What did the police do?

Write about 120 words.

# E Mediation

INTERNET

Ziele | Sehenswürdigkeiten | Tipps | Bilder | Kontakte

## Kapstadt und der Tafelberg

Kapstadt gilt als eine der schönsten Städte der Welt und ist immer eine Reise wert.

Das Kap der Guten Hoffnung (Cape of Good Hope), das nur 45 km von der Metropole entfernt liegt, hat der Stadt ihren Namen gegeben. Kapstadt wurde 1652 gegründet und war somit die erste Stadt, die in der Kolonialzeit entstand.

Deshalb wird sie auch Mutterstadt genannt.

Nicht nur die Lage der Stadt am Fuße des Tafelbergs, sondern auch ihre tollen Strände in der Camps Bay und in Clifton sowie zahlreiche weitere Sehenswürdigkeiten, locken jedes Jahr Touristen aus aller Welt an.

Die meisten der vielen Besucher zieht es auf den Tafelberg. Den Gipfel erreicht man bequem mit der Seilbahn oder für die Abenteuerlustigen auf zahlreichen Wanderwegen. Oben angekommen hat man einen einmaligen 360 Grad Blick über die ganze Stadt, den Ozean und die Bergspitzen der Kapregion.

In Kapstadt selbst finden sich viele weitere Sehenswürdigkeiten, wie z. B. die V & A Waterfront mit ihren zahlreichen Bars, Restaurants und kleinen Läden, die zum Bummeln und Verweilen einladen. Die Long Street mit ihren historischen Gebäuden und das Two Oceans Aquarium sind einen Besuch wert. Am Bloubergstrand kommen Wassersportfans auf ihre Kosten.

Für alle, die an der Geschichte Südafrikas interessiert sind, ist ein Besuch der ehemaligen Gefängnisinsel Robben Island ein Muss. Sie wurde von den Apartheid-Regierungen als Gefängnis für politische Häftlinge genutzt. Auch Nelson Mandela war hier inhaftiert.

You are on an exchange visit to Cape Town. You and your exchange partner have found this website, and he is interested in what it says about his hometown. Summarise the following facts for him in English.

- the history of Cape Town
- information about Table Mountain
- other important sights in the city
- information about Robben Island

T

## F Speaking

Partner A: Look at the sign for the Table Mountain Cableway. Explain to your partner what it is, where it is and what kind of information is given.

Partner B: Look at the sign for Robben Island Tours. Explain to your partner what it is, where it is and what kind of information is given.

Partner A + B: Discuss which sight you would visit if you could spend a day in Cape Town.

(A)

### Table Mountain Cableway

**Rates (in South African rand) valid from 1 Oct to 30 Sept (excludes 15 Dec – 15 Jan):**

| Ticket type | Return | One way |
|---|---|---|
| Adult | 255 rand | 135 rand |
| Child 4 – 17 years of age | 125 rand | 65 rand |
| Student (Fridays only at Ticket Office) | 130 rand | 70 rand |

**Operating Times**
The cable car operates weather permitting during the following times:

| Date | First car up | Last car down |
|---|---|---|
| 1 May – 31 August | 08:30 a.m. | 05:30 p.m. |
| 1 September – 31 October | 08:30 a.m. | 07:00 p.m. |

(B)

### Robben Island Tours

**Includes visit to Nelson Mandela's cell**

Tour times (weather permitting): Mon – Sat: 09:00 11:00 01:00 (p.m.)
Departs from: Nelson Mandela Gateway (V & A Waterfront)
Duration of tour: 4 hours
Duration of journey to island: 30 minutes
Transport to sights by bus. Tour guide on bus.

Price: 320 rand per adult
160 rand per child (under 18)

uc7j5b

# A Listening

You will listen to Marcus talking to his English friend, Alan, in a video chat. One month ago Marcus' family moved from a small town near London to live in Hong Kong.
You will hear the recordings twice.

2,32 **1** **Listen to part 1. Complete the sentences.**

1. Marcus hasn't learned much Cantonese, only a — .
2. The first thing he noticed in Hong Kong was that the streets — .
3. Everywhere there's the smell of food or — .
4. The shops are open from 10:00 in the morning until — .
5. The kids at Marcus' school come from all over — .
6. The new girl has an Indian — .

2,33 **2** **Listen to part 2. Which of these things does Marcus talk about?**

A

B

C

D

E

F

## B Reading

### High-density[1] living in Hong Kong

**A**

Hong Kong is a very big city – it's the home of over seven million people. Because Hong Kong consists of a group of mountainous islands, only about 25 % of the city can be used as building land. As a consequence, it's one of the most densely populated cities in the world. On average, over 6,000 people live on each square[2] kilometre. How does the city deal with this challenge?

**B**

Most inhabitants of Hong Kong live in skyscrapers. Visitors to Hong Kong are often amazed at the number and height of the skyscrapers, and Hong Kong has more skyscrapers than any other city in the world. At least 1,300 of its buildings are over 100 metres tall. The International Commerce Centre in Kowloon, with a height of 484 metres, is the tallest of them all.

**C**

The prices for flats in Hong Kong are among the highest in the world. So it's no surprise that inhabitants are forced to live in small spaces. Even people who earn good salaries can usually only afford to rent a small place. A lot of the flats seem extremely small compared to European sizes. Flats which are only twelve square metres big are not unusual.

**D**

It's especially difficult for poor people to find a place to live in Hong Kong. Tens of thousands have to live in 'cage homes[3]'. They look like large cages for animals with a bed in them. Usually there are twelve or more cage homes in a regular flat. They are very narrow[4], and an adult can hardly[5] sit or stand in them. There's little space for personal things either. The people who live there share the toilet and the kitchen. Cage homes are often dirty and not safe. But even they're not cheap.

Cage homes

**E**

Air pollution is another major problem that comes with the high population density. The pollution is mostly caused by heavy traffic in the city centre, especially by buses and lorries[6]. The power plants are also part of the problem. They produce the electricity that the huge population requires and add to the pollution. In addition, the tall buildings of the city stop the wind from carrying polluted air away.

1 density ['densɪti] – *Dichte;* 2 square [skweə] – *Quadrat-;* 3 cage home [ˌkeɪdʒ'həʊm] – *Bettunterkunft in Hongkong;* 4 narrow ['nærəʊ] – *eng;* 5 hardly ['hɑːdli] – *kaum;* 6 lorry ['lɒri] – *Lastwagen*

**F**

However, there are also positive effects of the high population density. Public transport, for example, is efficient. People only have to travel short distances for their daily activities. Only a couple of years ago the people in Hong Kong still seemed to be quite happy with their living conditions. In fact, they liked having a lot of people around them. But new surveys show that this has changed. Hong Kong has fallen in the list of happiest places in the world.

**G**

Although there are many problems in Hong Kong today, it will stay a crowded city because it will continue to attract people who want to live and work there. The biggest challenges for the government of the city are to increase the number of cheap homes and to reduce the amount of air pollution. Will the government be successful?

## 1 Match the headings with the paragraphs of the text.

1. The problem of air pollution
2. What people in Hong Kong think
3. So many people in one city
4. Homes of the poor
5. Challenges for the future
6. Tall buildings
7. High prices

## 2 Complete the table with the information from the text.

| | |
|---|---|
| 1. Number of people who live in Hong Kong | |
| 2. Number of buildings taller than 100 metres | |
| 3. Size of flats compared to flats in Europe | |
| 4. Number of people who live in cage homes | |
| 5. Main cause of air pollution | |
| 6. The two major challenges | |

T

## C Language

### Find suitable words to fill in the gaps.

Before you visit Hong Kong, there are a few things you need to know. As a citizen of an EU country, you … (1) stay in Hong Kong for up to 90 days without a visa. More … (2) 100 airlines offer flights to Hong Kong International Airport from all over the world.
Public transport in Hong Kong is fast and cheap. You can … (3) trains, buses or taxis to get … (4) the city centre. The Airport Express takes you to Hong Kong Island in only 25 minutes, for example. So you don't … (5) a car. Most shops … (6) credit cards, but it's good to have some cash too for the street markets. If you have any questions, visit one of the many tourist information centres.

## D Writing

Choose one of the following tasks.

### 1 Write an e-mail.

You and your family want to visit Hong Kong next month.
Write an e-mail to an English-speaking friend who knows the place.
Tell her or him what you are interested in and ask for tips about Hong Kong (cheap hotels, public transport, sights, …).

Write about 150 words.

**OR**

### 2 Write a short essay.

"Bikes are the best form of transport in a big city."
Write a short essay in which you either agree or disagree with this statement (Here are some ideas: parking, environment, traffic jams, dangerous, …).
Give examples to support your arguments.

Write about 150 words.

# E Mediation

Your mother has been sent to Hong Kong by her company. You and your dad have a meeting with a teacher at your new school. Your dad's English isn't very good, so you help him.

Teacher: Good morning. My name is Mr Turner. You must be Mr Grünwald. Welcome to our International School here in Hong Kong.
Your dad: Guten Morgen. Entschuldigen Sie bitte, ich spreche nicht so gut Englisch. Aber mein Sohn kann aushelfen.
You: ...

Teacher: Oh, I see. Well, first of all, here are some papers for registration that should be filled in. You can do that at home.
You: ...

Teacher: And this is your timetable. There is a meeting for all students at 7:45 every morning.
You: ...

Your dad: Frage ihn, wo sie stattfindet.
You: ...

Teacher: It's in room four near the main door. After the meeting one of our students will help you to find the classrooms.
You: ...

Your dad: Musst du eine Schuluniform tragen, und woher bekommen wir sie?
You: ...

Teacher: Yes, all students have to wear a uniform. You can buy it in the school shop.
You: ...

Your dad: Das ist gut zu wissen. Wie sieht es mit einem warmen Mittagessen aus?
You: ...

Teacher: Yes, you can get a warm meal in our cafeteria. But you must order it the day before.
You: ...

...

## F Speaking

Look at the photo and prepare a short three-minute talk about it.

First describe the picture:
- Who can you see in the picture?
- What are they doing?
- Where are they?

Then give your point of view:
- Why do people work in another country?
- Would you like to work in another country? Why? / Why not?
- What jobs would you go abroad for?
- Which country would you go to?

3,14

# Tornado by J. Townsend

I'm a joyrider[1]. I'm a twister[2].
Give up now. You can't resist[3].
Gun-slinger[4]. Car slinger too.
Watch out! I'll wake you and take you
and shake you about. Like a massive[5] bonfire
in the distance. I will not tolerate
resistance. Sharpshooter,
house looter[6], on the run.
Get in my way
and it won't be fun.
In my eye
it's as quiet
as a mouse.
Next minute
I'll destroy[7]
your house.
Hide in the
cellar. Hide
in the bath.
I'll find you
if you're in
my path.
I'm a tornado
bent on[8]
trouble.
Behind me
is only
a pile[9]
of rubble[10].

**INFO**

In poems writers use often rhythm and stylistic devices (Stilmittel) to show their ideas and how they feel.
Metaphors (Metaphern), personifications (Personifizierungen) and repetitions (Wiederholungen) help to make the writer's ideas about something clearer.
**Metaphor:** A metaphor claims that one thing is another thing. "I'm a joyrider." (line 1)
**Personification:** An animal or a thing is given human qualities. "I will not tolerate" (line 6)
**Repetition:** Words or sentences are repeated.

## 1 Work with the text.

1. Describe the shape of the poem.
2. Find the metaphors in the poem. Why does the writer use them?
3. Find the repetitions. Why are they used?
4. Why does the writer use personification in the poem?

1 joyrider ['dʒɔɪˌraɪdə] – *jemand, der mit einem gestohlenen Auto fährt*; 2 twister ['twɪstə] – *Wirbelsturm*; 3 to resist [rɪ'zɪst] – *widerstehen*; 4 gun-slinger ['gʌnˌslɪŋə] – *Revolverheld, Revolverheldin*; 5 massive ['mæsɪv] – *riesig*; 6 looter ['lu:tə] – *Plünderer, Plünderin*; 7 to destroy [dɪ'strɔɪ] – *zerstören*; 8 bent on ['bent‿'ɒn] – *auf etwas aus*; 9 pile [paɪl] – *Haufen*; 10 rubble ['rʌbl] – *Geröll*

3,15

# Stealing Stacey by L.R. Banks (2004)

*Stacey is a teenager from London. One December her Australian grandmother comes to stay and takes Stacey back to Australia with her to spend the Christmas holidays there – without telling Stacey's mum and dad.*
*The first few days are great, and they stay in a hotel in Perth, the only big city in the west of the country. But then they go to the 'bush', the Australian countryside …*

That evening Gran told me she had things to do in the morning, and that I was to pack and meet her in the lobby. "I'm ordering room service to bring you a lovely brekky in your room, then just come on down at ten. See ya!" I thought she had a funny smile, as if she had a surprise for me. Boy, did she.
When I came out of the lift next morning, I couldn't see her. There was a tall man in a leather hat standing at the reception desk. My eyes went right past, still looking for Gran. Suddenly the tall man turned round.
I got a real shock.
It wasn't a man, it was her!
She was wearing combat trousers[1], a khaki shirt, and cowboy boots. She looked completely different.
I came up to her slowly.
"Gran, is it you? What have you done to yourself?"
She laughed. "Well, sugar-puff[2], we're off to the bush! You don't expect me to wear town clothes for that, do you? Didn't I tell you there are two of me, a town person and a bushie? This is your bush Glendine!"
While we'd been in Perth we'd driven around in taxis. Now we went outside and waiting at the front of the hotel was one of those truck-things with an open back. Her luggage[3] was there, with a whole lot of other stuff. Gran said, "How d'you like my ute[4]?"
"Ute?"
"Utility. That's what we call 'em."
I looked at it. It was about the last kind of vehicle I'd've expected her to drive. It was so rusty and old.
There was a big metal bar[5] in front.
"That's a roo bar," said Gran.
"Rhubarb[6]?"
"No! Roo bar! It's so if you hit a roo – kangaroo – he doesn't damage the car."
I said, "Oh, please, don't hit one, Gran!"
She laughed and said, "They'd better keep out of my way then."

1 combat trousers ['kɒmbæt ˌtraʊzəz] – *Cargohose*; 2 sugar-puff ['ʃʊgə ˌpʌf] – *Kosename*; 3 luggage ['lʌgɪdʒ] – *Gepäck*; 4 utility vehicle (ute) [juː'tɪləti ˌvɪəkl, juːt] – *Geländewagen*; 5 bar [bɑː] – *hier: Stange*; 6 rhubarb ['ruːbɑːb] – *Rhabarber*

I soon saw what she meant.

We climbed up into the cabin. Then Gran just took off. I've never seen anyone drive so fast.

"Gran, slow down!" I yelled.

"No fear[1], lovie! We've got a long way to go!"

3,16 At first there was forest on each side that seemed to go on forever, but after that there were what looked like sheep and wheat farms. It was endless, endless driving. There were a few enormous[2] trucks with two or three containers attached. Gran called them road trains. But there wasn't much else on the road at all.

Then it changed. On either side were low banks of bright red earth, and trees and bushes. I said to Gran, "Is this it – the bush?"

"Well, you know what they say! The bush is always 50 kilometres on from where you are! But I'd call this the beginning of it."

I said, "I thought it would be more, like, desert."

"This is a sort of desert. It's very dry. But it's full of life. Snakes, goannas[3], emus … This is roo country. That reminds[4] me, I should slow down now." And she did. "Roos have got no road sense[5]. They just jump right out on to the road."

I saw a lot of birds fly up from a lump[6] at the side of the road. "Oh, look!" I said. "Is that a dead one?"

"Yeah. He's just roadkill now, poor old thing. And that was a wedge-tailed eagle[7], eating him," she said, pointing to a huge bird that was flying away. A real eagle!

On and on we drove. There was always something new to see. Gran said, "Pretty well everything here is different from everything anywhere else. It's because Australia was cut off from the rest of the world, millions of years ago. That's what makes this such an exciting, wonderful place. Aren't you glad I brought you?"

Well, I was. At least, I had been, till now. Now Gran had changed. I began to feel just a little bit uneasy[8]. It was pretty obvious[9] we weren't going back to the hotel that night. Maybe not at all.

After about five hours we stopped in a little town. Gran parked outside a bar and we went in. It was dark and dreary[10]. As soon as I walked into it, I wanted to leave, but I needed a pee like mad[11]!

When we set off again, I asked where we were going.

She shouted above the motor, "Can't you guess? We're going to my station."

I stared at her. I was thinking railway or tube stations. "You've got a station?"

1 No fear! [ˌnəʊ ˈfɪə] – *Keine Bange!*; 2 enormous [ɪˈnɔːməs] – *riesig*; 3 goanna [ɡəʊˈænə] – *Waran (Reptilienart)*; 4 to remind [rɪˈmaɪnd] – *erinnern an*; 5 sense [sens] – *Sinn*; 6 lump [lʌmp] – *Klumpen*; 7 eagle [ˈiːɡl] – *Adler*; 8 uneasy [ʌnˈizi] – *besorgt*; 9 obvious [ˈɒbviəs] – *offensichtlich*; 10 dreary [ˈdrɪəri] – *trostlos*; 11 like mad [ˌlaɪk ˈmæd] – *wie verrückt*

"Course I have! I told you about it."

She'd never mentioned a station. I'd have remembered.

I'd have asked her to tell me more, but the motor was roaring[1] and I felt too exhausted[2]. The country was more like desert now. There weren't so many trees, just these low bushes and tall grey grass. It was getting hotter and hotter. And dustier[3]. At last I fell asleep.

3,17 Gran woke me up. It was dark. We must've been driving all day.

"Right, Stacey-bell, out you get and help me make a fire."

I got out of the cabin and almost fell over a pair of wellies[4]. "Put those on," said Gran. "And take this torch. There's lots of wood around. But be sure you kick it before you pick it up."

"Why?"

"Why d'you think?"

I had no idea why anyone would kick wood. But then a terrible idea came into my head.

"Gran! Are there snakes around here?"

"There might be. But just remember, the snake that bites[5] you is the one you don't see, so keep a lookout."

I nearly fainted[6]. I hate snakes. I don't know why because I'd never seen one. They just give me the creeps[7].

I ran back into the cabin and sat there. Gran came round to my side. "Get out, Stacey," she said. I think that was the first time she'd called me by my name.

When I still didn't move, she said, "Don't be such a pom."

"What's a pom?" I asked.

"An English person is a pom. Poms have a bad name with us Aussies for being whingers[8]. I'm not having a whingeing pom for a granddaughter. Now get these boots on your feet and get me some wood or there'll be no food."

When I still didn't move, she said, "We must make a fire to keep the dingoes away."

I knew dingoes were wild dogs. Dingoes are fierce[9]. I've read about it. They eat babies.

I was so scared, I almost forgot about snakes. But I couldn't just sit there all night.

I *was* a bit hungry. And except for the torch, it was pitch dark. A fire would be good.

I slowly put my feet out. Gran pushed the wellies on, then pulled me out and put the torch into my hand.

"Go," she said.

1 to roar [rɔː] – *dröhnen*; 2 exhausted [ɪɡˈzɔːstɪd] – *erschöpft*; 3 dusty [ˈdʌsti] – *staubig*; 4 welly [ˈweli] – *Gummistiefel*; 5 to bite [baɪt] – *beißen*; 6 to faint [feɪnt] – *ohnmächtig werden*; 7 to give sb the creeps [kriːps] – *jmdm. Angst machen*; 8 whinger [ˈwɪndʒə] – *jemand, der sich oft beschwert*; 9 fierce [fɪəs] – *grimmig*

3,18 I shone the torch around and right away I saw some dead wood quite close by. I kicked it hard, twice. Nothing came out. I carefully picked up a branch[1].

"Here's a piece," I said.

She looked at it as if it was so small she couldn't see it. "Oh, that's amazing," she said. "Do you think you could possibly find me another one just like it? Then we can rub[2] them together and make sparks[3]."

I dropped[4] the piece and went back to the pile[5] I'd taken it from. I kicked it again. Bit by bit I carried or dragged all the wood to where Gran was. Before long she'd got a fire going. (Using matches[6] of course. I should've known she was having me on[7].) The wood was dry and it really burnt well.

By the time Gran thought we had enough wood, there were some hot embers[8]. She used a shovel[9] to put them in a hole she'd dug. Then she said, "Now be a love and bring me the Esky."

I went to the back of the ute. I'd no idea what an Esky was, but I soon guessed, because what do you put food in if it's going to be shone on by the sun all day? One of those cold-box things, right? And sure enough there was one. It was really heavy, but I dragged it to the fire.

Gran opened it and inside were six packages wrapped[10] in foil[11], with some tins of Coke. She put the packages on top of the red embers, then she put more embers on top. She covered the red place with earth.

The food took quite a while to cook in the embers. At last a really good smell started to come out of the ground. By the time Gran dug the food out I was like dying of hunger. She opened the packages. Inside were big chicken legs, baked potatoes, and sweetcorn[12]. We ate with our fingers by firelight. The food tasted well delicious. I drank Coke and she drank beer.

Then Gran stood up and said, "Right. Bed."

She made me close the Esky and put all the stuff away in a box. The fire was dying down. Nearly all my wood was gone. I said, "Who's going to keep the fire going?"

She said, "Well it's no use looking at Glendine. She's going to make big Zs."

I said, "But if we don't, the dingoes'll come!"

She said, "Listen, Stacey. There's no dingoes around here. Now help me with my bed."

I didn't say anything. I helped her lift a rusty[13] old iron[14] bed and a mattress off the back of the ute. It wasn't far off the ground … There was another mattress on the floor of the ute for me.

1 branch [brɑːnʃ] – *Zweig*; 2 to rub [rʌb] – *reiben*; 3 spark [spɑːk] – *Funke*; 4 to drop [drɒp] – *fallen (lassen)*; 5 pile [paɪl] – *Haufen*; 6 match [mætʃ] – *Streichholz*; 7 to have sb on [hæv‿ˈɒn] – *veräppeln*; 8 embers [embəz] – *Glut*; 9 shovel [ʃʌvl] – *Schaufel*; 10 wrapped [ræpt] – *eingepackt*; 11 foil [fɔɪl] – *(Alu-)folie*; 12 sweetcorn [ˈswiːtkɔːn] – *Zuckermais*; 13 rusty [ˈrʌsti] – *rostig*; 14 iron [aɪən] – *Eisen*

I said, "I need to go to the loo[1]." I know I sounded sulky[2]. I couldn't *believe it* about the dingoes, that she'd do that just to make me get out and help.

She picked up the shovel and the torch. "Go ahead," she said. "Over there, by those trees. Keep downwind, ha ha."

I stared at the shovel, thinking what it meant. I had to dig a hole, and ... No. It was too gross.

"Was it true about the snakes?" I said.

"Lovie, would I lie[3] to you? Of course there are snakes in the outback. Just keep shining the torch and stay where the ground's open. Oh, here's some dunny paper[4]. Be sure to bury[5] it, too. Now go on and do what you have to do."

So I did it. I managed[6] somehow. But the walk there into the darkness was the worst thing I'd ever done.

I was beginning to change my mind about Gran being the greatest. That's putting it nicely.

## 1 Work with the text.

Read the information in the box and answer the questions. Explain and give line numbers.

1. Is there a first-person or a third-person narrator in the text?
2. What is his or her perspective?

## 2 Write your own text.

Read lines 76-103 again. Rewrite the text telling this part of the story with Gran as the narrator. Start like this:

Stacey was still sleeping.

"Right, Stacey-bell, out you get and help me make a fire," I said.

She got out of the cabin and almost fell ...

**INFO**

There are different types of narrators in novels.

The **first-person narrator** uses 'I' or 'we' when telling the story.

The **third-person narrator** uses 'he' or 'she'.

Narrators can tell stories from different perspectives.

**Omniscient (allwissend):** The narrator knows more than each character. He or she knows about future events and is able to make comments about the whole story.

**Personal (personal):** The narrator takes part in the story as a character and describes the story from his or her perspective. The narrator can usually only comment on actions he or she takes part in.

1 to go to the loo [lu:] – *auf die Toilette gehen*; 2 sulky ['sʌlki] – *beleidigt*; 3 to lie [laɪ] – *lügen*; 4 dunny paper ['dʌni ˌpeipə] – *Toilettenpapier*; 5 to bury ['beri] – *begraben*; 6 to manage ['mænɪdʒ] – *schaffen*

3,19

# Nelson Mandela – the troublemaker[1]

Newspapers report the death of Nelson Mandela

In the evening of Thursday, 5th December 2013, President Jacob Zuma of South Africa announced[2] the news of Nelson Mandela's death. Although Mandela had been ill for a long time and was 95 when he died, the world was in shock. It was difficult to imagine life without the man who had faced violence, brutality and many years in prison as part of his struggle to make South Africa a better place.

When Nelson Mandela was born on 18th July 1918 in a small South African village, his father gave him the name 'Rolihlahla[3]', which means 'troublemaker' in his tribal[4] language. As a young boy, Mandela made a catapult[5] and hit birds out of the sky. He learned how to stick fight[6] with other boys and later he became interested in boxing. This 'troublemaker' would have a huge positive impact on human rights[7] around the world.

Mandela's father had four wives and thirteen children. Mandela was lucky. He was the first child in his family to go to school. At school Mandela's teacher gave him the name 'Nelson'. In his autobiography *Long Walk to Freedom* Mandela explains that white people believed it was more civilised to have a European name. Apart from that, most white people could not pronounce African names.

It was a tradition in Mandela's tribe for boys to be circumcised[8] in their teenage years. The operation was very painful[9], but it was a custom that changed a boy into a man. Mandela was 16 when he had the operation and he felt very scared.

1 troublemaker ['trʌblˌmeɪkə] – *Unruhestifter, Unruhestifterin*; 2 to announce [ə'naʊns] – *ankündigen, bekanntgeben*; 3 Rolihlahla [ˌxɒli'hlæhlə] – *südafrikanischer Vorname*; 4 tribal ['traɪbl] – *Stammes-*; 5 catapult ['kætəpʌlt] *Schleuder*; 6 stick fighting ['stɪk ˌfaɪtɪŋ] – *südafrikanischer Kampfsport*; 7 human rights [ˌhju:mən 'raɪts] – *Menschenrechte*; 8 to circumcise ['sɜ:kəmsaɪz] – *beschneiden*; 9 painful ['peɪnfl] – *schmerzhaft*

But he suffered the pain in silence. In his autobiography Mandela says, "A boy may cry. A man hides his pain." Mandela didn't know it then, but he would suffer many more painful experiences in the future.

Mandela making a speech

3,20 Mandela was growing up at a time when white people had almost total control in South Africa, but as a young village boy he was not yet aware[1] of this power. However, in 1939 Mandela went to study at the University College of Fort Hare, a university for black students, and he began to realize that South African society was not fair. When Mandela helped students to protest about poor quality food at the university in 1940, for example, he was forced to leave.

In 1943 Mandela went to study law[2] at the University of the Witwatersrand in Johannesburg. It was there that he met Evelyn Mase, a trainee nurse. They fell in love and married in 1944. At the same time Mandela joined the African National Congress (ANC), the party that was fighting for black people's rights and for equality between blacks and whites.

In 1948, while Nelson Mandela was living in Johannesburg and working as a lawyer[3], the government started to introduce the system of apartheid. This meant that everything was officially separated, including schools, hospitals, beaches, toilets, buses and even public benches. People who did not obey[4] the law were often arrested. They were put in prison and could be tortured[5] or even killed. Apartheid meant that whites now had complete power over black people. In addition, blacks were not allowed to vote in elections, and many were forced to leave their homes and move to 'townships' in other parts of the city.

1 to be aware of [bi‿ə'weə] – *sich einer Sache bewusst sein*; 2 law [lɔː] – *hier: Jura*; 3 lawyer ['lɔɪə] – *Anwalt, Anwältin*; 4 to obey [ə'beɪ] – *gehorchen*; 5 to torture ['tɔːtʃə] – *foltern*

The Sharpeville Massacre

3,21 Nelson Mandela became very involved with the ANC and their protests. However, he had always believed in peaceful protests and he had never wanted to use violence. But when peaceful protests didn't work, he changed his opinion. Then, in March 1960, a crowd of people gathered outside the police station in Sharpeville, near Johannesburg, in a protest about rights for black people. As more protesters arrived, the police suddenly began to shoot at the crowd. They continued to shoot even when the terrified people started to run away. That day the South African police killed 69 people and injured 180 others. Many of those who died were shot in the back. Many people who were at the scene said that the protest had been peaceful before the police shot at the crowd. Others reported that they had seen some people throw stones at the police. However, it became clear after the massacre that the protesters had not had guns. The news of the massacre spread[1] around the world and many countries realized that the situation in South Africa could no longer[2] be ignored.

After the Sharpeville Massacre, Mandela started an ANC military group. He visited different countries to get money to support[3] and train the group. The military group's aim[4] was to destroy[5] a number of government buildings, but not to kill people. Mandela was arrested for sabotage[6] in 1963 and in the following year he was sent to prison for life on Robben Island, near Cape Town.

1 to spread [spred] – *sich verbreiten*; 2 no longer [ˌnəʊ ˈlɒŋgə] – *nicht mehr*; 3 to support [səˈpɔːt] – *unterstützen*; 4 aim [eɪm] – *Ziel*; 5 to destroy [dɪˈstrɔɪ] – *zerstören*; 6 sabotage [ˈsæbətɑːʒ] – *Sabotage (bewusste Zerstörung von Geräten, Maschinen usw.)*

E

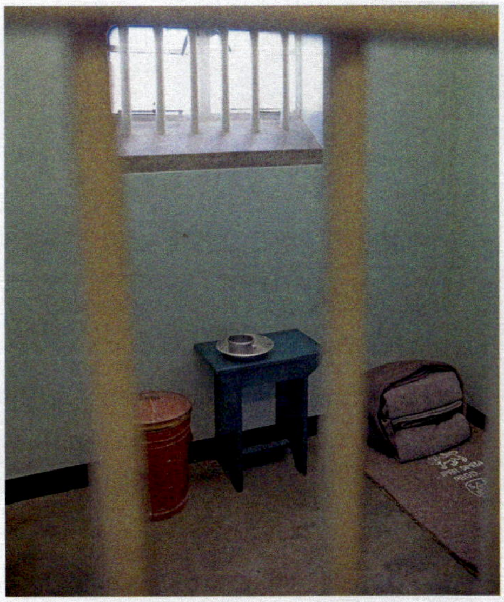

The prison on Robben Island

3,22 The years in prison were long and very hard. Mandela's marriage to Evelyn had ended in divorce[1] in 1958. In the same year he had married Winifred or 'Winnie' Madikizela. Mandela missed Winnie very much when he was in prison, and at first he was only allowed to write two letters a year to his family and friends (later he could write two letters a month). One of the worst moments was when his oldest son, Madiba, was killed in a car crash in 1969. Madiba had promised to look after the family while his father was in prison. Mandela was not allowed to go to the funeral[2].

However, Mandela never stopped fighting, even when he was in prison. He organized a hunger strike and found clever ways to send important news around the prison.

When Mandela was sent to prison, many people in the ANC had thought that change would come very soon. This didn't happen, and in the 1980s there were more bombings by the ANC's military group. This time people were killed in the attacks. In 1985 the South African government offered Mandela his freedom if he stopped the ANC violence and promised not to speak about apartheid after his release[3]. He refused[4] to do so. Mandela's fight became well-known in countries all around the world and this put a lot of pressure[5] on the government to end apartheid.

1 divorce [dɪ'vɔ:s] – *Scheidung*; 2 funeral ['fju:nrəl] – *Beerdigung*; 3 release [rɪ'li:s] – Entlassung; 4 to refuse [rɪ'fju:z] – *sich weigern, ablehnen*; 5 to put pressure on ['preʃə] – *Druck auf jdn ausüben*

Nelson and Winnie Mandela after Nelson Mandela's release from prison

Mandela was in prison for almost 27 years. Finally, in 1990, President F.W. de Klerk released Mandela without any conditions[1]. Many white South Africans had been afraid that they would lose their land and that they would have to leave the country if apartheid ended. But Nelson Mandela realized that hatred[2] would never heal[3] the country. He agreed to work with de Klerk to end apartheid peacefully. In 1993 they both won the Nobel Peace Prize for their determination[4] and hard work. Mandela and de Klerk continued to cooperate and in 1994 South Africa held its first free elections. It was then that the 'troublemaker', Rolihlahla Mandela, became the first black African president of South Africa.

3,23 In 1996 Mandela divorced Winnie Mandela. He married his third wife, Graca Machel, on his 80th birthday, in 1998. A year later he retired[5] as the president of South Africa, but Mandela did not retire from public life. He continued to work for peace in other African countries and around the world. As he grew older, his most important work became his fight against the disease AIDS. When his son Makgatho died in 2005, Mandela announced to the world that Makgatho had died of AIDS. This shocked people in Africa, who, until then, had refused to talk about the disease and tried to hide it. In a speech Mandela said, "Let us give publicity[6] to AIDS and not hide it, because the only way to make it appear like a normal illness[7] like TB, like cancer[8], is always to come out and to say somebody has died because of AIDS. And people will stop regarding[9] it as something extraordinary."

1 condition [kən'dɪʃn] – *Bedingung*; 2 hatred ['heɪtrəd] – *Hass*; 3 to heal [hi:l] – *heilen*; 4 determination [dɪˌtɜ:mɪn'eɪʃn] – *Entschlossenheit*; 5 to retire [rɪ'taɪə] – *zurücktreten, in den Ruhestand gehen*; 6 publicity [pʌb'lɪsəti] – *hier: öffentliche Aufmerksamkeit*; 7 illness ['ɪlnəs] – *Krankheit*; 8 cancer ['kænsə] – *Krebs*; 9 to regard [rɪ'ga:d] – *betrachten*

Mandela as an old man

In 2003 Mandela started a charity[1] named after his Robben Island prison number – 46664 – that raised money[2] through international pop concerts for AIDS victims. Many famous pop groups and musicians played concerts for the charity around the world between 2003 and 2008. Mandela also supported many other charities that work for AIDS awareness[3] and the victims of the disease.

Nelson Mandela overcame[4] huge challenges during his life and had many successes in his struggle for peace, equality and justice[5] in South Africa and the world. And Mandela's dream is still alive today. His grandson, Luvuyo Mandela, said, "We are all citizens of the world, and as citizens it is our duty[6] to help change it for the better."

## 1 Make a timeline.

Use the information in the text to make a timeline about Nelson Mandela and South Africa.
Start like this:
1918 (18th July): Mandela was born.
...

## 2 Talk about the text.

"Nelson Mandela's life was a journey from 'troublemaker' to 'peacemaker'."
Do you agree with this statement? Say why / why not. Give evidence from the text.

1 charity ['tʃærɪti] – *Wohlfahrtsorganisation, Wohltätigkeit*; 2 to raise money [ˌreɪz 'mʌni] – *Geld sammeln*; 3 awareness [ə'weənəs] – *Bewusstsein*; 4 to overcome [ˌəʊvə'kʌm] – *überwinden*; 5 justice ['dʒʌstɪs] – *Gerechtigkeit*; 6 duty ['dju:ti] – *Pflicht*

# S1 Doing better in tests

Sich besser auf Prüfungen vorbereiten

## 1 VOR dem Test

Du weißt oft schon lange im voraus, wann der nächste Test oder die nächste Klausur ansteht. Nimm dir daher genug Zeit zum Lernen. Wenn möglich, bildet Lerngruppen und fragt euch gegenseitig ab. Lege dir eine Liste mit den häufigsten Fehlern aus den vergangenen Arbeiten an. Sie kann dir helfen, diese Fehler zu vermeiden.

## 2 WÄHREND des Tests

- Konzentriere dich. Lass dich nicht ablenken.
- Überfliege die Testfragen und Texte einmal. So bekommst du einen guten Überblick.
- Lies jede Aufgabe genau durch. Vergiss die Aufgabenstellung nicht! Drehe das Aufgabenblatt um. Manchmal geht die Aufgabe dort weiter. Entscheide dich bei Wahlaufgaben für nur eine der beiden Aufgabenstellungen.

- Bearbeite zuerst die Aufgaben, die dir leicht fallen. Das motiviert.
- Versuche unbedingt, zu jeder Aufgabe etwas zu schreiben. Ein halber Punkt kann manchmal für deine Note entscheidend sein.
- Bleibe ruhig. Versuche ruhig zu atmen und dich darauf zu konzentrieren, was du gelernt hast.
- Sieh ab und zu auf die Uhr, um nicht plötzlich vom Ende der Testzeit überrascht zu werden.
- Lies dir in den letzten Minuten deinen Test noch einmal durch. Ändere nur Dinge, bei denen du dir völlig sicher bist.

## 3 NACH dem Test (ist VOR dem Test)

Geschafft! Vergleicht nicht eure Lösungen miteinander. Ändern könnt ihr eure Antworten jetzt sowieso nicht mehr. Manchmal täuscht auch das Gefühl. Gönnt euch eine Pause und „belohnt" euch. Nach dem Test oder der Klausur kannst du deine Fehlerliste ergänzen und für das nächste Mal zu Rate ziehen.
Viel Glück.

# S2 Collecting and structuring ideas

Ideen sammeln und ordnen

Eine Rede halten, eine Diskussion durchführen, einen Aufsatz oder eine Geschichte schreiben, ein Poster oder eine Computerpräsentation erstellen, … – der erste Schritt ist immer: Sammle Ideen und ordne sie.

## 1 Schreibe auf.

Schreibe alle deine Ideen zu deinem Thema in beliebiger Reihenfolge auf – so, wie sie dir in den Sinn kommen. Du kannst auf Deutsch, Englisch oder in beiden Sprachen schreiben.
Ihr könnt eure Ideen auch in Gruppen sammeln.

## 2 Wähle aus.

- Markiere die Ideen, die dir am wichtigsten erscheinen.
- Streiche die Ideen durch, die du nicht wichtig findest.
- Setze Ideen, bei denen du dir nicht sicher bist, in Klammern.

*In Gruppen könnt ihr die wichtigsten Ideen z. B. auch mit der Methode „Placemat“ (Platzdeckchen) auswählen.*

## 3 Ordne deine Ideen.

- Schreibe das Thema auf.
- Suche in deiner Ideen-Liste nach Oberbegriffen oder überlege, welche Ideen du unter einem Oberbegriff zusammenfassen kannst. Schreibe zunächst diese Oberbegriffe auf.
- Schreibe zu jedem Oberbegriff Unterbegriffe (Einzelheiten, Beispiele, …) auf.
- Prüfe, ob du alle wichtigen Punkte aus deiner Ideenliste verwendet hast.

Es gibt verschiedene Möglichkeiten, deine Ideen zu ordnen: Du kannst dafür z. B. eine Mind-Map, ein *Fishbone*-Diagramm oder eine Tabelle erstellen. Verwende zunächst einen Bleistift, damit du leichter etwas ändern kannst. Jetzt solltest du nur noch englische Begriffe verwenden. Schlage Wörter nach, die du nicht weißt. → S4, p. 141

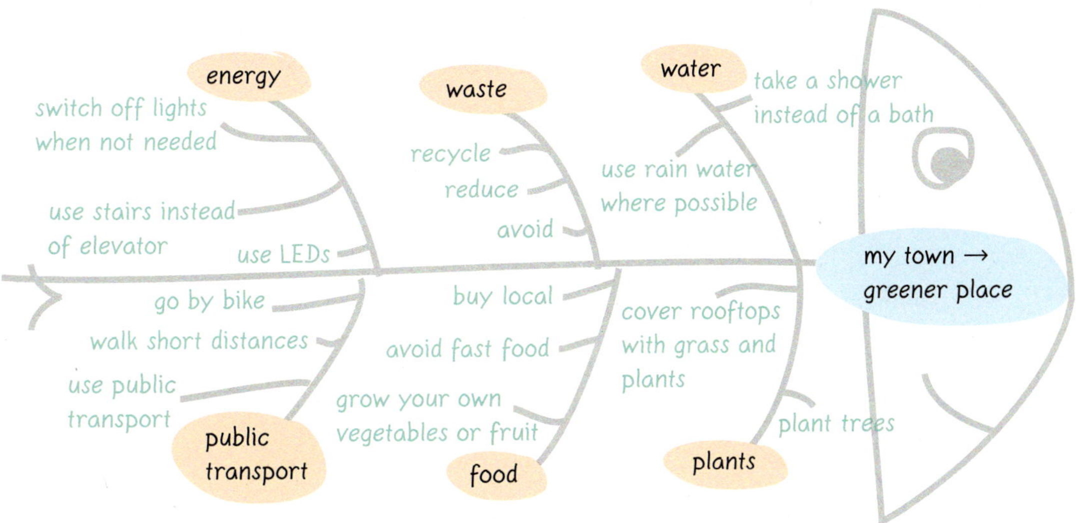

# S3 Finding information

Informationen beschaffen

Das Internet ist eine wertvolle Quelle für Informationen, die du für Referate, Präsentationen oder für die Vorbereitung auf eine Diskussion brauchst. Damit du deine Recherche möglichst zielgerichtet durchführen kannst, überlege dir im ersten Schritt immer: Was genau möchtest du wissen?
→ S2, p. 139

## 1 Suche gezielt Informationen.

- Finde klare und präzise Suchwörter. Eine Kombination von zwei bis drei Wörtern ist oft sinnvoller als nur ein Wort.
- Verwende bei deiner Recherche die englische Variante der Suchmaschine und arbeite mit englischen Seiten.
- Verwende bei unbekannten Wörtern ein digitales oder gedrucktes Wörterbuch.
- Vorsicht bei der Nutzung von Übersetzungsmaschinen: Durch die wortwörtliche Übersetzung fehlt oft der Zusammenhang, so dass der Sinn nicht immer klar wird.

Wenn du z. B. nach Tieren im Royal National Park in Australien suchst, beginne mit den Suchwörtern *animal* und *Royal National Park*. Wenn du genauere Informationen brauchst, verbinde die Wörter mit einem Pluszeichen (+) oder stelle der Suchmaschine deine Frage, z. B.:

Large animals + Royal National Park Australia

What animals are in the Royal National Park?

## 2 Prüfe die Informationen und wähle aus.

- Sieh dir die Internetseite genau an. Finde heraus, ob es sich um eine offizielle oder um eine private Seite, um Werbung oder um einen Blog handelt.
- Prüfe, wann die Seite zuletzt aktualisiert wurde.
- Vergleiche immer verschiedene Internetseiten und überprüfe, ob die Informationen und Fakten übereinstimmen.

Achte genau darauf, woher die Informationen stammen.

| offizielle Internetseite | Werbung | Blog |
|---|---|---|
| – Datum, Update<br>– Geschäfts- und Sicherheitsinformationen<br>– … | – Slogan<br>– kurz, einfach<br>– große Fotos<br>– … | – persönliche Meinung<br>– wie ein Journal oder Tagebuch<br>– … |

## 3 Gib die gefundenen Informationen wieder.

- Wenn du Informationen aus anderen Quellen entnimmst und diese wiedergibst, verwende dazu deine eigenen Worte und kopiere nicht einfach.
- Gib immer an, woher du die Informationen hast und zitiere die Quelle korrekt, v. a. dann, wenn du doch einmal Formulierungen wörtlich übernimmst. Mache Zitate durch Anführungszeichen kenntlich.
  Nenne den Link zur Seite und das Abfragedatum: http://www.national-park.gov.au (5th June 2017)

Weitere Möglichkeiten Informationen zu beschaffen, sind z. B. Bibliotheken, Archive oder Befragungen.

# S4 Using a dictionary

Ein Wörterbuch benutzen

Es gibt verschiedene Möglichkeiten, englische Wörter nachzuschlagen: Die genaueste und informativste Art ist es, ein Wörterbuch zu verwenden.

**Aufbau eines zweisprachigen Wörterbucheintrags:**

- Stammwort, auf das der gesamte Eintrag aufgebaut wird.
- So wird das Wort ausgesprochen.
- Hier wird die Wortart angegeben: Nomen (n), Adjektiv (adj), Verb (v), usw. Falls ein Verb unregelmäßig ist, werden die Formen hier in eckigen Klammern (<...>) angegeben.
- Die verschiedenen Bedeutungen des Wortes stehen jeweils hinter einer eigenen Ziffer. Nimm nicht gleich die erste Bedeutung, sondern prüfe zunächst die anderen Bedeutungen. Diese Hinweise helfen dir, die richtige Bedeutung zu finden.
- Häufige Wendungen und Phrasen, in denen das Wort vorkommt.

**share** [ʃeəʳ] **I.** *n* ❶ [An]teil *m;* **the lion's ~ of sth** der Löwenanteil von etw *dat;* **~ of the vote** Stimmenanteil *m* ❷ *usu pl (in company)* Aktie *f;* **stocks and ~s** Wertpapiere *pl* **II.** *vi* ❶ *(with others)* teilen ❷ **to ~ in sth** *(have part of)* an etw *dat* teilhaben; *(participate)* an etw *dat* beteiligt sein **III.** *vt* ❶ teilen; **to ~ responsibility** Verantwortung gemeinsam tragen ❷ *(have in common)* gemeinsam haben; **to ~ sb's concern** jds Besorgnis *f* teilen ❸ **to ~ a secret [with sb]** jdn in ein Geheimnis einweihen ▶ **a problem ~d is a problem halved** *(prov)* geteiltes Leid ist halbes Leid

**Übersetzungsbeispiele:**

Let me share this video with you. – *Lass mich dieses Video mit dir teilen.*

Everybody got their share of the prize money. – *Jeder bekam seinen Anteil am Preisgeld.*

**Aufbau und Vorteile eines einsprachigen Wörterbuchs:**

Einsprachige Wörterbücher geben dir noch weitere Zusatzinformationen, z. B.

... eine Definition für das Wort

... Beispielsätze

... ob ein Verb zusammen mit Wörtern wie with, by, on, ... verwendet wird (phrasal verbs)

Du erfährst außerdem,

... ob das Wort im britischen oder amerikanischen Englisch verwendet wird und ob es unterschiedliche Schreibweisen gibt.

... welche Synonyme es zu einem Wort gibt.

**shower¹** /ʃaʊəʳ/ *noun* [C] **1** WASH If you have or take a shower, you wash your whole body while standing under a flow of water *I got up, had a shower and got dressed.* **2** BATHROOM EQUIPMENT a piece of bathroom equipment that you stand under to wash your whole body *He likes to sing **in the shower**.* ➲See colour picture **The Bathroom** on page Centre 3 **3** RAIN a short period of rain **4 a shower of sth** a lot of small things in the air, especially falling through the air *a shower of glass*

**shower²** /ʃaʊəʳ/ *verb* [I] to wash standing under a shower

**shower sb with sth** *phrasal verb* to give a lot of something to someone *I was showered with gifts.*

Du kannst auch Online-Wörterbücher verwenden; die Suche geht dort meist sehr schnell und du kannst dir die Aussprache anhören.

# S5 Understanding spoken texts

Hörtexte verstehen / Höraufgaben bearbeiten

Radiosendungen, Nachrichten, Audioguides und Durchsagen sind Beispiele, in denen du Informationen nur übers Hören entnehmen kannst. Durchsagen werden immer wiederholt. Bei Audioguides kannst du meistens selbst entscheiden, ob du den Text noch einmal hören möchtest.

## 1 Bereite dich vor.

- Was erfährst du über das Thema und über die Personen, um die es geht?
  - Überschrift, Bilder und Aufgaben genau ansehen!
  - Bei mehreren Bildern: Worin unterscheiden sie sich?
- Worauf kommt es in der Aufgabenstellung an?
  - Globalverstehen: den Hauptgedanken verstehen.
  - Detailverstehen: Einzelheiten verstehen.
- Was weißt du schon über dieses Thema?
  - Welche Wörter kennst du zu diesem Thema?
  - Kannst du Fragen schon vor dem Hören beantworten? **Achtung:** Prüfe unbedingt, ob der Text die gleiche Antwort gibt.
- Stell dich auf folgende Dinge ein:
  - Die Antworten im Text sind meistens in der gleichen Reihenfolge wie in der Aufgabe.
  - Manchmal hörst du andere Wörter als in der Aufgabe, die aber das Gleiche bedeuten.
  - Die Sprecher können mit einem mehr oder weniger ausgeprägten Akzent sprechen.
  - Die Art, wie etwas gesagt wird, kann dir auch weiterhelfen: fröhlich, verärgert, gelangweilt, …

*Im Unterricht oder zu Hause kannst du einen Text auch in mehreren Abschnitten hören. So hast du mehr Zeit, dir Notizen zu machen.*

## 2 Höre den Text.

- Lass dich nicht ablenken. Schau auf deine Aufgaben und halte deinen Stift bereit.
- Schreibe nur englische Stichwörter oder Wortfetzen auf. Verwende Abkürzungen.

| | | | |
|---|---|---|---|
| + | and / yes | = | the same as, equals, means |
| – | not / no | ≠ | not the same as, does not equal |
| ++ | good / great | → | becomes, will be |
| e.g. | for example | | |

- Lass eine Leerzeile zwischen den einzelnen Aufgaben, damit du später etwas ergänzen kannst.
- Bei Multiple-Choice-Aufgaben: Markiere die richtige Antwort oder Antworten. Wenn du dich schwer tust, streiche die Antworten durch, von denen du weißt, dass sie falsch sind. Wenn du gar nicht weiterkommst, rate. Das ist immer besser, als gar keine Antwort zu geben.

## 3 Beantworte die Fragen.

Antworte mit Hilfe deiner Notizen in der Sprache, in der die Aufgaben gestellt sind.

## 4 Höre den Text ein zweites Mal.

- Konzentriere dich auf die Dinge, die du beim ersten Mal nicht verstanden hast.
- Überprüfe deine Antworten.

# S6 Understanding films

Filme verstehen

Um die Handlung eines Films begreifen zu können, musst du nicht nur die Sprache verstehen. Es gibt weitere Hinweise, die du nutzen kannst.

## 1 Vor dem Ansehen: Arten von Filmen

Es gibt unterschiedliche Arten von Filmen, z. B. Musikclip, Werbefilm, Spielfilm, Dokumentarfilm usw.

Was weißt du über die verschiedenen Filmarten? Was erwartest du von diesem Film?

## 2 Während des Ansehens: Filmische Mittel

Mache dir beim Ansehen Notizen zu den folgenden Punkten:

**Erstes Ansehen:**

- Wie wird der Schauplatz *(setting)* dargestellt?

  Achte auf Landschaften, Gebäude, Räume, Kleidung und Gegenstände.

- Wer sind die Hauptfiguren *(main characters)*?

  Achte darauf, wer den größten Redeanteil hat und am häufigsten auftaucht.

- Wie ist der Verlauf der Geschichte *(plot)*?

  Achte auf die Reihenfolge der Ereignisse: Werden sie der Reihe nach (chronologisch) erzählt, oder gibt es Zeitsprünge (Rückblenden)? Wer erzählt die Ereignisse und wie werden sie dargestellt?

**Zweites Ansehen:**

- Kameraeinstellungen verdeutlichen oft den Inhalt oder sie unterstreichen bestimmte Gefühle.

  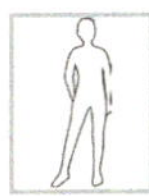
  Die Totale *(long / wide shot)* gibt einen Überblick über die Szene und den Schauplatz.

  Die Nahaufnahme *(close-up)* unterstreicht z. B. die Gefühle einer Person oder die Wichtigkeit eines Gegenstandes.

- Wie wird eine bestimmte Atmosphäre *(atmosphere / mood)* geschaffen?

  Achte auf Bilder, Licht, Farben, Musik und Geräusche.

- Wie stellen die Schauspieler die Figuren dar?

  Achte auf Sprache, Mimik und Gestik, Körperhaltung, Kleidung und Frisuren.

## 3 Nach dem Ansehen: Filme bewerten

- Ergänze deine Notizen.
- Hat dir der Film gefallen oder nicht? Nenne Gründe. → S15, p. 150

Wenn du Schwierigkeiten hast, englischsprachige Filme zu verstehen, blende die englischen Untertitel *(subtitles)* ein. Wenn du die Wörter geschrieben siehst, kannst du sie viel besser verstehen.

# S7 Understanding written texts

Lesetexte verstehen

Bei der Textarbeit ist es wichtig, zunächst zu klären, um welche Art von Text es sich handelt (z. B. Nachrichten, Werbung, Blog, Kommentar, Zeitschriftenartikel, Bedienungsanleitung, Geschichte usw.). Anschließend sollte man sich überlegen, welche Informationen man dem Text entnehmen will.

## Vorgehen beim Auswerten eines Textes

Lies den Text mindestens zweimal durch.
Halte dich dabei an die folgenden Schritte:

**Vor dem Lesen:**
- Lies zunächst die Überschrift. Worum könnte es in dem Text gehen?
- Falls es Zwischenüberschriften gibt, liefern diese weitere Informationen.
- Sieh dir auch die Fotos an. Sie können dir zusätzliche Hinweise geben.

**Während des ersten Lesens:**
- Mache dir unter folgenden Überschriften Notizen: *What? Who? When? Where?*
- Markiere wichtige Textstellen in verschiedenen Farben (z. B. Informationen zu Personen blau, inhaltliche Punkte grün und Zeit- und Ortsangaben gelb; *siehe Beispieltext).*
- Überlege bei unbekannten Wörtern, ob du bereits ähnliche Wörter im Englischen oder in anderen Sprachen kennst. Du kannst auch versuchen, sie aus dem Zusammenhang zu erschließen. Unterstreiche Wörter, die du nachschlagen musst. → S4, p. 141

**Während des zweiten Lesens:**
- Beantworte nun weitere Fragen, z. B. Warum und wie geschah etwas? Wer erzählt die Geschichte? Für welche Leser wurde der Text geschrieben?

## Verschiedene Lesetechniken

Abhängig davon, welche und wie viele Informationen du im Text finden willst, kannst du eine dieser Lesetechniken anwenden:

***Skimming*** **= orientierendes Lesen**
Beim *Skimming* überfliegst du den Text, um die wichtigsten Gedanken des Textes *(gist)* zusammenzufassen. Dabei ist es nicht nötig, jedes Wort zu verstehen.
- Lies die Überschrift. Sie verrät dir, worum es in dem Text geht.
- Achte auf zentrale Begriffe *(keywords)* oder wiederkehrende Personen. Auch Bilder können dir helfen, einzuschätzen, was wichtig ist und was nicht.
- Achte auf Zwischenüberschriften. Sie verraten dir, worum es im nächsten Abschnitt geht.

***Scanning*** **= suchendes Lesen**
Beim Scanning durchsuchst du den Text gezielt, um die Stellen mit der gesuchten Information *(details)* zu finden.
- Suche nach den passenden Stichwörtern *(keywords)*. Sie zeigen an, welche Teile du genauer lesen solltest, um mehr zu erfahren.
- Überlege, in welcher Form die gesuchte Information auftauchen könnte, z. B. als Zahlen oder kursiv oder fett gedruckt?

***Close-reading*** **= intensives Lesen**
Beim *Close-reading* entnimmst du dem Text alle Informationen, um wie z. B. bei einem Kochrezept oder in einer Bedienungsanleitung alle wichtigen Schritte bzw. Hinweise beachten zu können.

# Street art: Is it art or is it a crime?

What's the difference between a street artist and someone who just wants to write their name on a wall? If you draw a smiley on a window, are you a street artist, or are you a criminal? Street art is art in a city's public places and is getting more popular all the time. Often the artists aren't allowed to make art in these places, so they work at night and don't earn money for their work. These artists are often very talented, and they want to make people think about important topics.

## The history of street art

People have painted graffiti for hundreds of years, but street art probably started in New York in the 1980s. They painted graffiti on the subway trains, and instead of just writing their name or 'tag', they began painting amazing pictures. By painting in public places the artist could show people his or her work and message directly and not only in a museum. The first successful street artist was probably Keith Haring. He painted a wall as a present to the community in Houston Street, New York. This wall is one of the most famous street art walls in the world, and only artists who are invited can paint on it.

## The most famous street artist ever?

Today, the most famous street artist is probably Banksy. He started painting graffiti in the 1990s in Bristol, England. His works make people think about war and the power of money, and his pictures are funny and shocking at the same time. He likes to include children, old people, and animals in his work. One of his most famous pieces is probably *Keep it spotless*. This was originally a painting by another famous modern artist, and Banksy painted over it. It sold for $ 1,700,000. Banksy's work can now be found all over the world, from the UK to Israel and the US. Even today no one really knows who Banksy is.

What?
→ street art
- graffiti, painted pictures
- important topics
- direct messages

Who?
→ Keith Haring
→ Banksy (identity not clear)

When and where?
→ in public places, not only in a museum
→ graffiti has a long history, started in New York around the 1980s
→ today Banksy's work found all over the world

# S8 Analysing texts

Texte analysieren

Wenn du einen Text analysieren willst, finde zunächst heraus, um welche Art von Text es sich handelt.

## Fiktionale Texte

Fiktionale Texte sind z. B. Gedichte, Geschichten oder Romane. Sie erschaffen eine eigene Wirklichkeit, die so außerhalb der „Textwelt" zwar vorkommen kann, aber nicht muss. Fiktionale Texte haben zum Ziel, den Leser zu unterhalten.

**Erzähler *(narrator)***

Beschreibe, aus welcher Perspektive erzählt wird.

The story is told from a first-person point of view / by a third-person narrator.

**Schauplatz *(setting)***

Beschreibe, wo und wann die Handlung stattfindet.

The story is set in .... • The action takes place in 2008 / in a time when ....

**Figuren *(characters)***

- Beschreibe die wichtigsten Figuren der Geschichte.
- Beschreibe kurz ihr Äußeres und ihr Verhalten.
- Begründe, welche Rolle die jeweilige Figur für dich in der Geschichte spielt.

The main character(s) is / are .... • *(name)* is tall / small .... • *(name)* has dark / red / ... hair. • *(name)* seems to be a person who is happy / unhappy ... strong / weak ... clever / stupid .... • *(name)* seems to be the bad guy / hero / heroine of the story because in line ... he / she says / reacts in an annoying / a brave / ... way.

## Sachtexte

Sachtexte sind z. B. Zeitungsartikel, Bewerbungsschreiben, Lebensläufe *(CVs)*, Interviews usw. Sie handeln von einem bestimmten Thema und liefern dabei Fakten. Sachtexte haben zum Ziel, den Leser zu informieren.

**Textart, Thema und Aufbau**

- Nenne die Textart und das Thema.
- Erkläre den Aufbau des Texts.

The text is a report / interview / instruction / letter / advertisement .... • It tells the reader about .... • The text can be divided into ... parts. • The first / second / ... part is about ....

## Allgemeines

**Sprache und Stilmittel**

- Untersuche Sprache und Stilmittel.

The author presents his / her idea by using very clear / colourful / technical language. • He / she uses comparisons / alliteration / images / ....

**Persönlicher Eindruck**

- Wenn du deine Meinung zu einem Text äußern sollst, begründe sie.

I think the text is interesting / exciting / funny / great / awful because .... • In my opinion the author is right when he / she says that .... • All in all, I like / dislike the text / story / ... because ....

S

# S9 Describing charts

Diagramme beschreiben

Diagramme fassen komplexe Sachverhalte in vereinfachter Form zusammen. Welche Art von Darstellung verwendet wird, hängt davon ab, welche Information damit verdeutlicht werden soll. Wenn du ein Diagramm verstehen und auswerten willst, gehe schrittweise vor.

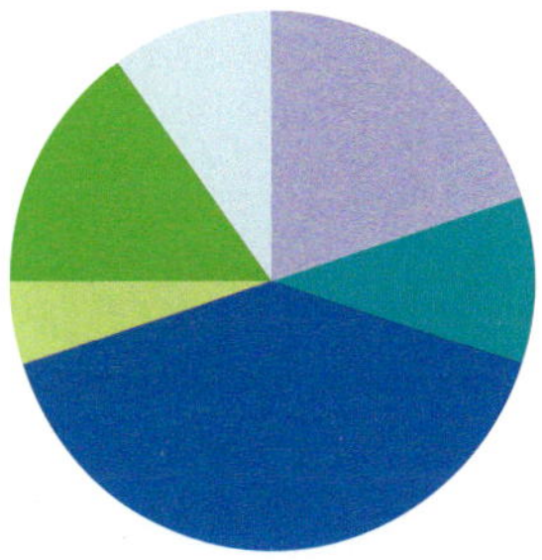

Mit einem Kuchen- oder Kreisdiagramm *(pie chart)* werden Prozentanteile verdeutlicht. Die einzelnen Stücke stellen die Anteile am ganzen Kreis (= 100 %) dar.

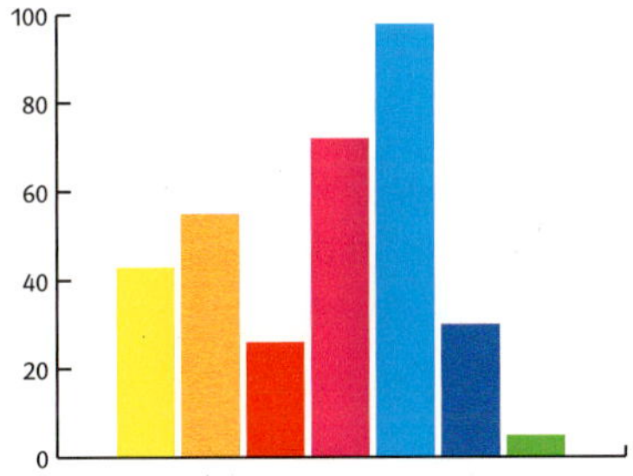


Säulen- oder Balkendiagramme *(bar chart)* verwendet man, um Zahlen direkt miteinander zu vergleichen.

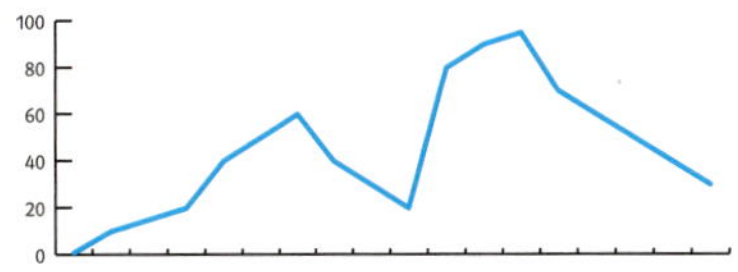


In einem Kurvendiagramm *(line graph)* kann man gut darstellen, wie sich etwas über einen längeren Zeitraum hinweg entwickelt hat.

## 1 Benenne, was dargestellt wird.

- Lies die Überschrift. Sie verrät dir, was im Diagramm, der Tabelle usw. dargestellt wird. Falls es keine Überschrift gibt, verraten dir die Beschriftung der Kreisstücke, die Achsen der Diagramme und die Spalten der Tabellen, was dargestellt wird.
- Sage, um welche Art von Diagramm es sich handelt und was damit dargestellt wird.
- Nenne die Quelle des Diagramms (z. B. Webseite, Zeitung, Zeitschrift) und den Zeitpunkt, an dem es veröffentlicht wurde.

This is a pie chart / bar chart / line graph / … . • It is about … / shows … / deals with … . • It was published by … in … .

## 2 Beschreibe.

- Beschreibe kurz, welche Informationen du aus dem Diagramm ablesen kannst.

The (next) largest group of … . • The majority / minority of … . • Half of … . • Most of … . • 40 percent of … .

- Wenn du aus dem Diagramm eine Entwicklung ablesen kannst, beschreibe diese kurz.

The number of … goes up / increases by … / drops / goes down / doesn't change.

## 3 Fasse zusammen.

- Fasse die wichtigsten Aussagen des Diagramms in ein bis zwei Sätzen zusammen.
- Beschreibe, welche Schlüsse du aus dem Diagramm ziehen kannst.

The chart / numbers / figures show / suggest that … . • We can draw the conclusion that … .

# S10 Writing and checking a text

Einen Text entwerfen und prüfen

## Vor dem Schreiben

Werde dir zunächst klar darüber, welche Textart (z. B. Zusammenfassung, Bericht, Brief, Geschichte usw.) du schreiben möchtest und für wen dein Text bestimmt sein soll.
→ S2, p. 139; → S4, p. 141

## 1 Plane deinen Text.

**Einleitung** ***(introduction / beginning)***
Informiere z. B. den Leser, worum es in deinem Text geht, bzw. wecke mit einem packenden Anfang Interesse.

**Hauptteil** ***(main part / middle)***
Gliedere den Hauptteil, indem du für jedes Argument oder jede Idee einen neuen Abschnitt beginnst.

**Schluss** ***(conclusion / ending)***
Fasse z. B. die Inhalte aus dem Hauptteil nochmals zusammen, bzw. finde einen ansprechenden Schluss.

## 2 Fertige einen Textentwurf an.

Nimm die Planung deines Textes als Grundlage für deinen ersten Entwurf.

## 3 Schreibe deinen Text.

- Verwende deinen Entwurf als Grundlage für deinen Text.
- Verbinde deine Sätze mit Bindewörtern. Das macht deinen Text verständlicher und leichter lesbar.

because … • for example … • therefore … • in addition … • as well as … • however … • in other words …

## 4 Überarbeite deinen Text.

- Lies deinen Entwurf noch einmal durch. Du kannst auch einen Mitschüler / eine Mitschülerin bitten, deinen Text zu lesen. Ist der Text verständlich und liest er sich flüssig?
- Korrigiere Fehler und holprige Formulierungen. Verwende dafür eine Checkliste.
- Achte auf *false friends*. Das sind Wörter, die im Deutschen und im Englischen ähnlich klingen, aber unterschiedliche Bedeutungen haben, z. B. *to become* = werden.

Lege dir eine persönliche Fehlerliste an. So kannst du Fehler, die dir immer wieder passieren, in Zukunft vermeiden.

## Checklisten

Wenn du einen Text geschrieben hast, ist es wichtig, dass du ihn am Ende noch einmal liest und die Wörter und die Grammatik überprüfst. Sieh dir das Beispiel auf dieser Seite an. Es enthält die Fehler, die am häufigsten vorkommen.

*A baeutiful place*

*Kruger National Park is south Africas oldest national park. There are plains and the landscape is flat. But the animal are fantastic. Most tourists go safari to see the elefant, the lion, the rhino, the leopard and the buffalo. They have to stay in their cars because the animals is dangerous. But they can take photos on the animals. The park was opened in 1926. Today rangers like Tony Okonwo work their You can go on tours, and the rangers help to conserve the animals and plants.*

*Kruger National Park is a beautiful place you will never forget*

- Achte auf vertauschte Buchstaben. ☐
- Eigennamen werden groß geschrieben. ☐
- Vergiss nicht den Apostroph beim Genitiv. ☐
- Steht ein Wort im Plural, hänge das -s an. ☐
- Überprüfe die richtige Schreibweise mit Hilfe eines Wörterbuchs. Manche Wörter sind dem Deutschen sehr ähnlich, werden aber anders geschrieben. ☐
- Lasse keine Wörter aus. ☐
- Setze die richtige Form des Verbs ein. ☐
- Achte auf die richtige Präposition. ☐
- Manche Wörter werden zwar gleich ausgesprochen, werden aber anders geschrieben und haben eine andere Bedeutung. ☐
- Vergiss die Satzzeichen nicht. ☐

*Wenn du deinen Text mit einem Textverarbeitungsprogramm schreibst, stelle die Sprache in deinem Programm auf Englisch um. Einige (aber nicht alle) Fehler werden dir rot und grün (für Grammatik) angestrichen.*

# S11 Writing a summary

Einen Text zusammenfassen

Bevor du einen Text zusammenfasst, beachte, dass du – je nach Textart – unterschiedlich vorgehen musst:

**Fiktionale Texte**
(Romane, Geschichten usw.)

Who is the text about?
What happens?
Where / When / Why does it happen?

**Nicht-Fiktionale Texte**
(Zeitungs- oder Fachartikel usw.)

What is the text about?
What are the main arguments?
Where / When / Why is it important?

## 1 Schreibe eine kurze Einleitung.

- Nenne Titel, Autor / Autorin und Herkunft des Textes.
- Sage, wovon der Text handelt.

The article / story / … *(title of text)* was written by *(author's name).* • It was published in *(name of magazine / book / …)* and is about … / deals with … / describes … .

## 2 Fasse den Hauptteil in ein paar Sätzen zusammen.

- Benutze hierfür deine Markierungen und Notizen. Verwende im Hauptteil immer das *simple present* und deine eigenen Worte.
- Verwende keine Zitate oder die direkte Rede.

In the first / second / … part, the author writes / points out / explains that / why … . • Then / Afterwards the author goes on with / discusses why … .

## 3 Schreibe einen Schlussteil.

Gib darin die Hauptaussagen des Textes wieder.

To sum up, … . • All in all, … . • I've come to the conclusion that … .

Summary of 'Just leave me alone!' ← **Überschrift**

The article 'Just leave me alone!' was written by Adam Harvey. It was published in *The Times* on 23rd May 2016 and deals with the topic of exam stress among teenagers. ← **Einleitung** Autor, Datum, Quelle, Thema

In the first part, the author explains that eight out of ten students feel stressed during exams. Most of them want their parents to leave them alone to study and not ask them lots of questions about their exams. ← **Hauptteil**

Then the author discusses how parents can support their children, for example cooking them their favourite meal. Students say it isn't helpful if parents always check if their children are studying or not.

Exam stress is a big problem, but there are certain ways in which parents can support stressed students. ← **Schluss**

# S12 Writing a letter

Einen Brief schreiben

Einen Brief oder eine E-Mail kannst du umgangssprachlich oder sachlich formulieren, je nachdem, wer der Adressat ist.
**Umgangssprachlich** schreibst du, wenn du jemanden persönlich gut kennst; unter Gleichaltrigen / Freunden (z. B. bei E-Mails, Post-, Dankes- oder Glückwunschkarten)
Einen **formellen** Stil verwendest du in einem Leserbrief *(siehe Beispiel)* oder Forumseintrag; bei einer Bewerbung; im Austausch mit Ämtern, Institutionen und Unternehmen; bei einer Beschwerde …

Schreibe **deine Adresse** oben rechts auf das Dokument.

Platziere **Adressat** und dessen **Anschrift** links.

Das **Datum** steht rechts.

**Betreff**: Fasse das Thema deines Briefes zusammen.

**Anrede:** Wenn dir der Adressat **bekannt** ist, beginne mit **Dear Ms … / Mr ….** Wenn er dir **unbekannt** ist, beginne mit **Dear Sir or Madam.**

Nenne zu Beginn den **Grund deines Schreibens.** Schildere dein Anliegen.

**Grußformel:** Wenn dir der Adressat **bekannt** ist, verwende **Yours sincerely.** Ist der Adressat **unbekannt**, verwende **Yours faithfully.**

**Unterschrift** und **Name**

Kartöfflestr. 123
70176 Stuttgart
Germany

Youthworld Magazine
Connor Street
London
SE4 6PH

6th June 2017

**Subject:** Your article 'Why are young people not interested in Work and Travel any more?' (April 2017)

Dear Sir or Madam,

I would like to comment on your article 'Why are young people not interested in Work and Travel any more?' (April 2017) because I think it is quite unfair towards young people.
In your article you write that many young people are only interested in taking holidays, and that they do not show much interest in working or understanding different cultures. This is an unfair statement. Of course young people like to have fun, but many are also interested in learning about other countries and cultures. Lots of young people want to help in social or environmental projects all around the world. For example, last summer I spent two weeks in South America helping in a wildlife project. I met many young people who were passionate about wildlife.
The article was unfair because it only showed one way to look at the topic. It would have been better to interview more young people and collect different opinions.

Yours faithfully,

*Julian Fischer*
Julian Fischer

*Verwende in einem formellen Schreiben keine Kurzformen.*

# S13 Writing a letter of application

Ein Bewerbungsschreiben verfassen

Für ein Bewerbungsschreiben gelten die gleichen Regeln wie bei einem formellen Schreiben. Füge außerdem folgende Inhalte hinzu:

→ S12, p. 151

**Briefkopf**

**Betreffzeile**

**Anrede**

**erster Abschnitt:**
- Stelle dich kurz vor.
- Sage, auf welche Stelle du dich bewirbst.
- Erwähne, wie / wo du von dieser Stelle erfahren hast.

**zweiter Abschnitt:**
- Zähle Qualifikationen und deine Erfahrungen auf, die für diese Stelle relevant sind.
- Nenne deine persönlichen Stärken.
- Sage, dass du in der Lage bist, die neuen Aufgaben gut zu erfüllen.
- Sage, warum du die richtige Person für die Stelle bist.
- Erkläre, warum du an der Stelle interessiert bist.

**Schluss:**
- Sage, dass du dich auf eine Antwort freust.

**Grußformel**

Kartöfflestr. 123
70176 Stuttgart
Germany

Ms Juliane Reed
Cruise Ships of the Caribbean
15 Handforth Road
London
SE34 7GH

6th August 2018

**Re:** Your job advertisement of July 2018

Dear Ms Reed,

Please find attached my application for the job as a waitress with Cruise Ships of the Caribbean as advertised in *Travel & Work Magazine* in July 2018.

After finishing school in June 2018, I am now looking forward to new challenges. I believe that I am well-qualified for this job. For the last three years I have worked as a help in a local restaurant during my summer holidays. Part of my job there was waiting tables, preparing food and cleaning the kitchen. I like being there for people. Also, my English is good, so I can deal with international guests.
I would like to spend a year working and travelling before I start a training programme to become a chef. The job that you are offering would give me the chance to get more work experience in service while travelling around the world.

Thank you for taking the time to consider this application. I look forward to hearing from you.

Yours sincerely,
*Hanna Fischer*
Hanna Fischer

Encl.: CV

Überprüfe dein Bewerbungsschreiben genau auf Rechtschreib- und Grammatikfehler.

# S14 Writing a CV

Einen Lebenslauf schreiben

Es gibt Unterschiede zwischen deutschen, britischen und amerikanischen Lebensläufen. Hier findest du ein Beispiel für einen Lebenslauf, wie er in Großbritannien geschrieben wird.

**Persönliche Daten**
- Name, Adresse, Telefonnummer, E-Mail
- Du kannst dein Geburtsdatum angeben, musst aber nicht.

**Persönliches Statement**
- Beschreibe dich kurz.
- Was ist deine Motivation?

**Schulbildung**
- Grundschule
- Weiterführende Schule (bei beiden: Name und Ort + Angabe der Jahreszahlen von … bis …)

**Prüfungen**
Name und Jahr der Prüfung

**Kenntnisse**
Fähigkeiten und Fertigkeiten, die du beherrschst, z. B. *computer*, *language* usw.

**Berufliche Erfahrungen**
Praktika und Jobs, die du gemacht hast: Was? Wo? Wann?

**Interessen**
Hobbys, Sport, ehrenamtliche Tätigkeiten usw.

Name: Hanna Fischer
Address: Kartöfflestraße 123, 70176 Stuttgart, Germany
Phone: + 49 123 456 7890
E-mail: fischer_h@online.de
Date of birth: 12th August 2002

A positive team player who is interested in travelling and being there for people.

Education:
2012 – 2018: Schloss-Realschule (Comprehensive school)
2006 – 2012: Fuchsweg-Schule (Primary school)

Qualifications:
2018: Mittlerer Schulabschluss (Secondary school leaving certificate), with special interest in English and Geography

Skills:
Very good communication skills and excellent team worker. Fluent English.

Experience:
2016 – 2018: Restaurant help during summer holidays
April 2017: Volunteer at a soup kitchen in the UK

Interests:
- Cooking – completed different cooking classes, e.g. French cooking
- Travelling and learning about other cultures – trips to North Africa and Thailand

References:
Available upon request

**Beachte außerdem folgende Regeln für deinen Lebenslauf auf Englisch:**
- Wenn möglich, verwende englische Ausdrücke für deutsche Begriffe (z. B. *comprehensive school* für Gesamtschule).
- Liste Kenntnisse und Fertigkeiten auf, die für den Job relevant sind.
- Schreibe nicht mehr als eine Seite.
- Überprüfe deinen Lebenslauf auf Fehler, bevor du ihn verschickst.
- Unterschreibe nicht am Ende.
- Füge kein Foto hinzu.

# S15 Writing a book or film review

Eine Buch- oder Filmkritik schreiben

Hat dir ein Buch oder ein Film gefallen oder nicht? Sollten andere dieses Buch lesen bzw. sich diesen Film ansehen oder nicht? In einer Kritik kannst du deine Meinung dazu äußern und begründen. Beachte dabei folgende Struktur:

## 1 Einleitung

- Schildere kurz deinen ersten Eindruck vom Film / Buch.
- Nenne Titel, Autor / Autorin / Regisseur / Regisseurin und das Erscheinungsjahr.
- Nenne das Genre und die wichtigsten Figuren.

The film / book *(title)* is one of the best / worst .... • I really liked / didn't like *(title)* .... • It is a comedy / drama / romance ... and was written / directed by *(author's / director's name)* in *(year)*. • It is about .... • The main characters are *(name)* ....

## 2 Inhalt des Buchs / Films

- Fasse kurz den Verlauf der Geschichte zusammen.
- Verwende das simple present.
- Verwende Adjektive, um deinen Text interessanter und aussagekräftiger zu machen.

The story starts in / takes place in / is about .... • The story is funny / simple / exciting / boring .... • One of the most surprising moments in the film / book is when .... • The story ends with ....

## 3 Deine Meinung

Sage, was dir an dem Film / Buch besonders gefallen oder missfallen hat.

The story is great / boring / silly / .... • The characters / stars are .... • Another thing I really liked / didn't like was .... • *(Title)* is a great / awful piece of writing / filmmaking.

## 4 Schlussfolgerung

Empfehle den Film / das Buch weiter oder rate davon ab.

Everybody / Nobody should see / read it. • I would / wouldn't watch / read it again • I would / wouldn't recommend it to anyone.

### Book Review: Jasper Jones

I really enjoyed *Jasper Jones* (2009) by Craig Silvey. It is a murder mystery, but it deals with racism too. ← **1. Einleitung**

The story takes place in Australia in 1965. The main characters are two teenagers, Charlie and Jasper. They find a girl's dead body and want to find out how she died. ← **2. Inhalt**

The most exciting moment is when they think they know who the murderer is because what happens is so unexpected! The ending is incredible: it's scary and beautiful at the same time. ← **3. Deine Meinung**

The story is fascinating and it never got boring. All in all, I'd recommend this book to my friends, and I give it 4 stars out of 5. ← **4. Schlussfolgerung**

# S16 Writing a report

Einen Bericht schreiben

In einem Bericht gibst du sachliche Informationen wieder. Wichtig dabei ist, dass die Informationen vollständig und verständlich sind. Im folgenden findest du ein Beispiel für einen Zeitungsbericht über einen Unfall:

**Beantworte zuerst die W-Fragen**
- Was geschah?
- Wer war beteiligt?
- Wann ist es passiert?
- Wo ist es passiert?
- Wie ist es abgelaufen?
- Warum geschah es?

## Big fire at the Falcon
### Shopping centre closed until 3rd May

Yesterday evening there was a fire at the Falcon Shopping Centre in Binder Street, Liverpool. It started at 8 p.m. One person was hurt, and four shops were badly damaged. The fire started in the electronics shop Power Up, but the cause is still unclear.

**Nenne die Quelle der Informationen.**

**Schildere Einzelheiten zum Geschehen.**

Adam Childs, one of the firefighters who helped to stop the fire, said it had taken 45 minutes to stop the fire completely. "It was lucky that all the shops were already closed. Only one person was hurt. She is the owner of the sweet shop next to the electronics shop," Childs explained. The woman spent last night in hospital but will be sent home today.

**Gib Informationen zu den Hintergründen.**

The Falcon Shopping Centre opened in 2001 and has 48 shops. It will be closed for the rest of this week and will open again on Monday, 4th May.

### Die ABC-Regel eines Berichtes:

**Accuracy** (= Genauigkeit)

Stelle sicher, dass alle Fakten (Personen, Orte, Gegenstände, Adressen usw.) genau stimmen.

**Brevity** (= Kürze)

Fasse dich kurz und beantworte gleichzeitig die wichtigsten W-Fragen (siehe oben).

**Clarity** (= Anschaulichkeit)

Schreibe so, dass der Leser ganz klar verstehen kann, was gemeint ist.

### Die Sprache eines Berichtes:

- In Berichten wird oft die Passivform der Verben verwendet. Das macht den Bericht sachlicher und schafft Distanz.
- Verwende Beispiele und / oder Zitate.
- Wer ist der Adressat deines Berichtes? Passe die Sprache dementsprechend an.

### Die Schlagzeile eines Berichtes:

Die Schlagzeile ist der wichtigste Teil eines Berichtes. Ist sie interessant, wird der Leser deinen Bericht lesen. Wenn nicht, blättert oder klickt er weiter. Wecke mit deiner Schlagzeile die Neugier des Lesers. Je kürzer die Schlagzeile, desto besser.

# S17 Writing an argumentative essay

Einen argumentativen Text schreiben

Ein argumentativer Text behandelt ein Thema, einen Text oder ein Zitat, zu dem es verschiedene Sichtweisen gibt.
→ S10, p. 148

## Der Aufbau deines Textes:

**Einleitung**

- Sage, warum das Thema wichtig ist.
- Stelle nun deine Sichtweise bzw. deine Fragestellung vor.

The topic of ... is one of great interest to .... • It is an important topic because .... • The question is: Should ... ?

**Hauptteil**

- Wenn du nur eine Sichtweise darstellen willst, beginne mit dem schwächsten und ende mit dem stärksten Argument.
- Willst du zwei oder mehrere Sichtweisen darstellen, kannst du aus zwei Varianten wählen:

Firstly / secondly ...

Moreover, ... • Either ..., or .... • not only ... but also .... • Another way to look at this is .... • On the other hand, ....

| | | |
|---|---|---|
| Einleitung ↓ | | Einleitung ↓ |
| Pro → Kontra ↓ | | Pro ↓ |
| Pro → Kontra ↓ | oder | Kontra ↓ |
| Pro → Kontra ↓ | | Schluss |
| Schluss | | |

Wenn du die Pro-Seite vertrittst, beginne mit den Kontra-Argumenten. Wenn du die Kontra-Seite vertrittst, beginne mit den Pro-Argumenten.

- Schreibe im ersten Satz dein Argument.
- Unterstütze dein Argument mit Fakten und anschaulichen Beispielen. Wenn möglich, präsentiere Hintergrundinformationen zu dem Thema. Das macht deinen Text überzeugend.

For example .... • A good example of this is .... • ... as in the following example .... • Statistics show that ....

*Wenn du den Leser von deiner Sichtweise überzeugen willst, drücke im Text deine Gefühle aus. Soll sich der Leser seine eigene Meinung bilden, bleibe sachlich.*

S

**Schluss**

- Verdeutliche deine persönliche Sichtweise bzw. überlasse es dem Leser, sich seine Meinung und / oder Schlussfolgerung zu bilden.

My conclusion is .... • In conclusion, .... • To sum up, .... • All in all, ....

Sieh dir dieses Beispiel an:

**'Schools don't need pens and paper any more: Students should only use tablets and laptops.' Do you agree with this statement?**

Today technology is used everywhere. Statistics show that almost 85% of workers in the US use a laptop or PC at work. But in most schools students still learn with books and write on paper. So, should schools still use pens and paper today?

← **Einleitung**

Beispiele
Fakten

Firstly, if students use computers from a very young age, their IT skills will develop more quickly. For example, Mark Zuckerberg learned programming early and developed his social media site while he was still at college. In addition, using computers could make life easier for students who find writing difficult. They could type their answers without worrying about their handwriting.

← **Hauptteil**

Argumente pro

But there are negative effects of using too much technology too. Science has shown that when you write something down by hand, you can remember it better. Also, when students use their hands, it helps them with other skills, like drawing.

Argumente kontra

In conclusion, I think that schools should use technology because students should learn skills which they will later need in a job. But it would be a bad idea to not use pens or paper at all because young children also need to develop other skills for daily life.

← **Schluss**

# S18 Writing a story

Eine Geschichte schreiben

Wenn du eine Geschichte schreibst, kann du diese völlig frei erfinden oder anhand eines vorgegebenen Themas verfassen. → S2, p. 139

*Brauchst du Ideen für deine Geschichte?
Denke an Geschehnisse oder Personen aus Büchern, Filmen oder aus deinem Alltag!*

## 1 Plane deine Geschichte

Wenn du eine Geschichte schreibst, musst du zuvor ein paar Entscheidungen treffen.

**Erzähler**

- Der Ich-Erzähler schildert die Geschichte aus seiner oder ihrer Sicht heraus.
- Ein Er- / Sie-Erzähler erzählt die Geschichte über andere Personen oder aus der Sicht einer anderen Person.

**Figuren**

- Wähle eine Hauptfigur, die ganz besondere Fähigkeiten hat (z. B. magische Kräfte besitzt).
- Für weitere Figuren lasse dich von Menschen aus deiner Umgebung inspirieren (jemand, der immer kichert, jemand, der sehr schnell / langsam spricht usw.).

**Ort**

Wähle einen Ort, an dem deine Geschichte spielt (ein altes Schloss, einen Zauberwald usw.).

**Zeit**

- Entscheide dich für eine Zeit, in der deine Geschichte spielt. Das kann gestern, letztes Jahr oder im nächsten Jahrhundert sein.

**Handlung**

- Anfang: Du kannst z. B. damit beginnen, die Hauptfigur vorzustellen; oder unmittelbar in die Handlung der Geschichte einsteigen.
- Hauptteil: Überlege dir, was die Handlung deiner Geschichte vorantreibt. Das könnte ein Konflikt oder ein Problem sein, ein lustiger oder überraschender Vorfall, eine zufällige Begegnung, …
- Schluss: Du kannst z. B. ein offenes Ende wählen, oder eines, das die Geschichte auflöst.

## 2 Schreibe deine Geschichte

Dieses Beispiel zeigt dir, wie deine Geschichte beginnen könnte. → S10, p. 148

*Verwende beim Erzählen die Vergangenheitsform.*
*Benutze Adjektive und Adverbien.*

It was evening and there were no cars or people on the street. I ran until I came to a big, old building, which looked dark and dirty. The sign said, 'Magic bought and sold here.' I pushed the door open.
"Good evening, young lady," said the old man behind the desk. He spoke very slowly and looked at me closely. I knew he was thinking, 'What has she got for me?'
"Buying or selling?" he asked curiously.
"Er … selling… I think." My voice sounded less nervous than I was. My father would go crazy if he knew I was here, talking to a man who could take some of my magic skills, put them into a bottle and sell them to a stranger. But we needed money, and this was the only way to get some fast. I hated this place, hated this man, but he had what I needed, and I had what he wanted.
"Show me what you've got for me then," he said.
Although I was really scared, I took a deep breath and showed him my hands. His eyes suddenly looked round and shocked. "I can't believe it," he said. …

# S19 Text-based writing

Schreiben zu einer Textvorlage

Wenn du einen vorhandenen Text weiterführen sollst, kann es sein, dass du z. B. das Ende eines Textes ergänzen oder eine Geschichte aus einer anderen Perspektive erzählen sollst. Manchmal wird auch ein Wechsel der Textsorte verlangt. Übliche Textvorlagen sind z. B. Dialoge, Tagebucheinträge, Blogs, Zeitungsberichte oder Geschichten.

## 1 Beachte die inhaltlichen und stilistischen Merkmale der Textsorten.

- Geschichte – Eine Geschichte ist wesentlich durch ihre Erzählperspektive, Figuren, Ort, Zeit und Handlung bestimmt. Sollst du ein Ende für eine Geschichte schreiben, achte darauf, Erzählperspektive und Stil beizubehalten und die Handlung so fortzusetzen, dass keine inhaltlichen Widersprüche entstehen.
- Interview – In einem Interview befragst du eine Person, um über sie oder ein bestimmtes Thema etwas zu erfahren. Interviews sind in der wörtlichen Rede geschrieben. Frage und Antwort wechseln sich ab.
- Dialog – Wenn du einen Dialog, z. B. für eine Filmszene schreibst, halte ihn kurz und verwende die wörtliche Rede. In den Regieanweisungen kannst du z. B. Anweisungen für Gesichtsausdrücke der Person(en) vorgeben.
- Tagebucheintrag – Ein Tagebucheintrag gibt Einblick in die persönlichen Erlebnisse einer Person. Benutze ausdrucksstarke Adjektive und Adverbien, wenn du Gedanken und Gefühle beschreibst.
- Blog – Blogs sind eine Art Online-Tagebuch. Es gibt verschiedene Arten, z. B. Nachrichtenblogs, Reiseblogs oder Sportblogs. Sie sind meistens in der Ich-Perspektive geschrieben und spiegeln die persönlichen Erlebnisse und Meinungen des Bloggers.

## 2 Mach dir Notizen.

- Wenn du eine Geschichte (weiter-) schreiben möchtest, achte z. B. auf Gedanken, Gefühle oder Ideen der Person(en).
- Bei Sachtexten musst du das Sprachniveau der Leser verwenden und sicherstellen, dass die Aussagen in deinem Text nicht dem Ausgangstext widersprechen.

## 3 Fertige einen ersten Entwurf an. Überarbeite ihn.

→ S10, p. 148

**Beispiel:**

*Dear Diary,*

*I can't believe it! Mum and Dad won't let me go to James' birthday party on Saturday night! They say that I have already been out too many nights this month, and I have to stay at home. ...*

**Notizen:**

**Merkmale der Textsorte:**
Tagebucheintrag:
umgangssprachlich,
Gefühle

S

# S20 Describing a picture

Ein Bild beschreiben

Wenn du ein Bild (z. B. ein Foto, eine Zeichnung, ein Gemälde) beschreiben willst, sieh es dir zuerst genau an. Die wichtigsten Inhalte sind meist leicht auszumachen. Nimm dir aber auch die Zeit, die Details zu entdecken.

## 1 Allgemeine Informationen

- Wer? Was? Wo? Wann?
- Überschrift / Bildunterschrift (falls vorhanden)

This photo / picture shows .... • In this picture you can see .... • This photo was taken in / at .... • The title / caption of this picture is ....

## 2 Genaue Beschreibung

Wähle eine sinnvolle Reihenfolge (z. B. Mitte – Vordergrund – Hintergrund oder von links oben nach rechts unten), um Einzelheiten zu beschreiben. Nicht alle Einzelheiten sind bei jedem Bild wichtig.

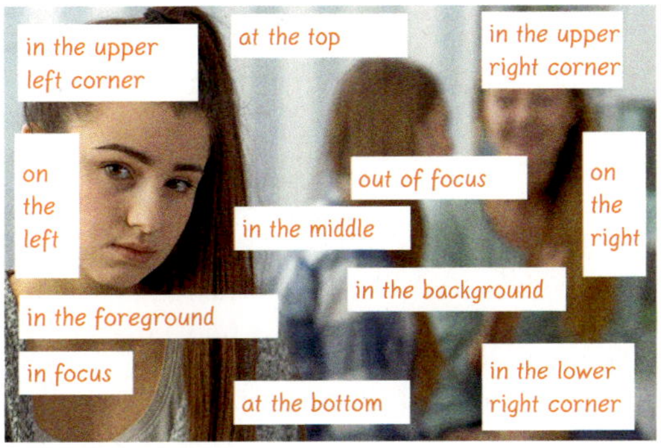


I need a true friend, now!

Beschreibe:

- wie die Personen aussehen

He / She is young / old / about 14 / .... • He / She has ... hair. • He / She is wearing .... • He / She is smiling / ....

- was die Personen tun (Zeitform: *present progressive*)

Two of the girls are talking to each other. • Another girl is looking at the camera.

- Vermutungen: was die Personen fühlen oder denken

The person looks happy / sad / worried / busy / lonely / relaxed .... • Maybe he / she is thinking about ....

- Sonstiges: Gegenstände beschreiben, Farben beschreiben, Ortsangaben

There is .... • It is / looks .... • black and white • colourful • next to • between • behind • over • in • on • in front of • under

## 3 Wirkung des Bildes

Wie wirkt das Bild auf dich?
Was denkst du über das Bild?

I think the picture is special / spectacular / shocking / realistic ... because .... • The picture makes me feel happy / sad / worried .... • I think the message of the picture is ....

## 4 Sonderfall Cartoon

Cartoons haben oft eine Bildunterschrift und / oder Sprechblasen. Ein Cartoon stellt meistens etwas Aktuelles dar und zwar in einer übertriebenen Weise. Auf welches Thema möchte der Cartoonist aufmerksam machen? Was denkst du darüber?

The caption of this picture says .... • The person / sign says ....
The cartoon is funny because .... • I think the cartoonist is criticising .... • I don't get the joke.
I agree / don't agree with the point the cartoonist is making because ....

# S21 Having a conversation

Ein Gespräch führen

Auf welche Weise man ein Gespräch führt, ist abhängig von der Situation, dem Thema und der Person, mit der du sprichst. Z. B. drückst du dich in einem Vorstellungsgespräch oder im Gespräch mit Älteren und Vorgesetzten formell aus. Wenn du jemanden gut kennst, oder unter Gleichaltrigen, verwendest du hingegen Umgangssprache.

**Ein Gespräch beginnen:**

| | |
|---|---|
| • sich begrüßen | Hi! / Hello! • Good morning. • How are you? • Nice to see you (again). |
| • sich vorstellen | My name is .... • I'm *(name)*, by the way. |
| • Smalltalk machen | Beautiful weather, isn't it? • How was your journey? • Have you been here before? • Did you see ... on TV last night? • I like your .... • It's great to be here. |

**Ein Gespräch am Laufen halten:**

| | |
|---|---|
| • Fragen stellen | Did you know that ...? • How do you like ...? • What do you think about ...? • Could I ask a question, please? • Could you tell me about ..., please? |
| • etwas über sich erzählen | It's my first time here in .... • Last year I .... • I'm interested in .... |
| • Interesse zeigen | I see. • Of course. • That sounds interesting. • Could you tell me more, please? • I can imagine that. • I know what you mean. |
| • höflich und taktvoll sein | ..., please. • Thank you. • You're welcome. • Sorry! • May I ...? • Would you ...? • I'd like .... • Yes, that's true but .... • Not exactly. |

*Sei nicht zu direkt. Eine Frage ist immer höflicher als eine Anweisung.*

| | |
|---|---|
| • nachfragen | Excuse me, could you say that again, please? • I'm sorry, but I didn't get that. • Could you explain that again, please? • I'm sorry, but I'm not sure what you mean. |
| • Vorschläge machen | Let's .... • Why don't we ...? • ... would be great. |
| • die eigene Meinung sagen | I think .... • In my opinion .... • If you ask me .... |
| • zustimmen | I agree. • You're right. • Absolutely. • That's a good idea / point. |
| • ablehnen | I'm sorry, but I don't think so. In my opinion .... • This is true, but .... • I see what you mean, but .... • Well, I'm not sure about that. |
| • Gefühle ausdrücken | I'm happy that .... • I'm worried about .... • Oh no! • What a shame! • How funny! • You're joking! • That's nice! • That's good to hear. |
| • Erstaunen ausdrücken | Really? • That's surprising! • I wouldn't have thought that! • Gosh! |

- Missverständnisse benennen — Sorry, let me make that clear: … . • I'm afraid that's not what I was trying to say.
- unterbrechen und unterbrochen werden — Sorry for interrupting, but … . • Could I just say something here? • Just a second, please, I haven't quite finished.
- das Thema wechseln und auf ein Thema zurückkommen — Oh, before I forget, … . • That reminds me: … . • By the way, … . • That's interesting, but could we get back to …, please? • Let's get back to the point. • What I really wanted to talk about was … . • As … said earlier, … . • I would like to come back to what … said about … . • I think it's more important to look at … .
- auf Zeit spielen — Well, I don't know. • Er, I'm not sure about that. • Let me think for a moment. • That's a very good question.

**Ein Gespräch beenden:** Well, I think that's everything. • It was nice talking to you! • Sorry, but I've got to go now. • Let's talk again another time. • Hope to see you again soon. • Take care. • Don't forget to say hello to … for me! • Goodbye. • Bye. • See you!

## Tipps zu besonderen Gesprächsformen:

### Das Vorstellungsgespräch

- Bereite dich darauf vor, über eigene Stärken, Schwächen, Arbeitserfahrungen usw. zu sprechen.
- Vermeide kurze Antworten wie „Yes.“, „No.“, „I don't know.“
- Stelle selbst Fragen.

I will be graduating from school in … . • During my time at school I did internships at … . • I already have some experience in … . • I'm a … person. • I have excellent … skills. • I'm quite good at … . • I might be less good at … . • I have good knowledge of … . • As you can see from my CV, … .

### Die Diskussion

Im Mittelpunkt einer Diskussion steht ein Streitthema.

- Mach dir vorab Notizen zum eigenen Standpunkt (Argumente und Beispiele)
- Strukturiere deine Rede klar. → S22, p. 164
- Bestimmt eine Diskussionsleitung: Sie eröffnet und beendet die Diskussion. Sie achtet darauf, dass die Regeln eingehalten werden und dass alle zu Wort kommen.
- Wählt eine Sitzordnung, bei der ihr euch gegenseitig anschauen könnt.
- Versucht, die andere Seite mit Argumenten zu überzeugen.
- Geht auf die andere Seite ein und widerlegt deren Argumente.
- Beachtet die Diskussionsregeln: andere ausreden lassen, höflich und sachlich sein; beim Thema bleiben.

Good morning. Welcome to today's discussion. • What's your opinion? • Please wait your turn. • Time is almost up. • Thank you for taking part in the discussion.

# S22 Making a speech

Eine Rede halten

Es gibt verschiedene Ziele von Reden: Informationen weitergeben; erklären, wie etwas funktioniert; die Zuhörer von etwas überzeugen. Der Inhalt einer Rede kann eine Person oder eine Sache sein. Wichtig ist, dass du dir am Anfang klar machst, was dein Thema und dein Ziel ist und was deine Zuhörer darüber schon wissen.
Wenn eine Rede mit Hilfe von Plakaten, Folien oder eines Computerprogrammes unterstützt wird, spricht man von einem Referat oder einer Präsentation.

→ S2, p. 139; → S3, p. 140

## Der Aufbau einer Rede

- **Einleitung:**
  Begrüße deine Zuhörer, stelle dich vor (falls sie dich noch nicht kennen). — Good morning. • Hello everyone. • My name is … .
  Nenne dein Thema und die einzelnen Punkte der Rede. — My presentation is about … . • I'm going to talk to you about … . • My topic today is … .
  Wecke Interesse für dein Thema (z. B. mit einem passenden Zitat, einem interessanten Bild, einer interessanten Frage, …). — As … said once, "…" • Have a look at this picture. It shows / says … . • Have you ever …?

- **Hauptteil:**
  Präsentiere dein Thema in 3 – 4 Hauptpunkten mit Hilfe von Beispielen. — First, I'd like to talk about … . • The reason is … . • Let me give you an example. • My next topic is … . • Another interesting point is … • My next point is … . • Finally, I'm going to talk about … .

- **Schluss:**
  Wiederhole die Hauptpunkte, bedanke dich bei deinen Zuhörern und lass sie Fragen stellen. — So what we have learned today is … . • To sum up, … . • That's the end of my presentation. Thank you for listening. Do you have any questions?

## Die Sprache einer Rede

- Sprich möglichst frei.
- Sprich die Zuhörer direkt an, z. B. indem du Fragen verwendest, auf ihre Befindlichkeiten eingehst oder sie aufforderst, etwas zu tun. — Have you ever thought of …? • Did you know that …? • I can see that you are surprised. • Let us ask ourselves … . • It's up to you / us.
- Sprich in einfachen, kurzen Sätzen.
- Sprich nicht zu schnell. Kurze Pausen sind OK.
- Betone wichtige Wörter.
- Wiederhole die wichtigsten Punkte. Das prägt sich ein.
- Verwende Vergleiche. Das macht deine Rede anschaulich und prägt sich gut ein. — … is 2,300 kilometres long. That's about the distance from London to Sicily. • … is like … . • … is as … as … .
- Erkläre unbekannte Wörter. — … is a kind of … . • It's something that … . • It's a person who … .

## Die Präsentationsform

Du kannst ein Poster, Folien für den Overhead-Projektor oder eine Computerpräsentation erstellen.
Wichtig ist: Diese Dinge ersetzen deine Rede nicht, sondern unterstützen sie.
Tipps:

- eine Folie pro Präsentationspunkt
- nur Stichwörter aufschreiben
- Schriftgröße: mindestens 16 Punkt
- Rechtschreibung kontrollieren
- anschauliches Bildmaterial verwenden (Fotos, Karten, Diagramme, Videoclips, ...)
- Bildgröße prüfen
- Farben und Effekte sparsam verwenden

## Hilfsmittel

Zusätzlich zu den Stichwörtern in der Präsentation kannst du weitere Stichwörter, Zahlen, Fakten und unbekannte Wörter, die du für deine Rede brauchst, notieren. Du kannst sie z. B. auf Karteikarten schreiben oder in der Computerpräsentation als Notizen einfügen.

## Weitere Tipps

- Übe deine Rede mehrmals.
- Achte auf die Zeit.
- Probiere das Material / Technik vorher aus.
- Halte Blickkontakt zu den Zuhörern (in den vorderen und hinteren Reihen).
- Schau freundlich drein.

## Nach der Rede

Hole dir von deinen Zuhörern Rückmeldung zu deiner Rede ein. → S23, p. 166

*Du kannst deine Rede daheim vor dem Spiegel üben, vor deiner Familie oder in der Schule vor einem Mitschüler / einer Mitschülerin oder einer kleinen Gruppe.*

In this picture you can see .... • That's a .... • These are ....
The poster / photo / map / diagram / video shows .... • Let's have a look at the photo / map / .... •
As you can see in this picture / video / diagram, ....

GENERAL FACTS
- Super Bowl: most famous sporting event
- first Sunday in February
- famous sporting event on TV
- unofficial national holiday
- final match of the season
- game first played in USA in 1869

CHEERLEADERS
- team of supporters
- motivate players and spectators
- today: 95% girls
- dance, jump, yell, do stunts
- 1–3 minutes per performance (= routine)

BASIC RULES
- team sport
- each team: 11 players on the field
- one game: 60 minutes (plus breaks)
- 4 quarters (one quarter = 15 minutes)

# S23 Giving feedback

Feedback geben

Feedbacks sind Rückmeldungen und Tipps, z. B. zu einer Präsentation, einem vorgetragenen Text oder einem Rollenspiel. Sich gegenseitig Feedback zu geben hilft euch, eure Arbeit zu verbessern. Bleibe dabei stets freundlich und respektvoll.

## Positives Feedback geben

- Beginne mit den Dingen, die du gut oder interessant fandest.

I really liked your … because … . • I was impressed by how you … . • I especially liked the beginning / end … because … .

- Beziehe dich auf die Art und Weise, wie der Inhalt präsentiert wurde und nicht auf die Person selbst.

I think it's good how you dealt with … because … . • I really liked how you presented … .

## Konstruktive Kritik äußern

- Vermeide Verallgemeinerungen wie "I didn't like the presentation", sondern sage genau, worauf sich deine Kritik bezieht.

In the third paragraph / section I thought … was missing. • I think you could try to … .

- Vermeide Sätze wie "I like it, but …" oder "You should have …".
- Denke daran, bei Kritik immer einen Verbesserungsvorschlag mitzugeben.

Maybe your work would be even better if you … . • The … of your work could be better if you … . • Sometimes I find … helpful … . • Maybe next time you should try … .

Ein Feedback-Bogen kann dir helfen, deine Eindrücke knapp zu notieren:

| **Feedback for your presentation** | Great! ☺ | OK 😐 | Could be better ☹ |
|---|---|---|---|
| Well-prepared | | | |
| Use of language | | | |
| Easy to understand | | | |
| Interesting | | | |
| Time | | | |

## Feedback erhalten

- Höre aufmerksam zu.

Thank you. • I understood that. • That's a good idea.

- Wenn du etwas nicht verstanden hast, frage nach.

Sorry, I didn't understand the last part / sentence / word. Could you repeat that for me, please?

- Wenn du nicht weißt, wie das Feedback gemeint ist, frage nach.

Can you give me an example? • Can you be more specific?

- Falls nötig, bitte um Verbesserungsvorschläge.

What could I do better next time?

- Auch wenn du das Feedback für unangemessen oder falsch hältst, bleibe trotzdem freundlich.

Thank you. I don't quite agree but I'll think about it.

# S24 Passing on information

Sprache vermitteln

Sprache vermitteln *(Mediation)* bedeutet, dass du wichtige Informationen von einer Sprache in eine andere überträgst, z. B. vom Englischen ins Deutsche oder umgekehrt. Manchmal kann es auch sein, dass du zwischen Gesprächspartnern vermittelst (s. unten). Dabei geht es nicht um eine wörtliche Übersetzung, sondern darum, nur die relevanten Informationen zu vermitteln. Beachte dabei folgende Punkte:

## Adressat

- Lies die Arbeitsanweisung aufmerksam durch und finde heraus, an wen du die Information vermitteln sollst.
- Überlege dir, wie viel dein Adressat schon weiß und wozu er die Information braucht.
- Gib nur die Informationen wieder, die für den Adressaten in der konkreten Situation wichtig sind.
- Übermittle die Informationen so, dass die Person sie gut verstehen kann. Verwende kurze Sätze.

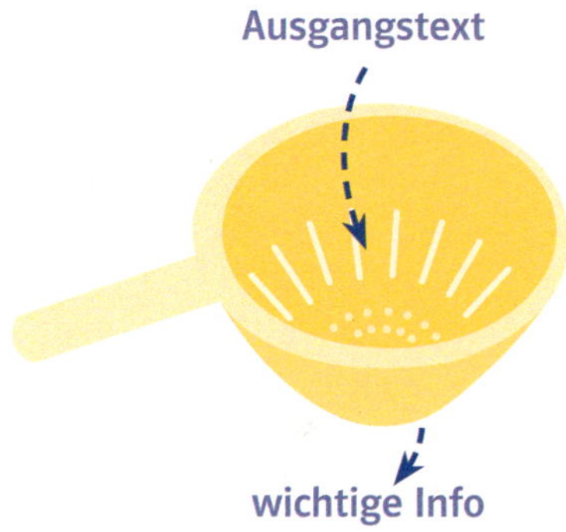


## Paraphrasieren

Wenn du die genaue Übersetzung für ein Wort in der Zielsprache nicht kennst, umschreibe es mit anderen Worten.

**Beispiel:**

My father always preaches to me and says that I should be on time. Every day he reminds me about it. I really don't want to hear it any more.

„Mein Vater erzählt mir jeden Tag, dass ich pünktlich sein soll. Ich kann es nicht mehr hören."

## Text in eigenen Worten zusammenfassen

Übersetze den Ausgangstext nicht wortwörtlich *(translation)*, sondern gib nur die wichtigen Informationen sinngemäß und in deinen eigenen Worten wieder *(summarising)*.

## Beispiel: Vermitteln zwischen zwei Gesprächspartnern

Patty, an Australian exchange student, is staying at your house. Your four-year-old sister wants to know more about Australia, but she can't speak English. Help Patty and your sister to understand each other.

Your little sister: Welche Tiere gibt es denn in Australien?
You: What kinds of animals are there in Australia?
Patty: Oh, we have lots of typical Australian animals, like kangaroos, koalas or emus.
You: Es gibt viele Tiere dort, z. B. Kängurus, Koalas oder Emus. Emus sind große Vögel, die nicht fliegen können.
Your sister: Wir könnten doch mal Patty in Australien besuchen. Ich will diese komischen Tiere sehen!
You: Could we visit you in Australia and see all those animals?
Patty: Sure. That would be nice.
You: Ja, sie würde sich freuen.

Erkläre Dinge, die dein Gesprächspartner / deine Gesprächspartnerin nicht wissen oder nicht verstehen kann.

Passe den Stil der Sprache so an, dass er zu deinem jeweiligen Gesprächspartner / deiner Gesprächspartnerin passt.

# Grammar

## G1

Mit G sind die Grammatikkapitel gekennzeichnet und der Reihe nach durchnummeriert. Eine Übersicht über alle Themen in diesem Band findest du unten auf der Seite.

### Language tip G5

Die Seiten kennzeichnen zusätzliche Grammatikkapitel. Du kannst dir die neuen Formen dort wie neue Vokabeln merken oder – wenn du es genau wissen willst – ein paar Regeln dazu lernen.

Hier stehen Besonderheiten und Tipps.

( TEST YOURSELF )

Hier kannst du üben.
Die Lösungen findest du auf S. 308.

( FÜR PROFIS )

Hier findest du knifflige Extras zum Thema.
R = Revision (Wiederholung)

G

# G1 R: Modale Hilfsverben und ihre Ersatzformen

Revision: Modal auxiliaries and their substitutes

Modale Hilfsverben kannst du nur im **simple present** verwenden. Für alle anderen Zeiten benötigst du **Ersatzformen**. Ausnahme **can**: Für **can** kannst du im **simple past** auch **could** verwenden.

Mit **can / could** und der Ersatzform **be able to** sagst du, was du **kannst** (Fähigkeit).

| Simple present | Simple past | Will-future |
|---|---|---|
| The guide **can / is able to** speak German. … kann … | He **could / was able to** read the text. … konnte … | I'm sure Tom **will be able to** help you. … kann … |
| She **can't / isn't able to** drive a truck. … kann nicht … | When he was seven, he **couldn't / wasn't able to** swim. … konnte … nicht … | He **won't be able to** repair his car himself. … kann … nicht … |

Mit **can / could** und der Ersatzform **be allowed to** sagst du, was du tun **darfst** (Erlaubnis).

| | | |
|---|---|---|
| Tourists **can / are allowed to** visit Uluru. … dürfen … | We **could / were allowed to** take photos. … durften … | You**'ll be allowed to** take photos. … darfst … |
| Tourists **can't / aren't allowed to / mustn't** go up Uluru. … dürfen nicht … | We **couldn't / weren't allowed to** catch fish. … durften keine … | You **won't be allowed to** make a fire. … darfst kein … |

Mit **must** und der Ersatzform **have to** sagst du, was du tun **musst** (Verpflichtung).

| | | |
|---|---|---|
| You **must / have to** write an application. … musst … | I **had to** write an application. … musste … | You**'ll have to** write an application. … musst … |
| You **don't have to** take part in the course. … musst nicht … | I **didn't have to** make breakfast. … musste nicht … | You **won't have to** wait for me. … musst nicht … |

Eine **Empfehlung** ausdrücken:

| | |
|---|---|
| Tourists **should / shouldn't** go by car. | Touristen **sollten / sollten nicht** mit dem Auto fahren. |

Sagen, das etwas **nicht notwendig** ist:

| | |
|---|---|
| You **needn't** pay for the course. | Du **brauchst** den Kurs **nicht** zu bezahlen. |

**( TEST YOURSELF ) Use the correct substitutes.**

1. Paul broke his leg last week, so he —— (not can) play football yesterday.
2. Last week Jane —— (must) wait for the plane to Perth for five hours.
3. Next week Koa —— (must) fly to Sydney.
4. If you go to Australia next summer, you —— (not can) bring in knives.
5. I —— (not must) pay for anything yesterday.
6. When Tom was ten, he —— (not can) read and write in English like he can today.

# G2 R: Steigerung und Vergleich von Adjektiven und Adverbien

Revision: Comparison of adjectives and adverbs

Ein **Adjektiv** beschreibt eine **Person** oder eine **Sache**, z. B.: Rob is a **good** surfer.

Adjektive mit **einer Silbe** oder **zweisilbige** mit der Endung **-y** steigerst du mit **-er / -est.**
Adjektive mit **zwei und mehr Silben** steigerst du, indem du **more** und the **most** davor setzt.

| | | |
|---|---|---|
| cheap | cheap**er** | the cheap**est** |
| easy | eas**ier** | the eas**iest** |
| expensive | **more** expensive | the **most** expensive |

Unregelmäßig gesteigert werden z. B.: good, **better**, the **best** und: bad, **worse**, the **worst**

So kannst du **Personen** oder **Dinge** miteinander vergleichen:

| | |
|---|---|
| New York is **bigger than** Berlin. | New York ist **größer als** Berlin. |
| My friend is **as** old **as** you. | Mein Freund ist **so** alt **wie** du. |
| Mobiles are **not as** expensive **as** laptops. | Handys sind **nicht so** teuer **wie** Laptops. |
| Mobiles are **less** expensive **than** laptops. | Handys sind **nicht so** teuer **wie** Laptops. |
| Nick's new laptop was **the most expensive.** | Nicks neues Laptop war **das teuerste.** |

Ein **Adverb** dagegen beschreibt, **wie** jemand etwas **tut** oder **wie** etwas **geschieht**. Man erkennt Adverbien im Englischen durch ein angehängtes **-ly**, z. B.: The actor spoke slow**ly** and clear**ly**.

Ein **Adverb** steigerst du mit **more** und (the) **most**.

| | | | |
|---|---|---|---|
| slowly | **more** slowly | (the) **most** slowly | langsam, langsamer, am langsamsten |

Einige unregelmäßige Adverbien wie **fast** und **hard** steigerst du wie einsilbige Adjektive:
You work **fast / hard**, she works **faster / harder**, he works (the) **fastest** / (the) **hardest**.

Achtung! **good**, better, (the) best (Adjektiv) wird zu: **well**, **better**, (the) **best** (Adverb).

So vergleichst du **Handlungen** miteinander:

| | |
|---|---|
| You speak **more clearly than** Colin. | Du sprichst **deutlicher als** Colin. |
| Kate works **as carefully as** Kim. | Kate arbeitet **so sorgfältig wie** Kim. |
| Ben doesn't write **as nicely as** Nora. | Ben schreibt **nicht so schön wie** Nora. |
| Amy dances (the) **most beautifully**. | Amy tanzt **am schönsten**. |

**( TEST YOURSELF )** **Use adverbs in the correct form.**

1. You write — (careful) than Bob.
2. Sally learns — (efficient) of all the girls.
3. You organized the meeting — (good) than your partners.
4. Nick speaks Chinese — (clear) than Sue.
5. Jay works — (hard) than anyone else.
6. A girl from Sydney won the race. She had sailed — (fast).

G

# G3 R: Relativsätze mit und ohne Relativpronomen

Revision: Relative clauses with and without relative pronouns (contact clauses)

Wenn du eine Person oder Sache genauer beschreiben willst, verwendest du die Relativpronomen **who** (für Personen), **which** (für Dinge) oder **that** (für Personen oder Dinge).

| | |
|---|---|
| He is the man **who / that** showed us the reef.<br>Look, that's the seafood **which / that** is sold on the Caribbean islands. | Er ist der Mann, **der** uns das Riff zeigte.<br>Schau, das sind die Meeresfrüchte, **die** auf den karibischen Inseln verkauft werden. |

Um Besitz und Zugehörigkeit auszudrücken, verwendest du **whose**.

| | |
|---|---|
| Bob Marley is a singer **whose** music is very famous.<br>That's the girl **whose** parents come from the Caribbean. | Bob Marley ist ein Sänger, **dessen** Musik sehr berühmt ist.<br>Das ist das Mädchen, **deren** Eltern aus der Karibik kommen. |

Folgt nach **who**, **which** oder **that** ein Personalpronomen wie **I**, **you**, **he**, **she**, **it**, **we**, **they** oder eine **Person**, kannst du **who**, **which** oder **that** auch weglassen. Diesen Satz nennt man **contact clause**.

| | |
|---|---|
| The dancer **(who)** <u>**we**</u> saw last night taught us a few moves.<br>The ferry **(which)** <u>**the guide**</u> chose was very slow. | Der Tänzer, **den wir** gestern Abend sahen, brachte uns ein paar Schritte bei.<br>Die Fähre, **die der Reiseleiter** auswählte, war sehr langsam. |

Das Relativpronomen **whom** leitet Relativsätze ein, die sich auf das Objekt (wen? wem?) des Hauptsatzes beziehen. Es gilt nur für Personen, wird vor allem in der Schriftsprache benutzt und klingt förmlich.

| | |
|---|---|
| I know **the boy** (<u>**whom**</u>) you met yesterday. | Ich kenne **den Jungen**, <u>**den**</u> du gestern getroffen hast. |

( TEST YOURSELF ) **Put in <u>who</u> or <u>which</u> where necessary.**

1. This is a photo — we took on the island of Dominica.
2. People — like hiking can find lots of interesting places in the Caribbean.
3. This is the boat — took us to an island.
4. Look, that's the diver — we met on our holiday.
5. They sell seafood — is from the Caribbean islands.
6. He showed us an old ship — had sunk in a storm.

( FÜR PROFIS )

I saw a postcard **which** (**that**) had a picture of a beach on it.
Dieser Relativsatz ist notwendig *(defining)*. Der Hauptsatz ergibt ohne ihn keinen Sinn.
Also: Keine Kommas! Hier kannst du **which** (oder **who**) durch **that** ersetzen.

Our instructor, **who** was very nice, showed us the reef.
Dieser Relativsatz ist <u>nicht</u> für das Verständnis notwendig *(non-defining)*. Er enthält zusätzliche Informationen. Deshalb stehen Kommas. **Who** (oder **which**) kann <u>nicht</u> durch **that** ersetzt werden.

# G4 Die Verlaufsform der Vergangenheit

The past progressive

While I was sleeping all morning, somebody put this umbrella next to me.

Mit dem **present progressive** kannst du ausdrücken, dass jemand gerade dabei ist, etwas zu tun. Du verwendest diese Form häufig, um Tätigkeiten auf einem Bild zu beschreiben.
So bildest du Aussagen im **present progressive: am / are / is + Verb + -ing**

| | |
|---|---|
| In the photo two children **are playing** in the street. A boy **is eating** an ice cream. | Auf dem Foto **spielen** (gerade) zwei Kinder auf der Straße. Ein Junge **isst** (gerade) ein Eis. |

Mit dem **past progressive** drückst du aus, dass etwas in der Vergangenheit über einen längeren Zeitraum passierte. So bildest du Aussagen im **past progressive: was / were + Verb + -ing**

| | |
|---|---|
| On Monday afternoon I **was visiting** Grandad. | Am Montagnachmittag **habe** ich Opa **besucht**. |
| What **were** you **doing** then? | Was **hast** du dann **gemacht**? |
| I **wasn't working** last Saturday. | Ich **habe** am letzten Samstag **nicht gearbeitet**. |

Das **past progressive** verwendest du auch, um eine Handlung zu beschreiben, die andauerte, als plötzlich eine neue eintrat. Das neue Ereignis wird mit dem **simple past** ausgedrückt.

| | |
|---|---|
| **While** she **was watching** a film, her mum suddenly **came** into the room. | **Während** sie (gerade) einen Film **anschaute**, **kam** plötzlich ihre Mutter ins Zimmer. |
| Tom **was painting** the walls **when** his friend **called** him. | Tom **strich** (gerade) die Wände, **als** sein Freund **anrief**. |

Liefen in der Vergangenheit zwei Handlungen zur gleichen Zeit und gleich lange, wird für beide Handlungen **past progressive** benutzt.

| | |
|---|---|
| **While** I **was repairing** my bike, Sue **was working** in the garden. | **Während** ich mein Fahrrad **reparierte**, **arbeitete** Sue im Garten. |

## ( TEST YOURSELF ) Use simple past or past progressive.

1. This time last week I — (not work), I — (sit) on a beach.
2. When I — (phone) my friend this morning, he — still — (have) breakfast.
3. I wanted to tell you something, but you — (talk) to somebody else.
4. What — you — (do) yesterday between 8 and 10 p.m.?
5. While we — (watch) a video, our neighbours — (call). They — (ask) for some salt.
6. Our dog — (sleep) on the sofa when a burglar — (try) to open the door.

G

# G5 Das Partizip Präsens

The present participle (after verbs of perception and instead of adverbial clauses)

We saw an elephant washing its baby elephant.

**Partizip Präsens nach Verben der Wahrnehmung** (after verbs of perception)

Verben wie **see**, **watch**, **notice**, **hear**, **feel** usw. drücken eine Wahrnehmung der Sinne aus. Wenn eine längere Handlung wahrgenommen wird, verwendest du nach diesen Verben das **present participle**: **verb + -ing**

| | |
|---|---|
| I **saw** the car **driving** towards the bus. | Ich sah, wie das Auto auf den Bus zufuhr.<br>Oder: Ich sah das Auto auf den Bus zufahren. |
| We **watched** the boys **playing** rugby. | Wir beobachteten die Jungs, wie sie Rugby spielten.<br>Oder: Wir beobachteten die Jungs beim Rugbyspielen. |

**Partizip Präsens anstelle von adverbialen Nebensätzen** (instead of adverbial clauses)

Sätze, die mit Partizipien (having / being … etc.) beginnen, findest du überwiegend in der Schriftsprache. Da die einleitenden Adverbialen (because, as, if, when usw.) fehlen, musst du versuchen, den Sinn aus dem Zusammenhang zu erschließen.

| | |
|---|---|
| **Being** poor and black, it's hard to get a job. | **Wenn** man arm und dunkelhäutig ist, ist es schwer, einen Job zu bekommen. |
| **Not knowing** the way to the station, she asked a policeman. | **Da** sie den Weg zum Bahnhof nicht kannte, fragte sie einen Polizisten. |

**( TEST YOURSELF ) Use present participles.**

1. I saw the rugby team —— (celebrate) after the game.
2. When I had that accident with my bike, I could feel everybody —— (stare) at me.
3. Did you hear him —— (talk) to his dad on the phone?
4. —— (grow) up in a gated community, she didn't see poor people very often.
5. When we were watching TV last night, we heard our neighbour —— (play) the drums.
6. —— (be) late, she had to run to get to the station.

# G6 R: Die Vorvergangenheit

Revision: The past perfect

Um über Ereignisse zu sprechen, die noch **vor** einem vergangenen Ereignis stattfanden, verwendest du die Vorvergangenheit, das **past perfect**:
**had / hadn't + 3. Form** des Verbs (past participle)

| Signalwörter | |
|---|---|
| after | nachdem |
| before | bevor |
| when | als |

Bei den regelmäßigen Verben hängst du für die 3. Form ein **-ed** an das Verb: visit → visit**ed**
Achte auf unregelmäßige Verben, z. B. go → **gone**; see → **seen**; be → **been** etc.

*Eine Liste der unregelmäßigen Verben findest du auf Seite 213.*

| | |
|---|---|
| **After** we **had lived** in Cape Town for two years, we moved to Pretoria. | **Nachdem** wir zwei Jahre in Kapstadt **gelebt hatten**, zogen wir nach Pretoria um. |
| **Before** school started, she **had heard** some bad news. | **Bevor** die Schule anfing, **hatte** sie schlechte Nachrichten **gehört**. |
| **When** the accident happened, the bus **had not arrived** yet. | **Als** der Unfall passierte, **war** der Bus noch **nicht angekommen**. |

Und so kannst du im **past perfect** Fragen stellen:

| | |
|---|---|
| **Had** you ever **been** to South Africa before you left the USA? | Yes, I **had**. No, I **hadn't**. |
| **Which** countries **had** you **visited** before you went to South Africa? | I **hadn't visited** any other countries. |

## ( TEST YOURSELF ) Put the verbs in the past perfect.

1. After we — (tidy) our flat, we ordered a pizza for lunch.
2. When I met Cebile at 11:30 a.m., she — (not have) breakfast.
3. A lot of guests — already — (go) home when we got to the party.
4. I couldn't remember anything about the text which I — (read) the week before.
5. What — you — (do) before you visited us that morning?
6. A snake got into our house yesterday because I — (not close) the door.

## ( FÜR PROFIS )

Wenn du die **Dauer** einer Handlung in der Vergangenheit betonen möchtest, verwendest du das **past perfect progressive: had been + -ing** (present participle).

| | |
|---|---|
| When I arrived at the party, my friends **had been waiting** for an hour. | Als ich auf der Party eintraf, **hatten** meine Freunde (schon) eine Stunde **gewartet**. |
| She **had been looking for** her shoes for hours when she finally found them under her bed. | Sie **hatte** (schon) stundenlang ihre Schuhe **gesucht**, als sie sie endlich unter ihrem Bett fand. |

G

# G7 R: Das Passiv (einfache Vergangenheit)

Revision: Passive voice (simple past)

Mit dem Passiv kannst du über eine Handlung Auskunft geben, ohne zu sagen, wer die Handlung ausführt. Im Vordergrund steht dabei die Sache.
So bildest du das Passiv im **simple present:**
**am / are / is + 3. Form** des Verbs (past participle)
English **is spoken** in a lot of countries. A lot of photos **are taken** in the park every day.

So bildest du das Passiv im **simple past:**
**was / were + 3. Form** des Verbs (past participle)

*Eine Liste der unregelmäßigen Verben findest du auf Seite 213.*

| | |
|---|---|
| The park **was named** after Paul Kruger. | Der Park **wurde** nach Paul Kruger **benannt**. |
| Roads and visitor centres **were built**. | Straßen und Besucherzentren **wurden gebaut**. |
| The park **wasn't opened** in 1910. | Der Park **wurde nicht** 1910 **eröffnet**. |

| | |
|---|---|
| **Was** the park **created** in 1926? | **Yes**, it **was**. |
| **Was** the park **named** after a singer? | **No**, it **wasn't**. |

So kannst du aus einem Aktivsatz einen Passivsatz machen. Die handelnden Personen müssen nicht immer genannt werden. Wenn doch, dann werden sie mit **by** angehängt.
Das Verb im Aktiv wird in der gleichen Zeit im Passiv gebildet.

| | |
|---|---|
| Aktiv: | South African workers built a new road. |
| Passiv: | A new road was built (**by** South African workers). |
| Aktiv: | Hunters killed elephants for their ivory. |
| Passiv: | Elephants were killed for their ivory (**by** hunters). |

## ( TEST YOURSELF ) Use the passive voice in the simple past.

1. The name 'Big Five' — first — (introduce) by big game hunters.
2. A visitor centre — (not build) before 1927.
3. — the park — (close) last year? No, it — .
4. The park — (not name) after a ranger.
5. Guides — (hire) to show tourists around.
6. — animals — (hunt) before the park — (found)? Yes, they — .

## ( FÜR PROFIS )

Auch eine **Person** kann **Subjekt** eines Passivsatzes sein („persönliches Passiv").

| | |
|---|---|
| First **I was given** my ticket. | Zuerst **wurde mir** meine Eintrittskarte **gegeben**.<br>Oder: Zuerst **gab man mir** meine Eintrittskarte. |
| Then **we were shown** some sights. | Dann **wurden uns** einige Sehenswürdigkeiten **gezeigt**.<br>Oder: Dann **zeigte man uns** einige Sehenswürdigkeiten. |

# G8 Indirekte Rede I (mit Zeitverschiebung → simple past)

Reported speech (with backshift → simple past)

My fitness instructor told me (that) some kind of sport was good for me.

Wenn du berichten willst, was jemand **vor einiger Zeit** gesagt hat, benutzt du die indirekte Rede. Du beginnst mit **He said that … / She told me that** … . usw. Das Wort **that** kann man auch weglassen. Das **Verb** des Satzes wird vom **simple present** in das **simple past** zurückgesetzt (**backshift**).

| Direkte Rede | Indirekte Rede |
|---|---|
| Kenneth: "I **work** a lot."<br>"Sneakerheads **are** a group of people with the same interest."<br>"I **hate** kids who **don't care** about their shoes." | Kenneth told me (that) he **worked** a lot.<br>He added (that) sneakerheads **were** a group of people with the same interest.<br>He said (that) he **hated** kids who **didn't care** about their shoes. |

Und so kannst du **Fragen** in der indirekten Rede wiedergeben:

Ohne Fragewort: **He asked if** … — Er fragte, **ob** …

Mit Fragewort: **She asked why / when / where** … — Sie fragte, **warum / wann / wo** …

| | |
|---|---|
| Cindy: "**Do** you **wear** the shoes?"<br>"**How many** pairs **do** you **own**?" | She asked **if** he **wore** the shoes.<br>She asked him **how many** pairs he **owned**. |

In der indirekten Rede ändern sich auch **Personalpronomen** und **Possessivbegleiter**!

| | |
|---|---|
| "I want to meet **my** friend Tom."<br>"**We** often help **our** neighbours in the garden." | He said (that) **he** wanted to meet **his** friend Tom.<br>She told me (that) **they** often helped **their** neighbours in the garden. |

## ( TEST YOURSELF ) Report what Kenneth said.

1. "I sometimes meet my girlfriend in Sneakers Street."
2. "She likes shopping, but she doesn't camp overnight in front of a shoe shop."
3. "I don't look for sneakers all the time."
4. "Do people in Germany collect shoes too?"
5. "Does Sue like sneakers?"
6. "What does she do at the weekend?"

G

# G9 Indirekte Rede II (mit Zeitverschiebung → past perfect)

Reported speech (with backshift → past perfect)

Yesterday Caty told me (that) she had been to a Chinese writing course.

Wenn du berichten willst, was jemand über **Vergangenes** erzählt hat, benutzt du die indirekte Rede so: Das **Verb** wird vom **simple past** in das **past perfect** (**had / hadn't + 3. Form**) zurückgesetzt.

| Direkte Rede | Indirekte Rede |
|---|---|
| Bob: "I **moved** to Hong Kong in 2010." | He told me (that) he **had moved** to Hong Kong in 2010. |
| "I **didn't like** Chinese food." | He added (that) he **hadn't liked** Chinese food. |
| "**Did** you **visit** New York?" | He asked **if** I **had visited** New York. |
| "**Where did** you **buy** the tickets?" | He asked **where** I **had bought** the tickets. |

Steht in der Aussage der direkten Rede **present perfect**, so wird das Verb in der indirekten Rede ebenfalls in das **past perfect** zurückgesetzt:

| | |
|---|---|
| "I **have been** to Sneakers Street only once." | She said (that) she **had been** to Sneakers Street only once. |
| "I **haven't seen** the new shopping centre yet." | She said (that) she **hadn't seen** the new shopping centre yet. |
| "**Have** you **been** to Hong Kong before?" | She asked **if** I **had been** to Hong Kong before. |

( TEST YOURSELF ) **Report what Linda said.**

1. "I visited Hong Kong in 2014."
2. "We had a great time."
3. "I went to an Asian restaurant, but I didn't like the food."
4. "I haven't seen Ben for two years."
5. "Have you ever been to France?"
6. "I travelled to Great Britain last summer. It didn't rain once."

( FÜR PROFIS )

Auch Aussagen über die Zukunft (**will-future**) kannst du in der indirekten Rede wiedergeben. Aus **will + Grundform** wird **would + Grundform**.

| | |
|---|---|
| "I'**ll meet** Tim on Friday." | He said (that) he **would meet** Tim on Friday. |
| "We **won't go** shopping at the weekend." | She told me (that) they **wouldn't go** shopping at the weekend. |

# G10 R: Zukunftszeiten (will und going to)

Revision: Future tenses (will-future and going to-future)

Wenn du über etwas sprechen möchtest, das in der Zukunft geschieht, kannst du das im Englischen auf verschiedene Weise tun. Die beiden häufigsten Zukunftszeiten sind das **will-future** und das **going to-future**. Zu weiteren Zeiten für die Zukunft siehe **G11**.

**Will-future**

Das **will-future** verwendest du

- allgemein für Zukünftiges
- für **Wünsche**, **Hoffnungen**, **Vorhersagen** (nach I hope, I think, I'm sure, probably, maybe etc.)
- für **spontane Entscheidungen**
- in **if-Sätzen Typ I**

Im Deutschen kann man über Zukünftiges mit der Zukunft oder der Gegenwart sprechen.

| | |
|---|---|
| I'**ll call** an ambulance. | Ich **rufe** einen Krankenwagen. (spontan) |
| I hope Rachel **will call** me soon. | Ich hoffe, Rachel **ruft** mich bald **an**. (Hoffnung) |
| Maybe we'**ll meet** the boys at the club. | Vielleicht **treffen** wir die Jungen im Klub. (Wunsch) |
| Don't worry, it **won't take** long. | Mach dir keine Sorgen, es **wird nicht** lange **dauern**. (spontan) |
| When **will** you **be** back from Hong Kong? | Wann **bist** du wieder zurück aus Hongkong? (Hoffnung) |
| If I meet Peter Lai, I **will talk** to him. | Wenn ich Peter Lai treffe, **werde** ich mit ihm **reden**. (if-Satz Typ I) |

**Going to-future**

Das **going to-future** verwendest du, wenn du beschreiben willst, was du in der Zukunft vorhast. Es drückt eine bestimmte **Absicht** oder einen **Plan** aus. Mit dem **going to-future** kannst du aber auch ausdrücken, dass etwas sicher eintreten wird, weil es schon **Anzeichen** dafür gibt.

| | |
|---|---|
| I'**m going to talk** to the boss tomorrow. | Ich **habe vor**, morgen mit dem Chef **zu sprechen**. (Absicht, Plan) |
| **Are** you **going to visit** Hong Kong? | **Habt** ihr **vor**, Hongkong **zu besuchen**? (Plan) |
| No, we **aren't going to travel** to Asia this year. | Nein, wir **haben** dieses Jahr **nicht vor**, nach Asien **zu reisen**. (Plan) |
| Look at those black clouds. It'**s going to rain** in a few minutes. | Schau dir diese schwarzen Wolken an. Es **wird** in ein paar Minuten **regnen**. (Anzeichen) |

( TEST YOURSELF ) **Use going to-future or will-future.**

1. If we go to Hong Kong, we — (visit) a night market.
2. Where — your sister — (spend) her holidays next year? What's her plan?
3. You are late. I hope you — (not miss) the flight to Hong Kong.
4. I have decided to go on holiday to Hong Kong. Maybe I — (hire) a car there.
5. Wait a moment. I — (help) you with your heavy bags.
6. Look at the sky. The sun — (come out) soon.

# G11 Zukunftszeiten (einfache Gegenwart und Verlaufsform der Gegenwart)

Future tenses (simple present and present progressive with future meaning)

The party starts at 7 p.m.
Are you coming?
Sorry, but I'm working until late.

**Simple present**

Wenn du über feste Termine in der Zukunft sprechen willst, kannst du das **simple present** verwenden. Dabei geht es meistens um genaue Zeitangaben aus Fahrplänen, Programmen, Stundenplänen usw.

| | |
|---|---|
| The next train from Fort Lauderdale to Miami Airport **leaves** at 6:08 p.m. | Der nächste Zug von Fort Lauderdale zum Flughafen Miami **fährt** um 18:08 Uhr. |
| Most shops in Miami **don't close** before 12 o'clock today. | In Miami **schließen** die meisten Geschäfte heute **nicht** vor 0 Uhr. |
| When **does** the flight to New York **leave**? | Wann **geht** der Flug nach New York? |

**Present progressive**

Wenn du für die Zukunft etwas fest geplant oder vereinbart hast, kannst du das **present progressive** verwenden.

| | |
|---|---|
| Tomorrow I'**m watching** a film at the cinema. | Morgen **schaue** ich mir einen Film im Kino **an**. |
| On Sunday we **are visiting** Liz in hospital. | Am Sonntag **besuchen** wir Liz im Krankenhaus. |
| I'**m not doing** anything special on Friday. | Am Freitag **mache** ich **nichts** Besonderes. |
| What **are** you **doing** at the weekend? | Was **machst** du am Wochenende? |

Achtung! Mit dem **present progressive** kann man sowohl eine **gegenwärtige** als auch eine **zukünftige** Handlung ausdrücken. Die Signalwörter zeigen den Unterschied!

| | |
|---|---|
| I'**m talking** to a blogger **at the moment**. | Ich **spreche gerade** mit einem Blogger. |
| I'**m talking** to a blogger **tomorrow**. | Ich **spreche morgen** mit einem Blogger. |

( TEST YOURSELF ) **Use simple present or present progressive.**

1. The film — (start) at 8:30 p.m.
2. We — (travel) to Florida next month.
3. When — the next plane to Miami — (leave)?
4. — you — (work) tomorrow? – Yes, I — .
5. What time — the concert — (start)?
6. — Jane — (meet) her friends at the weekend? – No, she — .

## Bus stop
(Lerntempoduett)

1. Bearbeite die Aufgabe zunächst allein. Schreibe deine Lösungen auf.
2. Wenn du fertig bist, gehe zum „bus stop“. Warte dort auf die nächste Person bzw. triff die Person, die dort schon wartet. Vergleicht und korrigiert eure Ergebnisse.
3. Gehe danach wieder zu deinem Platz zurück. Bearbeite die nächste Aufgabe.

## Dramatic reading
(Szenisches Lesen)

1. Verteilt die Rollen innerhalb eurer Gruppe.
2. Lies dir deinen Text lautlos oder ganz leise immer wieder vor, bis du ihn gut kennst.
3. Übt euren Text in der Gruppe mit der Methode „Read and look up“ (Seite 182).
4. Überlegt euch, wie ihr euch in der Rolle fühlt und wie ihr euch bewegen würdet. Tragt euren Text so frei wie möglich vor.

## Fishbowl
(Aquarium)

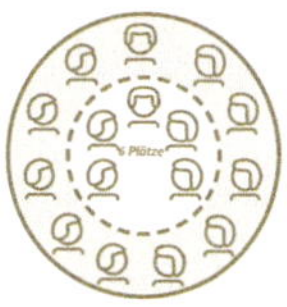

1. Bildet zwei Kreise: einen Stuhlkreis für 4 bis 6 Personen mit einem zusätzlichen, leeren Platz (Innenkreis) und einen Außenkreis für den Rest der Klasse.
2. Die Mitglieder des Innenkreises beginnen die Diskussion. Sie begründen ihre Meinungen, bringen Beispiele und gehen auf die Argumente der anderen ein.
3. Wer vom Außenkreis in die Diskussion einsteigen möchte, kann sich jederzeit auf den leeren Platz setzen. Die Mitglieder des Innenkreises können aber auch von sich aus den Stuhlkreis verlassen (immer nur einer). Im Verlauf der Diskussion sollte sich jeder mindestens einmal im Innenkreis äußern.
4. Wertet im Anschluss die Ergebnisse der Diskussion aus. Überlegt auch, was gut gelaufen ist und was ihr beim nächsten Mal besser machen könnt.

## Freeze frame
(Standbild)

1. Entscheidet euch in der Gruppe, welche Szene oder Personen ihr darstellen wollt. Verteilt die Rollen.
2. Probiert verschiedene Standbilder aus und entscheidet euch dann für eines. Denkt daran, ihr müsst euer Standbild eine Minute lang durchhalten. Keiner darf sich bewegen oder etwas sagen.
3. Präsentiert der Klasse euer Standbild. Die anderen beschreiben, was sie sehen.

## Gallery walk

1. Hängt nach eurer Gruppenarbeit euer Produkt gut sichtbar im Klassenzimmer auf.
2. Einer von euch, der „Experte“, bleibt bei eurem Produkt stehen und erklärt es den anderen. Die anderen gehen herum. Nach jedem Durchgang wechselt der Experte.
3. Seht euch die Produkte der anderen an und bewertet sie.
4. Wertet im Anschluss eure Ergebnisse in der Klasse aus.

## Jigsaw
(Gruppenpuzzle)

1. Bildet Stammgruppen („home groups“). Jedes Gruppenmitglied wählt einen Text aus, liest ihn und bearbeitet ihn. Macht euch Notizen dazu.
2. Trefft euch in Expertengruppen („expert groups“) mit den Mitgliedern der anderen Stammgruppen, die denselben Text wie ihr bearbeitet haben. Vergleicht eure Notizen, besprecht sie gemeinsam und ergänzt sie.
3. Geht zurück in eure Stammgruppe. Präsentiert dort die Informationen aus eurem Text. Macht euch Notizen zu den Texten der anderen, so dass am Ende jeder die Informationen aus allen Texten hat.

## Milling around
(Marktplatz)

1. Bearbeite die Aufgabe zunächst allein. Auf ein Zeichen vom Lehrer oder der Lehrerin steht ihr auf und geht durch den Raum. Nimm die Aufgabe und einen Stift mit.
2. Wenn ein Signal ertönt, bleibt ihr stehen. Besprecht mit der Person, die euch am nächsten steht, die Aufgabe.
3. Beim nächsten Signal trennt ihr euch und geht weiter durch den Raum. Wiederholt den Vorgang.

## Peer correction
(Partnerkontrolle)

1. Bearbeite die Aufgabe zunächst selbstständig.
2. Tausche deine Lösungen mit einem Partner / einer Partnerin. Kontrolliere seine oder ihre Lösungen.
3. Tauscht euch danach zu der Aufgabe aus und korrigiert den Text.

## Placemat
(Platzdeckchen)

1. Bildet Vierergruppen.
2. Teilt ein großes Blatt Papier in fünf Bereiche ein.
3. Setzt euch so hin, dass alle in eine Ecke des Blattes schreiben können.
4. Jedes Gruppenmitglied denkt allein über das Thema nach und schreibt Ideen auf seinen Teil des Blattes.
5. Tauscht euch über die Ideen aus. Einigt euch auf die besten Ideen und schreibt diese in die Mitte des Blattes.

## Read and look up
(Lesen und Aufschauen)

1. Schaue auf deinen Text und präge dir die erste Zeile oder den ersten Satz ein. Schaue hoch und sprich deine Zeile / deinen Satz lautlos oder leise vor dich hin. Nimm dir die nächste Zeile / den nächsten Satz vor.
2. Übe nun mit einer Partnerin / einem Partner. Erzähle deinen Text, Zeile für Zeile oder Satz für Satz. Dazwischen schaust du immer wieder nach unten auf deinen Text.
3. Wiederhole alles, bis es gut klappt. Überlege dir, wo du stehen und wie du dich bewegen willst.

## Reciprocal teaching
(Reziprokes Lesen)

1. Bildet Vierergruppen.
2. Bearbeitet den ersten Abschnitt des Textes allein. Jedes Gruppenmitglied übernimmt dabei eine bestimmte Aufgabe: A klärt unbekannte Wörter und unklare Textstellen. B fasst den Abschnitt in Stichpunkten zusammen. C stellt Fragen zum Inhalt. D formuliert Vermutungen über den weiteren Verlauf der Handlung oder über fehlende Informationen.
3. Tauscht euch in eurer Gruppe anhand eurer Ergebnisse über den Textabschnitt aus. Macht euch Notizen, um eure gemeinsamen Ergebnisse festzuhalten.
4. Bearbeitet den nächsten Textabschnitt. Jedes Gruppenmitglied übernimmt diesmal eine andere Aufgabe.
5. Wiederholt den Vorgang, bis ihr den ganzen Text bearbeitet habt und jeder alle Aufgaben mindestens einmal übernommen hat.
6. Wertet im Anschluss eure Gruppenergebnisse gemeinsam in der Klasse aus.

## Round robin
(Blitzlicht)

1. Bildet Gruppen und setzt euch in einen Kreis.
2. Jedes Gruppenmitglied überlegt sich kurz einen Satz, der seine persönliche Meinung zum Thema ausdrückt.
3. Wenn alle bereit sind, sagen die Gruppenmitglieder der Reihe nach ihre Meinung.
4. Die anderen Gruppenmitglieder dürfen die Sätze nicht kommentieren.

## Think – pair – share

1. Schreibe deine Ideen, Gedanken oder Lösungen zur Aufgabe auf.
2. Tauscht eure Notizen zu zweit aus und besprecht sie.
3. Präsentiert euer Ergebnis anderen Paaren oder der gesamten Klasse.

## Tip top

1. Sage zunächst, was dir gut gefallen hat – was „top“ war.
2. Sage nun, was noch nicht so gut war, und gib einen Tipp, was man noch verbessern könnte.

## Writers' conference
(Schreibwerkstatt)

1. Bildet Vierergruppen.
2. Lest euch eure Sätze / Texte gegenseitig vor.
3. Die anderen sagen, was ihnen gefallen hat.
4. Die Zuhörer machen Verbesserungsvorschläge.
5. Jede Gruppe wählt den besten Text aus und liest ihn der Klasse vor.

## 1-minute-presentation

1. Nimm ein Blatt DIN A4-Papier quer und falte es so, dass das untere Drittel nach hinten wegknickt.
2. Schreibe den Vortragstext auf die oberen zwei Drittel.
3. Streiche nun die wichtigsten Stichpunkte im Text an. Notiere sie noch einmal auf dem unteren Drittel. Das ist dein Spickzettel.
4. In deiner Präsentation verwendest du nur den Spickzettel. Wenn du steckenbleibst, darfst du ihn umknicken und kurz auf den Text oben schauen.

# Vocabulary

## Vocabulary tips

Um dich besser ausdrücken und noch mehr verstehen zu können, ist ein immer größerer Wortschatz nötig. Es gibt verschiedene Möglichkeiten, sich Wörter zu merken und dazu zu lernen.

**Erstelle Wortfelder.**
Wörter, die zu einem Wortfeld gehören, kannst du auf Lernkarten, z. B. als Mindmap aufschreiben. So erinnerst du dich leichter.

**Schreibe die Wörter auf.**
Du kannst neue Wörter einzeln aufschreiben. Es ist aber oft besser, Wörter in Sätzen oder Redewendungen aufzuschreiben.

**Zeichne mit und um Wörter herum.**
Zeichnungen helfen dem Gedächtnis, sich neue Wörter zu merken. Integriere ein Wort in ein Bild oder zeichne darum herum.

**Achte auf deine Umwelt.**
Englische Wörter begegnen dir im Alltag überall (Werbung, Durchsagen am Bahnhof …). Du wirst erstaunt sein, wie viele du findest und auch schon kennst.

**Bewege dich.**
Verbinde schwierige Wörter mit einfachen, immer gleichen Gesten oder Bewegungen.

**Schaue Serien und Filme im Original an.**
Sieh dir im Internet oder auf DVD das englische Original mit englischem Untertitel an. Durch das gleichzeitige Hören und Lesen wirst du sehr viel mehr verstehen und auch behalten.

**Höre englischen Liedern genau zu.**
Höre die Lieder an und lies den Text im Internet nach. Wenn du den Text verstanden hast, singe ihn mit.

**Rede einfach drauf los und frage nach.**
Versuche Wörter, die du nicht kennst, zu umschreiben. Verstehst du ein Wort nicht, frage bei anderen nach.

**Wortbildung und Worterschließung**
Man kann mit bestimmten Bausteinen neue Wörter bilden oder auch ihre Wortart erkennen. Hier findest du einige Beispiele:

| | |
|---|---|
| 1. Nomen: -ment, -tion, -ness, -ity, -ship | govern*ment*, inven*tion*, happi*ness*, electric*ity*, friend*ship* |
| 2. Personen: -er, -or, -ist, -ian | rid*er*; visit*or*; flor*ist*; histor*ian* |
| 3. Adjektive : -y, -ful, -able, -ible, -ive, -al, -ic, -ed, -ing | trick*y*, help*ful*, comfort*able*, flex*ible*, intens*ive*, nation*al*, athlet*ic*, excit*ed*, surpris*ing* |
| 4. Verben: -ize, -ise, -ate, -en | organ*ize*, summar*ise*, apprecia*te*, short*en* |
| 5. Adverben: -ly | slow*ly*, heavi*ly*, sad*ly* |

Beispiele:
organiza*tion* – organiz*er* – organiz*e* – organiz*ed*
read – read*er* – read*able*
music – music*ian* – music*al* – musical*ly*
enjoy – enjoy*ment* – enjoy*able*

Es gibt auch Fälle, in denen das Nomen und das Verb dieselbe Form haben (to smile – a smile, to walk – a walk).

# Vocabulary

Das *Vocabulary* enthält alle neuen Wörter und Wendungen. Sie stehen in der Reihenfolge, wie sie im Buch vorkommen.

Die **fett** gedruckten Wörter musst du lernen.
Die blau gedruckten Wörter kannst du lernen, musst du aber nicht.
Die Wörter aus den Checkpoints musst du nicht lernen.

Auf den *Word bank*-Seiten findest du nützlichen individuellen Wortschatz zum Thema der Unit, der dir hilft, über deine eigene Situation zu sprechen oder zu schreiben.

**Symbole und Abkürzungen:**

- 👄 Achte auf die Aussprache!
- ✎ Achte auf die Schreibung!
- ↔ ist das Gegenteil von
- → ist verwandt mit
- = entspricht
- sth something
- sb somebody
- *(sg)* Einzahl (Singular)
- *(pl)* Mehrzahl (Plural)
- [R] ähnlich wie im Russischen
- [T] ähnlich wie im Türkischen

## Zoom in

| | | | |
|---|---|---|---|
| p. 8 | **ladies and gentlemen** [ˌleɪdiz‿ən 'dʒentlmən] | meine Damen und Herren | Good evening **ladies and gentlemen**, boys and girls. |

## Unit 1 Exploring Australia

| | | | |
|---|---|---|---|
| p. 10 | to **explore** [ɪk'splɔ:] | erkunden; erforschen | Let's **explore** Australia together. |

### Way in

| | | | |
|---|---|---|---|
| | **Australian** [ɒs'treɪliən] | Australier; Australierin; australisch | **Australian** Australia |
| | **easy-going** [ˌi:zi'gəʊɪŋ] | gelassen; locker | Everyone is **easy-going** in Australia. |
| | **continent** ['kɒntɪnənt] | Kontinent; Erdteil | [R] континент |
| | **Antarctica** [æn'tɑ:ktɪkə] | Antarktis | Australia broke away from **Antarctica**. |
| | **isolation** *(no pl)* [ˌaɪsə'leɪʃn] | Isolation; Trennung | [R] изоляция [T] izolasyon |
| | **unusual** [ʌn'ju:ʒl] | ungewöhnlich; außergewöhnlich | **unusual** ↔ usual |
| | **species** ['spi:ʃi:z] | Art; Spezies | 👄 Achte auf die Aussprache! |
| | to **exist** [ɪg'zɪst] | existieren; bestehen | Koalas only **exist** in Australia. |
| | **koala** [kəʊ'ɑ:lə] | Koala | [R] коала [T] koala |
| | **kangaroo** [ˌkæŋgr'u:] | Känguru | [R] кенгуру [T] kanguru |
| p. 11 | **available** [ə'veɪləbl] | erhältlich; verfügbar | **available** unavailable |
| | **skilled** [skɪld] | qualifiziert; ausgebildet; Fach- | There are jobs available for **skilled** workers. |
| | **carpenter** ['kɑ:pəntə] | Zimmermann; Zimmerin; Tischler; Tischlerin | **Carpenters** make chairs, tables, houses, … |
| | **nurse** [nɜ:s] | Krankenschwester; Krankenpfleger | |

| | | |
|---|---|---|
| **Aboriginal people** [æbəˌrɪdʒnl 'pi:pl] | die Aborigines | **Aboriginal people** have been in Australia for over 50,000 years. |
| to **struggle** ['strʌgl] | kämpfen; ringen; sich anstrengen; Mühe haben | Aboriginal people **struggled** for their rights. |
| to **be known as** [bi: 'nəʊn‿əz] | bekannt sein als | Daniel Craig **is known as** James Bond. |
| **the outback** [ði 'aʊtbæk] | Outback *(australisches Hinterland)* | **The outback** is the area in the centre of Australia. |
| **great** [greɪt] | groß; riesig | **great** tiny, small |
| to **attend** [ə'tend] | teilnehmen; anwesend sein; besuchen | Children in the outback **attend** the School of the Air. |
| **satellite dish** ['sætlaɪt ˌdɪʃ] | Satellitenschüssel | The students need a **satellite dish**. |
| **necessary** ['nesəsri] | nötig; notwendig; erforderlich | **necessary** unnecessary |
| **up to** ['ʌp tə] | bis zu | We have to read the text **up to** page 46. |
| **boarding school** ['bɔ:dɪŋ ˌsku:l] | Internat | Peter will go to a **boarding school** next year. |
| **term** [tɜ:m] | Trimester; Semester | A school year has three **terms**. |
| **in addition** [ˌɪn‿ə'dɪʃn] | zusätzlich; außerdem | I play the piano **in addition** to the guitar. |

## Station 1

### Respect

| | | | |
|---|---|---|---|
| **disrespectful** [ˌdɪsrɪ'spektfl] | respektlos | to **compromise** ['kɒmprəmaɪz] | Kompromisse machen |
| **ignorant** ['ɪgnərnt] | ignorant; unwissend | **tolerant** ['tɒlrnt] | tolerant |
| to **ignore** [ɪg'nɔ:] | ignorieren; außer Acht lassen | **acceptable** [ək'septəbl] | akzeptabel; annehmbar |
| **offensive** [ə'fensɪv] | beleidigend; anstößig | **respectful** [rɪ'spektfl] | respektvoll |
| **politeness** [pə'laɪtnəs] | Höflichkeit | ignorance ['ɪgnərns] | Ignoranz; Unwissenheit |
| **rude** [ru:d] | unhöflich; unverschämt | acceptance [ək'septəns] | Akzeptanz; Zustimmung |
| **respect** [rɪ'spekt] | Respekt | tolerance ['tɒlrns] | Toleranz |
| **rudeness** ['ru:dnəs] | Unhöflichkeit; Unverschämtheit | compromising ['kɒmprəmaɪzɪŋ] | bloßstellend |
| **compromise** ['kɒmprəmaɪz] | Kompromiss | | |

| | | | |
|---|---|---|---|
| p. 12 | **sacred** ['seɪkrɪd] | heilig | The area around Uluru is **sacred**. |
| | **stunning** ['stʌnɪŋ] | überwältigend | The view from the tower is **stunning**. |
| | **whenever** [wen'evə] | wann immer; immer, wenn; so oft | I enjoy the view **whenever** I'm in London. |
| | **tribe** [traɪb] | Stamm; Volksstamm | My family is from an Aboriginal **tribe**. |
| | **generation** [ˌdʒenə'reɪʃn] | Generation | Achte auf die Aussprache! |
| | **official** [ə'fɪʃl] | offiziell | We won the game, it's **official**. |
| | **recognised** ['rekəgnaɪzd] | anerkannt | BE: **recognised** AE: recognized |
| | **tour guide** ['tʊə ˌgaɪd] | Reiseleiter; Reiseleiterin | Our **tour guide** knew lots about Australia. |
| | to **show sb around (a place)** [ˌʃəʊ‿ə'raʊnd] | jmdn. (an einem Ort) herumführen | The tour guide **showed us around** Uluru. |
| | to **send in** [send‿'ɪn] | einschicken; einsenden | I **sent in** my photos for the competition. |
| | **application** [ˌæplɪ'keɪʃn] | Bewerbung | **application** to apply |
| | **might** [maɪt] | könnten | We **might** see a wild animal. |
| | **legend** ['ledʒənd] | Legende; Sage | R легенда |
| | **creature** ['kri:tʃə] | Kreatur; Lebewesen; Geschöpf | We saw giant **creatures** in the zoo. |
| | to **create** [kri'eɪt] | schaffen; erschaffen; verursachen | The creatures **created** the mountains. |
| | **belief** [bɪ'li:f] | Glaube; Überzeugung | **belief** to believe |
| | **meaning** ['mi:nɪŋ] | Bedeutung | **meaning** to mean |
| | **protected** [prə'tektɪd] | geschützt | Uluru is sacred and needs to be **protected**. |
| | **ground** [graʊnd] | Boden; Erdboden | The man threw his rubbish on the **ground**. |
| | **path** [pɑ:θ] | Pfad; Weg | You have to walk on the **path**. |
| | to **keep sb happy** [ˌki:p 'hæpi] | jmdn. bei Laune halten | The tour guides **kept the tourists happy**. |
| | **by (+ gerund)** [baɪ] | indem | We did the exercise **by listening** carefully. |
| | **survival** [sə'vaɪvl] | Überleben; Überlebens- | **survival** to survive |
| | **desert** ['dezət] | Wüste |  |
| | **camel** ['kæml] | Kamel |  |
| | **painting** ['peɪntɪŋ] | Mal- | I took part in a **painting** workshop. |
| | **climbing** ['klaɪmɪŋ] | Klettern | **Climbing** can be dangerous. |
| p. 13 | to **realise** ['rɪəlaɪz] | erkennen; realisieren | BE: **to realise** AE: to realize |
| p. 14 | to **complete** [kəm'pli:t] | absolvieren; abschließen | I have to **complete** the course. |
| | to **pass** [pɑ:s] | bestehen | Koa has to **pass** a test to be a tour guide. |
| p. 15 | **climb** [klaɪm] | Aufstieg | Let's do the Sydney Harbour Bridge **Climb**. |
| | to **sit down** [ˌsɪt 'daʊn] | sich hinsetzen; sich setzen | **to sit down** to stand up |
| | **excuse** [ɪk'skju:s] | Entschuldigung; Ausrede | That is no **excuse** for forgetting your book. |

| | | |
|---|---|---|
| **to let sb know** [ˌlet ˈnəʊ] | jmdn. informieren; jmdm. Bescheid geben; jmdm. Bescheid sagen | **Let me know** if you can come. |

## Station 2

### Jobs

| | | | |
|---|---|---|---|
| **receptionist** [rɪˈsepʃnɪst] | Empfangschef; Empfangschefin | plumber [ˈplʌmə] | Installateur; Installateurin; Klempner; Klempnerin |
| **electrician** [ˌelɪkˈtrɪʃn] | Elektriker; Elektrikerin | mechanic [mɪˈkænɪk] | Mechaniker; Mechanikerin |
| **travel agent** [ˈtrævl‿ˌeɪdʒnt] | Reisebürokaufmann; Reisebürokauffrau | **bike courier** [ˈbaɪk ˌkʊriə] | Fahrradkurier; Fahrradkurierin |
| physiotherapist [ˌfɪziəˈθerəpɪst] | Physiotherapeut; Physiotherapeutin | | |

| | | | |
|---|---|---|---|
| p. 16 | **efficient** [ɪˈfɪʃnt] | effizient; leistungsfähig | **efficient** inefficient |
| | **to require** [rɪˈkwaɪə] | benötigen; erfordern | **to require** requirement |
| | **work experience** [ˈwɜːk‿ɪkˌspɪəriəns] | Praktikum; Berufserfahrung | I did **work experience** in a hotel. |
| | **customer service** [ˌkʌstəmə ˈsɜːvɪs] | Kundendienst; Kundenbetreuung | I go to **customer service** if I have a problem. |
| | **intermediate** [ɪntəˈmiːdiət] | Mittel-; mittleres Niveau | **intermediate** is in the middle |
| | **skill** [skɪl] | Kenntnis; Fertigkeit; Fähigkeit | Companies want to know about your **skills**. |
| | **native speaker** [ˌneɪtɪv ˈspiːkə] | Muttersprachler; Muttersprachlerin | I am a German **native speaker**. |
| | **certificate** [səˈtɪfɪkət] | Zertifikat; Bescheinigung; Urkunde; Zeugnis | ✎ Achtung Schreibweise! certificate |
| | **salary** [ˈsælri] | Gehalt | Your **salary** is what you earn. |
| | **on-the-job training** [ˌɒnðədʒɒb ˈtreɪnɪŋ] | Ausbildung am Arbeitsplatz | They said there is **on-the-job training**. |
| | **CV (= curriculum vitae)** [ˌsiːˈviː] | Lebenslauf | I have to send my **CV** with a photo on it. |
| | **letter of application** [ˌletər‿əv‿æplɪˈkeɪʃn] | Bewerbungsbrief | Send a **letter of application** and your CV. |
| | **personal statement** [ˌpɜːsnl ˈsteɪtmənt] | Motivationsschreiben | A **personal statement** is hard to write. |
| | **interest** [ˈɪntrəst] | Interesse | Don't forget to tell them your **interests**. |
| | **reference** [ˈrefrns] | Referenz; Referenzschreiben | Achte auf die Aussprache! |
| | **field** [fiːld] | Gebiet; Bereich | **field** = area |

| | | | |
|---|---|---|---|
| | **current** ['kʌrnt] | aktuell; derzeitig; gegenwärtig | What is your **current** job? |
| | **temporary** ['temprəri] | vorübergehend | I have a **temporary** job until September. |
| | to **check in** [ˌtʃek‿'ɪn] | einchecken | **to check in** ↔ to check out |
| | **permanent** ['pɜːmnənt] | unbefristet; permanent; dauerhaft | I'm looking for a **permanent** job. |
| | **communication** [kəˌmjuːnɪ'keɪʃn] | Kommunikation | **communication** → to communicate |
| | **administration** [ədˌmɪnɪ'streɪʃn] | Verwaltung | I have intermediate **administration** skills. |
| | to **qualify** ['kwɒlɪfaɪ] | qualifizieren; befähigen | I think my skills **qualify** me for the job. |
| | **attached** [ə'tætʃt] | angefügt; angehängt | Please find **attached** my CV. |
| | to **look forward to** (+ -ing) [ˌlʊk 'fɔːwəd tə] | sich freuen auf | I'm **looking forward to** visiting my grandma. |
| | **Yours sincerely,** [ˌjɔːz sɪn'sɪəli] | Mit freundlichen Grüßen | This can be used at the end of a formal letter. |
| | **teamwork** ['tiːmwɜːk] | Teamwork | I don't want to work alone. I like **teamwork**. |
| p. 17 | **preschool** ['priːskuːl] | Vorschule; Vorschul- | My mum is a **preschool** teacher. |
| | to **pay attention to sth** [ˌpeɪ‿ə'tenʃn tə] | seine Aufmerksamkeit auf etw. richten | Listen and **pay attention to detail**. |
| | **punctual** ['pʌŋktʃuəl] | pünktlich | **punctual** ↔ late |
| | **self-motivated** [ˌself'məʊtɪveɪtɪd] | eigenmotiviert | In some jobs you have to be **self-motivated**. |
| | **qualification** [ˌkwɒlɪfɪ'keɪʃn] | Qualifikation; Abschluss; Schulabschluss | **qualification** → to qualify |
| | **transport** ['trænspɔːt] | Transport; Beförderung | R транспорт |
| p. 18 | **experienced** [ɪk'spɪəriənst] | erfahren | **experienced** → experience → to experience |
| | to **go well** [ˌgəʊ 'wel] | gut laufen | **to go well** ↔ to go badly |
| | **of all the people** [əv‿'ɔːl ðə ˌpiːpl] | von allen Leuten | **Of all the people**, I worked best in a team. |
| p. 19 | **qualified** ['kwɒlɪfaɪd] | qualifiziert | **qualified** → to qualify → qualification |
| | **candidate** ['kændɪdət] | Kandidat; Kandidatin; Bewerber; Bewerberin | R кандидат |
| | **anybody else** [ˌenibədi 'els] | jeder andere | **anybody else** ↔ nobody else |
| | **requirement** [rɪ'kwaɪəmənt] | Voraussetzung; Anforderung | **requirement** → to require |

## Reading corner

| | | | |
|---|---|---|---|
| p. 20 | **danger** ['deɪndʒə] | Gefahr | **danger** dangerous |
| | **wonder** ['wʌndə] | Wunder | **wonder** wonderful  |
| | **underwater** [ˌʌndə'wɔ:tə] | Unterwasser- | |
| | **individual** [ˌɪndɪ'vɪdʒuəl] | einzeln; individuell | There are many **individual** islands near Scotland. |
| | **reef** [ri:f] | Riff | R риф T resif |
| | **Sicily** ['sɪsɪli] | Sizilien | R Сицилия T Sicilya |
| | **moon** [mu:n] | Mond |  |
| | **ecosystem** ['i:kəʊˌsɪstəm] | Ökosystem | This **ecosystem** is home to lots of fish. |
| | **coral** ['kɒrəl] | Koralle | R коралл  |
| | **to migrate** [maɪ'greɪt] | wandern; umherziehen | R мигрировать |
| | **turtle** ['tɜ:tl] | Schildkröte | **Turtles** live on land and under water. |
| | **uncertain** [ʌn'sɜ:tn] | ungewiss; unsicher | **uncertain** certain |
| | **most of** ['məʊst‿əv] | die meisten | **Most of** the coral has disappeared. |
| | **climate change** ['klaɪmət ˌtʃeɪndʒ] | Klimawandel | **Climate change** is a danger to the reef. |
| | **bleaching** ['bli:tʃɪŋ] | Bleichen; Ausbleichen | Coral **bleaching** is a problem. |
| | **threat** [θret] | Bedrohung; Gefahr | Climate change is the greatest **threat**. |
| | **increase** ['ɪnkri:s] | Zunahme; Wachstum; Anstieg | There is an **increase** in visitors to the reef. |
| | **temperature** ['temprətʃə] | Temperatur | R температура |
| | **to result in** [rɪ'zʌlt‿ɪn] | zur Folge haben; führen zu | The increase **resulted in** coral bleaching. |
| | **unknown** [ʌn'nəʊn] | unbekannt | **unknown** known |
| | **changing** ['tʃeɪndʒɪŋ] | wechselnd; sich verändernd | **changing** to change change |
| | **alga** *(sg)* ['ælgə], **algae** *(pl)* ['ældʒi:] | Alge | Warm water kills the **algae** on the coral. |
| | **death** [deθ] | Tod; Todesfall | The **death** of the algae kills the reef. |
| | **in turn** [ɪn 'tɜ:n] | dagegen; im Gegenzug | We all spoke **in turn** about our holidays. |
| | **diving** ['daɪvɪŋ] | Tauchen; Tauch- |  |
| | **snorkelling** ['snɔ:klɪŋ] | Schnorcheln |  |
| | **unfortunately** [ʌn'fɔ:tʃnətli] | leider; unglücklicherweise | **unfortunately** fortunately |
| | **damage** ['dæmɪdʒ] | Schaden; Beschädigung | The fire caused a lot of **damage**. |
| | **environment** [ɪn'vaɪrnmənt] | Umgebung; Umwelt | Tourists look at the reef **environment**. |
| | **platform** ['plætfɔ:m] | Plattform | Snorkelling **platforms** attract sea birds. |
| | **waste** [weɪst] | Abfall; *hier:* Exkremente | The sea birds' **waste** washes into the sea. |

| | | | |
|---|---|---|---|
| | **to pollute** [pə'lu:t] | verschmutzen; verunreinigen | The sea birds' waste **pollutes** the sea. |
| p. 21 | **oil spill** ['ɔɪl ˌspɪl] | Ölteppich | **Oil spills** happen when ships hit the reef. |
| | **cruise ship** ['kru:z ˌʃɪp] | Kreuzfahrtschiff |  |
| | **to damage** ['dæmɪdʒ] | beschädigen; schaden | The fire **damaged** a lot of houses. |
| | **to recover** [rɪ'kʌvə] | sich erholen | It will take years for the reef to **recover**. |
| | **tropical** ['trɒpɪkl] | tropisch | I love **tropical** fish. |
| | **rainy season** [ˌreɪni 'si:zn] | Regenzeit | The **rainy season** has just started. |
| | **chemical** ['kemɪkl] | Chemikalie | The rain washes the **chemicals** into the sea. |
| | **pesticide** ['pestɪsaɪd] | Pestizid; Schädlingsbekämpfungsmittel | **Pesticides** are chemicals used in farming. |
| | **to stop** [stɒp] | aufhalten; stoppen | **to stop** to start |
| | **decline** [dɪ'klaɪn] | Rückgang; Abnahme; Verschlechterung | The government doesn't stop the **decline**. |
| | **to control** [kən'trəʊl] | kontrollieren | **to control** control |
| | **shipping** ['ʃɪpɪŋ] | Schiffe | **shipping** ship |
| | **global** ['gləʊbl] | weltweit; global | R глобальный T global |
| | **to agree (on)** [ə'gri:] | sich einigen (auf) | **to agree (on)** to disagree (on) |
| | **to take action** [teɪk‿'ækʃn] | eingreifen; handeln | **to take action** = to do sth |
| | **to limit** ['lɪmɪt] | limitieren; begrenzen; beschränken | **to limit** limited |
| | **effect** [ɪ'fekt] | Effekt; Wirkung; Auswirkung | We have to limit the **effects** of pollution. |
| | **scientist** ['saɪəntɪst] | Wissenschaftler; Wissenschaftlerin | **Scientists** study the reef. |
| | **extinct** [ɪk'stɪŋkt] | ausgestorben | The reef might be **extinct** by 2030. |

## Film corner

| | | | |
|---|---|---|---|
| p. 23 | **whale shark** ['weɪl ˌʃɑ:k] | Walhai | **Whale sharks** live in the ocean. |
| | **saltwater crocodile** [sɔ:ltˌwɔ:tə 'krɒkədaɪl] | Salzwasserkrokodil | **Saltwater crocodiles** are very dangerous. |
| | **dolphin** ['dɒlfɪn] | Delfin | R дельфин  |
| | **manta ray** ['mæntə‿reɪ] | Teufelsrochen | The **manta ray** is a flat fish. |
| | **close** [kləʊs] | eng; nahe | The animals live in **close** family groups. |

## Word bank: Jobs and qualities

### Jobs

**baker** Bäcker / -in
**bank clerk / specialist** Bankkaufmann / -frau
**office assistant** Bürokaufmann / -frau
**electrician** Elektriker / -in
**receptionist** Empfangschef / -in
**nursery teacher** Erzieher / -in
**caterer** Fachkraft für Gastronomie
**food technology expert** Fachkraft für Lebensmitteltechnik
**vehicle painter** Fahrzeuglackierer / -in
**firefighter** Feuerwehrmann / -frau
**butcher** Fleischer / -in; Metzger / -in
**florist** Florist / -in
**aircraft mechanic** Fluggerätemechaniker / -in
**flight attendant** Flugzeugbegleiter / -in
**designer** Gestalter / -in; Designer / -in
**hotel assistant** Hotelfachmann / -frau
**industrial assistant** Industriekaufmann / -frau
**industrial mechanic** Industriemechaniker / -in
**plumber** Installateur / -in; Klempner / -in
**retail assistant** Kaufmann / -frau im Einzelhandel
**chef** Koch / Köchin
**beautician** Kosmetiker / -in
**nurse** Krankenpfleger / -schwester
**(landscape) gardener** (Landschafts)Gärtner / -in
**speech therapist** Logopäde / Logopädin
**bricklayer** Maurer / -in
**mechanic** Mechaniker / -in
**mechatronics technician** Mechatroniker / -in
**media designer** Mediengestalter / -in
**doctor's assistant** Medizinischer Fachangestellter / Medizinische Fachangestellte
**metalworker** Metallbauer / -in
**police officer** Polizeibeamter / -beamtin
**physiotherapist** Physiotherapeut / -in
**travel agent** Reisebürokaufmann / -frau
**secretary** Sekretär / -in; Assistent / -in
**plasterer** Stuckateur / -in
**telephonist** Telefonist / -in
**animal keeper** Tierpfleger / -in
**salesperson** Verkäufer / -in
**dentist's assistant** Zahnarzthelfer / -in
**carpenter** Zimmerer / Zimmerin

### Qualities needed

**be patient** Geduld haben
**be flexible** flexibel sein
**be interested in …** an … interessiert sein
**be understanding** verständnisvoll sein
**be willing to travel** bereit sein zu reisen
**be willing to work shifts** bereit sein, in Schichten zu arbeiten
**be well-organized** gut organisiert sein
**be willing to get up early** bereit sein, früh aufzustehen
**like to work outside / in an office** gerne im Freien / Büro arbeiten
**be able to work in a team** teamfähig sein
**be able to stay calm in difficult situations** in schwierigen Situationen ruhig bleiben können
**be able to take responsibility** Verantwortung übernehmen können

### Qualifications

**general school certificate** Hauptschulabschluss
**intermediate school certificate** Realschulabschluss
**school certificate for admission to college** Fachhochschulreife
**school certificate for admission to university** Abitur

### Work experience

**apprenticeship** Ausbildung
**work placement; internship** Berufspraktikum
**social placement** Sozialpraktikum
**holiday job** Ferienjob
**weekend job** Wochenendjob
**voluntary / gap year** Soziales Jahr

### Skills

**language skills** Sprachkenntnisse
(**advanced** fortgeschritten – **intermediate** mittel – **basic** Grundkenntnisse)
**communicate well** gut kommunizieren können

## Unit 2 Colourful Caribbean

| | | | |
|---|---|---|---|
| p. 28 | **the Caribbean** [ðə ˌkærɪ'biːən] | die Karibik | The weather is good in **the Caribbean**. |

### Way in

| | | | |
|---|---|---|---|
| | **to consist of** [kən'sɪst‿əv] | bestehen aus | The Caribbean **consists of** lots of islands. |
| | **inhabited** [ɪn'hæbɪtɪd] | bewohnt | **inhabited** uninhabited |
| | **sandy** ['sændi] | sandig | Let's go to the nice **sandy** beach. |
| | **autumn** ['ɔːtəm] | Herbst | September and October are in **autumn**. |
| | **hurricane** ['hʌrɪkən] | Orkan; Wirbelsturm | There are strong **hurricanes** in the autumn. |
| | **to threaten** ['θretn] | bedrohen | **to threaten** threat |
| | **tourist industry** ['tʊərɪst‿ ˌɪndəstri] | Tourismus | There are many jobs in the **tourist industry**. |
| p. 29 | **Caribbean** [ˌkærɪ'biːən] | karibisch; Karibisch; Karibe; Karibin | There are lots of **Caribbean** islands. |
| | **French** [frentʃ] | französisch; aus Frankreich | **French** France |
| | **Dutch** [dʌtʃ] | niederländisch; Niederländisch | **Dutch** people are from the Netherlands. |
| | **colony** ['kɒləni] | Kolonie | R колония T koloni |
| | **difference** ['dɪfrns] | Unterschied | **difference** different |
| | **all of** ['ɔːl‿əv] | alle | Nearly **all of** the fish are beautiful. |
| | **descendant** [dɪ'sendənt] | Abkömmling; Nachfahre; Nachfahrin | A lot of people are **descendants** of slaves. |
| | **all of them** ['ɔːl‿əv ˌðəm] | (sie) alle | Listen to the songs, **all of them** are good. |
| | **pirate** ['paɪrət] | Seeräuber; Seeräuberin; Pirat; Piratin | R пират  |
| | **to encourage** [ɪn'kʌrɪdʒ] | ermutigen; unterstützen | **to encourage** encouragement |
| | **rival** ['raɪvl] | Rivale; Rivalin; Konkurrent; Konkurrentin | Spain was a **rival** of the British. |
| | **international** [ˌɪntə'næʃnl] | international | Achte auf die Aussprache! |
| | **musician** [mjuː'zɪʃn] | Musiker; Musikerin | R музыкант T müzisyen |
| | **role model** ['rəʊl ˌmɒdl] | Vorbild | Bob Marley is Greg's **role model**. |
| | **return** [rɪ'tɜːn] | Rückkehr | We waited months for my brother's **return**. |
| | **full-time** [ˌfʊl'taɪm] | Vollzeit-; Ganztags- | **full-time** part-time |
| | **goal** [gəʊl] | Ziel; Tor | My **goal** is to be the best in the team. |

## Station 1

### Holiday words

| | | | |
|---|---|---|---|
| **ferry** ['feri] | Fähre | **lightning** *(no pl)* ['laɪtnɪŋ] | Blitz |
| **sand** [sænd] | Sand | **delay** [dɪ'leɪ] | Verzögerung; Verspätung |
| **diver** ['daɪvə] | Taucher; Taucherin | to **board** [bɔ:d] | an Bord gehen |
| **diving school** ['daɪvɪŋ ˌsku:l] | Tauchschule | **passport** ['pɑ:spɔ:t] | Pass; Reisepass |
| **accommodation** [əˌkɒmə'deɪʃn] | Unterbringung; Unterkunft | **couch surfing** ['kaʊtʃ ˌsɜ:fɪŋ] | Couchsurfing |
| **luxury resort** ['lʌkʃri rɪˌzɔ:t] | Luxusresort | **check-in** ['tʃekɪn] | Gepäckaufgabe; Einchecken |
| **resort** [rɪ'zɔ:t] | Ferienort; Ferienanlage | **breeze** [bri:z] | Brise |
| **hostel** ['hɒstl] | Herberge | **guest house** ['gest ˌhaʊs] | Gästehaus; Pension |
| **sunshine** ['sʌnʃaɪn] | Sonnenschein | **gate** [geɪt] | Gate; Ausgang |
| **departure** [dɪ'pɑ:tʃə] | Abflug; Abreise | **arrival** [ə'raɪvl] | Ankunft |
| **thunder** *(no pl)* ['θʌndə] | Donner | | |

| | | | |
|---|---|---|---|
| p. 30 | **hopping** ['hɒpɪŋ] | Hüpfen; Hopping | Island **hopping** is a good way to see more. |
| | **the Bahamas** [ðə bə'hɑ:məz] | die Bahamas *(Inselgruppe in der Karibik)* | There are many islands in **the Bahamas**. |
| | **nearby** [ˌnɪə'baɪ] | in der Nähe | **nearby** near |
| | **distant** ['dɪstnt] | entfernt; distanziert | You can take a flight to a **distant** island. |
| | **beauty** ['bju:ti] | Schönheit | **beauty** beautiful |
| | to **take one's breath away** [ˌteɪk wʌnz 'breθ‿əˌweɪ] | den Atem rauben | The view **took my breath away**. |
| | **art** [ɑ:t] | Kunst | Have you learned the **art** of doing nothing? |
| | to **discover** [dɪ'skʌvə] | entdecken | We **discovered** the underwater sea life. |
| | **by** [baɪ] | vorbei | A dolphin and a turtle swam **by**. |
| | **beginner** [bɪ'gɪnə] | Anfänger; Anfängerin | They offer courses for **beginners**. |
| | **shipwreck** ['ʃɪprek] | Schiffswrack |  |
| | **off** [ɒf] | von … weg; vor | The shipwreck is just **off** the coast. |
| | **the British Virgin Islands** [ðə ˌbrɪtɪʃ ˌvɜ:dʒɪn 'aɪləndz] | die Britischen Jungferninseln | The ship is near **the British Virgin Islands**. |
| | **Trinidad** ['trɪnɪdæd] | Trinidad *(Insel in der Karibik)* | R Тринидад T Trinidad |
| | to **party** ['pɑ:ti] | feiern | People really know how to **party** here. |
| | to **take place** [ˌteɪk 'pleɪs] | stattfinden | **to take place** = to happen |
| | **Ash Wednesday** [ˌæʃ 'wenzdeɪ] | Aschermittwoch | The carnival is before **Ash Wednesday**. |

| | | | |
|---|---|---|---|
| | **steelpan** ['sti:lpæn] | Steelpan *(Trommel aus Blech)* | The music from the **steelpans** is good. |
| | **seafood** ['si:fu:d] | Meeresfrüchte | The **seafood** is fresh and delicious. |
| | **volcano** *(sg)* [vɒl'keɪnəʊ], **volcanoes** *(pl)* [vɒl'keɪnəʊz] | Vulkan | R вулкан T volkan  |
| | **extraordinary** [ɪk'strɔ:dnri] | außergewöhnlich | **extraordinary** ordinary |
| | **colonial** [kə'ləʊniəl] | kolonial; Kolonial- | Achte auf die Aussprache! |
| p. 33 | **scared** [skeəd] | verängstigt | We were **scared** when the storm came. |

## Station 2

### Standards and values

| | | | |
|---|---|---|---|
| **lucky** ['lʌki] | glücklich; erfolgreich | **values** *(pl)* ['vælju:z] | Werte; Wertvorstellungen |
| **struggle** ['strʌgl] | Kampf; Anstrengung | **well-paid** [ˌwel'peɪd] | gut bezahlt |
| **bond** [bɒnd] | Bindung | **wealth** [welθ] | Reichtum |
| **complicated** ['kɒmplɪkeɪtɪd] | kompliziert | **health** [helθ] | Gesundheit |
| to **marry** ['mæri] | heiraten | **happiness** ['hæpɪnəs] | Glück; Zufriedenheit; Fröhlichkeit |
| **friendship** ['frendʃɪp] | Freundschaft | to **fit in** [ˌfɪt‿'ɪn] | hineinpassen |
| **religion** [rɪ'lɪdʒn] | Religion | **commitment** [kə'mɪtmənt] | Engagement; Einsatz |
| **disadvantaged** [ˌdɪsəd'vɑ:ntɪdʒd] | benachteiligt | **honesty** ['ɒnɪsti] | Ehrlichkeit |
| **faith** [feɪθ] | Glaube | **responsibility** [rɪˌspɒnsə'bɪləti] | Verantwortung |
| **privilege** ['prɪvlɪdʒ] | Privileg; (Vor)Recht | **solidarity** [ˌsɒlɪ'dærəti] | Solidarität |
| to **afford** [ə'fɔ:d] | sich leisten | | |
| **conservative** [ˌkən'sɜ:vətɪv] | konservativ | | |

| | | | |
|---|---|---|---|
| p. 34 | **last night** [ˌlɑ:st 'naɪt] | gestern Abend; gestern Nacht | At 8 o'clock **last night** I was asleep. |
| | **nursing** ['nɜ:sɪŋ] | Pflege; Krankenpflege | I was accepted for a **nursing** course. |
| | **violence** *(no pl)* ['vaɪəlns] | Gewalt | There's a lot of **violence** on the streets. |
| | to **break out** [ˌbreɪk‿'aʊt] | ausbrechen | Violence **breaks out** regularly. |
| | **street gang** ['stri:t ˌgæŋ] | Straßengang | I don't want to join a **street gang**. |
| | **shooting** ['ʃu:tɪŋ] | Schießerei | There are **shootings** every day. |
| | **drug** [drʌg] | Droge | Don't start taking **drugs**, they make you ill. |
| | **everywhere** ['evriweə] | überall | **everywhere** nowhere |
| | **constant** ['kɒnstənt] | ständig; konstant; stetig; permanent | Shootings are a **constant** problem. |

| | | | |
|---|---|---|---|
| | to **keep** [ki:p] | *hier:* bleiben | My family helps me to **keep** strong. |
| | **even though** [ˌi:vn ˈðəʊ] | auch wenn; obwohl | **Even though** I'm an adult, they help me. |
| | **else** [els] | andere; sonst | Everyone **else** helps me too. |
| | to **be involved** [bi: ɪnˈvɒlvd] | sich beteiligen; sich engagieren | Everyone **is involved** with the party. |
| | **including** [ɪnˈklu:dɪŋ] | einschließlich | Everyone is involved, **including** my friends. |
| | **free-time** [ˌfri:ˈtaɪm] | Freizeit- | Look at the list of **free-time** activities. |
| | **counsellor** [ˈkaʊnslə] | Berater; Beraterin | I always wanted to be a **counsellor**. |
| | to **wonder** [ˈwʌndə] | sich Gedanken machen; sich fragen | I **wonder** what living in Canada would be like. |
| | **fee** [fi:] | Gebühr | The school **fees** were too high. |
| | to **come out** [ˌkʌm‿ˈaʊt] | sich outen | My brother **came out** to my parents. |
| | **gay** [geɪ] | schwul; homosexuell | He's **gay**. He loves a man. |
| | **shock** [ʃɒk] | Schock | It was a **shock** for my family. |
| p. 37 | to **grow** [grəʊ] | ansteigen | Poverty **grows** fast in Jamaica. |
| | to **feed** [fi:d] | ernähren | Some parents can't **feed** their children. |
| | to shoot [ʃu:t] | erschießen | **to shoot** shooting |

## Reading corner

| | | | |
|---|---|---|---|
| p. 38 | to **lie** [laɪ], **lay** [leɪ], **lain** [leɪn] | liegen | Brighton **lies** on the southern coast. |
| | **position** [pəˈzɪʃn] | Position; Stelle | Achte auf die Aussprache! |
| | governess [ˈgʌvnəs] | Gouvernante; Hauslehrerin | She was **governess** to the children. |
| | **Barbados** [bɑ:ˈbeɪdɒs] | Barbados *(Inselstaat in der Karibik)* | R Барбадос T Barbados |
| p. 39 | to **wake** [weɪk], **woke** [wəʊk], **woken** [ˈwəʊkn] | wecken; aufwecken | I was **woken** by terrible shouts outside. |
| | **cannon** [ˈkænən] | Kanone |  |
| | porthole [ˈpɔ:thəʊl] | Bullauge; Luke | The windows on boats are called **portholes**. |
| | **brutal** [ˈbru:tl] | brutal | Blackheart was a **brutal** captain. |
| | **at that time** [ət ðæt ˈtaɪm] | damals; zu der Zeit | There were lots of attacks **at that time**. |
| | **perhaps** [pəˈhæps] | vielleicht | **perhaps** = maybe |
| | to **fly open** [ˌflaɪ‿ˈəʊpn] | auffliegen | Suddenly the door **flew open**. |
| | it took me a moment [ɪt ˌtʊk mi:‿ə ˈməʊmənt] | ich brauchte einen Moment | **It took me a moment** to see who it was. |
| | to **recognise** [ˈrekəgnaɪz] | erkennen; anerkennen | BE: **to recognise** AE: to recognize |
| | to **stop sb from sth** [ˈstɒp frəm] | jmdn. an etw. hindern; jmdn. von etw. abhalten | My sister didn't **stop** me **from leaving**. |

| | | | |
|---|---|---|---|
| | **not ... anyone** [nɒt ... 'eniwʌn] | niemand | I went, although I **didn't** know **anyone**. |
| p. 40 | **cabin** ['kæbɪn] | Kabine | A pirate followed Carol into her **cabin**. |
| | **look** [lʊk] | Ausdruck; Blick | He had an evil **look** on his face. |
| | **ugly** ['ʌgli] | hässlich | **ugly** beautiful |
| | **to open** ['əʊpn] | sich öffnen; aufgehen | Suddenly the door **opened**. |
| | **horror** ['hɒrə] | Horror; Schrecken; Entsetzen | Oh, the **horror** when I saw Blackheart. |
| | **punishment** ['pʌnɪʃmənt] | Bestrafung | **punishment** to punish |
| | **dagger** ['dægə] | Dolch |  |
| | **prisoner** ['prɪznə] | Gefangener; Gefangene |  |
| | **to resist** [rɪ'zɪst] | sich widersetzen; widerstehen | We couldn't **resist** looking at the food. |
| | **in order to** [ɪn‿'ɔ:də tə] | um ... zu; mit der Absicht | We left early **in order to** be on time. |
| | **to walk the plank** [ˌwɔ:k ðə 'plæŋk] | über eine Schiffsplanke ins Wasser getrieben werden | Pirates make people **walk the plank**. |
| | **smile** [smaɪl] | Lächeln |  |
| | **to continue** [kən'tɪnju:] | fortfahren; weitergehen | **to continue** to stop |
| | **to think of** ['θɪŋk‿əv] | sich ausdenken; sich einfallen lassen | **Think of** a number between 1 and 10. |
| | **to keep one's mouth shut** [ˌki:p wʌnz 'maʊθ ʃʌt] | den Mund halten | I **kept my mouth shut** and didn't say anything. |
| | **to give away** [ˌgɪv‿ə'weɪ] | *hier:* verraten | I was afraid my voice would **give** me **away**. |
| | **to fool sb** [fu:l] | jmdn. täuschen | Eliza **fooled the pirates**. |
| | **to cry** [kraɪ] | weinen; schreien; rufen | **to cry** to laugh |
| | **to be terrified (of sth)** [bi: 'terəfaɪd (əv)] | (große) Angst (vor etw.) haben | **to be terrified** = to be scared |
| p. 41 | **sky** [skaɪ] | Himmel |  |
| | **to hunt** [hʌnt] | jagen | **to hunt** hunter |
| | **to fire** [faɪə] | schießen mit; abfeuern | The pirate **fired** a cannon at the ship. |
| | **shot** [ʃɒt] | Schuss | The **shot** landed in the sea. |
| | **obviously** ['ɒbviəsli] | offensichtlich | The crew was **obviously** terrified. |
| | **to stop** [stɒp] | stehen bleiben; anhalten | The pirate who was with me **stopped**. |
| | **to get away (from sb)** [ˌget‿ə'weɪ frəm] | (jmdm.) entkommen; (von jmdm.) wegkommen | **to get away** = to escape |

## Film corner

| | | | |
|---|---|---|---|
| p. 43 | **fishing boat** ['fɪʃɪŋ ˌbəʊt] | Fischerboot | We went fishing in a **fishing boat**. |

Checkpoint

| | | | |
|---|---|---|---|
| rainforest ['reɪnˌfɒrɪst] | Regenwald | in conclusion [ˌɪn kən'klu:ʒn] | abschließend; zum Abschluss |
| furthermore [ˌfɜ:ðə'mɔ:] | überdies; außerdem | | |

## Word bank: Talking about travelling

### accommodation details

**single room** Einzelzimmer
**double room** Doppelzimmer
**en-suite bathroom** mit Bad
**dorm** Schlafsaal
**bunk bed** Doppelstockbett
**view** Blick
**clean** sauber
**modern** modern
**well-equipped** gut ausgestattet
**comfortable** bequem
**shared** Gemeinschafts-
**roomy** geräumig
**half-board** Halbpension
**full-board** Vollpension

### weather

**wet weather**
**rain** Regen
**drizzle** Nieselregen
**soaked** durchnässt
**showery** regnerisch
**humid** schwül; feucht
**overcast** bewölkt; bedeckt

**cold weather**
**chilly** kühl
**below zero** unter Null
**frost** Frost
**hail** Hagel
**freezing** eiskalt
**icy** eisig
**snow** Schnee

**good weather**
**sunny** sonnig
**sunshine** Sonnenschein
**heatwave** Hitzewelle
**mild** mild
**clear** klar

**windy weather**
**storm** Sturm
**gale** stürmischer Wind
**breezy** windig

### travel

**arrival** Ankunft
**departure** Abflug; Abreise
**delay** Verspätung
**cancellation** Stornierung; Annulierung
**destination** (Reise)Ziel
**(hand) luggage** (Hand)Gepäck
**passport** Reisepass
**ID card** (Personal)Ausweis
**visa** Visum; Einreisebewilligung
**boarding pass** Bordkarte
**single ticket** einfache Fahrkarte
**return ticket** Hin- und Rückfahrkarte
**to book** buchen
**to check in** einchecken
**to check out** auschecken
**to make a reservation** reservieren

### types

**B & B** Pension
**campsite** Campingplatz
**caravan** Wohnwagen
**hotel** Hotel
**tent** Zelt
**youth hostel** Jugendherberge

| | |
|---|---|
| **We stayed in a ....** | Wir haben in einem / einer ... übernachtet. |
| **We had a ... room with ....** | Wir hatten ein ... Zimmer mit .... |
| **The weather was ....** | Das Wetter war .... |
| **It rained / snowed / was sunny / ... every day.** | Es hat jeden Tag geregnet / geschneit. / Es war jeden Tag sonnig. / .... |
| **We travelled by ....** | Wir sind mit dem / der ... gefahren / angereist. |
| **Our ... was on time / late by ... minutes.** | Unsere / Unser ... war pünktlich / hatte ... Minuten Verspätung. |
| **The journey took ....** | Die Anreise dauerte .... |

## Unit 3 Around South Africa

| | | | |
|---|---|---|---|
| p. 48 | **South Africa** [ˌsaʊθ ˈæfrɪkə] | Südafrika | Sport is popular in **South Africa**. |

### Way in

| | | | |
|---|---|---|---|
| | **main** [meɪn] | Haupt- | The **main** capital city is Pretoria. |
| | **seat** [si:t] | Sitz | The president has his **seat** in Pretoria. |
| | **mixed race** [ˌmɪkst ˈreɪs] | gemischter Abstammung; Mischrasse | There are **mixed race** people in South Africa. |
| | **amount (of)** [əˈmaʊnt (əv)] | Menge; Summe | South Africa has large **amounts** of gold. |
| | **diamond** [ˈdaɪəmənd] | Diamant |  |
| | **safari** [səˈfɑ:ri] | Safari | Achte auf die Aussprache! |
| | **lion** [ˈlaɪən] | Löwe |  |
| | **rhino** [ˈraɪnəʊ] | Rhinozeros; Nashorn |  |
| | **national park** [ˌnæʃnl ˈpɑ:k] | Nationalpark | The US has lots of **national parks**. |
| | **nature reserve** [ˈneɪtʃə rɪˌzɜ:v] | Naturschutzgebiet | South Africa has lots of **nature reserves**. |
| | **scenery** [ˈsi:nri] | Landschaft | There is amazing **scenery** and wildlife. |
| p. 49 | **South African** [ˌsaʊθ ˈæfrɪkən] | Südafrikaner; Südafrikanerin; südafrikanisch; aus Südafrika | **South African** South Africa |
| | **the Dutch** [ðə ˈdʌtʃ] | die Niederländer | **The Dutch** are from the Netherlands. |
| | **apartheid** *(no pl)* [əˈpɑ:taɪt] | Apartheid *(Rassentrennung per Gesetz)* | **Apartheid** ended in 1994. |
| | **to separate** [ˈsepreɪt] | trennen | Black and white people were **separated**. |
| | **to build** [bɪld] | *hier:* gründen | Nelson Mandela **built** a new South Africa. |
| | **nation** [ˈneɪʃn] | Nation; Land; Staat | R нация |
| | **gated community** [ˌgeɪtɪd kəˈmju:nəti] | bewachte Wohnanlage; geschlossene Wohnanlage | Rich people live in **gated communities**. |
| | **security** [sɪˈkjʊərəti] | Sicherheit; Schutz; Wachdienst | Gated communities have high **security**. |
| | **township** [ˈtaʊnʃɪp] | Township *(Wohnsiedlungen für Schwarze in Südafrika)* | Poor people live in **townships**. |
| | **democratic** [ˌdeməˈkrætɪk] | demokratisch | R демократический T demokratik |
| | **election** [ɪˈlekʃn] | Wahl | **election** to elect |
| | **territory** [ˈterɪtri] | Gebiet; Revier; Territorium | The Dutch moved to a new **territory**. |
| | **war** [wɔ:] | Krieg | Armies fight each other in **wars**. |
| | **peace** [pi:s] | Frieden | **peace** war |
| | **constitution** [kɒnstɪˈtju:ʃn] | Verfassung | All countries have their **constitutions**. |

## Station 1

### Social differences

| | |
|---|---|
| **private** ['praɪvɪt] | Privat-; privat |
| **consequence** ['kɒnsɪkwəns] | Konsequenz; Folge; Auswirkung |
| **victim** ['vɪktɪm] | Opfer |
| to **drop out of** [ˌdrɒp‿'aʊt‿əv] | abbrechen |
| **health insurance** ['helθ‿ɪnˌʃʊərns] | Krankenversicherung |
| **well-educated** ['welˌedʒʊkeɪtɪd] | gebildet |
| **state school** ['steɪt ˌsku:l] | staatliche Schule; öffentliche Schule |
| **the rich** [ðə 'rɪtʃ] | die Reichen |
| to **be middle class** [bi: ˌmɪdl 'klɑ:s] | zur Mittelschicht gehören |
| **social** ['səʊʃl] | gesellschaftlich; sozial |
| **privileged** ['prɪvlɪdʒd] | privilegiert; bevorzugt |
| **equal** ['i:kwəl] | gleich; gleichberechtigt |
| **underprivileged** [ˌʌndə'prɪvlɪdʒd] | benachteiligt; unterprivilegiert |
| **fair** [feə] | gerecht; fair |
| **unequal** [ˌʌn'i:kwəl] | ungleich |
| **equality** [ɪ'kwɒləti] | Gleichberechtigung; Ebenbürtigkeit |
| **inequality** [ˌɪnɪ'kwɒləti] | Ungleichheit |
| **fairness** ['feənəs] | Gerechtigkeit |
| **unfairness** [ʌn'feənəs] | Ungerechtigkeit |
| **justice** ['dʒʌstɪs] | Gerechtigkeit; Justiz |
| **injustice** [ɪn'dʒʌstɪs] | Ungerechtigkeit |

| | | | |
|---|---|---|---|
| p. 50 | **central** ['sentrl] | zentral; im Mittelpunkt stehen | R центральный |
| | to **suffer** ['sʌfə] | leiden; erleiden | The driver **suffered** back injuries. |
| | **crash** [kræʃ] | Zusammenstoß |  |
| | **police station** [pə'li:s ˌsteɪʃn] | Polizeirevier; Polizeiwache | We all had to go to the **police station**. |
| | **questioning** ['kwestʃənɪŋ] | Verhör; Vernehmung | **questioning** question |
| | **Dear Sir or Madam,** [dɪə ˌsɜ:r‿ɔ: 'mædəm] | Sehr geehrte Damen und Herren, | This can be used at the start of a formal letter. |
| | **Yours faithfully,** [ˌjɔ:z 'feɪθfli] | Mit freundlichen Grüßen | This can be used at the end of a formal letter. |
| | to **swear** [sweə], **swore** [swɔ:], **sworn** [swɔ:n] | schwören | I **swear** I didn't do anything. |
| | **out of control** [ˌaʊt‿əv kən'trəʊl] | außer Kontrolle | The car was **out of control**. |
| | to **go on** [ˌgəʊ‿'ɒn] | weitermachen; weitergehen | We will decide how to **go on** later. |
| | **either ... or ...** ['aɪðə ... ɔ: ...] | entweder ... oder ... | **Either** I went to school **or** work. |
| | **further** ['fɜ:ðə] | weiter | There will be **further** questioning. |
| | **construction** [kən'strʌkʃn] | Bau; Konstruktion; Aufbau | I build houses, I work in **construction**. |
| | to **show up** [ˌʃəʊ‿'ʌp] | auftauchen; erscheinen | He **showed up** late for school. |
| p. 51 | **flashback** ['flæʃbæk] | Rückblende; Flashback | I often have **flashbacks** of the accident. |

| | | | |
|---|---|---|---|
| | **at night** [ˌət 'naɪt] | nachts | I can't sleep well **at night**. |
| | to **frighten the hell out of sb** [ˌfraɪtn ðə 'hel‿aʊt‿əv] | jmdn. zu Tode erschrecken | The crash **frightened the hell out of me**. |
| | **nightmare** ['naɪtmeə] | Albtraum | **nightmare** dream |
| | **guard** [gɑ:d] | Wache; Wächter; Wächterin |  |
| | **someone stupid** [ˌsʌmwʌn 'stju:pɪd] | irgendein Idiot | **Someone stupid** ruined my life. |
| | **fault** [fɔ:lt] | Schuld | Mama thinks it was her **fault**. |
| | **guilty** ['gɪlti] | schuldig | **guilty** innocent |
| | **journalist** ['dʒɜ:nlɪst] | Journalist; Journalistin | R журналист |
| | **treatment** ['tri:tmənt] | Behandlung | I needed **treatment** after the crash. |
| p. 52 | **console** ['kɒnsəʊl] | Konsole | Achte auf die Aussprache! |

## Station 2

### Landscapes

| | | | |
|---|---|---|---|
| **endless** ['endləs] | endlos | **marsh** [mɑ:ʃ] | Sumpf; Moor |
| **plain** [pleɪn] | Ebene | **pond** [pɒnd] | Teich; Tümpel |
| **fence** [fens] | Zaun | **valley** ['væli] | Tal |
| **mountain range** ['maʊntɪn ˌreɪndʒ] | Bergkette; Gebirge | | |

| | | | |
|---|---|---|---|
| p. 54 | **ranger** *(AE)* ['reɪndʒə] | Ranger; Rangerin | Tony is a **ranger** in a national park. |
| | **wide** [waɪd] | groß; weit; ausgedehnt | The field is 20 metres **wide**. |
| | **ever since** [ˌevə 'sɪns] | seitdem | The park has been a success **ever since**. |
| | to **conserve** [kən'sɜ:v] | erhalten; bewahren | The goal is to **conserve** the wildlife. |
| | **evidence** ['evɪdns] | Beweis; Beleg; Beweismaterial | **Evidence** of human life has been found. |
| | **mankind** [mæn'kaɪnd] | Menschheit | We looked at the history of **mankind**. |
| | **value** ['vælju:] | Wert | The **value** of tourism is now recognised. |
| | **ivory** ['aɪvri] | Elfenbein | **Ivory** comes from elephants. |
| | to **face** [feɪs] | gegenüberstehen; konfrontiert werden mit | **to face** face |
| | **challenge** ['tʃælɪndʒ] | Herausforderung | There are lots of **challenges** to face. |
| | to **regulate** ['regjəleɪt] | vorschreiben; bestimmen; regeln | Rules **regulate** what happens in the park. |
| | **leopard** ['lepəd] | Leopard; Leopardin | **Leopards** are big, wild cats. |
| | **buffalo** *(sg)* ['bʌfləʊ], **buffaloes** *(pl)* ['bʌfləʊz] | Büffel | We saw **buffaloes** at the zoo. |
| | **game** [geɪm] | Wild | **game**: elephant, lion, leopard, rhino, … |

| | | | |
|---|---|---|---|
| | **therefore** ['ðeəfɔ:] | deshalb; deswegen; daher; somit | Game is dangerous, we're **therefore** careful. |
| | to **treat** [tri:t] | behandeln | **to treat** treatment |
| | **caution** ['kɔ:ʃn] | Sorgfalt; Warnung; Vorsicht | We treat them with **caution.** |
| | to **take action** [ˌteɪk‿'ækʃn] | eingreifen; handeln | We **take action** against hunters. |
| | **poaching** ['pəʊtʃɪŋ] | Wilderei; Wildern | **Poaching** is against the law. |
| | **edition** [ɪ'dɪʃn] | Ausgabe; Auflage; Edition | Find out more in our next **edition.** |
| | **up** [ʌp] | abgelaufen | Sorry but the time is **up.** |
| | **chatroom** ['tʃætrʊm] | Chatroom | You can ask questions in our **chatroom.** |
| p. 55 | **opposite** ['ɒpəzɪt] | Gegenteil | Left is the **opposite** of right. |
| | to **recycle** [ˌri:'saɪkl] | recyceln; wiederverwerten | We can **recycle** the bottles and paper. |
| | to **reduce** [rɪ'dju:s] | reduzieren; vermindern; verringern | We must **reduce** the rubbish in our cities. |
| | to **go on** [ˌgəʊ‿'ɒn] | geschehen; passieren | Look what **goes on** in the national parks. |
| | **baby elephant** ['beɪbi ˌelɪfənt] | Elefantenbaby | This **baby elephant** is so cute. |
| | to **live** [lɪv] | überleben | Animals can't **live** without water. |
| | **category** ['kætəgri] | Kategorie | Achte auf die Aussprache! |
| p. 56 | to **leave** [li:v] | zurücklassen; vergessen | He **left** his bag on the bus. |
| | **closed** [kləʊzd] | geschlossen | The path was **closed** last week. |

## Reading corner

| | | | |
|---|---|---|---|
| p. 58 | **alive** [ə'laɪv] | belebt | **alive** dead |
| | to **skip** [skɪp] | hüpfen; springen; überspringen | The kids were **skipping** in the garden. |
| | **well-kept** [ˌwel'kept] | gut gepflegt | The garden had nice **well-kept** grass. |
| | **rough** [rʌf] | rau; grob; derb | The **rough** dry land separated the town. |
| | **primary school** ['praɪmri ˌsku:l] | Grundschule | You go to **primary school** first. |
| | **pupil** ['pju:pl] | Schüler; Schülerin | Rosa isn't a **pupil** at the primary school yet. |
| | to **take turns** [ˌteɪk 'tɜ:nz] | sich abwechseln | We **took turns** to use the classrooms. |
| | **classmate** ['klɑ:smeɪt] | Mitschüler; Mitschülerin | I have nice **classmates.** |
| | **no playground to speak of** [nəʊ ˌpleɪgraʊnd tə 'spi:k‿əv] | so gut wie kein(en) Schulhof | We had **no playground to speak of.** |
| | **cactus** ['kæktəs] | Kaktus | R кактус T kaktüs  |
| | **weekday** ['wi:kdeɪ] | Werktag | **weekdays**: Monday to Friday |

| | | | |
|---|---|---|---|
| | sandpit ['sænpɪt] | Sandkasten |  |
| | **sudden** ['sʌdn] | unerwartet; plötzlich | Our playing came to a **sudden** end. |
| | the two of them [ðə 'tu: əv ðəm] | die beiden | **The two of them** played together. |
| | sprinkler ['sprɪŋklə] | Rasensprenger | The **sprinkler** was fun to run through. |
| | to make funny faces [meɪk fʌni 'feɪsɪz] | lustige Grimassen schneiden | We **made funny faces** at each other. |
| | **lawn** [lɔ:n] | Rasen |  |
| | to **sweep (up)** [swi:p (ʌp)], **swept (up)** [swept (ʌp)], **swept (up)** [swept (ʌp)] | (hoch)heben; (auf)fegen | He **swept** him up in his arms. |
| | **bottom** ['bɒtəm] | Hintern; Po | Hennie's father hit his **bottom**. |
| | savage ['sævɪdʒ] | Wilder; Wilde | They were running round like **savages**. |
| p. 59 | **joy** [dʒɔɪ] | Freude; Vergnügen | We sang with **joy** in church. |
| | **unexpected** [ˌʌnɪk'spektɪd] | unerwartet | **unexpected** expected |
| | lap [læp] | Schoß | Rosa sat on her mother's **lap**. |
| | grey-haired [ˌgreɪ'heəd] | grauhaarig | My grandparents are **grey-haired**. |
| | smiling ['smaɪlɪŋ] | lächelnd | The man on TV had a nice **smiling** face. |
| | **all around** [ˌɔ:l‿ə'raʊnd] | rundherum; ringsumher; überall | **All around** me people were laughing. |
| | to **pray** [preɪ] | beten | Everyone **prayed** for the victims. |
| | to vote [vəʊt] | abstimmen; wählen | The black South Africans could also **vote**. |
| | **townsfolk** ['taʊnzfəʊk] | Bürger *(Pl.)*; Stadtbewohner *(Pl.)* | We waited with the other **townsfolk**. |
| | playing field ['pleɪɪŋ ˌfi:ld] | Sportplatz | We play football on the **playing field**. |
| | traffic light ['træfɪk ˌlaɪt] | (Verkehrs)Ampel | The cars waited at the **traffic lights**. |
| | to **protest** [prə'test] | protestieren | **to protest** protest |
| | **New Year** [ˌnju: 'jɪə] | Neujahr | The **New Year** starts on 1st January. |
| | **firm** [fɜ:m] | fest; standhaft | The police officer spoke to me **firmly**. |
| | **scream** [skri:m] | Schrei | **scream** to scream |
| | **black (person)** [blæk] | Schwarzer; Schwarze | |
| p. 60 | to argue ['ɑ:gju:] | argumentieren; streiten | A man was **arguing** with a teacher. |
| | **headteacher** [ˌhed'ti:tʃə] | Schulleiter; Schulleiterin | The **headteacher** spoke to the school. |
| | **anyone** ['eniwʌn] | irgendjemand *(in Fragesätzen)* | Has **anyone** seen my mother? |
| | to pick [pɪk] | pflücken | We **picked** some roses in the garden. |
| | **to leave sb alone** [ˌli:v‿ə'ləʊn] | jmdn. in Ruhe lassen | I told the others to **leave me alone**. |
| | fierceness ['fɪəsnəs] | Grimm; Heftigkeit; Wildheit | His voice had the **fierceness** I knew. |
| | **atmosphere** ['ætməsfɪə] | Atmosphäre; Stimmung | R атмосфера T atmosfer |
| | **to turn to sb** ['tɜ:n tə] | sich jmdm. zuwenden | He **turned to me** and laughed. |

| | | |
|---|---|---|
| to take notice [ˌteɪk ˈnəʊtɪs] | beachten; zur Kenntnis nehmen; aufmerksam werden | I **took** no **notice** of the signs. |
| to **pause** [pɔ:z] | (eine kurze) Pause machen; innehalten | He **paused** before reading the story. |
| **awkward** [ˈɔ:kwəd] | ungünstig; ungeschickt; unbeholfen; peinlich | Rosa felt **awkward** in the classroom. |
| to go red [ˌgəʊ ˈred] | rot werden | His face **went red.** |
| to chase [tʃeɪs] | jagen; verfolgen | Hennie and the boys **chased** the rugby ball. |
| **stare** [steə] | Starren; starrer Blick | He gave me a frightening **stare.** |
| to shake one's head [ˌʃeɪk wʌns ˈhed] | den Kopf schütteln | I **shook my head** and said "No!" |
| one step at a time [ˌwʌn step‿æt‿ə ˈtaɪm] | schrittweise; ein Schritt nach dem anderen | Mama said, "Take one step at a time." |
| to **take a deep breath** [ˌteɪk‿ə ˌdi:p ˈbreθ] | tief einatmen; tief Luft holen | I **took a deep breath** and then walked in. |

## Film corner

| | | | |
|---|---|---|---|
| p. 63 | **baboon** [bəˈbu:n] | Pavian | There is a **baboon** problem in Cape Town. |

### Checkpoint

| | | | |
|---|---|---|---|
| tasty [ˈteɪsti] | lecker; schmackhaft | to respond [rɪˈspɒnd] | reagieren; erwidern; antworten |
| right here [ˌraɪt ˈhɪə] | genau hier | rhetorical question [rɪˌtɒrɪkl ˈkwestʃən] | rhetorische Frage |
| right now [ˌraɪt ˈnaʊ] | jetzt gleich; sofort; gerade | | |

V

## Word bank: Social differences

### education and social status

**public / private school** Privatschule
**state school** staatliche Schule
**boarding school** Internat
**university** Universität
**rich** reich / **poor** arm
**(un)equal** (un)gleich
**(un)fairness** (Un)Gerechtigkeit
**equality** Gleichberechtigung; Ebenbürtigkeit
**inequality** Ungleichheit
**privileged** privilegiert; bevorzugt
**underprivileged** benachteiligt; unterprivilegiert
**(in)justice** (Un)Gerechtigkeit
**advantaged** bevorteilt
**disadvantaged** benachteiligt
**drop out of school** die Schule abbrechen

### where people live

**villa / mansion** Villa
**bungalow** Bungalow
**detached house** Einfamilienhaus
**semi-detached house** Doppelhaus
**terraced house** Reihenhaus
**flat** Wohnung
**gated community** bewachte Wohnanlage
**township** Township
**smart home** intelligentes Haus
**homeless shelter** Obdachlosenheim

### possessions

**car** Auto
**jewellery** Schmuck
**mobile phone** Handy
**games console** Spielekonsole

### adjectives for clothes

**smart** schick
**expensive** teuer / **cheap** billig
**fancy** modisch; ausgefallen
**scruffy** ungepflegt; dreckig
**patched** geflickt
**worn** getragen; abgenutzt
**torn** zerrissen

## Word bank: Nature

### kinds of plants

**tree** Baum
**bush** Busch; Strauch
**flower** Blume
**hedge** Hecke

### landscape features

**ditch** Graben
**mound** Hügel
**ridge** Erhöhung
**path / trail** Weg; Spur
**plain** Ebene
**mountain range** Bergkette; Gebirge
**marsh** Sumpf; Moor
**dune** Düne
**pond** Teich; Tümpel
**spring** Quelle
**valley** Tal
**fence** Zaun

### kinds of animals

**mammal** Säugetier
**reptile** Reptil
**insect** Insekt
**fish** Fisch(e)

### adjectives for landscape features

**dry** trocken / **wet** nass
**wide** breit / **narrow** eng
**steep** steil / **flat** flach
**overgrown** verwildert / **barren** karg
**rocky** felsig; steinig
**grassy** grasbewachsen
**sandy** sandig
**hilly** hügelig
**vast** gewaltig; riesig
**(un)polluted** (un)verschmutzt
**fenced off** eingezäunt
**restricted** begrenzt
**endless** endlos

### adjectives for plants and animals

**protected** geschützt
**endangered** gefährdet
**rare** rar; selten
**common** häufig; verbreitet
**extinct** ausgestorben

# Unit 4 Living in Hong Kong

## Way in

| | | | |
|---|---|---|---|
| p. 68 | **pro** [prəʊ] | Pro; Vorteil | What are the **pros** of living here? |
| | **con** [kɒn] | Kontra; Nachteil | Let's look at the pros and **cons** of the idea. |
| | **shopper** ['ʃɒpə] | Käufer; Käuferin; Einkäufer; Einkäuferin | **shopper** to shop shop shopping |
| | **luxurious** [lʌg'ʒʊəriəs] | luxuriös; Luxus- | **luxurious** luxury |
| | **mall** [mɔ:l] | Einkaufszentrum | I love shopping in a big **mall**. |
| | to **bargain** ['bɑ:gɪn] | handeln; verhandeln | **to bargain** bargain |
| | **specialist** ['speʃlɪst] | Spezial- | **specialist** special |
| | **electronic** [ˌelek'trɒnɪk] | elektronisch | R электронный T elektronik |
| | **stall** [stɔ:l] | Stand; Bude |  |
| | **noodle** ['nu:dl] | Nudel | Achte auf die Aussprache!  |
| | **fortune teller** ['fɔ:tʃu:n ˌtelə] | Wahrsager; Wahrsagerin | A **fortune teller** told me about my future. |
| p. 69 | **pollution** [pə'lu:ʃn] | Verschmutzung | **pollution** to pollute |
| | **thick** [θɪk] | dick | The air was **thick** with pollution. |
| | **smog** [smɒg] | Smog | R смог |
| | **health** [helθ] | Gesundheits-; gesundheitlich | This could cause serious **health** problems. |
| | **effort** ['efət] | Mühe; Bemühung; Versuch; Arbeitsaufwand | I made a big **effort** with my presentation. |
| | **busy** ['bɪzi] | rege; belebt; *hier:* aktiv | Hong Kong has a **busy** music scene. |
| | **media** ['mi:diə] | Medien- | Many people use social **media** sites. |
| | **martial art** [ˌmɑ:ʃl_'ɑ:t] | Kampfkunst; Kampfsportart | **Martial arts** films are made in Hong Kong. |
| | **mixture** ['mɪkstʃə] | Mischung | Hong Kong is a **mixture** of east and west. |
| | **pressure** ['preʃə] | Druck | My parents put me under **pressure**. |
| | **network** ['netwɜ:k] | Netzwerk | I have a good **network** of friends. |
| | **scale** [skeɪl] | Skala; Maßstab; Ausmaß | A **scale** from 1 to 5: 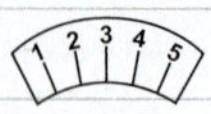 |
| | **hurry** ['hʌri] | Eile; Hast | I'm in a **hurry**, I don't want to be late. |
| | to **relax** [rɪ'læks] | sich entspannen; sich ausruhen | We **relaxed** on the beach in the sun. |

## Station 1

### Buying and selling

| | | | |
|---|---|---|---|
| **fashionable** [ˈfæʃnəbl] | modisch | **trading** [ˈtreɪdɪŋ] | Handel |
| **latest** [ˈleɪtɪst] | neueste | to **swap** [swɒp] | tauschen |
| to **browse** [braʊz] | durchstöbern | to **purchase** [ˈpɜːtʃəs] | kaufen; erwerben |
| **shop window** [ˌʃɒp ˈwɪndəʊ] | Schaufenster | to **stock** [stɒk] | führen; vorrätig haben |
| **must-have** [ˈmʌstˌhæv] | etwas, das man haben muss | **second-hand** [ˌseknd'hænd] | gebraucht; second-hand; aus zweiter Hand |
| to **make money** [ˌmeɪk ˈmʌni] | Geld verdienen | to **donate** [dəˈneɪt] | spenden; stiften |
| **brand-new** [ˌbrænd'njuː] | brandneu | to **contact** [ˈkɒntækt] | sich in Verbindung setzen; kontaktieren |
| to **resell** [ˌriːˈsel] | wiederverkaufen; weiterverkaufen | **discount** [ˈdɪskaʊnt] | Rabatt; Preisnachlass |

| | | | |
|---|---|---|---|
| p. 70 | **sneakerhead** [ˈsniːkəhed] | *Sammler von Sportschuhen* | somebody who collects sneakers |
| | **district** [ˈdɪstrɪkt] | Distrikt; Bezirk | I love going to the shopping **district**. |
| | **super** [ˈsuːpə] | super | The new band is **super** cool. |
| | **rare** [reə] | rar; selten | The book is **rare**, there aren't many of it. |
| | **pair** [peə] | Paar | I have got ten **pairs** of shoes. |
| | **row** [rəʊ] | Reihe; Zeile | There were **rows** and **rows** of shoes. |
| | **sneaker** *(AE)* [ˈsniːkə] | Sportschuh; Sneaker |  |
| | **line** [laɪn] | Schlange |  |
| | **to camp** [kæmp] | campen; kampieren; zelten | **to camp** camp |
| | **overnight** [ˌəʊvəˈnaɪt] | über Nacht | We camped **overnight** outside the shop. |
| | **particular** [pəˈtɪkjələ] | bestimmte | We wanted a **particular** pair of shoes. |
| | to **claim** [kleɪm] | behaupten; beanspruchen | He **claimed** his shoes were the best. |
| | to **go crazy** [ˌɡəʊ ˈkreɪzi] | ausflippen; durchdrehen; verrückt werden | I **go crazy** when I see him. |
| | **status symbol** [ˈsteɪtəs ˌsɪmbl] | Statussymbol | Sneakers were **status symbols** in the USA. |
| | to **nag sb** [næɡ] | jmdm. auf die Nerven gehen | Dave **nagged his parents** for new sneakers. |
| | **for ages** [fər‿ˈeɪdʒɪz] | ewig lange | The boy nagged his **parents for ages**. |
| | **pocket money** [ˈpɒkɪt ˌmʌni] | Taschengeld | I saved my **pocket money** to buy a bike. |
| | **grown-up** [ˌɡrəʊn‿ˈʌp] | Erwachsener; Erwachsene | **grown-up** child |
| | **a month** [ə ˈmʌnθ] | pro Monat | He buys ten pairs of shoes **a month**. |
| | to **keep a record of sth** [ˌkiːp‿ə ˈrekɔːd‿əv] | über etw. Buch führen | He **keeps a record of everything he buys**. |

| | | | |
|---|---|---|---|
| | **wore** [wɔ:] | simple past von *to wear* (tragen) | I **wore** = ich trug/ich habe getragen |
| | to **care** [keə] | sich interessieren; wichtig nehmen | I don't **care** if my shoes get dirty. |
| | **anyway** ['eniweɪ] | sowieso | The kids don't wear the shoes **anyway**. |
| | to **guess** [ges] | annehmen; vermuten; schätzen | 20 years ago things were hard, I **guess**. |
| p. 71 | **the poor** [ðə 'pɔ:] | die Armen | **the poor** the rich |
| p. 72 | **to reply** [rɪ'plaɪ] | antworten; erwidern | **to reply** = to answer |
| p. 73 | **article** ['ɑ:tɪkl] | Artikel; Bericht *(in einer Zeitung)* | I read a good **article** in the newspaper. |

## Station 2

### Verbs for effects

| | | | |
|---|---|---|---|
| to **do sth about sth** [ˌdu: ə'baʊt] | etw. gegen etw. unternehmen | to **convert** [ken'vɜ:t] | umwandeln |
| to **produce** [prə'dju:s] | erzeugen; herstellen; anbauen | to **improve** [ɪm'pru:v] | verbessern |
| to **increase** [ɪn'kri:s] | erhöhen; steigern | to **absorb** [əb'zɔ:b] | aufnehmen; absorbieren |
| to **advise sb** [əd'vaɪz] | beraten; jdm. etw. raten | to **decrease** [dɪ'kri:s] | vermindern; abnehmen |
| to **install** [ɪn'stɔ:l] | anschließen; installieren; einrichten | to **raise** [reɪz] | anheben; erhöhen |
| to **suggest** [sə'dʒest] | vorschlagen; nahelegen; andeuten | to **generate** ['dʒenreɪt] | generieren; erzeugen |

| | | | |
|---|---|---|---|
| p. 74 | **host** [həʊst] | Talkmaster; Gastgeber; Gastgeberin | Rachel is the **host** of a TV show. |
| | **renewable energy** [rɪˌnju:əbl‿'enədʒi] | erneuerbare Energie | Peter is an expert on **renewable energy**. |
| | **power plant** ['paʊə ˌplɑ:nt] | Kraftwerk |  |
| | **future** ['fju:tʃə] | Zukunfts-; zukünftig | He likes the **future** designs. |
| | **technology** [tek'nɒlədʒi] | Technologie | **Technology** changes very quickly. |
| | **mask** [mɑ:sk] | Maske | [R] маска [T] maske  |
| | **in the long run** [ˌɪn ðə 'lɒŋ rʌn] | langfristig; auf Dauer | **In the long run**, your idea is better. |
| | **individual** [ˌɪndɪ'vɪdʒuəl] | einzeln; individuell | There are lots of **individual** buildings. |
| | **audience** ['ɔ:diəns] | Publikum; Zuschauer *(Pl.)*; Zuhörer *(Pl.)* | the people who watch a show or concert |
| | **at present** [ət 'preznt] | augenblicklich; derzeit | **at present** = now |
| | **eco-friendly** ['i:kəʊˌfrendli] | umweltfreundlich | The school wants to be more **eco-friendly**. |
| | **solar panel** [ˌsəʊlə 'pænl] | Sonnenkollektor |  |

| | | | |
|---|---|---|---|
| | **motion sensor** [ˌməʊʃn ˈsensə] | Bewegungsmelder | We have **motion sensors** outside our house. |
| | **development** [dɪˈveləpmənt] | Entwicklung | **development** to develop |
| | **transparent** [trænˈspærnt] | durchsichtig; transparent | The window is **transparent**. |
| | **cell** [sel] | Zelle | Solar **cells** can be very efficient. |
| | **exhaust fumes** *(pl)* [ɪgˈzɔ:st ˌfju:mz] | Abgase *(von Fahrzeugen)* | **Exhaust fumes** cause pollution. |
| | **pod** [pɒd] | *hier:* Gondel; Kabine | The London Eye has **pods** on it. |
| | **ski lift** [ˈski: ˌlɪft] | Skilift | Achte auf die Aussprache!  |
| | to **drop off** [drɒp‿ˈɒf] | absetzen | The bus **dropped** us **off** at the park. |
| | **quality** [ˈkwɒləti] | Qualität; Eigenschaft; Merkmal | These shoes are really good **quality**. |
| p. 75 | **roof** [ru:f] | Dach |  |
| | **CO2 (carbon dioxide)** [ˌsi:əʊˈtu: (ˌkɑ:bn daɪˈɒksaɪd)] | Kohlendioxid | Grass and plants reduce **CO2**. |
| | to **tune in** [ˌtju:n‿ˈɪn] | einschalten | **Tune in** later for **more information.** |
| p. 76 | **aged** [eɪdʒd] | im Alter von | People **aged** 12-25 were asked. |
| | **bath** [bɑ:θ] | Bad; Badewanne |  |
| | **food waste** [ˈfu:d ˌweɪst] | Speisereste; Lebensmittelabfälle | We should produce less **food waste**. |
| | **chart** [tʃɑ:t] | Diagramm; Tabelle | The **chart** shows that most people agreed. |
| | **level** [ˈlevl] | Höhe; Grenze; Niveau | Pollution **levels** will be high tomorrow. |
| | to **clear** [klɪə] | aufklaren; sich aufhellen | The smog will **clear** in the afternoon. |

## Reading corner

| | | | |
|---|---|---|---|
| p. 78 | **truth** [tru:θ] | Wahrheit | Tell the **truth** about the accident. |
| | **out** [aʊt] | draußen; aus; außerhalb | **out** in |
| | to **be surrounded by sth/sb** [bi: səˈraʊndɪd baɪ] | umgeben sein von etw./jmdm. | I'**m surrounded by new information**. |
| | **never-ending** [ˌnevrˈendɪŋ] | endlos; unendlich | Pollution is a **never-ending** problem. |
| | **flood** [flʌd] | Flut; Hochwasser; Überschwemmung |  |
| | **whether** [ˈweðə] | ob | I'm leaving, **whether** you like it or not. |
| | **puzzle** [ˈpʌzl] | Rätsel; Puzzle | Achte auf die Aussprache! |
| | **press** [pres] | Presse | The musician never talks to the **press**. |
| | to **publish** [ˈpʌblɪʃ] | veröffentlichen; publizieren; verlegen | Look, the magazine **published** my report. |
| | to **punish** [ˈpʌnɪʃ] | bestrafen | **to punish** punishment |

| | | | |
|---|---|---|---|
| | **to abuse** [ə'bju:z] | missbrauchen; misshandeln; beschimpfen | Governments also **abuse** their power. |
| | **to oppress** [ə'pres] | unterdrücken | Governments often **oppress** people. |
| | **to observe** [əb'zɜ:v] | beobachten; beachten; befolgen | **to observe** observation |
| | **to censor** ['sensə] | zensieren | Some governments **censor** letters. |
| | **publisher** ['pʌblɪʃə] | Verlag; Herausgeber | **publisher** to publish |
| | **critical** ['krɪtɪkl] | kritisch | Some people are **critical** of others. |
| | **pro-** [prəʊ] | für; Pro- | **Pro**-China journalists kept their jobs. |
| | **flow** [fləʊ] | Fluss; Fließen; Strömung | The **flow** of information is controlled too. |
| p. 79 | **moral standards** *(pl)* [ˌmɒrl 'stændədz] | sittliche Werte *(Pl.)* | The site was a threat to **moral standards**. |
| | **blacklisted** ['blæklɪstɪd] | auf die schwarze Liste gesetzt | You can't use words that are **blacklisted**. |
| | **phrase** [freɪz] | Redewendung; Ausdruck; Satz | Some **phrases** you have to learn. |
| | **democracy** [dɪ'mɒkrəsi] | Demokratie | R демократия T demokrasi |
| | **oppression** [ə'preʃn] | Unterdrückung | **oppression** to oppress |
| | **human rights** *(pl)* [ˌhju:mən 'raɪts] | Menschenrechte *(Pl.)* | There was a protest for **human rights**. |
| | **freedom of speech** [ˌfri:dəm‿əv 'spi:tʃ] | Redefreiheit | Everyone here has **freedom of speech**. |
| | **to guarantee** [ˌgærn'ti:] | garantieren; gewährleisten | Our places at the front were **guaranteed**. |
| | **limit** ['lɪmɪt] | Limit; Grenze; Beschränkung | There are **limits** to freedom of speech. |
| | **to glorify** ['glɔ:rɪfaɪ] | verherrlichen | They tried to **glorify** the violence. |
| | **right-wing** [ˌraɪt'wɪŋ] | rechtsorientiert; Rechts-; rechts- | He posted **right-wing** comments. |
| | **extremism** [ɪk'stri:mɪzm] | Extremismus | R экстремизм |
| | **mind** [maɪnd] | Meinung; Geist; Verstand | The press influence people's **minds**. |
| | **objective** [əb'dʒektɪv] | sachlich; objektiv | Journalists should try to be **objective**. |
| | **to spread** [spred], **spread** [spred], **spread** [spred] | (sich) verbreiten | The news of the accident **spread** fast. |
| | **fear** [fɪə] | Angst; Furcht | There was **fear** among the passengers. |
| | **terrorist** ['terərɪst] | Terrorist; Terroristin | R террорист T terörist |
| | **unfiltered** [ʌn'fɪltəd] | ungefiltert | **Unfiltered** information is hard to control. |
| | **to take sth for granted** [ˌteɪk fə 'grɑ:ntɪd] | etw. als selbstverständlich hinnehmen; etw. als gegeben voraussetzen | You shouldn't **take everything for granted**. |
| | **access** *(no pl)* ['ækses] | Zugang; Zutritt | People have **access** to lots of sources. |
| | **restriction** [rɪ'strɪkʃn] | Beschränkung; Einschränkung | **Restrictions** won't stop people. |
| | **censorship** ['sensəʃɪp] | Zensur | In some countries there's **censorship**. |

V

### Film corner

| | | | |
|---|---|---|---|
| p. 81 | **glasses** *(pl only)* ['glɑ:sɪz] | Brille | I need **glasses** for reading. |
| | **speed limit** ['spi:d ˌlɪmɪt] | Geschwindigkeitsbeschränkung | What's the **speed limit** in towns? |
| | **mph (miles per hour)** [ˌempi:'eɪtʃ (ˌmaɪlz pər‿'aʊə)] | kmh (Kilometer pro Stunde) | The speed limit in towns is 30 **mph**. |
| | **floor** [flɔ:] | Stockwerk | The shopping centre has five **floors**. |

## Word bank: Environment

### environmental problems

**air pollution** Luftverschmutzung
**noise pollution** Lärmverschmutzung
**water pollution** Wasserverschmutzung
**smog** Smog
**waste** Abfall
**plastic bags / bottles** Plastiktüten / Plastikflaschen
**packaging** Verpackung
**exhaust fumes** Abgase (von Fahrzeugen)
**fine particles** Feinstaub
**fossil fuels** fossile Brennstoffe
**landfill site** Mülldeponie
**burning waste** Verbrennen von Müll

### projects

**sponsorship** Förderung
**support** Unterstützung
**sponsored walk** Sponsorenlauf
**charity event** Wohltätigkeitsveranstaltung
**jumble sale** Flohmarkt

### ways to improve things

**clean fuel** sauberer Treibstoff
**public transport** öffentliche Verkehrsmittel
**electric vehicle** Elektrofahrzeug
**windpark** Windpark
**renewable energy** erneuerbare Energie
**solar panel** Sonnenkollektor
**save energy** Energie sparen
**make eco-friendly / greener** umweltfreundlicher machen

### verbs for talking about the environment

**to avoid** vermeiden
**to reduce** reduzieren
**to increase** erhöhen
**to decrease** vermindern; abnehmen
**to generate** generieren; erzeugen
**to produce** erzeugen; herstellen; anbauen
**to convert** umwandeln
**to conserve** erhalten; schonen; einsparen
**to improve** verbessern
**to recycle** wiederverwerten
**to reuse** wiederverwenden
**to raise money** Geld aufbringen / sammeln
**to advise sb** jdm. etw. raten
**to install** anschließen; installieren; einrichten
**to suggest** vorschlagen
**to absorb** aufnehmen; absorbieren
**to raise** anheben; erhöhen

| | |
|---|---|
| **Our neighbourhood is eco-friendly / greener because ....** | Unser Viertel ist umweltfreundlicher, weil .... |
| **I read about a project in ....** | Ich habe über ein Projekt in ... gelesen. |
| **They did the following: ....** | Sie haben Folgendes getan: .... |
| **They had some good ideas about ....** | Sie hatten gute Ideen über / zu .... |
| **I wouldn't want to have ... where I live.** | Ich möchte keine / keinen ... haben, wo ich wohne. |
| **We need to ask ... about financial help.** | Wir müssen uns bei ... wegen finanzieller Unterstützung erkundigen. |
| **We can collect ....** | Wir können ... sammeln. |
| **We can organize a ....** | Wir können ein / eine ... organisieren. |
| **This will reduce / save ....** | Das wird ... reduzieren / sparen. |

# Instructions

*Arbeitsanweisungen mit Operatoren*

| | |
|---|---|
| **Act** the dialogue • the interview. | **Spielt** den Dialog • ein Bewerbungsgespräch. |
| **Add** more information. | **Ergänze** mehr Informationen. |
| **Analyse** the chart. | **Analysiere** das Diagramm. |
| **Answer** the questions. | **Beantworte** die Fragen. |
| **Ask** a partner. | **Frage** eine Partnerin / einen Partner. |
| **Check** your draft. | **Überprüfe** deinen Entwurf. |
| **Choose** one of the tasks • the right answer. | **Wähle** eine der Aufgaben • die richtige Antwort **aus**. |
| **Collect** ideas. | **Sammle** Ideen. |
| **Comment** on the article. | **Kommentiere** den Artikel. |
| **Compare** with your partner. | **Vergleicht** zu zweit. |
| **Complete** the sentences • the dialogue. | **Vervollständige** die Sätze • den Dialog. |
| **Continue** the story. | **Setze** die Geschichte **fort**. |
| **Copy** the table. | **Schreibe** die Tabelle **ab**. |
| **Correct** the mistakes. | **Verbessere** die Fehler. |
| **Decide** on the best order. | **Entscheide dich für** die beste Reihenfolge. |
| **Describe** the picture. | **Beschreibe** das Bild. |
| **Discuss** with a partner. | **Besprecht euch** zu zweit. |
| **Explain** the rules • the quotes. | **Erkläre** die Regeln • die Zitate. |
| **Fill in** the gaps. | **Fülle** die Lücken **aus**. |
| **Find** synonyms • it in the text. | **Finde** Synonyme. • es im Text. |
| **Finish** the sentences. | **Vervollständige** die Sätze. |
| **Give a presentation • evidence from the text.** | **Halte eine Präsentation. • Beweise es am Text.** |
| **Give reasons.** | **Gib Gründe an.** |
| **Join** the sentences. | **Verbinde** die Sätze. |
| **Listen to** the dialogue. | **Höre** dir den Dialog **an**. |
| **Look at** the photos • pictures (again). | **Schau** dir die Fotos • Bilder (noch einmal) **an**. |
| **Make** a list • a chart • a mind map. | **Erstelle** eine Liste • eine Tabelle • ein Wörternetz. |
| **Make** notes • pairs. | **Mache** dir **Stichpunkte** • Bilde Paare. |
| **Make up** rules. | **Denke dir** Regeln **aus**. |
| **Match** the sentences with the pictures. | **Ordne** den Bildern die richtigen Sätze **zu**. |
| **Name** the place. | **Nenne** den Ort. |
| **Practise with a partner.** | **Übe mit einer Partnerin / einem Partner.** |
| **Prepare a speech • a presentation.** | **Bereite eine Rede • eine Präsentation vor.** |
| **Present your profile to the class.** | **Stelle** dein Profil deiner Klasse vor. |
| **Put in** the right verbs • tenses. | **Setze** die richtigen Verben • Zeitformen **ein**. |
| Put the words **in the right order**. | **Bringe** die Wörter **in die richtige Reihenfolge**. |
| **Report** what ... • how .... | **Berichte**, was ... • wie .... |

| | |
|---|---|
| **Retell** the story. | **Erzähle** die Geschichte **nach.** |
| **Rewrite** the sentences. | **Schreibe** die Sätze **um.** |
| **Say** what these words mean. | **Sage**, was diese Wörter bedeuten. |
| **Sort** the words **into groups.** | **Sortiere** die Wörter **in Gruppen.** |
| **Take notes • turns.** | **Mache** dir **Notizen • Wechselt euch ab.** |
| **Talk about** the photos. | **Rede** über die Fotos. |
| **Think of** questions. | **Denke** dir Fragen **aus.** |
| True, false or not in the text? | Richtig, falsch oder nicht im Text? |
| **Use** a dictionary. | **Benutze** ein Wörterbuch. |
| **Write** a definition • a heading • a draft. | **Schreibe** eine Definition • einen Titel • einen Entwurf. |

## Classroom phrases

### You and your teacher

| | |
|---|---|
| I'm sorry I'm late. | Tut mir leid, dass ich mich verspätet habe. |
| I'm sorry I don't have my exercise book. | Tut mir leid, ich habe mein Heft nicht dabei. |
| What's the homework? | Was haben wir als Hausaufgabe auf? |
| Can you help me, please? | Können Sie / Kannst du mir bitte helfen? |
| Can you say that again, please? | Können Sie / Kannst du das bitte wiederholen? |
| Can I go to the toilet, please? | Kann ich bitte auf Toilette gehen? |
| Mr / Mrs / Miss ..., I don't feel well. | Herr / Frau ..., mir geht es nicht gut. |
| What page is it, please? | Auf welcher Seite ist das? |
| What's the German / English word for ...? | Was ist das deutsche / englische Wort für ...? |
| How do you spell ...? | Wie schreibt man ...? |
| What does that mean? | Was heißt / bedeutet das? |
| Sorry, I don't understand / I don't know. | Tut mir leid, ich verstehe das nicht / ich weiß es nicht. |

### Working together

| | |
|---|---|
| Can we work in pairs / groups? | Können wir zu zweit / in Gruppen arbeiten? |
| Do you want to work with me / us? | Willst du / Wollt ihr mit mir / uns arbeiten? |
| Let's make a / draw a ... | Lass(t) uns ein ... machen / zeichnen. |
| Whose turn is it? – It's my / your turn. | Wer ist dran? – Ich bin dran. / Du bist dran. |

### Your teacher can say ...

| | |
|---|---|
| Turn to page ... | Schlagt Seite ... auf. |
| Look at the board. | Schaut an die Tafel. |
| Put your hands up, please! | Meldet euch, bitte! |
| Try again! | Versuche es noch einmal. |

# List of irregular verbs

*Hier findest du alle unregelmäßigen Verben, die im Buch vorkommen. Die Liste enthält jeweils alle drei Formen, auch wenn sie noch nicht alle in den Units vorgekommen sind.*

| infinitive | simple past | past participle | German |
|---|---|---|---|
| be [bi:] | was, were [wɒz, wɜ:] | been [bi:n] | sein |
| beat [bi:t] | beat [bi:t] | beaten ['bi:tn] | schlagen; besiegen |
| become [bɪ'kʌm] | became [bɪ'keɪm] | become [bɪ'kʌm] | werden |
| begin [bɪ'gɪn] | began [bɪ'gæn] | begun [bɪ'gʌn] | beginnen; anfangen |
| bleed [bli:d] | bled [bled] | bled [bled] | bluten |
| break [breɪk] | broke [brəʊk] | broken ['brəʊkn] | brechen |
| bring [brɪŋ] | brought [brɔ:t] | brought [brɔ:t] | bringen; mitbringen |
| build [bɪld] | built [bɪlt] | built [bɪlt] | bauen |
| burn [bɜ:n] | burned / burnt [bɜ:nt] | burned / burnt [bɜ:nt] | brennen |
| buy [baɪ] | bought [bɔ:t] | bought [bɔ:t] | kaufen |
| choose [tʃu:z] | chose [tʃəʊz] | chosen ['tʃəʊzn] | auswählen; wählen |
| come [kʌm] | came [keɪm] | come [kʌm] | kommen |
| cost [kɒst] | cost [kɒst] | cost [kɒst] | kosten |
| cut [kʌt] | cut [kʌt] | cut [kʌt] | (sich) schneiden |
| deal (with) [di:l] | dealt [delt] | dealt [delt] | sich befassen mit; umgehen mit |
| dig [dɪg] | dug [dʌg] | dug [dʌg] | graben |
| do [du:] | did [dɪd] | done [dʌn] | machen; tun |
| draw [drɔ:] | drew [dru:] | drawn [drɔ:n] | zeichnen |
| dream [dri:m] | dreamed / dreamt [dremt] | dreamed / dreamt [dremt] | träumen |
| drink [drɪŋk] | drank [dræŋk] | drunk [drʌŋk] | trinken |
| drive [draɪv] | drove [drəʊv] | driven ['drɪvn] | fahren; treiben |
| eat [i:t] | ate [eɪt] | eaten ['i:tn] | essen |
| fall [fɔ:l] | fell [fel] | fallen ['fɔ:ln] | fallen; hinfallen |
| feed [fi:d] | fed [fed] | fed [fed] | füttern; ernähren |
| feel [fi:l] | felt [felt] | felt [felt] | (sich) fühlen |
| fight [faɪt] | fought [fɔ:t] | fought [fɔ:t] | kämpfen; streiten |
| find [faɪnd] | found [faʊnd] | found [faʊnd] | finden |
| fly [flaɪ] | flew [flu:] | flown [fləʊn] | fliegen |
| forget [fə'get] | forgot [fə'gɒt] | forgotten [fə'gɒtn] | vergessen |
| freeze [fri:z] | froze [frəʊz] | frozen ['frəʊzn] | frieren; gefrieren |
| get [get] | got [gɒt] | got [gɒt] | bekommen; werden |
| give [gɪv] | gave [geɪv] | given ['gɪvn] | geben |
| go [gəʊ] | went [went] | gone [gɒn] | gehen; fahren |
| grow [grəʊ] | grew [gru:] | grown [grəʊn] | anbauen; züchten; ziehen; wachsen; ansteigen |
| grow up [ˌgrəʊ‿'ʌp] | grew up [ˌgru:‿'ʌp] | grown up [ˌgrəʊn‿'ʌp] | aufwachsen |
| hang [hæŋ] | hung [hʌŋ] | hung [hʌŋ] | hängen |

| infinitive | simple past | past participle | German |
|---|---|---|---|
| have [hæv] | had [hæd] | had [hæd] | haben; besitzen |
| hear [hɪə] | heard [hɜ:d] | heard [hɜ:d] | hören |
| hide [haɪd] | hid [hɪd] | hidden ['hɪdn] | verstecken |
| hit [hɪt] | hit [hɪt] | hit [hɪt] | schlagen; treffen |
| hold [həʊld] | held [held] | held [held] | halten; festhalten |
| hurt [hɜ:t] | hurt [hɜ:t] | hurt [hɜ:t] | verletzen; weh tun |
| keep [ki:p] | kept [kept] | kept [kept] | halten |
| know [nəʊ] | knew [nju:] | known [nəʊn] | wissen; kennen |
| lay [leɪ] | laid [leɪd] | laid [leɪd] | legen; (den Tisch) decken |
| lead [li:d] | led [led] | led [led] | führen; anführen; leiten |
| leave [li:v] | left [left] | left [left] | verlassen; lassen; abfahren; vergessen; zurücklassen |
| lend [lend] | lent [lent] | lent [lent] | leihen; verleihen |
| lie [laɪ] | lay [leɪ] | lain [leɪn] | liegen |
| lose [lu:z] | lost [lɒst] | lost [lɒst] | verlieren |
| make [meɪk] | made [meɪd] | made [meɪd] | machen; tun; bilden |
| mean [mi:n] | meant [ment] | meant [ment] | bedeuten; meinen |
| meet [mi:t] | met [met] | met [met] | kennen lernen; (sich) treffen |
| pay [peɪ] | paid [peɪd] | paid [peɪd] | bezahlen |
| put [pʊt] | put [pʊt] | put [pʊt] | setzen; legen; stellen |
| read [ri:d] | read [red] | read [red] | lesen |
| ride [raɪd] | rode [rəʊd] | ridden ['rɪdn] | fahren; reiten |
| ring [rɪŋ] | rang [ræŋ] | rung [rʌŋ] | klingeln; läuten |
| run [rʌn] | ran [ræn] | run [rʌn] | laufen; rennen |
| say [seɪ] | said [sed] | said [sed] | sagen; sprechen |
| see [si:] | saw [sɔ:] | seen [si:n] | sehen |
| sell [sel] | sold [səʊld] | sold [səʊld] | verkaufen |
| send [send] | sent [sent] | sent [sent] | schicken; senden |
| shake [ʃeɪk] | shook [ʃʊk] | shaken ['ʃeɪkn] | schütteln |
| shine [ʃaɪn] | shone [ʃɒn] | shone [ʃɒn] | glänzen; scheinen |
| shoot [ʃu:t] | shot [ʃɒt] | shot [ʃɒt] | schießen |
| show [ʃəʊ] | showed [ʃəʊd] | shown [ʃəʊn] | zeigen |
| sing [sɪŋ] | sang [sæŋ] | sung [sʌŋ] | singen |
| sink [sɪŋk] | sank [sæŋk] | sunk [sʌŋk] | untergehen; sinken |
| sit [sɪt] | sat [sæt] | sat [sæt] | sitzen |
| sleep [sli:p] | slept [slept] | slept [slept] | schlafen |
| smell [smel] | smelled / smelt [smelt] | smelled / smelt [smelt] | riechen |
| speak [spi:k] | spoke [spəʊk] | spoken ['spəʊkn] | sprechen |
| spell [spel] | spelled / spelt [spelt] | spelled / spelt [spelt] | buchstabieren |
| spill [spɪl] | spilt [spɪlt] | spilt [spɪlt] | auslaufen; verschütten |

| infinitive | simple past | past participle | German |
|---|---|---|---|
| spend [spend] | spent [spent] | spent [spent] | ausgeben; verbringen |
| spread [spred] | spread [spred] | spread [spred] | (sich) verbreiten |
| stand [stænd] | stood [stʊd] | stood [stʊd] | stehen |
| steal [sti:l] | stole [stəʊl] | stolen ['stəʊlən] | stehlen |
| swear [sweə] | swore [swɔ:] | sworn [swɔ:n] | schwören |
| sweep [swi:p] | swept [swept] | swept [swept] | fegen |
| swim [swɪm] | swam [swæm] | swum [swʌm] | schwimmen |
| take [teɪk] | took [tʊk] | taken ['teɪkn] | nehmen; mitnehmen |
| tear (up) [teə] | tore [tɔ:] | torn [tɔ:n] | kaputt machen; (zer)reißen |
| tell [tel] | told [təʊld] | told [təʊld] | erzählen; sagen |
| think [θɪŋk] | thought [θɔ:t] | thought [θɔ:t] | denken; glauben |
| throw [θrəʊ] | threw [θru:] | thrown [θrəʊn] | werfen |
| understand [ˌʌndə'stænd] | understood [ˌʌndə'stʊd] | understood [ˌʌndə'stʊd] | verstehen |
| wake [weɪk] | woke [wəʊk] | woken ['wəʊkn] | wecken; aufwecken |
| wake up [weɪk‿'ʌp] | woke up [wəʊk‿'ʌp] | woken up [ˌwəʊkn‿'ʌp] | aufwachen |
| wear [weə] | wore [wɔ:] | worn [wɔ:n] | tragen |
| win [wɪn] | won [wʌn] | won [wʌn] | gewinnen; siegen |
| write [raɪt] | wrote [rəʊt] | written ['rɪtn] | schreiben |

# Dictionary

Im *Dictionary* sind alle wichtigen Wörter aus deinem Buch enthalten. Die Wörter stehen in alphabetischer Reihenfolge. Englische Wörter schlägst du ab S. 218 nach, deutsche Wörter ab S. 273.

Die Abkürzungen geben an, wo das Wort zum ersten Mal im Buch erscheint.

| | | | | | |
|---|---|---|---|---|---|
| to **afford** | [ə'fɔ:d] | sich leisten | V | U2 | 34 |
| englisches Wort | Aussprache | deutsche Übersetzung | Band 5 | Unit 2 | Seite 34 |

Die mit einem Sternchen (*) gekennzeichneten Verben sind unregelmäßige Verben (→ *List of irregular verbs*, S. 215–217).

Manche Wörter haben verschiedene Bedeutungen. Am besten liest du alle, bevor du dich für eine entscheidest.

**practice** ['præktɪs] Training; Übung I[1]
**basic** ['beɪsɪk] Grund- <V U4, 76>[3]
**although** [ɔ:l'ðəʊ] obwohl IV[1]
**accident** ['æksɪdnt] Unfall III[1]
**breeze** [bri:z] Brise V U2, 31[2]
**address** [ə'dres] Adresse II[2]

1 Lernwortschatz für alle: schwarz; 2 Differenzierungswortschatz: blau; 3 kein Lernwortschatz: < >

a

## A

**a** [ə] ein; eine I
a bit [ə 'bɪt] ein bisschen; ein wenig II
a few [ə 'fju:] ein paar; wenige; einige III
a little [ə 'lɪtl] ein bisschen II
a lot [ə 'lɒt] viel I; sehr II
a lot of [ə 'lɒt‿əv] viel(e); eine Menge I
a month [ə 'mʌnθ] pro Monat V U4, 70
a number of [ə 'nʌmbər‿əv] einige; mehrere IV
a pair of [ə 'peər‿əv] ein Paar II
a/one hundred ['hʌndrəd] einhundert; hundert I
a/one thousand [ə/wʌn 'θaʊznd] eintausend; tausend II
a five minute walk [ə 'faɪv mɪnɪt ˌwɔ:k] fünf Minuten zu Fuß III
**a.m.** [ˌeɪ'em] vormittags *(Uhrzeit)* II
*to be **able** to (do sth) [bi: 'eɪbl tə] (zu ew.) fähig sein; (etw.) können; (etw.) dürfen IV
to **abolish** [ə'bɒlɪʃ] abschaffen IV
**Aboriginal** [ˌæbə'rɪdʒnl] Aborigine- V U1, 11
Aboriginal people [æbəˌrɪdʒnl 'pi:pl] die Aborigines V U1, 11
**about** [ə'baʊt] über I; ungefähr; circa; etwa II
to be about [bi: ə'baʊt] gehen um; handeln von III
to do sth about sth [ˌdu: ə'baʊt] etw. gegen etw. unternehmen V U4, 74
out and about [ˌaʊt‿ən‿ə'baʊt] unterwegs I
**above** all [əbʌv‿'ɔ:l] vor allen Dingen; in erster Linie IV
**abroad** [ə'brɔ:d] im Ausland; ins Ausland IV
to **abseil** ['æbseɪl] sich abseilen II
**absolutely** [ˌæbsə'lu:tli] absolut; völlig IV
to **absorb** [əb'zɔ:b] aufnehmen; absorbieren V U4, 75
to **abuse** [ə'bju:z] missbrauchen; misshandeln; beschimpfen V U4, 78
**accent** ['æksnt] Akzent <III>
to **accept** [ək'sept] akzeptieren; annehmen; hinnehmen IV
**acceptable** [ək'septəbl] akzeptabel; annehmbar V U1, 13
**acceptance** [ək'septəns] Akzeptanz; Zustimmung V U1, 13
**access** *(no pl)* ['ækses] Zugang; Zutritt V U4, 79
**accident** ['æksɪdnt] Unfall III
**accommodation** [əˌkɒmə'deɪʃn] Unterbringung; Unterkunft V U2, 30
**according** to [ə'kɔ:dɪŋ tə] laut; gemäß III
**account** [ə'kaʊnt] Konto IV

stomach **ache** ['stʌmək ˌeɪk] Bauchweh; Bauchschmerzen II

**across** [ə'krɒs] über III; hinüber; herüber; quer durch IV

to come across (sb/sth) [ˌkʌm‿ə'krɒs] (jmd./etw.) vorfinden; (jmdm./etw.) zufällig begegnen; (jmdn./etw.) antreffen <V U4, 84>

to **act** [ækt] spielen II; handeln; sich verhalten <V U2, 41>

**acting** ['æktɪŋ] Schauspielen; Schauspielerei III

acting workshop ['æktɪŋ ˌwɜ:kʃɒp] Schauspielworkshop II

**action** ['ækʃn] Handlung; Action IV

to take action [ˌteɪk‿'ækʃn] eingreifen; handeln V U3, 54

**activity** [æk'tɪvəti] Aktivität I

activity centre [æk'tɪvəti ˌsentə] Jugendzentrum III

**actor** ['æktə] Schauspieler; Schauspielerin II

**actually** ['æktʃuəli] eigentlich; tatsächlich; wirklich III

**AD** (= Anno Domini) [ˌeɪ'di:] nach Christus III

to **adapt** (to) [ə'dæpt (tə)] sich anpassen IV

**adaptor** [ə'dæptə] Adapter III

to **add** [æd] hinzufügen; addieren IV

in **addition** [ˌɪn‿ə'dɪʃn] zusätzlich; außerdem V U1, 11

**address** [ə'dres] Adresse II

to **address** [ə'dres] ansprechen; adressieren <IV>

**adjective** ['ædʒɪktɪv] Adjektiv; Eigenschaftswort III

**administration** [ədˌmɪnɪ'streɪʃn] Verwaltung V U1, 16

**adult** ['ædʌlt] Erwachsene; Erwachsener III

**advanced** [əd'vɑ:nst] fortgeschritten <V U1, 192>

**advantaged** [əd'vɑ:ntɪdʒd] bevorteilt <V U3, 205>

**adventure** [əd'ventʃə] Abenteuer I

**adventurer** [əd'ventʃrə] Abenteurer; Abenteurerin IV

**adverb** ['ædvɜ:b] Adverb <III>

**ad(vert)** (= advertisement) ['æd(vɜ:t) (əd'vɜ:tɪsmənt)] Anzeige; Werbespot II; Annonce IV

**advertising** text ['ædvətaɪzɪŋ ˌtekst] Werbetext <IV>

**advice** [əd'vaɪs] Rat; Ratschlag III

to **advise** sb [əd'vaɪz] beraten; jdm. etw. raten V U4, 74

to **afford** [ə'fɔ:d] sich leisten V U2, 34

**afraid** [ə'freɪd] ängstlich II

to be afraid [bi: ə'freɪd] sich fürchten; Angst haben II

**African** ['æfrɪkən] afrikanisch; aus Afrika; Afrikaner; Afrikanerin IV

African American [ˌæfrɪkən ə'merɪkən] Afroamerikaner; Afroamerikanerin IV

South African [ˌsaʊθ‿'æfrɪkən] Südafrikaner; Südafrikanerin; südafrikanisch; aus Südafrika V U3, 49

**African-American** [ˌæfrɪkənə'merɪkən] afroamerikanisch IV

**Afrikaans** [ˌæfrɪ'kɑ:ns] Afrikaans *(Sprache in Südafrika)* <V U3, 62>

**after** ['ɑ:ftə] nach I; danach; später III

after all [ˌɑ:ftər‿'ɔ:l] schließlich; immerhin IV

after that [ˌɑ:ftə 'ðæt] danach I

**afternoon** [ˌɑ:ftə'nu:n] Nachmittag I

in the afternoon [ˌɪn ði ˌɑ:ftə'nu:n] nachmittags I

**again** [ə'gen] wieder; noch einmal II

again and again [ə'gen‿ən‿ə'gen] immer wieder <V U4, 83>

then again [ˌðen ə'gen] andererseits III

**against** [ə'genst] gegen II

**age** [eɪdʒ] Alter I

for ages [fər‿'eɪdʒɪz] ewig lange V U4, 70

**aged** [eɪdʒd] im Alter von V U4, 76

travel **agent** ['trævl‿ˌeɪdʒnt] Reisebürokaufmann; Reisebürokauffrau V U1, 17

**ago** [ə'gəʊ] vor II

to **agree** [ə'gri:] zustimmen II

to agree (on) [ə'gri:] sich einigen (auf) V U1, 21

to agree (with) [ə'gri:] einer Meinung sein (mit) III

right **ahead** [ˌraɪt‿ə'hed] geradeaus IV

**ahead of** [ə'hed‿əv] vor IV

**ahoy** [ə'hɔɪ] ahoi *(Seemannsruf)* V U2, 41

**air** [eə] Luft IV

**airboat** ['eəbəʊt] Propellerboot IV

**aircraft** ['eəkrɑ:ft] Fluggerät; Flugzeug <V U1, 192>

**airport** ['eəpɔ:t] Flughafen II

**alarm** clock [ə'lɑ:m ˌklɒk] Wecker I

**alcohol** *(no pl)* ['ælkəhɒl] Alkohol IV

**alga** *(sg)* ['ælgə], **algae** *(pl)* ['ældʒi:] Alge V U1, 20

**alien** ['eɪliən] Außerirdischer; Außerirdische I

**alive** [ə'laɪv] am Leben III; belebt V U3, 58

to be alive with … [bi: ə'laɪv wɪð] erfüllt sein von …; vor … wimmeln IV

**all** [ɔ:l] alle I; ganz II

above all [əbʌv‿'ɔ:l] vor allen Dingen; in erster Linie IV

after all [ˌɑ:ftər‿'ɔ:l] schließlich; immerhin IV

all alone [ˌɔ:l‿ə'ləʊn] ganz allein I

all around [ˌɔ:l‿ə'raʊnd] rundherum; ringsumher; überall V U3, 59

all day [ˌɔ:l 'deɪ] den ganzen Tag III

all in all [ˌɔ:l‿ɪn 'ɔ:l] alles in allem; insgesamt IV

all of ['ɔ:l‿əv] alle V U2, 29

all of them ['ɔ:l‿əv ˌðəm] (sie) alle V U2, 29

all over [ˌɔ:l‿'əʊvə] überall I

all the time [ˌɔ:l ðə 'taɪm] die ganze Zeit III

all around the world [ɔ:l‿əˌraʊnd ðə 'wɜ:ld] in aller Welt III

all right [ˌɔ:l 'raɪt] in Ordnung; alles klar II

of all the people [əv‿'ɔ:l ðə ˌpi:pl] von allen Leuten V U1, 18

**allegiance** [ə'li:dʒns] Treue IV

pledge of allegiance [ˌpledʒ‿əv‿ə'li:dʒns] Treueeid IV

**allergic** to [ə'lɜ:dʒɪk tə] allergisch gegen II

**allergy** ['ælədʒi] Allergie II

**alley** ['æli] Gasse; Weg IV

**alligator** ['ælɪgeɪtə] Alligator IV

to **allow** [ə'laʊ] erlauben; gestatten IV
to be allowed to (do sth) [bi: ə'laʊd tə] (etw.) dürfen IV
**allowance** *(AE)* [ə'laʊəns] Taschengeld; Unterhaltsgeld IV
**almost** ['ɔ:lməʊst] fast; beinahe III
**alone** [ə'ləʊn] allein I
all alone [ˌɔ:l‿ə'ləʊn] ganz allein I
to leave sb alone [ˌli:v‿ə'ləʊn] jmdn. in Ruhe lassen V U3, 60
**along** [ə'lɒŋ] entlang I
**alphabet** ['ælfəbet] Alphabet I
**already** [ɔ:l'redi] schon; bereits II
**alright** [ɔ:l'raɪt] okay IV
**also** ['ɔ:lsəʊ] auch I
**alternative** [ɔ:l'tɜ:nətɪv] alternativ; abwechselnd <IV>
**although** [ɔ:l'ðəʊ] obwohl IV
**aluminium** [ˌæljə'mɪniəm] Aluminium III
**always** ['ɔ:lweɪz] immer I
**amazed** [ə'meɪzd] erstaunt; verblüfft IV
**amazing** [ə'meɪzɪŋ] unglaublich; toll; erstaunlich II
**ambition** [æm'bɪʃn] Ziel III
**ambitious** [æm'bɪʃəs] ehrgeizig IV
**ambulance** ['æmbjələns] Krankenwagen III
**American** [ə'merɪkən] amerikanisch; Amerikanisch; aus Amerika; Amerikaner; Amerikanerin IV
Native American [ˌneɪtɪv‿ə'merɪkən] Ureinwohner Amerikas; Ureinwohnerin Amerikas; Indianer; Indianerin; indianisch IV
**Amish** ['ɑ:mɪʃ] amisch IV
the Amish [ði 'ɑ:mɪʃ] die Amischen IV
**among** [ə'mʌŋ] unter; inmitten III
**amount** (of) [ə'maʊnt (əv)] Menge; Summe V U3, 48
**amused** [ə'mju:zd] amüsiert; vergnügt IV
**an** [ən] ein; eine I
to **analyse** ['ænlaɪz] analysieren <V U4, 76>
**ancestor** ['ænsestə] Vorfahre; Vorfahrin <V U2, 46>
**ancient** ['eɪnʃnt] alt; altertümlich IV

**and** [ænd] und I
**angle** ['æŋgl] Winkel <III>
**angry** ['æŋgri] wütend; zornig; verärgert; böse II
**animal** ['ænɪml] Tier I
animal rescue shelter [ˌænɪml 'reskju: ˌʃeltə] Tierheim I
**ankle** ['æŋkl] Fußgelenk; Fußknöchel II
**announcement** [ə'naʊnsmənt] Durchsage; Ankündigung II
**annoyed** [ə'nɔɪd] verärgert III
**annual** ['ænjuəl] jährlich III
**another** [ə'nʌðə] ein anderer; noch ein II
one another [ˌwʌn‿ə'nʌðə] einander; gegenseitig <V U3, 62>
**answer** ['ɑ:nsə] Antwort II
to **answer** ['ɑ:nsə] antworten; beantworten I
to answer the phone [ˌɑ:nsə ðə 'fəʊn] ans Telefon gehen III
**antenna** [æn'tenə] Antenne III
**anthem** ['ænθəm] Hymne <V U3, 62>
**any** ['eni] irgendein; irgendwelche II; jede III
not … any [ˌnɒt … eni] kein II
**anybody** else [ˌenibədi 'els] jeder andere V U1, 19
**anyone** ['eniwʌn] irgendjemand *(in Fragesätzen)* V U3, 60
not … anyone [nɒt … 'eniwʌn] niemand V U2, 39
**anything** ['eniθɪŋ] irgendetwas II
anything (that) … ['eniθɪŋ (ðæt)] alles, was … <V U1, 27>
Anything else? ['eniθɪŋ ˌels] Darf es sonst noch etwas sein? I
anything to drink ['eniθɪŋ tə 'drɪŋk] etwas zu trinken II
**anyway** ['eniweɪ] trotzdem; jedenfalls III; eigentlich IV; sowieso V U4, 70
**apart** [ə'pɑ:t] auseinander; entfernt IV
**apartheid** *(no pl)* [ə'pɑ:taɪt] Apartheid *(Rassentrennung per Gesetz)* V U3, 49
**apostrophe** [ə'pɒstrəfi] Apostroph <III>
**appealing** [ə'pi:lɪŋ] ansprechend IV

to **appear** [ə'pɪə] auftauchen; erscheinen III; auftreten <V U3, 61>
**apple** crumble [ˌæpl 'krʌmbl] Apfelauflauf *(mit Streuseln bedeckt)* II
**applicant** ['æplɪkənt] Bewerber; Bewerberin <V U1, 24>
**application** [ˌæplɪ'keɪʃn] Bewerbung V U1, 12
letter of application [ˌletər‿əv‿æplɪ'keɪʃn] Bewerbungsbrief V U1, 16
to **apply** (for) [ə'plaɪ (fə)] sich bewerben (für/um) IV
to **appreciate** [ə'pri:ʃieɪt] schätzen; anerkennen; würdigen IV
**apprenticeship** [ə'prentɪʃɪp] Ausbildung <V U1, 192>
**April** ['eɪprl] April I
**architect** ['ɑ:kɪtekt] Architekt; Architektin IV
**architecture** ['ɑ:kɪtektʃə] Architektur <V U3, 63>
**archive** ['ɑ:kaɪv] Archiv II
**are** [ɑ:] bist; sind I
Are you serious? [ˌɑ: ju 'sɪəriəs] Im Ernst? III
**area** ['eəriə] Gegend; Gebiet; Areal III; Fläche; Bereich IV
to **argue** ['ɑ:gju:] argumentieren; streiten <IV>; V U3, 60
**argument** ['ɑ:gjəmənt] Auseinandersetzung; Streit II; Argument <IV>
**(argumentative) essay** [(ɑ:gjəˌmentətɪv) 'eseɪ] Erörterung <V U2, 44>
**arm** [ɑ:m] Arm I
**armour** ['ɑ:mə] Rüstung III
**army** ['ɑ:mi] Armee; Heer III
**around** [ə'raʊnd] herum; umher I; gegen; ungefähr um III; um … herum IV
all around [ˌɔ:l‿ə'raʊnd] rundherum; ringsumher; überall V U3, 59
around the house [ə'raʊnd ðə haʊs] im Haus I
to be around [bi: ə'raʊnd] geben; existieren IV
to get around [ˌget ə'raʊnd] herumkommen III

to show sb around (a place) [ˌʃəʊ‿əˈraʊnd] jmdn. (an einem Ort) herumführen V U1, 12
to turn around [ˌtɜːn‿əˈraʊnd] (sich) umdrehen III
to **arrange** [əˈreɪndʒ] arrangieren <IV>
to **arrest** [əˈrest] festnehmen; verhaften IV
**arrival** [əˈraɪvl] Ankömmling IV; Ankunft V U2, 31
to **arrive** [əˈraɪv] ankommen II
**art** [ɑːt] Kunst V U2, 30
martial art [ˌmɑːʃl‿ˈɑːt] Kampfkunst; Kampfsportart V U4, 69
**article** [ˈɑːtɪkl] Artikel; Bericht *(in einer Zeitung)* V U4, 73
make-up **artist** [ˈmeɪkʌp ˌɑːtɪst] Maskenbildner; Maskenbildnerin; Visagist; Visagistin <III>
**as** [æz] wie II; als III
as far as [ˌəz ˈfɑːr‿əz] soweit IV
as soon as [əz ˈsuːn‿əz] sobald IV
as … as [əz … əz] so … wie II
Ash Wednesday [ˌæʃ ˈwenzdeɪ] Aschermittwoch V U2, 30
to **ask** [ɑːsk] fragen I
to ask about [ˈɑːsk‿əˌbaʊt] sich erkundigen nach; fragen nach II
to ask for [ˈɑːsk fɔː] bitten um II
to ask sb out [ˌɑːsk … ˈaʊt] sich mit jmdm. verabreden IV
asking the way [ˈɑːskɪŋ ðə ˌweɪ] nach dem Weg fragen I
*to be **asleep** [biː əˈsliːp] schlafen III
to fall asleep [ˌfɔːl‿əˈsliːp] einschlafen III
**aspect** [ˈæspekt] Aspekt; Gesichtspunkt; Blickwinkel <IV>
**assistant** [əˈsɪstnt] Verkäufer; Verkäuferin III; Helfer; Helferin; Kaufmann; Kauffrau; Fachmann; Fachfrau <V U1, 192>
shop assistant [ˈʃɒp‿əˌsɪstnt] Verkäufer; Verkäuferin II
sales **associate** *(AE)* [ˌseɪlz əˈsəʊʃiət] Verkäufer; Verkäuferin IV
**astronomy** [əˈstrɒnəmi] Astronomie IV
**at** [æt] an; in; um; bei; auf I
at break [ət ˈbreɪk] in der Pause I
at first [ət ˈfɜːst] zuerst; zunächst IV
at home [ət ˈhəʊm] zu Hause I
at last [ət ˈlɑːst] endlich; zu guter Letzt II
at least [ət ˈliːst] wenigstens; mindestens III
at night [ət ˈnaɪt] nachts V U3, 51
at present [ət ˈpreznt] augenblicklich; derzeit V U4, 74
at school [ət ˈskuːl] in der Schule I
at that time [ət ðæt ˈtaɪm] damals; zu der Zeit V U2, 39
at the back [ət ðə ˈbæk] hinten; am Ende; im hinteren Teil IV
at the bottom [æt ðə ˈbɒtəm] unten III; ganz am Ende IV
at the front [ət ðə ˈfrʌnt] vorn <IV>
at the front of [ət ðə ˈfrʌnt‿əv] an der Spitze (von); im vorderen Bereich II
at the seaside [ət ðə ˈsiːsaɪd] am Meer I
at the top [æt ðə ˈtɒp] oben III
at the weekend [ˌət ðə ˈwiːkend] am Wochenende I
**ate** [eɪt] simple past von *to eat* II
**athlete** [ˈæθliːt] Leichtathlet; Leichtathletin <V U2, 47>
**atmosphere** [ˈætməsfɪə] Atmosphäre; Stimmung V U3, 60
to **attach** [əˈtætʃ] verbinden III
**attached** [əˈtætʃt] angefügt; angehängt V U1, 16
**attack** [əˈtæk] Angriff; Attacke IV
to **attack** [əˈtæk] angreifen IV
to **attend** [əˈtend] teilnehmen; anwesend sein; besuchen V U1, 11
**attention** [əˈtenʃn] Aufmerksamkeit <IV>
to catch sb's attention [ˌkætʃ‿əˈtenʃn] jmdn. auf sich aufmerksam machen <IV>
to pay attention to sth [ˌpeɪ‿əˈtenʃn tə] seine Aufmerksamkeit auf etw. richten V U1, 17
**attic** [ˈætɪk] Dachboden I
**attitude** [ˈætɪtjuːd] Einstellung; Haltung IV
to **attract** [əˈtrækt] anziehen IV
**attraction** [əˈtrækʃn] Attraktion; Sehenswürdigkeit <V U2, 28>
**audience** [ˈɔːdiəns] Publikum; Zuschauer *(Pl.)*; Zuhörer *(Pl.)* V U4, 74
**audition** [ɔːˈdɪʃn] Vorspielen; Vorsprechen; Vorsingen; Vortanzen II
**August** [ˈɔːgəst] August I
in August [ɪn ˈɔːgəst] im August I
**aunt** [ɑːnt] Tante II
**Australian** [ɒsˈtreɪliən] Australier; Australierin; australisch V U1, 10
**autograph** [ˈɔːtəgrɑːf] Autogramm IV
to sign autographs [ˌsaɪn ˈɔːtəgrɑːfs] Autogramme geben IV
**autumn** [ˈɔːtəm] Herbst V U2, 28
modal **auxiliary** [ˌməʊdl‿ɔːgˈzɪljri] modales Hilfsverb <V U1, 14>
**available** [əˈveɪləbl] erhältlich; verfügbar V U1, 11
**avenue** [ˈævənjuː] Allee; Boulevard IV
**average** [ˈævrɪdʒ] durchschnittlich IV
to **avoid** [əˈvɔɪd] vermeiden; meiden; aus dem Weg gehen; ausweichen IV
**awake** [əˈweɪk] bei Bewusstsein; wach III
**away** [əˈweɪ] weg; entfernt II
to get away (from sb) [ˌget‿əˈweɪ frəm] (jmdm.) entkommen; (von jmdm.) wegkommen V U2, 41
right away [ˌraɪt‿əˈweɪ] sofort; gleich IV
**awesome** [ˈɔːsəm] super; spitze IV
**awful** [ˈɔːfl] schrecklich; furchtbar I
**awkward** [ˈɔːkwəd] ungünstig; ungeschickt; unbeholfen; peinlich V U3, 60

## B

**baboon** [bəˈbuːn] Pavian V U3, 63
**baby** [ˈbeɪbi] Baby II
baby elephant [ˈbeɪbi ˌelɪfənt] Elefantenbaby V U3, 55
**babysitter** [ˈbeɪbɪˌsɪtə] Babysitter; Babysitterin IV
**back** [bæk] Rückseite <III>
**back** [bæk] zurück I; Hinter-; Rücken; Rückseite IV
at the back [ət ðə ˈbæk] hinten; am Ende; im hinteren Teil IV

back home [bæk 'həʊm] zu Hause II
back then ['bæk ˌðen] damals IV
**background** ['bækgraʊnd] Hintergrund III
in the background [ɪn ðə 'bækgraʊnd] im Hintergrund III
**backpack** ['bækpæk] Rucksack IV
**bad** [bæd] schlecht I
badly ['bædli] sehr; schwer III; dringend IV
**bag** [bæg] Tasche; Tüte; Sack I
**bagel** ['beɪgl] Bagel *(weiches, ringförmiges Brötchen)* IV
**bagpipes** *(pl)* ['bægpaɪps] Dudelsack III
pasta **bake** [ˌpæstə 'beɪk] Nudelauflauf II
**baker** ['beɪkə] Bäcker; Bäckerin III
baker's ['beɪkəz] Bäckerei III
**bald** eagle [ˌbɔ:ld 'i:gl] Weißkopfseeadler IV
**ball** [bɔ:l] Ball II
cannon ball ['kænən ˌbɔ:l] Kanonenkugel II
**balloon** [bə'lu:n] Luftballon I
**bamboo** [bæm'bu:] Bambus <V U4, 84>
to **ban** [bæn] verbannen; verbieten; sperren IV
**banana** [bə'nɑ:nə] Banane I
**band** [bænd] Band; Musikgruppe II
**bandage** ['bændɪdʒ] Verband III
**bank** clerk ['bæŋk ˌklɑ:k] Bankkaufmann; Bankkauffrau <V U1, 192>
**bank** specialist ['bæŋk ˌspeʃlɪst] Bankkaufmann; Bankkauffrau <V U1, 192>
**bar** chart ['bɑ: ˌtʃɑ:t] Balkendiagramm; Säulendiagramm <IV>
**bar** of chocolate [bɑ:r‿əv 'tʃɒklət] Tafel Schokolade I
**barbecue** ['bɑ:bɪkju:] Grill; Grillparty I
**bargain** ['bɑ:gɪn] Schnäppchen II
to **bargain** ['bɑ:gɪn] handeln; verhandeln V U4, 68
to **bark** [bɑ:k] bellen III
**barrel** ['bærl] Fass; Tonne IV
**barren** ['bærn] karg <V U3, 205>
**barrier** ['bæriə] Schranke; Barriere; Sperre <V U3, 66>

**baseball** ['beɪsbɔ:l] Baseball IV
**basic** ['beɪsɪk] Grund- <V U4, 76>
basically ['beɪsɪkli] eigentlich; grundsätzlich; im Grunde genommen IV
**basketball** ['bɑ:skɪtbɔ:l] Basketball II
**bat** [bæt] Fledermaus I
**bath** [bɑ:θ] Bad; Badewanne V U4, 76
Turkish bath [ˌtɜ:kɪʃ 'bɑ:θ] Dampfbad III
**bathroom** ['bɑ:θrʊm] Badezimmer; Bad I
**bathroom** *(AE)* ['bɑ:θrʊm] Toilette; Bad(ezimmer) IV
**battle** ['bætl] Schlacht; Kampf III
**bay** [beɪ] Bucht IV
*to **be** [bi:] sein I
to be able to (do sth) [bi: 'eɪbl tə] (zu ew.) fähig sein; (etw.) können; (etw.) dürfen IV
to be about [bi: ə'baʊt] gehen um; handeln von III
to be afraid [bi: ə'freɪd] sich fürchten; Angst haben II
to be alive with … [bi: ə'laɪv wɪð] erfüllt sein von …; vor … wimmeln IV
to be allowed to (do sth) [bi: ə'laʊd tə] (etw.) dürfen IV
to be around [bi: ə'raʊnd] geben; existieren IV
to be asleep [bi: ə'sli:p] schlafen III
to be born [bi: 'bɔ:n] geboren werden III
to be bullied [bi: 'bʊlid] gemobbt werden <V U4, 80>
to be called [bi: 'kɔ:ld] heißen; genannt werden II
to be fed up (with) [bi: fed‿'ʌp (wɪð)] die Nase voll haben (von); sauer sein III
to be good at [bi: 'gʊd‿ət] gut sein in/bei I
to be homesick [bi: 'həʊmsɪk] Heimweh haben III
to be included [bi: ɪn'klu:dɪd] enthalten sein III
to be interested in [bi: 'ɪntrəstɪd‿ɪn] sich interessieren für; interessiert sein an III

to be involved [bi: ɪn'vɒlvd] sich beteiligen; sich engagieren V U2, 34
to be known as [bi: 'nəʊn‿əz] bekannt sein als V U1, 11
to be located [bi: ləʊ'keɪtɪd] liegen III; gelegen sein; sich befinden IV
to be lucky [bi: 'lʌki] Glück haben III
to be made of [bi: 'meɪd‿əv] hergestellt sein aus III
to be middle class [bi: ˌmɪdl 'klɑ:s] zur Mittelschicht gehören V U3, 51
to be on fire [bi: ɒn 'faɪə] brennen II
to be patient [bi: 'peɪʃnt] Geduld haben <V U1, 192>
to be related to [bi: rɪ'leɪtɪd tə] verwandt sein mit; sich beziehen auf <V U4, 79>
to be right [bi: 'raɪt] recht haben II
to be scared [bi: 'skeəd] Angst haben; erschrocken sein II
to be sick [bi: 'sɪk] sich übergeben I
to be sorry [bi: 'sɒri] leidtun III
to be stuck [bi: 'stʌk] feststecken; nicht weg können; festsitzen; hängen bleiben IV
to be surrounded by sth/sb [bi: sə'raʊndɪd baɪ] umgeben sein von etw./jmdm. V U4, 78
to be terrified (of sth) [bi: 'terəfaɪd (əv)] (große) Angst (vor etw.) haben V U2, 40
to be understanding [bi: ˌʌndə'stændɪŋ] verständnisvoll sein <V U1, 192>
to be up to [bi: 'ʌp tə] vorhaben III
to be willing to do sth [bi: 'wɪlɪŋ] bereit sein, etw. zu tun; gewillt sein, etw. zu tun <V U1, 192>
to be worth [bi: 'wɜ:θ] wert sein III
to be wrong [bi: 'rɒŋ] unrecht haben; sich irren III
Be careful! [bi: 'keəfl] Sei vorsichtig! I
**beach** [bi:tʃ] Strand I
to go beach combing [gəʊ 'bi:tʃ ˌkəʊmɪŋ] den Strand nach Strandgut absuchen II

kidney **bean** ['kɪdni ˌbiːn] Kidneybohne II
soy **bean** ['sɔɪ ˌbiːn] Sojabohne IV
**bear** [beə] Bär I
*to **beat** [biːt] besiegen III
**beat** [biːt] simple past von *to beat* III
**beaten** ['biːtn] past participle von *to beat* III
**beautician** [bjuː'tɪʃn] Kosmetiker; Kosmetikerin <V U1, 192>
**beautiful** ['bjuːtɪfl] schön; hübsch I
**beauty** ['bjuːti] Schönheit V U2, 30
**beaver** ['biːvə] Biber <V U1, 27>
**became** [bɪ'keɪm] simple past von *to become* II
**because** [bɪ'kɒz] weil; da I
because of [bɪ'kɒz‿əv] wegen III
That's because ... [ˌðæts bɪ'kɒz] Das liegt daran, dass ... III
*to **become** [bɪ'kʌm] werden II
**become** [bɪ'kʌm] past participle von *to become* II
**bed** [bed] Bett I
bed and breakfast (B & B) [ˌbed‿ən 'brekfəst] Frühstückspension III
to go to bed [ˌgəʊ tə 'bed] ins Bett gehen I
**bedroom** ['bedrʊm] Schlafzimmer; Kinderzimmer I
**beef** [biːf] Rindfleisch II
**been** [biːn] past particple von *to be* II
**beer** [bɪə] Bier IV
**before** [bɪ'fɔː] bevor; bis zu; vorher; zuvor II; schon einmal III; vor IV
before that [bɪ'fɔː ðæt] davor III
**began** [bɪ'gæn] simple past von *to begin* IV
*to **begin** [bɪ'gɪn] beginnen; anfangen IV
**beginner** [bɪ'gɪnə] Anfänger; Anfängerin V U2, 30
**beginning** [bɪ'gɪnɪŋ] Anfang; Beginn III
**begun** [bɪ'gʌn] past participle von *to begin* IV
to **behave** [bɪ'heɪv] sich benehmen; sich verhalten IV
**behavior** *(AE)* [bɪ'heɪvjə] Verhalten IV
**behaviour** [bɪ'heɪvjə] Verhalten <IV>
**behind** [bɪ'haɪnd] hinter II
from behind [ˌfrəm bɪ'haɪnd] von hinten I
**belief** [bɪ'liːf] Glaube; Überzeugung V U1, 12
to **believe** [bɪ'liːv] glauben II
**bell** [bel] Glocke II
to **belong** (to) [bɪ'lɒŋ (tə)] gehören (zu) IV
**beloved** [bɪ'lʌvɪd] geliebt IV
**below** [bɪ'ləʊ] unter <V U2, 198>
**belt** [belt] Gürtel IV
**bench** [benʃ] Bank; Sitzbank III
**best** [best] beste II
best known [ˌbest 'nəʊn] weltberühmt IV
to like ... best [ˌlaɪk ... 'best] am meisten mögen; am liebsten mögen I
the best [ðə 'best] die besten II
Best wishes, [ˌbest 'wɪʃɪz] Viele Grüße, I
**best-paid** ['bestˌpeɪd] bestbezahlt IV
**best-paying** [ˌbest'peɪɪŋ] bestbezahlt IV
*to **bet** [bet] wetten (auf) III
**bet** [bet] simple past, past participle von *to bet* III
**better** ['betə] besser I
**between** [bɪ'twiːn] zwischen II
**big** [bɪg] groß I
big wheel [ˌbɪg 'wiːl] Riesenrad II
**bike** [baɪk] Fahrrad I
bike courier ['baɪk ˌkʊriə] Fahrradkurier; Fahrradkurierin V U1, 19
**bill** [bɪl] Rechnung III
to pay the bill [ˌpeɪ ðə 'bɪl] die Rechnung bezahlen III
**billion** ['bɪliən] Milliarde IV
**biography** [baɪ'ɒgrəfi] Biografie <III>
**Biology** [baɪ'ɒlədʒi] Biologie I
**bird** [bɜːd] Vogel I
bird watching ['bɜːd ˌwɒtʃɪŋ] Vogelbeobachtung III
**birthday** ['bɜːθdeɪ] Geburtstag I
Happy birthday! [ˌhæpi 'bɜːθdeɪ] Alles Gute zum Geburtstag! I
**biscuit** ['bɪskɪt] Keks II
a **bit** [ə 'bɪt] ein bisschen; ein wenig II
**bite** [baɪt] Biss <V U1, 27>
**black** [blæk] schwarz I
black (person) [blæk] Schwarzer; Schwarze V U3, 59
**blacklisted** ['blæklɪstɪd] auf die schwarze Liste gesetzt V U4, 79
**blanket** ['blæŋkɪt] Decke; Bettdecke; Wolldecke IV
**blast** [blɑːst] Wahnsinnsspaß IV
**bleaching** ['bliːtʃɪŋ] Bleichen; Ausbleichen V U1, 20
**bled** [bled] simple past, past participle von *to bleed* III
*to **bleed** [bliːd] bluten III
to **blind** [blaɪnd] blenden; verblenden <V U1, 26>
**block** [blɒk] Block; Häuserblock IV
**blog** [blɒg] Blog; Internettagebuch II
**blogger** ['blɒgə] Blogger; Bloggerin IV
**blouse** [blaʊz] Bluse I
**blue** [bluː] blau I
blue cheese [ˌbluː 'tʃiːs] Schimmelkäse II
**blues** [bluːz] Blues *(Musikrichtung)* IV
**board** [bɔːd] Tafel I
on board ['ɒn bɔːd] an Bord III
to **board** [bɔːd] an Bord gehen V U2, 31
**boarding pass** ['bɔːdɪŋ ˌpɑːs] Bordkarte <V U2, 198>
**boarding school** ['bɔːdɪŋ ˌskuːl] Internat V U1, 11
**boat** [bəʊt] Boot II
boat trip ['bəʊt ˌtrɪp] Bootsfahrt; Schiffsfahrt II
fishing boat ['fɪʃɪŋ ˌbəʊt] Fischerboot V U2, 43
**body** ['bɒdi] Körper III; Leiche IV
body language ['bɒdi ˌlæŋgwɪdʒ] Körpersprache <III>
body lotion ['bɒdi ˌləʊʃn] Körperlotion III
**bond** [bɒnd] Bindung V U2, 34
**bonus** ['bəʊnəs] Bonus; Prämie IV
**book** [bʊk] Buch; Heft I
exercise book ['eksəsaɪz ˌbʊk] Übungsheft I
to **book** [bʊk] buchen; reservieren IV
**booklet** ['bʊklət] Broschüre; Heft IV
to **bookmark** ['bʊkmɑːk] zu ... hinzufügen II

**boom** years ['bu:m ˌjɪəz] Blütezeit; fette Jahre *(ugs.)* IV
**boomtown** ['bu:mtaʊn] Boomtown *(eine Stadt, die sehr schnell wächst)* IV
**boot** [bu:t] Stiefel II
**border** ['bɔ:də] Grenze III
to cross the border [ˌkrɒs ðə 'bɔ:də] über die Grenze gehen; die Grenze überschreiten IV
**bored** [bɔ:d] gelangweilt IV
**boring** ['bɔ:rɪŋ] langweilig I
*to be **born** [bi: 'bɔ:n] geboren werden III
**borough** ['bʌrə] Stadtteil; Bezirk IV
to **borrow** ['bɒrəʊ] ausleihen II
**boss** [bɒs] Boss; Chef; Chefin II
**bossy** ['bɒsi] rechthaberisch IV
**both** [bəʊθ] beide III
both ... and ... ['bəʊθ ... ənd] sowohl ... als auch ... IV
to **bother** ['bɒðə] stören; belästigen; nerven IV
**bottle** ['bɒtl] Flasche I
bottle bank ['bɒtl bæŋk] Altglascontainer II
**bottom** ['bɒtəm] unterer Teil; Boden; Grund III; Hintern; Po V U3, 58
at the bottom [æt ðə 'bɒtəm] unten III; ganz am Ende IV
**bought** [bɔ:t] simple past von *to buy* I; past participle von *to buy* II
**bowl** [bəʊl] Schale; Schälchen; Schüssel II
**bowling** ['bəʊlɪŋ] Bowlen IV
**box** [bɒks] Box; Kiste; Schachtel I
telephone box ['telɪfəʊn ˌbɒks] Telefonzelle II
to **box** [bɒks] boxen <V U1, 26>
**boy** [bɔɪ] Junge I
**boyfriend** ['bɔɪfrend] Freund *(in einer Paarbeziehung)* IV
to **brainstorm** ['breɪnstɔ:m] brainstormen; sammeln <IV>
**brand** [brænd] Marke III
**brand-new** [ˌbrænd'nju:] brandneu V U4, 70
**brave** [breɪv] tapfer; mutig III
**bread** [bred] Brot II
sliced bread [ˌslaɪst 'bred] in Scheiben geschnittenes Brot III

**break** [breɪk] Pause I
at break [ət 'breɪk] in der Pause I
to take a break [ˌteɪk‿ə 'breɪk] Pause machen II
to take a short break [ˌteɪk‿ə 'ʃɔ:t breɪk] eine kurze Pause machen <V U3, 60>
*to **break** [breɪk] brechen; zerbrechen II
to break down [ˌbreɪk 'daʊn] zerstören; niederreißen <V U3, 66>
to break out [ˌbreɪk‿'aʊt] ausbrechen V U2, 34
**breakfast** ['brekfəst] Frühstück I
bed and breakfast (B & B) [ˌbed‿ən 'brekfəst] Frühstückspension III
to have breakfast [ˌhæv 'brekfəst] frühstücken I
**breath** [breθ] Atem; Atemzug V U2, 30
to take a deep breath [ˌteɪk‿ə ˌdi:p 'breθ] tief einatmen; tief Luft holen V U3, 60
to take one's breath away [ˌteɪk wʌnz 'breθ‿əˌweɪ] den Atem rauben V U2, 30
to **breathe** [bri:ð] atmen III
**breeze** [bri:z] Brise V U2, 31
**breezy** ['bri:zi] windig <V U2, 198>
**brick** [brɪk] Stein; Ziegelstein II
**bricklayer** ['brɪkleɪə] Maurer; Maurerin <V U1, 192>
**bridge** [brɪdʒ] Brücke II
**briefcase** ['bri:fkeɪs] Aktenkoffer; Aktentasche III
fire **brigade** ['faɪə brɪˌgeɪd] Feuerwehr <III>
**bright** [braɪt] hell; leuchtend; strahlend IV
**brilliant** ['brɪliənt] toll I
*to **bring** [brɪŋ] bringen; mitbringen II
to bring to life [ˌbrɪŋ tə‿'laɪf] zum Leben erwecken; veranschaulichen IV
**British** ['brɪtɪʃ] britisch II
**broadcast** ['brɔ:dkɑ:st] Sendung; Ausstrahlung; Übertragung <IV>
**brochure** ['brəʊʃə] Broschüre; Prospekt III
**broke** [brəʊk] simple past von *to break* II

**broken** ['brəʊkn] past participle von *to break* II; gebrochen; kaputt IV
**brother** ['brʌðə] Bruder I
**brought** [brɔ:t] simple past von *to bring* II
**brown** [braʊn] braun I
to **browse** [braʊz] durchstöbern V U4, 70
**brutal** ['bru:tl] brutal V U2, 39
speech **bubble** ['spi:tʃ ˌbʌbl] Sprechblase <III>
thought **bubble** ['θɔ:t ˌbʌbl] Denkblase; Gedankenblase <IV>
**bucket** of water ['bʌkɪt‿əv ˌwɔ:tə] Eimer Wasser I
**buddy** *(infml)* ['bʌdi] Kumpel IV
**buffalo** *(sg)* ['bʌfləʊ], **buffaloes** *(pl)* ['bʌfləʊz] Büffel V U3, 54
**buffet** ['bʊfeɪ] Büfett III
*to **build** [bɪld] bauen II; gründen V U3, 49
**builder** ['bɪldə] Bauarbeiter; Bauarbeiterin II
ship builder ['ʃɪp ˌbɪldə] Schiffsbauer; Schiffsbauerin III
**building** ['bɪldɪŋ] Gebäude II
**built** [bɪlt] simple past, past participle von *to build* II
light **bulb** ['laɪt ˌbʌlb] Glühbirne III
**bullet** ['bʊlɪt] Kugel; Geschoss IV
*to be **bullied** [bi: 'bʊlid] gemobbt werden <V U4, 80>
**bungalow** ['bʌŋgləʊ] Bungalow <V U3, 205>
**bunk** bed ['bʌŋk ˌbed] Doppelstockbett <V U2, 198>
**burger** ['bɜ:gə] Hamburger II
**burglar** ['bɜ:glə] Einbrecher; Einbrecherin I
*to **burn** [bɜ:n] verbrennen; brennen III
to burn down [bɜ:n 'daʊn] niederbrennen; verbrennen II
**burnt** [bɜ:nt] simple past, past participle von *to burn* III
**bus** [bʌs] Bus I
bus stop ['bʌs ˌstɒp] Bushaltestelle II
on the bus [ˌɒn ðə 'bʌs] im Bus II
**bush** [bʊʃ] Busch; Strauch <V U3, 205>

**bushman** ['bʊʃmən] Buschmann <V U1, 27>
**business** ['bɪznɪs] Geschäft; Branche IV; Geschäftswelt <V U3, 62>
**businessman** ['bɪznɪsmæn] Geschäftsmann IV
**busy** ['bɪzi] beschäftigt; arbeitsreich I; belebt; voller Menschen <III>; rege; aktiv V U4, 69
a busy day [ə ˌbɪzi 'deɪ] ein ausgefüllter Tag I
**but** [bʌt] aber I
**butcher** ['bʊtʃə] Fleischer; Fleischerin; Metzger; Metzgerin <V U1, 192>
butcher's ['bʊtʃəz] Metzgerei III
**butter** ['bʌtə] Butter I
peanut butter [ˌpiːnʌt 'bʌtə] Erdnussbutter III
*to **buy** [baɪ] kaufen I
**by** [baɪ] von II; bis (spätestens) III; vorbei V U2, 30; an IV
by (+ gerund) [baɪ] indem V U1, 12
by *(train)* [baɪ] mit *(dem Zug)* I
by far [baɪ 'fɑː] bei weitem <V U2, 46>
by heart [ˌbaɪ 'hɑːt] auswendig <V U4, 83>
by the end [ˌbaɪ ði 'end] am Schluss II
by yourself [baɪ 'jɔːself] allein II
**Bye.** [baɪ] Tschüss. I
**by-product** ['baɪˌprɒdʌkt] Nebenprodukt <V U2, 46>

## C

**cabbage** ['kæbɪdʒ] Kohl; Kraut II
**cabin** ['kæbɪn] Kabine V U2, 40
**cable car** ['keɪbl ˌkɑː] Seilbahn IV
**cactus** ['kæktəs] Kaktus V U3, 58
**café** ['kæfeɪ] Café I
**cafeteria** [kæfə'tɪəriə] Cafeteria; Mensa I
**cage** [keɪdʒ] Käfig I
**cake** [keɪk] Kuchen I
to make a cake [ˌmeɪk‿ə 'keɪk] einen Kuchen backen I
piece of cake ['piːs‿əv keɪk] einfach <IV>
**calculator** ['kælkjəleɪtə] Rechner; Taschenrechner I
**calendar** ['kæləndə] Kalender IV
**call** [kɔːl] Anruf; Ruf III
phone call ['fəʊn ˌkɔːl] Telefonanruf I
to **call** [kɔːl] rufen; anrufen I; nennen III
to be called [biː 'kɔːld] heißen; genannt werden II
**caller** ['kɔːlə] Anrufer; Anruferin II
**calm** [kɑːm] ruhig; friedlich <V U1, 192>
to keep calm [ˌkiːp 'kɑːm] Ruhe bewahren; ruhig bleiben <IV>
**came** [keɪm] simple past von *to come* I
**camel** ['kæml] Kamel V U1, 12
**camera** ['kæmrə] Fotoapparat; Kamera <III>
camera operator ['kæmrə ˌɒpreɪtə] Kameramann; Kamerafrau <III>
**camp** [kæmp] Camp; Lager II
to **camp** [kæmp] campen; kampieren; zelten V U4, 70
**campaign** [kæm'peɪn] Kampagne; Aktion <V U1, 21>
**camping** ['kæmpɪŋ] Camping; Zelten III
to go camping [ˌgəʊ 'kæmpɪŋ] campen gehen; zelten II
**campsite** ['kæmpsaɪt] Campingplatz; Zeltplatz III
**campus** ['kæmpəs] Campus; Schulgelände IV
**can** [kæn] können; Dose I
can't [kɑːnt] nicht können I
**canary** [kə'neəri] Kanarienvogel III
**cancellation** [ˌkænsl'eɪʃn] Stornierung; Annulierung <V U2, 198>
**candidate** ['kændɪdət] Kandidat; Kandidatin; Bewerber; Bewerberin V U1, 19
**candle** ['kændl] Kerze I
**cannibal** ['kænɪbl] Kannibale; Kannibalin <V U2, 46>
**cannon** ['kænən] Kanone V U2, 39
cannon ball ['kænən ˌbɔːl] Kanonenkugel II
**cannot** ['kænɒt] nicht können III
**canoeing** [kə'nuːɪŋ] Kanufahren I
**Cantonese** [ˌkæntə'niːz] Kantonesisch; kantonesisch <V U4, 84>
**cap** [kæp] Kappe; Mütze I
**Cape Dutch** [ˌkeɪp 'dʌtʃ] kapholländisch <V U3, 63>
**capital** (city) ['kæpɪtl (sɪti)] Hauptstadt III
**capital** letter [ˌkæpɪtl 'letə] Großbuchstabe <III>
**captain** ['kæptɪn] Kapitän; Kapitänin I
**caption** ['kæpʃn] Untertitel; Bildunterschrift <II>
**car** [kɑː] Auto I
**caravan** ['kærəvæn] Wohnwagen III
**carbon** dioxide (CO2) [ˌkɑːbn daɪ'ɒksaɪd (ˌsiːəʊ'tuː)] Kohlendioxid V U4, 75
**card** [kɑːd] Karte; Spielkarte I
ID card [ˌaɪ'diː ˌkɑːd] Ausweis; Personalausweis <V U2, 198>
prompt card ['prɒmt ˌkɑːd] Stichwortkarte <IV>
**cardboard** ['kɑːdbɔːd] Pappe; Karton III
to **care** [keə] sich interessieren; wichtig nehmen V U4, 70
to take care of sb [ˌteɪk 'keər‿əv] sich um jmdn. kümmern; für jmdn. sorgen IV
to care (for) ['keə (fɔː)] sich kümmern (um) III
**career** [kə'rɪə] Beruf; Laufbahn; Karriere IV
**careful** ['keəfl] vorsichtig; sorgfältig II
Be careful! [biː 'keəfl] Sei vorsichtig! I
**caretaker** ['keəˌteɪkə] Hausmeister; Hausmeisterin I
**cargo** ship ['kɑːgəʊ ˌʃɪp] Frachtschiff <V U2, 39>
**Carib** ['kærɪb] Karibe <V U2, 46>
**Caribbean** [ˌkærɪ'biːən] karibisch; Karibisch; Karibe; Karibin V U2, 29
**carnival** ['kɑːnɪvl] Karneval; Fasching IV
**carpenter** ['kɑːpəntə] Zimmermann; Zimmerin; Tischler; Tischlerin V U1, 11
**carpet** ['kɑːpɪt] Teppich I
**carrot** ['kærət] Karotte II
to **carry** ['kæri] tragen; befördern II
**cart** [kɑːt] Stand IV

**cartoon** [kɑːˈtuːn] Cartoon; Zeichentrickfilm <IV>
**case** [keɪs] Fall; Verhandlung IV
court case [ˈkɔːt ˌkeɪs] Gerichtsverhandlung; Rechtsfall IV
pencil case [ˈpensl ˌkeɪs] Federmäppchen I
**cash** [kæʃ] Bargeld II
**cast** [kɑːst] Gips III
**castle** [ˈkɑːsl] Schloss; Burg II
**cat** [kæt] Katze I
*to **catch** [kætʃ] fangen II
to catch fire [ˌkætʃ ˈfaɪə] Feuer fangen <V U1, 26>
to catch sb's attention [ˌkætʃ‿əˈtenʃn] jmdn. auf sich aufmerksam machen <IV>
to catch up with [kætʃ‿ˈʌp wɪð] einholen IV
**catchy** [ˈkætʃi] eingängig; einprägsam IV
**category** [ˈkætəgri] Kategorie V U3, 55
**caterer** [ˈkeɪtərə] Fachkraft für Gastronomie <V U1, 192>
**catering** college [ˈkeɪtərɪŋ ˌkɒlɪdʒ] Hotelfachschule II
**Catholic** [ˈkæθlɪk] katholisch; Katholik; Katholikin III
**cattle** *(pl only)* [ˈkætl] Vieh; Rindvieh <V U1, 26>
**caught** [kɔːt] simple past, past participle von *to catch* II
to **cause** [kɔːz] verursachen IV
**'cause** (= because) [kɒz] weil <V U2, 35>
**caution** [ˈkɔːʃn] Sorgfalt; Warnung; Vorsicht V U3, 54
**cautious** [ˈkɔːʃəs] vorsichtig; behutsam III
**cave** [keɪv] Höhle II
**ceiling** [ˈsiːlɪŋ] Zimmerdecke IV
to **celebrate** [ˈseləbreɪt] feiern I
**celebration** [ˌseləˈbreɪʃn] Feier IV
**celebrity** [səˈlebrəti] Prominenter; Prominente; berühmte Person IV
**cell** [sel] Zelle V U4, 74
cell phone *(AE)* [ˈsel fəʊn] Mobiltelefon; Handy IV
to **censor** [ˈsensə] zensieren V U4, 78
**censorship** [ˈsensəʃɪp] Zensur V U4, 79
**cent** [sent] Cent *(Währung)* III
**center** *(AE)* [ˈsentə] Zentrum; Mitte; Center IV
**centimetre** (cm) [ˈsentɪˌmiːtə] Zentimeter (cm) I
**central** [ˈsentrl] zentral; im Mittelpunkt stehen V U3, 50
**centre** [ˈsentə] Zentrum; Mitte; Center III
activity centre [ækˈtɪvəti ˌsentə] Jugendzentrum III
city centre [ˌsɪti ˈsentə] Stadtzentrum; Stadtmitte III
shopping centre [ˈʃɒpɪŋ ˌsentə] Einkaufszentrum I
in the centre of [ˌɪn ðə ˈsentər‿əv] in der Mitte von III
**century** [ˈsenʃri] Jahrhundert III
**cereal** [ˈsɪəriəl] Müsli; Cornflakes III
**certain** [ˈsɜːtn] bestimmte IV
certainly [ˈsɜːtnli] allerdings IV
**certificate** [səˈtɪfɪkət] Zertifikat; Bescheinigung; Urkunde; Zeugnis V U1, 16
**chain** [tʃeɪn] Kette <III>
**chair** [tʃeə] Stuhl I
**challenge** [ˈtʃælɪndʒ] Herausforderung V U3, 54
**champion** [ˈtʃæmpiən] Sieger; Siegerin; Champion <V U2, 47>
**chance** [tʃɑːns] Chance; Gelegenheit II; Möglichkeit IV
**change** [tʃeɪndʒ] Münzgeld; Wechselgeld II; Änderung; Veränderung; Wechsel <V U3, 59>
climate change [ˈklaɪmət ˌtʃeɪndʒ] Klimawandel V U1, 20
to **change** [tʃeɪndʒ] wechseln II; (sich) ändern; verändern; umsteigen III
to change one's mind [ˌtʃeɪndʒ wʌnz ˈmaɪnd] seine Meinung ändern III
**changing** [ˈtʃeɪndʒɪŋ] wechselnd; sich verändernd V U1, 20
**chant** [tʃɑːnt] Sprechgesang <I>
**chapter** [ˈtʃæptə] Kapitel <IV>
**character** [ˈkærəktə] Charakter; Figur <III>
**charades** [ʃəˈrɑːdz] Scharaden <II>
**charger** [ˈtʃɑːdʒə] Ladegerät III
**charity** event [ˈtʃærɪti ɪˌvent] Wohltätigkeitsveranstaltung <V U4, 212>
**chart** [tʃɑːt] Diagramm; Tabelle V U4, 76
bar chart [ˈbɑː ˌtʃɑːt] Balkendiagramm; Säulendiagramm <IV>
pie chart [ˈpaɪ ˌtʃɑːt] Kuchendiagramm; Tortendiagramm <IV>
**charts** *(pl only)* [tʃɑːts] Hitparade IV
to **chase** [tʃeɪs] jagen; verfolgen V U3, 60
**chaser** [ˈtʃeɪsə] Jäger; Jägerin; Verfolger; Verfolgerin IV
video **chat** [ˈvɪdiəʊ ˌtʃæt] Video-Chat III
to **chat** [tʃæt] chatten; plaudern II
**chatroom** [ˈtʃætrʊm] Chatroom V U3, 54
**cheap** [tʃiːp] billig II
**check** [tʃek] Kontrolle IV
check-in [ˈtʃekɪn] Gepäckaufgabe; Einchecken V U2, 31
spell check [ˈspel ˌtʃek] Rechtschreibprüfprogramm <III>
to **check** [tʃek] überprüfen; kontrollieren III
to check in [ˌtʃek‿ˈɪn] einchecken V U1, 16
to check out [ˌtʃek‿ˈaʊt] auschecken III; anschauen; ausprobieren IV; abchecken <V U3, 67>
**checklist** [ˈtʃeklɪst] Checkliste <I>
**cheeky** [ˈtʃiːki] frech III
to **cheer** sb up [ˌtʃɪər‿ˈʌp] jmdn. aufheitern; jmdn. aufmuntern III
**cheerleader** [ˈtʃɪəˌliːdə] Cheerleader *(Mädchen, das in einer Gruppe eine Sportmannschaft anfeuert)* IV
**cheerleading** [ˈtʃɪəˌliːdɪŋ] Cheerleading *(Aktivitäten der Cheerleader)* IV
**cheese** [tʃiːz] Käse I
blue cheese [ˌbluː ˈtʃiːs] Schimmelkäse II
**cheesecake** [ˈtʃiːskeɪk] Käsekuchen II
**chef** [ʃef] Koch; Köchin II
head chef [ˈhed ʃef] Chefkoch II; Chefköchin II
**chemical** [ˈkemɪkl] Chemikalie V U1, 21
**chewing** gum [ˈtʃuːɪŋ ˌgʌm] Kaugummi I
**chic** [ʃɪk] schick; elegant I
**chicken** [ˈtʃɪkɪn] Huhn I; Hähnchen IV
**child** [tʃaɪld] Kind II

child labour [ˌtʃaɪld ˈleɪbə] Kinderarbeit <IV>

**children** *(pl)* [ˈtʃɪldrn] Kinder II

to **chill out** [ˌtʃɪlˈaʊt] chillen; sich entspannen IV

**chilli** [ˈtʃɪli] Chili II

**chilly** [ˈtʃɪli] kühl <V U2, 198>

**china** [ˈtʃaɪnə] Porzellan III

**Chinese** [tʃaɪˈniːz] chinesisch; Chinesisch; aus China; Chinese; Chinesin IV

the Chinese [ðə ˈtʃaɪniːz] die Chinesen <V U4, 84>

**chips** *(pl)* [tʃɪps] Pommes frites I

**chocolate** [ˈtʃɒklət] Schokolade I; Praline IV

**choice** [tʃɔɪs] Auswahl; Wahl IV

*to **choose** [tʃuːz] auswählen; wählen II

**chorus** [ˈkɔːrəs] Refrain <I>

**chose** [tʃəʊz] simple past von *to choose* II

**chosen** [ˈtʃəʊzn] past participle von *to choose* II

**Christian** [ˈkrɪstʃn] christlich IV; Christ; Christin <V U2, 46>

**Christianity** [ˌkrɪstiˈænəti] Christentum <V U2, 46>

**Christmas** [ˈkrɪsməs] Weihnachten I

**chronological** [ˌkrɒnəˈlɒdʒɪkl] chronologisch <III>

**church** [tʃɜːtʃ] Kirche II

**cinema** [ˈsɪnəmə] Kino I

**circle** [ˈsɜːkl] Kreis; Ring III

to **cite** [saɪt] zitieren; anführen <IV>

**citizen** [ˈsɪtɪzn] Staatsbürger; Staatsbürgerin; Staatsangehöriger; Staatsangehörige IV

**city** [ˈsɪti] Stadt; Großstadt II

city centre [ˌsɪti ˈsentə] Stadtzentrum; Stadtmitte III

**civil rights** *(pl)* [ˌsɪvl ˈraɪts] Bürgerrechte IV

to **claim** [kleɪm] behaupten; beanspruchen V U4, 70

to **clap** [klæp] klatschen <I>

**class** [klɑːs] Unterricht I; Klasse III; Unterrichtsstunde; Kurs IV

**classical** [ˈklæsɪkl] klassisch *(Musik)* III

**classmate** [ˈklɑːsmeɪt] Klassenkamerad; Klassenkameradin <II>; Mitschüler; Mitschülerin V U3, 58

**classroom** [ˈklɑːsrʊm] Klassenzimmer I

relative **clause** [ˈrelətɪv ˌklɔːz] Relativsatz <V U2, 33>

to **clean** [kliːn] sauber machen; putzen I

**clean** [kliːn] sauber I

vacuum **cleaner** [ˈvækjuːm ˌkliːnə] Staubsauger IV

to **clear** [klɪə] abräumen; ausräumen IV; aufklaren; sich aufhellen V U4, 76

to clear the table [ˌklɪə ðə ˈteɪbl] den Tisch abräumen II

**clear** [klɪə] klar; deutlich; eindeutig IV

**clever** [ˈklevə] schlau; klug; intelligent I

to **click** [klɪk] klicken I

**climate** [ˈklaɪmət] Klima V U1, 20

climate change [ˈklaɪmət ˌtʃeɪndʒ] Klimawandel V U1, 20

**climb** [klaɪm] Aufstieg V U1, 15

to **climb** [klaɪm] besteigen; steigen; klettern III

**climbing** [ˈklaɪmɪŋ] Kletter- IV; Klettern V U1, 12

rock climbing [ˈrɒk ˌklaɪmɪŋ] Klettern I

**clip** [klɪp] Clip; Ausschnitt; Kurzfilm IV

**clock** [klɒk] Uhr II

alarm clock [əˈlɑːm ˌklɒk] Wecker I

clock tower [ˈklɒk ˌtaʊə] Uhrenturm II

o'clock [əˈklɒk] Uhr *(Zeitangabe bei vollen Stunden)* I

to **close** [kləʊz] schließen; zumachen I

**close** [kləʊs] genau <III>; eng; nahe V U1, 23

**closed** [kləʊzd] geschlossen V U3, 56

**clothes** *(pl)* [kləʊðz] Kleider *(Pl.)*; Kleidung I

**cloud** [klaʊd] Wolke IV

**cloudy** [ˈklaʊdi] wolkig I

**club** [klʌb] Klub; Verein II

**clubhouse** [ˈklʌbhaʊs] Klubhaus; Vereinsheim IV

**clue** [kluː] Hinweis; Spur I

**co-worker** [ˈkəʊˌwɜːkə] Arbeitskollege; Arbeitskollegin IV

**CO2** (carbon dioxide) [ˌsiːəʊˈtuː (ˌkɑːbn daɪˈɒksaɪd)] Kohlendioxid V U4, 75

**coach** [kəʊtʃ] Trainer; Trainerin <III>

**coal** [kəʊl] Kohle III

**coast** [kəʊst] Küste III

on the coast [ˌɒn ðə ˈkəʊst] an der Küste III

**coastal** [ˈkəʊstl] Küsten- <V U3, 67>

roller **coaster** [ˈrəʊlə ˌkəʊstə] Achterbahn II

**coastguard** [ˈkəʊstgɑːd] Küstenwache <III>

**coat** [kəʊt] Jacke I

**coconut** [ˈkəʊkənʌt] Kokosnuss II

dress **code** [ˈdres ˌkəʊd] Kleiderordnung; Bekleidungsvorschriften IV

**coffee** [ˈkɒfi] Kaffee IV

**coin** [kɔɪn] Münze III

**coke** [kəʊk] Cola I

**cold** [kəʊld] kalt I

to get cold [ˌget ˈkəʊld] frieren III

**collage** [kɒlˈɑːʒ] Collage <V U1, 21>

**collar** [ˈkɒlə] Halsband I

to **collect** [kəˈlekt] sammeln I

**collection** [kəˈlekʃn] Sammlung; Kollektion IV

**college** *(AE)* [ˈkɒlɪdʒ] Universität; Institut; College IV

catering college [ˈkeɪtərɪŋ ˌkɒlɪdʒ] Hotelfachschule II

**colonial** [kəˈləʊniəl] kolonial; Kolonial- V U2, 30

**colony** [ˈkɒləni] Kolonie V U2, 29

**color** *(AE)* [ˈkʌlə] Farbe IV

**colour** [ˈkʌlə] Farbe I

colourful [ˈkʌləfl] bunt II

**comb** [kəʊm] Kamm III

**combination** [ˌkɒmbɪˈneɪʃn] Kombination II

to **combine** [kəmˈbaɪn] kombinieren; verbinden <V U4, 83>

*to **come** [kʌm] kommen I

to come across (sb/sth) [ˌkʌm əˈkrɒs] (jmd./etw.) vorfinden;

(jmdm./etw.) zufällig begegnen; (jmdn./etw.) antreffen <V U4, 84>
to come out [ˌkʌm‿ˈaʊt] sich outen V U2, 34
to come to mind [ˌkʌm tə ˈmaɪnd] einem einfallen; zufällig einfallen <IV>
to come true [ˌkʌm ˈtruː] wahr werden; in Erfüllung gehen IV
to come up [ˌkʌm‿ˈʌp] bevorstehen III
Come on! [ˌkʌm‿ˈɒn] Komm jetzt! I; Komm schon! III
**comedy** [ˈkɒmədi] Komödie III
**comfortable** [ˈkʌmftəbl] bequem; angenehm III
**comic** [ˈkɒmɪk] Comic(heft) II
comic strip [ˈkɒmɪk strɪp] Comic <III>
**comment** [ˈkɒment] Kommentar IV
to put a comment [ˌpʊt‿ə ˈkɒment] einen Kommentar schreiben <I>
to **comment** (on) [ˈkɒment (ɒn)] kommentieren <IV>
**commitment** [kəˈmɪtmənt] Engagement; Einsatz V U2, 35
**common** [ˈkɒmən] häufig; verbreitet <V U3, 205>
commonly [ˈkɒmənli] üblich; gewöhnlich; gebräuchlich <V U3, 62>
to **communicate** [kəˈmjuːnɪkeɪt] kommunizieren; sich verständigen IV
**communication** [kəˌmjuːnɪˈkeɪʃn] Kommunikation V U1, 16
**community** [kəˈmjuːnəti] Gemeinde; Gemeinschaft IV
gated community [ˌgeɪtɪd kəˈmjuːnəti] bewachte Wohnanlage; geschlossene Wohnanlage V U3, 49
**commuter** [kəˈmjuːtə] Pendler; Pendlerin IV
**company** [ˈkʌmpəni] Gesellschaft; Firma II
**comparative** [kəmˈpærətɪv] Komparativ <V U1, 18>
to **compare** [kəmˈpeə] vergleichen I
**comparison** [kəmˈpærɪsn] Vergleich <IV>
**competition** [ˌkɒmpəˈtɪʃn] Wettbewerb II; Konkurrenz IV
**competitive** [kəmˈpetɪtɪv] wettkampforientiert; leistungsorientiert III
**competitor** [kəmˈpetɪtə] Teilnehmer; Teilnehmerin; Mitbewerber; Mitbewerberin <V U3, 67>
to **complain** [kəmˈpleɪn] sich beschweren; sich beklagen III
**complaint** [kəmˈpleɪnt] Beschwerde III
to **complete** [kəmˈpliːt] vervollständigen I; fertigstellen IV; absolvieren; abschließen V U1, 14
**complete** [kəmˈpliːt] vollständig IV
completely [kəmˈpliːtli] völlig III
**complex** [ˈkɒmpleks] komplexe <V U2, 33>
**complicated** [ˈkɒmplɪkeɪtɪd] kompliziert V U2, 34
**compromise** [ˈkɒmprəmaɪz] Kompromiss V U1, 13
to **compromise** [ˈkɒmprəmaɪz] sich einigen; Kompromisse schließen IV; Kompromisse eingehen V U1, 13
**compromising** [ˈkɒmprəmaɪzɪŋ] bloßstellend V U1, 13
**computer** [ˌkəmˈpjuːtə] Computer I
computer science [kəmˌpjuːtə ˈsaɪəns] Informatik <III>
**con** [kɒn] Kontra; Nachteil V U4, 68
to **concentrate** [ˈkɒnsntreɪt] (sich) konzentrieren IV
**concert** [ˈkɒnsət] Konzert II
**conclusion** [kənˈkluːʒn] Schlussfolgerung; Schluss III
in conclusion [ˌɪn kənˈkluːʒn] abschließend; zum Abschluss <V U2, 45>
**concrete** [ˈkɒŋkriːt] Beton III
**condition** [kənˈdɪʃn] Bedingung; Zustand IV
working conditions *(pl only)* [ˈwɜːkɪŋ kənˌdɪʃnz] Arbeitsbedingungen <V U1, 18>
**confident** [ˈkɒnfɪdnt] selbstsicher; selbstbewusst III
to **confirm** [kənˈfɜːm] bestätigen; bekräftigen IV
**conflict** [ˈkɒnflɪkt] Auseinandersetzung; Konflikt <III>
to **confront** [kənˈfrʌnt] konfrontieren; entgegentreten; sich stellen IV
**confused** [kənˈfjuːzd] verwirrt; wirr III
**Congratulations!** [ˌkəŋgrætjʊˈleɪʃnz] Glückwunsch! II
to **connect** [kəˈnekt] verbinden III
**connecting** [kəˈnektɪŋ] verbindend <II>
**connective** [kəˈnektɪv] Bindewort <III>
**consequence** [ˈkɒnsɪkwəns] Konsequenz; Folge; Auswirkung V U3, 50
**conservative** [ˌkənˈsɜːvətɪv] konservativ V U2, 34
to **conserve** [kənˈsɜːv] erhalten; bewahren V U3, 54
to **consist** of [kənˈsɪst‿əv] bestehen aus V U2, 28
**console** [ˈkɒnsəʊl] Konsole V U3, 52
**constant** [ˈkɒnstənt] ständig; konstant; stetig; permanent V U2, 34
**constitution** [kɒnstɪˈtjuːʃn] Verfassung V U3, 49
**construction** [kənˈstrʌkʃn] Bau; Konstruktion; Aufbau V U3, 50
construction site [kənˈstrʌkʃn ˌsaɪt] Baustelle IV
**contact** [ˈkɒntækt] Kontakt IV
to **contact** [ˈkɒntækt] sich in Verbindung setzen; kontaktieren V U4, 71
**content** [ˈkɒntent] Inhalt III
**context** [ˈkɒntekst] Kontext; Zusammenhang <V U1, 21>
**continent** [ˈkɒntɪnənt] Kontinent; Erdteil V U1, 10
to **continue** [kənˈtɪnjuː] fortfahren; weitergehen V U2, 40; andauern; weitermachen; fortsetzen IV
pro and **contra** [ˌprəʊ ən ˈkɒntrə] für und wider <IV>
**contradiction** [ˌkɒntrəˈdɪkʃn] Widerspruch; Widersprüchlichkeit <V U2, 41>
**control** [kənˈtrəʊl] Kontrolle; Steuerung IV
out of control [ˌaʊt‿əv kənˈtrəʊl] außer Kontrolle V U3, 50
to **control** [kənˈtrəʊl] kontrollieren V U1, 21
**controversial** [ˌkɒntrəˈvɜːʃl] umstritten; strittig <IV>

**conversation** [ˌkɒnvəˈseɪʃn] Konversation; Gespräch; Unterhaltung III
**to convert** [kenˈvɜ:t] umwandeln V U4, 74
**to convince** [kənˈvɪns] überzeugen <IV>
**convinced** [kənˈvɪnst] überzeugt IV
**convincing** [kənˈvɪnsɪŋ] überzeugend III
**to cook** [kʊk] kochen II
**cooking** [ˈkʊkɪŋ] Kochen II
**to cool** [ku:l] kühlen III
**cool** [ku:l] cool; super; kühl I
  to keep cool [ˌki:p ˈku:l] Ruhe bewahren <III>
**cooperative** [kəʊˈɒprətɪv] kooperativ; hilfsbereit IV
**copy** [ˈkɒpi] Kopie II; Abschrift <III>; Exemplar IV
**to copy** [ˈkɒpi] kopieren II; abschreiben <III>
**coral** [ˈkɒrəl] Koralle V U1, 20
**core subject** [ˌkɔ: ˈsʌbdʒɪkt] Pflichtfach IV
**corn** [kɔ:n] Korn; Mais; Getreide IV
**corner** [ˈkɔ:nə] Ecke III
  corner shop [ˈkɔ:nə ˌʃɒp] Tante-Emma-Laden I
**Cornish** [ˈkɔ:nɪʃ] kornisch; aus Cornwall II
**to correct** [kəˈrekt] verbessern I
**correct** [kəˈrekt] richtig; korrekt IV
**corridor** [ˈkɒrɪdɔ:] Gang; Flur II
*to **cost** [kɒst] kosten III
**cost** [kɒst] simple past, past participle von *to cost* III
**costume** [ˈkɒstju:m] Kostüm I
**cosy** [ˈkəʊzi] gemütlich III
**cottage** [ˈkɒtɪdʒ] Häuschen III
**cotton** [ˈkɒtn] Baumwolle III
**couch surfing** [ˈkaʊtʃ ˌsɜ:fɪŋ] Couchsurfing V U2, 31
**to cough** [kɒf] husten III
**could** [kʊd] konnte; könnte III
**counsellor** [ˈkaʊnslə] Berater; Beraterin V U2, 34
**to count** [kaʊnt] zählen IV
**countdown** [ˈkaʊntdaʊn] Countdown <I>
**country** [ˈkʌntri] ländliche Gegend; Land I
  home country [ˌhəʊm ˈkʌntri] Heimat; Heimatland IV
  in the country [ɪn ðə ˈkʌntri] auf dem Land I
**countryside** [ˈkʌntrɪsaɪd] Land; Landschaft III
(a) **couple of** [ə ˈkʌpl‿əv] (ein) paar IV
**courage** [ˈkʌrɪdʒ] Mut; Tapferkeit; Courage IV
bike **courier** [ˈbaɪk ˌkʊriə] Fahrradkurier; Fahrradkurierin V U1, 19
**course** [kɔ:s] Kurs III
  main course [ˌmeɪn ˈkɔ:s] Hauptgericht II
of **course** [əv ˈkɔ:s] natürlich; selbstverständlich I
**court** [kɔ:t] Spielfeld III; Gericht IV
  court case [ˈkɔ:t ˌkeɪs] Gerichtsverhandlung; Rechtsfall IV
**cousin** [ˈkʌzn] Cousin; Cousine II
**cover** [ˈkʌvə] Cover; Titelblatt <V U3, 61>
**to cover** [ˈkʌvə] bedecken; abdecken IV
  to cover in flour [ˌkʌvər‿ɪn ˈflaʊə] in Mehl wenden IV
**cow** [kaʊ] Kuh III
**crash** [kræʃ] Zusammenstoß V U3, 50
**crazy** [ˈkreɪzi] verrückt I
  to drive sb crazy [ˌdraɪv … ˈkreɪzi] jmdn. verrückt machen III
  to go crazy [ˌgəʊ ˈkreɪzi] ausflippen; durchdrehen; verrückt werden V U4, 70
ice **cream** [ˌaɪs ˈkri:m] Eiscreme; Eis I
**to create** [kriˈeɪt] schaffen; erschaffen; verursachen V U1, 12
**creature** [ˈkri:tʃə] Kreatur; Lebewesen; Geschöpf V U1, 12
**credit card** [ˈkredɪt ˌkɑ:d] Kreditkarte <IV>
**creepy** [ˈkri:pi] gruselig IV
**Creole** [ˈkri:əʊl] Kreolisch; kreolisch <V U2, 35>
**crew** [kru:] Crew; Besatzung; Mannschaft III
**cricket** [ˈkrɪkɪt] Kricket II
**crisp** [krɪsp] Kartoffelchip I
**critical** [ˈkrɪtɪkl] kritisch V U4, 78
**crocodile** [ˈkrɒkədaɪl] Krokodil V U1, 23
  saltwater crocodile [sɔ:ltˌwɔ:tə ˈkrɒkədaɪl] Salzwasserkrokodil V U1, 23
**to cross** [krɒs] überqueren III
  to cross the border [ˌkrɒs ðə ˈbɔ:də] über die Grenze gehen; die Grenze überschreiten IV
**crossed** [krɒst] verschränkt <IV>
**crossing** [ˈkrɒsɪŋ] Überfahrt; Überquerung IV
**crossroads** *(pl only)* [ˈkrɒsrəʊdz] Kreuzung <IV>
**crowd** [kraʊd] Menschenmenge II
**crowded** [ˈkraʊdɪd] überfüllt IV
**crown-of-thorns** starfish [ˌkraʊn‿əv ðɔ:nz ˈstɑ:fɪʃ] Dornenkronenseestern <V U1, 21>
**cruise** [kru:z] Kreuzfahrt <V U2, 47>
  cruise ship [ˈkru:z ˌʃɪp] Kreuzfahrtschiff V U1, 21
**to cry** [kraɪ] weinen; schreien; rufen V U2, 40
**Cuban** [ˈkju:bən] kubanisch; aus Kuba; Kubaner; Kubanerin IV
**cuddler** [ˈkʌdlə] Schmuser; Schmuserin <V U1, 24>
**cuddly** [ˈkʌdli] knuddelig III
  cuddly toy [ˈkʌdli ˌtɔɪ] Kuscheltier III
**cultural** [ˈkʌltʃrl] kulturell IV
  cultural movement [ˌkʌltʃrl ˈmu:vmənt] Kulturbewegung IV
**culture** [ˈkʌltʃə] Kultur IV
**cup** [kʌp] Tasse II; Pokal; Kelch <V U3, 66>
**cupboard** [ˈkʌbəd] Schrank III
**curious** [ˈkjʊəriəs] neugierig <IV>
**currency** [ˈkʌrnsi] Währung IV
**current** [ˈkʌrnt] aktuell; derzeitig; gegenwärtig V U1, 16
**curry** [ˈkʌri] Curry II
**custard** [ˈkʌstəd] Vanillesauce II
**custom** [ˈkʌstəm] Brauch; Sitte IV
**customer** [ˈkʌstəmə] Kunde; Kundin III
  customer service [ˌkʌstəmə ˈsɜ:vɪs] Kundendienst; Kundenbetreuung V U1, 16
*to **cut** [kʌt] (sich) schneiden II
**cut** [kʌt] simple past, past participle von *to cut* II

**cute** [kju:t] niedlich; süß I
**CV** (= curriculum vitae) [ˌsi:ˈvi:] Lebenslauf V U1, 16
**cyberbullying** [ˈsaɪbəˌbʊliɪŋ] Cyber-Mobbing IV
to **cycle** [ˈsaɪkl] Fahrrad fahren <V U3, 67>
**cycling** [ˈsaɪklɪŋ] Radfahren III
**cyclist** [ˈsaɪklɪst] Radfahrer; Radfahrerin <V U3, 67>

## D

**dad** [dæd] Papa I
**dagger** [ˈdægə] Dolch V U2, 40
**daily** [ˈdeɪli] täglich IV
**damage** [ˈdæmɪdʒ] Schaden; Beschädigung V U1, 20
to **damage** [ˈdæmɪdʒ] beschädigen; schaden V U1, 21
**dance** [dɑ:ns] Tanz III; Tanzveranstaltung; Ball IV
to **dance** [dɑ:ns] tanzen I
**dancer** [ˈdɑ:nsə] Tänzer; Tänzerin III
**dancing** [ˈdɑ:nsɪŋ] Tanzen; Tanz- IV
**danger** [ˈdeɪndʒə] Gefahr V U1, 20
**dangerous** [ˈdeɪndʒrəs] gefährlich III
**daredevil** [ˈdeəˌdevl] Draufgänger; Draufgängerin IV
**dark** [dɑ:k] dunkel I
the dark [ðə ˈdɑ:k] Dunkelheit III
**data** [ˈdeɪtə] Daten; Angaben <IV>
**date** [deɪt] Datum I; Verabredung; Date IV
**daughter** [ˈdɔ:tə] Tochter I
**day** [deɪ] Tag I
a day off [ə ˌdeɪ‿ˈɒf] ein freier Tag III
all day [ˌɔ:l ˈdeɪ] den ganzen Tag III
in the old days [ɪn ði ˈəʊld ˌdeɪz] früher III
lucky day [ˌlʌki ˈdeɪ] Glückstag II
one day [wʌn ˈdeɪ] eines Tages III
a busy day [ə ˌbɪzi ˈdeɪ] ein ausgefüllter Tag I
four hours a day [ˌaʊəz‿ə ˈdeɪ] vier Stunden täglich I
**dead** [ded] tot III
deadly [ˈdedli] tod-; tödlich III
**deaf** [def] gehörlos; schwerhörig; taub III

*to **deal** (with) [di:l (wɪð)] sich befassen (mit); umgehen (mit) IV
**dealt** (with) [delt (wɪð)] simple past, past participle von *to deal with* IV
**Dear** …, [dɪə] Liebe/Lieber …, *(Anrede in Briefen)* I
Dear Sir or Madam, [dɪə ˌsɜ:r‿ɔ: ˈmædəm] Sehr geehrte Damen und Herren, V U3, 50
**death** [deθ] Tod; Todesfall V U1, 20
**debate** [dɪˈbeɪt] Diskussion; Debatte IV
**December** [dɪˈsembə] Dezember I
to **decide** [dɪˈsaɪd] (sich) entscheiden III
**decision** [dɪˈsɪʒn] Entscheidung IV
to make a decision [ˌmeɪk‿ə dɪˈsɪʒn] eine Entscheidung treffen <III>
**deck** [dek] Schiffsdeck IV
**decline** [dɪˈklaɪn] Rückgang; Abnahme; Verschlechterung V U1, 21
**decoration** [ˌdekˈreɪʃn] Schmuck; Dekoration <V U4, 85>
to **decrease** [dɪˈkri:s] vermindern; abnehmen V U4, 75
**deep** [di:p] tief IV
to take a deep breath [ˌteɪk‿ə ˌdi:p ˈbreθ] tief einatmen; tief Luft holen V U3, 60
**definition** [ˌdefɪˈnɪʃn] Definition <III>
**degree** [dɪˈgri:] Grad IV
**delay** [dɪˈleɪ] Verzögerung; Verspätung V U2, 31
**delicious** [dɪˈlɪʃəs] köstlich II
**deluxe** [dɪˈlʌks] Luxus- IV
**democracy** [dɪˈmɒkrəsi] Demokratie V U4, 79
**democratic** [ˌdeməˈkrætɪk] demokratisch V U3, 49
**dense** [dens] dicht IV
**dentist** [ˈdentɪst] Zahnarzt; Zahnärztin <V U1, 192>
**department** [dɪˈpɑ:tmənt] Abteilung II
department store [dɪˈpɑ:tmənt ˌstɔ:] Kaufhaus II
**departure** [dɪˈpɑ:tʃə] Abflug; Abreise V U2, 31

**descendant** [dɪˈsendənt] Abkömmling; Nachfahre; Nachfahrin V U2, 29
to **describe** [dɪˈskraɪb] beschreiben IV
**description** [dɪˈskrɪpʃn] Beschreibung <IV>
**desert** [ˈdezət] Wüste V U1, 12
to **deserve** [dɪˈzɜ:v] verdienen IV
**design** [dɪˈzaɪn] Design; Gestaltung IV
Design Technology (DT) [dɪˌzaɪn tekˈnɒlədʒi, ˌdi:ˈti:] Technik I
to **design** [dɪˈzaɪn] entwerfen; gestalten <III>
**designer** [dɪˈzaɪnə] Gestalter; Gestalterin; Designer; Designerin <V U1, 192>
**desk** [desk] Schreibtisch IV
information desk [ɪnfəˈmeɪʃn ˌdesk] Information II
**desperately** [ˈdesprətli] dringend; verzweifelt IV
**dessert** [dɪˈzɜ:t] Nachspeise II
**destination** [ˌdestɪˈneɪʃn] Ziel; Reiseziel IV
to **destroy** [dɪˈstrɔɪ] zerstören <V U1, 26>
**destructive** [dɪˈstrʌktɪv] destruktiv; zerstörerisch <V U1, 26>
**detached** house [dɪˈtætʃt ˌhaʊs] Einfamilienhaus <V U3, 205>
**detail** [ˈdi:teɪl] Detail; Einzelheit IV
language **detectives** [ˈlæŋgwɪdʒ ˌdɪtektɪvz] Sprachdetektive <I>
**detector** [dɪˈtektə] Detektor III
**detention** [dɪˈtenʃn] Nachsitzen IV
to **develop** [dɪˈveləp] (sich) entwickeln IV
**development** [dɪˈveləpmənt] Entwicklung V U4, 74
**device** [dɪˈvaɪs] Gerät; Vorrichtung IV
stylistic device [staɪˌlɪstɪk dɪˈvaɪs] Stilmittel <V U3, 65>
**diagram** [ˈdaɪəgræm] Diagramm <V U4, 82>
**dialect** [ˈdaɪəlekt] Dialekt <IV>
**dialogue** [ˈdaɪəlɒg] Dialog; Gespräch <III>
**diamond** [ˈdaɪəmənd] Diamant V U3, 48
**diary** [ˈdaɪəri] Tagebuch I

**dictionary** [ˈdɪkʃnri] Wörterbuch <III>
**did** [dɪd] simple past von *to do* I
to **die** [daɪ] sterben III
**difference** [ˈdɪfrns] Unterschied V U2, 29
**different** [ˈdɪfrnt] anders; unterschiedlich I
**difficult** [ˈdɪfɪklt] schwierig III
*to **dig** [dɪg] graben; schürfen IV
**dining room** [ˈdaɪnɪŋ ˌrʊm] Esszimmer I
**dinner** [ˈdɪnə] Abendessen II; Essen IV
**direct** [dɪˈrekt] direkt <III>
direct speech [dɪˌrekt ˈspiːtʃ] direkte Rede <IV>
**direction** [dɪˈrekʃn] Richtung IV
**directions** *(pl)* [dɪˈrekʃnz] Anweisungen; Wegbeschreibung <III>
**director** [dɪˈrektə] Regisseur; Regisseurin II
**dirty** [ˈdɜːti] dreckig; schmutzig I
**disadvantaged** [ˌdɪsədˈvɑːntɪdʒd] benachteiligt V U2, 34
to **disagree** [ˌdɪsəˈgriː] anderer Meinung sein; nicht einverstanden sein II
to **disappear** [ˌdɪsəˈpɪə] verschwinden IV
**disaster** [dɪˈzɑːstə] Desaster; Katastrophe; Unglück III
**discount** [ˈdɪskaʊnt] Rabatt; Preisnachlass V U4, 71
to **discover** [dɪˈskʌvə] entdecken V U2, 30
**discovery** [dɪˈskʌvri] Entdeckung IV
**discrimination** [dɪˌskrɪmɪˈneɪʃn] Diskriminierung IV
to **discuss** [dɪˈskʌs] diskutieren <III>
**discussion** [dɪˈskʌʃn] Diskussion <V U3, 66>
**disease** [dɪˈziːz] Krankheit IV
**dish** [dɪʃ] Gericht; Speise II
satellite dish [ˈsætlaɪt ˌdɪʃ] Satellitenschüssel V U1, 11
**dishwasher** [ˈdɪʃˌwɒʃə] Spülmaschine IV
to **dislike** [dɪˈslaɪk] nicht mögen IV
**disorganized** [ˌdɪsˈɔːgənaɪzd] unorganisiert; ungeordnet IV
**disrespectful** [ˌdɪsrɪˈspektfl] respektlos V U1, 12
**distance** [ˈdɪstns] Entfernung; Distanz IV
in the distance [ˌɪn ðə ˈdɪstns] in der Ferne IV
**distant** [ˈdɪstnt] entfernt; distanziert V U2, 30
to **distract** sb (from sth) [dɪˈstrækt (frəm)] jmdn. (von etw.) ablenken <IV>
**district** [ˈdɪstrɪkt] Distrikt; Bezirk V U4, 70
**ditch** [dɪtʃ] Graben <V U3, 205>
**diver** [ˈdaɪvə] Taucher; Taucherin V U2, 30
to **divide** (up) [dɪˈvaɪd (ʌp)] teilen; aufteilen; unterteilen <IV>
**diving** [ˈdaɪvɪŋ] Tauchen; Tauch- V U1, 20
diving school [ˈdaɪvɪŋ ˌskuːl] Tauchschule V U2, 30
*to **do** [duː] machen; tun I
to do homework [ˌduː ˈhəʊmwɜːk] Hausaufgabe(n) machen I
to do sth about sth [ˌduː əˈbaʊt] etw. gegen etw. unternehmen V U4, 74
to do the right thing [ˌduː ðə ˈraɪt θɪŋ] das Richtige tun III
to do the shopping [ˌduː ðə ˈʃɒpɪŋ] Einkäufe machen; Besorgungen machen II
to do the washing up [ˌduː ðə ˈwɒʃɪŋ ˌʌp] abspülen II
to **dock** [dɒk] andocken IV
**doctor** [ˈdɒktə] Arzt; Ärztin II
**documentary** [ˌdɒkjəˈmentri] Dokumentarfilm <V U1, 23>
**dog** [dɒg] Hund I
dog walker [ˈdɒg ˌwɔːkə] Hundeausführer; Hundeausführerin IV
**dollar** [ˈdɒlə] Dollar *(amer. Währungseinheit)* IV
**dolphin** [ˈdɒlfɪn] Delfin V U1, 23
**dome** [dəʊm] Kuppel II
to **donate** [dəˈneɪt] spenden; stiften V U4, 71
**done** [dʌn] past participle von *to do* II
**door** [dɔː] Tür I
**doorbell** [ˈdɔːbel] Türklingel IV
**doorstep** [ˈdɔːstep] Türschwelle <V U2, 35>
**dorm** [dɔːm] Schlafsaal <V U2, 198>
**double** [ˈdʌbl] Doppel- <V U2, 198>
to **double-check** [ˌdʌblˈtʃek] genau nachprüfen <III>
to **doubt** [daʊt] bezweifeln IV
**down** [daʊn] entlang; herunter; hinunter; deprimiert III
to break down [ˌbreɪk ˈdaʊn] zerstören; niederreißen <V U3, 66>
down there [ˌdaʊn ˈðeə] dahin; da unten IV
down under [ˌdaʊn ˈʌndə] in Australien <V U1, 26>
to **download** [ˌdaʊnˈləʊd] herunterladen II
**downtown** *(AE)* [ˌdaʊnˈtaʊn] im Stadtzentrum IV
**Dr** [ˈdɒktə] Dr. *(Anrede)* III
**draft** [drɑːft] Entwurf <II>
**drafting** [ˈdrɑːftɪŋ] Formulieren <III>
to **drag** [dræg] schleppen; schleifen; ziehen IV
**dragon** [ˈdrægn] Drache <V U4, 84>
**drama** [ˈdrɑːmə] Theater II; Drama III
**drank** [dræŋk] simple past von *to drink* II
*to **draw** [drɔː] zeichnen II
**drawing** [ˈdrɔːɪŋ] Zeichnung; Bild <IV>
**drawn** [drɔːn] past participle von *to draw* II
**dreadful** [ˈdredfl] furchtbar III
**dream** [driːm] Traum I
*to **dream** [driːm] träumen III
**dreamt** [dremt] simple past, past participle von *to dream* III
**dress** [dres] Kleid I
dress code [ˈdres ˌkəʊd] Kleiderordnung; Bekleidungsvorschriften IV
fancy dress [ˌfænsi ˈdres] Verkleidung; Kostüm I
**dressed** [drest] angezogen; verkleidet III
to get dressed [ˌget ˈdrest] sich anziehen II
**drew** [druː] simple past von *to draw* II
**drink** [drɪŋk] Getränk II
*to **drink** [drɪŋk] trinken II

anything to drink ['eniθɪŋ tə 'drɪŋk] etwas zu trinken II

*to **drive** [draɪv] fahren; treiben IV

to drive sb crazy [ˌdraɪv … 'kreɪzi] jmdn. verrückt machen III

**driven** ['drɪvn] past participle von *to drive* IV

**driver** ['draɪvə] Fahrer; Fahrerin III

driver's license *(AE)* ['draɪvəz ˌlaɪsns] Führerschein IV

lorry driver ['lɒri ˌdraɪvə] LKW-Fahrer; LKW-Fahrerin II

**drizzle** ['drɪzl] Nieselregen <V U2, 198>

to **drop** off [drɒp‿'ɒf] absetzen V U4, 74

to **drop** out of sth [ˌdrɒp‿'aʊt‿əv] etw. abbrechen V U3, 50

**drove** [drəʊv] simple past von *to drive* IV

**drug** [drʌg] Droge V U2, 34

**drum** [drʌm] Trommel <III>

**drumming** ['drʌmɪŋ] Trommel- III

**drunk** [drʌŋk] past participle von *to drink* II; betrunken IV

… to keep them drunk [tə ˌki:p ðəm 'drʌŋk] … dass sie betrunken bleiben IV

to **dry** [draɪ] trocknen IV

**dry** [draɪ] trocken III

**dryer** ['draɪə] Wäschetrockner IV

**duck** [dʌk] Ente <V U1, 27>

**dug** [dʌg] simple past, past participle von *to dig* IV

**dull** [dʌl] langweilig; matt IV

**dumpling** ['dʌmplɪŋ] Kloß II

**dune** [dju:n] Düne <V U3, 205>

**during** ['djʊərɪŋ] während III

to **dust** [dʌst] abstauben; Staub wischen IV

**Dutch** [dʌtʃ] niederländisch; Niederländisch V U2, 29

the Dutch [ðə 'dʌtʃ] die Niederländer V U3, 49

## E

**e.g.** (= for example) [ˌi:'dʒi:] z. B. (= zum Beispiel) <V U3, 64>

**each** [i:tʃ] jeder <I>; pro Stück II

each other [ˌi:tʃ‿'ʌðə] einander; sich; sich gegenseitig III

**bald eagle** [ˌbɔ:ld 'i:gl] Weißkopfseeadler IV

**ear** [ɪə] Ohr II

**early** ['ɜ:li] früh I

to **earn** [ɜ:n] verdienen IV

**earth** [ɜ:θ] die Erde; Boden; Erde; Erdboden IV

**east** [i:st] Osten III

east of ['i:st‿əv] östlich von IV

**easy** ['i:zi] einfach; leicht I

**easy-going** [ˌi:zi'gəʊɪŋ] gelassen; locker V U1, 10

*to **eat** [i:t] essen I

**eaten** ['i:tn] past participle von *to eat* II

**eco-friendly** ['i:kəʊˌfrendli] umweltfreundlich V U4, 74

**ecosystem** ['i:kəʊˌsɪstəm] Ökosystem V U1, 20

**editing** ['edɪtɪŋ] Kontrolle <III>

**edition** [ɪ'dɪʃn] Ausgabe; Auflage; Edition V U3, 54

**education** [ˌedʒʊ'keɪʃn] Ausbildung; Erziehung; Bildung IV

**effect** [ɪ'fekt] Effekt; Wirkung; Auswirkung V U1, 21

**efficient** [ɪ'fɪʃnt] effizient; leistungsfähig V U1, 16

**effort** ['efət] Mühe; Bemühung; Versuch; Arbeitsaufwand V U4, 69

**egg** [eg] Ei I

scrambled egg [ˌskræmbld‿'eg] Rührei II

**eight** [eɪt] acht I

**eighteen** [ˌeɪ'ti:n] achtzehn I

**eighty** ['eɪti] achtzig I

not … **either** [nɒt … 'aɪðə] auch nicht III

**either** … or … ['aɪðə … ɔ: …] entweder … oder … V U3, 50

**elderly** ['eldəli] älter IV

to **elect** [ɪ'lekt] wählen <IV>

**election** [ɪ'lekʃn] Wahl V U3, 49

**elective** [ɪ'lektɪv] Wahlfach IV

**electric** [ɪ'lektrɪk] elektrisch IV

**electrician** [ˌelɪk'trɪʃn] Elektriker; Elektrikerin V U1, 17

**electricity** [ˌelɪk'trɪsəti] Strom; Elektrizität III

**electronic** [ˌelek'trɒnɪk] elektronisch V U4, 68

**element** ['elɪmənt] Element <IV>

**elephant** ['elɪfənt] Elefant I

baby elephant ['beɪbi ˌelɪfənt] Elefantenbaby V U3, 55

**elevator** *(AE)* ['elɪveɪtə] Aufzug; Lift IV

**eleven** [ɪ'levn] elf I

**else** [els] andere; sonst V U2, 34

**e-mail** ['i:meɪl] E-Mail I

**embarrassed** [ɪm'bærəst] verlegen II

**embarrassing** [ɪm'bærəsɪŋ] peinlich IV

**emergency** [ɪ'mɜ:dʒnsi] Notfall III

emergency call [ɪ'mɜ:dʒnsi ˌkɔ:l] Notruf III

emergency service [ɪ'mɜ:dʒnsi ˌsɜ:vɪs] Notdienst; Rettungsdienst III

to **emigrate** ['emɪgreɪt] auswandern; emigrieren IV

**emotion** [ɪ'məʊʃn] Gefühl; Emotion <IV>

to **emphasize** ['emfəsaɪz] betonen <IV>

**empire** ['empaɪə] Reich; Kaiserreich III

**empty** ['emti] leer IV

**emu** ['i:mju:] Emu <V U1, 26>

to **encourage** [ɪn'kʌrɪdʒ] ermutigen; unterstützen V U2, 29

**encyclopedia** [ɪnˌsaɪklə'pi:diə] Enzyklopädie; Lexikon IV

**end** [end] Ende; Schluss II

by the end [ˌbaɪ ði 'end] am Schluss II

endless ['endləs] endlos V U3, 54

in the end [ɪn ði 'end] schließlich; zum Schluss II

to **end** [end] enden; beenden; aufhören IV

**endangered** [ɪn'deɪndʒəd] gefährdet <V U3, 205>

**ending** ['endɪŋ] Schluss; Ende III; Endung <V U1, 13>

happy ending [ˌhæpi 'endɪŋ] Happy End <III>

**enemy** ['enəmi] Feind; Feindin III

**energetic** [ˌenə'dʒetɪk] tatkräftig IV

**energy** ['enədʒi] Energie; Kraft V U4, 74

renewable energy [rɪˌnju:əbl‿ 'enədʒi] erneuerbare Energie V U4, 74

**engine** ['endʒɪn] Motor IV

fire engine ['faɪər‿ˌendʒɪn] Feuerwehrauto II

search engine ['sɜ:tʃ‿ˌendʒɪn] Suchmaschine <IV>

steam engine ['sti:m‿ˌendʒɪn] Dampfmaschine III

**engineer** [ˌendʒɪ'nɪə] Ingenieur; Ingenieurin; Techniker; Technikerin II

**English** ['ɪŋglɪʃ] englisch; Englisch; aus England I

the English [ðɪ 'ɪŋglɪʃ] die Engländer III

to **enjoy** [ɪn'dʒɔɪ] genießen II; mögen III

to enjoy oneself [ɪn'dʒɔɪ] Spaß haben; sich amüsieren III

**enough** [ɪ'nʌf] genug; genügend III

**en-suite** bathroom [ˌɒnswi:t 'bɑ:θrʊm] mit Bad <V U2, 198>

to **enter** ['entə] hineingehen; hereinkommen; betreten; eintreten IV

**entertainment** *(no pl)* [ˌentə'teɪnmənt] Unterhaltung <V U4, 85>

**entry** ['entri] Eintrag IV

entry form ['entri ˌfɔ:m] Anmeldeformular II

**envelope** ['envələʊp] Umschlag; Briefumschlag <V U4, 85>

**environment** [ɪn'vaɪrnmənt] Umgebung; Umwelt V U1, 20

**environmental** [ɪnˌvaɪrn'mentl] Umwelt- <V U4, 212>

**equal** ['i:kwəl] gleich; gleichberechtigt V U3, 52

**equality** [ɪ'kwɒləti] Gleichberechtigung; Ebenbürtigkeit V U3, 52

**equipment** [ɪ'kwɪpmənt] Ausrüstung III

Victorian **era** [vɪkˌtɔ:riən 'ɪərə] viktorianisches Zeitalter III

**eraser** [ɪ'reɪzə] Radiergummi I

**escalator** ['eskəleɪtə] Rolltreppe II

to **escape** [ɪ'skeɪp] entkommen; fliehen; entfliehen; flüchten IV

**especially** [ɪ'speʃli] besonders; vor allem IV

**essay** ['eseɪ] Aufsatz <V U2, 44>

(argumentative) essay [(ɑ:gjəˌmentətɪv) 'eseɪ] Erörterung <V U2, 44>

**establishing shot** [ɪ'stæblɪʃɪŋ ˌʃɒt] Anfangsszene; Eingangsszene <IV>

**euro** ['jʊərəʊ] Euro *(Währung)* III

**European** [ˌjʊərə'pi:ən] europäisch; Europäisch; aus Europa; Europäer; Europäerin IV

**even** ['i:vn] noch; sogar II; lieber IV

even though [ˌi:vn 'ðəʊ] auch wenn; obwohl V U2, 34

**evening** ['i:vnɪŋ] Abend I

in the evenings [ɪn ði 'i:vnɪŋz] abends III

**event** [ɪ'vent] Ereignis; Veranstaltung IV

**ever** ['evə] jemals II

ever since [ˌevə 'sɪns] seitdem V U3, 54

**every** ['evri] jeder I

**everybody** ['evriˌbɒdi] jeder; alle IV

**everyday** ['evrideɪ] alltäglich <IV>

**everyone** ['evriwʌn] jeder I; zusammen; alle II

**everything** ['evriθɪŋ] alles II

**everywhere** ['evriweə] überall V U2, 34

**evidence** ['evɪdns] Beweis; Beleg; Beweismaterial V U3, 54

**evil** ['i:vl] böse; schlecht IV

**exact** [ɪg'zækt] exakt; genau III

**exactly** [ɪg'zæktli] genau IV

**exam** [ɪg'zæm] Prüfung; Examen <IV>

**example** [ɪg'zɑ:mpl] Beispiel IV

for example [fər‿ɪg'zɑ:mpl] zum Beispiel IV

**excellent** ['ekslnt] exzellent; hervorragend IV

**except** [ɪk'sept] außer III

**exchange** [ɪks'tʃeɪndʒ] Austausch IV

to **exchange** [ɪks'tʃeɪndʒ] tauschen; austauschen <III>

**excited** [ɪk'saɪtɪd] aufgeregt; begeistert II

**excitement** [ɪk'saɪtmənt] Aufregung IV

**exciting** [ɪk'saɪtɪŋ] spannend; aufregend I

**excuse** [ɪk'skju:s] Entschuldigung; Ausrede V U1, 15

Excuse me! [ɪk'skju:z mi] Entschuldigung! I

**exercise** ['eksəsaɪz] Übung I

exercise book ['eksəsaɪz ˌbʊk] Übungsheft I

**exhaust fumes** *(pl)* [ɪg'zɔ:st ˌfju:mz] Abgase *(von Fahrzeugen)* V U4, 74

**exhausted** [ɪg'zɔ:stɪd] erschöpft III

**exhibition** [ˌeksɪ'bɪʃn] Ausstellung III

to **exist** [ɪg'zɪst] existieren; bestehen V U1, 10

to **expect** [ɪk'spekt] erwarten III

**expensive** [ɪk'spensɪv] teuer II

**experience** [ɪk'spɪəriəns] Erfahrung; Erlebnis IV

work experience ['wɜ:k‿ɪkˌspɪəriəns] Praktikum; Berufserfahrung V U1, 16

to **experience** [ɪk'spɪəriəns] erleben; erfahren IV

**experienced** [ɪk'spɪəriənst] erfahren V U1, 18

**experiment** [ɪk'sperɪmənt] Versuch II

**expert** ['ekspɜ:t] Experte; Expertin IV

to **explain** [ɪk'spleɪn] erklären III

**explanation** [ˌeksplə'neɪʃn] Erklärung; Erläuterung <IV>

to **explode** [ɪk'spləʊd] explodieren III

to **explore** [ɪk'splɔ:] erkunden; erforschen V U1, 10

**explosion** [ɪk'spləʊʒn] Explosion III

to **express** [ɪk'spres] ausdrücken <III>

**expression** [ɪk'spreʃn] Ausdruck; Wendung; Äußerung <IV>

facial expression ['feɪʃl ɪkˌspreʃn] Gesichtsausdruck; Mimik <IV>

**extinct** [ɪk'stɪŋkt] ausgestorben V U1, 21

**extra** ['ekstrə] zusätzlich; Zusatz- II

extra activities ['ekstrə ˌæktɪvətiz] Zusatzaktivitäten <I>

**extracurricular** [ˌekstrəkə'rɪkjələ] außerhalb des Lehrplans; außerunterrichtlich *(Zusatzunterricht)* IV

**extraordinary** [ɪk'strɔ:dnri] außergewöhnlich V U2, 30

**extremely** [ɪk'stri:mli] äußerst; sehr IV

**extremism** [ɪk'stri:mɪzm] Extremismus V U4, 79
**eye** [aɪ] Auge II
**eye-catching** ['aɪˌkætʃɪŋ] auffallend; plakativ <IV>

## F

**fable** ['feɪbl] Fabel; Märchen III
**face** [feɪs] Gesicht IV
to make funny **faces** [meɪk fʌni 'feɪsɪz] lustige Grimassen schneiden V U3, 58
to **face** [feɪs] gegenüberstehen; konfrontiert werden mit V U3, 54
**facial** expression ['feɪʃl ɪkˌspreʃn] Gesichtsausdruck; Mimik <IV>
**facilities** *(pl)* [fə'sɪlətiz] Einrichtungen <V U2, 47>
**fact** [fækt] Fakt; Tatsache II
in **fact** [ɪn 'fækt] eigentlich; tatsächlich; genau genommen III
**factory** ['fæktri] Fabrik; Werk III
to **fail** [feɪl (ət)] versagen (in/bei); ausfallen; fehlschlagen IV
**fair** [feə] gerecht; fair V U3, 52
**fairness** ['feənəs] Gerechtigkeit V U3, 52
**faith** [feɪθ] Glaube V U2, 34
Yours **faithfully**, [ˌjɔ:z 'feɪθfli] Mit freundlichen Grüßen V U3, 50
**fall** *(AE)* [fɔ:l] Herbst IV
*to **fall** [fɔ:l] fallen I
to **fall** (over) [ˌfɔ:l‿'əʊvə] fallen; hinfallen; umfallen III
to **fall** asleep [ˌfɔ:l‿ə'sli:p] einschlafen III
to **fall** in love (with) [ˌfɔ:l‿ɪn 'lʌv] sich verlieben (in) III
to **fall** off [ˌfɔ:l‿'ɒf] fallen; herunterfallen III
to **fall** out of [ˌfɔ:l‿'aʊt‿əv] herausfallen aus IV
**false** [fɔ:ls] falsch <II>
**familiar** [fə'mɪliə] vertraut; bekannt IV
**family** ['fæmli] Familie I
host **family** ['həʊst ˌfæmli] Gastfamilie IV
**famous** ['feɪməs] berühmt I
**fan** [fæn] Fan I; Ventilator IV
**fancy** ['fænsi] modisch; ausgefallen <V U3, 205>
**fancy** dress [ˌfænsi 'dres] Verkleidung; Kostüm I
**fantastic** [fæn'tæstɪk] fantastisch; großartig II
**fantasy** ['fæntəsi] Fantasie; Fantasy II
**FAQ** (= frequently asked questions) [ˌefeɪ'kju: (ˌfri:kwəntli ˌɑ:skt 'kwestʃənz)] häufig gestellte Fragen <V U4, 80>
**far** [fɑ:] weit III
as **far** as [ˌəz 'fɑ:r‿əz] soweit IV
by **far** [baɪ 'fɑ:] bei weitem <V U2, 46>
so **far** [ˌsəʊ 'fɑ:] bis jetzt IV
**fare** [feə] Fahrpreis III
**farewell** speech [feə'wel spi:tʃ] Abschiedsrede II
**farm** [fɑ:m] Bauernhof I
wind **farm** ['wɪnd fɑ:m] Windpark III
**farmer** ['fɑ:mə] Landwirt; Landwirtin; Bauer; Bäuerin I
**farming** ['fɑ:mɪŋ] Landwirtschaft; Ackerbau IV
**farmland** ['fɑ:mlænd] Ackerland; Ackerboden; Landwirtschaftsflächen IV
**fascinating** ['fæsɪneɪtɪŋ] faszinierend IV
**fashion** *(no pl)* ['fæʃn] Mode IV
out of **fashion** [ˌaʊt‿əv 'fæʃn] altmodisch; nicht mehr aktuell IV
**fashionable** ['fæʃnəbl] modisch V U4, 70
**fast** [fɑ:st] schnell II
**fast** food [ˌfɑ:st 'fu:d] Fastfood I
**fast** food restaurant [ˌfɑ:st fu:d 'restrɒnt] Fastfood-Restaurant I
**fast-paced** ['fɑ:stˌpeɪst] flott; temporeich <V U4, 82>
**father** ['fɑ:ðə] Vater I
**fault** [fɔ:lt] Schuld V U3, 51
**favorite** *(AE)* ['feɪvrɪt] Lieblings- IV
**favourite** ['feɪvrɪt] Lieblings- I; Favorit; Favoritin <V U3, 66>
**fear** [fɪə] Angst; Furcht V U4, 79
**feature** ['fi:tʃə] Merkmal <III>
**February** ['februri] Februar I
**fed** [fed] simple past von *to feed* I; past participle von *to feed* II
*to be **fed** up (with) [bi: fed‿'ʌp (wɪð)] die Nase voll haben (von); sauer sein III
**fee** [fi:] Gebühr V U2, 34
*to **feed** [fi:d] füttern I; ernähren V U2, 37
**feedback** ['fi:dbæk] Feedback; Rückmeldung <II>
*to **feel** [fi:l] (sich) fühlen II
to **feel** sick [ˌfi:l 'sɪk] Übelkeit verspüren; sich schlecht fühlen IV
to **feel** sorry for [ˌfi:l 'sɒri fə] Mitleid haben mit; bedauern III
to make sb **feel** like sth [ˌmeɪk … 'fi:l laɪk] jmdm. das Gefühl geben, etw. zu sein III
**feeling** ['fi:lɪŋ] Gefühl <III>
**fell** [fel] simple past von *to fall* I
**felt** [felt] simple past von *to feel* II
**felt-tip** [ˌfelt'tɪp] Filzstift I
**fence** [fens] Zaun V U3, 54
**fenced** off [ˌfenst‿'ɒf] eingezäunt <V U3, 205>
**feng shui** [ˌfeŋ 'ʃu:i] Feng Shui <V U4, 84>
**ferry** ['feri] Fähre V U2, 30
**festival** ['festɪvl] Festival; Fest III
**fever** ['fi:və] Fieber IV
**few** [fju:] wenige IV
a **few** [ə 'fju:] ein paar; wenige; einige III
science **fiction** [ˌsaɪəns 'fɪkʃn] Science-Fiction I
**fictional** ['fɪkʃnl] fiktiv; fiktional <V U2, 28>
**field** [fi:ld] Feld; Wiese; Weide IV; Gebiet; Bereich V U1, 16
playing **field** ['pleɪɪŋ ˌfi:ld] Sportplatz V U3, 59
**fierceness** ['fɪəsnəs] Grimm; Heftigkeit; Wildheit V U3, 60
**fifteen** [ˌfɪf'ti:n] fünfzehn I
**fifty** ['fɪfti] fünfzig I
**fight** [faɪt] Kampf; Streit III
*to **fight** [faɪt] kämpfen; (sich) streiten III
toy **figure** [ˌtɔɪ 'fɪgə] Spielzeugfigur <V U3, 61>
**file** [faɪl] Datei II

**to fill** [fɪl] (sich) füllen III
to fill in [ˌfɪl‿ˈɪn] ausfüllen <V U1, 15>
**film** [fɪlm] Film I
film maker [ˈfɪlm ˌmeɪkə] Filmemacher; Filmemacherin <III>
**to film** [fɪlm] filmen; drehen <III>
**filming** [ˈfɪlmɪŋ] Filmen; Drehen <IV>
**final** [ˈfaɪnl] letzte <V U1, 23>; endgültig <V U2, 45>
finally [ˈfaɪnli] schließlich; zum Schluss II; endlich; letztlich; zuletzt IV
**financial** [faɪˈnænʃl] finanziell; Finanz- IV
*to **find** [faɪnd] finden; herausfinden I
to find out [ˌfaɪnd‿ˈaʊt] herausfinden I
**fine** [faɪn] schön; gut; in Ordnung II
fine particles [ˌfaɪn ˈpɑːtɪklz] Feinstaub <V U4, 212>
**finger** [ˈfɪŋgə] Finger III
**fingerprint** [ˈfɪŋgəprɪnt] Fingerabdruck II
**to finish** [ˈfɪnɪʃ] beenden; enden; aufhören; fertigstellen; vervollständigen II
**fire** [faɪə] Feuer I
to be on fire [biː ɒn ˈfaɪə] brennen II
to catch fire [ˌkætʃ ˈfaɪə] Feuer fangen <V U1, 26>
fire brigade [ˈfaɪə brɪˌgeɪd] Feuerwehr <III>
fire engine [ˈfaɪər‿ˌendʒɪn] Feuerwehrauto II
**to fire** [faɪə] schießen mit; abfeuern V U2, 41
**fired** [ˈfaɪəd] gefeuert; hinausgeworfen III
**firefighter** [ˈfaɪəˌfaɪtə] Feuerwehrmann; Feuerwehrfrau <V U1, 192>
**firm** [fɜːm] fest; standhaft V U3, 59
**first** [fɜːst] zuerst; als Erstes; erste I
at first [ət ˈfɜːst] zuerst; zunächst IV
first name [ˌfɜːst ˈneɪm] Vorname <III>
**fish** *(sg)* [fɪʃ], **fish** *(pl)* [fɪʃ] Fisch I
**fishing** [ˈfɪʃɪŋ] Angeln; Fischen IV
fishing boat [ˈfɪʃɪŋ ˌbəʊt] Fischerboot V U2, 43
**to fit** [fɪt] passen II
to fit in [ˌfɪt‿ˈɪn] hineinpassen V U2, 35
**fit** [fɪt] fit; in Form III
**fitness centre** [ˈfɪtnəs ˌsentə] Fitness-Studio; Fitnesscenter <V U2, 47>
**jumping fitness** [ˈdʒʌmpɪŋ ˌfɪtnəs] Jumping Fitness *(Trendsportart)* IV
**five** [faɪv] fünf I
**flag** [flæg] Flagge; Fahne II
**flame** [fleɪm] Flamme III
**flamingo** [fləˈmɪŋgəʊ] Flamingo I
**flashback** [ˈflæʃbæk] Rückblende; Flashback V U3, 51
**flat** [flæt] Wohnung I; flach; platt IV
**flew** [fluː] simple past von *to fly* II
**flexible** [ˈfleksɪbl] flexibel <IV>
**flight** [flaɪt] Flug II
flight attendant [ˈflaɪt‿əˌtendnt] Flugbegleiter; Flugbegleiterin <V U1, 192>
**flood** [flʌd] Flut; Hochwasser; Überschwemmung V U4, 78
**floor** [flɔː] Fußboden I; Stockwerk V U4, 81
**florist** [ˈflɒrɪst] Florist; Floristin <V U1, 192>
**flour** [flaʊə] Mehl II
to cover in flour [ˌkʌvər‿ɪn ˈflaʊə] in Mehl wenden IV
**flow** [fləʊ] Fluss; Fließen; Strömung V U4, 78
**flower** [ˈflaʊə] Blume III
**flown** [fləʊn] past participle von *to fly* II
**fluent** [ˈfluːənt] fließend; flüssig III
*to **fly** [flaɪ] fliegen II
to fly open [ˌflaɪ‿ˈəʊpn] auffliegen V U2, 39
**flyer** [ˈflaɪə] Flyer; Faltblatt II
**to focus (on)** [ˈfəʊkəs (ɒn)] sich konzentrieren (auf) <IV>
**fog** [fɒg] Nebel IV
**foggy** [ˈfɒgi] neblig I
**to fold** [fəʊld] falten; klappen IV
**folder** [ˈfəʊldə] Ordner; Mappe <III>
**to follow** [ˈfɒləʊ] folgen; befolgen IV
**follower** [ˈfɒləʊə] Follower; Followerin; Anhänger; Anhängerin IV
**food** [fuːd] Essen; Nahrung; Lebensmittel I
food stall [ˈfuːd ˌstɔːl] Essensstand II
food technology expert [fuːd tekˌnɒlədʒi ˈekspɜːt] Fachkraft für Lebensmitteltechnik <V U1, 192>
food waste [ˈfuːd ˌweɪst] Speisereste; Lebensmittelabfälle V U4, 76
**to fool sb** [fuːl] jmdn. täuschen V U2, 40
**foot** [fʊt] Fuß *(Längenmaß: 30,48 cm)* IV
on foot [ɒn ˈfʊt] zu Fuß I
**foot** *(sg)* [fʊt], **feet** *(pl)* [fiːt] Fuß I
**football** [ˈfʊtbɔːl] Fußball I
**for** [fɔː] für I; seit IV
for ages [fər‿ˈeɪdʒɪz] ewig lange V U4, 70
for a start [ˌfɔːr‿ə ˈstɑːt] zunächst III
for five months [fə ˈfaɪv ˌmʌnθs] fünf Monate lang I
for fun [fə ˈfʌn] zum Spaß III
**forbidden** [fəˈbɪdn] verboten IV
**to force** [fɔːs] zwingen IV
**foreground** [ˈfɔːgraʊnd] Vordergrund III
in the foreground [ɪn ðə ˈfɔːgraʊnd] im Vordergrund III
**foreign** [ˈfɒrɪn] fremd; ausländisch IV
foreign language [ˌfɒrɪn ˈlæŋgwɪdʒ] Fremdsprache <V U4, 84>
**forest** [ˈfɒrɪst] Wald IV
*to **foretell** [fɔːˈtel] vorhersagen III
**forever** [fəˈrevə] für immer; ewig II
*to **forget** [fəˈget] vergessen I
**forgot** [fəˈgɒt] simple past von *to forget* I
**forgotten** [fəˈgɒtn] past participle von *to forget* II
**fork** [fɔːk] Gabel II
**form** [fɔːm] Form <III>
entry form [ˈentri ˌfɔːm] Anmeldeformular II
**to form** [fɔːm] bilden <III>
**former** [ˈfɔːmə] ehemalige; frühere IV
**fortune** [ˈfɔːtʃuːn] Vermögen; Reichtum IV
fortune teller [ˈfɔːtʃuːn ˌtelə] Wahrsager; Wahrsagerin V U4, 68
**forty** [ˈfɔːti] vierzig I

forty

**forum** ['fɔ:rəm] Forum <V U4, 73>
to look **forward** to (+ -ing) [ˌlʊk 'fɔ:wəd tə] sich freuen auf V U1, 16
**fossil** fuel ['fɒsl ˌfju:əl] fossiler Brennstoff <V U4, 75>
**fought** [fɔ:t] simple past, past participle von *to fight* III
to **found** [faʊnd] gründen IV
**found** [faʊnd] simple past von *to find* I
**four** [fɔ:] vier I
**fourteen** [ˌfɔ:'ti:n] vierzehn I
**fourth** [fɔ:θ] vierte I
**free** [fri:] kostenlos III; frei IV
free-time [ˌfri:'taɪm] Freizeit- V U2, 34
free range [ˌfri: 'reɪndʒ] Freiland- II
free time [ˌfri: 'taɪm] Freizeit I
land of the free [ˌlænd‿əv ðə 'fri:] Land der Freien IV
**freedom** *(no pl)* ['fri:dəm] Freiheit; Unabhängigkeit IV
freedom of speech [ˌfri:dəm‿əv 'spi:tʃ] Redefreiheit V U4, 79
*to **freeze** [fri:z] frieren; gefrieren III
**freeze** frame ['fri:z ˌfreɪm] Standbild <I>
**freezing** ['fri:zɪŋ] eiskalt; gefrierend IV
**French** [frentʃ] Französisch I; französisch; aus Frankreich V U2, 29
the French [ðə 'frenʃ] die Franzosen IV
**fresh** [freʃ] frisch II
**freshman** *(AE)* ['freʃmən] Neuntklässler; Neuntklässlerin IV
**Friday** ['fraɪdeɪ] Freitag I
**fridge** [frɪdʒ] Kühlschrank III
**fried** [fraɪd] (in der Pfanne) gebraten II
**friend** [frend] Freund; Freundin I
to make friends [ˌmeɪk 'frendz] Freundschaften schließen I
to see friends [si: 'frendz] Freunde treffen I
to **friend** [frend] befreunden *(jmdn. zu seiner Freundesliste hinzufügen)* IV
**friendly** ['frendli] freundlich; nett III
**friendship** ['frendʃɪp] Freundschaft V U2, 34

to **frighten** the hell out of sb [ˌfraɪtn ðə 'hel‿aʊt‿əv] jmdn. zu Tode erschrecken V U3, 51
**frightening** ['fraɪtnɪŋ] furchterregend IV
**frisbee** ['frɪzbi] Frisbee; Frisbeescheibe I
**from** [frɒm] aus; von I
from behind [ˌfrəm bɪ'haɪnd] von hinten I
at the **front** [ət ðə 'frʌnt] vorn <IV>
at the **front** of [ət ðə 'frʌnt‿əv] an der Spitze (von); im vorderen Bereich II
in **front** of [ɪn 'frʌnt‿əv] vor; davor II
**frost** [frɒst] Frost <V U2, 198>
**froze** [frəʊz] simple past von *to freeze* III
**frozen** ['frəʊzn] past participle von *to freeze* III
**fruit** [fru:t] Frucht; Obst I
to **fry** [fraɪ] braten; frittieren IV
**fuel** ['fju:əl] Brennstoff; Treibstoff <V U4, 212>
fossil fuel ['fɒsl ˌfju:əl] fossiler Brennstoff <V U4, 75>
**full** [fʊl] voll III
full stop [ˌfʊl 'stɒp] Punkt <III>
full length [ˌfʊl 'leŋθ] volle Länge; ganze Länge <IV>
**full-board** [ˌfʊl'bɔ:d] Vollpension <V U2, 198>
**full-time** [ˌfʊl'taɪm] Vollzeit-; Ganztags- V U2, 29
exhaust **fumes** *(pl)* [ɪg'zɔ:st ˌfju:mz] Abgase *(von Fahrzeugen)* V U4, 74
**fun** [fʌn] Freude; Spaß I
for fun [fə 'fʌn] zum Spaß III
**funny** ['fʌni] lustig; witzig I; merkwürdig; seltsam II
to make funny faces [meɪk fʌni 'feɪsɪz] lustige Grimassen schneiden V U3, 58
**fur** [fɜ:] Fell; Pelz <V U1, 27>
**furious** ['fjʊəriəs] wütend III
**further** ['fɜ:ðə] weiter V U3, 50
**furthermore** [ˌfɜ:ðə'mɔ:] überdies; außerdem <V U2, 45>
**future** ['fju:tʃə] Zukunft III; Zukunfts-; zukünftig V U4, 74

## G

**gale** [geɪl] stürmischer Wind <V U2, 198>
**game** [geɪm] Spiel I; Wild V U3, 54
**gamer** ['geɪmə] Spieler *(Computer)*; Spielerin *(Computer)* II
**gaming** ['geɪmɪŋ] Computerspiele- IV
street **gang** ['stri:t ˌgæŋ] Straßengang V U2, 34
**gap** year ['gæp ˌjɪə] Soziales Jahr <V U1, 192>
**garden** ['gɑ:dn] Garten I
**gardener** ['gɑ:dnə] Gärtner; Gärtnerin <V U1, 192>
**garlic** ['gɑ:lɪk] Knoblauch II
**gas** [gæs] Gas III
**gate** [geɪt] Tor III; Gate; Ausgang V U2, 31
**gated** community [ˌgeɪtɪd kə'mju:nəti] bewachte Wohnanlage; geschlossene Wohnanlage V U3, 49
**gateway** ['geɪtweɪ] Tor; Eingangstor IV
to **gather** ['gæðə] (sich) sammeln IV
**gave** [geɪv] simple past von *to give* II
**gay** [geɪ] schwul; homosexuell V U2, 34
**gel** [dʒel] Gel III
hair gel ['heə ˌdʒel] Haargel III
shower gel ['ʃaʊə ˌdʒel] Duschgel III
**general** ['dʒenrl] allgemein <III>
general school certificate [ˌdʒenrl sku:l sə'tɪfɪkət] Hauptschulabschluss <V U1, 192>
in general [ɪn 'dʒenrl] allgemein; generell IV
to **generate** ['dʒenreɪt] generieren; erzeugen V U4, 75
**generation** [ˌdʒenə'reɪʃn] Generation V U1, 12
**generous** ['dʒenrəs] großzügig IV
**genre** ['ʒɑ̃:nrə] Gattung <V U4, 85>
ladies and **gentlemen** [ˌleɪdiz‿ən 'dʒentlmən] meine Damen und Herren V ZI 8
**geocaching** ['dʒiəʊkæʃɪŋ] Geocaching I
**Geography** [dʒi'ɒgrəfi] Geografie; Erdkunde I
**German** ['dʒɜ:mən] Deutsch I; deutsch; aus Deutschland III

**gesture** ['dʒestʃə] Geste; Gebärde <IV>
*to **get** [get] bekommen; werden I; holen II; verstehen III
to get around [ˌget əˈraʊnd] herumkommen III
to get away (from sb) [ˌget‿əˈweɪ frəm] (jmdm.) entkommen; (von jmdm.) wegkommen V U2, 41
to get cold [ˌget ˈkəʊld] frieren III
to get dressed [ˌget ˈdrest] sich anziehen II
to get in [ˈget‿ɪn] hereinkommen I
to get into [ˌget‿ˈɪntə] hineinkommen; hineingelangen IV
to get lost [ˌget ˈlɒst] sich verirren I
to get married [ˌget ˈmærɪd] heiraten II
to get off [ˌget‿ˈɒf] aussteigen II
to get on [ˌget‿ˈɒn] einsteigen III
to get on one's nerves [ˌget‿ɒn wʌnz ˈnɜːvz] auf die Nerven gehen III
to get out [ˌget ˈaʊt] herauskommen III
to get ready [ˌget ˈredi] sich vorbereiten; sich fertig machen IV
to get sth [get] etw. verstehen IV
to get stuck [ˌget ˈstʌk] stecken bleiben IV
to get there [ˈget‿ðeə] hinkommen III
to get tired of sth [ˌget ˈtaɪəd‿əv] etw. sattbekommen; etw. satthaben IV
to get to [ˈget tə] hinkommen zu; gelangen IV
to get to know [ˌget tə ˈnəʊ] kennen lernen II
to get together [ˌge‿təˈgəðə] zusammenkommen; zusammenfinden IV
to get up [ˌget‿ˈʌp] aufstehen I
to get used to (sth) [ˌget ˈjuːzd tə] sich an (etw.) gewöhnen IV
**ghost** [gəʊst] Geist II
ghost town [ˈgəʊst ˌtaʊn] Geisterstadt IV
**giant** [dʒaɪənt] Riesen-; riesig; Riese III
**giraffe** [dʒɪˈrɑːf] Giraffe I
**girl** [gɜːl] Mädchen I
**girlfriend** [ˈgɜːlfrend] Freundin *(in einer Paarbeziehung)* IV
**gist** [dʒɪst] das Wesentliche <III>
*to **give** [gɪv] geben I
to give a speech [gɪv‿ə ˈspiːtʃ] einen Vortrag halten <V U3, 65>
to give a talk [ˌgɪv‿ə ˈtɔːk] einen Vortrag halten <III>
to give away [ˌgɪv‿əˈweɪ] verraten V U2, 40
to give reasons [ˌgɪv ˈriːznz] Gründe nennen; Gründe angeben III
to give sth a miss [ˌgɪv sʌmθɪŋ‿ə ˈmɪs] auf etw. verzichten; etw. bleiben lassen III
to give up [ˌgɪv‿ˈʌp] aufgeben III
**glad** [glæd] froh IV
**glamor** *(AE) (no pl)* [ˈglæmə] Glanz; Zauber IV
**glass** [glɑːs] Glas II
**glasses** *(pl only)* [ˈglɑːsɪz] Brille V U4, 81
**global** [ˈgləʊbl] weltweit; global V U1, 21
to **glorify** [ˈglɔːrɪfaɪ] verherrlichen V U4, 79
**glue** [gluː] Klebstoff I
*to **go** [gəʊ] gehen; fahren I
to go ahead [ˌgəʊ əˈhed] fortfahren; loslegen; vorangehen IV
to go beach combing [gəʊ ˈbiːtʃ ˌkəʊmɪŋ] den Strand nach Strandgut absuchen II
to go camping [ˌgəʊ ˈkæmpɪŋ] campen gehen; zelten II
to go crazy [ˌgəʊ ˈkreɪzi] ausflippen; durchdrehen; verrückt werden V U4, 70
to go on [ˌgəʊ‿ˈɒn] hineingehen II; weitergehen; weitermachen V U3, 50; geschehen; passieren V U3, 55; angehen V U4, 74
to go out [ˌgəʊ‿ˈaʊt] ausgehen III
to go quiet [ˌgəʊ ˈkwaɪət] still werden III
to go red [ˌgəʊ ˈred] rot werden V U3, 60
to go shopping [ˌgəʊ ˈʃɒpɪŋ] einkaufen gehen II
to go sightseeing [gəʊ ˈsaɪtsiːɪŋ] eine Besichtigungstour machen II
to go swimming [ˌgəʊ ˈswɪmɪŋ] schwimmen gehen I
to go to bed [ˌgəʊ tə ˈbed] ins Bett gehen I
to go viral [gəʊ ˈvaɪrl] rasend schnell bekannt werden <V U1, 24>
to go well [ˌgəʊ ˈwel] gut laufen V U1, 18
to go without sth [ˌgəʊ wɪˈðaʊt] ohne etw. auskommen <V U1, 26>
**goal** [gəʊl] Ziel; Tor V U2, 29
**goat** [gəʊt] Ziege III
**God** [gɒd] Gott <IV>
**goddess** [ˈgɒdes] Göttin IV
**gold** [gəʊld] Gold; golden; Gold- III
gold rush [ˈgəʊld ˌrʌʃ] Goldrausch IV
**golden** [ˈgəʊldn] golden; Gold- IV
**gone** [gɒn] past participle von *to go* II
**gonna** (= going to) [ˈgɒnə] werden <V U2, 35>
**good** [gʊd] gut I
to be good at [biː ˈgʊd‿ət] gut sein in/bei I
Good morning. [ˌgʊd ˈmɔːnɪŋ] Guten Morgen. II
good luck [ˌgʊd ˈlʌk] viel Glück II
**Goodbye.** [gʊdˈbaɪ] Auf Wiedersehen. I
**goods** *(no pl)* [gʊdz] Güter; Waren IV
**gospel** [ˈgɒspl] Gospel *(Musikrichtung)* IV
**gossip** [ˈgɒsɪp] Klatsch; Tratsch; Gerede IV
**got** [gɒt] simple past von *to get* I
to have got [hæv ˈgɒt] besitzen; haben II
**governess** [ˈgʌvnəs] Gouvernante; Hauslehrerin V U2, 38
**government** [ˈgʌvnmənt] Regierung IV
state government [ˈsteɪt ˌgʌvnmənt] Landesregierung IV
**GPS** *(Global Positioning System)* [ˌdʒiːpiːˈes] GPS I
to **grab** [græb] schnappen; greifen; ergreifen III
**grade** *(AE)* [greɪd] Note; Klasse IV

**grammar** ['græmə] Grammatik <I>
**grammatical** [grə'mætɪkl] grammatikalisch <IV>
**grand** [grænd] großartig III
**grandad** ['grændæd] Opa III
**grandfather** ['græn,fɑ:ðə] Großvater II
**grandma** ['grænmɑ:] Oma II
**grandmother** ['græn,mʌðə] Großmutter III
**grandparent** ['græn,peərənt] Großelternteil <III>
**grandparents** *(pl)* ['græn,peərənts] Großeltern II
*to take sth for **granted** [,teɪk fə 'grɑ:ntɪd] etw. als selbstverständlich hinnehmen; etw. als gegeben voraussetzen V U4, 79
**graph** [grɑ:f] Diagramm; Schaubild <V U4, 76>
**grass** [grɑ:s] Gras I
**grassy** ['grɑ:si] grasbewachsen <V U3, 205>
**grave** [greɪv] Grab III
**great** [greɪt] großartig; toll I; groß; riesig V U1, 11
**great-grandparents** [,greɪt'græn,peərənts] Urgroßeltern IV
**Greek** [gri:k] griechisch; Griechisch; aus Griechenland IV
**green** [gri:n] grün I; umweltfreundlich <V U4, 212>
**greengrocer's** ['gri:n,grəʊsəz] Obst- und Gemüseladen III
**grew** [gru:] simple past von *to grow* IV
**grey** [greɪ] grau I
grey-haired [,greɪ'heəd] grauhaarig V U3, 59
**grid** [grɪd] Gitter; Raster IV
to **grin** [grɪn] grinsen IV
**groceries** *(pl)* ['grəʊsriz] Lebensmittel IV
**ground** [graʊnd] Boden; Erdboden V U1, 12
**grounds** *(pl)* [graʊndz] Gelände; Gebiet IV
**group** [gru:p] Gruppe I
tutor group ['tju:tə ,gru:p] Klasse *(in einer englischen Schule)* I

*to **grow** [grəʊ] anbauen; züchten; ziehen; wachsen IV; ansteigen V U2, 37
to grow up [,grəʊ_'ʌp] aufwachsen III
**grown** [grəʊn] past participle von *to grow* IV
**grown-up** [,grəʊn_'ʌp] Erwachsener; Erwachsene V U4, 70
to **guarantee** [,gærn'ti:] garantieren; gewährleisten V U4, 79
**guard** [gɑ:d] Wache; Wächter; Wächterin V U3, 51
**guarded** ['gɑ:dɪd] vorsichtig; zurückhaltend III
to **guess** [ges] erraten; raten; überlegen II; vermuten; schätzen IV; annehmen V U4, 70
**guest** [gest] Gast III
guest house ['gest ,haʊs] Gästehaus; Pension V U2, 31
**guestbook** ['gestbʊk] Gästebuch <I>
**guide** [gaɪd] Führer; Führerin II
tour guide ['tʊə ,gaɪd] Reiseleiter; Reiseleiterin V U1, 12
**guided** tour ['gaɪdɪd ,tɔ:] Führung <IV>
**guilty** ['gɪlti] schuldig V U3, 51
**guinea** pig ['gɪni ,pɪg] Meerschweinchen I
**guitar** [gɪ'tɑ:] Gitarre III
**gun** [gʌn] Schusswaffe IV
**guy** [gaɪ] Typ; Kerl IV
**guys** *(pl)* [gaɪz] Leute II
**gym**(nasium) [dʒɪm('neɪziəm)] Turnhalle IV
**gymnasium** [dʒɪm'neɪziəm] Fitnessraum III

## H

**habit** ['hæbɪt] Gewohnheit <V U4, 72>
**had** [hæd] simple past von *to have* I; past participle von *to have* II
**hail** [heɪl] Hagel <V U2, 198>
**hair** [heə] Haar; Haare III
hair gel ['heə dʒel] Haargel III
hair straightener ['heə ,streɪtnə] Haarglätter IV
**hairbrush** ['heəbrʌʃ] Haarbürste III
**haircut** ['heəkʌt] Haarschnitt II
to have a haircut ['heəkʌt] sich die Haare schneiden lassen II
**hairdresser** ['heə,dresə] Friseur; Friseurin II
**hairdryer** ['heə,draɪə] Fön III
**half** *(sg)* [hɑ:f], **halves** *(pl)* [hɑ:vz] (die) Hälfte IV
**half** [hɑ:f] halb III
half past (two) [,hɑ:f 'pɑ:st] halb (drei) I
half a million [,hɑ:f_ə 'mɪljən] eine halbe Million III
**half-board** [,hɑ:f'bɔ:d] Halbpension <V U2, 198>
**hall** [hɔ:l] Flur; Diele; Korridor IV
town hall [,taʊn 'hɔ:l] Rathaus II
**ham** [hæm] Schinken II
**hand** [hænd] Hand I
*to **hang** [hæŋ] hängen II; erhängen IV
to hang out (with) [,hæŋ_'aʊt (wɪð)] rumhängen (mit); sich treffen (mit); sich herumtreiben (mit) IV
to **happen** ['hæpn] geschehen; passieren II
**happiness** ['hæpɪnəs] Glück; Zufriedenheit; Fröhlichkeit V U2, 35
**happy** ['hæpi] glücklich I
happy ending [,hæpi 'endɪŋ] Happy End <III>
to keep sb happy [,ki:p 'hæpi] jmdn. bei Laune halten V U1, 12
Happy birthday! [,hæpi 'bɜ:θdeɪ] Alles Gute zum Geburtstag! I
**harbor** *(AE)* ['hɑ:bə] Hafen IV
**harbour** ['hɑ:bə] Hafen II
**hard** [hɑ:d] hart; schwer; schwierig II
**hard-working** [,hɑ:d'wɜ:kɪŋ] fleißig IV
**harp** [hɑ:p] Harfe <III>
**harvest** ['hɑ:vɪst] Ernte <IV>
**hat** [hæt] Hut II
to **hate** [heɪt] hassen; nicht mögen I
*to **have** [hæv] haben I; essen II
to have a haircut ['heəkʌt] sich die Haare schneiden lassen II
to have a look [,hæv_ə 'lʊk] anschauen II
to have breakfast [,hæv 'brekfəst] frühstücken I
to have got [hæv 'gɒt] besitzen; haben II

to have no idea [hæv ˌnəʊ aɪ'dɪə] keine Ahnung haben IV
to have to ['hæv tə] müssen II
Have a seat. [ˌhæv‿ə 'siːt] Setzen Sie sich.; Setz dich. IV
**he** [hiː] er I
**head** [hed] Kopf II
head chef ['hed ʃef] Chefkoch II; Chefköchin II
head first ['hed fɜːst] kopfüber III
to shake one's head [ˌʃeɪk wʌns 'hed] den Kopf schütteln V U3, 60
**headache** ['hedeɪk] Kopfschmerzen; Kopfweh II
**heading** ['hedɪŋ] Überschrift; Titel <III>
**headline** ['hedlaɪn] Schlagzeile; Überschrift IV
**headphones** *(pl)* ['hedfəʊnz] Kopfhörer IV
**headteacher** [ˌhed'tiːtʃə] Schulleiter; Schulleiterin V U3, 60
**health** [helθ] Gesundheit V U2, 35; Gesundheits-; gesundheitlich V U4, 69
health insurance ['helθ‿ɪnˌʃʊərns] Krankenversicherung V U3, 51
**healthy** ['helθi] gesund III
*to **hear** [hɪə] hören I
**heard** [hɜːd] simple past von *to hear* I; past participle von *to hear* II
**heart** [hɑːt] Herz III
by heart [ˌbaɪ 'hɑːt] auswendig <V U4, 83>
**heat** [hiːt] Hitze IV
**heatwave** ['hiːtˌweɪv] Hitzewelle <V U2, 198>
**heavy** ['hevi] schwer; stark II
**hectic** ['hektɪk] hektisch <IV>
**hedge** [hedʒ] Hecke <V U3, 205>
**height** [haɪt] Höhe II
**held** [held] simple past, past participle von *to hold* III
**helicopter** ['helɪkɒptə] Helikopter; Hubschrauber IV
to frighten the **hell** out of sb [ˌfraɪtn ðə 'hel‿aʊt‿əv] jmdn. zu Tode erschrecken V U3, 51
**Hello.** [hə'ləʊ] Hallo. I
Hello there. [hə'ləʊ ˌðeə] Hallo.; Grüß dich. I
**helmet** ['helmət] Helm III

**help** [help] Hilfe II
helpful ['helpfl] hilfreich; nützlich III; hilfsbereit IV
to **help** [help] helfen I
to help oneself [ˌhelp wʌn'self] sich bedienen III
I couldn't help but ... [ˌaɪ kʊdnt 'help bʌt] Ich konnte nicht anders als ... III
**helper** ['helpə] Helfer; Helferin IV
**her** [hɜː] ihr; ihre; sie I
**here** [hɪə] hier I
right here [ˌraɪt 'hɪə] genau hier <V U3, 65>
Here you are. [ˌhɪə ju‿'ɑː] Bitte schön. I
**hero** *(sg)* ['hɪərəʊ], **heroes** *(pl)* ['hɪərəʊz] Held III
**hers** [hɜːz] ihre II
**herself** [hɜː'self] sie selbst; sich (selbst) III
**Hi.** [haɪ] Hi.; Hallo. I
to say hi to [ˌseɪ 'haɪ tə] grüßen; Grüße ausrichten I
**hid** [hɪd] simple past von *to hide* III
**hidden** ['hɪdn] past participle von *to hide* III
*to **hide** [haɪd] (sich) verstecken III
**high** [haɪ] hoch; groß I
high school ['haɪ ˌskuːl] Highschool *(weiterführende Schule, Oberstufe)* IV
**highlighted** ['haɪlaɪtɪd] hervorgehoben <III>
**high-tech** [ˌhaɪ'tek] Hightech- IV
to **hijack** ['haɪdʒæk] kapern; entführen <V U2, 39>
to **hike** [haɪk] wandern II
**hiking** ['haɪkɪŋ] Wandern III
**hill** [hɪl] Berg; Hügel IV
hilly ['hɪli] hügelig <V U3, 205>
**him** [hɪm] ihm; ihn I
**himself** [hɪm'self] sich (selbst); er selbst III
to **hire** [haɪə] mieten; anheuern; einstellen IV
**his** [hɪz] sein I; seins; seiner II
**historic** [hɪ'stɒrɪk] historisch IV
**historical** [hɪ'stɒrɪkl] historisch; geschichtlich <III>
**history** ['hɪstri] Geschichte III

**hit** [hɪt] Hit; Treffer IV
*to **hit** [hɪt] treffen; schlagen II; (sich) stoßen; anstoßen; fahren gegen III
**hit** [hɪt] simple past, past participle von *to hit* II
**hobby** ['hɒbi] Hobby III
*to **hold** [həʊld] halten; festhalten III
**hole** [həʊl] Loch I
**holiday** ['hɒlədeɪ] Ferien; Urlaub I; Feiertag III
holiday job ['hɒlədeɪ ˌdʒɒb] Ferienjob <V U1, 192>
**home** [həʊm] Zuhause; Heim; nach Hause I; Heimat <V U1, 23>
at home [ət 'həʊm] zu Hause I
back home [bæk 'həʊm] zu Hause II
home country [ˌhəʊm 'kʌntri] Heimat; Heimatland IV
to make oneself at home [ˌmeɪk wʌnself ət 'həʊm] sich wie zu Hause fühlen III
**Homecoming** *(AE)* ['həʊmˌkʌmɪŋ] Ehemaligentreffen IV
**homeless shelter** [ˌhəʊmləs 'ʃeltə] Obdachlosenheim <V U3, 205>
**homepage** ['həʊmpeɪdʒ] Homepage III
**homeroom** ['həʊmruːm] erste Stunde *(in der Schule)* IV
**homeschooled** ['həʊmˌskuːld] zu Hause unterrichtet <IV>
**homeschooling** ['həumˌskuːlɪŋ] Hausunterricht <IV>
*to be **homesick** [biː 'həʊmsɪk] Heimweh haben III
**homework** ['həʊmwɜːk] Hausaufgabe(n) I
to do homework [ˌduː 'həʊmwɜːk] Hausaufgabe(n) machen I
**honest** ['ɒnɪst] ehrlich III
honestly ['ɒnɪstli] ehrlich IV
**honesty** ['ɒnɪsti] Ehrlichkeit V U2, 35
**honor** *(AE)* ['ɒnə] Ehre IV
to **hoover** ['huːvə] staubsaugen II
to **hop** [hɒp] hüpfen <V U1, 26>
**hope** [həʊp] Hoffnung IV
hopeful ['həʊpfl] hoffnungsvoll III
to **hope** [həʊp] hoffen I
**hopping** ['hɒpɪŋ] Hüpfen; Hopping V U2, 30

**horrible** ['hɒrəbl] schrecklich; furchtbar III
horror ['hɒrə] Horror; Schrecken; Entsetzen V U2, 40
**horse** [hɔːs] Pferd I
horse riding ['hɔːs ˌraɪdɪŋ] Reiten I
**hospital** ['hɒspɪtl] Hospital; Krankenhaus I
**host** [həʊst] Talkmaster; Gastgeber; Gastgeberin V U4, 74
host family ['həʊst ˌfæmli] Gastfamilie IV
to **host** [həʊst] ausrichten <V U3, 66>
**hostel** ['hɒstl] Herberge V U2, 30
youth hostel ['juːθ ˌhɒstl] Jugendherberge III
**hot** [hɒt] heiß I
hot dog ['hɒt ˌdɒg] Hot Dog *(Würstchen im Brötchen)* IV
**hotel** [həʊ'tel] Hotel II
**hour** [aʊə] Stunde I
rush hour ['rʌʃ ˌaʊə] Hauptverkehrszeit IV
working hours *(pl)* ['wɜːkɪŋ ˌaʊəz] Arbeitszeit IV
**house** [haʊs] Haus I
around the house [ə'raʊnd ðə haʊs] im Haus I
State House *(AE)* ['steɪt ˌhaʊs] Regierungsgebäude IV
**how** [haʊ] wie I
How about …? [ˌhaʊ‿ə'baʊt] Wie wäre es mit … ? II
How are you doing? [ˌhaʊ‿ə jə 'duːɪŋ] Wie geht's dir? IV
How are you? [ˌhaʊ‿'ɑː jə] Wie geht es dir? I
How do I get there? [ˌhaʊ du aɪ 'get ðeə] Wie komme ich dahin? III
how many [ˌhaʊ 'meni] wie viele II
how much [ˌhaʊ 'mʌtʃ] wie sehr III
How much (is/are) …? [ˌhaʊ 'mʌtʃ‿ɪz/ɑː] Wie viel (kostet/kosten) …? I
How old are you? [haʊ‿'əʊld‿ə juː] Wie alt bist du? I
How's it going? [ˌhaʊz‿ɪt 'gəʊɪŋ] Wie geht's?; Wie läuft's? IV
**however** [haʊ'evə] jedoch III
**huge** [hjuːdʒ] riesig; riesengroß IV
**human** ['hjuːmən] menschlich III
human rights *(pl)* [ˌhjuːmən 'raɪts] Menschenrechte *(Pl.)* V U4, 79
**humid** ['hjuːmɪd] schwül; feucht <V U2, 198>
a/one **hundred** ['hʌndrəd] einhundert; hundert I
**hung** [hʌŋ] simple past, past participle von *to hang* II
**hungry** ['hʌŋgri] hungrig I
to **hunt** [hʌnt] jagen V U2, 41
**hunter** ['hʌntə] Jäger; Jägerin IV
**hurricane** ['hʌrɪkən] Orkan; Wirbelsturm V U2, 28
**hurry** ['hʌri] Eile; Hast V U4, 69
to **hurry** ['hʌri] sich beeilen II
*to **hurt** [hɜːt] weh tun; verletzen II
**hurt** [hɜːt] simple past, past participle von *to hurt* II; verletzt II
**husband** ['hʌzbənd] Ehemann IV

# I

**I** [aɪ] ich I
I don't know! [ˌaɪ ˌdəʊnt 'nəʊ] Ich weiß (es) nicht! I
I wouldn't like (to) … [aɪ 'wʊdnt laɪk (tə)] Ich möchte nicht …; Ich würde nicht gerne … I
I'd like (to) … (= I would like to) [aɪd 'laɪk (tə)] Ich möchte …; Ich würde gerne … I
I'd love to … (= I would love to) [aɪd 'lʌv tə] Ich würde sehr gern … III
I'd rather [aɪd 'rɑːðə] ich würde lieber III
I'm from … ['aɪm ˌfrɒm] Ich komme aus … I
I'm sorry. [aɪm 'sɒrɪ] Es tut mir leid.; Entschuldigung. I
**ice** [aɪs] Eis IV
ice cream [ˌaɪs 'kriːm] Eiscreme; Eis I
ice rink ['aɪs ˌrɪŋk] Eislaufbahn <IV>
**iceberg** ['aɪsbɜːg] Eisberg III
**ice-cold** [aɪs'kəʊld] eiskalt IV
**icy** ['aɪsi] eisig <V U2, 198>
**ID** [ˌaɪ'diː] Ausweis; Personalausweis III
ID card [ˌaɪ'diː ˌkɑːd] Ausweis; Personalausweis <V U2, 198>
**idea** [aɪ'dɪə] Idee; Ahnung I
to have no idea [hæv ˌnəʊ aɪ'dɪə] keine Ahnung haben IV
**identity** [aɪ'dentəti] Identität IV
**if** [ɪf] wenn; falls II
**ignorance** ['ɪgnərns] Ignoranz; Unwissenheit V U1, 13
**ignorant** ['ɪgnərnt] ignorant; unwissend V U1, 12
to **ignore** [ɪg'nɔː] ignorieren; außer Acht lassen V U1, 12
**ill** [ɪl] krank; schlecht II
**image** ['ɪmɪdʒ] Bild; Image <V U3, 63>
to **imagine** (sth) [ɪ'mædʒɪn] sich (etw.) vorstellen IV
**immigrant** ['ɪmɪgrənt] Immigrant; Immigrantin; Einwanderer; Einwanderin IV
to **immigrate** ['ɪmɪgreɪt] einwandern; immigrieren IV
**immigration** [ˌɪmɪ'greɪʃn] Immigration; Einwanderung; Zuwanderung IV
**impact** ['ɪmpækt] Einfluss; Auswirkung IV
speech **impaired** ['spiːtʃ ɪmˌpeəd] sprachbehindert IV
**imperative** [ɪm'perətɪv] Imperativ <III>
**import** [ɪm'pɔːt] Importprodukt <V U1, 26>
to **import** [ɪm'pɔːt] importieren; einführen <V U4, 75>
**important** [ɪm'pɔːtnt] wichtig; einflussreich II
**impossible** [ɪm'pɒsəbl] unmöglich III
to **impress** [ɪm'pres] beeindrucken III
**impression** [ɪm'preʃn] Eindruck <IV>
to **improve** [ɪm'pruːv] verbessern V U4, 74
**in** [ɪn] in I; drinnen II
in addition [ˌɪn‿ə'dɪʃn] zusätzlich; außerdem V U1, 11
in conclusion [ˌɪn kən'kluːʒn] abschließend; zum Abschluss <V U2, 45>
in fact [ɪn 'fækt] eigentlich; tatsächlich; genau genommen III
in order to [ɪn‿'ɔːdə tə] um … zu; mit der Absicht V U2, 40

in the background [ɪn ðə 'bækgraʊnd] im Hintergrund III
in the distance [ˌɪn ðə 'dɪstns] in der Ferne IV
in the foreground [ɪn ðə 'fɔ:graʊnd] im Vordergrund III
in the long run [ˌɪn ðə 'lɒŋ rʌn] langfristig; auf Dauer V U4, 74
in the middle [ɪn ðə 'mɪdl] in der Mitte III
in tow [ɪn 'təʊ] im Schlepptau IV
in turn [ɪn 'tɜ:n] dagegen; im Gegenzug V U1, 20
in August [ɪn 'ɔ:gəst] im August I
in front of [ɪn 'frʌnt‿əv] vor; davor II
in my opinion [ɪn 'maɪ‿əˌpɪnjən] meiner Meinung nach III
in the afternoon [ˌɪn ði ˌɑ:ftə'nu:n] nachmittags I
in the centre of [ˌɪn ðə 'sentər‿əv] in der Mitte von III
in the country [ɪn ðə 'kʌntri] auf dem Land I
in the end [ɪn ði 'end] schließlich; zum Schluss II
in the evenings [ɪn ði 'i:vnɪŋz] abends III
in the south of [ˌɪn ðə 'saʊθ‿əv] im Süden von III
in the world [ɪn ðə 'wɜ:ld] auf der Welt II
in time [ɪn 'taɪm] rechtzeitig I
to **include** [ɪn'klu:d] enthalten; beinhalten IV; einbeziehen; aufnehmen; einbinden; einschließen <V U4, 73>
*to be **included** [bi: ɪn'klu:dɪd] enthalten sein III
**including** [ɪn'klu:dɪŋ] einschließlich V U2, 34
**increase** ['ɪnkri:s] Zunahme; Wachstum; Anstieg V U1, 20
to **increase** [ɪn'kri:s] zunehmen; vergrößern IV; erhöhen; steigern V U4, 74
**independence** [ˌɪndɪ'pendəns] Unabhängigkeit IV
**Indian** ['ɪndiən] indisch II
**individual** [ˌɪndɪ'vɪdʒuəl] einzeln; individuell V U4, 74
**indoor** [ˌɪn'dɔ:] Hallen-; Innen- III
**industrial** [ɪn'dʌstriəl] Industrie-; industriell <V U1, 192>
Industrial Revolution [ɪnˌdʌstriəl revl'u:ʃn] industrielle Revolution III
**industry** ['ɪndəstri] Industrie III
tourist industry ['tʊərɪst‿ˌɪndəstri] Tourismus V U2, 28
**inequality** [ˌɪnɪ'kwɒləti] Ungleichheit V U3, 52
**influence** ['ɪnfluəns] Einfluss IV
to **influence** ['ɪnfluəns] beeinflussen IV
**information** *(no pl)* [ˌɪnfə'meɪʃn] Information; Informationen I
information desk [ɪnfə'meɪʃn ˌdesk] Information II
**informative** [ɪn'fɔ:mətɪv] informativ IV
*to keep sb **informed** [ˌki:p‿ɪn'fɔ:md] jmdn. auf dem Laufenden halten IV
**ingredient** [ɪn'gri:diənt] Zutat II
**inhabitant** [ɪn'hæbɪtnt] Einwohner; Einwohnerin; Bewohner; Bewohnerin III
**inhabited** [ɪn'hæbɪtɪd] bewohnt V U2, 28
**injection** [ɪn'dʒekʃn] Spritze III
**injury** ['ɪndʒri] Verletzung III
**injustice** [ɪn'dʒʌstɪs] Ungerechtigkeit V U3, 52
**innocent** ['ɪnəsnt] unschuldig IV
**innovation** [ˌɪnə'veɪʃn] Innovation; Neuheit IV
**insect** ['ɪnsekt] Insekt III
**inside** [ˌɪn'saɪd] in … hinein II; in; innen in; im Innern III; innen; drinnen IV
**inspection** [ɪn'spekʃn] Inspektion; Kontrolle; Überprüfung IV
to **inspire** [ɪn'spaɪə] inspirieren; anregen <V U3, 66>
to **install** [ɪn'stɔ:l] anschließen; installieren; einrichten V U4, 74
**instead** [ɪn'sted] stattdessen IV
**instructor** [ɪn'strʌktə] Lehrer; Lehrerin III
**instrument** ['ɪnstrəmənt] Instrument <III>
**insurance** [ɪn'ʃʊərns] Versicherung V U3, 51
health insurance ['helθ‿ɪnˌʃʊərns] Krankenversicherung V U3, 51
**intelligent** [ɪn'telɪdʒnt] intelligent; klug; vernünftig III
**interact** [ˌɪntə'ræk] interagieren; zusammenspielen <IV>
**interest** ['ɪntrəst] Interesse V U1, 16
**interest (in)** ['ɪntrəst (ɪn)] Interesse (an) <III>
to **interest** ['ɪntrəst] interessieren <IV>
*to be **interested** in [bi: 'ɪntrəstɪd‿ɪn] sich interessieren für; interessiert sein an III
**interesting** ['ɪntrəstɪŋ] interessant I
**intermediate** [ɪntə'mi:diət] Mittel-; mittleres Niveau V U1, 16
intermediate school certificate [ˌɪntəmi:diət sku:l sə'tɪfɪkət] Realschulabschluss <V U1, 192>
**international** [ˌɪntə'næʃnl] international V U2, 29
**internet** ['ɪntənet] Internet II
to surf the internet [ˌsɜ:f ði 'ɪntənet] im Internet surfen II
**internship** ['ɪntɜ:nʃɪp] Berufspraktikum <V U1, 192>
to **interrupt** [ˌɪntə'rʌpt] unterbrechen IV
**intersection** *(AE)* [ˌɪntə'sekʃn] Kreuzung IV
**interview** ['ɪntəvju:] Interview; Befragung II; Vorstellungsgespräch IV
to **interview** ['ɪntəvju:] interviewen; befragen I
**interviewee** [ˌɪntəvju'i:] Befragter; Befragte <V U1, 25>
**interviewer** ['ɪntəvju:ə] Interviewer; Interviewerin; Befrager; Befragerin IV
**into** ['ɪntu] in; hinein IV
to **introduce** [ˌɪntrə'dju:s] vorstellen III; einführen; einleiten IV
**introduction** [ˌɪntrə'dʌkʃn] Einleitung; Einführung III; Vorstellung <IV>
to **invade** [ɪn'veɪd] einmarschieren (in); eindringen (in) III
to **invent** [ɪn'vent] erfinden III
**invention** [ɪn'venʃn] Erfindung III

**inventor** [ɪn'ventə] Erfinder; Erfinderin III
**invitation** [ˌɪnvɪ'teɪʃn] Einladung I
to **invite** [ɪn'vaɪt] einladen I
*to be **involved** [bi: ɪn'vɒlvd] sich beteiligen; sich engagieren V U2, 34
**Irish** ['aɪrɪʃ] irisch; Irisch III
the Irish [ði 'aɪrɪʃ] die Iren III
to **iron** [aɪən] bügeln IV
**is** [ɪz] ist I
**island** ['aɪlənd] Insel II
**isn't it?** ['ɪznt‿ɪt] nicht wahr?; stimmt's? II
**isolation** *(no pl)* [ˌaɪs'leɪʃn] Isolation; Trennung V U1, 10
**it** [ɪt] es I
**IT** (Information Technology) [ˌaɪ'ti:, ɪnfəˌmeɪʃn tek'nɒlədʒi] Informatik; Informationstechnik I
**Italian** [ɪ'tæliən] italienisch; Italienisch; Italiener; Italienerin II
**its** [ɪts] sein; ihr III
**itself** [ɪt'self] (sich) selbst III
**ivory** ['aɪvri] Elfenbein V U3, 54

## J

**jacket** ['dʒækɪt] Jacke II
jacket potato [ˌdʒækɪt pə'teɪtəʊ] Ofenkartoffel II
**jail** [dʒeɪl] Gefängnis IV
**jam** [dʒæm] Marmelade; Konfitüre III
traffic jam ['træfɪk ˌdʒæm] Stau IV
**Jamaican** [dʒə'meɪkən] jamaikanisch II
**January** ['dʒænjuri] Januar I
**Japanese** [ˌdʒæpən'i:z] japanisch; Japanisch; aus Japan; Japaner; Japanerin IV
**jar** [dʒɑ:] Glas III
**jazz** [dʒæz] Jazz *(Musikrichtung)* IV
**jealous** ['dʒeləs] eifersüchtig; neidisch II
**jeans** *(pl)* [dʒi:nz] Jeans I
**jersey** ['dʒɜ:zi] Trikot <V U3, 66>
**jeweller's** ['dʒu:ələz] Juwelierladen III
**jewellery** ['dʒu:əlri] Schmuck II
**job** [dʒɒb] Job I; Aufgabe; Tätigkeit; Arbeit; Beruf II
job title ['dʒɒb ˌtaɪtl] Stellenbezeichnung; Berufsbezeichnung IV
to **join** [dʒɔɪn] sich anschließen III; verbinden <V U2, 33>
**joke** [dʒəʊk] Witz I
to **joke** [dʒəʊk] Witze machen; scherzen III
**journalism** ['dʒɜ:nlɪzm] Journalistik; Journalismus IV
**journalist** ['dʒɜ:nlɪst] Journalist; Journalistin V U3, 51
**journey** ['dʒɜ:ni] Fahrt; Reise III
to **joust** [dʒaʊst] einen Turnierzweikampf austragen; turnieren III
**jousting** ['dʒaʊstɪŋ] Turnierzweikampf III
**joy** [dʒɔɪ] Freude; Vergnügen V U3, 59
**judge** [dʒʌdʒ] Juror; Jurorin II
**juice** [dʒu:s] Saft II
**July** [dʒʊ'laɪ] Juli I
**jumble sale** ['dʒʌmbl ˌseɪl] Flohmarkt II
to **jump** [dʒʌmp] zusammenzucken; erschrecken III; springen IV
jumping fitness ['dʒʌmpɪŋ ˌfɪtnəs] Jumping Fitness *(Trendsportart)* IV
**June** [dʒu:n] Juni I
**jungle** ['dʒʌŋgl] Dschungel IV
**just** [dʒʌst] gerade (eben); soeben; nur II; einfach IV
**justice** ['dʒʌstɪs] Gerechtigkeit; Justiz V U3, 52

## K

**kangaroo** [ˌkæŋgr'u:] Känguru V U1, 10
*to **keep** [ki:p] halten II; aufbewahren; behalten IV; bleiben V U2, 34
to keep a record of sth [ˌki:p‿ə 'rekɔ:d‿əv] über etw. Buch führen V U4, 70
to keep calm [ˌki:p 'kɑ:m] Ruhe bewahren; ruhig bleiben <IV>
to keep cool [ˌki:p 'ku:l] Ruhe bewahren <III>
to keep going [ki:p 'gəʊɪŋ] weitergehen; weitermachen IV
to keep in mind [ˌki:p‿ɪn 'maɪnd] nicht vergessen; im Auge behalten <V U1, 25>
to keep in touch [ˌki:p‿ɪn 'tʌtʃ] in Verbindung bleiben II
to keep one's mouth shut [ˌki:p wʌnz 'maʊθ ˌʃʌt] den Mund halten V U2, 40
to keep out [ˌki:p‿'aʊt] draußen halten III
to keep quiet [ˌki:p 'kwaɪət] ruhig sein <III>
to keep safe [ˌki:p 'seɪf] schützen III
to keep sb happy [ˌki:p 'hæpi] jmdn. bei Laune halten V U1, 12
to keep sb informed [ˌki:p‿ɪn'fɔ:md] jmdn. auf dem Laufenden halten IV
… to keep them drunk [tə ˌki:p ðəm 'drʌŋk] … dass sie betrunken bleiben IV
**keeper** ['ki:pə] Pfleger; Pflegerin <V U1, 192>
**kept** [kept] simple past, past participle von *to keep* II
**ketchup** ['ketʃʌp] Ketchup II
**key** [ki:] Legende <IV>
**keyword** ['ki:ˌwɜ:d] Stichwort; Schlüsselbegriff <III>
to **kick** [kɪk] schießen; treten III
**kid** [kɪd] Kind II
**kidney** bean ['kɪdni ˌbi:n] Kidneybohne II
to **kill** [kɪl] töten III
**killing** ['kɪlɪŋ] Tötung; Ermordung IV
**kilogram** (kg) ['kɪləgræm] Kilogramm (kg) I
**kilometre** (km) [kɪ'lɒmɪtə] Kilometer (km) I
**kilt** [kɪlt] Schottenrock; Kilt III
**kind** [kaɪnd] freundlich; nett II; Art; Sorte III
**king** [kɪŋ] König III
**kiss** [kɪs] Kuss II
to **kiss** [kɪs] küssen III
**kitchen** ['kɪtʃɪn] Küche I
**knee** [ni:] Knie III
**knew** [nju:] simple past von *to know* IV
**knife** *(sg)* [naɪf], **knives** *(pl)* [naɪvz] Messer II
**knight** [naɪt] Ritter III
to **knock down** [ˌnɒk 'daʊn] niederreißen; abreißen <V U4, 84>

*to **know** [nəʊ] wissen; kennen I; verstehen IV
to get to know [ˌget tə ˈnəʊ] kennen lernen II
to let sb know [ˌlet ˈnəʊ] jmdn. informieren; jmdm. Bescheid geben; jmdm. Bescheid sagen V U1, 15
I don't know! [ˌaɪ ˌdəʊnt ˈnəʊ] Ich weiß (es) nicht! I

**known** [nəʊn] past participle von *to know* IV
to be known as [biː ˈnəʊn‿əz] bekannt sein als V U1, 11
best known [ˌbest ˈnəʊn] weltberühmt IV

**koala** [kəʊˈɑːlə] Koala V U1, 10

**kookaburra** [ˈkʊkəˌbʌrə] Jägerliest *(australische Vogelart)* <V U1, 27>

**kung fu** [ˌkʊŋ ˈfuː] Kung-Fu <V U4, 85>

## L

**label** [ˈleɪbl] Etikett; Beschriftung <IV>

to **label** [ˈleɪbl] beschriften <III>

**labour** [ˈleɪbə] Arbeitskräfte <V U2, 46>
child labour [ˌtʃaɪld ˈleɪbə] Kinderarbeit <IV>

**ladder** [ˈlædə] Leiter I

**lady** [ˈleɪdi] Dame; Frau II
ladies and gentlemen [ˌleɪdiz‿ən ˈdʒentlmən] meine Damen und Herren V ZI 8

**laid** [leɪd] simple past, past participle von *to lay* II

**lain** [leɪn] past participle von *to lie* V U2, 38

**lake** [leɪk] See III

**lamb** [læm] Lamm II

**lame** [leɪm] lahm; schwach IV

**lamp** [læmp] Lampe I

**land** [lænd] Land II
land of the free [ˌlænd‿əv ðə ˈfriː] Land der Freien IV

to **land** [lænd] landen IV

**landfill site** [ˌlænfɪl ˈsaɪt] Mülldeponie <V U4, 212>

**landlord** [ˈlændlɔːd] Eigentümer II

**landmark** [ˈlænmɑːk] Wahrzeichen IV

**landowner** [ˈlændˌəʊnə] Grundbesitzer; Grundbesitzerin IV

**landscape** [ˈlændskeɪp] Landschaft IV

**lane** [leɪn] Fahrspur; Weg; Gasse IV

**language** [ˈlæŋgwɪdʒ] Sprache II
body language [ˈbɒdi ˌlæŋgwɪdʒ] Körpersprache <III>
foreign language [ˌfɒrɪn ˈlæŋgwɪdʒ] Fremdsprache <V U4, 84>
language detectives [ˈlæŋgwɪdʒ ˌdɪtektɪvz] Sprachdetektive <I>
language tip [ˌlæŋgwɪdʒ ˈtɪp] Grammatikhinweis <I>
official language [əˌfɪʃl ˈlæŋgwɪdʒ] Amtssprache <V U3, 62>
sign language [ˈsaɪn ˌlæŋgwɪdʒ] Gebärdensprache; Zeichensprache III

**lantern** [ˈlæntən] Laterne <V U4, 85>

**lap** [læp] Schoß V U3, 59

**laptop** [ˈlæptɒp] Laptop I

**large** [lɑːdʒ] groß II

**lasagne** [ləˈzænjə] Lasagne II

to **last** [lɑːst] dauern; andauern; anhalten IV

**last** [lɑːst] letzte I; als letztes; zuletzt <V U4, 83>
at last [ət ˈlɑːst] endlich; zu guter Letzt II
last night [ˌlɑːst ˈnaɪt] gestern Abend; gestern Nacht V U2, 34

**late** [leɪt] (zu) spät I
later [ˈleɪtə] später I

**latest** [ˈleɪtɪst] neueste V U4, 70

**laugh** [lɑːf] Lachen IV

to **laugh** [lɑːf] lachen II

**laughter** [ˈlɑːftə] Gelächter; Lachen <V U1, 27>

**law** [lɔː] Gesetz III

**lawn** [lɔːn] Rasen V U3, 58

*to **lay** [leɪ] legen; decken II
to lay the table [ˌleɪ ðə ˈteɪbl] den Tisch decken II

**lay** [leɪ] past participle von *to lie* V U2, 38

**layout** [ˈleɪaʊt] Layout; Anordnung IV

**lazy** [ˈleɪzi] faul IV

**lead** [liːd] Leine I

*to **lead** [liːd] führen; anführen IV; leiten V U3, 58

**leader** [ˈliːdə] Anführer; Anführerin; Führer; Führerin III

**leaf** *(sg)* [liːf], **leaves** *(pl)* [liːvz] Blatt IV

**league** [liːg] Liga IV

to **learn** [lɜːn] lernen II; erfahren; herausfinden IV
to learn about sth [ˌlɜːn əˈbaʊt] etwas erfahren über III

**least** [liːst] geringste; am wenigsten <IV>
at least [ət ˈliːst] wenigstens; mindestens III

**leather** [ˈleðə] Leder III

*to **leave** [liːv] lassen; verlassen; abfahren II; gehen IV; zurücklassen; vergessen V U3, 56
to leave out [ˌliːv‿ˈaʊt] weglassen <III>
to leave sb alone [ˌliːv‿əˈləʊn] jmdn. in Ruhe lassen V U3, 60

**leaving** [ˈliːvɪŋ] Abschieds- II

**led** [led] simple past, past participle von *to lead* IV

**left** [left] simple past, past participle von *to leave* II; links; übrig III
to turn left [ˌtɜːn ˈleft] (nach) links abbiegen I
on the left [ɒn ðə ˈleft] auf der linken Seite; links I

**leg** [leg] Bein II

**legend** [ˈledʒənd] Legende; Sage V U1, 12

**lemon** [ˈlemən] Zitrone II

**lemonade** [ˌleməˈneɪd] Limonade II

*to **lend** [lend] leihen; verleihen II

**length** *(no pl)* [leŋθ] Länge; Dauer IV
full length [ˌfʊl ˈleŋθ] volle Länge; ganze Länge <IV>

**lent** [lent] simple past von *to lend* II

**leopard** [ˈlepəd] Leopard; Leopardin V U3, 54

**less** [les] weniger III

**lesson** [ˈlesn] Schulstunde; Unterricht I; Lektion; Lehre IV

*to **let** [let] lassen III
to let sb know [ˌlet ˈnəʊ] jmdn. informieren; jmdm. Bescheid geben; jmdm. Bescheid sagen V U1, 15

**let** [let] simple past, past participle von *to let* III
**letter** ['letə] Buchstabe; Brief III
capital letter [ˌkæpɪtl 'letə] Großbuchstabe <III>
letter of application [ˌletər‿əv‿æplɪ'keɪʃn] Bewerbungsbrief V U1, 16
**lettuce** ['letɪs] Kopfsalat II
**level** ['levl] Höhe; Grenze; Niveau V U4, 76
**library** ['laɪbri] Bibliothek; Bücherei III
**licence** ['laɪsns] Lizenz; Erlaubnis <IV>
**license** *(BE)* ['laɪsns] Lizenz; Erlaubnis <IV>
driver's license *(AE)* ['draɪvəz ˌlaɪsns] Führerschein IV
*to **lie** [laɪ] liegen V U2, 38
**life** *(sg)* [laɪf], **lives** *(pl)* [laɪvz] Leben I
to bring to life [ˌbrɪŋ tə‿'laɪf] zum Leben erwecken; veranschaulichen IV
way of life [ˌweɪ əv 'laɪf] Lebensart; Lebensweise IV
**lifeboat** ['laɪfbəʊt] Rettungsboot III
**lifestyle** ['laɪfstaɪl] Lebensart; Lifestyle IV
**lifetime** ['laɪftaɪm] Leben; Lebenszeit IV
ski **lift** ['ski: ˌlɪft] Skilift V U4, 74
**light** [laɪt] Licht IV; leicht <V U4, 84>
light bulb ['laɪt ˌbʌlb] Glühbirne III
lights [laɪts] Ampel IV
traffic light ['træfɪk ˌlaɪt] (Verkehrs-)Ampel V U3, 59
*to **light** [laɪt] anzünden <V U1, 26>
**lighting** ['laɪtɪŋ] Beleuchtung <III>
**lightning** *(no pl)* ['laɪtnɪŋ] Blitz V U2, 31
to **like** [laɪk] mögen I
to like ... best [ˌlaɪk ... 'best] am meisten mögen; am liebsten mögen I
would like [wʊd 'laɪk] würde(n) gern; hätte(n) gern II
I wouldn't like (to) ... [aɪ 'wʊdnt laɪk (tə)] Ich möchte nicht ...; Ich würde nicht gerne ... I
I'd like (to) ... (= I would like to) [aɪd 'laɪk (tə)] Ich möchte ...; Ich würde gerne ... I
Would you like (to) ...? [ˌwʊd jə 'laɪk (tə)] Möchtest du? I
**like** [laɪk] wie I
like this [laɪk 'ðɪs] so; auf diese Weise I; ähnlich <III>
**lime** [laɪm] Limette <V U2, 46>
**limit** ['lɪmɪt] Limit; Grenze; Beschränkung V U4, 79
speed limit ['spi:d ˌlɪmɪt] Geschwindigkeitsbeschränkung V U4, 81
to **limit** ['lɪmɪt] limitieren; begrenzen; beschränken V U1, 21
**limited** ['lɪmɪtɪd] begrenzt; beschränkt; limitiert <V U4, 82>
**line** [laɪn] Zeile; Linie II; Schlange V U4, 70
**lines** *(pl)* [laɪnz] Text II
**link** [lɪŋk] Link; Verbindung IV
to **link** [lɪŋk] verbinden IV
**linking** word [ˌlɪŋkɪŋ 'wɜ:d] Verbindungswort <IV>
**lion** ['laɪən] Löwe V U3, 48
**list** [lɪst] Liste II
ranking list ['ræŋkɪŋ ˌlɪst] Rangliste; Rangfolge <IV>
shopping list ['ʃɒpɪŋ ˌlɪst] Einkaufszettel I
to **list** [lɪst] auflisten <V U2, 38>
to **listen** (to) ['lɪsn] zuhören; anhören; hören I
**listener** ['lɪsənə] Zuhörer; Zuhörerin II
**listening** ['lɪsnɪŋ] Hörverstehen <I>
**little** ['lɪtl] klein II; wenig; kaum IV
a little [ə 'lɪtl] ein bisschen II
a little something [ə ˌlɪtl 'sʌmθɪŋ] eine Kleinigkeit IV
to **live** [lɪv] wohnen; leben I; überleben V U3, 55
**lively** ['laɪvli] lebhaft; lebendig <IV>
**living** ['lɪvɪŋ] Wohnen; Leben <V U4, 76>
living room ['lɪvɪŋ ˌrʊm] Wohnzimmer I
**loaf** *(sg)* [ləʊf], **loaves** *(pl)* [ləʊvz] Brotlaib III
**lobster** ['lɒbstə] Hummer IV
**local** ['ləʊkl] hiesig; lokal; örtlich III
*to be **located** [bi: ləʊ'keɪtɪd] liegen III; gelegen sein; sich befinden IV
**location** [ləʊ'keɪʃn] Drehort; Lage III; Aufenthaltsort <IV>
**loch** [lɒk] See *(in Schottland)* III
to **lock** [lɒk] abschließen I
**locker** ['lɒkə] Schließfach; Spind IV
**lonely** ['ləʊnli] einsam III
**long** [lɒŋ] lang I
in the long run [ˌɪn ðə 'lɒŋ rʌn] langfristig; auf Dauer V U4, 74
**look** [lʊk] Ausdruck; Blick V U2, 40
to have a look [ˌhæv‿ə 'lʊk] anschauen II
to **look** [lʊk] schauen; nachschauen I; aussehen; sehen II
to look after [ˌlʊk‿'ɑ:ftə] aufpassen; hüten II
to look at ['lʊk‿ət] anschauen I
to look for ['lʊk fə] suchen nach II
to look forward to (+ -ing) [ˌlʊk 'fɔ:wəd tə] sich freuen auf V U1, 16
to look up [ˌlʊk‿'ʌp] aufschauen; nachschauen II
Look ... [lʊk] Schau mal ...; Schau ... nach. I
**lookout** point ['lʊkaʊt ˌpɔɪnt] Aussichtspunkt II
**loose** [lu:s] locker; lose II
**lorry** driver ['lɒri ˌdraɪvə] LKW-Fahrer; LKW-Fahrerin II
*to **lose** [lu:z] verlieren II
**lost** [lɒst] simple past von *to lose* II; past participle von *to lose* III
to get lost [ˌget 'lɒst] sich verirren I
a **lot** [ə 'lɒt] viel I; sehr II
a **lot** of [ə 'lɒt‿əv] viel(e); eine Menge I
body **lotion** ['bɒdi ˌləʊʃn] Körperlotion III
**lots** [lɒts] viel; jede Menge III
lots of ['lɒts‿əv] viel; jede Menge I
**loud** [laʊd] laut III
**love** [lʌv] Liebe IV
to fall in love (with) [ˌfɔ:l‿ɪn 'lʌv] sich verlieben (in) III
to **love** [lʌv] lieben; gern mögen I
I'd love to ... (= I would love to) [aɪd 'lʌv tə] Ich würde sehr gern ... III

**lovely** ['lʌvli] schön; herrlich; hübsch II

**loving** ['lʌvɪŋ] liebend; liebevoll IV

**low** [ləʊ] niedrig II

**lower** ['ləʊə] untere III

good **luck** [ˌgʊd 'lʌk] viel Glück II

**luckily** ['lʌkɪli] glücklicherweise IV

**lucky** ['lʌki] glücklich; erfolgreich V U2, 34

to be lucky [bi: 'lʌki] Glück haben III

lucky day [ˌlʌki 'deɪ] Glückstag II

lucky number [ˌlʌki 'nʌmbə] Glückszahl I

**luggage** ['lʌgɪdʒ] Gepäck <V U2, 198>

**lunch** [lʌnʃ] Mittagessen I

packed lunch [ˌpækt 'lʌnʃ] Lunchpaket; Vesper II

**lunchtime** ['lʌnʃtaɪm] Mittagszeit; Mittagspause I

**luxurious** [lʌg'ʒʊəriəs] luxuriös; Luxus- V U4, 68

**luxury** ['lʌkʃri] Luxus; Luxus- V U2, 30

**lyrics** *(pl)* ['lɪrɪks] Liedtext <II>

## M

**machine** [mə'ʃi:n] Automat; Maschine II

payment machine ['peɪmənt ˌməʃi:n] Bezahlautomat II

Dear Sir or **Madam**, [dɪə ˌsɜ:r‿ɔ: 'mædəm] Sehr geehrte Damen und Herren, V U3, 50

**made** [meɪd] simple past von *to make* I; past participle von *to make* II

**magazine** [ˌmægə'zi:n] Zeitschrift I

**magic** ['mædʒɪk] Magie; magisch; Zauberei; Zauber- II

**magician** [mə'dʒɪʃn] Zauberer; Zauberin; Magier; Magierin IV

**main** [meɪn] Haupt- V U3, 48

main course [ˌmeɪn 'kɔ:s] Hauptgericht II

**mainland** ['meɪnlənd] Festland <V U4, 75>

**major** ['meɪdʒə] Haupt-; wichtig; bedeutend IV

**majority** [mə'dʒɒrəti] Mehrheit; Mehrzahl IV

*to **make** [meɪk] erstellen; machen; tun; bilden I

to be made of [bi: 'meɪd‿əv] hergestellt sein aus III

to make a cake [ˌmeɪk‿ə 'keɪk] einen Kuchen backen I

to make a decision [ˌmeɪk‿ə dɪ'sɪʒn] eine Entscheidung treffen <III>

to make a reservation [ˌmeɪk‿ə 'rezəveɪʃn] reservieren III

to make friends [ˌmeɪk 'frendz] Freundschaften schließen I

to make funny faces [meɪk fʌni 'feɪsɪz] lustige Grimassen schneiden V U3, 58

to make it ['meɪk‿ɪt] es schaffen IV

to make money [ˌmeɪk 'mʌni] Geld verdienen V U4, 70

to make one's point [ˌmeɪk wʌnz 'pɔɪnt] seinen Standpunkt deutlich machen <V U4, 73>

to make oneself at home [ˌmeɪk wʌnself ət 'həʊm] sich wie zu Hause fühlen III

to make room [ˌmeɪk 'ru:m] Platz machen <V U4, 84>

to make sb feel like sth [ˌmeɪk … 'fi:l laɪk] jmdm. das Gefühl geben, etw. zu sein III

to make sense [ˌmeɪk 'sens] Sinn ergeben; einleuchten <III>

to make sth up [ˌmeɪk‿'ʌp] erfinden; sich ausdenken <V U1, 25>

to make sure [ˌmeɪk 'ʃɔ:] dafür sorgen; sich versichern III

to make up [ˌmeɪk‿'ʌp] erfinden; sich ausdenken <III>

**maker** ['meɪkə] Macher; Macherin <IV>

film maker ['fɪlm ˌmeɪkə] Filmemacher; Filmemacherin <III>

**make-up** ['meɪkʌp] Make-up; Schminke IV

make-up artist ['meɪkʌp ˌɑ:tɪst] Maskenbildner; Maskenbildnerin; Visagist; Visagistin <III>

**mall** [mɔ:l] Einkaufszentrum V U4, 68

shopping mall ['ʃɒpɪŋ ˌmɔ:l] Einkaufszentrum IV

**mama** ['mæmə] Mama II

**mammal** ['mæml] Säugetier <V U3, 205>

**man** *(sg)* [mæn], **men** *(pl)* [men] Mann I

**manager** ['mænɪdʒə] Manager; Managerin; Geschäftsführer; Geschäftsführerin IV

**Mandarin** ['mændrɪn] Mandarin <V U4, 84>

**mankind** [mæn'kaɪnd] Menschheit V U3, 54

**mansion** ['mænʃn] Villa; Herrenhaus <V U3, 205>

**manta** ray ['mæntə‿ˌreɪ] Teufelsrochen V U1, 23

**many** ['meni] viele II

how many [ˌhaʊ 'meni] wie viele II

**map** [mæp] Stadtplan; Landkarte III; Karte; Plan IV

mind map ['maɪnd ˌmæp] Wörternetz <I>

**marathon** ['mærəθn] Marathon <IV>

**March** [mɑ:tʃ] März I

**marijuana** [ˌmærɪ'wɑ:nə] Marihuana <V U2, 46>

to **mark** [mɑ:k] markieren; kennzeichnen III

**market** ['mɑ:kɪt] Markt II

*to get **married** [ˌget 'mærɪd] heiraten II

to **marry** ['mæri] heiraten V U2, 34

**marsh** [mɑ:ʃ] Sumpf; Moor V U3, 55

**martial** art [ˌmɑ:ʃl‿'ɑ:t] Kampfkunst; Kampfsportart V U4, 69

**mascot** ['mæskət] Maskottchen <III>

**mashed** potatoes [ˌmæʃt pə'teɪtəʊz] Kartoffelbrei II

**mask** [mɑ:sk] Maske V U4, 74

**match** [mætʃ] Spiel I

to **match** [mætʃ] zuordnen I; zusammenpassen <IV>

**material** [mə'tɪəriəl] Material; Stoff III; materiell <V U2, 46>

**Math** *(AE)* [mæθ] Mathematik; Mathe IV

**Maths** [mæθs] Mathematik; Mathe I

It doesn't **matter**. [ɪt ˌdʌznt 'mætə] Es ist egal. II

**May** [meɪ] Mai I

**may** [meɪ] vielleicht; können; dürfen II

**maybe** ['meɪbi] vielleicht I
**mayonnaise** [ˌmeɪə'neɪz] Mayonnaise II
**me** [mi:] mich; ich; mir I
**meal** [mi:l] Essen; Mahlzeit II
*to **mean** [mi:n] bedeuten; meinen III
**mean** [mi:n] gemein IV
**meaning** ['mi:nɪŋ] Bedeutung V U1, 12
**meant** [ment] simple past, past participle von *to mean* III
**meat** [mi:t] Fleisch I
**mechanic** [mɪ'kænɪk] Mechaniker; Mechanikerin V U1, 17
**mechatronics** technician [mekə'trɒnɪks tekˌnɪʃn] Mechatroniker; Mechatronikerin <V U1, 192>
**medal** ['medl] Medaille <V U2, 47>
**media** ['mi:diə] Medien IV; Medien- V U4, 69
media designer ['mi:diə dɪˌzaɪnə] Mediengestalter; Mediengestalterin <V U1, 192>
social media [ˌsəʊʃl 'mi:diə] soziale Medien IV
**mediation** [ˌmi:di'eɪʃn] Sprachmittlung <I>
**medical** ['medɪkl] medizinisch; ärztlich IV
**medicine** ['medsn] Medikamente; Medizin III
*to **meet** [mi:t] kennen lernen; treffen I
to meet requirements [ˌmi:t rɪ'kwaɪəmənts] Voraussetzungen erfüllen <V U1, 16>
**melody** ['melədi] Melodie <V U2, 35>
**member** ['membə] Mitglied IV
**mental** ['mentl] geistig IV
to **mention** ['menʃn] erwähnen <IV>
**menu** ['menju:] Speisekarte II
**mess** [mes] Unordnung; Durcheinander I
**message** ['mesɪdʒ] Botschaft; Nachricht; SMS II
morning message ['mɔ:nɪŋ ˌmesɪdʒ] morgendliche Ansprache IV
text message ['tekst ˌmesɪdʒ] SMS II
**met** [met] simple past von *to meet* I
**metal** ['metl] Metall III
**metalworker** ['metlwɜ:kə] Metallbauer; Metallbauerin <V U1, 192>
**method** ['meθəd] Methode II
**metre** ['mi:tə] Meter I
**microwave** ['maɪkrəweɪv] Mikrowelle IV
**middle** ['mɪdl] Mitte III
to be middle class [bi: ˌmɪdl 'klɑ:s] zur Mittelschicht gehören V U3, 51
in the middle [ɪn ðə 'mɪdl] in der Mitte III
**midnight** ['mɪdnaɪt] Mitternacht III
**might** [maɪt] könnte IV; könnten V U1, 12
to **migrate** [maɪ'greɪt] wandern; umherziehen V U1, 20
**mild** [maɪld] mild I
**mile** [maɪl] Meile II
mph (miles per hour) [ˌempi:'eɪtʃ (ˌmaɪlz pər‿'aʊə)] kmh (Kilometer pro Stunde) V U4, 81
square mile (= sq. mi.) [ˌskweə 'maɪl] Quadratmeile IV
**milk** [mɪlk] Milch I
to **milk** [mɪlk] melken III
**milkshake** ['mɪlkˌʃeɪk] Milchmischgetränk; Milchshake III
**million** ['mɪljən] Million III
half a million [ˌhɑ:f‿ə 'mɪljən] eine halbe Million III
**mind** [maɪnd] Meinung; Geist; Verstand V U4, 79
to come to mind [ˌkʌm tə 'maɪnd] einem einfallen; zufällig einfallen <IV>
to keep in mind [ˌki:p‿ɪn 'maɪnd] nicht vergessen; im Auge behalten <V U1, 25>
mind map ['maɪnd ˌmæp] Wörternetz <I>
Never mind. [ˌnevə 'maɪnd] Macht nichts.; Schon gut.; Mach dir nichts draus. II
**mine** [maɪn] meins; meine II; Bergwerk III
of mine [əv 'maɪn] von mir II
**miner** ['maɪnə] Bergarbeiter; Bergarbeiterin III
**mineral** water ['mɪnrl ˌwɔ:tə] Mineralwasser III
**minimum** ['mɪnɪməm] Minimum; minimal; Mindest- IV
**minority** [maɪ'nɒrəti] Minderheit IV
**minute** ['mɪnɪt] Minute II
**mirror** ['mɪrə] Spiegel III
**miserable** ['mɪzrəbl] elend; armselig; jämmerlich III
*to give sth a **miss** [ˌgɪv sʌmθɪŋ‿ə 'mɪs] auf etw. verzichten; etw. bleiben lassen III
to **miss** [mɪs] verpassen; vermissen II
**missing** ['mɪsɪŋ] fehlend; verschwunden <V U1, 13>
**mistake** [mɪ'steɪk] Fehler <III>
to **mix** [mɪks] mischen; vermischen; mixen IV
**mixed** [mɪkst] gemischt V U3, 48
mixed race [ˌmɪkst 'reɪs] gemischter Abstammung; Mischrasse V U3, 48
**mixture** ['mɪkstʃə] Mischung V U4, 69
**mobile** ['məʊbaɪl] mobil; tragbar; beweglich IV
mobile (phone) ['məʊbaɪl (ˌfəʊn)] Handy; Mobiltelefon I
**modal** auxiliary [ˌməʊdl‿ɔ:g'zɪljri] modales Hilfsverb <V U1, 14>
role **model** ['rəʊl ˌmɒdl] Vorbild V U2, 29
**modern** ['mɒdn] modern I
**mom** *(AE)* [mɒm] Mama IV
**moment** ['məʊmənt] Moment; Augenblick II
it took me a moment [ɪt ˌtʊk mi:‿ə 'məʊmənt] ich brauchte einen Moment V U2, 39
**Monday** ['mʌndeɪ] Montag I
**money** ['mʌni] Geld I
to make money [ˌmeɪk 'mʌni] Geld verdienen V U4, 70
pocket money ['pɒkɪt ˌmʌni] Taschengeld V U4, 70
**monkey** ['mʌŋki] Affe I
**monster** ['mɒnstə] Ungeheuer; Monster III
**month** [mʌnθ] Monat I
a month [ə 'mʌnθ] pro Monat V U4, 70
monthly ['mʌnθli] monatlich III
**monument** ['mɒnjəmənt] Denkmal II
**mood** [mu:d] Stimmung; Laune <III>

**moon** [muːn] Mond V U1, 20
**moral standards** ***(pl)*** [ˌmɒrl ˈstændədz] sittliche Werte *(Pl.)* V U4, 79
**more** [mɔː] mehr I
**morning** [ˈmɔːnɪŋ] Morgen; Vormittag I
Good morning. [ˌɡʊd ˈmɔːnɪŋ] Guten Morgen. II
morning message [ˈmɔːnɪŋ ˌmesɪdʒ] morgendliche Ansprache IV
**mosque** [mɒsk] Moschee II
**most** [məʊst] die meisten; die Mehrheit I; am meisten II
most of [ˈməʊst‿əv] die meisten V U1, 20
mostly [ˈməʊstli] meistens; hauptsächlich IV
**mother** [ˈmʌðə] Mutter I
**motion sensor** [ˌməʊʃn ˈsensə] Bewegungsmelder V U4, 74
**motivated** [ˈməʊtɪveɪtɪd] motiviert IV
**motorbike** [ˈməʊtəbaɪk] Motorrad I
**mound** [maʊnd] Hügel <V U3, 205>
**mountain** [ˈmaʊntɪn] Berg III
in the mountains [ˌɪn ðə ˈmaʊntɪnz] in den Bergen III
mountain range [ˈmaʊntɪn ˌreɪndʒ] Bergkette; Gebirge V U3, 55
**mouse** ***(sg)*** [maʊs], **mice** ***(pl)*** [maɪs] Maus I
**moussaka** [muˈsɑːkə] Moussaka II
**mouth** [maʊθ] Mund II
to keep one's mouth shut [ˌkiːp wʌnz ˈmaʊθ ʃʌt] den Mund halten V U2, 40
**move** [muːv] Bewegung III
to **move** [muːv] (sich) bewegen III
to move (house) [muːv] umziehen II
**movement** [ˈmuːvmənt] Bewegung IV
cultural movement [ˌkʌltʃrl ˈmuːvmənt] Kulturbewegung IV
**movie** [ˈmuːvi] Film I
movie theater *(AE)* [ˈmuːvi ˌθiːətə] Kino IV
**the movies** ***(AE)*** [ðə ˈmuːviz] Kino IV
**mph** (miles per hour) [ˌempiːˈeɪtʃ (ˌmaɪlz pər‿ˈaʊə)] kmh (Kilometer pro Stunde) V U4, 81

**Mr** [ˈmɪstə] Herr *(Anrede)* I
**Mrs** [ˈmɪsɪz] Frau *(Anrede)* I
**Ms** [mɪz] Frau *(Anrede)* I
**much** [mʌtʃ] viel I
so much [ˈsəʊ ˌmʌtʃ] so sehr III
too much [ˌtuː ˈmʌtʃ] zu sehr II
how much [ˌhaʊ ˈmʌtʃ] wie sehr III
**mud** [mʌd] Schlamm; Matsch III
**muddy** [ˈmʌdi] schlammig I
**multicultural** [ˌmʌltiˈkʌltʃrl] multikulturell IV
**multilingual** [ˌmʌltiˈlɪŋɡwəl] mehrsprachig <V U3, 62>
**multiracial** [ˌmʌltiˈreɪʃl] gemischtrassig <V U3, 59>
**mum** [mʌm] Mama I
**mural** [ˈmjʊərəl] Wandgemälde III
**murderer** [ˈmɜːdrə] Mörder; Mörderin III
**museum** [mjuːˈziːəm] Museum II
**music** [ˈmjuːzɪk] Musik I
**musical** [ˈmjuːzɪkl] Musik-; musikalisch III
**musician** [mjuːˈzɪʃn] Musiker; Musikerin V U2, 29
**Muslim** [ˈmʊzlɪm] Muslim; Muslimin I
**must** [mʌst] müssen I
must not/never [ˌmʌst ˈnɒt/ˈnevə] nicht/nie dürfen III
mustn't [ˈmʌsnt] nicht dürfen III
**mustard** [ˈmʌstəd] Senf II
**must-have** [ˈmʌstˌhæv] *etwas, das man haben muss* V U4, 70
**my** [maɪ] mein; meine I
My name is ... [maɪ ˈneɪm‿ɪz] Ich heiße ... I
**myself** [maɪˈself] selbst; selber III
**mystery** [ˈmɪstri] Rätsel; Geheimnis I
mystery story [ˈmɪstri ˌstɔːri] Krimi (= Kriminalgeschichte); Detektivgeschichte IV
**myth** [mɪθ] Mythos <V U1, 26>

## N

to **nag** [næɡ] nörgeln; meckern III; auf die Nerven gehen V U4, 70
**nail** [neɪl] Nagel III
nail scissors *(pl)* [ˈneɪl ˌsɪzəz] Nagelschere III

**name** [neɪm] Name I
first name [ˌfɜːst ˈneɪm] Vorname <III>
to **name** [neɪm] benennen IV
**napkin** [ˈnæpkɪn] Serviette II
**narrator** [nəˈreɪtə] Erzähler; Erzählerin I
**narrow** [ˈnærəʊ] eng <V U3, 205>
**nation** [ˈneɪʃn] Nation; Land; Staat V U3, 49
**national** [ˈnæʃnl] National-; national III
national park [ˌnæʃnl ˈpɑːk] Nationalpark V U3, 48; Naturpark <IV>
**nationality** [ˌnæʃnˈæləti] Nationalität; Staatsangehörigkeit <IV>
**native** [ˈneɪtɪv] eingeboren; einheimisch IV
Native American [ˌneɪtɪv‿əˈmerɪkən] Ureinwohner Amerikas; Ureinwohnerin Amerikas; Indianer; Indianerin; indianisch IV
native speaker [ˌneɪtɪv ˈspiːkə] Muttersprachler; Muttersprachlerin V U1, 16
**naturally** [ˈnætʃrli] natürlich <IV>
**nature** [ˈneɪtʃə] Natur III
nature reserve [ˈneɪtʃə rɪˌzɜːv] Naturschutzgebiet V U3, 48
**naughty** [ˈnɔːti] frech; böse III
**near** [nɪə] in der Nähe von I; nah III
**nearby** [ˌnɪəˈbaɪ] in der Nähe V U2, 30
**nearly** [ˈnɪəli] fast; beinahe; annähernd IV
**neat** [niːt] ordentlich; hübsch; gepflegt <IV>
**necessarily** [ˈnesəsrli] zwangsläufig <V U3, 62>
**necessary** [ˈnesəsri] nötig; notwendig; erforderlich V U1, 11
to **need** [niːd] brauchen I
to need to [ˈniːd ˌtə] müssen IV
needn't [ˈniːdnt] nicht brauchen; nicht müssen I
with special **needs** [wɪð ˌspeʃl ˈniːdz] mit Behinderung III
**negative** [ˈneɡətɪv] negativ IV
**neighbor** ***(AE)*** [ˈneɪbə] Nachbar; Nachbarin IV
**neighbour** [ˈneɪbə] Nachbar; Nachbarin III

**neighbourhood** [ˈneɪbəhʊd] Nachbarschaft <V U4, 77>
**neither** … nor … [ˈniːðə … nɔː] weder … noch … <V U4, 84>
*to get on one's **nerves** [ˌget_ɒn wʌnz ˈnɜːvz] auf die Nerven gehen III
**nervous** [ˈnɜːvəs] nervös; aufgeregt II
**net** [net] Netz IV
safety net [ˈseɪfti ˌnet] Sicherheitsnetz IV
**netball** [ˈnetbɔːl] Korbball I
**network** [ˈnetwɜːk] Netzwerk V U4, 69
**never** [ˈnevə] nie; niemals I
Never mind. [ˌnevə ˈmaɪnd] Macht nichts.; Schon gut.; Mach dir nichts draus. II
**never-ending** [ˌnevrˈendɪŋ] endlos; unendlich V U4, 78
**new** [njuː] neu I
New Year [ˌnjuː ˈjɪə] Neujahr V U3, 59
**news** [njuːz] Neuigkeit(en); Nachricht(en) II
**newsagent's** [ˈnjuːzˌeɪdʒnts] Zeitschriftenladen III
**newspaper** [ˈnjuːsˌpeɪpə] Zeitung II
**next** [nekst] nächste I; als Nächstes II
next to [ˈnekst tə] neben I
**nice** [naɪs] schön; nett I; lecker; gut III
**nickname** [ˈnɪkneɪm] Spitzname IV
**niece** [niːs] Nichte III
**night** [naɪt] Nacht I
at night [ət ˈnaɪt] nachts V U3, 51
last night [ˌlɑːst ˈnaɪt] gestern Abend; gestern Nacht V U2, 34
night walk [ˌnaɪt ˈwɔːk] Nachtwanderung I
that night [ˌðæt ˈnaɪt] an jenem Abend; in jener Nacht II
**nightmare** [ˈnaɪtmeə] Albtraum V U3, 51
**nine** [naɪn] neun I
**nineteen** [ˌnaɪnˈtiːn] neunzehn I
**ninety** [ˈnaɪnti] neunzig I
**no** [nəʊ] kein; keine; nein I
no one [ˈnəʊ wʌn] niemand I
**nobody** [ˈnəʊbədi] niemand III
**noise** [nɔɪz] Geräusch I; Lärm <V U4, 212>
**noisy** [ˈnɔɪzi] laut III
**non-** [nɒn] nicht- IV
**noodle** [ˈnuːdl] Nudel V U4, 68
**neither** … **nor** … [ˈniːðə … nɔː] weder … noch … <V U4, 84>
**north** [nɔːθ] Norden III
north of [ˈnɔːθ_əv] nördlich von IV
to the north of [ˌtə ðə ˈnɔːθ_əv] nördlich von III
**northeast** [ˌnɔːθˈiːst] Nordosten III
**northern** [ˈnɔːðən] nördlich III
**northwest** [ˌnɔːθˈwest] Nordwesten III
northwest of [ˌnɔːθˈwest_əv] nordwestlich III
**nose** [nəʊz] Nase I
**not** [nɒt] nicht I
not at all [ˌnɒt_ət_ˈɔːl] überhaupt nicht; gar nicht II
not … any [ˌnɒt … eni] kein II
not … any more [ˌnɒt … eni ˈmɔː] nicht mehr III
not … either [nɒt … ˈaɪðə] auch nicht III
not … yet [nɒt … ˈjet] noch nicht II
not possibly [nɒt ˈpɒsəbli] unmöglich III
**note** [nəʊt] Geldschein II; Notiz <III>
**nothing** [ˈnʌθɪŋ] nichts IV
*to take **notice** [ˌteɪk ˈnəʊtɪs] beachten; zur Kenntnis nehmen; aufmerksam werden V U3, 60
**to notice** [ˈnəʊtɪs] bemerken; wahrnehmen III
**noun** [naʊn] Nomen; Hauptwort <I>
**novel** [ˈnɒvl] Roman IV
**November** [nəˈvembə] November I
**now** [naʊ] jetzt; nun I; heutzutage II
right now [ˌraɪt ˈnaʊ] jetzt gerade III; jetzt gleich; sofort; gerade <V U3, 65>
**nowadays** [ˈnaʊədeɪz] heutzutage IV
**nowhere** [ˈnəʊweə] nirgendwo; nirgendwohin IV
**nuclear** [ˈnjuːkliə] nuklear; Atom- <V U4, 75>
**number** [ˈnʌmbə] Nummer; Zahl I; Anzahl IV
a number of [ə ˈnʌmbər_əv] einige; mehrere IV
lucky number [ˌlʌki ˈnʌmbə] Glückszahl I
ordinal number [ˌɔːdɪnəl ˈnʌmbə] Ordinalzahl <I>
phone number [ˈfəʊn ˌnʌmbə] Telefonnummer III
**to number** [ˈnʌmbə] nummerieren <V U2, 44>
**nurse** [nɜːs] Krankenschwester; Krankenpfleger V U1, 11
**nursery** teacher [ˈnɜːsri ˌtiːtʃə] Erzieher; Erzieherin <V U1, 192>
**nursing** [ˈnɜːsɪŋ] Pflege; Krankenpflege V U2, 34
**nut** [nʌt] Nuss I

## O

o'clock [əˈklɒk] Uhr *(Zeitangabe bei vollen Stunden)* I
**oat** [əʊt] Hafer III
**object** [ˈɒbdʒɪkt] Objekt; Gegenstand <III>
**objective** [əbˈdʒektɪv] sachlich; objektiv V U4, 79
**to observe** [əbˈzɜːv] beobachten; beachten; befolgen V U4, 78
**obviously** [ˈɒbviəsli] offensichtlich V U2, 41
**ocean** [ˈəʊʃn] Ozean; Meer IV
**October** [ɒkˈtəʊbə] Oktober I
the **odd** one out [ˌɒd wʌn_ˈaʊt] das Wort, das nicht in die Gruppe passt <III>
**of** [ɒv] von I
of course [əv ˈkɔːs] natürlich; selbstverständlich I
of mine [əv ˈmaɪn] von mir II
of all the people [əv_ˈɔːl ðə ˌpiːpl] von allen Leuten V U1, 18
**off** [ɒf] von … weg; vor V U2, 30
a day off [ə ˌdeɪ_ˈɒf] ein freier Tag III
to set off [ˌset_ˈɒf] aufbrechen; sich aufmachen; auslösen IV
to turn off [ˌtɜːn_ˈɒf] abschalten; ausschalten <IV>
Off we went. [ˈɒf wi went] Nichts wie weg. III
**offensive** [əˈfensɪv] beleidigend; anstößig V U1, 12
**offer** [ˈɒfə] Angebot <V U2, 44>
special offer [ˌspeʃl_ˈɒfə] Sonderangebot III
**to offer** [ˈɒfə] anbieten; bieten IV

**office** ['ɒfɪs] Büro II
post office ['pəʊst͜ˌɒfɪs] Postamt I
**officer** ['ɒfɪsə] Beamter; Beamtin <IV>
police officer [pə'li:s͜ˌɒfɪsə] Polizeibeamter; Polizeibeamtin I
**official** [ə'fɪʃl] offiziell V U1, 12
official language [əˌfɪʃl 'læŋgwɪdʒ] Amtssprache <V U3, 62>
officially [ə'fɪʃli] offiziell <III>
**often** ['ɒfn] oft; häufig I
**oh** [əʊ] null *(bei Uhrzeiten und Telefonnummern)* I
**oil** [ɔɪl] Öl IV
oil spill ['ɔɪl ˌspɪl] Ölteppich V U1, 21
**OK** [əʊ'keɪ] okay I
**old** [əʊld] alt I
in the old days [ɪn ði 'əʊld ˌdeɪz] früher III
**old-fashioned** [ˌəʊld'fæʃnd] altmodisch IV
**Olympic** [ə'lɪmpɪk] Olympia-; olympisch <V U2, 47>
**on** [ɒn] auf; an I
on board ['ɒn bɔ:d] an Bord III
on time [ɒn 'taɪm] pünktlich III
on weekdays [ɒn 'wi:kdeɪz] unter der Woche; an Werktagen III
to try on [ˌtraɪ͜'ɒn] anprobieren II
on foot [ɒn 'fʊt] zu Fuß I
on purpose [ɒn 'pɜ:pəs] absichtlich II
on 7th July [ɒn ðə 'sevnθ əv ˌdʒʊlaɪ] am 7. Juli I
on the bus [ˌɒn ðə 'bʌs] im Bus II
on the left [ɒn ðə 'left] auf der linken Seite; links I
on the one hand [ɒn ðə͜'wʌn ˌhænd] einerseits IV
on the right [ɒn ðə 'raɪt] auf der rechten Seite; rechts I
on the way [ˌɒn ðə ˌ'weɪ] auf dem Weg; unterwegs I
on Tuesday [ˌɒn 'tju:zdeɪ] am Dienstag I
on TV [ɒn ˌti:'vi:] im Fernsehen IV
on Wednesdays [ɒn 'wenzdeɪz] mittwochs I
**once** [wʌns] einst; einmal IV
once-in-a-lifetime [ˌwʌns͜ɪn͜ə 'laɪftaɪm] einmalig; einmal im Leben <V U2, 42>
once more ['wʌns ˌmɔ:] noch einmal II
**one** [wʌn] eins I
one another [ˌwʌn͜ə'nʌðə] einander; gegenseitig <V U3, 62>
one day [wʌn 'deɪ] eines Tages III
**one(s)** [wʌn(z)] *Platzhalter für ein Nomen* III
**onion** ['ʌnjən] Zwiebel II
**online** [ˌɒn'laɪn] online II
**only** ['əʊnli] nur I; einzige III
**on-the-job** training [ˌɒnðədʒɒb 'treɪnɪŋ] Ausbildung am Arbeitsplatz V U1, 16
to **open** ['əʊpn] öffnen; aufmachen I; sich öffnen; aufgehen V U2, 40
**open** ['əʊpn] offen; geöffnet III
to fly open [ˌflaɪ͜'əʊpn] auffliegen V U2, 39
**opening** ['əʊpnɪŋ] Anfang; Eröffnung <IV>
opening times ['əʊpnɪŋ ˌtaɪmz] Öffnungszeiten IV
**open-water** swim [ˌəʊpnwɔ:tə 'swɪm] Freiwasserschwimmen <V U3, 67>
**operation** [ˌɒpr'eɪʃn] Operation III
**operator** ['ɒpreɪtə] Vermittlung III
camera operator ['kæmrə ˌɒpreɪtə] Kameramann; Kamerafrau <III>
**opinion** [ə'pɪnjən] Meinung III
in my opinion [ɪn 'maɪ͜əˌpɪnjən] meiner Meinung nach III
**opium** ['əʊpiəm] Opium <V U4, 84>
**opportunity** [ˌɒpə'tju:nəti] Gelegenheit; Chance IV
**opposite** ['ɒpəzɪt] gegenüber I; Gegenteil <II>; V U3, 55
to **oppress** [ə'pres] unterdrücken V U4, 78
**oppression** [ə'preʃn] Unterdrückung V U4, 79
**optimistic** [ˌɒptɪ'mɪstɪk] optimistisch III
**option** ['ɒpʃn] Möglichkeit; Wahl; Option IV
**or** [ɔ:] oder I
either … or … ['aɪðə … ɔ: …] entweder … oder … V U3, 50
**oral** ['ɔ:rl] mündlich <IV>
**orange** ['ɒrɪndʒ] orange; Orange I
**orchestra** ['ɔ:kɪstrə] Orchester III
**order** ['ɔ:də] Reihenfolge <III>
in order to [ɪn͜'ɔ:də tə] um … zu; mit der Absicht V U2, 40
to **order** ['ɔ:də] bestellen II
**ordinal** number [ˌɔ:dɪnəl 'nʌmbə] Ordinalzahl <I>
**organisation** [ˌɔ:gnaɪ'zeɪʃn] Organisation <V U3, 66>
**organization** [ˌɔ:gnaɪ'zeɪʃn] Organisation <IV>
to **organize** ['ɔ:gənaɪz] organisieren II
**origin** ['ɒrɪdʒɪn] Ursprung; Herkunft <V U1, 26>
**original** [ə'rɪdʒnl] original; ursprünglich IV
to **originate** [ə'rɪdʒneɪt] entstehen IV
**other** ['ʌðə] andere; weitere I
each other [ˌi:tʃ͜'ʌðə] einander; sich; sich gegenseitig III
on the other (hand) [ɒn ði 'ʌðə (hænd)] andererseits IV
**others** ['ʌðəz] andere II
the others [ði͜'ʌðəz] die anderen I
**otter** ['ɒtə] Otter <V U1, 27>
**our** [aʊə] unser; unsere I
**ours** [aʊəz] unsere III
**ourselves** [ˌaʊə'selvz] selber; selbst III
**out** [aʊt] heraus II; draußen; aus; außerhalb V U4, 78
to ask sb out [ˌɑ:sk … 'aʊt] sich mit jmdm. verabreden IV
to check out [tʃek͜'aʊt] abchecken <V U3, 67>
to come out [ˌkʌm͜'aʊt] sich outen V U2, 34
to drop out of sth [ˌdrɒp͜'aʊt͜əv] etw. abbrechen V U3, 50
to fall out of [ˌfɔ:l͜'aʊt͜əv] herausfallen aus IV
to go out [ˌgəʊ͜'aʊt] ausgehen III
to keep out [ˌki:p͜'aʊt] draußen halten III
out and about [ˌaʊt͜ən͜ə'baʊt] unterwegs I
out of ['aʊt͜əv] aus … heraus II
out of control [ˌaʊt͜əv kən'trəʊl] außer Kontrolle V U3, 50
out of fashion [ˌaʊt͜əv 'fæʃn] altmodisch; nicht mehr aktuell IV
the **outback** [ði 'aʊtbæk] Outback *(australisches Hinterland)* V U1, 11

**outdated** [ˌaʊtˈdeɪtɪd] veraltet IV
**outdoor** [ˌaʊtˈdɔː] Freiluft-; Outdoor- III
**the outdoors** [ˌðiː ˈaʊtdɔːz] die freie Natur IV
**outfit** [ˈaʊtfɪt] Outfit; Kleidung III
**outnumbered** [ˌaʊtˈnʌmbəd] in der Unterzahl IV
**outside** [ˌaʊtˈsaɪd] draußen; im Freien II; außerhalb IV
outside world [ˌaʊtsaɪd ˈwɜːld] Außenwelt IV
**oven** [ˈʌvn] Backofen II
**over** [ˈəʊvə] über III; vorbei IV
over there [ˌəʊvə ˈðeə] da drüben; dort drüben II
**overcast** [ˈəʊvəkɑːst] bewölkt; bedeckt <V U2, 198>
**overfishing** [ˌəʊvəˈfɪʃɪŋ] Überfischung <V U1, 21>
**overgrown** [ˌəʊvəˈgrəʊn] verwildert <V U3, 205>
**overnight** [ˌəʊvəˈnaɪt] über Nacht V U4, 70
to **owe** [əʊ] schulden III
to **own** [əʊn] besitzen II
**own** [əʊn] eigene II
**owner** [ˈəʊnə] Besitzer; Besitzerin IV

## P

**p.m.** [ˌpiːˈem] nachmittags *(Uhrzeit)* II
to **pack** [pæk] packen; einpacken II
to pack up [ˈpæk‿ʌp] packen; einpacken II
**package** [ˈpækɪdʒ] Paket IV
**packaging** [ˈpækɪdʒɪŋ] Verpackung <V U4, 212>
**packed lunch** [ˌpækt ˈlʌnʃ] Lunchpaket; Vesper II
**packet** [ˈpækɪt] Packung; Tüte I
**paella** [paɪˈelə] Paella IV
**page** [peɪdʒ] Seite I
**paid** [peɪd] simple past, past participle von *to pay* II
to **paint** [peɪnt] streichen; anmalen; malen IV
**painting** [ˈpeɪntɪŋ] Mal- V U1, 12
**pair** [peə] Paar V U4, 70
a pair of [ə ˈpeər‿əv] ein Paar II
to **pan** [pæn] schwenken <IV>
**pancake** [ˈpænkeɪk] Pfannkuchen II
solar **panel** [ˌsəʊlə ˈpænl] Sonnenkollektor V U4, 74
to **panic** [ˈpænɪk] panisch werden II
**pantomime** [ˈpæntəmaɪm] Weihnachtstheaterstück II
**pants** *(pl) (AE)* [pænts] Hose IV
**paper** [ˈpeɪpə] Papier III
**paperboy** [ˈpeɪpəˌbɔɪ] Zeitungsausträger IV
**papergirl** [ˈpeɪpəˌgɜːl] Zeitungsausträgerin IV
**parade** [pəˈreɪd] Parade; Umzug III
**paradise** [ˈpærədaɪs] Paradies IV
**paragraph** [ˈpærəgrɑːf] Paragraf; Absatz <IV>
to **paraphrase** [ˈpærəfreɪz] paraphrasieren; umschreiben <V U2, 42>
**pardon** [ˈpɑːdn] Begnadigung; Entschuldigung; Verzeihung IV
Pardon? [ˈpɑːdn] Wie bitte? I
to **pardon** [ˈpɑːdn] begnadigen; entschuldigen; verzeihen IV
**parents** *(pl)* [ˈpeərnts] Eltern II
**park** [pɑːk] Park I
national park [ˌnæʃnl ˈpɑːk] Nationalpark V U3, 48; Naturpark <IV>
theme park [ˈθiːm ˌpɑːk] Freizeitpark I; Themenpark II
**parking** lot *(AE)* [ˈpɑːkɪŋ ˌlɒt] Parkplatz IV
**parrot** [ˈpærət] Papagei I
**part** [pɑːt] Rolle; Teil II
to take part (in) [ˌteɪk ˈpɑːt] teilnehmen (an) II
**particular** [pəˈtɪkjələ] bestimmte V U4, 70
**partner** [ˈpɑːtnə] Partnerin; Partner III
**part-time** [ˌpɑːtˈtaɪm] Teilzeit-; Halbtags- IV
**party** [ˈpɑːti] Party; Feier I
to **party** [ˈpɑːti] feiern V U2, 30
**pass** [pɑːs] Ausweis; Pass IV
boarding pass [ˈbɔːdɪŋ ˌpɑːs] Bordkarte <V U2, 198>
to **pass** [pɑːs] reichen II; vorbeigehen; durchgehen IV; bestehen V U1, 14
to pass on [ˌpɑːs‿ˈɒn] weitergeben <III>
**passenger** [ˈpæsndʒə] Passagier; Passagierin II
**passive** [ˈpæsɪv] Passiv; Passiv- <IV>
**passport** [ˈpɑːspɔːt] Pass; Reisepass V U2, 31
**past** [pɑːst] Vergangenheit III
past perfect [ˌpɑːst ˈpɜːfɪkt] Plusquamperfekt <IV>
past progressive [ˌpɑːst prəˈgresɪv] Verlaufsform der Vergangenheit <V U2, 37>
simple past [ˌsɪmpl ˈpɑːst] einfache Vergangenheit <III>
**past** [pɑːst] nach *(bei Uhrzeitangaben)* II; vorbei (an) III
half past (two) [ˌhɑːf ˈpɑːst] halb (drei) I
**pasta** [ˈpæstə] Pasta; Nudeln II
pasta bake [ˌpæstə ˈbeɪk] Nudelauflauf II
to **paste** [peɪst] einfügen II
**pasty** [ˈpæsti] Pastete II
**patched** [pætʃt] geflickt <V U3, 205>
**path** [pɑːθ] Pfad; Weg V U1, 12
**patient** [ˈpeɪʃnt] Patient; Patientin II; geduldig III
**patterned** [ˈpætənd] gemustert II
**pause** [pɔːz] Pause <V U3, 55>
to **pause** [pɔːz] (eine kurze) Pause machen; innehalten V U3, 60
**pay** [peɪ] Bezahlung; Lohn; Gehalt IV
**pay** phone [ˈpeɪ fəʊn] Münztelefon III
*to **pay** [peɪ] bezahlen II
to pay attention to sth [ˌpeɪ‿əˈtenʃn tə] seine Aufmerksamkeit auf etw. richten V U1, 17
to pay back [ˌpeɪ ˈbæk] zurückzahlen II
to pay the bill [ˌpeɪ ðə ˈbɪl] die Rechnung bezahlen III
**payment** machine [ˈpeɪmənt ˌməʃiːn] Bezahlautomat II
**PE** (Physical Education) [ˌpiːˈiː, ˌfɪzɪkl edʒʊˈkeɪʃn] Sportunterricht I
**peace** [piːs] Frieden V U3, 49
peaceful [ˈpiːsfl] friedlich IV
**peach** [piːtʃ] Pfirsich I
**peanut** butter [ˌpiːnʌt ˈbʌtə] Erdnussbutter III
**pecan** [ˈpiːkæn] Pekannuss IV
**pen** [pen] Füller; Stift I

**pence** *(pl)* [pens], **penny** *(sg)* ['peni] Pence *(brit. Währungseinheit)* I

**pencil** ['pensl] Bleistift; Buntstift I

pencil case ['pensl ˌkeɪs] Federmäppchen I

pencil sharpener ['pensl ˌʃɑ:pnə] Anspitzer I

**penguin** ['peŋgwɪn] Pinguin I

**people** ['pi:pl] Leute; Menschen I; Volk V U1, 11

Aboriginal people [æbəˌrɪdʒnl 'pi:pl] die Aborigines V U1, 11

of all the people [əv‿'ɔ:l ðə ˌpi:pl] von allen Leuten V U1, 18

**pepper** ['pepə] Pfeffer II

**per** [pɜ:] pro IV

**percent** (%) [pə'sent] Prozent IV

**percentage** [pə'sentɪdʒ] Prozentsatz; prozentualer Anteil <V U3, 66>

**perfect** ['pɜ:fɪkt] perfekt; vollkommen IV

past perfect [ˌpɑ:st 'pɜ:fɪkt] Plusquamperfekt <IV>

present perfect [ˌpreznt 'pɜ:fɪkt] das Perfekt <III>

to **perform** [pə'fɔ:m] auftreten; aufführen III

**perfume** ['pɜ:fju:m] Parfüm III

**perhaps** [pə'hæps] vielleicht V U2, 39

**period** ['pɪəriəd] Stunde; Unterrichtsstunde IV

period of time [ˌpɪəriəd‿əv 'taɪm] Zeitraum <IV>

study hall period ['stʌdi hɔ:l ˌpɪəriəd] Freistunde IV

**permanent** ['pɜ:mnənt] unbefristet; permanent; dauerhaft V U1, 16

**person** ['pɜ:sn] Person; Mensch II

**personal** ['pɜ:snl] persönlich III

personal statement [ˌpɜ:snl 'steɪtmənt] Motivationsschreiben V U1, 16

**personality** [ˌpɜ:sn'æləti] Persönlichkeit <III>

**perspective** [pə'spektɪv] Perspektive; Blickwinkel <IV>

to **persuade** [pə'sweɪd] überreden <III>

**pesticide** ['pestɪsaɪd] Pestizid; Schädlingsbekämpfungsmittel V U1, 21

**pet** [pet] Haustier I

pet shop ['pet ʃɒp] Tierhandlung III

**phone** [fəʊn] Telefon II

to answer the phone [ˌɑ:nsə ðə 'fəʊn] ans Telefon gehen III

cell phone *(AE)* ['sel fəʊn] Mobiltelefon; Handy IV

mobile (phone) ['məʊbaɪl (ˌfəʊn)] Handy; Mobiltelefon I

pay phone ['peɪ fəʊn] Münztelefon III

phone call ['fəʊn ˌkɔ:l] Telefonanruf I

phone number ['fəʊn ˌnʌmbə] Telefonnummer III

to **phone** [fəʊn] anrufen; telefonieren II

**photo** ['fəʊtəʊ] Foto I

to take a photo [ˌteɪk‿ə 'fəʊtəʊ] ein Foto machen I

to take photos [ˌteɪk 'fəʊtəʊz] fotografieren; Fotos machen II

**phrase** [freɪz] Redewendung; Ausdruck; Satz V U4, 79

PE (**Physical** Education) [ˌpi:'i:, ˌfɪzɪkl edʒʊ'keɪʃn] Sportunterricht I

**physical** ['fɪzɪkl] physisch; körperlich IV

**physiotherapist** [ˌfɪziə'θerəpɪst] Physiotherapeut; Physiotherapeutin V U1, 17

**pic** (picture) [pɪk ('pɪktʃə)] Foto IV

to **pick** [pɪk] auswählen; aussuchen; nehmen <IV>; pflücken V U3, 60

to pick up [ˌpɪk‿'ʌp] aufheben II; aufgreifen <III>; abholen IV; aufnehmen <V U2, 41>

**pick-up** ['pɪkʌp] Abholung; Pick-up IV

**picnic** ['pɪknɪk] Picknick I

**picture** ['pɪktʃə] Bild II

**pie** [paɪ] Kuchen; Pastete II

pie chart ['paɪ ˌtʃɑ:t] Kuchendiagramm; Tortendiagramm <IV>

**piece** [pi:s] Stück II

piece of cake ['pi:s‿əv keɪk] einfach <IV>

**pierogi** [pjɜ'rɔgi] Pirogge II

**pig** [pɪg] Schwein <V U2, 42>

guinea pig ['gɪni ˌpɪg] Meerschweinchen I

**pile** [paɪl] Stapel; Haufen <V U1, 26>

**pilot** ['paɪlət] Pilot; Pilotin IV

**pinch** [pɪntʃ] Prise II

**pineapple** ['paɪnæpl] Ananas III

**pinhead** ['pɪnhed] Trottel IV

**pink** [pɪŋk] pink; rosa I

**pipe** [paɪp] Rohr III

**pirate** ['paɪrət] Seeräuber; Seeräuberin; Pirat; Piratin V U2, 29

to **pitch** [pɪtʃ] zwitschern <V U2, 35>

it's a **pity** [ˌɪts‿ə 'pɪti] (es ist) schade IV

**pizza** ['pi:tsə] Pizza I

**place** [pleɪs] Platz; Stelle; Ort I

to take place [ˌteɪk 'pleɪs] stattfinden V U2, 30

**plain** [pleɪn] schlicht; einfach II; Ebene V U3, 54

**plan** [plæn] Plan II

to **plan** [plæn] planen III

**plane** [pleɪn] Flugzeug II

**plank** [plæŋk] Brett; Planke II

to walk the plank [ˌwɔ:k ðə 'plæŋk] über eine Schiffsplanke ins Wasser getrieben werden V U2, 40

**plant** [plɑ:nt] Pflanze I

power plant ['paʊə ˌplɑ:nt] Kraftwerk V U4, 74

**plantain** ['plænteɪn] Kochbanane II

**plantation** [plæn'teɪʃn] Plantage IV

**planter** ['plɑ:ntə] Pflantagenbesitzer; Pflantagenbesitzerin <V U2, 46>

**plaster** ['plɑ:stə] Pflaster III

**plasterer** ['plɑ:stərə] Stuckateur; Stuckateurin <V U1, 192>

**plastic** ['plæstɪk] Plastik; Kunststoff III

**plate** [pleɪt] Teller II

**platform** ['plætfɔ:m] Plattform V U1, 20

**platypus** ['plætɪpəs] Schnabeltier <V U1, 27>

**play** [pleɪ] Theaterstück II

role play ['rəʊl ˌpleɪ] Rollenspiel <II>

to **play** [pleɪ] spielen I

**player** ['pleɪə] Spieler; Spielerin II

**playground** ['pleɪgraʊnd] Schulhof; Pausenhof; Spielplatz I

no playground to speak of [nəʊ ˌpleɪgraʊnd tə 'spi:k‿əv] so gut wie kein(en) Schulhof V U3, 58

**playing field** ['pleɪɪŋ ˌfi:ld] Sportplatz V U3, 59

**please** [pli:z] bitte I
**pledge** [pledʒ] Versprechen IV
  pledge of allegiance [ˌpledʒ‿əv‿əˈli:dʒns] Treueeid IV
**plot** [plɒt] Handlung <III>
**plumber** [ˈplʌmə] Installateur; Installateurin; Klempner; Klempnerin V U1, 17
**plural** [ˈplʊərl] Mehrzahl; Plural <IV>
**poaching** [ˈpəʊtʃɪŋ] Wilderei; Wildern V U3, 54
**pocket** [ˈpɒkɪt] Tasche; Hosentasche II
  pocket money [ˈpɒkɪt ˌmʌni] Taschengeld V U4, 70
**pod** [pɒd] Gondel; Kabine V U4, 74
**podcast** [ˈpɒdkɑ:st] Podcast IV
**poem** [ˈpəʊɪm] Gedicht III
**point** [pɔɪnt] Punkt IV
  lookout point [ˈlʊkaʊt ˌpɔɪnt] Aussichtspunkt II
  to make one's point [ˌmeɪk wʌnz ˈpɔɪnt] seinen Standpunkt deutlich machen <V U4, 73>
  starting point [ˈstɑ:tɪŋ ˌpɔɪnt] Ausgangspunkt <III>
  turning point [ˈtɜ:nɪŋ ˌpɔɪnt] Wendepunkt <III>
**to point** (at) [ˌpɔɪnt‿ˈət] zeigen (auf) I
  to point out [ˌpɔɪnt‿ˈaʊt] zeigen; darauf hinweisen IV
**pointless** [ˈpɔɪntləs] sinnlos IV
**poisonous** [ˈpɔɪznəs] giftig <V U1, 27>
**police** [pəˈli:s] Polizei III
  police officer [pəˈli:s‿ɒfɪsə] Polizeibeamter; Polizeibeamtin I
  police station [pəˈli:s ˌsteɪʃn] Polizeirevier; Polizeiwache V U3, 50
**Polish** [ˈpəʊlɪʃ] polnisch; Polnisch; aus Polen IV
**polite** [pəˈlaɪt] höflich II
  politeness [pəˈlaɪtnəs] Höflichkeit V U1, 13
**political** [pəˈlɪtɪkl] politisch IV
**politics** *(pl only)* [ˈpɒlətɪks] Politik <V U3, 62>
**to pollute** [pəˈlu:t] verschmutzen; verunreinigen V U1, 20
**polluted** [pəˈlu:tɪd] verschmutzt <V U3, 205>
**pollution** [pəˈlu:ʃn] Verschmutzung V U4, 69
**pond** [pɒnd] Teich; Tümpel V U3, 55
swimming **pool** [ˈswɪmɪŋ ˌpu:l] Schwimmbad I
**poor** [pɔ:] arm IV
  the poor [ðə ˈpɔ:] die Armen V U4, 71
**popcorn** [ˈpɒpkɔ:n] Popcorn I
**popular** [ˈpɒpjələ] beliebt III; weit verbreitet <V U2, 46>
**populated** [ˈpɒpjəleɪtɪd] bevölkert; besiedelt IV
**population** *(no pl)* [ˌpɒpjəˈleɪʃn] Bevölkerung; Einwohner; Einwohnerzahl III
**pork** [pɔ:k] Schweinefleisch II
**porridge** [ˈpɒrɪdʒ] Haferbrei III
**port** [pɔ:t] Hafen IV
**porthole** [ˈpɔ:thəʊl] Bullauge; Luke V U2, 39
**Portuguese** [ˌpɔ:tʃəˈgi:z] portugiesisch; Portugiesisch; aus Portugal; Portugiese; Portugiesin <V U4, 84>
**position** [pəˈzɪʃn] Position; Stelle V U2, 38
**positive** [ˈpɒzətɪv] positiv III
**possession** [pəˈzeʃn] Eigentum <V U3, 205>
**possessive** pronoun [pəˈsesɪv ˌprəʊnaʊn] Possessivpronomen <III>
**possible** [ˈpɒsəbl] möglich <V U2, 33>
not **possibly** [nɒt ˈpɒsəbli] unmöglich III
**post** [pəʊst] Post *(online gestellte Nachricht)* IV
  post office [ˈpəʊst‿ɒfɪs] Postamt I
**to post** [pəʊst] aufgeben *(einen Brief)*; abschicken *(einen Brief)* III; online stellen; posten IV
**postcard** [ˈpəʊstkɑ:d] Postkarte I
**poster** [ˈpəʊstə] Poster I
**pot** [pɒt] Topf III
**potato** *(sg)* [pəˈteɪtəʊ], **potatoes** *(pl)* [pəˈteɪtəʊz] Kartoffel II
  jacket potato [ˌdʒækɪt pəˈteɪtəʊ] Ofenkartoffel II
  mashed potatoes [ˌmæʃt pəˈteɪtəʊz] Kartoffelbrei II
**pouch** [paʊtʃ] Beutel <V U1, 26>
**pound** [paʊnd] Pfund *(brit. Währungseinheit)* I
**poverty** [ˈpɒvəti] Armut IV
**power** [ˈpaʊə] Energie; Kraft; Macht III
  power plant [ˈpaʊə ˌplɑ:nt] Kraftwerk V U4, 74
  powerful [ˈpaʊəfl] stark; mächtig; bedeutend; beeindruckend IV
**practical** [ˈpræktɪkl] praktisch IV
**practice** [ˈpræktɪs] Training; Übung I
**to practise** [ˈpræktɪs] üben; trainieren III; ausüben; praktizieren <V U2, 46>
**to pray** [preɪ] beten V U3, 59
**prayer** [preə] Gebet IV
**precise** [prɪˈsaɪs] genau <IV>
**to prefer** [prɪˈfɜ:] vorziehen II
**to prepare** [prɪˈpeə] zubereiten; (sich) vorbereiten III
**preposition** [ˌprepəˈzɪʃn] Präposition <III>
**preschool** [ˈpri:sku:l] Vorschule; Vorschul- V U1, 17
**present** [ˈpreznt] Geschenk I; Gegenwart; Präsens <IV>
  present perfect [ˌpreznt ˈpɜ:fɪkt] das Perfekt <III>
  present progressive [ˌpreznt prəˈgresɪv] Verlaufsform der Gegenwart <III>
  simple present [ˌsɪmpl ˈpreznt] Gegenwart; Präsens <III>
at **present** [ət ˈpreznt] augenblicklich; derzeit V U4, 74
**to present** [prɪˈzent] vorstellen I; präsentieren IV; überreichen <V U3, 66>; darstellen <V U4, 76>
**presentation** [ˌpreznˈteɪʃn] Präsentation; Vortrag IV
**president** [ˈprezɪdnt] Sprecher; Sprecherin; Präsident; Präsidentin IV
**press** [pres] Presse V U4, 78
**pressure** [ˈpreʃə] Druck V U4, 69
**pretty** [ˈprɪti] hübsch II; ziemlich; ganz schön IV
**prewriting** [pri:ˈraɪtɪŋ] vor dem Schreiben <III>
**price** [praɪs] Preis II
**pride** [praɪd] Stolz IV

**primary** school ['praɪmri ˌsku:l] Grundschule V U3, 58
**principal** *(AE)* ['prɪnsɪpl] Schulleiter; Schulleiterin IV
**prison** ['prɪzn] Gefängnis II
**prisoner** ['prɪznə] Gefangener; Gefangene V U2, 40
**private** ['praɪvɪt] Privat-; privat V U3, 50
**privilege** ['prɪvlɪdʒ] Privileg; Recht; Vorrecht V U2, 34
privileged ['prɪvlɪdʒd] privilegiert; bevorzugt V U3, 52
**prize** [praɪz] Preis II
**pro** [prəʊ] Pro; Vorteil V U4, 68
**pro** and contra [ˌprəʊ ən 'kɒntrə] für und wider <IV>
**pro-** [prəʊ] für; Pro- V U4, 78
**probably** ['prɒbəbli] wahrscheinlich III
**problem** ['prɒbləm] Problem I
to **produce** [prə'dju:s] hervorbringen; produzieren III; anbauen; erzeugen; herstellen V U4, 74
**production** [prə'dʌkʃn] Produktion; Herstellung <III>
**profile** ['prəʊfaɪl] Profil; Steckbrief <III>
**programme** ['prəʊgræm] Programm; Sendung I
past **progressive** [ˌpa:st prə'gresɪv] Verlaufsform der Vergangenheit <V U2, 37>
present **progressive** [ˌpreznt prə'gresɪv] Verlaufsform der Gegenwart <III>
**project** ['prɒdʒekt] Projekt III
to **promise** ['prɒmɪs] versprechen IV
**prompt** card ['prɒmt ˌka:d] Stichwortkarte <IV>
**pronoun** ['prəʊnaʊn] Pronomen; Fürwort <IV>
possessive pronoun [pə'sesɪv ˌprəʊnaʊn] Possessivpronomen <III>
to **pronounce** [prə'naʊns] aussprechen <IV>
**pronunciation** [prəˌnʌnsi'eɪʃn] Aussprache <IV>
**prop** [prɒp] Requisit III
to **protect** [prə'tekt] schützen III
**protected** [prə'tektɪd] geschützt V U1, 12
**protest** ['prəʊtest] Protest; Demonstration IV
to **protest** [prə'test] protestieren V U3, 59
**Protestant** ['prɒtɪstnt] protestantisch; Protestant; Protestantin III
**protester** [prə'testə] Gegner; Gegnerin IV
**proud** (of) [praʊd (əv)] stolz (auf) III
to **prove** [pru:v] beweisen IV
**pub** [pʌb] Kneipe; Gasthaus III
**public** ['pʌblɪk] öffentlich <V U3, 62>
public holiday [ˌpʌblɪk 'hɒlədeɪ] Feiertag <V U4, 85>
public school [ˌpʌblɪk 'sku:l] Privatschule <V U3, 205>
public transport [ˌpʌblɪk 'trænspɔ:t] öffentliche Verkehrsmittel III
to **publish** ['pʌblɪʃ] veröffentlichen; publizieren; verlegen V U4, 78
**publisher** ['pʌblɪʃə] Verlag; Herausgeber V U4, 78
**pudding** ['pʊdɪŋ] Nachspeise; Pudding II
to **puke** [pju:k] erbrechen; sich übergeben IV
to **pull** [pʊl] ziehen I
**punctual** ['pʌŋktʃuəl] pünktlich V U1, 17
**punctuation** [ˌpʌŋktʃu'eɪʃn] Zeichensetzung; Interpunktion <III>
to **punish** ['pʌnɪʃ] bestrafen V U4, 78
**punishment** ['pʌnɪʃmənt] Bestrafung V U2, 40
**pupil** ['pju:pl] Schüler; Schülerin V U3, 58
**puppet** ['pʌpɪt] Puppe; Handpuppe <V U3, 63>
to **purchase** ['pɜ:tʃəs] kaufen; erwerben V U4, 71
**pure** [pjʊə] rein; pur <V U2, 35>
**purple** ['pɜ:pl] lila; violett I
on **purpose** [ɒn 'pɜ:pəs] absichtlich II
to **push** [pʊʃ] schieben; drücken I; schubsen; drängeln III
*to **put** [pʊt] setzen; legen; stellen I
to put a comment [ˌpʊt‿ə 'kɒment] einen Kommentar schreiben <I>
to put in [ˌpʊt‿'ɪn] einsetzen I
to put in the right order [ˌpʊt‿ɪn ðə 'raɪt ɔ:də] in die richtige Reihenfolge bringen I
to put on [ˌpʊt‿'ɒn] anlegen; anziehen III
to put up [ˌpʊt‿'ʌp] aufstellen; errichten IV
**put** [pʊt] simple past von to put I
**puzzle** ['pʌzl] Rätsel; Puzzle V U4, 78

## Q

**qualification** [ˌkwɒlɪfɪ'keɪʃn] Qualifikation; Abschluss; Schulabschluss V U1, 17
**qualified** ['kwɒlɪfaɪd] qualifiziert V U1, 19
to **qualify** ['kwɒlɪfaɪ] qualifizieren; befähigen V U1, 16
**quality** ['kwɒləti] Qualität; Eigenschaft; Merkmal V U4, 74
**quarter** past ['kwɔ:tə pa:st] Viertel nach I
**quarter** to ['kwɔ:tə tə] Viertel vor I
**queen** [kwi:n] Königin III
**question** ['kwestʃən] Frage I
rhetorical question [rɪˌtɒrɪkl 'kwestʃən] rhetorische Frage <V U3, 65>
**questioning** ['kwestʃənɪŋ] Verhör; Vernehmung V U3, 50
**queue** [kju:] Warteschlange II
**quick** [kwɪk] schnell II
**quiet** ['kwaɪət] ruhig; leise; still III
to go quiet [ˌgəʊ 'kwaɪət] still werden III
to keep quiet [ˌki:p 'kwaɪət] ruhig sein <III>
**quite** [kwaɪt] ziemlich III
**quiz** [kwɪz] Quiz; Rätsel <I>
**quota** ['kwəʊtə] Quote; Quoten- <V U3, 66>
**quote** [kwəʊt] Zitat <IV>

## R

**rabbit** ['ræbɪt] Kaninchen <V U1, 26>
**raccoon** [rə'ku:n] Waschbär I
**race** [reɪs] Wettrennen; Rennen I; Rasse V U3, 48

mixed race [ˌmɪkst ˈreɪs] gemischter Abstammung; Mischrasse V U3, 48
**racial** [ˈreɪʃl] Rassen- <V U3, 66>
**racing** [ˈreɪsɪŋ] Rennen <V U3, 67>
**racism** [ˈreɪsɪzm] Rassismus IV
**radiator** [ˈreɪdieɪtə] Heizkörper IV
**radio** [ˈreɪdiəʊ] Radio II
**rafting** [ˈrɑːftɪŋ] Rafting III
**railway** [ˈreɪlweɪ] Eisenbahn IV
railway track [ˈreɪlweɪ ˌtræk] Gleis IV
**rain** [reɪn] Regen III
to **rain** [reɪn] regnen I
**rainbow** [ˈreɪnbəʊ] Regenbogen III
**raincoat** [ˈreɪnkəʊt] Regenmantel III
**rainforest** [ˈreɪnˌfɒrɪst] Regenwald <V U2, 44>
**rainy** [ˈreɪni] regnerisch I
rainy season [ˌreɪni ˈsiːzn] Regenzeit V U1, 21
to **raise** [reɪz] anheben; erhöhen V U4, 75
to raise money [ˌreɪz ˈmʌni] Geld aufbringen; Geld sammeln <V U4, 212>
**ran** [ræn] simple past von *to run* III
**rang** [ræŋ] simple past von *to ring* III
mountain **range** [ˈmaʊntɪn ˌreɪndʒ] Bergkette; Gebirge V U3, 55
**ranger** *(AE)* [ˈreɪndʒə] Ranger; Rangerin V U3, 54
to **rank** [ræŋk] einstufen <IV>
**ranking** list [ˈræŋkɪŋ ˌlɪst] Rangliste; Rangfolge <IV>
**rap** [ræp] Rap <I>
to **rap** [ræp] rappen II
**rapper** [ˈræpə] Rapper; Rapperin III
**rare** [reə] rar; selten V U4, 70
**raspberry** [ˈrɑːzbri] Himbeere III
**Rastafarianism** [ˌræstəˈfeəriənɪzm] Rastafarianismus *(Glaubensrichtung)* <V U2, 46>
to **rate** [reɪt] bewerten; einstufen III
I'd **rather** [aɪd ˈrɑːðə] ich würde lieber III
**rating** [ˈreɪtɪŋ] Bewertung <III>
**ration** [ˈræʃn] Ration <V U2, 46>
**razor** [ˈreɪzə] Rasierer; Rasierapparat IV

**RE** (Religious Education) [ˌɑːˈriː, rɪˌlɪdʒəs‿edʒʊˈkeɪʃn] Religionsunterricht I
to **reach** [riːtʃ] erreichen IV
to **react** [riˈækt] reagieren IV
**reaction** [riˈækʃn] Reaktion IV
*to **read** [riːd] lesen I
**reader** [ˈriːdə] Leser; Leserin IV
**reading** [ˈriːdɪŋ] Lesen <I>
**ready** [ˈredi] fertig; bereit I
to get ready [ˌget ˈredi] sich vorbereiten; sich fertig machen IV
**real** [rɪəl] echt; richtig; wirklich II
to **realise** [ˈrɪəlaɪz] erkennen; realisieren V U1, 13
**really** [ˈrɪəli] wirklich I; echt II
**reason** [ˈriːzn] Grund III
to give reasons [ˌgɪv ˈriːznz] Gründe nennen; Gründe angeben III
**receipt** [riˈsiːt] Quittung II
**receptionist** [rɪˈsepʃnɪst] Empfangschef; Empfangschefin V U1, 16
**recess** *(AE)* [ˈriːses] Pause IV
**recipe** [ˈresɪpi] Rezept II
to **recognise** [ˈrekəgnaɪz] erkennen; anerkennen V U2, 39
**recognised** [ˈrekəgnaɪzd] anerkannt V U1, 12
*to keep a **record** of sth [ˌkiːp‿ə ˈrekɔːd‿əv] über etw. Buch führen V U4, 70
to **record** [rɪˈkɔːd] aufnehmen <III>
**recording** [rɪˈkɔːdɪŋ] Aufnahme <III>
recording studio [rɪˈkɔːdɪŋ ˌstjuːdiəʊ] Tonstudio I
to **recover** [rɪˈkʌvə] sich erholen V U1, 21
to **recycle** [ˌriːˈsaɪkl] recyceln; wiederverwerten V U3, 55
**red** [red] rot I
to go red [ˌgəʊ ˈred] rot werden V U3, 60
to **reduce** [rɪˈdjuːs] reduzieren; vermindern; verringern V U3, 55
**redwood** (tree) [ˈredwʊd (triː)] Mammutbaum IV
**reef** [riːf] Riff V U1, 20
**reference** [ˈrefrns] Referenz; Referenzschreiben V U1, 16

to **refuse** [rɪˈfjuːz] sich weigern; ablehnen IV
**region** [ˈriːdʒn] Region; Gegend IV
to **register** [ˈredʒɪstə] sich registrieren lassen; sich eintragen; sich anmelden <V U4, 80>
**registration** [ˌredʒɪˈstreɪʃn] Überprüfung der Anwesenheit I; Anmeldung II
to **regret** [rɪˈgret] bedauern IV
**regular** [ˈregjələ] regelmäßig; normal; üblich; gleichmäßig IV
to **regulate** [ˈregjəleɪt] vorschreiben; bestimmen; regeln V U3, 54
to **reject** [rɪˈdʒekt] zurückweisen; ablehnen IV
*to be **related** to [biː rɪˈleɪtɪd tə] verwandt sein mit; sich beziehen auf <V U4, 79>
**relationship** [rɪˈleɪʃnʃɪp] Beziehung <V U3, 60>
**relative** clause [ˈrelətɪv ˌklɔːz] Relativsatz <V U2, 33>
to **relax** [rɪˈlæks] sich entspannen; sich ausruhen V U4, 69
**relaxed** [rɪˈlækst] entspannt; locker; gelassen IV
**relaxing** [rɪˈlæksɪŋ] entspannend; erholsam III
to **release** [rɪˈliːs] veröffentlichen; herausgeben; freigeben; freisetzen; loslassen IV
**reliable** [rɪˈlaɪəbl] verlässlich; zuverlässig; vertrauenswürdig IV
**religion** [rɪˈlɪdʒn] Religion V U2, 34
**religious** [rɪˈlɪdʒəs] religiös; gläubig IV
RE (Religious Education) [ˌɑːˈriː, rɪˌlɪdʒəs‿edʒʊˈkeɪʃn] Religionsunterricht I
to **remain** [rɪˈmeɪn] übrig bleiben; bleiben <V U4, 84>
to **remember** [rɪˈmembə] sich merken; sich erinnern (an) II
to **remove** [rɪˈmuːv] entfernen IV
**renewable** [rɪˈnjuːəbl] erneuerbar; verlängerbar V U4, 74
renewable energy [rɪˌnjuːəbl‿ˈenədʒi] erneuerbare Energie V U4, 74
**rent** [rent] Miete II

**to rent** [rent] mieten III
**to repair** [rɪ'peə] reparieren III
**to repeat** [rɪ'pi:t] wiederholen III
**to replace** [rɪ'pleɪs] ersetzen IV
**to reply** [rɪ'plaɪ] antworten; erwidern V U4, 72
**report** [rɪ'pɔ:t] Bericht IV
**to report (on)** [rɪ'pɔ:t (ɒn)] berichten (über) IV
**reported** speech [rɪˌpɔ:tɪd 'spi:tʃ] indirekte Rede <IV>
**reporter** [rɪ'pɔ:tə] Reporter; Reporterin III
**to represent** [ˌreprɪ'zent] repräsentieren; stehen für; darstellen <V U3, 52>
**reptile** ['reptaɪl] Reptil <V U3, 205>
**republic** [rɪ'pʌblɪk] Republik III
**reputation** [ˌrepjə'teɪʃn] Ruf; Ansehen IV
**request** [rɪ'kwest] Anfrage IV
**to require** [rɪ'kwaɪə] benötigen; erfordern V U1, 16
**requirement** [rɪ'kwaɪəmənt] Voraussetzung; Anforderung V U1, 19
to meet requirements [ˌmi:t rɪ'kwaɪəmənts] Voraussetzungen erfüllen <V U1, 16>
*to **re-read** [ˌri:'ri:d] erneut lesen <V U3, 60>
animal **rescue** shelter [ˌænɪml 'reskju: ˌʃeltə] Tierheim I
**to research** [rɪ'sɜ:tʃ] recherchieren; erforschen; untersuchen <V U1, 27>; recherchieren; erforschen; untersuchen <V U3, 61>
*to **resell** [ˌri:'sel] wiederverkaufen; weiterverkaufen V U4, 70
**to resent** [rɪ'zent] übelnehmen; verübeln IV
**reservation** [ˌrezə'veɪʃn] Reservierung; Reservat IV
to make a reservation [ˌmeɪk‿ə 'rezəveɪʃn] reservieren III
nature **reserve** ['neɪtʃə rɪˌzɜ:v] Naturschutzgebiet V U3, 48
**to resist** [rɪ'zɪst] sich widersetzen; widerstehen V U2, 40
**resort** [rɪ'zɔ:t] Ferienort; Ferienanlage V U2, 30
**respect** [rɪ'spekt] Respekt V U1, 13
respectful [rɪ'spektfl] respektvoll V U1, 13
**to respect** [rɪ'spekt] respektieren IV
**to respond** [rɪ'spɒnd] reagieren; erwidern; antworten <V U3, 65>
**responsibility** [rɪˌspɒnsə'bɪləti] Verantwortung <V U1, 192>; V U2, 35
**responsible** [rɪs'pɒnsəbl] verantwortlich; verantwortungsvoll IV
the **rest** [ðə 'rest] der Rest IV
**to rest** [rest] rasten; ausruhen; liegen IV
**restaurant** ['restrɒnt] Restaurant II
**restricted** [rɪ'strɪktɪd] begrenzt <V U3, 205>
**restriction** [rɪ'strɪkʃn] Beschränkung; Einschränkung V U4, 79
**restroom** *(AE)* ['restrʊm] Toilette IV
**result** [rɪ'zʌlt] Ergebnis II
**to result** in [rɪ'zʌlt‿ɪn] zur Folge haben; führen zu V U1, 20
**retail** ['ri:teɪl] Einzelhandel <V U1, 192>
*to **retell** [ˌri:'tel] nacherzählen; nochmals erzählen <IV>
**return** [rɪ'tɜ:n] Rückkehr V U2, 29
return ticket [rɪ'tɜ:n ˌtɪkɪt] Hin- und Rückfahrkarte III
**to return** [rɪ'tɜ:n] zurückkehren; zurückgeben IV
**to reuse** [ˌri:'ju:z] wiederverwenden <V U4, 212>
**review** [rɪ'vju:] Kritik III
**revising** [rɪ'vaɪzɪŋ] Überarbeitung <III>
Industrial **Revolution** [ɪnˌdʌstriəl revl'u:ʃn] industrielle Revolution III
*to **rewrite** [ˌri:'raɪt] umschreiben; neu schreiben <V U2, 32>
**rhetorical** question [rɪˌtɒrɪkl 'kwestʃən] rhetorische Frage <V U3, 65>
**rhino** ['raɪnəʊ] Rhinozeros; Nashorn V U3, 48
**to rhyme** [raɪm] (sich) reimen III
**rhythm** ['rɪðm] Rhythmus III
**rice** [raɪs] Reis II
**rich** [rɪtʃ] reich III
the rich [ðə 'rɪtʃ] die Reichen V U3, 51
**ridden** ['rɪdn] past participle von *to ride* II
**ride** [raɪd] Fahrt; Ritt IV
to take a ride [ˌteɪk‿ə 'raɪd] fahren IV
*to **ride** [raɪd] fahren; reiten II
**ridge** [rɪdʒ] Erhöhung <V U3, 205>
horse **riding** ['hɔ:s ˌraɪdɪŋ] Reiten I
**right** [raɪt] Recht IV
civil rights *(pl)* [ˌsɪvl 'raɪts] Bürgerrechte IV
human rights *(pl)* [ˌhju:mən 'raɪts] Menschenrechte *(Pl.)* V U4, 79
**right** [raɪt] richtig; korrekt I; also II; rechts III; gerade; genau; in dem Moment als IV
to be right [bi: 'raɪt] recht haben II
to do the right thing [ˌdu: ðə 'raɪt θɪŋ] das Richtige tun III
right ahead [ˌraɪt‿ə'hed] geradeaus IV
right away [ˌraɪt‿ə'weɪ] sofort; gleich IV
right here [ˌraɪt 'hɪə] genau hier <V U3, 65>
right now [ˌraɪt 'naʊ] jetzt gerade III; jetzt gleich; sofort; gerade <V U3, 65>
right there [ˌraɪt 'ðeə] genau vor dir <III>
to turn right [ˌtɜ:n 'raɪt] (nach) rechts abbiegen I
all right [ɔ:l 'raɪt] in Ordnung; alles klar II
on the right [ɒn ðə 'raɪt] auf der rechten Seite; rechts I
You're right. [jɔ:‿'raɪt] Du hast recht. I
**right-wing** [ˌraɪt'wɪŋ] rechtsorientiert; Rechts-; rechts- V U4, 79
*to **ring** [rɪŋ] läuten; klingeln III
ice **rink** ['aɪs ˌrɪŋk] Eislaufbahn <IV>
*to **rise up** [ˌraɪz‿'ʌp] aufstehen <V U2, 35>
**risin'** ['raɪzɪn] aufgehende <V U2, 35>
**to risk** [rɪsk] riskieren <IV>
**ritual** ['rɪtjuəl] Ritual <V U2, 46>
**rival** ['raɪvl] Rivale; Rivalin; Konkurrent; Konkurrentin V U2, 29
**river** ['rɪvə] Fluss I
**road** [rəʊd] Straße I

**roadwork** *(AE)* ['rəʊdwɜ:k] Straßenbauarbeiten IV
to **rob** [rɒb] ausrauben; rauben; berauben <V U2, 39>
**rock** [rɒk] Fels; Stein; Rock *(Musik)* III
rock climbing ['rɒk ˌklaɪmɪŋ] Klettern I
rock climbing wall [ˌrɒk klaɪmɪŋ 'wɔ:l] Kletterwand <V U2, 47>
rocky ['rɒki] felsig; steinig <V U3, 205>
**rode** [rəʊd] simple past von *to ride* II
**role** [rəʊl] Rolle IV
role model ['rəʊl ˌmɒdl] Vorbild V U2, 29
role play ['rəʊl ˌpleɪ] Rollenspiel <II>
to **roll** up [ˌrəʊl‿'ʌp] zusammenrollen; aufrollen; aufkrempeln IV
**roller** coaster ['rəʊlə ˌkəʊstə] Achterbahn II
**romance** ['rəʊmæns] Liebesgeschichte III
**roo** [ru:] Känguru *(ugs.)* <V U1, 26>
**roof** [ru:f] Dach V U4, 75
**room** [ru:m] Zimmer; Raum I
to make room [ˌmeɪk 'ru:m] Platz machen <V U4, 84>
roomy ['ru:mi] geräumig <V U2, 198>
**root** [ru:t] Wurzel IV
root word [ˌru:t 'wɜ:d] Stammwort <III>
**rope** [rəʊp] Seil I
**rose** [rəʊz] Rose IV
**rough** [rʌf] rau; grob; derb V U3, 58
**route** [ru:t] Strecke; Route <V U3, 67>
sea route ['si: ˌru:t] Seeweg <V U2, 39>
**row** [rəʊ] Reihe; Zeile V U4, 70
**royal** ['rɔɪəl] königlich II
**rubber** ['rʌbə] Gummi III
**rubbish** ['rʌbɪʃ] Müll; Abfall II
**rude** [ru:d] unhöflich; unverschämt V U1, 13
**rudeness** ['ru:dnəs] Unhöflichkeit; Unverschämtheit V U1, 13
**rugby** ['rʌgbi] Rugby III
to **ruin** ['ru:ɪn] ruinieren; zerstören II
**rule** [ru:l] Regel III; Herrschaft IV
**ruler** ['ru:lə] Lineal I
**rum** [rʌm] Rum <V U2, 46>
*to **run** [rʌn] rennen; laufen I; betreiben III
to run about ['rʌn‿əˌbaʊt] herumrennen II
to run away [ˌrʌn‿ə'weɪ] weglaufen III
to run out of [ˌrʌn‿'aʊt‿əv] ausgehen *(Ware)* III
**run** [rʌn] past participle von *to run* III
**rung** [rʌŋ] past participle von *to ring* III
gold **rush** ['gəʊld ˌrʌʃ] Goldrausch IV
to **rush** [rʌʃ] eilen; sich beeilen; stürzen III
to rush down [rʌʃ 'daʊn] hinuntereilen II
rush hour ['rʌʃ ˌaʊə] Hauptverkehrszeit IV
**Russian** ['rʌʃn] russisch; Russisch; aus Russland; Russe; Russin IV
to **rust** [rʌst] rosten IV

## S

**sacred** ['seɪkrɪd] heilig V U1, 12
**sad** [sæd] traurig III
**safari** [sə'fɑ:ri] Safari V U3, 48
**safe** [seɪf] in Sicherheit; sicher III
to keep safe [ˌki:p 'seɪf] schützen III
**safety** ['seɪfti] Sicherheit IV
safety net ['seɪfti ˌnet] Sicherheitsnetz IV
**said** [sed] simple past von *to say* I
to **sail** [seɪl] segeln IV
**sailor** ['seɪlə] Seemann; Matrose <V U2, 42>
**salad** ['sæləd] Salat II
**salary** ['sælri] Gehalt V U1, 16
**sale** [seɪl] Schlussverkauf; Ausverkauf II
jumble sale ['dʒʌmbl ˌseɪl] Flohmarkt II
**sales** associate *(AE)* [ˌseɪlz ə'səʊʃiət] Verkäufer; Verkäuferin IV
**salesperson** ['seɪlzˌpɜ:sn] Verkäufer; Verkäuferin <V U1, 192>
**salt** [sɔ:lt] Salz II
**saltwater** crocodile [sɔ:ltˌwɔ:tə 'krɒkədaɪl] Salzwasserkrokodil V U1, 23
**the same** [ðə 'seɪm] derselbe; gleich II
**sample** ['sɑ:mpl] Probe <V U1, 24>
**sand** [sænd] Sand V U2, 30
**sandpit** ['sænpɪt] Sandkasten V U3, 58
**sandwich** ['sænwɪdʒ] Sandwich; belegtes Brot I
**sandy** ['sændi] sandig V U2, 28
**sang** [sæŋ] simple past von *to sing* II
**sank** [sæŋk] simple past von *to sink* III
**sat** [sæt] simple past, past participle von *to sit* IV
**satellite** ['sætlaɪt] Satellit V U1, 11
satellite dish ['sætlaɪt ˌdɪʃ] Satellitenschüssel V U1, 11
**satnav** ['sætnæv] Navi I
**Saturday** ['sætədeɪ] Samstag I
**sauce** [sɔ:s] Soße II
**sausage** ['sɒsɪdʒ] Wurst; Bratwurst II
sausage roll [ˌsɒsɪdʒ 'rəʊl] Blätterteig mit Wurstfüllung II
**savage** ['sævɪdʒ] Wilder; Wilde V U3, 58
to **save** [seɪv] speichern II; retten; bergen III; sparen; aufheben IV
**saw** [sɔ:] simple past von *to see* I
**saxophone** ['sæksəfəʊn] Saxofon I
*to **say** [seɪ] nachsprechen; nennen; sagen; sprechen I
to say hi to [ˌseɪ 'haɪ tə] grüßen; Grüße ausrichten I
to say sorry [ˌseɪ 'sɒri] sich entschuldigen II
**scaffolding** ['skæfldɪŋ] Gerüst <V U4, 84>
**scale** [skeɪl] Skala; Maßstab; Ausmaß V U4, 69
to **scan** [skæn] scannen; nach Details durchsuchen <III>
to **scare** [skeə] erschrecken II
**scared** [skeəd] verängstigt V U2, 33
to be scared [bi: 'skeəd] Angst haben; erschrocken sein II
**scarf** *(sg)* [skɑ:f], **scarves** *(pl)* [skɑ:vz] Schal; Tuch I
**scary** ['skeəri] gruselig; beängstigend I
**scene** [si:n] Szene II
to set the scene [ˌset ðə 'si:n] beste Voraussetzungen schaffen <IV>

**scenery** [ˈsiːnri] Landschaft V U3, 48
**schedule** *(AE)* [ˈskedʒuːl] Stundenplan; Fahrplan IV
**school** [skuːl] Schule I
at school [ət ˈskuːl] in der Schule I
boarding school [ˈbɔːdɪŋ ˌskuːl] Internat V U1, 11
diving school [ˈdaɪvɪŋ ˌskuːl] Tauchschule V U2, 30
high school [ˈhaɪ ˌskuːl] Highschool *(weiterführende Schule, Oberstufe)* IV
primary school [ˈpraɪmri ˌskuːl] Grundschule V U3, 58
school certificate for admission to college [ˌskuːl sətɪfɪkət fər‿ədmɪʃn tə ˈkɒlɪdʒ] Fachhochschulreife <V U1, 192>
school certificate for admission to university [ˌskuːl sətɪfɪkət fər‿ədmɪʃn tə ˌjuːnɪˈvɜːsəti] Abitur <V U1, 192>
school life [ˈskuː‿ˌlaɪf] Schulalltag <I>
school trip [ˌskuːl ˈtrɪp] Klassenfahrt I
state school [ˈsteɪt ˌskuːl] staatliche Schule; öffentliche Schule V U3, 51
**Science** [saɪəns] Wissenschaft; Naturwissenschaft I
computer science [kəmˌpjuːtə ˈsaɪəns] Informatik <III>
science fiction [ˌsaɪəns ˈfɪkʃn] Science-Fiction I
**scientist** [ˈsaɪəntɪst] Wissenschaftler; Wissenschaftlerin V U1, 21
**scissors** *(pl)* [ˈsɪzəz] Schere III
nail scissors *(pl)* [ˈneɪl ˌsɪzəz] Nagelschere III
**scone** [skɒn] Scone *(eine Art süßes Brötchen)* II
**score** [skɔː] Punktestand II
**Scot** [skɒt] Schotte; Schottin III
**Scottish** [ˈskɒtɪʃ] schottisch III
**scrambled** egg [ˌskræmbld‿ˈeg] Rührei II
**scream** [skriːm] Schrei V U3, 59
to **scream** [skriːm] schreien; kreischen III
**script** [skrɪpt] Drehbuch; Skript <III>
**scriptwriter** [ˈskrɪptˌraɪtə] Drehbuchautor; Drehbuchautorin <III>
**scruffy** [ˈskrʌfi] ungepflegt; dreckig <V U3, 205>
**sea** [siː] Meer I
sea route [ˈsiː ˌruːt] Seeweg <V U2, 39>
**seafood** [ˈsiːfuːd] Meeresfrüchte V U2, 30
**seal** [siːl] Seehund; Robbe <III>
**search** [sɜːtʃ] Suche <IV>
search engine [ˈsɜːtʃ‿ˌendʒɪn] Suchmaschine <IV>
to **search** [sɜːtʃ] durchsuchen; suchen IV
to search for [ˈsɜːtʃ fə] suchen nach <III>
at the **seaside** [ət ðə ˈsiːsaɪd] am Meer I
**season** [ˈsiːzn] Saison; Jahreszeit IV
rainy season [ˌreɪni ˈsiːzn] Regenzeit V U1, 21
**seat** [siːt] Sitz V U3, 48; Sitzplatz; Platz IV
Have a seat. [ˌhæv‿ə ˈsiːt] Setzen Sie sich.; Setz dich. IV
**second** [ˈseknd] zweite I; Sekunde II; zweitens IV
**second-hand** [ˌsekndˈhænd] gebraucht; secondhand; aus zweiter Hand V U4, 71
**secret** [ˈsiːkrət] geheim; Geheimnis II
**secretary** [ˈsekrətri] Sekretär; Sekretärin; Assistent; Assistentin <V U1, 192>
**section** [ˈsekʃn] Abschnitt <III>
**security** [sɪˈkjʊərəti] Sicherheit; Schutz; Wachdienst V U3, 49
*to **see** [siː] sehen I
to see friends [siː ˈfrendz] Freunde treffen I
See you later. [ˌsiː jə ˈleɪtə] Tschüss.; Bis bald. I
See you. [ˈsiː ˌjuː] Tschüss.; Bis bald. I
to **seem** [siːm] scheinen III
**seen** [siːn] past participle von *to see* II
**segregated** [ˈsegrɪgeɪtɪd] getrennt IV
**segregation** [ˌsegrɪˈgeɪʃn] Rassentrennung; Trennung IV
**self** [self] selbst; sich III
**selfie** [ˈselfi] Selfie IV
**selfish** [ˈselfɪʃ] selbstsüchtig IV
**self-motivated** [ˌselfˈməʊtɪveɪtɪd] eigenmotiviert V U1, 17
*to **sell** [sel] verkaufen III
**semi-detached** house [ˌsemɪdɪˈtætʃt ˌhaʊs] Doppelhaus <V U3, 205>
*to **send** [send] schicken; senden I
to send in [ˌsend‿ˈɪn] einschicken; einsenden V U1, 12
*to make **sense** [ˌmeɪk ˈsens] Sinn ergeben; einleuchten <III>
motion **sensor** [ˌməʊʃn ˈsensə] Bewegungsmelder V U4, 74
**sent** [sent] simple past von *to send* I; past participle von *to send* II
**sentence** [ˈsentəns] Satz <I>
to **separate** [ˈsepreɪt] trennen V U3, 49
**separate** [ˈseprət] getrennt; separat; verschieden IV
**September** [sepˈtembə] September I
**sequence** [ˈsiːkwəns] Sequenz; Szene; Abfolge <IV>
**serious** [ˈsɪəriəs] schwer; ernst III
to take sth seriously [ˌteɪk ˈsɪəriəsli] etw. ernst nehmen IV
Are you serious? [ˌɑː ju ˈsɪəriəs] Im Ernst? III
to **serve** [sɜːv] servieren IV
**service** [ˈsɜːvɪs] Dienst III
customer service [ˌkʌstəmə ˈsɜːvɪs] Kundendienst; Kundenbetreuung V U1, 16
emergency service [ɪˈmɜːdʒnsi ˌsɜːvɪs] Notdienst; Rettungsdienst III
**Sesotho** [sɪˈsuːtuː] Sesotho *(Sprache)* <V U3, 62>
*to **set off** [ˌset‿ˈɒf] aufbrechen; sich aufmachen; auslösen IV
*to **set the scene** [ˌset ðə ˈsiːn] beste Voraussetzungen schaffen <IV>
**setting** [ˈsetɪŋ] Schauplatz <III>
to **settle** [ˈsetl] besiedeln; sich niederlassen IV
**settler** [ˈsetlə] Siedler; Siedlerin IV
**seven** [ˈsevn] sieben I
**seventeen** [ˌsevnˈtiːn] siebzehn I
**seventy** [ˈsevnti] siebzig I

**several** ['sevrl] einige; mehrere; verschiedene IV

*to **shake** [ʃeɪk] schütteln V U3, 60

to shake one's head [ˌʃeɪk wʌns 'hed] den Kopf schütteln V U3, 60

**shaken** ['ʃeɪkn] past participle von *to shake* V U3, 60

**shampoo** [ʃæm'pu:] Shampoo III

**shamrock** ['ʃæmrɒk] Kleeblatt III

**shape** [ʃeɪp] Form <V U4, 85>

to **share** [ʃeə] teilen III

**shared** [ʃeəd] Gemeinschafts- <V U2, 198>

**shark** [ʃɑ:k] Hai I

whale shark ['weɪl ˌʃɑ:k] Walhai V U1, 23

pencil **sharpener** ['pensl ˌʃɑ:pnə] Anspitzer I

**she** [ʃi:] sie I

**sheep** *(sg)* [ʃi:p], **sheep** *(pl)* [ʃi:p] Schaf I

**shelf** *(sg)* [ʃelf], **shelves** *(pl)* [ʃelvz] Regal; Regalbrett I

animal rescue **shelter** [ˌænɪml 'reskju: ˌʃeltə] Tierheim I

**shift** [ʃɪft] Schicht <V U1, 192>

*to **shine** [ʃaɪn] scheinen; glänzen IV

**shiny** ['ʃaɪni] glänzend IV

**ship** [ʃɪp] Schiff I

cargo ship ['kɑ:gəʊ ˌʃɪp] Frachtschiff <V U2, 39>

cruise ship ['kru:z ˌʃɪp] Kreuzfahrtschiff V U1, 21

ship builder ['ʃɪp ˌbɪldə] Schiffsbauer; Schiffsbauerin III

**shipping** ['ʃɪpɪŋ] Schiffe V U1, 21

**shipwreck** ['ʃɪprek] Schiffswrack V U2, 30

**shipyard** ['ʃɪpjɑ:d] Werft III

**shirt** [ʃɜ:t] Hemd; Shirt I

**shock** [ʃɒk] Schock V U2, 34

**shoe** [ʃu:] Schuh I

**shone** [ʃɒn] simple past, past participle von *to shine* IV

**shook** [ʃʊk] simple past von *to shake* V U3, 60

*to **shoot** [ʃu:t] erschießen V U2, 37

to shoot (a film) [ˌʃu:t (ə 'fɪlm)] (einen Film) drehen <III>

to shoot (at) [ʃu:t (ət)] schießen (auf) IV

**shooting** ['ʃu:tɪŋ] Schießerei V U2, 34

**shop** [ʃɒp] Laden; Geschäft I

shop assistant ['ʃɒp əˌsɪstnt] Verkäufer; Verkäuferin II

shop window [ˌʃɒp 'wɪndəʊ] Schaufenster V U4, 70

sports shop ['spɔ:ts ˌʃɒp] Sportgeschäft I

**shopper** ['ʃɒpə] Käufer; Käuferin; Einkäufer; Einkäuferin V U4, 68

**shopping** ['ʃɒpɪŋ] Einkaufen I

to do the shopping [ˌdu: ðə 'ʃɒpɪŋ] Einkäufe machen; Besorgungen machen II

to go shopping [ˌgəʊ 'ʃɒpɪŋ] einkaufen gehen II

shopping centre ['ʃɒpɪŋ ˌsentə] Einkaufszentrum I

shopping list ['ʃɒpɪŋ ˌlɪst] Einkaufszettel I

shopping mall ['ʃɒpɪŋ ˌmɔ:l] Einkaufszentrum IV

**short** [ʃɔ:t] kurz II

shortly ['ʃɔ:tli] kurz III

**shorts** *(pl)* [ʃɔ:ts] Shorts; kurze Hose I

**shot** [ʃɒt] Schuss V U2, 41; Einstellung; Aufnahme; simple past, past participle von *to shoot* IV; Kameraeinstellung <V U4, 81>

establishing shot [ɪ'stæblɪʃɪŋ ˌʃɒt] Anfangsszene; Eingangsszene <IV>

**shotgun** ['ʃɒtgʌn] Schrotflinte; Jagdgewehr IV

**should** [ʃʊd] sollte III

**shout** [ʃaʊt] Schrei I

to **shout** [ʃaʊt] schreien; rufen II

**show** [ʃəʊ] Show; Wettbewerb I; Schau; Aufführung IV

slide show ['slaɪd ˌʃəʊ] Folienpräsentation <V U4, 82>

talent show ['tælənt ˌʃəʊ] Talentwettbewerb I

talk show ['tɔ:k ˌʃəʊ] Talkshow <IV>

TV show [ˌti: 'vi: ˌʃəʊ] Fernsehsendung II

*to **show** [ʃəʊ] zeigen II

to show sb around (a place) [ˌʃəʊ‿ə'raʊnd] jmdn. (an einem Ort) herumführen V U1, 12

to show up [ˌʃəʊ‿'ʌp] auftauchen; erscheinen V U3, 50

**show-business** ['ʃəʊˌbɪznɪs] Showbusiness; Showgeschäft; Unterhaltungsindustrie IV

**shower** ['ʃaʊə] Dusche III

shower gel ['ʃaʊə ˌdʒel] Duschgel III

**showery** ['ʃaʊəri] regnerisch <V U2, 198>

*to **shut** up [ˌʃʌt‿'ʌp] die Klappe halten IV

*to keep one's mouth **shut** [ˌki:p wʌnz 'maʊθ ˌʃʌt] den Mund halten V U2, 40

**shy** [ʃaɪ] schüchtern IV

**sick** [sɪk] krank III

to be sick [bi: 'sɪk] sich übergeben I

to feel sick [ˌfi:l 'sɪk] Übelkeit verspüren; sich schlecht fühlen IV

**side** [saɪd] Seite I

**sidewalk** *(AE)* ['saɪdwɔ:k] Gehweg; Bürgersteig IV

**sight** [saɪt] Sehenswürdigkeit II

**sightseeing** ['saɪtsi:ɪŋ] Besichtigungstour IV

to go sightseeing [gəʊ 'saɪtsi:ɪŋ] eine Besichtigungstour machen II

**sign** [saɪn] Schild; Zeichen III

sign language ['saɪn ˌlæŋgwɪdʒ] Gebärdensprache; Zeichensprache III

star sign ['stɑ: ˌsaɪn] Sternzeichen IV

to **sign** [saɪn] unterschreiben; unterzeichnen IV

to sign autographs [ˌsaɪn 'ɔ:təgrɑ:fs] Autogramme geben IV

**signal** ['sɪgnl] Empfang; Signal; Zeichen III

signal word ['sɪgnl ˌwɜ:d] Signalwort <III>

**silence** ['saɪləns] Stille; Schweigen; Ruhe III

**silent** ['saɪlənt] schweigsam; stumm III

**silk** [sɪlk] Seide III

**silly** ['sɪli] albern II; dumm; doof III

**similar** ['sɪmɪlə] ähnlich <III>

**simple** ['sɪmpl] einfach III

simple past [ˌsɪmpl 'pɑ:st] einfache Vergangenheit <III>

simple present [ˌsɪmpl ˈpreznt] Gegenwart; Präsens <III>
**simply** [ˈsɪmpli] einfach nur IV
**since** [sɪns] seit; seitdem IV
ever since [ˌevə ˈsɪns] seitdem V U3, 54
Yours **sincerely**, [jɔ:z sɪnˈsɪəli] Mit freundlichen Grüßen V U1, 16
*to **sing** [sɪŋ] singen I
**singer** [ˈsɪŋə] Sänger; Sängerin I
**singing** [ˈsɪŋɪŋ] Gesangs- III
**single** [ˈsɪŋgl] einzeln <III>
single ticket [ˈsɪŋgl ˌtɪkɪt] einfache Fahrkarte III
*to **sink** [sɪŋk] untergehen; sinken III
**sinking** [ˈsɪŋkɪŋ] Untergang III
Dear **Sir** or Madam, [dɪə ˌsɜ:r‿ɔ: ˈmædəm] Sehr geehrte Damen und Herren, V U3, 50
**sister** [ˈsɪstə] Schwester I
*to **sit** [sɪt] sitzen I
to sit down [ˌsɪt ˈdaʊn] sich hinsetzen; sich setzen V U1, 15
**site** [saɪt] Seite *(im Internet)* IV
construction site [kənˈstrʌkʃn ˌsaɪt] Baustelle IV
**situation** [ˌsɪtjuˈeɪʃn] Situation II
**six** [sɪks] sechs I
**sixteen** [ˌsɪkˈsti:n] sechzehn I
**sixty** [ˈsɪksti] sechzig I
**size** [saɪz] Größe II
**skateboard** [ˈskeɪtbɔ:d] Skateboard III
**sketch** [sketʃ] Zeichnung; Skizze <IV>
**ski lift** [ˈski: ˌlɪft] Skilift; Sesselbahn V U4, 74
to **ski** [ski:] Ski fahren II
**skiing** [ˈski:ɪŋ] Skifahren III
**skill** [skɪl] Fertigkeit; Kenntnis; Fähigkeit V U1, 16
**skilled** [skɪld] qualifiziert; ausgebildet; Fach- V U1, 11
to **skim** [skɪm] überfliegen <III>
**skin** [skɪn] Haut <V U3, 66>
to **skip** [skɪp] hüpfen; springen; überspringen V U3, 58
**skirt** [skɜ:t] Rock I
**sky** [skaɪ] Himmel V U2, 41
**skyline** [ˈskaɪlaɪn] Skyline IV
**skyscraper** [ˈskaɪskreɪpə] Wolkenkratzer IV
to **slap** [slæp] einen Klaps geben; schlagen IV
**slave** [sleɪv] Sklave; Sklavin IV
**slavery** [ˈsleɪvri] Sklaverei <IV>
**sleep** [sli:p] Schlaf III
*to **sleep** [sli:p] schlafen I
**sleepover** [ˈsli:pˌəʊvə] Übernachtung I
**slept** [slept] simple past, past participle von *to sleep* II
**sliced** bread [ˌslaɪst ˈbred] in Scheiben geschnittenes Brot III
**slide** [slaɪd] Folie <V U4, 82>
slide show [ˈslaɪd ˌʃəʊ] Folienpräsentation <V U4, 82>
**slogan** [ˈsləʊgən] Slogan; Werbespruch IV
to **slow** to a walk [ˌsləʊ tʊ‿ə ˈwɔ:k] in Schritttempo verfallen IV
**slow** [sləʊ] langsam III
**small** [smɔ:l] klein I
small talk [ˈsmɔ:l ˌtɔ:k] Smalltalk <IV>
**smart** [smɑ:t] schlau; klug; intelligent III; gepflegt; schick <V U1, 25>
smart home [ˌsmɑ:t ˈhəʊm] intelligentes Haus <V U3, 205>
**smartphone** [ˈsmɑ:tˌfəʊn] Smartphone IV
**smell** [smel] Geruch III
**smelly** [smeli] stinkend; übelriechend IV
**smile** [smaɪl] Lächeln V U2, 40
to **smile** [smaɪl] lächeln III
**smiling** [ˈsmaɪlɪŋ] lächelnd V U3, 59
**smog** [smɒg] Smog V U4, 69
**smoke** [sməʊk] Rauch III
**smuggler** [ˈsmʌglə] Schmuggler; Schmugglerin II
**smurf** [smɜ:f] Schlumpf I
**snack** [snæk] Snack; Imbiss I
**snake** [sneɪk] Schlange I
**sneaker** *(AE)* [ˈsni:kə] Sportschuh; Sneaker V U4, 70
**sneakerhead** [ˈsni:kəhed] *Sammler von Sportschuhen* V U4, 70
**snorkelling** [ˈsnɔ:klɪŋ] Schnorcheln V U1, 20
**snow** [snəʊ] Schnee IV
**so** [səʊ] deshalb; also I; so II
so far [ˌsəʊ ˈfɑ:] bis jetzt IV
so much [ˈsəʊ ˌmʌtʃ] so sehr III
so that [səʊ ˈðæt] damit; so dass IV
**soaked** [səʊkt] durchnässt <V U2, 198>
**soap** [səʊp] Seife III
**social** [ˈsəʊʃl] gesellschaftlich; sozial V U3, 51
social media [ˌsəʊʃl ˈmi:diə] soziale Medien IV
social placement [ˌsəʊʃl ˈpleɪsmənt] Sozialpraktikum <V U1, 192>
Social Studies [ˈsəʊʃl ˌstʌdiz] Gesellschaftslehre; Sozialkunde I
**society** [səˈsaɪəti] Gesellschaft IV
**sociogram** [ˌsəʊʃiəˈgræm] Soziogramm <V U3, 60>
**sock** [sɒk] Socke I
**sofa** [ˈsəʊfə] Sofa II
**soft** [sɒft] weich; sanft <V U1, 27>
**software** [ˈsɒftweə] Software II
**solar** [ˈsəʊlə] Sonnen-; Solar-; solar III
solar panel [ˌsəʊlə ˈpænl] Sonnenkollektor V U4, 74
**sold** [səʊld] simple past, past participle von *to sell* III
**soldier** [ˈsəʊldʒə] Soldat; Soldatin III
**solid** [ˈsɒlɪd] fest III
**solidarity** [ˌsɒlɪˈdærəti] Solidarität V U2, 35
**solution** [səˈlu:ʃn] Lösung IV
to **solve** [sɒlv] lösen I
**some** [sʌm] manch V U4, 72
**some** [sʌm] einige; ein paar I; etwas II
**somebody** [ˈsʌmbədi] jemand III
somebody else [ˌsʌmbədi ˈels] jemand anderes II
**someone** [ˈsʌmwʌn] jemand <V ZI, 8>
someone stupid [ˌsʌmwʌn ˈstju:pɪd] irgendein Idiot V U3, 51
**something** [ˈsʌmθɪŋ] etwas I
a little something [ə ˌlɪtl ˈsʌmθɪŋ] eine Kleinigkeit IV
**sometimes** [ˈsʌmtaɪmz] manchmal I
**somewhere** [ˈsʌmweə] irgendwo <III>
**son** [sʌn] Sohn III
**song** [sɒŋ] Lied I
**soon** [su:n] bald II
as soon as [əz ˈsu:n‿əz] sobald IV
**sore** [sɔ:] schmerzhaft; wund II
sore throat [ˌsɔ: ˈθrəʊt] Halsschmerzen II

**Sorry.** ['sɒri] Tut mir leid.; Entschuldigung. I
to be sorry [bi: 'sɒri] leidtun III
to feel sorry for [ˌfi:l 'sɒri fə] Mitleid haben mit; bedauern III
I'm sorry. [aɪm 'sɒrɪ] Es tut mir leid.; Entschuldigung. I
Sorry about … ['sɒri əˌbaʊt] Es tut mir leid wegen … I
**sort** [sɔ:t] Sorte; Art II
to **sort** [sɔ:t] sortieren IV
**sound** [saʊnd] Ton; Laut; Geräusch III
to **sound** [saʊnd] klingen II
**soup** [su:p] Suppe II
**source** [sɔ:s] Quelle IV
**south** [saʊθ] Süden III
South African [ˌsaʊθ‿'æfrɪkən] Südafrikaner; Südafrikanerin; südafrikanisch; aus Südafrika V U3, 49
in the south of [ˌɪn ðə 'saʊθ‿əv] im Süden von III
south of ['saʊθ‿əv] südlich von IV
**southern** ['sʌðən] südlich IV
**Southerner** ['sʌðnə] Südstaatler; Südstaatlerin IV
**southwest** [ˌsaʊθ'west] Südwesten III
**souvenir** [ˌsu:vn'ɪə] Souvenir; Andenken III
souvenir shop ['su:vnɪə ˌʃɒp] Souvenirladen III
**soy** bean ['sɔɪ ˌbi:n] Sojabohne IV
**space** [speɪs] Ort; Stelle; Platz; Raum; Fläche IV
**spaghetti** [spə'geti] Spaghetti II
**Spanish** ['spænɪʃ] spanisch; Spanisch; aus Spanien IV
*to **speak** [spi:k] sprechen II
native **speaker** [ˌneɪtɪv 'spi:kə] Muttersprachler; Muttersprachlerin V U1, 16
**speaking** ['spi:kɪŋ] Sprechen <I>
**special** ['speʃl] besonders; speziell I
special offer [ˌspeʃl‿'ɒfə] Sonderangebot III
with special needs [wɪð ˌspeʃl 'ni:dz] mit Behinderung III
**specialist** ['speʃlɪst] Spezial- V U4, 68
**species** ['spi:ʃi:z] Art; Spezies V U1, 10
**specific** [spə'sɪfɪk] spezifisch; speziell <III>

**spectacular** [spek'tækjələ] spektakulär III
**spectator** [spek'teɪtə] Zuschauer; Zuschauerin <V U3, 67>
**speech** [spi:tʃ] Sprache; Rede III
direct speech [dɪˌrekt 'spi:tʃ] direkte Rede <IV>
farewell speech [feə'wel spi:tʃ] Abschiedsrede II
freedom of speech [ˌfri:dəm‿əv 'spi:tʃ] Redefreiheit V U4, 79
to give a speech [gɪv‿ə 'spi:tʃ] einen Vortrag halten <V U3, 65>
reported speech [rɪˌpɔ:tɪd 'spi:tʃ] indirekte Rede <IV>
speech bubble ['spi:tʃ ˌbʌbl] Sprechblase <III>
speech impaired ['spi:tʃ ɪmˌpeəd] sprachbehindert IV
speech therapist ['spi:tʃ ˌθerəpɪst] Logopäde; Logopädin <V U1, 192>
**speed** [spi:d] Geschwindigkeit V U4, 81
speed limit ['spi:d ˌlɪmɪt] Geschwindigkeitsbeschränkung V U4, 81
**spell** check ['spel ˌtʃek] Rechtschreibprüfprogramm <III>
*to **spell** [spel] buchstabieren I
**spelling** ['spelɪŋ] Rechtschreibung I
*to **spend** [spend] ausgeben *(Geld)*; verbringen *(Zeit)* II
**spent** [spent] simple past, past participle von *to spend* II
**spice** [spaɪs] Gewürz II
**spicy** ['spaɪsi] würzig; pikant II
**spider** ['spaɪdə] Spinne III
oil **spill** ['ɔɪl ˌspɪl] Ölteppich V U1, 21
*to **spill** [spɪl] auslaufen; verschütten IV
**spilt** [spɪlt] simple past, past participle von *to spill* IV
**spirit** ['spɪrɪt] Stimmung; Geist IV
**splash** [splæʃ] Platsch I
**spoke** [spəʊk] simple past von *to speak* II
**spoken** ['spəʊkn] past participle von *to speak* II
**sponsored** walk ['spɒnsəd ˌwɔ:k] Sponsorenlauf <V U4, 212>
**sponsorship** ['spɒnsəʃɪp] Förderung <V U4, 212>

**spoon** [spu:n] Löffel II
**sport** [spɔ:t] Sport I; Sportart III
sports shop ['spɔ:ts ˌʃɒp] Sportgeschäft I
to **sprain** [spreɪn] verstauchen; verrenken III
**sprang up** [ˌspræŋ‿'ʌp] simple past von *to spring up* IV
*to **spread** [spred] (sich) verbreiten V U4, 79
**spread** [spred] simple past, past participle von *to spread* V U4, 79
**spring** [sprɪŋ] Quelle <V U3, 205>
spring roll [ˌsprɪŋ 'rəʊl] Frühlingsrolle II
*to **spring up** [ˌsprɪŋ‿'ʌp] entstehen; entspringen IV
**sprinkler** ['sprɪŋklə] Rasensprenger V U3, 58
to **sprint** [sprɪnt] sprinten; spurten <V U2, 47>
**sprung up** [ˌsprʌŋ‿'ʌp] past participle von *to spring up* IV
**squad** [skwɒd] Gruppe; Team; Mannschaft IV
**square** [skweə] Platz II; quadratisch <V U4, 84>
square mile (= sq. mi.) [ˌskweə 'maɪl] Quadratmeile IV
to **squeeze** [skwi:z] drücken; pressen; quetschen IV
**stadium** ['steɪdiəm] Stadion II
**staff** *(no pl)* [stɑ:f] Personal; Belegschaft; Kollegium IV
**stage** [steɪdʒ] Bühne II
**stairs** *(pl)* [steəz] Treppe II
**stall** [stɔ:l] Stand; Bude V U4, 68
food stall ['fu:d ˌstɔ:l] Essensstand II
**stallholder** ['stɔ:lˌhəʊldə] Standinhaber; Standinhaberin II
**stamp** [stæmp] Briefmarke III
to **stamp** [stæmp] stampfen <V U1, 26>
*to **stand** [stænd] stehen II; ertragen; ausstehen IV
to stand out ['stænd‿aʊt] auffallen; herausragen; herausstechen IV
to stand up [ˌstænd‿'ʌp] aufstehen IV

**standard** [ˈstændəd] Standard <V U2, 28>

moral standards *(pl)* [ˌmɒrl ˈstændədz] sittliche Werte *(Pl.)* V U4, 79

**star** [stɑː] Star I; Stern III

star sign [ˈstɑː ˌsaɪn] Sternzeichen IV

**stare** [steə] Starren; starrer Blick V U3, 60

to **stare** [steə] starren III

**start** [stɑːt] Start; Anfang III

for a start [ˌfɔːr‿ə ˈstɑːt] zunächst III

to **start** [stɑːt] anfangen; beginnen; starten II; gründen III

starting point [ˈstɑːtɪŋ ˌpɔɪnt] Ausgangspunkt <III>

**starter** [ˈstɑːtə] Vorspeise II

**state** [steɪt] Staat; Bundesstaat; Land; Zustand IV

state government [ˈsteɪt ˌɡʌvnmənt] Landesregierung IV

State House *(AE)* [ˈsteɪt ˌhaʊs] Regierungsgebäude IV

state school [ˈsteɪt ˌskuːl] staatliche Schule; öffentliche Schule V U3, 51

**statement** [ˈsteɪtmənt] Aussage; Behauptung; Erklärung IV

personal statement [ˌpɜːsnl ˈsteɪtmənt] Motivationsschreiben V U1, 16

**state-of-the-art** [ˌsteɪtəvðiːˈɑːt] hochmodern; auf dem neuesten Stand der Technik <V U2, 47>

**station** [ˈsteɪʃn] Haltestelle; Station; Bahnhof III

police station [pəˈliːs ˌsteɪʃn] Polizeirevier; Polizeiwache V U3, 50

**statistical** [stəˈtɪstɪkl] statistisch <IV>

**statistics** *(no pl)* [stəˈtɪstɪks] Statistik IV

**status** [ˈsteɪtəs] Status IV

status symbol [ˈsteɪtəs ˌsɪmbl] Statussymbol V U4, 70

to **stay** [steɪ] übernachten; bleiben II

to stay up [steɪ ˈʌp] aufbleiben IV

*to **steal** [stiːl] stehlen IV

**steam** engine [ˈstiːm‿endʒɪn] Dampfmaschine III

**steamship** [ˈstiːmʃɪp] Dampfschiff; Dampfer IV

**steel** [stiːl] Stahl III

**steelpan** [ˈstiːlpæn] Steelpan *(Trommel aus Blech)* V U2, 30

**steep** [stiːp] steil <V U3, 205>

**step** [step] Schritt III; Stufe II

one step at a time [ˌwʌn step‿æt‿ə ˈtaɪm] schrittweise; ein Schritt nach dem anderen V U3, 60

to **step** [step] treten; steigen IV

**stereotype** [ˈsteriəʊtaɪp] Stereotyp; Klischee <IV>

**stick** [stɪk] Stock II

**sticker** [ˈstɪkə] Aufkleber II

**still** [stɪl] noch; immer noch; dennoch III; still <V U3, 65>

**sting** [stɪŋ] Stachel; Spitze <V U1, 27>

to **stir** [stɜː] rühren; umrühren II

to **stock** [stɒk] führen; vorrätig haben V U4, 71

**stocks** [stɒks] Pranger III

**stole** [stəʊl] simple past von *to steal* IV

**stolen** [ˈstəʊlən] past participle von *to steal* IV

**stomach** [ˈstʌmək] Magen; Bauch II

stomach ache [ˈstʌmək ˌeɪk] Bauchweh; Bauchschmerzen II

**stone** [stəʊn] Stein III

**stood** [stʊd] simple past, past participle von *to stand* II

**stop** [stɒp] Haltestelle; Halt II

bus stop [ˈbʌs ˌstɒp] Bushaltestelle II

full stop [ˌfʊl ˈstɒp] Punkt <III>

to **stop** [stɒp] aufhören I; aufhalten; stoppen V U1, 21; stehen bleiben; anhalten V U2, 41

to stop sb from sth [ˈstɒp frəm] jmdn. an etw. hindern; jmdn. von etw. abhalten V U2, 39

**stopwatch** [ˈstɒpwɒtʃ] Stoppuhr <V U4, 83>

**store** *(AE)* [stɔː] Laden; Geschäft IV

department store [dɪˈpɑːtmənt ˌstɔː] Kaufhaus II

**storm** [stɔːm] Sturm IV

**story** [ˈstɔːri] Geschichte I

mystery story [ˈmɪstri ˌstɔːri] Krimi (= Kriminalgeschichte); Detektivgeschichte IV

story-telling [ˈstɔːriˌtelɪŋ] Geschichtenerzählen <IV>

**story** *(AE)* [ˈstɔːri] Stock; Stockwerk; Etage IV

**straight** [streɪt] gerade <IV>; direkt <V U3, 63>

straight on [streɪt‿ˈɒn] geradeaus I

hair **straightener** [ˈheə ˌstreɪtnə] Haarglätter IV

**straightforward** [ˌstreɪtˈfɔːwəd] aufrichtig; geradlinig III

**strange** [streɪndʒ] merkwürdig; seltsam II; fremd IV

**straw** [strɔː] Trinkhalm II

**strawberry** [ˈstrɔːbri] Erdbeere II

to **stream** [striːm] streamen *(im Internet)* IV

**street** [striːt] Straße III

street gang [ˈstriːt ˌɡæŋ] Straßengang V U2, 34

**strength** [streŋθ] Stärke; Kraft IV

**stress** [stres] Stress IV

to **stretch** [stretʃ] sich strecken; erstrecken; dehnen IV

**strict** [strɪkt] streng; strikt IV

**striking** [ˈstraɪkɪŋ] bemerkenswert; auffallend III

comic **strip** [ˈkɒmɪk strɪp] Comic <III>

to **stroll** [strəʊl] schlendern; bummeln IV

**strong** [strɒŋ] stark III

**structure** [ˈstrʌktʃə] Struktur; Aufbau III

to **structure** [ˈstrʌktʃə] strukturieren; gliedern <IV>

**struggle** [ˈstrʌɡl] Kampf; Anstrengung V U2, 34

to **struggle** [ˈstrʌɡl] kämpfen; ringen; sich anstrengen; **Mühe** haben V U1, 11

**stubborn** [ˈstʌbən] eigensinnig; störrisch IV

*to be **stuck** [biː ˈstʌk] festsitzen; feststecken; nicht weg können; hängen bleiben IV

*to get **stuck** [ˌɡet ˈstʌk] stecken bleiben IV

**student** [ˈstjuːdnt] Schüler; Schülerin; Student; Studentin I

**studio** [ˈstjuːdiəʊ] Studio IV

recording studio [rɪ'kɔ:dɪŋ ˌstju:diəʊ] Tonstudio I
TV studio [ˌti:'vi: ˌstju:diəʊ] Fernsehstudio II
**study** ['stʌdi] Untersuchung; Studie <V U2, 46>
study hall period ['stʌdi hɔ:l ˌpɪəriəd] Freistunde IV
study skills [ˌstʌdi 'skɪlz] Fertigkeit Lern- und Arbeitstechniken <I>
to **study** ['stʌdi] studieren; lernen IV
**stuff** [stʌf] Zeug IV
**stunning** ['stʌnɪŋ] überwältigend V U1, 12
**stuntman** ['stʌntmæn] Stuntman IV
**stupid** ['stju:pɪd] dumm; blöd V U3, 51
someone stupid [ˌsʌmwʌn 'stju:pɪd] irgendein Idiot V U3, 51
**style** [staɪl] Stil III
**stylistic device** [staɪˌlɪstɪk dɪ'vaɪs] Stilmittel <V U3, 65>
**subject** ['sʌbdʒɪkt] Schulfach I
core subject [ˌkɔ: 'sʌbdʒɪkt] Pflichtfach IV
**submarine** [ˌsʌbmr'i:n] U-Boot I
to **subscribe** [səb'skraɪb] abonnieren IV
**suburb** ['sʌbɜ:b] Vorort IV
**subway** *(AE)* ['sʌbweɪ] U-Bahn IV
to **succeed** (in) [sək'si:d (ɪn)] Erfolg haben (mit/bei); nachfolgen IV
**success** [sək'ses] Erfolg III
successful [sək'sesfl] erfolgreich III
**such** [sʌtʃ] solch IV
**such** as ['sʌtʃ‿əz] wie <V U2, 47>
**sudden** ['sʌdn] unerwartet; plötzlich V U3, 58
suddenly ['sʌdnli] plötzlich; auf einmal II
to **suffer** ['sʌfə] leiden; erleiden V U3, 50
**sugar** ['ʃʊgə] Zucker I
to **suggest** [sə'dʒest] vorschlagen; nahelegen; andeuten V U4, 74
**suggestion** [sə'dʒestʃn] Vorschlag; Anregung <V U2, 42>
to **suit** [su:t] stehen; passen II
**suitable** ['su:təbl] geeignet; passend <IV>
**suitcase** ['su:tkeɪs] Koffer II
trolley suitcase ['trɒli ˌsu:tkeɪs] Rollkoffer III
to **sum up** [ˌsʌm‿'ʌp] zusammenfassen IV
to **summarise** ['sʌmraɪz] zusammenfassen <IV>
**summary** ['sʌmri] Zusammenfassung <III>
**summer** ['sʌmə] Sommer II
**sun** [sʌn] Sonne III
to **sunbathe** ['sʌnbeɪð] sonnenbaden II
**Sunday** ['sʌndeɪ] Sonntag I
**sunglasses** *(pl)* ['sʌnˌglɑ:sɪz] Sonnenbrille II
**sunk** [sʌŋk] past participle von *to sink* III
**sunny** ['sʌni] sonnig I
**sunshine** ['sʌnʃaɪn] Sonnenschein V U2, 31
**super** ['su:pə] super V U4, 70
**superhero** ['su:pəˌhɪərəʊ] *(sg)*, **superheroes** ['su:pəˌhɪərəʊz] *(pl)* Superheld IV
**superlative** [su:'pɜ:lətɪv] Superlativ <V U1, 18>
**supermarket** ['su:pəˌmɑ:kɪt] Supermarkt II
**superstition** [ˌsu:pə'stɪʃn] Aberglaube <V U4, 84>
**support** [sə'pɔ:t] Unterstützung; Hilfe IV
to **support** [sə'pɔ:t] unterstützen IV
**supporter** [sə'pɔ:tə] Anhänger; Anhängerin; Fan <V U3, 66>
**sure** [ʃʊə] sicher I
to make sure [ˌmeɪk 'ʃɔ:] dafür sorgen; sich versichern III
sure of oneself ['ʃʊər‿əv ˌwʌnself] selbstsicher III
to **surf** [sɜ:f] surfen; wellenreiten II
to surf the internet [ˌsɜ:f ði 'ɪntənet] im Internet surfen II
**surface** ['sɜ:fɪs] Oberfläche IV
**surfer** ['sɜ:fə] Wellenreiter; Wellenreiterin; Surfer; Surferin IV
**surfing** ['sɜ:fɪŋ] Surfen; Wellenreiten III
couch surfing ['kaʊtʃ ˌsɜ:fɪŋ] Couchsurfing V U2, 31
**surprise** [sə'praɪz] Überraschung I
surprised [sə'praɪzd] überrascht II
to **surprise** [sə'praɪz] überraschen <III>
*to be **surrounded** by sth/sb [bi: sə'raʊndɪd baɪ] umgeben sein von etw./jmdm. V U4, 78
**survey** ['sɜ:veɪ] Umfrage II
**survival** [sə'vaɪvl] Überleben; Überlebens- V U1, 12
to **survive** [sə'vaɪv] überleben III
**sushi** ['su:ʃi] Sushi IV
**suspense** [sə'spens] Spannung <III>
**swam** [swæm] simple past von *to swim* II
**swamp** [swɒmp] Sumpf IV
to **swap** [swɒp] tauschen V U4, 71
*to **swear** [sweə] schwören V U3, 50
**sweatshirt** ['swetʃɜ:t] Sweatshirt I
*to **sweep** [swi:p] fegen II
*to **sweep** (up) [swi:p (ʌp)] (hoch)heben; (auf)fegen V U3, 58
**sweet** [swi:t] süß III; Süßigkeit; Bonbon I
**swept** [swept] simple past, past participle von *to sweep* II
open-water **swim** [ˌəʊpnwɔ:tə 'swɪm] Freiwasserschwimmen <V U3, 67>
*to **swim** [swɪm] schwimmen II
**swimmer** ['swɪmə] Schwimmer; Schwimmerin IV
**swimming** ['swɪmɪŋ] schwimmend <V U2, 42>
to go swimming [ˌgəʊ 'swɪmɪŋ] schwimmen gehen I
swimming pool ['swɪmɪŋ ˌpu:l] Schwimmbad I
**Swiss** [swɪs] schweizerisch; aus der Schweiz; Schweizer; Schweizerin IV
to **switch** off [ˌswɪtʃ‿'ɒf] ausschalten <V U1, 25>
**sword** [sɔ:d] Schwert III
**swore** [swɔ:] simple past von *to swear* V U3, 50
**sworn** [swɔ:n] past participle von *to swear* V U3, 50
**swum** [swʌm] past participle von *to swim* II
**symbol** ['sɪmbl] Symbol IV
status symbol ['steɪtəs ˌsɪmbl] Statussymbol V U4, 70

**synonym** ['sɪnənɪm] Synonym <V U4, 75>
**system** ['sɪstəm] System IV

## T

**table** ['teɪbl] Tisch I; Tabelle <III>
table tennis ['teɪbl ˌtenɪs] Tischtennis II
**tablet** ['tæblət] Tablette II; Tablet IV
**tactic** ['tæktɪk] Taktik; Vorgehensweise III
**tail** [teɪl] Schwanz; Schweif <V U1, 27>
**take** [teɪk] Aufnahme <III>
*to **take** [teɪk] nehmen; mitnehmen I; hinbringen II; dauern III
to take a break [ˌteɪk‿ə 'breɪk] Pause machen II
to take a deep breath [ˌteɪk‿ə ˌdi:p 'breθ] tief einatmen; tief Luft holen V U3, 60
to take a photo [ˌteɪk‿ə 'fəʊtəʊ] ein Foto machen I
to take a ride [ˌteɪk‿ə 'raɪd] fahren IV
to take a short break [ˌteɪk‿ə 'ʃɔ:t breɪk] eine kurze Pause machen <V U3, 60>
to take a trip [ˌteɪk‿ə 'trɪp] eine Fahrt machen III
to take action [ˌteɪk‿'ækʃn] eingreifen; handeln V U3, 54
to take care of sb [ˌteɪk 'keər‿əv] sich um jmdn. kümmern; für jmdn. sorgen IV
to take notes [ˌteɪk 'nəʊts] sich Notizen machen I
to take notice [ˌteɪk 'nəʊtɪs] beachten; zur Kenntnis nehmen; aufmerksam werden V U3, 60
to take off [ˌteɪk‿'ɒf] ausziehen III; durchstarten; abheben IV; abnehmen; herunternehmen V U1, 13
to take one's breath away [ˌteɪk wʌnz 'breθ‿əˌweɪ] den Atem rauben V U2, 30
to take out [ˌteɪk‿'aʊt] herausnehmen I
to take part (in) [ˌteɪk 'pɑ:t] teilnehmen (an) II
to take photos [ˌteɪk 'fəʊtəʊz] fotografieren; Fotos machen II
to take place [ˌteɪk 'pleɪs] stattfinden V U2, 30
to take sth for granted [ˌteɪk fə 'grɑ:ntɪd] etw. als selbstverständlich hinnehmen; etw. als gegeben voraussetzen V U4, 79
to take sth seriously [ˌteɪk 'sɪəriəsli] etw. ernst nehmen IV
to take the dog for a walk [ˌteɪk ðə ˌdɒg fər‿ə 'wɔ:k] den Hund spazieren führen II
to take turns [ˌteɪk 'tɜ:nz] sich abwechseln V U3, 58
Take care. ['teɪk ˌkeə] Macht's gut. I
**takeaway** ['teɪkəweɪ] zum Mitnehmen; Essen zum Mitnehmen II
**taken** ['teɪkn] past participle von *to take* II
**talent** ['tælənt] Talent I
talent show ['tælənt ˌʃəʊ] Talentwettbewerb I
talented ['tæləntɪd] begabt; talentiert III
**talk** [tɔ:k] Gerede II; Vortrag; Rede <III>
to give a talk [ˌgɪv‿ə 'tɔ:k] einen Vortrag halten <III>
small talk ['smɔ:l ˌtɔ:k] Smalltalk <IV>
talk show ['tɔ:k ˌʃəʊ] Talkshow <IV>
to **talk** (to) ['tɔ:k tə] sprechen (mit); reden (mit) I
to talk about ['tɔ:k‿əˌbaʊt] sprechen über II
**tall** [tɔ:l] groß; hoch II
**task** [tɑ:sk] Aufgabe; Auftrag <I>
**tasty** ['teɪsti] lecker; schmackhaft III
**taught** [tɔ:t] simple past, past participle von *to teach* III
**taxi** ['tæksi] Taxi II
**tea** [ti:] Tee; (frühes) Abendessen I
*to **teach** [ti:tʃ] beibringen; unterrichten; lehren III
**teacher** ['ti:tʃə] Lehrer; Lehrerin I
**team** [ti:m] Team; Mannschaft I
**teamwork** ['ti:mwɜ:k] Teamwork V U1, 16
*to **tear** (up) [teər (ʌp)] kaputt machen; reißen; zerreißen IV
to **tease** [ti:z] hänseln; sticheln; reizen IV
**teaspoon** ***(tsp)*** ['ti:spu:n] Teelöffel *(TL)* II
**technology** [tek'nɒlədʒi] Technologie V U4, 74
Design Technology (DT) [dɪˌzaɪn tek'nɒlədʒi, ˌdi:'ti:] Technik I
**teen** [ti:n] Jugend-; Teenager; Jugendliche; Jugendlicher II
**teenage** ['ti:neɪdʒ] jugendlich IV
**teenager** ['ti:nˌeɪdʒə] Teenager; Jugendliche; Jugendlicher III
**telephone** ['telɪfəʊn] Telefon III
telephone box ['telɪfəʊn ˌbɒks] Telefonzelle II
*to **tell** [tel] erzählen; sagen I
**temperature** ['temprətʃə] Temperatur V U1, 20
**temporary** ['temprəri] vorübergehend V U1, 16
**ten** [ten] zehn I
**tennis** ['tenɪs] Tennis I
**tense** [tens] Zeit; Zeitform <III>
**tent** [tent] Zelt II
**term** [tɜ:m] Trimester; Semester V U1, 11
**terraced house** [ˌterɪst 'haʊs] Reihenhaus <V U3, 205>
**terrible** ['terəbl] schrecklich; schlimm; furchtbar I
*to be **terrified** (of sth) [bi: 'terəfaɪd (əv)] (große) Angst (vor etw.) haben V U2, 40
**terrifying** ['terəfaɪɪŋ] furchterregend; erschreckend IV
**territory** ['terɪtri] Gebiet; Revier; Territorium V U3, 49
**terrorist** ['terərɪst] Terrorist; Terroristin V U4, 79
**test** [test] Test; Klassenarbeit I
to **test** [test] testen; prüfen II
**text** [tekst] Text II
advertising text ['ædvətaɪzɪŋ ˌtekst] Werbetext <IV>
text message ['tekst ˌmesɪdʒ] SMS II
to **text** [tekst] eine SMS schreiben II
**texter** ['tekstə] SMS-Schreiber; SMS-Schreiberin II
**than** [ðæn] als II

**Thank you.** ['θæŋk ju] Danke. I
**thankful** ['θæŋkfl] dankbar IV
**thanks** [θæŋks] danke I
Thanks so much. [ˌθæŋk‿səʊ 'mʌtʃ] Vielen Dank.; Herzlichen Dank. IV
**Thanksgiving** [ˌθæŋks'gɪvɪŋ] Erntedankfest IV
**that** [ðæt] das I; so *(Betonung)*; dass III
after that [ˌɑ:ftə 'ðæt] danach I
so that [səʊ 'ðæt] damit; so dass IV
that night [ˌðæt 'naɪt] an jenem Abend; in jener Nacht II
That's because … [ˌðæts bɪ'kɒz] Das liegt daran, dass … III
that's why ['ðæts waɪ] deswegen III
**the** [ðə] der; die *(auch Pl.)*; das I
**theater** *(AE)* ['θɪətə] Theater IV
movie theater *(AE)* ['mu:vi ˌθi:ətə] Kino IV
**theatre** ['θɪətə] Theater II
**their** [ðeə] ihr *(Pl.)*; ihre *(Pl.)* I
**theirs** [ðeəz] ihre III
**them** [ðem; ðəm] sie *(Pl.)*; ihnen I
the two of them [ðə 'tu: əv ðəm] die beiden V U3, 58
**theme** [θi:m] Thema; Motto <IV>
theme park ['θi:m ˌpɑ:k] Freizeitpark I; Themenpark II
**themselves** [ðəm'selvz] selber; sie selbst; sich selbst; selbst III
**then** [ðen] dann; danach I; damals III
then again [ˌðen ə'gen] andererseits III
**there** [ðeə] da; dort I
down there [ˌdaʊn 'ðeə] dahin; da unten IV
over there [ˌəʊvə 'ðeə] da drüben; dort drüben II
there are [ðeər‿'ɑ:] da sind; es gibt I
there is [ðeə 'ɪz] da ist; dort ist; es gibt I
**therefore** ['ðeəfɔ:] deshalb; deswegen; daher; somit V U3, 54
**these** [ði:z] diese (hier) II
**they** [ðeɪ] sie *(Pl.)* I
**thick** [θɪk] dick V U4, 69
**thing** [θɪŋ] Sache; Ding I
*to **think** [θɪŋk] denken; glauben I
to think of ['θɪŋk‿əv] sich ausdenken; sich etwas einfallen lassen <III>; sich einfallen lassen V U2, 40
**a third** [ə 'θɜ:d] ein Drittel <V U2, 46>
**third** [θɜ:d] dritte I
**thirsty** ['θɜ:sti] durstig II
**thirteen** [θɜ:'ti:n] dreizehn I
**thirty** ['θɜ:ti] dreißig I
**this** [ðɪs] das; dies I
like this [laɪk 'ðɪs] ähnlich <III>
this way [ðɪs 'weɪ] in diese Richtung II; auf diese Weise <III>
**those** [ðəʊz] jene II
**though** [ðəʊ] jedoch III
even though [ˌi:vn 'ðəʊ] auch wenn; obwohl V U2, 34
**thought** [θɔ:t] simple past, past participle von *to think* II; Gedanke IV
thought bubble ['θɔ:t ˌbʌbl] Denkblase; Gedankenblase <IV>
a/one **thousand** [ə/wʌn 'θaʊznd] eintausend; tausend II
**threat** [θret] Bedrohung; Gefahr V U1, 20
to **threaten** ['θretn] bedrohen V U2, 28
**three** [θri:] drei I
**threw** [θru:] simple past von *to throw* IV
**throat** [θrəʊt] Hals II
sore throat [ˌsɔ: 'θrəʊt] Halsschmerzen II
**through** [θru:] durch II
*to **throw** [θrəʊ] werfen IV
**thrown** [θrəʊn] past participle von *to throw* IV
**thunder** *(no pl)* ['θʌndə] Donner V U2, 31
**Thursday** ['θɜ:zdeɪ] Donnerstag I
**ticket** ['tɪkɪt] Karte II; Fahrschein; Eintrittskarte III
return ticket [rɪ'tɜ:n ˌtɪkɪt] Hin- und Rückfahrkarte III
single ticket ['sɪŋgl ˌtɪkɪt] einfache Fahrkarte III
to **tidy** (up) [ˌtaɪdi 'ʌp] aufräumen; in Ordnung bringen II
to **tie** [taɪ] binden; zubinden; fesseln IV
**tiger** ['taɪgə] Tiger I
**tight** [taɪt] eng; fest II
to **tilt** [tɪlt] neigen; kippen <V U4, 81>
**time** [taɪm] Zeit; Uhrzeit I; Mal III
all the time [ˌɔ:l ðə 'taɪm] die ganze Zeit III
at that time [ət ðæt 'taɪm] damals; zu der Zeit V U2, 39
free time [ˌfri: 'taɪm] Freizeit I
on time [ɒn 'taɪm] pünktlich III
period of time [ˌpɪəriəd‿əv 'taɪm] Zeitraum <IV>
time travel ['taɪm ˌtrævl] Zeitreise III
time zone ['taɪm ˌzəʊn] Zeitzone IV
in time [ɪn 'taɪm] rechtzeitig I
one step at a time [ˌwʌn step‿æt‿ə 'taɪm] schrittweise; ein Schritt nach dem anderen V U3, 60
opening times ['əʊpnɪŋ ˌtaɪmz] Öffnungszeiten IV
**timeline** ['taɪmˌlaɪn] Zeitstrahl <III>
**timetable** ['taɪmˌteɪbl] Stundenplan I; Fahrplan III
**tin** [tɪn] Dose; Büchse; Mülleimer IV
**tiny** ['taɪni] klein; winzig III
**tip** [tɪp] Tipp; Ratschlag II
**tired** [taɪəd] müde I
to get tired of sth [ˌget 'taɪəd‿əv] etw. sattbekommen; etw. satthaben IV
**tissue** ['tɪʃu:] Taschentuch III
**title** ['taɪtl] Titel; Überschrift <II>
job title ['dʒɒb ˌtaɪtl] Stellenbezeichnung; Berufsbezeichnung IV
**to** [tʊ] in; nach; zu; vor *(bei Uhrzeitangaben)* I; bis II
to the north of [ˌtə ðə 'nɔ:θ‿əv] nördlich von III
**toast** [təʊst] Toast II
**today** [tə'deɪ] heute I
**together** [tə'geðə] zusammen; gemeinsam I
to get together [ˌge‿tə'gəðə] zusammenkommen; zusammenfinden IV
**toilet** ['tɔɪlət] Toilette I
**told** [təʊld] simple past von *to tell* I
**tolerance** ['tɒlrns] Toleranz V U1, 13
**tolerant** ['tɒlrnt] tolerant V U1, 13
to **tolerate** ['tɒlreɪt] tolerieren; dulden IV
**tomato** *(sg)* [tə'mɑ:təʊ], **tomatoes** *(pl)* [tə'mɑ:təʊz] Tomate II

**tomorrow** [tə'mɒrəʊ] morgen II
**ton** [tʌn] Tonne *(Gewicht)* IV
**tone** [təʊn] Ton <IV>
**tongue twister** ['tʌŋ ˌtwɪstə] Zungenbrecher <III>
**tonight** [tə'naɪt] heute Abend; heute Nacht II
**tonne** [tʌn] Tonne II
**too** [tu:] auch I; zu II
too much [ˌtu: 'mʌtʃ] zu sehr II
**took** [tʊk] simple past von *to take* II
**tool** [tu:l] Werkzeug; Gerät II
**tooth** *(sg)* [tu:θ], **teeth** *(pl)* [ti:θ] Zahn III
**toothbrush** ['tu:θbrʌʃ] Zahnbürste III
**toothpaste** ['tu:θpeɪst] Zahnpasta III
**toothpick** ['tu:θpɪk] Zahnstocher II
**top** [tɒp] Top; Oberteil II; oberer Teil; oberes Ende III; Spitze IV
at the top [æt ðə 'tɒp] oben III
**top-class** ['tɒpklɑ:s] Spitzen <V U3, 67>
**topic** ['tɒpɪk] Thema IV
**torch** [tɔ:tʃ] Taschenlampe I
**tore (up)** [tɔ:r (ʌp)] simple past von *to tear up* IV
**torn (up)** [tɔ:n (ʌp)] past participle von *to tear up* IV
**torn** [tɔ:n] zerrissen; aufgerissen IV
**tornado** [tɔ:'neɪdəʊ] Tornado; Wirbelsturm IV
**total** ['təʊtl] Gesamt-; gesamt; komplett <IV>
***to keep in touch** [ˌki:p‿ɪn 'tʌtʃ] in Verbindung bleiben II
**to touch** [tʌtʃ] berühren III
**tough** [tʌf] hart III
**tour** [tʊə] Tour; Fahrt; Reise IV
guided tour ['gaɪdɪd ˌtɔ:] Führung <IV>
tour guide ['tʊə ˌgaɪd] Reiseleiter; Reiseleiterin V U1, 12
**tourism** ['tʊərɪzm] Tourismus IV
**tourist** ['tʊərɪst] Tourist; Touristin I
tourist industry ['tʊərɪst‿ˌɪndəstri] Tourismus V U2, 28
Tourist Information Centre ['tʊərɪst ɪnfə'meɪʃn ˌsentə] Touristeninformation I
**in tow** [ɪn 'təʊ] im Schlepptau IV
**towards** [tə'wɔ:dz] in Richtung; auf … zu IV
**towel** ['taʊəl] Handtuch III
**tower** ['taʊə] Turm II
clock tower ['klɒk ˌtaʊə] Uhrenturm II
**town** [taʊn] Stadt I
ghost town ['gəʊst ˌtaʊn] Geisterstadt IV
town hall [ˌtaʊn 'hɔ:l] Rathaus II
**townsfolk** ['taʊnzfəʊk] Bürger *(Pl.)*; Stadtbewohner *(Pl.)* V U3, 59
**township** ['taʊnʃɪp] Township *(Wohnsiedlungen für Schwarze in Südafrika)* V U3, 49
**toy** [tɔɪ] Spielzeug III
cuddly toy ['kʌdli ˌtɔɪ] Kuscheltier III
toy figure [ˌtɔɪ 'fɪgə] Spielzeugfigur <V U3, 61>
**track** [træk] Strecke IV
railway track ['reɪlweɪ ˌtræk] Gleis IV
**tractor** ['træktə] Traktor I
**trade** [treɪd] Handel; Gewerbe <V U4, 84>
**to trade** [treɪd] Handel treiben; handeln <V U4, 84>
**trading** ['treɪdɪŋ] Handel V U4, 70
**tradition** [trə'dɪʃn] Tradition III
**traditional** [trə'dɪʃnl] traditionell III
**traffic light** ['træfɪk ˌlaɪt] (Verkehrs-)Ampel V U3, 59
**traffic** ['træfɪk] Verkehr III
traffic jam ['træfɪk ˌdʒæm] Stau IV
**trail** [treɪl] Wanderweg; Spur IV
**train** [treɪn] Zug I
**trainer** ['treɪnə] Turnschuh I; Trainer; Trainerin IV
**training** ['treɪnɪŋ] Training III; Ausbildung V U1, 16
on-the-job training [ˌɒnðədʒɒb 'treɪnɪŋ] Ausbildung am Arbeitsplatz V U1, 16
**tram** [træm] Straßenbahn III
**transcontinental** [ˌtrænsˌkɒntɪ'nentl] transkontinental *(über den Kontinent hinweg)* IV
**transfer** [træns'fɜ:] Transport; Transfer IV
**to translate** [trænz'leɪt] übersetzen IV
**translation** [trænz'leɪʃn] Übersetzung <III>
**transparency** [træn'spærnsi] Folie <IV>
**transparent** [træn'spærnt] durchsichtig; transparent V U4, 74
**transport** ['trænspɔ:t] Verkehrs- IV; Transport; Beförderung V U1, 17
public transport [ˌpʌblɪk 'trænspɔ:t] öffentliche Verkehrsmittel III
**trash** (AE) [træʃ] Abfall; Müll IV
**travel** ['trævl] (das) Reisen <V U2, 198>; Reise- <V U3, 57>
time travel ['taɪm ˌtrævl] Zeitreise III
travel agent ['trævl‿ˌeɪdʒnt] Reisebürokaufmann; Reisebürokauffrau V U1, 17
travelling ['trævlɪŋ] (das) Reisen <IV>
**to travel** ['trævl] reisen II; fahren III; bewegen <V U1, 26>
**tray** [treɪ] Tablett II
**treasure** ['treʒə] Schatz II
**to treat** [tri:t] behandeln V U3, 54
**treatment** ['tri:tmənt] Behandlung V U3, 51
**tree** [tri:] Baum I
**trend** [trend] Trend; Entwicklung; Richtung IV
trendy ['trendi] trendy; modisch IV
**trending** ['trendɪŋ] trendsetzend IV
**tribe** [traɪb] Stamm; Volksstamm V U1, 12
**trick** [trɪk] Trick; Streich I; Kunststück III
Trick or treat! [ˌtrɪk‿ə 'tri:t] Süßes, sonst gibt's Saures! I
**tricky** ['trɪki] schwierig; knifflig IV
**trip** [trɪp] Ausflug I; Trip; Fahrt; Reise III
boat trip ['bəʊt ˌtrɪp] Bootsfahrt; Schiffsfahrt II
school trip [ˌsku:l 'trɪp] Klassenfahrt I
to take a trip [ˌteɪk‿ə 'trɪp] eine Fahrt machen III
**trolley suitcase** ['trɒli ˌsu:tkeɪs] Rollkoffer III
**tropical** ['trɒpɪkl] tropisch V U1, 21
**trouble** ['trʌbl] Schwierigkeiten; Problem; Ärger III
**trousers** *(pl)* ['traʊzəz] Hose I

**truck** [trʌk] Wagen; Karre III
**true** [tru:] wahr II; treu IV
to come true [ˌkʌm ˈtru:] wahr werden; in Erfüllung gehen IV
to **trust** [trʌst] vertrauen IV
**truth** [tru:θ] Wahrheit V U4, 78
to **try** [traɪ] probieren; versuchen II
to try on [ˌtraɪ‿ˈɒn] anprobieren II
to try out [ˌtraɪ‿ˈaʊt] ausprobieren III
**T-shirt** [ˈti:ʃɜ:t] T-Shirt I
**tube** [tju:b] Schlauch; Rohr III
**Tuesday** [ˈtju:zdeɪ] Dienstag I
on Tuesday [ˌɒn ˈtju:zdeɪ] am Dienstag I
**tuna** [ˈtju:nə] Thunfisch II
to **tune** in [ˌtju:n‿ˈɪn] einschalten V U4, 75
**tunnel** [ˈtʌnl] Tunnel III
(wind) **turbine** [(wɪnd) ˈtɜ:baɪn] Windrad III
**turbulent** [ˈtɜ:bjələnt] unruhig <V U4, 84>
**turkey** [ˈtɜ:ki] Truthahn; Pute IV
**Turkish** [ˈtɜ:kɪʃ] türkisch; Türkisch; aus der Türkei IV
Turkish bath [ˌtɜ:kɪʃ ˈbɑ:θ] Dampfbad III
**turn** [tɜ:n] Drehung IV
in turn [ɪn ˈtɜ:n] dagegen; im Gegenzug V U1, 20
to take turns [ˌteɪk ˈtɜ:nz] sich abwechseln V U3, 58
to **turn** [tɜ:n] abbiegen III
to turn around [ˌtɜ:n‿əˈraʊnd] (sich) umdrehen III
to turn left [ˌtɜ:n ˈleft] (nach) links abbiegen I
to turn off [ˌtɜ:n‿ˈɒf] abschalten; ausschalten <IV>
to turn on [ˌtɜ:n‿ˈɒn] einschalten IV
to turn right [ˌtɜ:n ˈraɪt] (nach) rechts abbiegen I
to turn to sb [ˈtɜ:n tə] sich jmdm. zuwenden V U3, 60
**turning** point [ˈtɜ:nɪŋ ˌpɔɪnt] Wendepunkt <III>
**turtle** [ˈtɜ:tl] Schildkröte V U1, 20
**tutor** [ˈtju:tə] Klassenlehrer; Klassenlehrerin I
tutor group [ˈtju:tə ˌgru:p] Klasse *(in einer englischen Schule)* I
**tutorial** [tju:ˈtɔ:riəl] Anleitung; Tutorial IV
**TV** [ˌti:ˈvi:] Fernseher; Fernsehen I
TV show [ˌti: ˈvi: ˌʃəʊ] Fernsehsendung II
TV studio [ˌti:ˈvi: ˌstju:diəʊ] Fernsehstudio II
to watch TV [ˌwɒtʃ ti:ˈvi:] fernsehen I
on TV [ɒn ˌti:ˈvi:] im Fernsehen IV
**twelve** [twelv] zwölf I
**twenty** [ˈtwenti] zwanzig I
twenty-one [ˌtwentiˈwʌn] einundzwanzig I
**twice** [twaɪs] zweimal; doppelt IV
to **twist** [twɪst] verdrehen; verzerren II
**two** [tu:] zwei I
the two of them [ðə ˈtu: əv ðəm] die beiden V U3, 58
**type** [taɪp] Sorte; Typ; Art III
to **type** [taɪp] tippen <III>
**typical** [ˈtɪpɪkl] typisch <IV>
**tyre** [taɪə] Reifen III

## U

**ugly** [ˈʌgli] hässlich V U2, 40
**umbrella** [ʌmˈbrelə] Regenschirm II
**umpire** [ˈʌmpaɪə] Schiedsrichter; Schiedsrichterin <III>
**unappealing** [ˌʌnəˈpi:lɪŋ] uninteressant IV
**uncertain** [ʌnˈsɜ:tn] ungewiss; unsicher V U1, 20
**uncle** [ˈʌŋkl] Onkel I
**uncomfortable** [ʌnˈkʌmftəbl] unbequem; unangenehm II
**under** [ˈʌndə] unter I
down under [ˌdaʊn‿ˈʌndə] in Australien <V U1, 26>
**underground** [ˈʌndəgraʊnd] U-Bahn II
**underlined** [ˌʌndəˈlaɪnd] unterstrichen <III>
**underprivileged** [ˌʌndəˈprɪvlɪdʒd] benachteiligt; unterprivilegiert V U3, 52
*to **understand** [ˌʌndəˈstænd] verstehen II
**understood** [ˌʌndəˈstʊd] simple past von *to understand* II
**underwater** [ˌʌndəˈwɔ:tə] Unterwasser- V U1, 20
**unemployed** [ˌʌnɪmˈplɔɪd] arbeitslos IV
**unequal** [ˌʌnˈi:kwəl] ungleich V U3, 52
**unexpected** [ˌʌnɪkˈspektɪd] unerwartet V U3, 59
**unfair** [ʌnˈfeə] unfair III
unfairness [ʌnˈfeənəs] Ungerechtigkeit V U3, 52
**unfashionable** [ʌnˈfæʃnəbl] unmodisch II
**unfiltered** [ˌʌnˈfɪltəd] ungefiltert V U4, 79
**unfortunately** [ʌnˈfɔ:tʃnətli] leider; unglücklicherweise V U1, 20
to **unfriend** [ʌnˈfrend] entfreunden *(jmdn. von seiner Freundesliste streichen)* IV
**unfriendly** [ʌnˈfrendli] unfreundlich III
**unhappy** [ʌnˈhæpi] unglücklich II
**uniform** [ˈju:nɪfɔ:m] Uniform I
**unit** [ˈju:nɪt] Lektion; Kapitel <I>
to **unite** [ju:ˈnaɪt] vereinen; vereinigen <V U3, 66>
**university** [ˌju:nɪˈvɜ:səti] Universität III
**unjust** [ʌnˈdʒʌst] ungerecht IV
**unknown** [ʌnˈnəʊn] unbekannt V U1, 20
**unlike** [ʌnˈlaɪk] anders als; im Gegensatz zu III
**unlucky** [ʌnˈlʌki] Unglücks- <V U4, 84>
**unmotivated** [ˌʌnˈməʊtɪveɪtɪd] unmotiviert IV
**unofficial** [ˌʌnəˈfɪʃl] inoffiziell <V U3, 62>
**unpleasant** [ʌnˈpleznt] unangenehm; unerfreulich IV
**unpolluted** [ˌʌnpəˈlu:tɪd] unverschmutzt <V U3, 205>
**unpopular** [ʌnˈpɒpjələ] unpopulär; unbeliebt III
**until** [ʌnˈtɪl] bis I
**unusual** [ʌnˈju:ʒl] ungewöhnlich; außergewöhnlich V U1, 10



p pen • b bed • t ten • d dad • k cat • g grey • tʃ chair • dʒ joke • f fan • v very • θ three • ð the

**up** [ʌp] hinauf; oben II; abgelaufen V U3, 54
up to ['ʌp tə] bis zu V U1, 11
**update** [ʌp'deɪt] Aktualisierung <IV>
to **update** ['ʌpdeɪt] updaten; auf den neuesten Stand bringen IV
to **upload** ['ʌpləʊd] hochladen; ins Internet stellen II
**upper** ['ʌpə] obere III
**upset** [ʌp'set] aufgebracht; bestürzt I
**upwards** ['ʌpwədz] aufwärts <V U4, 81>
**US** [ˌju:'es] US-amerikanisch IV
**us** [ʌs] wir; uns I
**use** [ju:s] Nutzen; Verwendung; Gebrauch <V U2, 46>
useful ['ju:sfl] nützlich; hilfreich III
to **use** [ju:z] benutzen; verwenden II
*to get **used** to (sth) [ˌget 'ju:zd tə] sich an (etw.) gewöhnen IV
**used** to (live) ['ju:st tə] (wohnte) früher III
**usual** ['ju:ʒl] üblich <V U4, 84>
usually ['ju:ʒli] normalerweise; gewöhnlich II

## V

**vacation** *(AE)* [və'keɪʃn] Ferien; Urlaub IV
**vacuum** cleaner ['vækju:m ˌkli:nə] Staubsauger IV
**valid** ['vælɪd] gültig III
**valley** ['væli] Tal V U3, 55
**value** ['vælju:] Wert V U3, 54
**values** *(pl)* ['vælju:z] Werte; Wertvorstellungen V U2, 34
**van** [væn] Lieferwagen; Transporter III
**vast** [vɑ:st] gewaltig; riesig <V U3, 205>
**veganism** *(no pl)* ['vi:gənɪzm] Veganismus IV
**vegetable** (veg) ['vedʒtəbl] Gemüse II
**vegetarian** [ˌvedʒɪ'teəriən] Vegetarier; Vegetarierin I
**vehicle** ['vɪəkl] Fahrzeug <V U4, 212>
vehicle painter ['vɪəkl ˌpeɪntə] Fahrzeuglackierer; Fahrzeuglackiererin <V U1, 192>
**verb** [vɜ:b] Verb <III>
**verse** [vɜ:s] Vers; Strophe <III>
**version** ['vɜ:ʃn] Version <III>
**very** ['veri] sehr I
**vet** [vet] Tierarzt; Tierärztin III
**victim** ['vɪktɪm] Opfer V U3, 50
**Victorian** era [vɪkˌtɔ:riən 'ɪərə] viktorianisches Zeitalter III
**video** ['vɪdiəʊ] Video IV
video chat ['vɪdiəʊ ˌtʃæt] Video-Chat III
**Vietnamese** [ˌvjetnə'mi:z] vietnamesisch; Vietnamesisch; aus Vietnam; Vietnamese; Vietnamesin IV
**view** [vju:] Aussicht; Sicht; Ausblick; Blick IV
**viewing** ['vju:ɪŋ] Hör-/Sehverstehen <I>
**Viking** ['vaɪkɪŋ] Wikinger- III
**villa** ['vɪlə] Villa <V U3, 205>
**village** ['vɪlɪdʒ] Dorf III
**violence** *(no pl)* ['vaɪəlns] Gewalt V U2, 34
*to go **viral** [gəʊ 'vaɪrl] rasend schnell bekannt werden <V U1, 24>
**visa** ['vi:zə] Visum; Einreisebewilligung <V U2, 198>
**visit** ['vɪzɪt] Besuch III
to **visit** ['vɪzɪt] besuchen II
**visitor** ['vɪzɪtə] Besucher; Besucherin II
**vitamin** ['vɪtəmɪn] Vitamin <V U2, 46>
**vocabulary** [və'kæbjələri] Vokabular; Wortschatz II
**voice** [vɔɪs] Stimme III
**volcano** *(sg)* [vɒl'keɪnəʊ], **volcanoes** *(pl)* [vɒl'keɪnəʊz] Vulkan V U2, 30
**volleyball** ['vɒlibɔ:l] Volleyball IV
**voluntary** year ['vɒləntri ˌjɪə] Soziales Jahr <V U1, 192>
**volunteer** [ˌvɒlən'tɪə] Freiwilliger; Freiwillige; ehrenamtlicher Helfer; ehrenamtliche Helferin III
**Voodoo** ['vu:du:] Voodoo *(westafrikanische Religion)* <V U2, 46>
to **vote** [vəʊt] abstimmen; wählen V U3, 59
to vote for ['vəʊt fə] abstimmen über; wählen IV
**voyage** ['vɔɪɪdʒ] Reise; Fahrt III
**vuvuzela** [ˌvu:vu:'zeɪlə] Vuvuzela *(Plastikhorn)* <V U3, 66>

## W

**wage** [weɪdʒ] Lohn IV
**wagon** ['wægən] Waggon; Planwagen IV
to **wait** [weɪt] warten II
to wait for ['weɪt fɔ:] warten auf II
**waiter** ['weɪtə] Kellner II
**waitress** ['weɪtrəs] Kellnerin; Bedienung IV
*to **wake** [weɪk] wecken; aufwecken V U2, 39
to wake up [ˌweɪk‿'ʌp] aufwachen II
**walk** [wɔ:k] Spaziergang III
night walk [ˌnaɪt 'wɔ:k] Nachtwanderung I
to slow to a walk [ˌsləʊ tʊ‿ə 'wɔ:k] in Schritttempo verfallen IV
to take the dog for a walk [ˌteɪk ðə ˌdɒg fər‿ə 'wɔ:k] den Hund spazieren führen II
a five minute walk [ə 'faɪv mɪnɪt ˌwɔ:k] fünf Minuten zu Fuß III
to **walk** [wɔ:k] gehen I; laufen II
to walk the plank [ˌwɔ:k ðə 'plæŋk] über eine Schiffsplanke ins Wasser getrieben werden V U2, 40
dog **walker** ['dɒg ˌwɔ:kə] Hundeausführer; Hundeausführerin IV
**walking** ['wɔ:kɪŋ] Wandern III
**wall** [wɔ:l] Mauer; Wand II
rock climbing wall [ˌrɒk klaɪmɪŋ 'wɔ:l] Kletterwand <V U2, 47>
**wallet** ['wɒlɪt] Brieftasche; Geldbörse III
to **want** (to) [wɒnt (tə)] wollen I
**war** [wɔ:] Krieg V U3, 49
**wardrobe** ['wɔ:drəʊb] Kleiderschrank I
**warm** [wɔ:m] warm I
to **warn** [wɔ:n] warnen III
**warning** ['wɔ:nɪŋ] Warnung <V U4, 76>
**was** [wɒz] simple past von *to be* I
to **wash** [wɒʃ] (sich) waschen; spülen III
*to do the **washing** up [ˌdu: ðə 'wɒʃɪŋ‿ʌp] abspülen II
**waste** [weɪst] Abfall; Exkremente V U1, 20
food waste ['fu:d ˌweɪst] Speisereste; Lebensmittelabfälle V U4, 76

to **waste** [weɪst] verschwenden IV
to **watch** [wɒtʃ] anschauen; ansehen I; aufpassen auf; zuschauen; beobachten II
to watch TV [ˌwɒtʃ tiːˈviː] fernsehen I
bird **watching** [ˈbɜːd ˌwɒtʃɪŋ] Vogelbeobachtung III
whale **watching** [ˈweɪl ˌwɒtʃɪŋ] Walbeobachtung IV
**water** [ˈwɔːtə] Wasser I
bucket of water [ˈbʌkɪt‿əv ˌwɔːtə] Eimer Wasser I
mineral water [ˈmɪnrl ˌwɔːtə] Mineralwasser III
**wave** [weɪv] Welle IV
to **wave** [weɪv] winken II
**way** [weɪ] Weg; Art und Weise III
way in [ˌweɪ ˈɪn] Einstieg <I>
way of life [ˌweɪ əv ˈlaɪf] Lebensart; Lebensweise IV
asking the way [ˈɑːskɪŋ ðə ˌweɪ] nach dem Weg fragen I
on the way [ˌɒn ðə ˈweɪ] auf dem Weg; unterwegs I
this way [ðɪs ˈweɪ] in diese Richtung II; auf diese Weise <III>
way to go [ˈweɪ tə ˌɡəʊ] super II
**we** [wiː] wir I
**weak** [wiːk] schwach III
**weakness** [ˈwiːknəs] Schwäche IV
**wealth** [welθ] Reichtum V U2, 35
*to **wear** [weə] tragen *(Kleidung)* I
**weather** [ˈweðə] Wetter I
**web** [web] Spinnennetz; Netz III
**website** [ˈwebsaɪt] Website II
**wedding** [ˈwedɪŋ] Hochzeit II
**Wednesday** [ˈwenzdeɪ] Mittwoch I
Ash Wednesday [ˌæʃ ˈwenzdeɪ] Aschermittwoch V U2, 30
on Wednesdays [ɒn ˈwenzdeɪz] mittwochs I
**week** [wiːk] Woche I
**weekday** [ˈwiːkdeɪ] Werktag V U3, 58
on weekdays [ɒn ˈwiːkdeɪz] unter der Woche; an Werktagen III
**weekend** [ˈwiːkend] Wochenende I
at the weekend [ˌət ðə ˈwiːkend] am Wochenende I
**weekly** [ˈwiːkli] wöchentlich III
to **weigh** [weɪ] wiegen II
**weight** [weɪt] Gewicht <IV>
to **welcome** [ˈwelkəm] begrüßen; willkommen heißen IV
**welcome** (to) [ˈwelkəm (tʊ)] willkommen (bei/in) I
You're **welcome.** [jɔː ˈwelkəm] Gern geschehen. I
**well** [wel] na ja I; gut II
to go well [ˌɡəʊ ˈwel] gut laufen V U1, 18
Well done! [ˌwel ˈdʌn] Gut gemacht! I
**well-educated** [ˈwelˌedʒʊkeɪtɪd] gebildet V U3, 51
**well-equipped** [ˌwelɪˈkwɪpt] gut ausgestattet <V U2, 198>
**well-informed** [ˌwelɪnˈfɔːmd] gut informiert <IV>
**well-kept** [ˌwelˈkept] gut gepflegt V U3, 58
**well-organized** [ˈwelˌɔːɡnaɪzd] gut organisiert <IV>
**well-paid** [ˌwelˈpeɪd] gut bezahlt V U2, 34
**well-prepared** [ˌwelprɪˈpeəd] gut vorbereitet <V U4, 82>
**welly** [ˈweli] Gummistiefel I
**Welsh** [welʃ] walisisch; Walisisch; Waliser; Waliserin III
**went** [went] simple past von *to go* I
**were** [wɜː] simple past von *to be* I
**west** [west] Westen III
west of [ˈwest‿əv] westlich von IV
**wet** [wet] nass I
**whale** [weɪl] Wal IV
whale shark [ˈweɪl ˌʃɑːk] Walhai V U1, 23
whale watching [ˈweɪl ˌwɒtʃɪŋ] Walbeobachtung IV
**what** [wɒt] was I; welche II; wie III
What about you? [ˌwɒt‿əbaʊt ˈjuː] Und du? II
What about …? [ˈwɒt‿əˌbaʊt] Was ist mit …? I
What a … [ˈwɒt‿ə] Was für ein/eine … I
what else [ˌwɒt‿ˈels] was sonst; was noch III
What else can you …? [ˌwɒt‿ˈels kæn juː] Was kannst du noch …? <I>
What have you been up to? [ˌwɒt‿əv juː biːn ˈʌp tə] Was hast du (in letzter Zeit) gemacht?; Wie läuft's bei dir? IV
What time is it? [ˌwɒt ˈtaɪm‿ɪz‿ɪt] Wie spät ist es?; Wie viel Uhr ist es? I
What's up? [ˌwɒts‿ˈʌp] Wie geht's? IV
What's your name? [ˌwɒts jə ˈneɪm] Wie heißt du? I
**whatever** [wɒtˈevə] egal was; egal welche <V U3, 67>
**wheel** [wiːl] Rad II
big wheel [ˌbɪɡ ˈwiːl] Riesenrad II
**wheelchair** [ˈwiːltʃeə] Rollstuhl III
**when** [wen] wann I; wenn; als II
**whenever** [wenˈevə] wann immer; immer, wenn; so oft V U1, 12
**where** [weə] wo; wohin; woher I
Where are you from? [ˌweər‿ə ju ˈfrɒm] Woher kommst du? I
**wherever** [weəˈrevə] wo(hin) auch immer; egal wo(hin); überall wo(hin) III
**whether** [ˈweðə] ob V U4, 78
**which** [wɪtʃ] welche II; die; der; dem; den; das III
a **while** [ə ˈwaɪl] eine Weile IV
**while** [waɪl] während II
to **whisper** [ˈwɪspə] flüstern <IV>
**white** [waɪt] weiß I
**who** [huː] wer I; die; welche II; der; dem; den III
**whole** [həʊl] ganz III
**whom** [huːm] wen; wem III
**whose** [huːz] dessen; deren III
**why** [waɪ] warum I
that's why [ˈðæts waɪ] deswegen III
**wide** [waɪd] breit IV; groß; weit; ausgedehnt V U3, 54
**wife** *(sg)* [waɪf], **wives** *(pl)* [waɪvz] Ehefrau III
**wild** [waɪld] wild III
the wild [ðə ˈwaɪld] Wildnis; freie Wildbahn IV
**wilderness** [ˈwɪldənəs] Wildnis IV
**wildlife** [ˈwaɪldlaɪf] Tierwelt *(in freier Wildbahn)* IV
**will** [wɪl] werden II
**willing** [ˈwɪlɪŋ] bereitwillig IV

*to **win** [wɪn] gewinnen; siegen I
**wind** [wɪnd] Wind I
wind farm ['wɪnd fɑ:m] Windpark III
windy ['wɪndi] windig I
**window** ['wɪndəʊ] Fenster I
shop window [ˌʃɒp 'wɪndəʊ] Schaufenster V U4, 70
**windscreen** wiper ['wɪnskri:n ˌwaɪpə] Scheibenwischer III
**wine** [waɪn] Wein IV
**winner** ['wɪnə] Sieger; Siegerin; Gewinner; Gewinnerin I
**winter** ['wɪntə] Winter I
windscreen **wiper** ['wɪnskri:n ˌwaɪpə] Scheibenwischer III
**wire** ['waɪə] Draht; Kabel III
**wish** [wɪʃ] Wunsch <IV>
Best wishes, [ˌbest 'wɪʃɪz] Viele Grüße, I
to **wish** [wɪʃ] wünschen III
**witch** [wɪtʃ] Hexe I
**with** [wɪð] mit I
**within** [wɪ'ðɪn] innerhalb <V U3, 62>
**without** [wɪ'ðaʊt] ohne III
**witness** ['wɪtnəs] Zeuge; Zeugin IV
**woke** [wəʊk] simple past von *to wake* V U2, 39
**woken** ['wəʊkn] past participle von *to wake* V U2, 39
**woman** *(sg)* ['wʊmən], **women** *(pl)* ['wɪmɪn] Frau I
**wombat** ['wɒmbæt] Beutelmaus <V U1, 24>
**won** [wʌn] simple past von *to win* I; past participle von *to win* II
**won't** (= will not) [wəʊnt] nicht werden II
**wonder** ['wʌndə] Wunder V U1, 20
wonderful ['wʌndəfl] wunderbar III
to **wonder** ['wʌndə] sich Gedanken machen; sich fragen V U2, 34
**wood** [wʊd] Holz; Wald III
**wool** [wʊl] Wolle I
**word** [wɜ:d] Wort IV
linking word [ˌlɪŋkɪŋ 'wɜ:d] Verbindungswort <IV>
root word [ˌru:t 'wɜ:d] Stammwort <III>
signal word ['sɪgnl ˌwɜ:d] Signalwort <III>
**wore** [wɔ:] simple past von *to wear* V U4, 70
**work** [wɜ:k] Arbeit I
work experience ['wɜ:k‿ɪkˌspɪəriəns] Praktikum; Berufserfahrung V U1, 16
work placement [ˌwɜ:k 'pleɪsmənt] Berufspraktikum <V U1, 192>
to **work** [wɜ:k] arbeiten I; funktionieren II
to work off [ˌwɜ:k‿'ɒf] abarbeiten IV
**workbook** ['wɜ:kbʊk] Arbeitsheft I
**worker** ['wɜ:kə] Arbeiter; Arbeiterin II
**working** conditions *(pl only)* ['wɜ:kɪŋ kənˌdɪʃnz] Arbeitsbedingungen <V U1, 18>
**working** hours *(pl)* ['wɜ:kɪŋ ˌaʊəz] Arbeitszeit IV
**workshop** ['wɜ:kʃɒp] Workshop II
acting workshop ['æktɪŋ ˌwɜ:kʃɒp] Schauspielworkshop II
**world** [wɜ:ld] Welt II
outside world [ˌaʊtsaɪd 'wɜ:ld] Außenwelt IV
all around the world [ɔ:l‿əˌraʊnd ðə 'wɜ:ld] in aller Welt III
in the world [ɪn ðə 'wɜ:ld] auf der Welt II
**worn** [wɔ:n] past participle von *to wear* II; getragen; abgenutzt <V U3, 205>
**worried** ['wʌrid] beunruhigt; besorgt II
to **worry** ['wʌri] sich Sorgen machen I
**worst** [wɜ:st] schlimmste; schlechteste III
*to be **worth** [bi: 'wɜ:θ] wert sein III
**would** [wʊd] würde(n) II
would like [wʊd 'laɪk] würde(n) gern; hätte(n) gern II
I wouldn't like (to) … [aɪ 'wʊdnt laɪk (tə)] Ich möchte nicht …; Ich würde nicht gerne … I
I'd love to … (= I would love to) [aɪd 'lʌv tə] Ich würde sehr gern … III
Would you like (to) …? [ˌwʊd jə 'laɪk (tə)] Möchtest du? I
**wrap** [ræp] Wrap II
**wrist** [rɪst] Handgelenk IV
*to **write** [raɪt] schreiben I
**writer** ['raɪtə] Schriftsteller; Schriftstellerin II; Verfasser; Verfasserin; Autor; Autorin III
**writing** ['raɪtɪŋ] Schreiben <I>
**wrong** [rɒŋ] falsch I
to be wrong [bi: 'rɒŋ] unrecht haben; sich irren III
**wrote** [rəʊt] simple past von *to write* I

## X

**Xhosa** ['kɔ:sə] Xhosa *(Sprache)* <V U3, 62>

## Y

**year** [jɪə] Jahr; Jahrgangsstufe; Klasse I
New Year [ˌnju: 'jɪə] Neujahr V U3, 59
boom years ['bu:m ˌjɪəz] Blütezeit; fette Jahre *(ugs.)* IV
**year-old** [ˌjɪər‿'əʊld] jährig; Jahre alt IV
**yellow** ['jeləʊ] gelb I
**yes** [jes] ja I
**yesterday** ['jestədeɪ] gestern I
**yet** [jet] schon II
not … yet [nɒt … 'jet] noch nicht II
**yogurt** ['jɒgət] Joghurt II
**you** [ju:] du; Sie; ihr; euch; dich; dir; Ihnen I
You're right. [jɔ:‿'raɪt] Du hast recht. I
You're welcome. [jɔ: 'welkəm] Gern geschehen. I
**young** [jʌŋ] jung II
**your** [jɔ:] dein; deine; euer; eure; Ihr; Ihre I
**yours** [jɔ:z] deine; eure; Ihre I
**Yours,** [jɔ:z] Eure *(als Briefabschluss)* I
Yours faithfully, [ˌjɔ:z 'feɪθfli] Mit freundlichen Grüßen V U3, 50
Yours sincerely, [ˌjɔ:z sɪn'sɪəli] Mit freundlichen Grüßen V U1, 16
**yourself** [jɔ:'self] dich selbst II
by yourself [baɪ 'jɔ:self] allein II
**yourselves** [jɔ:'selvz] selber; ihr/euch/Sie/sich (selbst) III

**youth** *(no pl)* [juːθ] Jugend-; Jugend III
youth hostel [ˈjuːθ ˌhɒstl] Jugendherberge III

## Z

**zebra** [ˈzebrə] Zebra I
**zero** [ˈzɪərəʊ] null I
**zip** line [ˈzɪp ˌlaɪn] Seilrutsche III
time **zone** [ˈtaɪm ˌzəʊn] Zeitzone IV
**zoo** [zuː] Zoo; Tierpark I
**zookeeper** [ˌzuːˈkiːpə] Tierpfleger; Tierpflegerin I
to **zoom** in [ˈzuːm‿ɪn] heranzoomen <I>
**Zulu** [ˈzuːluː] Zulu *(Sprache)* <V U3, 62>

## Boys' names

**Aman** [əˈmɑːn] V U2, 35
**Andy** [ˈændi] <V U2, 43>
**Carlie** [ˈkɑːli] V U3, 54
**Christian** [ˈkrɪstʃn] V U4, 69
**Clayton** [ˈkleɪtn] <V U2, 42>
**Frankie** [ˈfræŋki] V U2, 34
**Greg** [greg] V U1, 18
**Hennie** [ˈheni] V U3, 58
**Jack** [dʒæk] V U1, 19
**James** [dʒeɪmz] V U3, 54
**Jeff** [dʒef] V U4, 73
**Jesper** [ˈjespə] V ZI 8
**Kenneth** [ˈkenɪθ] V U4, 70
**Koa** [kəʊˈɑː] V U1, 12
**Lefa** [ˈleːfa] V U3, 50
**Len** [len] V U1, 15
**Marc** [mɑːk] V U4, 73
**Neil** [niːl] V U4, 73
**Oliver** [ˈɒlɪvə] V U1, 19
**Piet** [pit] V U3, 50
**Steven** [ˈstiːvn] V U4, 73
**Tinus** [ˈtiːnʊs] V U3, 50
**Tony** [ˈtəʊni] V U3, 54
**Willem** [ˈwɪləm] V U3, 58
**Yong Guang** [jɒŋ ˈgwæŋ] V U4, 69

## Girls' names

**Alison** [ˈælɪsn] V U4, 69
**Beverley** [ˈbevli] V U3, 58
**Cebile** [ˈsebɪlə] V U3, 50
**Cindy** [ˈsɪndi] V U4, 70
**Danielle** [ˌdæniˈel] V U2, 34
**Dawn** [dɔːn] V U3, 51
**Eleni** [ˈeləni] V ZI 8
**Eliza** [ɪˈlaɪzə] V U2, 38
**Fran** [fræn] V U4, 73
**Ida** [ˈaɪdə] V U4, 77
**Jen** [dʒen] V U4, 72
**Kagiso** [kəˈhiːsəʊ] V U3, 50
**Layla** [ˈleɪlə] V U2, 34
**Rosa** [ˈrəʊzə] V U3, 58
**Rosie** [ˈrəʊzi] V U2, 33
**Serena** [səˈriːnə] V U2, 34
**Tara** [ˈtɑːrə] V U2, 34
**Tina** [ˈtiːnə] V U1, 15
**Trish** [trɪʃ] V U4, 71

## Surnames

**Austin** [ˈɔːstɪn] V U2, 38
**Blackbeard** [ˈblækbɪəd] V U2, 41
**Blackheart** [ˈblækhɑːt] V U2, 39
**Botha** [ˈbɒːta] V U3, 50
**Chan** [tʃæn] V U4, 70
**Chow** [tʃaʊ] V U4, 78
**Clarke** [klɑːk] V U2, 34
**Ho** [həʊ] V U4, 74
**Jansen** [ˈjansən] V U3, 50
**Keita** [kɛjˈta] V U3, 54
**Lai** [leɪ] V U4, 74
**Moloi** [ˈmələɪ] V U3, 58
**Naidoo** [ˈneɪduː] V U3, 58
**Okonwo** [ɔˈkɒnwoː] V U3, 54
**Pitt** [pɪt] V U1, 16
**Sekibo** [səˈkiːbəʊ] V U3, 50
**Wessels** [ˈwɛslz] V U3, 56
**White** [waɪt] V U1, 17
**Wong** [wɒŋ] V U4, 71
**Wynner** [ˈwɪnə] V U1, 16

## Place names

**Africa** [ˈæfrɪkə] Afrika II
**Alice Springs** [ˌælɪs ˈsprɪŋz] *Stadt in Australien* V U1, 12
**America** [əˈmerɪkə] Amerika II
**Antarctica** [ænˈtɑːktɪkə] Antarktis V U1, 10
**Asia** [ˈeɪʒə] Asien IV
**Australia** [ɒsˈtreɪliə] Australien I
the **Bahamas** [ðə bəˈhɑːməz] die Bahamas *(Inselgruppe in der Karibik)* V U2, 30
**Barbados** [bɑːˈbeɪdɒs] Barbados *(Inselstaat in der Karibik)* V U2, 38
**Bloemfontein** [ˈbluːmfənteɪn] *Hauptstadt Südafrikas* V U3, 48
**Bo-Kaap** [ˌbəʊˈkæp] *Stadtteil von Kapstadt* <V U3, 63>
**Boston** [ˈbɒstən] *Stadt in den USA* III
The **British Isles** [ðə ˌbrɪtɪʃ ˈaɪlz] die Britischen Inseln III
the **British Virgin Islands** [ðə ˌbrɪtɪʃ ˌvɜːdʒɪn ˈaɪləndz] die Britischen Jungferninseln V U2, 30
**Canada** [ˈkænədə] Kanada III
**Cape Peninsula** [ˌkeɪp pəˈnɪnsjələ] Kap-Halbinsel <V U3, 67>
**Cape Town** [ˈkeɪp ˌtaʊn] Kapstadt *(Hauptstadt Südafrikas)* V U3, 48
the **Caribbean** [ðə ˌkærɪˈbiːən] die Karibik V U2, 28
**China** [ˈtʃaɪnə] China IV
**Cuba** [ˈkjuːbə] Kuba IV
The **Czech Republic** [ðə ˌtʃek rɪˈpʌblɪk] Tschechien II
**Denmark** [ˈdenmɑːk] Dänemark III
**Dominica** [dəˈmɪnɪkə] Dominica *(Inselstaat in der Karibik)* V U2, 30
The **Dominican Republic** [ðə dəˌmɪnɪkn rɪˈpʌblɪk] Dominikanische Republik IV
**Durban** [ˈdɜːbən] *Stadt in Südafrika* V U3, 50
**Eastern Europe** [ˈiːstn ˌjʊərəp] Osteuropa IV
**England** [ˈɪŋglənd] England I
**Europe** [ˈjʊərəp] Europa II
**Exuma** [ɪksˈjuːmə] Exuma *(Inselgruppe der Bahamas)* <V U2, 42>
**France** [frɑːns] Frankreich II
**Germany** [ˈdʒɜːməni] Deutschland I
**Great Britain** [ˌgreɪt ˈbrɪtn] Großbritannien III
**Greece** [griːs] Griechenland IV
**Grenada** [grəˈneɪdə] Grenada *(Insel in der Karibik)* V U2, 43
**Haiti** [ˈheɪti] Haiti *(Insel in der Karibik)* <V U2, 46>
**Havana** [həˈvænə] *Hauptstadt Kubas* V U2, 30

**Hong Kong** [ˌhɒŋ ˈkɒŋ] Hongkong V U1, 15
**India** [ˈɪndiə] Indien I
**Italy** [ˈɪtəli] Italien II
**Jamaica** [dʒəˈmeɪkə] Jamaika II
**Kingston** [ˈkɪŋstən] *Stadt auf Jamaika* V U2, 31
**London** [ˈlʌndən] *Hauptstadt von England* I
**Malaysia** [məˈleɪziə] *Staat in Südostasien* <V U3, 63>
**Melbourne** [ˈmelbən] *Stadt in Australien* V U1, 16
**Mexico** [ˈmeksɪkəʊ] Mexiko IV
The **Netherlands** [ðə ˈneðələndz] die Niederlande II
**New Zealand** [ˌnjuː ˈziːlənd] Neuseeland <V U3, 66>
**North America** [ˌnɔːθ‿əˈmerɪkə] Nordamerika IV
**Northern Ireland** [ˌnɔːðn‿ˈaɪələnd] Nordirland III
**Norway** [ˈnɔːweɪ] Norwegen III
**Perth** [pɜːθ] *Stadt in Australien* V U1, 10
The **Philippines** [ˌðə ˈfɪlɪpiːnz] die Philippinen IV
**Poland** [ˈpəʊlənd] Polen II
**Pretoria** [prɪˈtɔːriə] *Hauptstadt Südafrikas* V U3, 48
**Puerto Rico** [ˌpwɜːtə ˈriːkəʊ] Puerto Rico <V U2, 46>
**Queensland** [ˈkwiːnzlənd] *Bundesstaat in Australien* V U1, 10
The **Republic of Ireland** [ðə rɪˌpʌblɪk‿əv‿ˈaɪələnd] Irland III
**Rio de Janeiro** [ˌriːəʊ dədʒəˈnɪərəʊ] *brasilianische Stadt* <V U2, 47>
**Robben Island** [ˌrɒbn ˈaɪlənd] *Insel mit Gefängnis vor Südafrika* V U3, 63
**Russia** [ˈrʌʃə] Russland IV
**Scandinavia** [ˌskændɪˈneɪviə] Skandinavien IV
**Scotland** [ˈskɒtlənd] Schottland III
**Sicily** [ˈsɪsɪli] Sizilien V U1, 20
**South Africa** [ˌsaʊθ‿ˈæfrɪkə] Südafrika V U3, 48
**Spain** [speɪn] Spanien II
**Sydney** [ˈsɪdni] *Stadt in Australien* V U1, 10
**Tasmania** [tæzˈmeɪniə] Tasmanien <V U1, 24>
**Titjikala** [ˌtɪtjiˈkɑːlə] *Ort in Australien* V U1, 12
**Toronto** [təˈrɒntəʊ] *Stadt in Kanada* V U2, 34
**Trinidad** [ˈtrɪnɪdæd] Trinidad *(Insel in der Karibik)* V U2, 30
**Turkey** [ˈtɜːki] Türkei II
**Umlazi** [ʊmˈlɑːzi] *Stadtteil von Durban* V U3, 50
The **United Kingdom (UK)** [ðə juːˌnaɪtɪd ˈkɪŋdəm] Vereinigtes Königreich von Großbritannien und Nordirland III
**USA (United States of America)** [ˌjuːesˈeɪ (juːˌnaɪtɪd ˌsteɪts‿əv əˈmerɪkə)] USA (Vereinigte Staaten von Amerika) III
**Vietnam** [ˌvjetˈnæm] Vietnam IV
**Wales** [weɪlz] Wales III

## Other names

**All Blacks** [ˌɔːl ˈblæks] *neuseeländisches Rugby-Team* <V U3, 66>
**Amagwinya** [ˌɑːmaˈgwɪnja] *südafrikanisches frittiertes Hefebrötchen* V U3, 52
**Atlantic Ocean** [ətˌlæntɪk ˈəʊʃn] Atlantischer Ozean V U2, 39
the **Big Five** [ˌðə bɪg ˈfaɪv] *die bedeutendsten Großtierarten Afrikas: Leopard, Löwe, Nashorn, Büffel, Elefant* V U3, 54
Usain **Bolt** [ˌjuːzeɪn ˈbəʊlt] *jamaikanischer Sprinter* <V U2, 47>
**Bridge Climb** [ˌbrɪdʒ ˈklaɪm] *touristische Brückenbesteigung in Sydney* V U1, 15
**Cape Town Cycle Tour** [keɪp ˌtaʊn ˈsaɪkl ˌtʊə] *Name eines Radrennens* <V U3, 67>
the **Caribbean Sea** [ðə ˌkærɪbiːən ˈsiː] das Karibische Meer V U2, 29
**Certificate in Advanced English** [səˌtɪfɪkət‿ɪn ədvɑːnst‿ˈɪŋglɪʃ] *Sprachtest* V U1, 16
Jackie **Chan** [ˌdʒæki ˈtʃæn] *chinesischer Schauspieler* <V U4, 85>
the **Creator** [kriˈeɪtə] der Schöpfer <V U1, 26>
Lood **de Jager** [ˌluːd də ˈjɛːgɐ] *Rugbyspieler* V U3, 55
**Dreamtime** [ˈdriːmtaɪm] **Traumzeit** *(Entstehungsgeschichte der australischen Ureinwohner)* V U1, 12
**Flying Emu Lodge** [ˌflaɪɪŋ ˌiːmjuː ˈlɒdʒ] *Name eines Hotels* V U1, 16
**Great Barrier Reef** [ˌgreɪt ˌbæriə ˈriːf] *Korallenriff vor der Küste Australiens* V U1, 10
**Gulf of Mexico** [ˌgʌlf‿əv ˈmeksɪkəʊ] Golf von Mexiko <V U2, 39>
**HMS Revenge** [ˌeɪdʒemes rɪˈvendʒ] *Schiffsname* V U2, 41
**Indian Ocean** [ˌɪndiən ˈəʊʃn] Indischer Ozean <V U2, 39>
Michael **Jordan** [ˌmaɪkl ˈdʒɔːdn] *ehemaliger amerik. Basketballspieler* V U4, 70
**Kakadu National Park** [ˌkækəduː ˌnæʃnl ˈpɑːk] *Name eines Nationalparks in Australien* V U1, 23
**Kowloon Park** [ˌkaʊˈluːn ˌpɑːk] *Park in Hongkong* V U4, 71
Paul **Kruger** [ˌpɔːl ˈkruːgə] *südafrikanischer Präsident (1882-1902)* V U3, 54
**Kruger National Park** [ˌkruːgə ˌnæʃnl ˈpɑːk] *Nationalpark in Südafrika* V U3, 48
**Lady Margaret** [ˌleɪdi ˈmɑːgrət] *Schiffsname* V U2, 39
**Lord Winton** [ˌlɔːd ˈwɪntən] *Personenname* V U2, 38
**Malva pudding** [ˌmælvə ˈpʊdɪŋ] *südafrikanischer Nachtisch* V U3, 52
Bob **Marley** [bɒb ˈmɑːli] *jamaikanischer Sänger* V U2, 29
**Midmar Mile** [ˌmɪdmɑː ˈmaɪl] *Schwimmwettbewerb* <V U3, 67>
**Nelson Mandela** [ˌnelsn mænˈdelə] *Präsident von Südafrika (1994–1999)* V U3, 49
the **Olympics** *(Olympic Games)* [ði‿əˈlɪmpɪks (əˌlɪmpɪk ˈgeɪmz)] Olympiade; Olympische Spiele <V U2, 47>

**Oranje Primary School** [ˌorаɲə ˈpraɪmri ˌsku:l] *Name einer Grundschule in Südafrika* V U3, 58
**Panama Canal** [ˌpænəmɑ: ˈkənæl] Panamakanal <V U2, 39>
**PRT** (Personal Rapid Transit) [ˌpi:a:ˈti: (ˌpɜ:snl ræpɪd ˈtrænsɪt)] *Name eines Personentransportsystems* V U4, 74
**Radio Cape Gold FM** [ˌreɪdiəʊ keɪp gəʊld‿ef‿ˈem] *Radiostation* V U3, 54
**Redhill School** [ˌredhɪl ˈsku:l] *Name einer Schule* V U3, 50
**RMS Rhone** [ɑ:remes ˈrəʊn] *gesunkenes Kreuzfahrtschiff* V U2, 30
**Royal Flying Doctor Service** [ˌrɔɪəl ˌflaɪɪŋ ˌdɒktə ˈsɜ:vɪs] *Fliegender Ärtzedienst in Australien* V U1, 11
**Royal Navy** [ˌrɔɪəl ˈneɪvi] *Kriegsmarine des Vereinigten Königreichs* V U2, 41
**School of the Air** [ˌsku:l‿əv ði‿ˈeə] *Fernunterricht in Australien* V U1, 11
**Seven Mile Beach** [ˌsevn ˌmaɪl ˈbi:tʃ] *Sandstrand in Jamaika* V U2, 30
**Sneakers Street** [ˌsni:kəz ˈstri:t] *Straßenname* V U4, 70
The **Springboks** [ðə ˈsprɪŋbɒks] *afrikanisches Rugby-Team* <V U3, 66>
**Sydney Harbour Bridge** [ˌsɪdni ˌhɑ:bə ˈbrɪdʒ] *ein Wahrzeichen von Sydney* V U1, 15
**Jinjin Tong** [ˌdʒɪndʒɪn ˈtɒŋ] *Personenname* V U4, 81
**Uluru** [u:ˈlu:ru:] Uluru = Ayers Rock *(heiliger Berg der Aborigines)* V U1, 12
The **Union of South Africa** [ðə ˌju:njən‿əv ˌsaʊθ‿ˈæfrɪkə] Südafrikanische Union V U3, 49
**Victoria Peak** [ˈvɪktɔ:riə ˌpi:k] *bekanntester Berg Hongkongs* <V U4, 81>
**Waterfront Hotel** [ˌwɔ:təfrʌnt həʊˈtel] *Name eines Hotels* V U1, 16
John **Woo** [ˌdʒɒn ˈwu:] *chinesischer Regisseur* <V U4, 85>
**World Cup** [ˌwɜ:ld ˈkʌp] Weltmeisterschaft <V U3, 66>

## A

**abarbeiten** to work off IV
**abbiegen** to turn III
etw. **abbrechen** to drop out of sth V U3, 50
**abdecken** to cover IV
**Abend** evening I
gestern Abend last night V U2, 34
an jenem Abend that night II
heute Abend tonight II
**Abendessen** dinner II
(frühes) Abendessen tea I
**abends** in the evenings III
**Abenteuer** adventure I
**Abenteurer** adventurer IV
**Abenteurerin** adventurer IV
**aber** but I
**abfahren** to leave II
**Abfall** rubbish II; trash (AE) IV; waste V U1, 20
**abfeuern** to fire V U2, 41
**Abflug** departure V U2, 31
**Abgase** *(von Fahrzeugen)* exhaust fumes *(pl)* V U4, 74
**abgelaufen** up V U3, 54
jmdn. von etw. **abhalten** to stop sb from sth V U2, 39
**abheben** to take off IV
**abholen** to pick up IV
**Abholung** pick-up IV
**Abkömmling** descendant V U2, 29
**ablehnen** to reject; to refuse IV
**Abnahme** decline V U1, 21
**abnehmen** to take off V U1, 13; to decrease V U4, 75
**abonnieren** to subscribe IV
die **Aborigines** Aboriginal people V U1, 11
**Aborigine-** Aboriginal V U1, 11
**abräumen** to clear IV
den Tisch abräumen to clear the table II
**Abreise** departure V U2, 31
**abschaffen** to abolish IV
**abschicken** *(einen Brief)* to post III
**Abschieds-** leaving II
**Abschiedsrede** farewell speech II
**abschließen** to lock I; to complete V U1, 14
**Abschluss** qualification V U1, 17
sich **abseilen** to abseil II
**absetzen** to drop off V U4, 74
mit der **Absicht** in order to V U2, 40
**absichtlich** on purpose II
**absolut** absolutely IV
**absolvieren** to complete V U1, 14
**absorbieren** to absorb V U4, 75
**abspülen** to do the washing up II
gemischter **Abstammung** mixed race V U3, 48
**abstauben** to dust IV
**abstimmen** to vote V U3, 59
abstimmen über to vote for IV
**Abteilung** department II
sich **abwechseln** to take turns V U3, 58
außer **Acht** lassen to ignore V U1, 12
**acht** eight I
**Achterbahn** roller coaster II
**achtzehn** eighteen I
**achtzig** eighty I
**Ackerbau** farming IV
**Ackerboden** farmland IV
**Ackerland** farmland IV
**Action** action IV
**Adapter** adaptor III
**addieren** to add IV
**Adjektiv** adjective III
**Adresse** address II
**Affe** monkey I
**Afrikaner** African IV
**Afrikanerin** African IV
**afrikanisch** African IV
**Afroamerikaner** African American IV
**Afroamerikanerin** African American IV
**afroamerikanisch** African-American IV
**Ahnung** idea I
keine Ahnung haben to have no idea IV
**ahoi** *(Seemannsruf)* ahoy V U2, 41
**Aktenkoffer** briefcase III
**Aktentasche** briefcase III
**aktiv** busy V U4, 69
**Aktivität** activity I
**aktuell** current V U1, 16
nicht mehr aktuell out of fashion IV
**akzeptabel** acceptable V U1, 13
**Akzeptanz** acceptance V U1, 13
**akzeptieren** to accept IV
**albern** silly II
**Albtraum** nightmare V U3, 51
**Alge** alga V U1, 20
**Alkohol** alcohol *(no pl)* IV
**alle** all I; everyone II; everybody IV; all of V U2, 29
(sie) alle all of them V U2, 29
von allen Leuten of all the people V U1, 18
**Allee** avenue IV
**allein** alone I; by yourself II
ganz allein all alone I
**allerdings** certainly IV
**allererste** very first III
**Allergie** allergy II
**allergisch** gegen allergic to II
**alles** everything II
alles in allem all in all IV
alles klar all right II
**allgemein** in general IV
**Alligator** alligator IV
**Alphabet** alphabet I
**als** when; than II; as III
**also** so I; right II
**alt** old I; ancient IV
**Alter** age I
im Alter von aged V U4, 76
**älter** elderly IV
**altertümlich** ancient IV
**Altglascontainer** bottle bank II
**altmodisch** old-fashioned; out of fashion IV
**Aluminium** aluminium III
**am** Dienstag on Tuesday I
**am** Schluss by the end II
**am** Wochenende at the weekend I
**Amerikaner** American IV
**Amerikanerin** American IV
**Amerikanisch** American IV
**amerikanisch** American IV
**amisch** Amish IV
die **Amischen** the Amish IV
**Ampel** lights IV
(Verkehrs)**Ampel** traffic light V U3, 59
sich **amüsieren** to enjoy oneself III
**amüsiert** amused IV
**an** on; at I; by IV
an Bord on board III
an der Spitze (von) at the front of II
**Ananas** pineapple III

**anbauen** to grow IV; to produce V U4, 74
**anbieten** to offer IV
**andauern** to last; to continue IV
**Andenken** souvenir III
**andere** other I; others II; else V U2, 34
ein anderer another II
jeder andere anybody else V U1, 19
die anderen the others I
anderer Meinung sein to disagree II
**andererseits** then again III; on the other (hand) IV
seine Meinung **ändern** to change one's mind III
(sich) **ändern** to change III
**anders** different I
anders als unlike III
**andeuten** to suggest V U4, 74
**andocken** to dock IV
**anerkannt** recognised V U1, 12
**anerkennen** to appreciate IV; to recognise V U2, 39
**Anfang** start; beginning III
**anfangen** to start II
**Anfänger** beginner V U2, 30
**Anfängerin** beginner V U2, 30
**Anforderung** requirement V U1, 19
**Anfrage** request IV
**anführen** to lead IV
**Anführer** leader III
**Anführerin** leader III
**angefügt** attached V U1, 16
**angehängt** attached V U1, 16
**angehen** to go on V U4, 74
**Angeln** fishing IV
**angenehm** comfortable III
**angezogen** dressed III
**angreifen** to attack IV
**Angriff** attack IV
**Angst** fear V U4, 79
Angst haben to be scared; to be afraid II
(große) Angst (vor etw.) haben to be terrified (of sth) V U2, 40
**ängstlich** afraid II
**anhalten** to stop V U2, 41
**Anhänger** follower IV
**Anhängerin** follower IV
**anheben** to raise V U4, 75
**anheuern** to hire IV
**anhören** to listen (to) I
**ankommen** to arrive II
**Ankömmling** arrival IV
**Ankündigung** announcement II
**Ankunft** arrival V U2, 31
**anlegen** to put on III
**Anleitung** tutorial IV
**anmalen** to paint IV
**Anmeldeformular** entry form II
**Anmeldung** registration II
**annähernd** nearly IV
**annehmbar** acceptable V U1, 13
**annehmen** to guess V U4, 70; to accept IV
**Annonce** ad(vert) (= advertisement) IV
**Anordnung** layout IV
sich **anpassen** to adapt (to) IV
**anprobieren** to try on II
**Anruf** call III
**anrufen** to call I; to phone II
**Anrufer** caller II
**Anruferin** caller II
**anschauen** to watch; to look at I; to have a look II; to check out IV
**anschließen** to install V U4, 74
sich anschließen to join III
**Ansehen** reputation IV
**ansehen** to watch I
**Anspitzer** pencil sharpener I
**ansprechend** appealing IV
**ansteigen** to grow V U2, 37
**Anstieg** increase V U1, 20
**anstoßen** to hit III
**anstößig** offensive V U1, 12
sich **anstrengen** to struggle V U1, 11
**Anstrengung** struggle V U2, 34
**Antenne** antenna III
**Antwort** answer II
**antworten** to answer I; to reply V U4, 72
**anwesend** sein to attend V U1, 11
**Anzahl** number IV
**Anzeige** ad(vert) (= advertisement); advertisement II
**anziehen** to put on III; to attract IV
sich anziehen to get dressed II
**Apartheid** *(Rassentrennung per Gesetz)* apartheid *(no pl)* V U3, 49
**April** April I
**Arbeit** work I; job II
**arbeiten** to work I
**Arbeiter** worker II
**Arbeiterin** worker II
**Arbeitsaufwand** effort V U4, 69
**Arbeitsheft** workbook I
**Arbeitskollege** co-worker IV
**Arbeitskollegin** co-worker IV
**arbeitslos** unemployed IV
Ausbildung am **Arbeitsplatz** on-the-job training V U1, 16
**arbeitsreich** busy I
**Arbeitszeit** working hours *(pl)* IV
**Architekt** architect IV
**Architektin** architect IV
**Archiv** archive II
**Areal** area III
**Ärger** trouble III
**argumentieren** to argue V U3, 60
**Arm** arm I
**arm** poor IV
die **Armen** the poor V U4, 71
**Armee** army III
**armselig** miserable III
**Armut** poverty IV
**Art** sort II; type; kind III; species V U1, 10
Art und Weise way III
**Artikel** article V U4, 73
**Arzt** doctor II
**Ärztin** doctor II
**ärztlich** medical IV
**Aschermittwoch** Ash Wednesday V U2, 30
**Astronomie** astronomy IV
**Atem** breath V U2, 30
den Atem rauben to take one's breath away V U2, 30
**Atemzug** breath V U2, 30
**atmen** to breathe III
**Atmosphäre** atmosphere V U3, 60
**Attacke** attack IV
**auch** too; also I
auch nicht not ... either III
auch wenn even though V U2, 34
**auf** on; at I
auf dem Weg on the way I
auf der linken Seite on the left I
auf der rechten Seite on the right I
auf einmal suddenly II
Auf Wiedersehen! Goodbye. I
auf ... zu towards IV

auf Dauer in the long run V U4, 74
auf dem Land in the country I
auf der Welt in the world II
**Aufbau** structure III; construction V U3, 50
**aufbewahren** to keep IV
**aufbleiben** to stay up IV
**aufbrechen** to set off IV
**auffallen** to stand out IV
**auffallend** striking III
**auffliegen** to fly open V U2, 39
**aufführen** to perform III
**Aufführung** show IV
**Aufgabe** job II
**aufgeben** to give up III
**aufgeben** *(einen Brief)* to post III
**aufgebracht** upset I
**aufgehen** to open V U2, 40
**aufgeregt** excited; nervous II
**aufgerissen** torn IV
**aufhalten** to stop V U1, 21
**aufheben** to pick up II; to save IV
jmdn. **aufheitern** to cheer sb up III
sich **aufhellen** to clear V U4, 76
**aufhören** to stop I; to finish II; to end IV
**aufklaren** to clear V U4, 76
**Aufkleber** sticker II
**aufkrempeln** to roll up IV
**Auflage** edition V U3, 54
**aufmachen** to open I
sich aufmachen to set off IV
**aufmerksam** werden to take notice V U3, 60
seine **Aufmerksamkeit** auf etw. richten to pay attention to sth V U1, 17
jmdn. **aufmuntern** to cheer sb up III
**aufnehmen** to absorb V U4, 75
**aufpassen** to look after II
aufpassen auf to watch II
**aufräumen** to tidy (up) II
**aufregend** exciting I
**Aufregung** excitement IV
**aufrichtig** straightforward III
**aufrollen** to roll up IV
**aufschauen** to look up II
**aufstehen** to get up I; to stand up IV
**aufstellen** to put up IV
**Aufstieg** climb V U1, 15
**auftauchen** to appear III; to show up V U3, 50
**auftreten** to perform III
**aufwachen** to wake up II
**aufwachsen** to grow up III
**aufwecken** to wake V U2, 39
**Aufzug** elevator *(AE)* IV
**Auge** eye II
**Augenblick** moment II
**augenblicklich** at present V U4, 74
**August** August I
im August in August I
**aus** from I; out V U4, 78
aus dem Weg gehen to avoid IV
aus … heraus out of II
**Ausbildung** education IV; training V U1, 16
Ausbildung am Arbeitsplatz on-the-job training V U1, 16
**Ausbleichen** bleaching V U1, 20
**Ausblick** view IV
**ausbrechen** to break out V U2, 34
**auschecken** to check out III
sich **ausdenken** to think of V U2, 40
**Ausdruck** look V U2, 40; phrase V U4, 79
**auseinander** apart IV
**Auseinandersetzung** argument II
**ausfallen** to fail IV
**ausflippen** to go crazy V U4, 70
**Ausflug** trip I
**Ausgabe** edition V U3, 54
**ausgeben** *(Geld)* to spend II
**ausgebildet** skilled V U1, 11
**ausgedehnt** wide V U3, 54
ein **ausgefüllter** Tag a busy day I
**ausgehen** to go out III
**ausgehen** *(Ware)* to run out of III
**ausgestorben** extinct V U1, 21
im **Ausland** abroad IV
ins **Ausland** abroad IV
**ausländisch** foreign IV
**auslaufen** to spill IV
**ausleihen** to borrow II
**auslösen** to set off IV
**Ausmaß** scale V U4, 69
**ausprobieren** to try out III; to check out IV
**ausräumen** to clear IV
**Ausrede** excuse V U1, 15
**ausruhen** to rest IV
sich ausruhen to relax V U4, 69
**Ausrüstung** equipment III
**Aussage** statement IV
**Ausschnitt** clip IV
**aussehen** to look II
**Außenwelt** outside world IV
**außer** except III
außer Acht lassen to ignore V U1, 12
**außerdem** in addition V U1, 11
**außergewöhnlich** unusual V U1, 10; extraordinary V U2, 30
**außerhalb** outside IV; out V U4, 78
außerhalb des Lehrplans extracurricular IV
**Außerirdische** alien I
**Außerirdischer** alien I
**äußerst** extremely IV
**außerunterrichtlich** *(Zusatzunterricht)* extracurricular IV
**Aussicht** view IV
**Aussichtspunkt** lookout point II
**ausstehen** to stand IV
**aussteigen** to get off II
**Ausstellung** exhibition III
**Austausch** exchange IV
**Australier** Australian V U1, 10
**Australierin** Australian V U1, 10
**australisch** Australian V U1, 10
**Ausverkauf** sale II
**Auswahl** choice IV
**auswählen** to choose II
**auswandern** to emigrate IV
**ausweichen** to avoid IV
**Ausweis** ID III; pass IV
**Auswirkung** impact IV; effect V U1, 21; consequence V U3, 50
**ausziehen** to take off III
**Auto** car I
**Autogramm** autograph IV
Autogramme geben to sign autographs IV
**Automat** machine II
**Autor** writer III
**Autorin** writer III

## B

**Baby** baby II
**Babysitter** babysitter IV
**Babysitterin** babysitter IV
einen Kuchen **backen** to make a cake I

**Bäcker** baker III
**Bäckerei** baker's III
**Bäckerin** baker III
**Backofen** oven II
**Bad** bathroom I; bath V U4, 76
**Badewanne** bath V U4, 76
**Badezimmer** bathroom I; bathroom *(AE)* IV
**Bahnhof** station I
**bald** soon II
**Ball** ball II; dance IV
**Banane** banana I
**Band** band II
**Bank** bench III
**Bär** bear I
**Bargeld** cash II
**Baseball** baseball IV
**Basketball** basketball II
**Bau** construction V U3, 50
**Bauarbeiter** builder II
**Bauarbeiterin** builder II
**Bauch** stomach II
**Bauchschmerzen** stomach ache II
**Bauchweh** stomach ache II
**bauen** to build II
**Bauer** farmer I
**Bäuerin** farmer I
**Bauernhof** farm I
**Baum** tree I
**Baumwolle** cotton III
**Baustelle** construction site IV
**beachten** to take notice V U3, 60; to observe V U4, 78
**beängstigend** scary I
**beanspruchen** to claim V U4, 70
**beantworten** to answer I
**bedauern** to feel sorry for III; to regret IV
**bedecken** to cover IV
**bedeuten** to mean III
**bedeutend** major; powerful IV
**Bedeutung** meaning V U1, 12
sich **bedienen** to help oneself III
**Bedienung** waitress IV
**Bedingung** condition IV
**bedrohen** to threaten V U2, 28
**Bedrohung** threat V U1, 20
sich **beeilen** to hurry II; to rush III
**beeindrucken** to impress III
**beeindruckend** powerful IV
**beeinflussen** to influence IV
**beenden** to finish II; to end IV
**befähigen** to qualify V U1, 16
sich **befassen** (mit) to deal (with) IV
sich **befinden** to be located IV
**befolgen** to observe V U4, 78
**befördern** to carry II
**Beförderung** transport V U1, 17
**befragen** to interview I
**Befrager** interviewer IV
**Befragerin** interviewer IV
**Befragung** interview II
**befreunden** *(jmdn. zu seiner Freundesliste hinzufügen)* to friend IV
**begabt** talented III
**begeistert** excited II
**Beginn** beginning III
**beginnen** to start II; to begin IV
**begnadigen** to pardon IV
**Begnadigung** pardon IV
**begrenzen** to limit V U1, 21
**begrüßen** to welcome IV
**behalten** to keep IV
**behandeln** to treat V U3, 54
**Behandlung** treatment V U3, 51
**behaupten** to claim V U4, 70
**Behauptung** statement IV
mit **Behinderung** with special needs III
**behutsam** cautious III
**bei** at I
bei Bewusstsein awake III
**beibringen** to teach III
**beide** both III
die beiden the two of them V U3, 58
**Bein** leg II
**beinahe** almost III; nearly IV
**beinhalten** to include IV
**Beispiel** example IV
zum Beispiel for example IV
**bekannt** familiar IV
**bekannt sein als** to be known as V U1, 11
sich **beklagen** to complain III
**Bekleidungsvorschriften** dress code IV
**bekommen** to get I
**bekräftigen** to confirm IV
**belästigen** to bother IV
**belebt** alive V U3, 58; busy V U4, 69
**Beleg** evidence V U3, 54
**Belegschaft** staff *(no pl)* IV
**beleidigend** offensive V U1, 12
**beliebt** popular III
**bellen** to bark III
**bemerken** to notice III
**bemerkenswert** striking III
**Bemühung** effort V U4, 69
**benachteiligt** disadvantaged V U2, 34; underprivileged V U3, 52
sich **benehmen** to behave IV
**benennen** to name IV
**benötigen** to require V U1, 16
**benutzen** to use II
**beobachten** to watch II; to observe V U4, 78
**bequem** comfortable III
**beraten** to advise sb V U4, 74
**Berater** counsellor V U2, 34
**Beraterin** counsellor V U2, 34
**Bereich** area IV; field V U1, 16
**bereit** ready I
**bereits** already II
**bereitwillig** willing IV
**Berg** mountain III; hill IV
in den Bergen in the mountains III
**Bergarbeiter** miner III
**Bergarbeiterin** miner III
**bergen** to save III
**Bergkette** mountain range V U3, 55
**Bergwerk** mine III
**Bericht** report IV
**Bericht** *(in einer Zeitung)* article V U4, 73
**berichten** (über) to report (on) IV
**Beruf** job II; career IV
**Berufsbezeichnung** job title IV
**Berufserfahrung** work experience V U1, 16
**berühmt** famous I
berühmte Person celebrity IV
**berühren** to touch III
**Besatzung** crew III
**beschädigen** to damage V U1, 21
**Beschädigung** damage V U1, 20
**beschäftigt** busy I
jmdm. **Bescheid** geben to let sb know V U1, 15
jmdm. **Bescheid** sagen to let sb know V U1, 15
**Bescheinigung** certificate V U1, 16
**beschimpfen** to abuse V U4, 78

**beschränken** to limit V U1, 21
**Beschränkung** restriction; limit V U4, 79
**beschreiben** to describe IV
**Beschwerde** complaint III
sich **beschweren** to complain III
**Besichtigungstour** sightseeing IV
eine Besichtigungstour machen to go sightseeing II
**besiedeln** to settle IV
**besiedelt** populated IV
**besitzen** to own; to have got II
**Besitzer** owner IV
**Besitzerin** owner IV
**besonders** special I; especially IV
**besorgt** worried II
**Besorgungen** machen to do the shopping II
**besser** better I
**bestätigen** to confirm IV
**bestbezahlt** best-paid; best-paying IV
**beste** best II
die besten the best II
**bestehen** to exist V U1, 10; to pass V U1, 14
bestehen aus to consist of V U2, 28
**besteigen** to climb III
**bestellen** to order II
**bestimmen** to regulate V U3, 54
**bestimmte** certain IV; particular V U4, 70
**bestrafen** to punish V U4, 78
**Bestrafung** punishment V U2, 40
**bestürzt** upset I
**Besuch** visit III
**besuchen** to visit II; to attend V U1, 11
**Besucher** visitor II
**Besucherin** visitor II
sich **beteiligen** to be involved V U2, 34
**beten** to pray V U3, 59
**Beton** concrete III
**betreiben** to run III
**betreten** to enter IV
**betrunken** drunk IV
**Bett** bed I
ins Bett gehen to go to bed I
**Bettdecke** blanket IV
**beunruhigt** worried II
**bevölkert** populated IV
**Bevölkerung** population *(no pl)* III

**bevor** before II
**bevorstehen** to come up III
**bevorzugt** privileged V U3, 52
**bewachte** Wohnanlage gated community V U3, 49
**bewahren** to conserve V U3, 54
(sich) **bewegen** to move III
**beweglich** mobile IV
**Bewegung** move III; movement IV
**Bewegungsmelder** motion sensor V U4, 74
**Beweis** evidence V U3, 54
**beweisen** to prove IV
**Beweismaterial** evidence V U3, 54
sich **bewerben** (für/um) to apply (for) IV
**Bewerber** candidate V U1, 19
**Bewerberin** candidate V U1, 19
**Bewerbung** application V U1, 12
**Bewerbungsbrief** letter of application V U1, 16
**bewerten** to rate III
**Bewohner** inhabitant III
**Bewohnerin** inhabitant III
**bewohnt** inhabited V U2, 28
bei **Bewusstsein** awake III
**Bezahlautomat** payment machine II
**bezahlen** to pay II
gut **bezahlt** well-paid V U2, 34
**Bezahlung** pay IV
**Bezirk** borough IV; district V U4, 70
**bezweifeln** to doubt IV
**Bibliothek** library III
**Bier** beer IV
**bieten** to offer IV
**Bild** picture II
**bilden** to make I
**Bildung** education IV
**billig** cheap II
**binden** to tie IV
**Bindung** bond V U2, 34
**Biologie** Biology I
**bis** until I; to II
bis (spätestens) by III
bis jetzt so far IV
bis zu before II; up to V U1, 11
ein **bisschen** a little; a bit II
**bitte** please I
Bitte schön. Here you are. I
**bitten** um to ask for II
**Blatt** leaf IV

**blau** blue I
**bleiben** to stay II; to keep V U2, 34
etw. bleiben lassen to give sth a miss III
hängen bleiben to be stuck IV
in Verbindung bleiben to keep in touch II
**Bleichen** bleaching V U1, 20
**Bleistift** pencil I
**Blick** view IV; look V U2, 40
starrer Blick stare V U3, 60
**Blitz** lightning *(no pl)* V U2, 31
**Block** block IV
**blöd** stupid V U3, 51
**Blog** blog II
**Blogger** blogger IV
**Bloggerin** blogger IV
**bloßstellend** compromising V U1, 13
**Blume** flower III
**Bluse** blouse I
**bluten** to bleed III
**Blütezeit** boom years IV
**Boden** ground V U1, 12; bottom III; earth IV
**Bonbon** sweet I
**Bonus** bonus IV
**Boot** boat II
**Bootsfahrt** boat trip II
an **Bord** on board III
an **Bord** gehen to board V U2, 31
**böse** angry II; naughty III; evil IV
**Boss** boss II
**Botschaft** message II
**Boulevard** avenue IV
**Bowlen** bowling IV
**Box** box I
**Branche** business IV
**brandneu** brand-new V U4, 70
**braten** to fry IV
**Bratwurst** sausage II
**Brauch** custom IV
**brauchen** to need I
nicht brauchen needn't I
**braun** brown I
**brechen** to break II
**breit** wide IV
**brennen** to be on fire II; to burn III
**Brett** plank II
**Brief** letter III
**Briefmarke** stamp III
**Brieftasche** wallet III

**Brille** glasses *(pl only)* V U4, 81
**bringen** to bring II
**Brise** breeze V U2, 31
**britisch** British II
**Broschüre** brochure III; booklet IV
**Brot** bread II
belegtes Brot sandwich I
**Brotlaib** loaf III
**Brücke** bridge II
**Bruder** brother I
**brutal** brutal V U2, 39
**Buch** book I
über etw. Buch führen to keep a record of sth V U4, 70
**buchen** to book IV
**Bücherei** library III
**Büchse** tin IV
**Buchstabe** letter III
**buchstabieren** to spell I
**Bucht** bay IV
**Bude** stall V U4, 68
**Büfett** buffet III
**Büffel** buffalo V U3, 54
**bügeln** to iron IV
**Bühne** stage II
**Bullauge** porthole V U2, 39
**bummeln** to stroll IV
**Bundesstaat** state IV
**bunt** colourful II
**Buntstift** pencil I
**Burg** castle II
**Bürger** *(Pl.)* townsfolk V U3, 59
**Bürgerrechte** civil rights *(pl)* IV
**Bürgersteig** sidewalk *(AE)* IV
**Büro** office II
**Bus** bus I
im Bus on the bus II
**Bushaltestelle** bus stop II
**Butter** butter I

## C

**Café** café I
**Cafeteria** cafeteria I
**Camp** camp II
**campen** to camp V U4, 70
campen gehen to go camping II
**Camping** camping III
**Campingplatz** campsite III
**Campus** campus IV
**Cent** *(Währung)* cent III
**Center** centre III; center *(AE)* IV
**Chance** chance II; opportunity IV
**Chatroom** chatroom V U3, 54
**chatten** to chat II
**Cheerleader** *(Mädchen, das in einer Gruppe eine Sportmannschaft anfeuert)* cheerleader IV
**Cheerleading** *(Aktivitäten der Cheerleader)* cheerleading IV
**Chef** boss II
**Chefin** boss II
**Chefkoch** head chef II
**Chefköchin** head chef II
**Chemikalie** chemical V U1, 21
**Chili** chilli II
**chillen** to chill out IV
**Chinese** Chinese IV
**Chinesin** Chinese IV
**Chinesisch** Chinese IV
**chinesisch** Chinese IV
**christlich** Christian IV
nach **Christus** AD (= Anno Domini) III
**circa** about II
**Clip** clip IV
**Cola** coke I
**College** college *(AE)* IV
**Comic(heft)** comic II
**Computer** computer I
**Computerspiele-** gaming IV
**Cornflakes** cereal III
**Couchsurfing** couch surfing V U2, 31
**Courage** courage IV
**Cousin** cousin II
**Cousine** cousin II
**Crew** crew III
**Curry** curry II
**Cyber-Mobbing** cyberbullying IV

## D

**da** there; because I
da drüben over there II
da unten down there IV
da ist there is I
da sind there are I
**Dach** roof V U4, 75
**Dachboden** attic I
**dagegen** in turn V U1, 20
**daher** therefore V U3, 54
**dahin** down there IV
**damals** then III; back then IV; at that time V U2, 39
**Dame** lady II
meine Damen und Herren ladies and gentlemen V ZI 8
Sehr geehrte Damen und Herren, Dear Sir or Madam, V U3, 50
**damit** so that IV
**Dampfbad** Turkish bath III
**Dampfer** steamship IV
**Dampfmaschine** steam engine III
**Dampfschiff** steamship IV
**danach** then; after that I; after III
**dankbar** thankful IV
**danke** thanks I
**Danke.** Thank you. I
**dann** then I
**das** the; this; that I; which III
**dass** that III
**Datei** file II
**Datum** date I
**Dauer** length *(no pl)* IV
auf Dauer in the long run V U4, 74
**dauerhaft** permanent V U1, 16
**dauern** to take III; to last IV
**davor** in front of II; before that III
**Debatte** debate IV
**Decke** blanket IV
**decken** to lay II
**dehnen** to stretch IV
**dein** your I
**deine** your; yours I
**Delfin** dolphin V U1, 23
**dem** who; which III
**Demokratie** democracy V U4, 79
**demokratisch** democratic V U3, 49
**Demonstration** protest IV
**den** who; which III
**denken** to think I
**Denkmal** monument II
**dennoch** still III
**deprimiert** down III
**der** the I; who; which III
**derb** rough V U3, 58
**deren** whose III
**derselbe** the same II
**derzeit** at present V U4, 74
**derzeitig** current V U1, 16
**Desaster** disaster III
**deshalb** so I; therefore V U3, 54
**Design** design IV
**dessen** whose III

**deswegen** that's why III; therefore V U3, 54
**Detail** detail IV
**Detektivgeschichte** mystery story IV
**Detektor** detector III
**deutlich** clear IV
**Deutsch** German I
**deutsch** German III
**Dezember** December I
**Diagramm** chart V U4, 76
**Diamant** diamond V U3, 48
**dich** you I
dich selbst yourself II
**dicht** dense IV
**dick** thick V U4, 69
**die** who II; which III
**die** *(auch Pl.)* the I
**Diele** hall IV
**Dienst** service III
**Dienstag** Tuesday I
am Dienstag on Tuesday I
**dies** this I
**diese** (hier) these II
**Ding** thing I
vor allen Dingen above all IV
**dir** you I
**Diskriminierung** discrimination IV
**Diskussion** debate IV
**Distanz** distance IV
**distanziert** distant V U2, 30
**Distrikt** district V U4, 70
**Dolch** dagger V U2, 40
**Dollar** *(amer. Währungseinheit)* dollar IV
**Donner** thunder *(no pl)* V U2, 31
**Donnerstag** Thursday I
**doof** silly III
**doppelt** twice IV
**Dorf** village III
**dort** there I
dort drüben over there II
dort ist there is I
**Dose** can I; tin IV
**Dr.** *(Anrede)* Dr III
**Draht** wire III
**Drama** drama III
**drängeln** to push III
**Draufgänger** daredevil IV
**Draufgängerin** daredevil IV
**draußen** outside II; out V U4, 78
draußen halten to keep out III
**dreckig** dirty I
**Drehort** location III
**Drehung** turn IV
**drei** three I
**dreißig** thirty I
**dreizehn** thirteen I
**dringend** badly; desperately IV
**drinnen** in II; inside IV
**dritte** third I
**Droge** drug V U2, 34
da **drüben** over there III
**Druck** pressure V U4, 69
**drücken** to push I; to squeeze IV
**Dschungel** jungle IV
**du** you I
**Dudelsack** bagpipes *(pl)* III
**dulden** to tolerate IV
**dumm** silly III; stupid V U3, 51
**dunkel** dark I
**Dunkelheit** the dark III
**durch** through II
quer durch across IV
**durchdrehen** to go crazy V U4, 70
**Durcheinander** mess I
**durchgehen** to pass IV
**Durchsage** announcement II
**durchschnittlich** average IV
**durchsichtig** transparent V U4, 74
**durchstarten** to take off IV
**durchstöbern** to browse V U4, 70
**durchsuchen** to search IV
**dürfen** may II; to be able to; to be allowed to IV
nicht dürfen mustn't III
nicht/nie dürfen must not/never III
Darf es sonst noch etwas sein? Anything else? I
**durstig** thirsty II
**Dusche** shower III
**Duschgel** shower gel III

## E

**Ebenbürtigkeit** equality V U3, 52
**Ebene** plain V U3, 54
**echt** really; real II
**Ecke** corner III
**Edition** edition V U3, 54
**Effekt** effect V U1, 21
**effizient** efficient V U1, 16
Es ist **egal**. It doesn't matter. II
**egal** wo(hin) wherever III
**Ehefrau** wife III
**ehemalige** former IV
**Ehemaligentreffen** Homecoming *(AE)* IV
**Ehemann** husband IV
**Ehre** honor *(AE)* IV
**ehrenamtliche** Helferin volunteer III
**ehrenamtlicher** Helfer volunteer III
**ehrgeizig** ambitious IV
**ehrlich** honest III; honestly IV
**Ehrlichkeit** honesty V U2, 35
**Ei** egg I
**eifersüchtig** jealous II
**eigene** own II
**eigenmotiviert** self-motivated V U1, 17
**Eigenschaft** quality V U4, 74
**Eigenschaftswort** adjective III
**eigensinnig** stubborn IV
**eigentlich** actually; in fact III; anyway; basically IV
**Eigentümer** landlord II
**Eile** hurry V U4, 69
**eilen** to rush III
**Eimer** Wasser bucket of water I
**ein** a; an I
ein bisschen a bit II
ein paar a few III
ein wenig a bit II
**einander** each other III
tief **einatmen** to take a deep breath V U3, 60
**Einbrecher** burglar I
**Einbrecherin** burglar I
**Einchecken** check-in V U2, 31
**einchecken** to check in V U1, 16
**eindeutig** clear IV
**eindringen** (in) to invade III
**eine** a; an I
**einerseits** on the one hand IV
**einfach** easy I; plain II; simple III; just IV
einfach nur simply IV
einfache Fahrkarte single ticket III
sich **einfallen** lassen to think of V U2, 40
**Einfluss** impact; influence IV
**einflussreich** important II
**einfügen** to paste II

**einführen** to introduce IV
**Einführung** introduction III
**eingängig** catchy IV
**Eingangstor** gateway IV
**eingeboren** native IV
Kompromisse **eingehen** to compromise V U1, 13
**eingreifen** to take action V U3, 54
**einheimisch** native IV
**einholen** to catch up with IV
**einhundert** a/one hundred I
**einige** some I; a few III; several; a number of IV
sich **einigen** to compromise IV
sich **einigen** (auf) to agree (on) V U1, 21
**Einkäufe** machen to do the shopping II
**Einkaufen** shopping I
**einkaufen** gehen to go shopping II
**Einkäufer** shopper V U4, 68
**Einkäuferin** shopper V U4, 68
**Einkaufszentrum** shopping centre I; shopping mall IV; mall V U4, 68
**Einkaufszettel** shopping list I
**einladen** to invite I
**Einladung** invitation I
**einleiten** to introduce IV
**Einleitung** introduction III
**einmal** once IV
noch einmal once more II
**einmarschieren** (in) to invade III
**einpacken** to pack; to pack up II
**einprägsam** catchy IV
**einrichten** to install V U4, 74
**eins** one I
**einsam** lonely III
**Einsatz** commitment V U2, 35
**einschalten** to turn on IV; to tune in V U4, 75
**einschicken** to send in V U1, 12
**einschlafen** to fall asleep III
**einschließlich** including V U2, 34
**Einschränkung** restriction V U4, 79
**einsenden** to send in V U1, 12
**einsetzen** to put in I
**einst** once IV
**einsteigen** to get on III
**einstellen** to hire IV
**Einstellung** attitude IV
**einstufen** to rate III

**Eintrag** entry IV
**eintreten** to enter IV
**Eintrittskarte** ticket III
nicht **einverstanden** sein to disagree II
**Einwanderer** immigrant IV
**Einwanderin** immigrant IV
**einwandern** to immigrate IV
**Einwohner** inhabitant; population *(no pl)* III
**Einwohnerin** inhabitant III
**Einwohnerzahl** population *(no pl)* III
**Einzelheit** detail IV
**einzeln** individual V U4, 74
**einzige** only III
**Eis** ice cream I; ice IV
**Eisberg** iceberg III
**Eiscreme** ice cream I
**Eisenbahn** railway IV
**eiskalt** freezing; ice-cold IV
**Elefant** elephant I
**Elefantenbaby** baby elephant V U3, 55
**elegant** chic I
**Elektriker** electrician V U1, 17
**Elektrikerin** electrician V U1, 17
**elektrisch** electric IV
**Elektrizität** electricity III
**elektronisch** electronic V U4, 68
**elend** miserable III
**elf** eleven I
**Elfenbein** ivory V U3, 54
**Eltern** parents *(pl)* II
**E-Mail** e-mail I
**emigrieren** to emigrate IV
**Empfang** signal III
**Empfangschef** receptionist V U1, 16
**Empfangschefin** receptionist V U1, 16
**Ende** end II; ending III
am Ende at the back IV
ganz am Ende at the bottom IV
oberes Ende top III
**enden** to finish II; to end IV
**endlich** at last II; finally IV
**endlos** endless V U3, 54; never-ending V U4, 78
**Energie** power III; energy V U4, 74
erneuerbare Energie renewable energy V U4, 74
**eng** tight II
**Engagement** commitment V U2, 35

sich **engagieren** to be involved V U2, 34
die **Engländer** the English III
**Englisch** English I
**englisch** English I
**entdecken** to discover V U2, 30
**Entdeckung** discovery IV
**entfernen** to remove IV
**entfernt** away II; apart IV; distant V U2, 30
**Entfernung** distance IV
**entfliehen** to escape IV
**entfreunden** *(jmdn. von seiner Freundesliste streichen)* to unfriend IV
**entgegentreten** to confront IV
**enthalten** to include IV
enthalten sein to be included III
**entkommen** to escape IV
(jmdm.) **entkommen** to get away (from sb) V U2, 41
**entlang** along I; down III
(sich) **entscheiden** to decide III
**Entscheidung** decision IV
**entschuldigen** to pardon IV
sich entschuldigen to say sorry II
**Entschuldigung** pardon IV; excuse V U1, 15
Entschuldigung! Excuse me! I
Entschuldigung. Sorry.; I'm sorry. I
**Entsetzen** horror V U2, 40
sich **entspannen** to chill out IV; to relax V U4, 69
**entspannend** relaxing III
**entspannt** relaxed IV
**entspringen** to spring up IV
**entstehen** to spring up; to originate IV
**entweder** … oder … either … or … V U3, 50
(sich) **entwickeln** to develop IV
**Entwicklung** trend IV; development V U4, 74
**Enzyklopädie** encyclopedia IV
**er** he I
**erbrechen** to puke IV
**Erdbeere** strawberry II
**Erdboden** ground V U1, 12; earth IV
**Erde** earth IV
die Erde earth IV
**Erdkunde** Geography I
**Erdnussbutter** peanut butter III

**Erdteil** continent V U1, 10
**Ereignis** event IV
**erfahren** to learn; to experience IV
etwas erfahren über to learn about sth III
**erfahren** experienced V U1, 18
**Erfahrung** experience IV
**erfinden** to invent III
**Erfinder** inventor III
**Erfinderin** inventor III
**Erfindung** invention III
**Erfolg** success III
Erfolg haben (mit/bei) to succeed (in) IV
**erfolgreich** successful III; lucky V U2, 34
**erforderlich** necessary V U1, 11
**erfordern** to require V U1, 16
**erforschen** to explore V U1, 10
**erfüllt** sein von ... to be alive with ... IV
in **Erfüllung** gehen to come true IV
**Ergebnis** result II
**ergreifen** to grab III
**erhalten** to conserve V U3, 54
**erhältlich** available V U1, 11
**erhängen** to hang IV
**erhöhen** to increase V U4, 74; to raise V U4, 75
sich **erholen** to recover V U1, 21
**erholsam** relaxing III
sich **erinnern** (an) to remember II
**erkennen** to realise V U1, 13; to recognise V U2, 39
**erklären** to explain III
**Erklärung** statement IV
**erkunden** to explore V U1, 10
sich **erkundigen** nach to ask about II
**erlauben** to allow IV
**erleben** to experience IV
**Erlebnis** experience IV
**erleiden** to suffer V U3, 50
**Ermordung** killing IV
**ermutigen** to encourage V U2, 29
**ernähren** to feed V U2, 37
**erneuerbar** renewable V U4, 74
erneuerbare Energie renewable energy V U4, 74
**ernst** serious III
etw. ernst nehmen to take sth seriously IV
Im Ernst? Are you serious? III
**Erntedankfest** Thanksgiving IV
**erraten** to guess II
**erreichen** to reach IV
**errichten** to put up IV
**erschaffen** to create V U1, 12
**erscheinen** to appear III; to show up V U3, 50
**erschießen** to shoot V U2, 37
**erschöpft** exhausted III
**erschrecken** to scare II; to jump III
jmdn. zu Tode erschrecken to frighten the hell out of sb V U3, 51
**erschreckend** terrifying IV
**erschrocken** sein to be scared II
**ersetzen** to replace IV
**erstaunlich** amazing II
**erste** first I
erste Stunde *(in der Schule)* homeroom IV
**erstellen** to make I
als **Erstes** first I
**erstrecken** to stretch IV
**ertragen** to stand IV
**Erwachsene** adult III; grown-up V U4, 70
**Erwachsener** adult III; grown-up V U4, 70
**erwarten** to expect III
**erwerben** to purchase V U4, 71
**erwidern** to reply V U4, 72
**erzählen** to tell I
**Erzähler** narrator I
**Erzählerin** narrator I
**erzeugen** to produce V U4, 74; to generate V U4, 75
**Erziehung** education IV
**es** it I
es gibt there are; there is I
**Essen** food I; meal II; dinner IV
Essen zum Mitnehmen takeaway II
**essen** to eat I; to have II
**Essensstand** food stall II
**Esszimmer** dining room I
**Etage** story *(AE)* IV
**etwa** about II
**etwas** something I; some II
*etwas, das man haben muss* must-have V U4, 70
**euch** you I
**euer** your I
**eure** your; yours I
**Eure** *(als Briefabschluss)* Yours, I
**Euro** *(Währung)* euro III
**Europäisch** European IV
**europäisch** European IV
**ewig** forever II
ewig lange for ages V U4, 70
**exakt** exact III
**Exemplar** copy IV
**existieren** to be around IV; to exist V U1, 10
**Exkremente** waste V U1, 20
**Experte** expert IV
**Expertin** expert IV
**explodieren** to explode III
**Explosion** explosion III
**Extremismus** extremism V U4, 79
**exzellent** excellent IV

## F

**Fabel** fable III
**Fabrik** factory III
**Fach-** skilled V U1, 11
**Fähigkeit** skill V U1, 16
**Fahne** flag II
**Fähre** ferry V U2, 30
**fahren** to go I; to ride II; to travel III; to drive; to take a ride IV
fahren gegen to hit III
Ski fahren to ski II
**Fahrer** driver III
**Fahrerin** driver III
einfache **Fahrkarte** single ticket III
**Fahrplan** timetable III; schedule *(AE)* IV
**Fahrpreis** fare III
**Fahrrad** bike I
**Fahrradkurier** bike courier V U1, 19
**Fahrradkurierin** bike courier V U1, 19
**Fahrschein** ticket III
**Fahrspur** lane IV
**Fahrt** ride; trip; voyage; journey III; tour IV
eine Fahrt machen to take a trip III
**fair** fair V U3, 52
**Fakt** fact II
**Fall** case IV

**fallen** to fall I; to fall (over); to fall off III
**falls** if II
**falsch** wrong I
**Faltblatt** flyer II
**falten** to fold IV
**Familie** family I
**Fan** fan I
**fangen** to catch II
**Fantasie** fantasy II
**fantastisch** fantastic II
**Fantasy** fantasy II
**Farbe** colour I; color *(AE)* IV
**Fasching** carnival IV
**Fass** barrel IV
**fast** almost III; nearly IV
**Fastfood** fast food I
**faszinierend** fascinating IV
**faul** lazy IV
**Februar** February I
**Federmäppchen** pencil case I
(auf)**fegen** to sweep (up) V U3, 58
**fegen** to sweep II
**fehlschlagen** to fail IV
**Feier** party I; celebration IV
**feiern** to celebrate I; to party V U2, 30
**Feiertag** holiday III
**Feind** enemy III
**Feindin** enemy III
**Feld** field IV
**Fels** rock III
**Fenster** window I
**Ferien** holiday I; vacation *(AE)* IV
**Ferienanlage** resort V U2, 30
**Ferienort** resort V U2, 30
in der **Ferne** in the distance IV
**Fernsehen** TV I
  im Fernsehen on TV IV
**fernsehen** to watch TV I
**Fernseher** TV I
**Fernsehsendung** TV show II
**Fernsehstudio** TV studio II
**fertig** ready I
  sich fertig machen to get ready IV
**Fertigkeit** skill V U1, 16
**fertigstellen** to finish II; to complete IV
**fesseln** to tie IV
**Fest** festival III
**fest** tight II; solid III; firm V U3, 59
**festhalten** to hold III
**Festival** festival III
**festnehmen** to arrest IV
**festsitzen** to be stuck IV
**feststecken** to be stuck IV
**fette** Jahre *(ugs.)* boom years IV
**Feuer** fire I
**Feuerwehrauto** fire engine II
**Fieber** fever IV
**Film** film; movie I
**Filzstift** felt-tip I
**Finanz-** financial IV
**finanziell** financial IV
**finden** to find I
**Finger** finger III
**Fingerabdruck** fingerprint II
**Firma** company II
**Fisch** fish I
**Fischen** fishing IV
**Fischerboot** fishing boat V U2, 43
**fit** fit III
**Fitnessraum** gymnasium III
**flach** flat IV
**Fläche** area; space IV
**Flagge** flag II
**Flamingo** flamingo I
**Flamme** flame III
**Flasche** bottle I
**Flashback** flashback V U3, 51
**Fledermaus** bat I
**Fleisch** meat I
**fleißig** hard-working IV
**fliegen** to fly II
**fliehen** to escape IV
**Fließen** flow V U4, 78
**fließend** fluent III
**Flohmarkt** jumble sale II
**flüchten** to escape IV
**Flug** flight II
**Flughafen** airport II
**Flugzeug** plane II
**Flur** hall IV; corridor II
**Fluss** river I; flow V U4, 78
**flüssig** fluent III
**Flut** flood V U4, 78
**Flyer** flyer II
**Folge** consequence V U3, 50
  zur Folge haben to result in V U1, 20
**folgen** to follow IV
**Follower** follower IV
**Followerin** follower IV
**Fön** hairdryer III
in **Form** fit III
**fortfahren** to go ahead IV; to continue V U2, 40
**fortsetzen** to continue IV
**Foto** photo I
  ein Foto machen to take a photo I
  Fotos machen to take photos II
**fotografieren** to take photos II
**Frage** question I
**fragen** to ask I
  fragen nach to ask about II
  sich fragen to wonder V U2, 34
die **Franzosen** the French IV
**Französisch** French I
**französisch** French V U2, 29
**Frau** woman I; lady II
**Frau** *(Anrede)* Mrs; Ms I
**frech** cheeky; naughty III
**frei** free IV
  ein freier Tag a day off III
  freie Wildbahn the wild IV
  die freie Natur the outdoors IV
  Land der Freien land of the free IV
**freigeben** to release IV
**Freiheit** freedom *(no pl)* IV
**Freiland-** free range II
**Freiluft-** outdoor III
**freisetzen** to release IV
**Freistunde** study hall period IV
**Freitag** Friday I
**Freiwillige** volunteer III
**Freiwilliger** volunteer III
**Freizeit** free time I
**Freizeit-** free-time V U2, 34
**Freizeitpark** theme park I
**fremd** strange; foreign IV
**Freude** fun I; joy V U3, 59
sich **freuen** auf to look forward to (+ -ing) V U1, 16
**Freund** friend I
  Freunde treffen to see friends I
**Freund** *(in einer Paarbeziehung)* boyfriend IV
**Freundin** friend I
**Freundin** *(in einer Paarbeziehung)* girlfriend IV
**freundlich** kind II; friendly III
**Freundschaft** friendship V U2, 34
  Freundschaften schließen to make friends I

**Frieden** peace V U3, 49
**friedlich** peaceful IV
**frieren** to freeze; to get cold III
**Frisbee** frisbee I
**Frisbeescheibe** frisbee I
**frisch** fresh II
**Friseur** hairdresser II
**Friseurin** hairdresser II
**frittieren** to fry IV
**froh** glad IV
**Fröhlichkeit** happiness V U2, 35
**Frucht** fruit I
**früh** early I
früher in the old days III
(wohnte) früher used to (live) III
**frühere** former IV
**Frühlingsrolle** spring roll II
**Frühstück** breakfast I
**frühstücken** to have breakfast I
**Frühstückspension** bed and breakfast (B & B) III
(sich) **fühlen** to feel II
sich schlecht fühlen to feel sick IV
sich wie zu Hause fühlen to make oneself at home III
**führen** to run III; to lead IV; to stock V U4, 71
führen zu to result in V U1, 20
**Führer** guide II; leader III
**Führerin** guide II; leader III
**Führerschein** driver's license *(AE)* IV
(sich) **füllen** to fill III
**Füller** pen I
**fünf** five I
**fünfzehn** fifteen I
**fünfzig** fifty I
**funktionieren** to work II
**für** for I; pro- V U4, 78
für immer forever II
**Furcht** fear V U4, 79
**furchtbar** awful; terrible I; horrible; dreadful III
sich **fürchten** to be afraid II
**furchterregend** terrifying; frightening IV
**Fuß** foot I
zu Fuß on foot I
**Fuß** *(Längenmaß: 30,48 cm)* foot IV
**Fußball** football I
**Fußboden** floor I
**Fußgelenk** ankle II
**Fußknöchel** ankle II
**füttern** to feed I

## G

**Gabel** fork II
**Gang** corridor II
**ganz** all II; whole III
ganz allein all alone I
ganz am Ende at the bottom IV
den ganzen Tag all day III
**Ganztags-** full-time V U2, 29
**gar** nicht not at all II
**garantieren** to guarantee V U4, 79
**Garten** garden I
**Gas** gas III
**Gasse** alley; lane IV
**Gast** guest III
**Gästehaus** guest house V U2, 31
**Gastfamilie** host family IV
**Gastgeber** host V U4, 74
**Gastgeberin** host V U4, 74
**Gasthaus** pub III
**Gebärdensprache** sign language III
**Gebäude** building II
**geben** to give I; to be around IV
Autogramme geben to sign autographs IV
einen Klaps geben to slap IV
jmdm. Bescheid geben to let sb know V U1, 15
jmdm. das Gefühl geben, etw. zu sein to make sb feel like sth III
es gibt there are; there is I
**Gebet** prayer IV
**Gebiet** area III; grounds *(pl)* IV; field V U1, 16; territory V U3, 49
**gebildet** well-educated V U3, 51
**Gebirge** mountain range V U3, 55
**geboren** werden to be born III
(in der Pfanne) **gebraten** fried II
**gebraucht** second-hand V U4, 71
**gebrochen** broken IV
**Gebühr** fee V U2, 34
**Geburtstag** birthday I
**Gedanke** thought IV
sich Gedanken machen to wonder V U2, 34
**Gedicht** poem III
**geduldig** patient III
Sehr **geehrte** Damen und Herren, Dear Sir or Madam, V U3, 50
**Gefahr** danger; threat V U1, 20
**gefährlich** dangerous III
**Gefangene** prisoner V U2, 40
**Gefangener** prisoner V U2, 40
**Gefängnis** prison II; jail IV
**gefeuert** fired III
**gefrieren** to freeze III
**gefrierend** freezing IV
jmdm. das **Gefühl** geben, etw. zu sein to make sb feel like sth III
etw. als **gegeben** voraussetzen to take sth for granted V U4, 79
**gegen** against II; around III
fahren gegen to hit III
**Gegend** area III; region IV
im **Gegensatz** zu unlike III
sich **gegenseitig** each other III
**Gegenteil** opposite V U3, 55
**gegenüber** opposite I
**gegenüberstehen** to face V U3, 54
**gegenwärtig** current V U1, 16
im **Gegenzug** in turn V U1, 20
**Gegner** protester IV
**Gegnerin** protester IV
**Gehalt** pay IV; salary V U1, 16
**geheim** secret II
**Geheimnis** mystery I; secret II
**gehen** to go; to walk I
aus dem Weg gehen to avoid IV
gehen um to be about III
ins Bett gehen to go to bed I
über die Grenze gehen to cross the border IV
**gehören** (zu) to belong (to) IV
**gehörlos** deaf III
**Gehweg** sidewalk *(AE)* IV
**Geist** ghost II; spirit IV; mind V U4, 79
**Geisterstadt** ghost town IV
**geistig** mental IV
**Gel** gel III
**Gelände** grounds *(pl)* IV
**gelangweilt** bored IV
**gelassen** relaxed IV; easy-going V U1, 10
**gelb** yellow I
**Geld** money I
Geld verdienen to make money V U4, 70
**Geldbörse** wallet III

**Geldschein** note II
**gelegen** sein to be located IV
**Gelegenheit** chance II; opportunity IV
**geliebt** beloved IV
**gemäß** according to III
**gemein** mean IV
**Gemeinde** community IV
**gemeinsam** together I
**Gemeinschaft** community IV
**gemischt** mixed V U3, 48
gemischter Abstammung mixed race V U3, 48
**Gemüse** vegetable (veg) II
Obst- und **Gemüseladen** greengrocer's III
**gemustert** patterned II
**gemütlich** cosy III
**genannt** werden to be called II
**genau** exact III; right; exactly IV
genau genommen in fact III
**Generation** generation V U1, 12
**generell** in general IV
**generieren** to generate V U4, 75
**genießen** to enjoy II
**genug** enough III
**genügend** enough III
**Geocaching** geocaching I
**geöffnet** open III
**Geografie** Geography I
**Gepäckaufgabe** check-in V U2, 31
**gerade** right IV
gerade (eben) just II
**geradeaus** straight on I; right ahead IV
**geradlinig** straightforward III
**Gerät** tool II; device IV
**Geräusch** noise I; sound III
**gerecht** fair V U3, 52
**Gerechtigkeit** fairness; justice V U3, 52
**Gerede** talk II; gossip IV
**Gericht** dish II; court IV
**Gerichtsverhandlung** court case IV
**Gern** geschehen. You're welcome. I
**gern** mögen to love I
**Geruch** smell III
**gesamt** total IV
**Gesamt-** total IV
**Gesangs-** singing III
**Geschäft** shop I; store *(AE)*; business IV
**Geschäftsführer** manager IV
**Geschäftsführerin** manager IV
**Geschäftsmann** businessman IV
**geschehen** to happen II; to go on V U3, 55
**Geschenk** present I
**Geschichte** story I; history III
**geschlossen** closed V U3, 56
geschlossene Wohnanlage gated community V U3, 49
**Geschöpf** creature V U1, 12
**Geschoss** bullet IV
**geschützt** protected V U1, 12
**Geschwindigkeit** speed V U4, 81
**Geschwindigkeitsbeschränkung** speed limit V U4, 81
**Gesellschaft** company II; society IV
**gesellschaftlich** social V U3, 51
**Gesellschaftslehre** Social Studies I
**Gesetz** law III
**Gesicht** face IV
**Gespräch** conversation III
**Gestaltung** design IV
**gestatten** to allow IV
**gestern** yesterday I
gestern Abend last night V U2, 34
gestern Nacht last night V U2, 34
**gesund** healthy III
**Gesundheit** health V U2, 35
**gesundheitlich** health V U4, 69
**Gesundheits-** health V U4, 69
**Getränk** drink II
**Getreide** corn IV
**getrennt** segregated; separate IV
**gewährleisten** to guarantee V U4, 79
**Gewalt** violence *(no pl)* V U2, 34
**gewinnen** to win I
**Gewinner** winner I
**Gewinnerin** winner I
sich an (etw.) **gewöhnen** to get used to (sth) IV
**gewöhnlich** usually II
**Gewürz** spice II
**Gips** cast III
**Giraffe** giraffe I
**Gitarre** guitar III
**Gitter** grid IV
**Glanz** glamor *(AE) (no pl)* IV
**glänzen** to shine IV
**glänzend** shiny IV
**Glas** glass II; jar III
**Glaube** belief V U1, 12; faith V U2, 34
**glauben** to think I; to believe II
**gläubig** religious IV
**gleich** the same II; right away IV; equal V U3, 52
**gleichberechtigt** equal V U3, 52
**Gleichberechtigung** equality V U3, 52
**gleichmäßig** regular IV
**Gleis** railway track IV
**global** global V U1, 21
**Glocke** bell II
**Glück** happiness V U2, 35
Glück haben to be lucky III
viel Glück good luck II
**glücklich** happy I; lucky V U2, 34
**glücklicherweise** luckily IV
**Glückstag** lucky day II
**Glückszahl** lucky number I
**Glückwunsch**! Congratulations! II
**Glühbirne** light bulb III
**Gold** gold III
**Gold-** gold III; golden IV
**golden** gold III; golden IV
**Goldrausch** gold rush IV
**Gondel** pod V U4, 74
**Göttin** goddess IV
**Gouvernante** governess V U2, 38
**Grab** grave III
**graben** to dig IV
**Grad** degree IV
**Gras** grass I
**grau** grey I
**grauhaarig** grey-haired V U3, 59
**greifen** to grab III
**Grenze** border III; level V U4, 76; limit V U4, 79
die Grenze überschreiten to cross the border IV
über die Grenze gehen to cross the border IV
**Griechisch** Greek IV
**griechisch** Greek IV
**Grill** barbecue I
**Grillparty** barbecue I
lustige **Grimassen** schneiden to make funny faces V U3, 58
**Grimm** fierceness V U3, 60
**grinsen** to grin IV
**grob** rough V U3, 58

**groß** big; high I; tall; large II; great V U1, 11; wide V U3, 54
**großartig** great I; fantastic II; grand III
**Größe** size II
**Großeltern** grandparents *(pl)* II
**Großmutter** grandmother III
**Großstadt** city II
**Großvater** grandfather II
**großzügig** generous IV
**grün** green I
**Grund** reason; bottom III
Gründe angeben to give reasons III
Gründe nennen to give reasons III
im Grunde genommen basically IV
**Grundbesitzer** landowner IV
**Grundbesitzerin** landowner IV
**gründen** to start III; to found IV; to build V U3, 49
**grundsätzlich** basically IV
**Grundschule** primary school V U3, 58
**Gruppe** group I; squad IV
**gruselig** scary I; creepy IV
Mit freundlichen **Grüßen** Yours sincerely, V U1, 16; Yours faithfully, V U3, 50
**Grüße** ausrichten to say hi to I
Viele **Grüße**, Best wishes, I
**grüßen** to say hi to I
**gültig** valid III
**Gummi** rubber III
**Gummistiefel** welly I
**Gürtel** belt IV
**gut** good I; fine; well II; nice III
gut bezahlt well-paid V U2, 34
gut gepflegt well-kept V U3, 58
gut laufen to go well V U1, 18
gut sein in/bei to be good at I
Gut gemacht! Well done! I
**Guten** Morgen. Good morning. II
**Güter** goods *(no pl)* IV

## H

**Haar** hair III
**Haarbürste** hairbrush III
**Haare** hair III
sich die Haare schneiden lassen to have a haircut II
**Haargel** hair gel III
**Haarglätter** hair straightener IV
**Haarschnitt** haircut II
**haben** to have I
hätte(n) gern would like II
keine Ahnung haben to have no idea IV
Spaß haben to enjoy oneself III
**Hafen** harbour II; harbor *(AE)*; port IV
**Hafer** oat III
**Haferbrei** porridge III
**Hähnchen** chicken IV
**Hai** shark I
**halb** half III
halb (drei) half past (two) I
**Halbtags-** part-time IV
(die) **Hälfte** half IV
**Hallen-** indoor III
**Hallo.** Hello.; Hi.; Hello there. I
**Hals** throat II
**Halsband** collar I
**Halsschmerzen** sore throat II
**Halt** stop II
**halten** to keep II; to hold III
die Klappe halten to shut up IV
**Haltestelle** stop II
**Haltung** attitude IV
**Hamburger** burger II
**Hand** hand I
**Handel** trading V U4, 70
**handeln** to take action V U3, 54; to bargain V U4, 68
handeln von to be about III
**Handgelenk** wrist IV
**Handlung** action IV
**Handtuch** towel III
**Handy** mobile (phone) I; cell phone *(AE)* IV
**hängen** to hang II
hängen bleiben to be stuck IV
**hänseln** to tease IV
**hart** hard II; tough III
**hassen** to hate I
**hässlich** ugly V U2, 40
**Hast** hurry V U4, 69
**häufig** often I
**Haupt-** major IV; main V U3, 48
**Hauptgericht** main course II
**hauptsächlich** mostly IV
**Hauptstadt** capital (city) III
**Hauptverkehrszeit** rush hour IV
**Haus** house I
im Haus around the house I
nach Hause home I
sich wie zu Hause fühlen to make oneself at home III
zu Hause at home I
**Hausaufgabe**(n) homework I
Hausaufgabe(n) machen to do homework I
**Häuschen** cottage III
**Häuserblock** block IV
**Hauslehrerin** governess V U2, 38
**Hausmeister** caretaker I
**Hausmeisterin** caretaker I
**Haustier** pet I
(hoch)**heben** to sweep (up) V U3, 58
**Heer** army III
**Heft** book I; booklet IV
**Heftigkeit** fierceness V U3, 60
**heilig** sacred V U1, 12
**Heim** home I
**Heimat** home country IV
**Heimatland** home country IV
**Heimweh** haben to be homesick III
**heiraten** to get married II; to marry V U2, 34
**heiß** hot I
**heißen** to be called II
willkommen heißen to welcome IV
**Heizkörper** radiator IV
**Held** hero III
**helfen** to help I
**Helfer** helper IV
**Helferin** helper IV
**Helikopter** helicopter IV
**hell** bright IV
**Helm** helmet III
**Hemd** shirt I
**heraus** out II
aus … heraus out of II
**herausfallen** aus to fall out of IV
**herausfinden** to find; to find out I; to learn IV
**Herausforderung** challenge V U3, 54
**herausgeben** to release IV
**Herausgeber** publisher V U4, 78
**herauskommen** to get out III
**herausnehmen** to take out I
**herausragen** to stand out IV
**herausstechen** to stand out IV
**Herberge** hostel V U2, 30

**Herbst** fall *(AE)* IV; autumn V U2, 28
**hereinkommen** to get in I; to enter IV
**hergestellt** sein aus to be made of III
**Herr** *(Anrede)* Mr I
meine Damen und Herren ladies and gentlemen V ZI 8
Sehr geehrte Damen und Herren, Dear Sir or Madam, V U3, 50
**herrlich** lovely II
**Herrschaft** rule IV
**herstellen** to produce V U4, 74
**herüber** across IV
**herum** around I
jmdn. (an einem Ort) **herumführen** to show sb around (a place) V U1, 12
**herumkommen** to get around III
**herumrennen** to run about II
sich **herumtreiben** (mit) to hang out (with) IV
**herunter** down III
**herunterfallen** to fall off III
**herunterladen** to download II
**herunternehmen** to take off V U1, 13
**hervorbringen** to produce III
**hervorragend** excellent IV
**Herz** heart III
**Herzlichen** Dank. Thanks so much. IV
**heute** today I
heute Abend tonight II
heute Nacht tonight II
**heutzutage** now II; nowadays IV
**Hexe** witch I
**Hi.** Hi. I
**hier** here I
**hiesig** local III
**Highschool** *(weiterführende Schule, Oberstufe)* high school IV
**Hightech-** high-tech IV
**Hilfe** help II; support IV
**hilfreich** useful; helpful III
**hilfsbereit** cooperative; helpful IV
**Himbeere** raspberry III
**Himmel** sky V U2, 41
**Hin-** und Rückfahrkarte return ticket III
**hinauf** up II
**hinausgeworfen** fired III
**hinbringen** to take II
jmdn. an etw. **hindern** to stop sb from sth V U2, 39
**hinein** into IV
in … hinein inside II
**hineingehen** to go on II; to enter IV
**hineingelangen** to get into IV
**hineinkommen** to get into IV
**hineinpassen** to fit in V U2, 35
**hinfallen** to fall (over) III
**hinkommen** to get there III
hinkommen zu to get to IV
**hinnehmen** to accept IV
etw. als selbstverständlich hinnehmen to take sth for granted V U4, 79
sich **hinsetzen** to sit down V U1, 15
**hinten** at the back IV
im hinteren Teil at the back IV
**hinter** behind II
**Hinter-** back IV
**Hintergrund** background III
im Hintergrund in the background III
**Hintern** bottom V U3, 58
**hinüber** across IV
**hinunter** down III
**hinuntereilen** to rush down II
**Hinweis** clue I
darauf **hinweisen** to point out IV
**hinzufügen** to add IV
zu … hinzufügen to bookmark II
**historisch** historic IV
**Hit** hit IV
**Hitparade** charts *(pl only)* IV
**Hitze** heat IV
**Hobby** hobby III
**hoch** high I; tall II
**hochladen** to upload II
**Hochwasser** flood V U4, 78
**Hochzeit** wedding II
**hoffen** to hope I
**Hoffnung** hope IV
**hoffnungsvoll** hopeful III
**höflich** polite II
**Höflichkeit** politeness V U1, 13
**Höhe** height II; level V U4, 76
**Höhle** cave II
**holen** to get II
**Holz** wood III
**Homepage** homepage III
**homosexuell** gay V U2, 34
**Hopping** hopping V U2, 30
**hören** to listen (to); to hear I
**Horror** horror V U2, 40
**Hose** trousers *(pl)* I; pants *(pl) (AE)* IV
kurze Hose shorts *(pl)* I
**Hosentasche** pocket II
**Hospital** hospital I
**Hot** Dog *(Würstchen im Brötchen)* hot dog IV
**Hotel** hotel II
**Hotelfachschule** catering college II
**hübsch** beautiful I; pretty; lovely II
**Hubschrauber** helicopter IV
**Hügel** hill IV
**Huhn** chicken I
**Hühnchen** chicken II
**Hummer** lobster IV
**Hund** dog I
**Hundeausführer** dog walker IV
**Hundeausführerin** dog walker IV
**hundert** a/one hundred I
**hungrig** hungry I
**Hüpfen** hopping V U2, 30
**hüpfen** to skip V U3, 58
**husten** to cough III
**Hut** hat II
**hüten** to look after II

# I

**ich** I; me I
Ich heiße … My name is … I
Ich komme aus … I'm from … I
Ich weiß (es) nicht! I don't know! I
ich würde lieber I'd rather III
**Idee** idea I
**Identität** identity IV
**ignorant** ignorant V U1, 12
**Ignoranz** ignorance V U1, 13
**ignorieren** to ignore V U1, 12
**ihm** him I
**ihn** him I
**Ihnen** you I
**ihnen** them I
**ihr** you; her I; its III
**Ihr** your I
**ihr** *(Pl.)* their I
**ihre** *(Pl.)* their I
**ihre** her I; hers II; theirs III
**Ihre** your; yours I
**im** August in August I

**im** Bus on the bus II
**Im** Ernst? Are you serious? III
**im** Freien outside II
**im** Haus around the house I
**im** Schlepptau in tow IV
**im** Stadtzentrum downtown *(AE)* IV
**im** Süden von in the south of III
**im** vorderen Bereich at the front of II
**Imbiss** snack I
**immer** always I
für immer forever II
immer noch still III
immer, wenn whenever V U1, 12
**immerhin** after all IV
**Immigrant** immigrant IV
**Immigrantin** immigrant IV
**Immigration** immigration IV
**immigrieren** to immigrate IV
**in** in; to; at I; inside III; into IV
in der Pause at break I
in der Schule at school I
in Form fit III
in Richtung towards IV
in ... hinein inside II
in der Ferne in the distance IV
in der Mitte von in the centre of III
in der Unterzahl outnumbered IV
in Ordnung fine; all right II
**indem** by (+ gerund) V U1, 12
**Indianer** Native American IV
**Indianerin** Native American IV
**indianisch** Native American IV
**indisch** Indian II
**individuell** individual V U4, 74
**Industrie** industry III
**industrielle** Revolution Industrial Revolution III
**Informatik** IT (Information Technology) I
**Information** information *(no pl)* I; information desk II
**Informationen** information *(no pl)* I
**informativ** informative IV
jmdn. **informieren** to let sb know V U1, 15
**Ingenieur** engineer II
**Ingenieurin** engineer II
**Inhalt** content III
**inmitten** among III
**innehalten** to pause V U3, 60
**innen** inside IV
innen in inside III
**Innen-** indoor III
im **Innern** inside III
**Innovation** innovation IV
**Insekt** insect III
**Insel** island II
**insgesamt** all in all IV
**Inspektion** inspection IV
**Installateur** plumber V U1, 17
**Installateurin** plumber V U1, 17
**installieren** to install V U4, 74
**Institut** college *(AE)* IV
**intelligent** clever I; smart; intelligent III
**interessant** interesting I
**Interesse** interest V U1, 16
sich **interessieren** to care V U4, 70
sich interessieren für to be interested in III
**interessiert** sein an to be interested in III
**Internat** boarding school V U1, 11
**international** international V U2, 29
**Internet** internet II
im Internet surfen to surf the internet II
ins Internet stellen to upload II
**Internettagebuch** blog II
**Interview** interview II
**interviewen** to interview I
**Interviewer** interviewer IV
**Interviewerin** interviewer IV
die **Iren** the Irish III
**irgendein** any II
**irgendein** Idiot someone stupid V U3, 51
**irgendetwas** anything II
**irgendjemand** *(in Fragesätzen)* anyone V U3, 60
**irgendwelche** any II
**Irisch** Irish III
**irisch** Irish III
sich **irren** to be wrong III
**Isolation** isolation *(no pl)* V U1, 10
**Italiener** Italian II
**Italienerin** Italian II
**Italienisch** Italian II
**italienisch** Italian II

## J

**ja** yes I
na ja well I
**Jacke** coat I; jacket II
**Jagdgewehr** shotgun IV
**jagen** to hunt V U2, 41; to chase V U3, 60
**Jäger** chaser; hunter IV
**Jägerin** chaser; hunter IV
**Jahr** year I
Jahre alt year-old IV
fette Jahre *(ugs.)* boom years IV
**Jahreszeit** season IV
**Jahrgangsstufe** year I
**Jahrhundert** century III
**jährig** year-old IV
**jährlich** annual III
**jamaikanisch** Jamaican II
**jämmerlich** miserable III
**Januar** January I
**Japaner** Japanese IV
**Japanerin** Japanese IV
**Japanisch** Japanese IV
**japanisch** Japanese IV
**Jeans** jeans *(pl)* I
**jede** any III
**jedenfalls** anyway III
**jeder** every; everyone I; everybody IV
jeder andere anybody else V U1, 19
**jedoch** however; though III
**jemals** ever II
**jemand** somebody III
jemand anderes somebody else II
**jene** those II
**jetzt** now I
jetzt gerade right now III
**Job** job I
**Joghurt** yogurt II
**Journalismus** journalism IV
**Journalist** journalist V U3, 51
**Journalistik** journalism IV
**Journalistin** journalist V U3, 51
**Jugend** youth *(no pl)* III
**Jugend-** teen II; youth *(no pl)* III
**Jugendherberge** youth hostel III
**jugendlich** teenage IV
**Jugendliche** teen II; teenager III
**Jugendlicher** teen II; teenager III
**Jugendzentrum** activity centre III
**Juli** July I
**jung** young II

**Junge** boy I
**Juni** June I
**Juror** judge II
**Jurorin** judge II
**Justiz** justice V U3, 52
**Juwelierladen** jeweller's III

## K

**Kabel** wire III
**Kabine** cabin V U2, 40; pod V U4, 74
**Kaffee** coffee IV
**Käfig** cage I
**Kaiserreich** empire III
**Kaktus** cactus V U3, 58
**Kalender** calendar IV
**kalt** cold I
**Kamel** camel V U1, 12
**Kamm** comb III
**Kampf** battle; fight III; struggle V U2, 34
**kämpfen** to fight III; to struggle V U1, 11
**Kampfkunst** martial art V U4, 69
**Kampfsportart** martial art V U4, 69
**kampieren** to camp V U4, 70
**Kanarienvogel** canary III
**Kandidat** candidate V U1, 19
**Kandidatin** candidate V U1, 19
**Känguru** kangaroo V U1, 10
**Kanone** cannon V U2, 39
**Kanonenkugel** cannon ball II
**Kanufahren** canoeing I
**Kapitän** captain I
**Kapitänin** captain I
**Kappe** cap I
**kaputt** broken IV
kaputt machen to tear (up) IV
**Karibe** Caribbean V U2, 29
**Karibin** Caribbean V U2, 29
**Karibisch** Caribbean V U2, 29
**karibisch** Caribbean V U2, 29
**Karneval** carnival IV
**Karotte** carrot II
**Karre** truck III
**Karriere** career IV
**Karte** card I; ticket II; map IV
**Kartoffel** potato II
**Kartoffelbrei** mashed potatoes II
**Kartoffelchip** crisp I
**Karton** cardboard III
**Käse** cheese I
**Käsekuchen** cheesecake II
**Katastrophe** disaster III
**Kategorie** category V U3, 55
**Katholik** Catholic III
**Katholikin** Catholic III
**katholisch** Catholic III
**Katze** cat I
**kaufen** to buy I; to purchase V U4, 71
**Käufer** shopper V U4, 68
**Käuferin** shopper V U4, 68
**Kaufhaus** department store II
**Kaugummi** chewing gum I
**kaum** little IV
**kein** no I; not … any II
**keine** no I
keine Ahnung haben to have no idea IV
**Keks** biscuit II
**Kellner** waiter II
**Kellnerin** waitress IV
**kennen** to know I
kennen lernen to meet I; to get to know II
**Kenntnis** skill V U1, 16
zur Kenntnis nehmen to take notice V U3, 60
**kennzeichnen** to mark III
**Kerl** guy IV
**Kerze** candle I
**Ketchup** ketchup II
**Kidneybohne** kidney bean II
**Kilogramm** (kg) kilogram (kg) I
**Kilometer** (km) kilometre (km) I
kmh (Kilometer pro Stunde) mph (miles per hour) V U4, 81
**Kilt** kilt III
**Kind** child; kid II
**Kinder** children *(pl)* II
**Kinderzimmer** bedroom I
**Kino** cinema I; the movies *(AE)*; movie theater *(AE)* IV
**Kirche** church II
**Kiste** box I
die **Klappe** halten to shut up IV
**klappen** to fold IV
einen **Klaps** geben to slap IV
**klar** clear IV
alles klar all right II
**Klasse** year I; class III; grade *(AE)* IV
**Klasse** *(in einer englischen Schule)* tutor group I
**Klassenarbeit** test I
**Klassenfahrt** school trip I
**Klassenlehrer** tutor I
**Klassenlehrerin** tutor I
**Klassenzimmer** classroom I
**klassisch** *(Musik)* classical III
**Klatsch** gossip IV
**Klebstoff** glue I
**Kleeblatt** shamrock III
**Kleid** dress I
**Kleider** *(Pl.)* clothes *(pl)* I
**Kleiderordnung** dress code IV
**Kleiderschrank** wardrobe I
**Kleidung** clothes *(pl)* I; outfit III
**klein** small I; little II; tiny III
eine **Kleinigkeit** a little something IV
**Klempner** plumber V U1, 17
**Klempnerin** plumber V U1, 17
**Kletter-** climbing IV
**Klettern** rock climbing I; climbing V U1, 12
**klettern** to climb III
**klicken** to click I
**Klima** climate V U1, 20
**Klimawandel** climate change V U1, 20
**klingeln** to ring III
**klingen** to sound II
**Kloß** dumpling II
**Klub** club II
**Klubhaus** clubhouse IV
**klug** clever I; smart; intelligent III
**kmh** (Kilometer pro Stunde) mph (miles per hour) V U4, 81
**Kneipe** pub III
**Knie** knee III
**knifflig** tricky IV
**Knoblauch** garlic II
**knuddelig** cuddly III
**Koala** koala V U1, 10
**Koch** chef II
**Kochbanane** plantain II
**Kochen** cooking II
**kochen** to cook II
**Köchin** chef II
**Koffer** suitcase II
**Kohl** cabbage II
**Kohle** coal III
**Kohlendioxid** $CO_2$ (carbon dioxide) V U4, 75

## L

**Laden** shop I; store *(AE)* IV
**Lage** location III
**Lager** camp II
**lahm** lame IV
**Lamm** lamb II
**Lampe** lamp I
**Land** country I; land II; countryside III; state IV; nation V U3, 49
auf dem Land in the country I
Land der Freien land of the free IV
**landen** to land IV
**Landesregierung** state government IV
**Landkarte** map III
**ländliche Gegend** country I
**Landschaft** countryside III; landscape IV; scenery V U3, 48
**Landwirt** farmer I
**Landwirtin** farmer I
**Landwirtschaft** farming IV
**Landwirtschaftsflächen** farmland IV
**lang** long I
**Länge** length *(no pl)* IV
**langfristig** in the long run V U4, 74
**langsam** slow III
**langweilig** boring I; dull IV
**Laptop** laptop I
**Lasagne** lasagne II
**lassen** to leave II; to let III
**Laufbahn** career IV
**laufen** to run I; to walk II
gut laufen to go well V U1, 18
Wie läuft's? How's it going? IV
jmdn. auf dem **Laufenden** halten to keep sb informed IV
jmdn. bei **Laune** halten to keep sb happy V U1, 12
**Laut** sound III
**laut** noisy; loud; according to III
**läuten** to ring III
**Layout** layout IV
**Leben** life I; lifetime IV
am Leben alive III
zum Leben erwecken to bring to life IV
**leben** to live I
**Lebensart** lifestyle; way of life IV
**Lebenslauf** CV (= curriculum vitae) V U1, 16
**Lebensmittel** food I; groceries *(pl)* IV
**Lebensmittelabfälle** food waste V U4, 76
**Lebensweise** way of life IV
**Lebenszeit** lifetime IV
**Lebewesen** creature V U1, 12
**lecker** nice; tasty III
**Leder** leather III
**leer** empty IV
**legen** to put I; to lay II
**Legende** legend V U1, 12
**Lehre** lesson IV
**lehren** to teach III
**Lehrer** teacher I; instructor III
**Lehrerin** teacher I; instructor III
**Leiche** body IV
**leicht** easy I
Es tut mir **leid** wegen … Sorry about … I
Es tut mir **leid**. I'm sorry. I
Tut mir **leid**. Sorry. I
**leiden** to suffer V U3, 50
**leider** unfortunately V U1, 20
**leidtun** to be sorry III
**leihen** to lend II
**Leine** lead I
**leise** quiet III
sich **leisten** to afford V U2, 34
**leistungsfähig** efficient V U1, 16
**leistungsorientiert** competitive III
**leiten** to run III; to lead V U3, 58
**Leiter** ladder I
**Lektion** lesson IV
**Leopard** leopard V U3, 54
**Leopardin** leopard V U3, 54
**lernen** to learn II; to study IV
kennen lernen to get to know II
**lesen** to read I
**Leser** reader IV
**Leserin** reader IV
zu guter **Letzt** at last II
**letzte** last I
**letztlich** finally IV
**leuchtend** bright IV
**Leute** people I; guys *(pl)* II
von allen Leuten of all the people V U1, 18
**Lexikon** encyclopedia IV
**Licht** light IV
**Liebe/Lieber** …, *(Anrede in Briefen)* Dear …, I
**Liebe** love IV
**lieben** to love I
**liebend** loving IV
**lieber** even IV
ich würde lieber I'd rather III
**Liebesgeschichte** romance III
**liebevoll** loving IV
**Lieblings-** favourite I; favorite *(AE)* IV
**Lied** song I
**Lieferwagen** van III
**liegen** to be located III; to rest IV; to lie V U2, 38
**Lifestyle** lifestyle IV
**Lift** elevator *(AE)* IV
**Liga** league IV
**lila** purple I
**Limit** limit V U4, 79
**limitieren** to limit V U1, 21
**Limonade** lemonade II
**Lineal** ruler I
**Linie** line II
in erster Linie above all IV
**Link** link IV
**links** on the left I; left III
**Liste** list II
auf die schwarze Liste gesetzt blacklisted V U4, 79
**LKW-Fahrer** lorry driver II
**LKW-Fahrerin** lorry driver II
**Loch** hole I
**locker** relaxed IV; loose II; easy-going V U1, 10
**Löffel** spoon II
**Lohn** wage; pay IV
**lokal** local III
**lose** loose II
**lösen** to solve I
**loslassen** to release IV
**loslegen** to go ahead IV
**Lösung** solution IV
**Löwe** lion V U3, 48
**Luft** air IV
tief Luft holen to take a deep breath V U3, 60
**Luftballon** balloon I
**Luke** porthole V U2, 39
**Lunchpaket** packed lunch II
**lustig** funny I
lustige Grimassen schneiden to make funny faces V U3, 58
**luxuriös** luxurious V U4, 68
**Luxus** luxury V U2, 30

**Luxus-** deluxe IV; luxury V U2, 30; luxurious V U4, 68

## M

**machen** to do; to make I
ein Foto machen to take a photo I
Hausaufgabe(n) machen to do homework I
kaputt machen to tear (up) IV
sich Notizen machen to take notes I
Gut gemacht! Well done! I
Mach dir nichts draus. Never mind. II
Macht nichts. Never mind. II
Macht's gut. Take care. I
**Macht** power III
**mächtig** powerful IV
**Mädchen** girl I
**Magen** stomach II
**Magie** magic II
**Magier** magician IV
**Magierin** magician IV
**magisch** magic II
**Mahlzeit** meal II
**Mai** May I
**Mais** corn IV
**Make-up** make-up IV
**Mal** time III
**Mal-** painting V U1, 12
**malen** to paint IV
**Mama** mum I; mama II; mom *(AE)* IV
**Mammutbaum** redwood (tree) IV
**Manager** manager IV
**Managerin** manager IV
**manch** some V U4, 72
**manchmal** sometimes I
**Mann** man I
**Mannschaft** team I; crew III; squad IV
**Märchen** fable III
**Marke** brand III
**markieren** to mark III
**Markt** market II
**Marmelade** jam III
**März** March I
**Maschine** machine II
**Maske** mask V U4, 74
**Maßstab** scale V U4, 69
**Material** material III
**Mathe** Maths I; Math *(AE)* IV
**Mathematik** Maths I; Math *(AE)* IV
**Matsch** mud III
**matt** dull IV
**Mauer** wall II
**Maus** mouse I
**Mayonnaise** mayonnaise II
**Mechaniker** mechanic V U1, 17
**Mechanikerin** mechanic V U1, 17
**meckern** to nag III
**Medien** media IV
soziale Medien social media IV
**Medien-** media V U4, 69
**Medikamente** medicine III
**Medizin** medicine III
**medizinisch** medical IV
**Meer** sea I; ocean IV
am Meer at the seaside I
**Meeresfrüchte** seafood V U2, 30
**Meerschweinchen** guinea pig I
**Mehl** flour II
in Mehl wenden to cover in flour IV
**mehr** more I
nicht mehr not … any more III
**mehrere** several; a number of IV
**Mehrheit** majority IV
die Mehrheit most I
**Mehrzahl** majority IV
**meiden** to avoid IV
**Meile** mile II
**mein** my I
**meine** my I; mine II
**meinen** to mean III
**Meinung** opinion III; mind V U4, 79
einer Meinung sein (mit) to agree (with) III
seine Meinung ändern to change one's mind III
anderer Meinung sein to disagree II
meiner Meinung nach in my opinion III
am **meisten** most II
die **meisten** most I; most of V U1, 20
**meistens** mostly IV
**melken** to milk III
**Menge** amount (of) V U3, 48
eine Menge a lot of I
jede Menge lots of I; lots III
**Mensa** cafeteria I
**Mensch** person II
**Menschen** people I
**Menschenmenge** crowd II
**Menschenrechte** *(Pl.)* human rights *(pl)* V U4, 79
**Menschheit** mankind V U3, 54
**menschlich** human III
sich **merken** to remember II
**Merkmal** quality V U4, 74
**merkwürdig** strange; funny II
**Messer** knife II
**Metall** metal III
**Meter** metre I
**Methode** method II
**Metzgerei** butcher's III
**mich** me I
**Miete** rent II
**mieten** to rent III; to hire IV
**Mikrowelle** microwave IV
**Milch** milk I
**Milchmischgetränk** milkshake III
**Milchshake** milkshake III
**mild** mild I
**Milliarde** billion IV
**Million** million III
eine halbe Million half a million III
**Minderheit** minority IV
**Mindest-** minimum IV
**mindestens** at least III
**Mineralwasser** mineral water III
**minimal** minimum IV
**Minimum** minimum IV
**Minute** minute II
**mir** me I
von mir of mine II
**mischen** to mix IV
**Mischrasse** mixed race V U3, 48
**Mischung** mixture V U4, 69
**missbrauchen** to abuse V U4, 78
**misshandeln** to abuse V U4, 78
**mit** with I
mit *(dem Zug)* by *(train)* I
**mitbringen** to bring II
**Mitglied** member IV
**Mitleid** haben mit to feel sorry for III
zum **Mitnehmen** takeaway II
**mitnehmen** to take I
**Mitschüler** classmate V U3, 58
**Mitschülerin** classmate V U3, 58
**Mittagessen** lunch I

**Mittagspause** lunchtime I
**Mittagszeit** lunchtime I
**Mitte** centre; middle III; center *(AE)* IV
in der Mitte in the middle III
in der Mitte von in the centre of III
**Mittel-** intermediate V U1, 16
im **Mittelpunkt** stehen central V U3, 50
zur **Mittelschicht** gehören to be middle class V U3, 51
**Mitternacht** midnight III
**mittleres** Niveau intermediate V U1, 16
**Mittwoch** Wednesday I
**mittwochs** on Wednesdays I
**mixen** to mix IV
**mobil** mobile IV
**Mobiltelefon** mobile (phone) I; cell phone *(AE)* IV
**Mode** fashion *(no pl)* IV
**modern** modern I
**modisch** fashionable V U4, 70; trendy IV
**mögen** to like I; to enjoy III
am liebsten mögen to like ... best I
am meisten mögen to like ... best I
gern mögen to love I
nicht mögen to hate I; to dislike IV
Ich möchte nicht ... I wouldn't like (to) ... I
Ich möchte ... I'd like (to) ... (= I would like to) I
Möchtest du? Would you like (to) ...? I
**Möglichkeit** chance; option IV
**Moment** moment II
in dem Moment als right IV
ich brauchte einen Moment it took me a moment V U2, 39
**Monat** month I
pro Monat a month V U4, 70
**monatlich** monthly III
**Mond** moon V U1, 20
**Monster** monster III
**Montag** Monday I
**Moor** marsh V U3, 55
**Mörder** murderer III
**Mörderin** murderer III

**Morgen** morning I
Guten Morgen. Good morning. II
**morgen** tomorrow II
**morgendliche** Ansprache morning message IV
**Moschee** mosque II
**Motivationsschreiben** personal statement V U1, 16
**motiviert** motivated IV
**Motor** engine IV
**Motorrad** motorbike I
**Moussaka** moussaka II
**müde** tired I
**Mühe** effort V U4, 69
Mühe haben to struggle V U1, 11
**Müll** rubbish II; trash (AE) IV
**Mülleimer** tin IV
**multikulturell** multicultural IV
**Mund** mouth II
den Mund halten to keep one's mouth shut V U2, 40
**Münze** coin III
**Münzgeld** change II
**Münztelefon** pay phone III
**Museum** museum II
**Musik** music I
**Musik-** musical III
**musikalisch** musical III
**Musiker** musician V U2, 29
**Musikerin** musician V U2, 29
**Musikgruppe** band II
**Müsli** cereal III
**Muslim** Muslim I
**Muslimin** Muslim I
**müssen** must I; to have to II
nicht müssen needn't I
**Mut** courage IV
**mutig** brave III
**Mutter** mother I
**Muttersprachler** native speaker V U1, 16
**Muttersprachlerin** native speaker V U1, 16
**Mütze** cap I

## N

**nach** to; after I
nach Hause home I
nach dem Weg fragen asking the way I

**nach** *(bei Uhrzeitangaben)* past II
**Nachbar** neighbour III
**Nachbarin** neighbour III
**Nachfahre** descendant V U2, 29
**Nachfahrin** descendant V U2, 29
**nachfolgen** to succeed (in) IV
**Nachmittag** afternoon I
**nachmittags** in the afternoon I
nachmittags *(Uhrzeit)* p.m. II
**Nachricht** message II
**Nachricht(en)** news II
**nachschauen** to look I; to look up II
**Nachsitzen** detention IV
**Nachspeise** dessert; pudding II
**nachsprechen** to say I
**nächste** next I
als **Nächstes** next II
**Nacht** night I
gestern Nacht last night V U2, 34
heute Nacht tonight II
in jener Nacht that night II
über Nacht overnight V U4, 70
**Nachteil** con V U4, 68
**nachts** at night V U3, 51
**Nachtwanderung** night walk I
**Nagel** nail III
**Nagelschere** nail scissors *(pl)* III
**nah** near III
in der **Nähe** nearby V U2, 30
in der Nähe von near I
**nahe** close V U1, 23
**nahelegen** to suggest V U4, 74
**Nahrung** food I
**Name** name I
**Nase** nose I
die Nase voll haben (von) to be fed up (with) III
**Nashorn** rhino V U3, 48
**nass** wet I
**Nation** nation V U3, 49
**national** national III
**National-** national III
**Nationalpark** national park V U3, 48
**Natur** nature III
die freie Natur the outdoors IV
**natürlich** of course I
**Naturschutzgebiet** nature reserve V U3, 48
**Naturwissenschaft** Science I
**Navi** satnav I
**Nebel** fog IV

**neben** next to I
**neblig** foggy I
**negativ** negative IV
**nehmen** to take I
etw. ernst nehmen to take sth seriously IV
**neidisch** jealous II
**nein** no I
**nennen** to say I; to call III
auf die **Nerven** gehen to get on one's nerves III; to nag V U4, 70
**nerven** to bother IV
**nervös** nervous II
**nett** nice I; kind II; friendly III
**Netz** web III; net IV
**Netzwerk** network V U4, 69
**neu** new I
**neueste** latest V U4, 70
**Neuheit** innovation IV
**Neuigkeit(en)** news II
**Neujahr** New Year V U3, 59
**neun** nine I
**Neuntklässler** freshman *(AE)* IV
**Neuntklässlerin** freshman *(AE)* IV
**neunzehn** nineteen I
**neunzig** ninety I
**nicht** not I
auch nicht not ... either III
nicht brauchen needn't I
nicht dürfen mustn't III
nicht können can't I; cannot III
nicht mögen to hate I; to dislike IV
nicht müssen needn't I
nicht weg können to be stuck IV
nicht werden won't (= will not) II
nicht einverstanden sein to disagree II
nicht mehr not ... any more III
nicht wahr? isn't it? II
**nicht-** non- IV
**Nichte** niece III
**nichts** nothing IV
**nie** never I
**niederbrennen** to burn down II
die **Niederländer** the Dutch V U3, 49
**Niederländisch** Dutch V U2, 29
**niederländisch** Dutch V U2, 29
sich **niederlassen** to settle IV
**niedlich** cute I
**niedrig** low II
**niemals** never I
**niemand** no one I; nobody III; not ... anyone V U2, 39
**nirgendwo** nowhere IV
**nirgendwohin** nowhere IV
**Niveau** level V U4, 76
mittleres Niveau intermediate V U1, 16
**noch** still III; even II
noch ein another II
noch einmal again; once more II
noch nicht not ... yet II
**Norden** north III
**nördlich** northern III
nördlich von to the north of III; north of IV
**Nordosten** northeast III
**Nordwesten** northwest III
**nordwestlich** northwest of III
**nörgeln** to nag III
**normal** regular IV
**normalerweise** usually II
**Notdienst** emergency service III
**Note** grade *(AE)* IV
**Notfall** emergency III
**nötig** necessary V U1, 11
sich **Notizen** machen to take notes I
**Notruf** emergency call III
**notwendig** necessary V U1, 11
**November** November I
**Nudel** noodle V U4, 68
**Nudelauflauf** pasta bake II
**Nudeln** pasta II
**null** zero I
null *(bei Uhrzeiten und Telefonnummern)* oh I
**Nummer** number I
**nun** now I
**nur** only I; just II
**Nuss** nut I
**nützlich** useful; helpful III

## O

**ob** whether V U4, 78
**oben** up II; at the top III
**obere** upper III
oberer Teil top III
oberes Ende top III
**Oberfläche** surface IV
**Oberteil** top II
**objektiv** objective V U4, 79
**Obst** fruit I
Obst- und Gemüseladen greengrocer's III
**obwohl** although IV; even though V U2, 34
**oder** or I
entweder ... oder ... either ... or ... V U3, 50
**Ofenkartoffel** jacket potato II
**offen** open III
**offensichtlich** obviously V U2, 41
**öffentliche** Schule state school V U3, 51
**öffentliche** Verkehrsmittel public transport III
**offiziell** official V U1, 12
**öffnen** to open I
sich öffnen to open V U2, 40
**Öffnungszeiten** opening times IV
**oft** often I
**ohne** without III
**Ohr** ear II
**okay** OK I; alright IV
**Ökosystem** ecosystem V U1, 20
**Oktober** October I
**Öl** oil IV
**Ölteppich** oil spill V U1, 21
**Oma** grandma II
**Onkel** uncle I
**online** online II
online stellen to post IV
**Opa** grandad III
**Operation** operation III
**Opfer** victim V U3, 50
**optimistisch** optimistic III
**Option** option IV
**Orange** orange I
**orange** orange I
**Orchester** orchestra III
in **Ordnung** fine; all right II
in Ordnung bringen to tidy (up) II
**organisieren** to organize II
**original** original IV
**Orkan** hurricane V U2, 28
**Ort** place I; space IV
**örtlich** local III
**Osten** east III
**östlich** von east of IV
**Outback** *(australisches Hinterland)* the outback V U1, 11
**Outdoor-** outdoor III

sich **outen** to come out V U2, 34
**Outfit** outfit III
**Ozean** ocean IV

## P

**Paar** pair V U4, 70
ein Paar a pair of II
ein **paar** some I; a few III
(ein) **paar** (a) couple of IV
**packen** to pack; to pack up II
**Packung** packet I
**Paella** paella IV
**Paket** package IV
**panisch** werden to panic II
**Papa** dad I
**Papagei** parrot I
**Papier** paper III
**Pappe** cardboard III
**Parade** parade III
**Paradies** paradise IV
**Parfüm** perfume III
**Park** park I
**Parkplatz** parking lot *(AE)* IV
**Partner** partner III
**Partnerin** partner III
**Party** party I
**Pass** pass IV
**Passagier** passenger II
**Passagierin** passenger II
**passen** to suit; to fit II
**passieren** to happen II; to go on V U3, 55
**Pasta** pasta II
**Pastete** pasty; pie II
**Patient** patient II
**Patientin** patient II
**Pause** break I; recess *(AE)* IV
(eine kurze) Pause machen to pause V U3, 60
in der Pause at break I
Pause machen to take a break II
**Pausenhof** playground I
**Pavian** baboon V U3, 63
**peinlich** embarrassing IV; awkward V U3, 60
**Pekannuss** pecan IV
**Pence** *(brit. Währungseinheit)* pence I
**Pendler** commuter IV
**Pendlerin** commuter IV
**Pension** guest house V U2, 31
**perfekt** perfect IV
**permanent** permanent V U1, 16; constant V U2, 34
**Person** person II
berühmte Person celebrity IV
**Personal** staff *(no pl)* IV
**Personalausweis** ID III
**persönlich** personal III
**Pestizid** pesticide V U1, 21
**Pfad** path V U1, 12
**Pfannkuchen** pancake II
**Pfeffer** pepper II
**Pferd** horse I
**Pfirsich** peach I
**Pflanze** plant I
**Pflaster** plaster III
**Pflege** nursing V U2, 34
**Pflichtfach** core subject IV
**pflücken** to pick V U3, 60
**Pfund** *(brit. Währungseinheit)* pound I
**Physiotherapeut** physiotherapist V U1, 17
**Physiotherapeutin** physiotherapist V U1, 17
**physisch** physical IV
**Picknick** picnic I
**Pick-up** pick-up IV
**pikant** spicy II
**Pilot** pilot IV
**Pilotin** pilot IV
**Pinguin** penguin I
**pink** pink I
**Pirat** pirate V U2, 29
**Piratin** pirate V U2, 29
**Pirogge** pierogi II
**Pizza** pizza I
**Plan** plan II; map IV
**planen** to plan III
**Planke** plank II
**Plantage** plantation IV
**Planwagen** wagon IV
**Plastik** plastic III
**Platsch** splash I
**platt** flat IV
**Plattform** platform V U1, 20
**Platz** place I; square II; space; seat IV
**plaudern** to chat II
**plötzlich** suddenly II; sudden V U3, 58
**Po** bottom V U3, 58
**Podcast** podcast IV
**politisch** political IV
**Polizei** police III
**Polizeibeamter** police officer I
**Polizeibeamtin** police officer I
**Polizeirevier** police station V U3, 50
**Polizeiwache** police station V U3, 50
**Polnisch** Polish IV
**polnisch** Polish IV
**Pommes frites** chips *(pl)* I
**Popcorn** popcorn I
**Porzellan** china III
**Position** position V U2, 38
**positiv** positive III
**Post** *(online gestellte Nachricht)* post IV
**Postamt** post office I
**Poster** poster I
**Postkarte** postcard I
**Praktikum** work experience V U1, 16
**praktisch** practical IV
**Praline** chocolate IV
**Prämie** bonus IV
**Pranger** stocks III
**Präsentation** presentation IV
**präsentieren** to present IV
**Präsident** president IV
**Präsidentin** president IV
**Preis** prize; price II
**Preisnachlass** discount V U4, 71
**Presse** press V U4, 78
**pressen** to squeeze IV
**Prise** pinch II
**privat** private V U3, 50
**Privat-** private V U3, 50
**Privileg** privilege V U2, 34
**privilegiert** privileged V U3, 52
**Pro** pro V U4, 68
**pro** per IV
pro Monat a month V U4, 70
pro Stück each II
**probieren** to try II
**Problem** problem I; trouble III
**produzieren** to produce III
**Programm** programme I
**Projekt** project III
**Prominente** celebrity IV
**Prominenter** celebrity IV
**Propellerboot** airboat IV
**Prospekt** brochure III
**Protest** protest IV
**Protestant** Protestant III

**Protestantin** Protestant III
**protestantisch** Protestant III
**protestieren** to protest V U3, 59
**Prozent** percent (%) IV
**prüfen** to test II
**Publikum** audience V U4, 74
**publizieren** to publish V U4, 78
**Pudding** pudding II
**Punkt** point IV
**Punktestand** score II
**pünktlich** on time III; punctual V U1, 17
**Pute** turkey IV
**putzen** to clean I
**Puzzle** puzzle V U4, 78

## Q

**Quadratmeile** square mile (= sq. mi.) IV
**Qualifikation** qualification V U1, 17
**qualifizieren** to qualify V U1, 16
**qualifiziert** skilled V U1, 11; qualified V U1, 19
**Qualität** quality V U4, 74
**Quelle** source IV
**quer** durch across IV
**quetschen** to squeeze IV
**Quittung** receipt II

## R

**Rabatt** discount V U4, 71
**Rad** wheel II
**Radfahren** cycling III
**Radiergummi** eraser I
**Radio** radio II
**Rafting** rafting III
**Ranger** ranger *(AE)* V U3, 54
**Rangerin** ranger *(AE)* V U3, 54
**rappen** to rap II
**Rapper** rapper III
**Rapperin** rapper III
**rar** rare V U4, 70
**Rasen** lawn V U3, 58
**Rasensprenger** sprinkler V U3, 58
**Rasierapparat** razor IV
**Rasierer** razor IV
**Rasse** race V U3, 48
**Rassentrennung** segregation IV
**Rassismus** racism IV
**rasten** to rest IV
**Raster** grid IV
**Rat** advice III
**raten** to guess II
jdm. etw. raten to advise sb V U4, 74
**Rathaus** town hall II
**Ratschlag** advice III; tip II
**Rätsel** mystery I; puzzle V U4, 78
**rau** rough V U3, 58
den Atem **rauben** to take one's breath away V U2, 30
**Rauch** smoke III
**Raum** room I; space IV
**reagieren** to react IV
**Reaktion** reaction IV
**realisieren** to realise V U1, 13
**Rechner** calculator I
**Rechnung** bill III
**Recht** right IV; privilege V U2, 34
**recht** haben to be right II
**rechthaberisch** bossy IV
**rechts** on the right I; right III
**Rechts-** right-wing V U4, 79
**rechts-** right-wing V U4, 79
**Rechtschreibung** spelling I
**Rechtsfall** court case IV
**rechtsorientiert** right-wing V U4, 79
**rechtzeitig** in time I
**recyceln** to recycle V U3, 55
**Rede** speech III
**Redefreiheit** freedom of speech V U4, 79
**reden** (mit) to talk (to) I
**Redewendung** phrase V U4, 79
**reduzieren** to reduce V U3, 55
**Referenz** reference V U1, 16
**Referenzschreiben** reference V U1, 16
**Regal** shelf I
**Regalbrett** shelf I
**rege** busy V U4, 69
**Regel** rule III
**regelmäßig** regular IV
**regeln** to regulate V U3, 54
**Regen** rain III
**Regenbogen** rainbow III
**Regenmantel** raincoat III
**Regenschirm** umbrella II
**Regenzeit** rainy season V U1, 21
**Regierung** government IV
**Regierungsgebäude** State House *(AE)* IV
**Region** region IV
**Regisseur** director II
**Regisseurin** director II
**regnen** to rain I
**regnerisch** rainy I
**Reich** empire III
**reich** rich III
die **Reichen** the rich V U3, 51
**reichen** to pass II
**Reichtum** wealth V U2, 35; fortune IV
**Reifen** tyre III
**Reihe** row V U4, 70
in die richtige **Reihenfolge** bringen to put in the right order I
(sich) **reimen** to rhyme III
**Reis** rice II
**Reise** trip; voyage; journey III; tour IV
**Reisebürokauffrau** travel agent V U1, 17
**Reisebürokaufmann** travel agent V U1, 17
**Reiseleiter** tour guide V U1, 12
**Reiseleiterin** tour guide V U1, 12
**reisen** to travel II
**Reiseziel** destination IV
**reißen** to tear (up) IV
**Reiten** horse riding I
**reiten** to ride II
**reizen** to tease IV
**Religion** religion V U2, 34
**Religionsunterricht** RE (Religious Education) I
**religiös** religious IV
**rennen** to run I
**reparieren** to repair III
**Reporter** reporter III
**Reporterin** reporter III
**Republik** republic III
**Requisit** prop III
**Reservat** reservation IV
**reservieren** to make a reservation III; to book IV
**Reservierung** reservation IV
**Respekt** respect V U1, 13
**respektieren** to respect IV
**respektlos** disrespectful V U1, 12
**respektvoll** respectful V U1, 13
der **Rest** the rest IV
**Restaurant** restaurant II

**retten** to save III
**Rettungsboot** lifeboat III
**Rettungsdienst** emergency service III
**Revier** territory V U3, 49
industrielle **Revolution** Industrial Revolution III
**Rezept** recipe II
**Rhinozeros** rhino V U3, 48
**Rhythmus** rhythm III
**richtig** right I; real II; correct IV
das **Richtige** tun to do the right thing III
**Richtung** direction; trend IV
in Richtung towards IV
in diese Richtung this way II
**Riese** giant III
**Riesen-** giant III
**riesengroß** huge IV
**Riesenrad** big wheel II
**riesig** huge IV; giant III; great V U1, 11
**Riff** reef V U1, 20
**Rindfleisch** beef II
**Ring** circle III
**ringen** to struggle V U1, 11
**ringsumher** all around V U3, 59
**Ritt** ride IV
**Ritter** knight III
**Rivale** rival V U2, 29
**Rivalin** rival V U2, 29
**Rock** skirt I
**Rock** *(Musik)* rock III
**Rohr** tube; pipe III
**Rolle** part II; role IV
**Rollkoffer** trolley suitcase III
**Rollstuhl** wheelchair III
**Rolltreppe** escalator II
**Roman** novel IV
**rosa** pink I
**Rose** rose IV
**rosten** to rust IV
**rot** red I
rot werden to go red V U3, 60
**Rückblende** flashback V U3, 51
**Rücken** back IV
Hin- und **Rückfahrkarte** return ticket III
**Rückgang** decline V U1, 21
**Rückkehr** return V U2, 29
**Rucksack** backpack IV
**Rückseite** back IV
**Ruf** call III; reputation IV
**rufen** to call I; to shout II; to cry V U2, 40
**Rugby** rugby III
**Ruhe** silence III
jmdn. in Ruhe lassen to leave sb alone V U3, 60
**ruhig** quiet III
**Rührei** scrambled egg II
**rühren** to stir II
**ruinieren** to ruin II
**rumhängen** (mit) to hang out (with) IV
**rundherum** all around V U3, 59
**Russe** Russian IV
**Russin** Russian IV
**Russisch** Russian IV
**russisch** Russian IV
**Rüstung** armour III

## S

**Sache** thing I
**sachlich** objective V U4, 79
**Sack** bag I
**Safari** safari V U3, 48
**Saft** juice II
**Sage** legend V U1, 12
**sagen** to say; to tell I
jmdm. Bescheid sagen to let sb know V U1, 15
**Saison** season IV
**Salat** salad II
**Salz** salt II
**Salzwasserkrokodil** saltwater crocodile V U1, 23
**sammeln** to collect I
(sich) sammeln to gather IV
**Sammlung** collection IV
**Samstag** Saturday I
**Sand** sand V U2, 30
**sandig** sandy V U2, 28
**Sandkasten** sandpit V U3, 58
**Sandwich** sandwich I
**Sänger** singer I
**Sängerin** singer I
**Satellit** satellite V U1, 11
**Satellitenschüssel** satellite dish V U1, 11
etw. **sattbekommen** to get tired of sth IV
etw. **satthaben** to get tired of sth IV
**Satz** phrase V U4, 79
**sauber** clean I
sauber machen to clean I
**sauer** sein to be fed up (with) III
**Saxofon** saxophone I
**Schachtel** box I
(es ist) **schade** it's a pity IV
**Schaden** damage V U1, 20
**schaden** to damage V U1, 21
**Schädlingsbekämpfungsmittel** pesticide V U1, 21
**Schaf** sheep I
**schaffen** to create V U1, 12
es schaffen to make it IV
**Schal** scarf I
**Schälchen** bowl II
**Schale** bowl II
**Schatz** treasure II
**schätzen** to guess; to appreciate IV
**Schau** show IV
**schauen** to look I
**Schaufenster** shop window V U4, 70
**Schauspielen** acting III
**Schauspieler** actor II
**Schauspielerei** acting III
**Schauspielerin** actor II
**Schauspielworkshop** acting workshop II
**Scheibenwischer** windscreen wiper III
**scheinen** to seem III; to shine IV
**Schere** scissors *(pl)* III
**scherzen** to joke III
**schick** chic I
**schicken** to send I
**schieben** to push I
**schießen** to kick III
schießen (auf) to shoot (at) IV
schießen mit to fire V U2, 41
**Schießerei** shooting V U2, 34
**Schiff** ship I
**Schiffe** shipping V U1, 21
**Schiffsbauer** ship builder III
**Schiffsbauerin** ship builder III
**Schiffsdeck** deck IV
**Schiffsfahrt** boat trip II
über eine **Schiffsplanke** ins Wasser getrieben werden to walk the plank V U2, 40
**Schiffswrack** shipwreck V U2, 30

**Schild** sign III
**Schildkröte** turtle V U1, 20
**Schimmelkäse** blue cheese II
**Schinken** ham II
**Schlacht** battle III
**Schlaf** sleep III
**schlafen** to sleep I; to be asleep III
**Schlafzimmer** bedroom I
**schlagen** to hit II; to beat III; to slap IV
**Schlagzeile** headline IV
**Schlamm** mud III
**schlammig** muddy I
**Schlange** snake I; line V U4, 70
**schlau** clever I; smart III
**Schlauch** tube III
**schlecht** bad I; ill II; evil IV
sich schlecht fühlen to feel sick IV
**schlechteste** worst III
**schleifen** to drag IV
**schlendern** to stroll IV
**schleppen** to drag IV
im **Schlepptau** in tow IV
**schlicht** plain II
**schließen** to close I
Kompromisse schließen to compromise IV
**Schließfach** locker IV
**schließlich** in the end; finally II; after all IV
**schlimm** terrible I
**schlimmste** worst III
**Schloss** castle II
**Schlumpf** smurf I
**Schluss** end II; ending; conclusion III
am Schluss by the end II
zum Schluss in the end; finally II
**Schlussfolgerung** conclusion III
**Schlussverkauf** sale II
**schmackhaft** tasty III
**schmerzhaft** sore II
**Schminke** make-up IV
**Schmuck** jewellery II
**Schmuggler** smuggler II
**Schmugglerin** smuggler II
**schmutzig** dirty I
**Schnäppchen** bargain II
**schnappen** to grab III
**Schnee** snow IV
(sich) **schneiden** to cut II
lustige Grimassen schneiden to make funny faces V U3, 58
sich die Haare schneiden lassen to have a haircut II
**schnell** fast; quick II
**Schnorcheln** snorkelling V U1, 20
**Schock** shock V U2, 34
**Schokolade** chocolate I
Tafel Schokolade bar of chocolate I
**schön** nice; beautiful I; fine; lovely II
ganz schön pretty IV
**schon** already; yet II
schon einmal before III
**Schönheit** beauty V U2, 30
**Schoß** lap V U3, 59
**Schotte** Scot III
**Schottenrock** kilt III
**Schottin** Scot III
**schottisch** Scottish III
**Schrank** cupboard III
**Schrecken** horror V U2, 40
**schrecklich** awful; terrible I; horrible III
**Schrei** shout I; scream V U3, 59
**schreiben** to write I
eine SMS schreiben to text II
**Schreibtisch** desk IV
**schreien** to shout II; to scream III; to cry V U2, 40
**Schriftsteller** writer II
**Schriftstellerin** writer II
**Schritt** step III
ein Schritt nach dem anderen one step at a time V U3, 60
in **Schritttempo** verfallen to slow to a walk IV
**schrittweise** one step at a time V U3, 60
**Schrotflinte** shotgun IV
**schubsen** to push III
**schüchtern** shy IV
**Schuh** shoe I
**Schulabschluss** qualification V U1, 17
**Schuld** fault V U3, 51
**schulden** to owe III
**schuldig** guilty V U3, 51
**Schule** school I
in der Schule at school I
öffentliche Schule state school V U3, 51
staatliche Schule state school V U3, 51
**Schüler** student I; pupil V U3, 58
**Schülerin** student I; pupil V U3, 58
**Schulfach** subject I
**Schulgelände** campus IV
**Schulhof** playground I
so gut wie kein(en) Schulhof no playground to speak of V U3, 58
**Schulleiter** principal *(AE)* IV; headteacher V U3, 60
**Schulleiterin** principal *(AE)* IV; headteacher V U3, 60
**Schulstunde** lesson I
**schürfen** to dig IV
**Schuss** shot V U2, 41
**Schüssel** bowl II
**Schusswaffe** gun IV
**schütteln** to shake V U3, 60
den Kopf schütteln to shake one's head V U3, 60
**Schutz** security V U3, 49
**schützen** to keep safe; to protect III
**schwach** weak III; lame IV
**Schwäche** weakness IV
**schwarz** black I
auf die schwarze Liste gesetzt blacklisted V U4, 79
**Schwarze** black (person) V U3, 59
**Schwarzer** black (person) V U3, 59
**Schweigen** silence III
**schweigsam** silent III
**Schweinefleisch** pork II
**Schweizer** Swiss IV
**Schweizerin** Swiss IV
**schweizerisch** Swiss IV
**schwer** heavy; hard II; badly; serious III
**schwerhörig** deaf III
**Schwert** sword III
**Schwester** sister I
**schwierig** difficult III; hard II; tricky IV
**Schwierigkeiten** trouble III
**Schwimmbad** swimming pool I
**schwimmen** to swim II
schwimmen gehen to go swimming I
**Schwimmer** swimmer IV
**Schwimmerin** swimmer IV
**schwören** to swear V U3, 50

**schwul** gay V U2, 34
**Science**-Fiction science fiction I
**Scone** *(eine Art süßes Brötchen)* scone II
**sechs** six I
**sechzehn** sixteen I
**sechzig** sixty I
**secondhand** second-hand V U4, 71
**See** lake III
**Seeräuber** pirate V U2, 29
**Seeräuberin** pirate V U2, 29
**segeln** to sail IV
**sehen** to see I; to look II
**Sehenswürdigkeit** sight II
**Sehr** geehrte Damen und Herren, Dear Sir or Madam, V U3, 50
**sehr** very I; a lot II; badly III; extremely IV
so sehr so much III
zu sehr too much II
**Seide** silk III
**Seife** soap III
**Seil** rope I
**Seilrutsche** zip line III
**sein** his; to be I; its III
**seit** since; for IV
**seitdem** since IV; ever since V U3, 54
**Seite** page; side I
Seite *(im Internet)* site IV
**Sekunde** second II
**selber** myself; ourselves; yourselves; themselves III
**selbst** myself; self III
dich selbst yourself II
er selbst himself III
ihr/euch/Sie/sich (selbst) yourselves III
sie selbst herself; themselves III
**selbstbewusst** confident III
**selbstsicher** confident; sure of oneself III
**selbstsüchtig** selfish IV
**selbstverständlich** of course I
etw. als selbstverständlich hinnehmen to take sth for granted V U4, 79
**selten** rare V U4, 70
**seltsam** strange; funny II
**Semester** term V U1, 11
**senden** to send I
**Sendung** programme I
**Senf** mustard II
**separat** separate IV
**September** September I
**servieren** to serve IV
**Serviette** napkin II
**setzen** to put I
sich setzen to sit down V U1, 15
Setz dich. Have a seat. IV
Setzen Sie sich. Have a seat. IV
**Shampoo** shampoo III
**Shirt** shirt I
**Shorts** shorts *(pl)* I
**Show** show I
**Showbusiness** show-business IV
**Showgeschäft** show-business IV
**sich** each other; self III
sich gegenseitig each other III
**sicher** sure I; safe III
**Sicherheit** safety IV; security V U3, 49
in Sicherheit safe III
**Sicherheitsnetz** safety net IV
**Sicht** view IV
**Sie** you I
**sie** her; she I
**sie** *(Pl.)* they; them I
**sieben** seven I
**siebzehn** seventeen I
**siebzig** seventy I
**Siedler** settler IV
**Siedlerin** settler IV
**siegen** to win I
**Sieger** winner I
**Siegerin** winner I
**Signal** signal III
**singen** to sing I
**sinken** to sink III
**sinnlos** pointless IV
**Sitte** custom IV
**sittliche Werte** *(Pl.)* moral standards *(pl)* V U4, 79
**Situation** situation II
**Sitz** seat V U3, 48
**Sitzbank** bench III
**sitzen** to sit I
**Sitzplatz** seat IV
**Skala** scale V U4, 69
**Skateboard** skateboard III
**Ski** fahren to ski II
**Skifahren** skiing III
**Skilift** ski lift V U4, 74
**Sklave** slave IV
**Sklavin** slave IV
**Skyline** skyline IV
**Slogan** slogan IV
**Smartphone** smartphone IV
**Smog** smog V U4, 69
**SMS** message; text message II
eine SMS schreiben to text II
**SMS-Schreiber** texter II
**SMS-Schreiberin** texter II
**Snack** snack I
**Sneaker** sneaker *(AE)* V U4, 70
**so** like this I; so II
so dass so that IV
so oft whenever V U1, 12
so sehr so much III
so … wie as … as II
**sobald** as soon as IV
**Socke** sock I
**soeben** just II
**Sofa** sofa II
**sofort** right away IV
**Software** software II
**sogar** even II
**Sohn** son III
**Sojabohne** soy bean IV
**solar** solar III
**Solar-** solar III
**solch** such IV
**Soldat** soldier III
**Soldatin** soldier III
**Solidarität** solidarity V U2, 35
**sollte** should III
**somit** therefore V U3, 54
**Sommer** summer II
**Sonderangebot** special offer III
**Sonne** sun III
**Sonnen-** solar III
**sonnenbaden** to sunbathe II
**Sonnenbrille** sunglasses *(pl)* II
**Sonnenkollektor** solar panel V U4, 74
**Sonnenschein** sunshine V U2, 31
**sonnig** sunny I
**Sonntag** Sunday I
**sonst** else V U2, 34
sich **Sorgen** machen to worry I
dafür **sorgen** to make sure III
für jmdn. **sorgen** to take care of sb IV
**Sorgfalt** caution V U3, 54
**sorgfältig** careful II
**Sorte** sort II; type; kind III
**sortieren** to sort IV

**Soße** sauce II
**Souvenir** souvenir III
**Souvenirladen** souvenir shop III
**soweit** as far as IV
**sowieso** anyway V U4, 70
**sowohl** ... als auch ...
both ... and ... IV
**sozial** social V U3, 51
**soziale** Medien social media IV
**Sozialkunde** Social Studies I
**Spaghetti** spaghetti II
**spanisch** Spanish IV
**Spanisch** Spanish IV
**spannend** exciting I
**sparen** to save IV
**Spaß** fun I
Spaß haben to enjoy oneself III
zum Spaß for fun III
(zu) **spät** late I
**später** later I; after III
den Hund **spazieren** führen to take the dog for a walk II
**Spaziergang** walk III
**speichern** to save II
**Speise** dish II
**Speisekarte** menu II
**Speisereste** food waste V U4, 76
**spektakulär** spectacular III
**spenden** to donate V U4, 71
**sperren** to ban IV
**Spezial-** specialist V U4, 68
**speziell** special I
**Spezies** species V U1, 10
**Spiegel** mirror III
**Spiel** match; game I
**spielen** to play I; to act II
**Spieler** player; gamer II
**Spielerin** player; gamer II
**Spielfeld** court III
**Spielkarte** card I
**Spielplatz** playground I
**Spielzeug** toy III
**Spind** locker IV
**Spinne** spider III
**Spinnennetz** web III
**Spitze** top IV
an der Spitze (von) at the front of II
**spitze** awesome IV
**Spitzname** nickname IV
**Sport** sport I
**Sportart** sport III
**Sportgeschäft** sports shop I
**Sportplatz** playing field V U3, 59
**Sportschuh** sneaker *(AE)* V U4, 70
**Sportunterricht** PE (Physical Education) I
**sprachbehindert** speech impaired IV
**Sprache** language II; speech III
**sprechen** to say I; to speak II
sprechen (mit) to talk (to) I
sprechen über to talk about II
**springen** to jump IV; to skip V U3, 58
**Spritze** injection III
**spülen** to wash III
**Spülmaschine** dishwasher IV
**Spur** clue I; trail IV
**Staat** state IV; nation V U3, 49
**staatliche** Schule state school V U3, 51
**Staatsangehörige** citizen IV
**Staatsangehöriger** citizen IV
**Staatsbürger** citizen IV
**Staatsbürgerin** citizen IV
**Stadion** stadium II
**Stadt** town I; city II
**Stadtbewohner** *(Pl.)* townsfolk V U3, 59
**Stadtmitte** city centre III
**Stadtplan** map III
**Stadtteil** borough IV
**Stadtzentrum** city centre III
im Stadtzentrum downtown *(AE)* IV
**Stahl** steel III
**Stamm** tribe V U1, 12
**Stand** cart IV; stall V U4, 68
**standhaft** firm V U3, 59
**ständig** constant V U2, 34
**Standinhaber** stallholder II
**Standinhaberin** stallholder II
**Star** star I
**stark** heavy II; powerful IV
**Stärke** strength IV
**starrer** Blick stare V U3, 60
**Starren** stare V U3, 60
**starren** to stare III
**Start** start III
**starten** to start II
**Statistik** statistics *(no pl)* IV
**stattdessen** instead IV
**stattfinden** to take place V U2, 30
**Status** status IV
**Statussymbol** status symbol V U4, 70
**Stau** traffic jam IV
**Staub** wischen to dust IV
**staubsaugen** to hoover II
**Staubsauger** vacuum cleaner IV
**stecken** bleiben to get stuck IV
**Steelpan** *(Trommel aus Blech)* steelpan V U2, 30
**stehen** to suit; to stand II
stehen bleiben to stop V U2, 41
**stehlen** to steal IV
**steigen** to climb III; to step IV
**steigern** to increase V U4, 74
**Stein** brick II; rock; stone III
**Stelle** place I; space IV; position V U2, 38
**stellen** to put I
online stellen to post IV
sich stellen to confront IV
**Stellenbezeichnung** job title IV
**sterben** to die III
**Stern** star III
**Sternzeichen** star sign IV
**stetig** constant V U2, 34
**Steuerung** control IV
**sticheln** to tease IV
**Stiefel** boot II
**Stift** pen I
**stiften** to donate V U4, 71
**Stil** style III
**still** quiet III
still werden to go quiet III
**Stille** silence III
**Stimme** voice III
**stimmt's?** isn't it? II
**Stimmung** spirit IV; atmosphere V U3, 60
**stinkend** smelly IV
**Stock** stick II; story *(AE)* IV
**Stockwerk** floor V U4, 81; story *(AE)* IV
**Stoff** material III
**Stolz** pride IV
**stolz** (auf) proud (of) III
**stoppen** to stop V U1, 21
**stören** to bother IV
**störrisch** stubborn IV
(sich) **stoßen** to hit III
**strahlend** bright IV
**Strand** beach I

den Strand nach Strandgut absuchen to go beach combing II
**Straße** road I; street III
**Straßenbahn** tram III
**Straßenbauarbeiten** roadwork *(AE)* IV
**Straßengang** street gang V U2, 34
**streamen** *(im Internet)* to stream IV
**Strecke** track IV
sich **strecken** to stretch IV
**Streich** trick I
**streichen** to paint IV
**Streit** argument II; fight III
**streiten** to argue V U3, 60
(sich) streiten to fight III
**streng** strict IV
**Stress** stress IV
**strikt** strict IV
**Strom** electricity III
**Strömung** flow V U4, 78
**Struktur** structure III
**Stück** piece II
pro Stück each II
**Student** student I
**Studentin** student I
**studieren** to study IV
**Studio** studio IV
**Stufe** step II
**Stuhl** chair I
**stumm** silent III
**Stunde** hour I; period IV
erste Stunde *(in der Schule)* homeroom IV
**Stundenplan** timetable I; schedule *(AE)* IV
**Stuntman** stuntman IV
**Sturm** storm IV
**suchen** to search IV
suchen nach to look for II
**Südafrikaner** South African V U3, 49
**Südafrikanerin** South African V U3, 49
**südafrikanisch** South African V U3, 49
**Süden** south III
im Süden von in the south of III
**südlich** southern IV
südlich von south of IV
**Südstaatler** Southerner IV
**Südstaatlerin** Southerner IV
**Südwesten** southwest III
**Summe** amount (of) V U3, 48
**Sumpf** swamp IV; marsh V U3, 55
**super** cool I; super V U4, 70; way to go II; awesome IV
**Superheld** superhero IV
**Supermarkt** supermarket II
**Suppe** soup II
**Surfen** surfing III
**surfen** to surf II
im Internet surfen to surf the internet II
**Surfer** surfer IV
**Surferin** surfer IV
**Sushi** sushi IV
**süß** sweet III; cute I
**Süßes**, sonst gibt's Saures! Trick or treat! I
**Süßigkeit** sweet I
**Sweatshirt** sweatshirt I
**Symbol** symbol IV
**System** system IV
**Szene** scene II

## T

**Tabelle** chart V U4, 76
**Tablet** tablet IV
**Tablett** tray II
**Tablette** tablet II
**Tafel** board I
Tafel Schokolade bar of chocolate I
**Tag** day I
ein freier Tag a day off III
eines Tages one day III
den ganzen Tag all day III
ein ausgefüllter Tag a busy day I
**Tagebuch** diary I
**täglich** daily IV
**Taktik** tactic III
**Tal** valley V U3, 55
**Talent** talent I
**talentiert** talented III
**Talentwettbewerb** talent show I
**Talkmaster** host V U4, 74
**Tante** aunt II
**Tanz** dance III
**Tanz-** dancing IV
**Tanzen** dancing IV
**tanzen** to dance I
**Tänzer** dancer III
**Tänzerin** dancer III
**Tanzveranstaltung** dance IV
**tapfer** brave III
**Tapferkeit** courage IV
**Tasche** bag I; pocket II
**Taschengeld** allowance *(AE)* IV; pocket money V U4, 70
**Taschenlampe** torch I
**Taschenrechner** calculator I
**Taschentuch** tissue III
**Tasse** cup II
**Tätigkeit** job II
**tatkräftig** energetic IV
**Tatsache** fact II
**tatsächlich** actually; in fact III
**taub** deaf III
**Tauch-** diving V U1, 20
**Tauchen** diving V U1, 20
**Taucher** diver V U2, 30
**Taucherin** diver V U2, 30
**Tauchschule** diving school V U2, 30
jmdn. **täuschen** to fool sb V U2, 40
**tauschen** to swap V U4, 71
**tausend** a/one thousand II
**Taxi** taxi II
**Team** team I; squad IV
**Teamwork** teamwork V U1, 16
**Technik** Design Technology (DT) I
**Techniker** engineer II
**Technikerin** engineer II
**Technologie** technology V U4, 74
**Tee** tea I
**Teelöffel** *(TL)* teaspoon *(tsp)* II
**Teenager** teen II; teenager III
**Teich** pond V U3, 55
**Teil** part II
oberer Teil top III
unterer Teil bottom III
**teilen** to share III
**teilnehmen** to attend V U1, 11
**teilnehmen** (an) to take part (in) II
**Telefon** phone II; telephone III
ans Telefon gehen to answer the phone III
**Telefonanruf** phone call I
**telefonieren** to phone II
**Telefonnummer** phone number III
**Telefonzelle** telephone box II
**Teller** plate II
**Temperatur** temperature V U1, 20
**Tennis** tennis I
**Teppich** carpet I
**Territorium** territory V U3, 49

**Terrorist** terrorist V U4, 79
**Terroristin** terrorist V U4, 79
**Test** test I
**testen** to test II
**teuer** expensive II
**Teufelsrochen** manta ray V U1, 23
**Text** lines *(pl)*; text II
**Theater** theatre; drama II
**Theaterstück** play II
**Thema** topic IV
**Themenpark** theme park II
**Thunfisch** tuna II
**tief** deep IV
  tief einatmen to take a deep breath V U3, 60
  tief Luft holen to take a deep breath V U3, 60
**Tier** animal I
**Tierarzt** vet III
**Tierärztin** vet III
**Tierhandlung** pet shop III
**Tierheim** animal rescue shelter I
**Tierpark** zoo I
**Tierpfleger** zookeeper I
**Tierpflegerin** zookeeper I
**Tierwelt** *(in freier Wildbahn)* wildlife IV
**Tiger** tiger I
**Tipp** tip II
**Tisch** table I
  den Tisch decken to lay the table II
**Tischler** carpenter V U1, 11
**Tischlerin** carpenter V U1, 11
**Tischtennis** table tennis II
**Toast** toast II
**Tochter** daughter I
**Tod** death V U1, 20
  jmdn. zu Tode erschrecken to frighten the hell out of sb V U3, 51
**tod-** deadly III
**Todesfall** death V U1, 20
**tödlich** deadly III
**Toilette** toilet I; bathroom *(AE)*; restroom *(AE)* IV
**tolerant** tolerant V U1, 13
**Toleranz** tolerance V U1, 13
**tolerieren** to tolerate IV
**toll** great; brilliant I; amazing II
**Tomate** tomato II
**Ton** sound III
**Tonne** tonne II; barrel IV
**Tonne** *(Gewicht)* ton IV
**Tonstudio** recording studio I
**Top** top II
**Topf** pot III
**Tor** gate III; gateway IV; goal V U2, 29
**Tornado** tornado IV
**tot** dead III
**töten** to kill III
**Tötung** killing IV
**Tour** tour IV
**Tourismus** tourism IV; tourist industry V U2, 28
**Tourist** tourist I
**Touristin** tourist I
**Touristeninformation** Tourist Information Centre I
**Township** *(Wohnsiedlungen für Schwarze in Südafrika)* township V U3, 49
**Tradition** tradition III
**traditionell** traditional III
**tragbar** mobile IV
**tragen** to carry II
**tragen** *(Kleidung)* to wear I
**Trainer** trainer IV
**Trainerin** trainer IV
**trainieren** to practise III
**Training** practice I; training III
**Traktor** tractor I
**Transfer** transfer IV
**transkontinental** *(über den Kontinent hinweg)* transcontinental IV
**transparent** transparent V U4, 74
**Transport** transfer IV; transport V U1, 17
**Transporter** van III
**Tratsch** gossip IV
**Traum** dream I
**träumen** to dream III
**traurig** sad III
**treffen** to meet I; to hit II
  Freunde treffen to see friends I
  sich treffen (mit) to hang out (with) IV
**treiben** to drive IV
**Trend** trend IV
**trendsetzend** trending IV
**trendy** trendy IV
**trennen** to separate V U3, 49
**Trennung** segregation IV; isolation *(no pl)* V U1, 10
**Treppe** stairs *(pl)* II
**treten** to kick III; to step IV
**treu** true IV
**Treue** allegiance IV
**Treueeid** pledge of allegiance IV
**Trick** trick I
**Trimester** term V U1, 11
**trinken** to drink II
**Trinkhalm** straw II
**Trip** trip III
**trocken** dry III
**trocknen** to dry IV
**Trommel-** drumming III
**tropisch** tropical V U1, 21
**Trottel** pinhead IV
**trotzdem** anyway III
**Truthahn** turkey IV
**Tschüss.** See you later.; Bye.; See you. I
**T-Shirt** T-shirt I
**Tuch** scarf I
**Tümpel** pond V U3, 55
**tun** to do; to make I
  Tut mir leid. Sorry. I
**Tunnel** tunnel III
**Tür** door I
**Türkisch** Turkish IV
**türkisch** Turkish IV
**Türklingel** doorbell IV
**Turm** tower II
**Turnhalle** gym(nasium) IV
**turnieren** to joust III
**Turnierzweikampf** jousting III
**Turnschuh** trainer I
**Tüte** bag; packet I
**Tutorial** tutorial IV
**Typ** type III; guy IV

## U

**U-Bahn** underground II; subway *(AE)* IV
**Übelkeit** verspüren to feel sick IV
**übelnehmen** to resent IV
**übelriechend** smelly IV
**üben** to practise III
**über** about I; over; across III
  über die Grenze gehen to cross the border IV

über Nacht overnight V U4, 70
**überall** all over I; everywhere V U2, 34; all around V U3, 59
überall wo(hin) wherever III
**Überfahrt** crossing IV
**überfüllt** crowded IV
sich **übergeben** to be sick I; to puke IV
**überhaupt** nicht not at all II
**Überleben** survival V U1, 12
**überleben** to survive III; to live V U3, 55
**Überlebens-** survival V U1, 12
**überlegen** to guess II
**übernachten** to stay II
**Übernachtung** sleepover I
**überprüfen** to check III
**Überprüfung** inspection IV
Überprüfung der Anwesenheit registration I
**überqueren** to cross III
**Überquerung** crossing IV
**überrascht** surprised II
**Überraschung** surprise I
die Grenze **überschreiten** to cross the border IV
**Überschrift** headline IV
**Überschwemmung** flood V U4, 78
**übersetzen** to translate IV
**überspringen** to skip V U3, 58
**überwältigend** stunning V U1, 12
**überzeugend** convincing III
**überzeugt** convinced IV
**Überzeugung** belief V U1, 12
**üblich** regular IV
**U-Boot** submarine I
**übrig** left III
**Übung** exercise; practice I
**Übungsheft** exercise book I
**Uhr** clock II
Uhr *(Zeitangabe bei vollen Stunden)* o'clock I
**Uhrenturm** clock tower II
**Uhrzeit** time I
**um** at I
um … zu in order to V U2, 40
um … herum around IV
(sich) **umdrehen** to turn around III
**umfallen** to fall (over) III
**Umfrage** survey II
**umgeben** sein von etw./jmdm. to be surrounded by sth/sb V U4, 78
**Umgebung** environment V U1, 20
**umgehen** (mit) to deal (with) IV
**umher** around I
**umherziehen** to migrate V U1, 20
**umrühren** to stir II
**umsteigen** to change III
**umwandeln** to convert V U4, 74
**Umwelt** environment V U1, 20
**umweltfreundlich** eco-friendly V U4, 74
**umziehen** to move (house) II
**Umzug** parade III
**Unabhängigkeit** independence; freedom *(no pl)* IV
**unangenehm** uncomfortable II; unpleasant IV
**unbefristet** permanent V U1, 16
**unbeholfen** awkward V U3, 60
**unbekannt** unknown V U1, 20
**unbeliebt** unpopular III
**unbequem** uncomfortable II
**und** and I
**unendlich** never-ending V U4, 78
**unerfreulich** unpleasant IV
**unerwartet** sudden V U3, 58; unexpected V U3, 59
**unfair** unfair III
**Unfall** accident III
**unfreundlich** unfriendly III
**ungefähr** about II
ungefähr um around III
**ungefiltert** unfiltered V U4, 79
**Ungeheuer** monster III
**ungeordnet** disorganized IV
**ungerecht** unjust IV
**Ungerechtigkeit** unfairness; injustice V U3, 52
**ungeschickt** awkward V U3, 60
**ungewiss** uncertain V U1, 20
**ungewöhnlich** unusual V U1, 10
**unglaublich** amazing II
**ungleich** unequal V U3, 52
**Ungleichheit** inequality V U3, 52
**Unglück** disaster III
**unglücklich** unhappy II
**unglücklicherweise** unfortunately V U1, 20
**ungünstig** awkward V U3, 60
**unhöflich** rude V U1, 13
**Unhöflichkeit** rudeness V U1, 13
**Uniform** uniform I
**uninteressant** unappealing IV
**Universität** university III; college *(AE)* IV
**unmodisch** unfashionable II
**unmöglich** impossible; not possibly III
**unmotiviert** unmotivated IV
**Unordnung** mess I
**unorganisiert** disorganized IV
**unpopulär** unpopular III
**unrecht** haben to be wrong III
**uns** us I
**unschuldig** innocent IV
**unser** our I
**unsere** our I; ours III
**unsicher** uncertain V U1, 20
**unten** at the bottom III
da unten down there IV
**unter** under I; among III
**unterbrechen** to interrupt IV
**Unterbringung** accommodation V U2, 30
**unterdrücken** to oppress V U4, 78
**Unterdrückung** oppression V U4, 79
**untere** lower III
unterer Teil bottom III
**Untergang** sinking III
**untergehen** to sink III
**Unterhaltsgeld** allowance *(AE)* IV
**Unterhaltung** conversation III
**Unterhaltungsindustrie** show-business IV
**Unterkunft** accommodation V U2, 30
**unterprivilegiert** underprivileged V U3, 52
**Unterricht** class; lesson I
**unterrichten** to teach III
**Unterrichtsstunde** class; period IV
**unterschiedlich** different I
**unterschreiben** to sign IV
**unterstützen** to support IV; to encourage V U2, 29
**Unterstützung** support IV
**Unterwasser-** underwater V U1, 20
**unterwegs** on the way; out and about I
in der **Unterzahl** outnumbered IV
**unterzeichnen** to sign IV
**unverschämt** rude V U1, 13

Unverschämtheit rudeness V U1, 13
unwissend ignorant V U1, 12
Unwissenheit ignorance V U1, 13
updaten to update IV
Ureinwohner Amerikas Native American IV
Ureinwohnerin Amerikas Native American IV
Urgroßeltern great-grandparents IV
Urkunde certificate V U1, 16
Urlaub holiday I; vacation *(AE)* IV
ursprünglich original IV
US-amerikanisch US IV

## V

**Vanillesauce** custard II
**Vater** father I
**Veganismus** veganism *(no pl)* IV
**Vegetarier** vegetarian I
**Vegetarierin** vegetarian I
**Ventilator** fan IV
sich mit jmdm. **verabreden** to ask sb out IV
**Verabredung** date IV
**veraltet** outdated IV
**verändern** to change III
sich **verändernd** changing V U1, 20
**verängstigt** scared V U2, 33
**veranschaulichen** to bring to life IV
**Veranstaltung** event IV
**verantwortlich** responsible IV
**Verantwortung** responsibility V U2, 35
**verantwortungsvoll** responsible IV
**verärgert** angry II; annoyed III
**Verband** bandage III
**verbannen** to ban IV
**verbessern** to correct I; to improve V U4, 74
**verbieten** to ban IV
**verbinden** to attach; to connect III; to link IV
**Verbindung** link IV
in Verbindung bleiben to keep in touch II
sich in Verbindung setzen to contact V U4, 71
**verblüfft** amazed IV
**verboten** forbidden IV
(sich) **verbreiten** to spread V U4, 79
**verbrennen** to burn down II; to burn III
**verbringen** *(Zeit)* to spend II
**verdienen** to deserve IV
Geld verdienen to make money V U4, 70
**verdrehen** to twist II
**Verein** club II
**Vereinsheim** clubhouse IV
**Verfasser** writer III
**Verfasserin** writer III
**Verfassung** constitution V U3, 49
**verfolgen** to chase V U3, 60
**Verfolger** chaser IV
**Verfolgerin** chaser IV
**verfügbar** available V U1, 11
**Vergangenheit** past III
**vergessen** to forget I; to leave V U3, 56
**vergleichen** to compare I
**Vergnügen** joy V U3, 59
**vergnügt** amused IV
**vergrößern** to increase IV
**verhaften** to arrest IV
**Verhalten** behavior *(AE)* IV
sich **verhalten** to behave IV
**verhandeln** to bargain V U4, 68
**Verhandlung** case IV
**verherrlichen** to glorify V U4, 79
**Verhör** questioning V U3, 50
sich **verirren** to get lost I
**verkaufen** to sell III
**Verkäufer** shop assistant II; assistant III; sales associate *(AE)* IV
**Verkäuferin** shop assistant II; assistant III; sales associate *(AE)* IV
**Verkehr** traffic III
**(Verkehrs)Ampel** traffic light V U3, 59
**Verkehrs-** transport IV
öffentliche **Verkehrsmittel** public transport III
**verkleidet** dressed III
**Verkleidung** fancy dress I
**Verlag** publisher V U4, 78
**verlängerbar** renewable V U4, 74
**verlassen** to leave II
**verlässlich** reliable IV
**verlegen** embarrassed II; to publish V U4, 78
**verletzen** to hurt II
**verletzt** hurt II
**Verletzung** injury III
sich **verlieben** (in) to fall in love (with) III
**verlieren** to lose II
**vermeiden** to avoid IV
**vermindern** to reduce V U3, 55; to decrease V U4, 75
**vermischen** to mix IV
**vermissen** to miss II
**Vermittlung** operator III
**Vermögen** fortune IV
**vermuten** to guess IV
**Vernehmung** questioning V U3, 50
**vernünftig** intelligent III
**veröffentlichen** to release IV; to publish V U4, 78
**verpassen** to miss II
**verraten** to give away V U2, 40
**verrenken** to sprain III
**verringern** to reduce V U3, 55
**verrückt** crazy I
jmdn. verrückt machen to drive sb crazy III
verrückt werden to go crazy V U4, 70
**versagen** (in/bei) to fail IV
**verschieden** separate IV
**verschiedene** several IV
**Verschlechterung** decline V U1, 21
**verschmutzen** to pollute V U1, 20
**Verschmutzung** pollution V U4, 69
**verschwenden** to waste IV
**verschwinden** to disappear IV
sich **versichern** to make sure III
**Versicherung** insurance V U3, 51
**Verspätung** delay V U2, 31
**versprechen** to promise IV
**Verstand** mind V U4, 79
sich **verständigen** to communicate IV
**verstauchen** to sprain III
(sich) **verstecken** to hide III
**verstehen** to understand II; to get III; to know IV
etw. verstehen to get sth IV
**Versuch** experiment II; effort V U4, 69
**versuchen** to try II
**vertrauen** to trust IV
**vertrauenswürdig** reliable IV
**vertraut** familiar IV
**verübeln** to resent IV
**verunreinigen** to pollute V U1, 20

**verursachen** to cause IV; to create V U1, 12
**vervollständigen** to complete I; to finish II
**Verwaltung** administration V U1, 16
**verwenden** to use II
**verwirrt** confused III
**verzeihen** to pardon IV
**Verzeihung** pardon IV
**verzerren** to twist II
auf etw. **verzichten** to give sth a miss III
**Verzögerung** delay V U2, 31
**verzweifelt** desperately IV
**Vesper** packed lunch II
**Video** video IV
**Video-Chat** video chat III
**viel** a lot; much; lots of I; lots III
viel(e) a lot of I
viel Glück good luck II
**viele** many II
Viele Grüße, Best wishes, I
Vielen Dank. Thanks so much. IV
wie viele how many II
**vielleicht** maybe I; may II; perhaps V U2, 39
**vier** four I
**vierte** fourth I
**Viertel** nach quarter past I
**Viertel** vor quarter to I
**vierzehn** fourteen I
**vierzig** forty I
**Vietnamese** Vietnamese IV
**Vietnamesin** Vietnamese IV
**Vietnamesisch** Vietnamese IV
**vietnamesisch** Vietnamese IV
**viktorianisches** Zeitalter Victorian era III
**violett** purple I
**Vogel** bird I
**Vogelbeobachtung** bird watching III
**Vokabular** vocabulary II
**Volk** people V U1, 11
**Volksstamm** tribe V U1, 12
**voll** full III
**Volleyball** volleyball IV
**völlig** completely III; absolutely IV
**vollkommen** perfect IV
**vollständig** complete IV
**von** from; of I; by II
von hinten from behind I
von … weg off V U2, 30
**vor** ago; in front of II; ahead of; before IV; off V U2, 30
vor *(bei Uhrzeitangaben)* to I
vor allem especially IV
vor … wimmeln to be alive with … IV
**vorangehen** to go ahead IV
etw. als gegeben **voraussetzen** to take sth for granted V U4, 79
**Voraussetzung** requirement V U1, 19
**vorbei** over IV
vorbei (an) past III
**vorbeigehen** to pass IV
(sich) **vorbereiten** to prepare III
sich vorbereiten to get ready IV
**Vorbild** role model V U2, 29
**Vordergrund** foreground III
im Vordergrund in the foreground III
**Vorgehensweise** tactic III
**vorhaben** to be up to III
**vorher** before II
**vorhersagen** to foretell III
**Vormittag** morning I
**vormittags** *(Uhrzeit)* a.m. II
**Vorort** suburb IV
**vorrätig** haben to stock V U4, 71
**Vorrecht** privilege V U2, 34
**Vorrichtung** device IV
**vorschlagen** to suggest V U4, 74
**vorschreiben** to regulate V U3, 54
**Vorschul-** preschool V U1, 17
**Vorschule** preschool V U1, 17
**Vorsicht** caution V U3, 54
**vorsichtig** careful II; cautious; guarded III
Sei vorsichtig! Be careful! I
**Vorsingen** audition II
**Vorspeise** starter II
**Vorspielen** audition II
**Vorsprechen** audition II
**vorstellen** to present I; to introduce III
sich (etw.) vorstellen to imagine (sth) IV
**Vorstellungsgespräch** interview IV
**Vortanzen** audition II
**Vorteil** pro V U4, 68
**Vortrag** presentation IV
**vorübergehend** temporary V U1, 16
**vorziehen** to prefer II
**Vulkan** volcano V U2, 30

## W

**wach** awake III
**Wachdienst** security V U3, 49
**Wache** guard V U3, 51
**wachsen** to grow IV
**Wachstum** increase V U1, 20
**Wächter** guard V U3, 51
**Wächterin** guard V U3, 51
**Wagen** truck III
**Waggon** wagon IV
**Wahl** option; choice IV; election V U3, 49
**wählen** to choose II; to vote for IV; to vote V U3, 59
**Wahlfach** elective IV
**Wahnsinnsspaß** blast IV
**wahr** true II
wahr werden to come true IV
**während** while II; during III
**Wahrheit** truth V U4, 78
**wahrnehmen** to notice III
**Wahrsager** fortune teller V U4, 68
**Wahrsagerin** fortune teller V U4, 68
**wahrscheinlich** probably III
**Währung** currency IV
**Wahrzeichen** landmark IV
**Wal** whale IV
**Walbeobachtung** whale watching IV
**Wald** wood III; forest IV
**Walhai** whale shark V U1, 23
**Waliser** Welsh III
**Waliserin** Welsh III
**Walisisch** Welsh III
**walisisch** Welsh III
**Wand** wall II
**Wandern** hiking; walking III
**wandern** to hike II; to migrate V U1, 20
**Wanderweg** trail IV
**Wandgemälde** mural III
**wann** when I
wann immer whenever V U1, 12
**Waren** goods *(no pl)* IV
**warm** warm I
**warnen** to warn III
**Warnung** caution V U3, 54
**warten** to wait II

warten auf to wait for II
**Warteschlange** queue II
**warum** why I
**was** what I
was noch what else III
Was für ein/eine … What a … I
Was hast du (in letzter Zeit) gemacht? What have you been up to? IV
Was ist los? What's wrong? II
Was ist mit …? What about …? I
was sonst what else III
Was stimmt nicht? What's wrong? II
**Waschbär** raccoon I
(sich) **waschen** to wash III
**Wäschetrockner** dryer IV
**Wasser** water I
Eimer Wasser bucket of water I
**Website** website II
**Wechselgeld** change II
**wechseln** to change II
**wechselnd** changing V U1, 20
**wecken** to wake V U2, 39
**Wecker** alarm clock I
**Weg** way III; alley; lane IV; path V U1, 12
auf dem Weg on the way I
aus dem Weg gehen to avoid IV
**weg** away II
nicht weg können to be stuck I
**wegen** because of III
(von jmdm.) **wegkommen** to get away (from sb) V U2, 41
**weglaufen** to run away III
**weh** tun to hurt II
**Weide** field IV
sich **weigern** to refuse IV
**Weihnachten** Christmas I
**Weihnachtstheaterstück** pantomime II
**weil** because I
eine **Weile** a while IV
**Wein** wine IV
**weinen** to cry V U2, 40
Art und **Weise** way III
auf diese **Weise** like this I
**weiß** white I
**Weißkopfseeadler** bald eagle IV
**weit** far III; wide V U3, 54
**weiter** further V U3, 50
**weitere** other I
**weitergehen** to keep going IV; to continue V U2, 40; to go on V U3, 50
**weitermachen** to keep going; to continue IV; to go on V U3, 50
**weiterverkaufen** to resell V U4, 70
**welche** which; what; who II
**Welle** wave IV
**Wellenreiten** surfing III
**wellenreiten** to surf II
**Wellenreiter** surfer IV
**Wellenreiterin** surfer IV
**Welt** world II
auf der Welt in the world II
in aller Welt all around the world III
**weltberühmt** best known IV
**weltweit** global V U1, 21
**wem** whom III
**wen** whom III
in Mehl **wenden** to cover in flour IV
**wenig** little IV
ein wenig a bit II
**wenige** a few III; few IV
**weniger** less III
**wenigstens** at least III
**wenn** when; if II
**wer** who I
**Werbespot** ad(vert) (= advertisement); advertisement II
**Werbespruch** slogan IV
**werden** to get I; will; to become II
genannt werden to be called II
nicht werden won't (= will not) II
rot werden to go red V U3, 60
wahr werden to come true IV
Ich würde nicht gerne … I wouldn't like (to) … I
**werfen** to throw IV
**Werft** shipyard III
**Werk** factory III
**Werktag** weekday V U3, 58
an **Werktagen** on weekdays III
**Werkzeug** tool II
**Wert** value V U3, 54
sittliche Werte *(Pl.)* moral standards *(pl)* V U4, 79
**wert** sein to be worth III
**Werte** values *(pl)* V U2, 34
**Wertvorstellungen** values *(pl)* V U2, 34
**Westen** west III
**westlich** von west of IV
**Wettbewerb** show I; competition II
**wetten** (auf) to bet III
**Wetter** weather I
**wettkampforientiert** competitive III
**wichtig** important II; major IV
wichtig nehmen to care V U4, 70
sich **widersetzen** to resist V U2, 40
**widerstehen** to resist V U2, 40
**wie** like; how I; as II; what III
so … wie as … as II
Wie alt bist du? How old are you? I
Wie bitte? Pardon? I
Wie geht es dir? How are you? I
Wie geht's dir? How are you doing? IV
Wie geht's? What's up?; How's it going? IV
Wie heißt du? What's your name? I
Wie läuft's bei dir? What have you been up to? IV
Wie läuft's? How's it going? IV
wie sehr how much III
Wie spät ist es? What time is it? I
Wie viel (kostet/kosten) …? How much (is/are) …? I
Wie viel Uhr ist es? What time is it? I
wie viele how many II
Wie wäre es mit … ? How about …? II
**wieder** again II
**wiederholen** to repeat III
Auf **Wiedersehen**. Goodbye. I
**wiederverkaufen** to resell V U4, 70
**wiederverwerten** to recycle V U3, 55
**wiegen** to weigh II
**Wiese** field IV
**Wikinger-** Viking III
**Wild** game V U3, 54
**wild** wild III
freie **Wildbahn** the wild IV
**Wilde** savage V U3, 58
**Wilder** savage V U3, 58
**Wilderei** poaching V U3, 54
**Wildern** poaching V U3, 54
**Wildheit** fierceness V U3, 60
**Wildnis** wilderness; the wild IV
**willkommen** (bei/in) welcome (to) I

willkommen heißen to welcome IV
vor … **wimmeln** to be alive with … IV
**Wind** wind I
**windig** windy I
**Windpark** wind farm III
**Windrad** (wind) turbine III
**winken** to wave II
**Winter** winter I
**winzig** tiny III
**wir** we; us I
**Wirbelsturm** tornado IV; hurricane V U2, 28
**wirklich** really I; real II; actually III
**Wirkung** effect V U1, 21
**wirr** confused III
Staub **wischen** to dust IV
**wissen** to know I
Ich weiß (es) nicht! I don't know! I
**Wissenschaft** Science I
**Wissenschaftler** scientist V U1, 21
**Wissenschaftlerin** scientist V U1, 21
**Witz** joke I
Witze machen to joke III
**witzig** funny I
**wo** where I
**Woche** week I
unter der Woche on weekdays III
**Wochenende** weekend I
am Wochenende at the weekend I
**wöchentlich** weekly III
**woher** where I
Woher kommst du? Where are you from? I
**wohin** where I
wo(hin) auch immer wherever III
bewachte **Wohnanlage** gated community V U3, 49
geschlossene **Wohnanlage** gated community V U3, 49
**wohnen** to live I
**Wohnung** flat I
**Wohnwagen** caravan III
**Wohnzimmer** living room I
**Wolke** cloud IV
**Wolkenkratzer** skyscraper IV
**wolkig** cloudy I
**Wolldecke** blanket IV
**Wolle** wool I
**wollen** to want (to) I
**Workshop** workshop II
**Wort** word IV
**Wortschatz** vocabulary II
**Wrap** wrap II
**wund** sore II
**Wunder** wonder V U1, 20
**wunderbar** wonderful III
**wünschen** to wish III
Ich **würde** gerne … I'd like (to) … (= I would like to) I
**würde(n)** would II
würde(n) gern would like II
**würdigen** to appreciate IV
**Wurst** sausage II
**Wurzel** root IV
**würzig** spicy II
**Wüste** desert V U1, 12
**wütend** angry II; furious III

## Z

**Zahl** number I
**zählen** to count IV
**Zahn** tooth III
**Zahnbürste** toothbrush III
**Zahnpasta** toothpaste III
**Zahnstocher** toothpick II
**Zauber** glamor *(AE)* *(no pl)* IV
**Zauber-** magic II
**Zauberei** magic II
**Zauberer** magician IV
**Zauberin** magician IV
**Zaun** fence V U3, 54
**Zebra** zebra I
**zehn** ten I
**Zeichen** sign; signal III
**Zeichensprache** sign language III
**zeichnen** to draw II
**zeigen** to show II; to point out IV
**Zeile** line II; row V U4, 70
**Zeit** time I
die ganze Zeit all the time III
zu der Zeit at that time V U2, 39
viktorianisches **Zeitalter** Victorian era III
**Zeitreise** time travel III
**Zeitschrift** magazine I
**Zeitschriftenladen** newsagent's III
**Zeitung** newspaper II
**Zeitungsausträger** paperboy IV
**Zeitungsausträgerin** papergirl IV
**Zeitzone** time zone IV
**Zelle** cell V U4, 74
**Zelt** tent II
**Zelten** camping III
**zelten** to go camping II; to camp V U4, 70
**Zeltplatz** campsite III
**zensieren** to censor V U4, 78
**Zensur** censorship V U4, 79
**Zentimeter** (cm) centimetre (cm) I
**zentral** central V U3, 50
**Zentrum** centre III; center *(AE)* IV
**zerbrechen** to break II
**zerreißen** to tear (up) IV
**zerrissen** torn IV
**zerstören** to ruin II
**Zertifikat** certificate V U1, 16
**Zeug** stuff IV
**Zeuge** witness IV
**Zeugin** witness IV
**Zeugnis** certificate V U1, 16
**Ziege** goat III
**Ziegelstein** brick II
**ziehen** to pull I; to grow; to drag IV
**Ziel** ambition III; destination IV; goal V U2, 29
**ziemlich** quite III; pretty IV
**Zimmer** room I
**Zimmerdecke** ceiling IV
**Zimmerin** carpenter V U1, 11
**Zimmermann** carpenter V U1, 11
**Zitrone** lemon II
**Zoo** zoo I
**zornig** angry II
**zu** to I; too II
auf … zu towards IV
zu Fuß on foot I
zu Hause at home I; back home II
zu sehr too much II
**zubereiten** to prepare III
**zubinden** to tie IV
**züchten** to grow IV
**Zucker** sugar I
**zuerst** first I; at first IV
**Zufriedenheit** happiness V U2, 35
**Zug** train I
**Zugang** access *(no pl)* V U4, 79
**Zuhause** home I
**zuhören** to listen (to) I
**Zuhörer** listener II
**Zuhörer** *(Pl.)* audience V U4, 74

**Zuhörerin** listener II
**Zukunft** future III
**zukünftig** future V U4, 74
**Zukunfts-** future V U4, 74
**zuletzt** finally IV
**zum** Schluss finally II
**zum** Spaß for fun III
**zumachen** to close I
**zunächst** for a start III; at first IV
**Zunahme** increase V U1, 20
**zunehmen** to increase IV
**zuordnen** to match I
**zurück** back I
**zurückgeben** to return IV
**zurückhaltend** guarded III
**zurückkehren** to return IV
**zurücklassen** to leave V U3, 56
**zurückweisen** to reject IV
**zurückzahlen** to pay back II
**zusammen** together I; everyone II
**zusammenfassen** to sum up IV
**zusammenfinden** to get together IV
**zusammenkommen** to get together IV
**zusammenrollen** to roll up IV
**Zusammenstoß** crash V U3, 50
**zusammenzucken** to jump III
**Zusatz-** extra II
**zusätzlich** extra II
**zusätzlich** in addition V U1, 11
**zuschauen** to watch II
**Zuschauer** *(Pl.)* audience V U4, 74
**Zustand** condition; state IV
**zustimmen** to agree II
**Zustimmung** acceptance V U1, 13
**Zutat** ingredient II
**Zutritt** access *(no pl)* V U4, 79
**zuverlässig** reliable IV
**zuvor** before II
**Zuwanderung** immigration IV
sich jmdm. **zuwenden** to turn to sb V U3, 60
**zwanzig** twenty I
**zwei** two I
**zweimal** twice IV
**zweite** second I
aus **zweiter** Hand second-hand V U4, 71
**zweitens** second IV
**Zwiebel** onion II
**zwingen** to force IV
**zwischen** between II
**zwölf** twelve I

# Lösungen Grammatik – TEST YOURSELF

**G1**
1. could not / couldn't; was not / wasn't able to
2. had to
3. will have to
4. will not / won't be allowed to
5. did not / didn't have to
6. could not / couldn't; was not / wasn't able to

**G2**
1. more carefully
2. (the) most efficiently
3. better
4. more clearly
5. harder
6. (the) fastest

**G3**
1. –
2. who / that
3. which / that
4. –
5. which / that
6. which / that

**G4**
1. was not / wasn't working; was sitting
2. phoned; was … having
3. were talking
4. were … doing
5. were watching; called; asked
6. was sleeping; tried

**G5**
1. celebrating
2. staring
3. talking
4. Growing
5. playing
6. Being

**G6**
1. had tidied
2. had not / hadn't had
3. had … gone
4. had read
5. had … done
6. had not / hadn't closed

**G7**
1. was … introduced
2. was not / wasn't built
3. Was … closed; wasn't
4. was not / wasn't named
5. were hired
6. Were … hunted; was founded; were

**G8**
1. He said (that) he sometimes met his girlfriend in Sneakers Street.
2. He said (that) she liked shopping, but she didn't camp overnight in front of a shoe shop.
3. He said (that) he didn't look for sneakers all the time.
4. He asked if people in Germany collected shoes too.
5. He asked if Sue liked sneakers.
6. He asked what she did at the weekend.

**G9**
1. Linda said (that) she had visited Hong Kong in 2014.
2. She said (that) they had had a great time.
3. She added (that) she had gone to an Asian restaurant but (that) she hadn't liked the food.
4. She said (that) she hadn't seen Ben for two years.
5. She asked me if I had ever been to France.
6. She said (that) she had travelled to Great Britain last summer and (that) it hadn't rained once.

**G10**
1. will / 'll visit
2. is … going to spend
3. will not / won't miss
4. will / 'll hire
5. will / 'll help
6. is going to come out

**G11**
1. starts
2. are / 're travelling
3. does … leave
4. Are … working; am
5. does … start
6. Is … meeting; isn't

**Quellennachweis**

**1** plainpicture GmbH & Co. KG (Jim Erickson), Hamburg; **2** Corbis (Shaun Egan/JAI), Berlin; **2.1** Getty Images (Universal Images Group), München; **3.1** Alamy stock photo (Prisma by Dukas Presseagentur GmbH), Abingdon, Oxon; **3.2** shutterstock (Gil.K), New York, NY; **4.1** shutterstock (Sean Pavone), New York, NY; **5.1** Thinkstock (shalamov), München; **5.2** shutterstock (Baiterek Media), New York, NY; **10.1** Getty Images (E+/Justin Horrocks), München; **10.2** Getty Images (Universal Images Group), München; **11.1** Getty Images (The Image Bank), München; **11.2** Getty Images (National Geographic), München; **11.3** Getty Images (Universal Images Group), München; **12.1** Getty Images (age fotostock), München; **12.2** Getty Images (Gerry Ellis/ Minden Pictures), München; **12.3** Alamy stock photo (Andrew Watson), Abingdon, Oxon; **13.1** www.CartoonStock.com (Coleman, Ron), Bath; **15.1** Destination NSW (Bridgeclimb Sydney/James Morgan), Sydney NSW 2000; **17.1** iStockphoto (ferlistockphoto), Calgary, Alberta; **17.2** iStockphoto (monkeybusinessimages), Calgary, Alberta; **17.3** iStockphoto (Geber86), Calgary, Alberta; **17.4** shutterstock (Basyn), New York, NY; **17.5** shutterstock (Phovoir), New York, NY; **17.6** shutterstock (Dima Sidelnikov), New York, NY; **18.1** shutterstock (Dmitry Kalinovsky), New York, NY; **18.2** shutterstock (Iakov Filimonov), New York, NY; **18.3** shutterstock (Dmitry Kalinovsky), New York, NY; **20.1** shutterstock (Kristina Vackova), New York, NY; **20.2** shutterstock (buttchi 3 Sha Life), New York, NY; **21.1** shutterstock (Edward Haylan), New York, NY; **22.1** Thinkstock (vanbeets), München; **22.2** Getty Images (Photolibrary), München; **22.3** Getty Images (Lonely Planet), München; **22.4** Getty Images (Lonely Planet), München; **22.6** Getty Images (imageBROKER), München; **22.7** Fotolia.com (Jan Schuler), New York; **22.8** Alamy stock photo (imageBROKER/Kurt Möbus), Abingdon, Oxon; **23.1** © BBC Motion Gallery — British Broadcasting Corporation — Media Centre, London; **23.2** © BBC Motion Gallery — British Broadcasting Corporation — Media Centre, London; **23.3** © BBC Motion Gallery — British Broadcasting Corporation — Media Centre, London; **23.4** © BBC Motion Gallery — British Broadcasting Corporation — Media Centre, London; **24.1** Alamy stock photo (a-train215 / Stockimo), Abingdon, Oxon; **25.1** shutterstock (Photographee.eu), New York, NY; **26.1** Thinkstock (JohnCarnemolla), München; **26.2** Alamy stock photo (Marc Anderson), Abingdon, Oxon; **26.3** Getty Images (Moment Open/2016 Jose A. Bernat), München; **26.4** Getty Images (Glowimages), München; **27.1** Alamy stock photo (Rob Walls), Abingdon, Oxon; **27.2** Alamy stock photo (Dave Watts), Abingdon, Oxon; **27.3** Getty Images (Moment/Boy_Anupong), München; **27.4** Getty Images (Glowimages), München; **28.1** shutterstock (Sean Pavone), New York, NY; **28.2** Alamy stock photo (Greg Balfour Evans), Abingdon, Oxon; **29.1** Alamy stock photo (Prisma by Dukas Presseagentur GmbH), Abingdon, Oxon; **29.2** Alamy stock photo (Pictorial Press Ltd), Abingdon, Oxon; **29.3** Getty Images (2013 Frans Sellies/Moment), München; **30.1** iStockphoto (AlpamayoPhoto), Calgary, Alberta; **30.2** iStockphoto (ultramarinfoto), Calgary, Alberta; **30.3** iStockphoto (salimoctober), Calgary, Alberta; **32.1** shutterstock (Olga Bogatyrenko), New York, NY; **32.2** shutterstock (Aztec Images), New York, NY; **32.3** Thinkstock (diverroy), München; **32.4** iStockphoto (alxpin), Calgary, Alberta; **32.5** Alamy stock photo (Andrew Rubtsov), Abingdon, Oxon; **32.6** Alamy stock photo (Tony Thorogood), Abingdon, Oxon; **33.1** Thinkstock (Xavier Marchant), München; **34.1** shutterstock (Daniel M Ernst), New York, NY; **35** "Three Little Birds" (written by Bob Marley) © 1977 Fifty-Six Hope Road Music Ltd & Blackwell Fuller Music Publishing LLC. Copyright Renewed. All Rights Reserved. Used By Permission. All rights administered by Blue Mountain Music Ltd.; **42.1** Thinkstock (shalamov), München; **43.1** © BBC Motion Gallery — British Broadcasting Corporation — Media Centre, London; **43.2** © BBC Motion Gallery — British Broadcasting Corporation — Media Centre, London; **44.1** shutterstock (Iakov Kalinin), New York, NY; **44.2** shutterstock (Gail Johnson), New York, NY; **46.1** Alamy stock photo (Hilke Maunder), Abingdon, Oxon; **46.2** shutterstock (HandmadePictures), New York, NY; **46.3** Getty Images (Glowimages), München; **47.1** Picture-Alliance (AP Photo), Frankfurt; **47.2** shutterstock (NAN728), New York, NY; **47.3** Getty Images (Glowimages), München; **48.1** shutterstock (michaeljung), New York, NY; **48.2** shutterstock (JONATHAN PLEDGER), New York, NY; **49.1** shutterstock (Mai Groves), New York, NY; **49.2** shutterstock (Gil.K), New York, NY; **49.3** Alamy stock photo (Africa Media Online), Abingdon, Oxon; **50.1** shutterstock (Svetlana Arapova), New York, NY; **51.1** iStockphoto (AfricaImages), Calgary, Alberta; **51.2** iStockphoto (nini), Calgary, Alberta; **51.3** iStockphoto (Clarissa Leahy), Calgary, Alberta; **52.1** Alamy stock photo (Tim Hill), Abingdon, Oxon; **52.2** Alamy stock photo (Simon Reddy), Abingdon, Oxon; **53.1** Getty Images (Stone), München; **53.2** iStockphoto (olaser), Calgary, Alberta; **54.1** shutterstock (Naeblys), New York, NY; **55.1** shutterstock (patjo), New York, NY; **55.2** shutterstock (Arndale), New York, NY; **55.3** shutterstock (byggarn.se), New York, NY; **55.4** shutterstock (iko), New York, NY; **55.5** Thinkstock (pavel_klimenko), München; **55.6** Thinkstock (wrangel), München; **57.1** shutterstock (Arab), New York, NY; **58 ff.** from OUT OF BOUNDS by Beverley Naidoo. Copyright © Beverley Naidoo, 1999; **62** Die Stem van Suid-Afrika by Cornelis Jacobus Langenhoven † 1932, Nkosi Sikelel' iAfrika by Enoch Mankayi Sontonga †1905,; **63.1** © BBC Motion Gallery — British Broadcasting Corporation — Media Centre, London; **64.1** Alamy stock photo (hans engbers), Abingdon, Oxon; **66.1** Getty Images (AFP), München; **66.2** Picture-Alliance (EPA/GERRY PENNY), Frankfurt; **66.3** Getty Images (Glowimages), München; **67.1** Getty Images (Lee Warren/ Gallo Images), München; **67.2** Picture-Alliance (dpa), Frankfurt; **67.3** Getty Images (Glowimages), München; **68.1** shutterstock (cozyta), New York, NY; **68.2** Alamy stock photo (robertharding), Abingdon, Oxon; **69.1** Alamy stock photo (Dinendra Haria), Abingdon, Oxon; **69.2** iStockphoto (George Clerk), Calgary, Alberta; **69.3** shutterstock (Baiterek Media), New York, NY; **70.1** Alamy stock photo (RosaIreneBetancourt 3), Abingdon, Oxon; **72.1** Alamy stock photo (Hero Images Inc.), Abingdon, Oxon; **74.1** Alamy stock photo (Maurice Savage), Abingdon, Oxon; **76.1** iStockphoto (baona), Calgary, Alberta; **77.1** Alamy stock photo (MBI), Abingdon, Oxon; **78.1** shutterstock (Blend Images), New York, NY; **78.2** shutterstock (coloursinmylife), New York, NY; **79.1** www.CartoonStock.com (Kinsella, Paul), Bath; **80.1** Thinkstock (Highwaystarz-Photography), München; **81.1** © BBC Motion Gallery — British Broadcasting Corporation — Media Centre, London; **82.1** Alamy stock photo (Piotr Marcinski), Abingdon, Oxon; **82.2** iStockphoto (AlexandrBognat), Calgary, Alberta; **82.3** shutterstock (Steve Lagreca), New York, NY; **84.1** Alamy stock photo (Sean Pavone), Abingdon, Oxon; **84.2** iStockphoto (Joe_Potato), Calgary, Alberta; **84.3** iStockphoto (PeJo29), Calgary, Alberta; **84.4** Getty

Images (Glowimages), München; **85.1** Alamy stock photo (United Archives GmbH), Abingdon, Oxon; **85.2** Alamy stock photo (Tetra Images), Abingdon, Oxon; **85.3** Getty Images (Glowimages), München; **86.1** www.CartoonStock.com (Coleman, Ron), Bath; **87.1** Destination NSW (Bridgeclimb Sydney/James Morgan), Sydney NSW 2000; **89.1** iStockphoto (ferlistockphoto), Calgary, Alberta; **89.2** iStockphoto (monkeybusinessimages), Calgary, Alberta; **89.3** iStockphoto (Geber86), Calgary, Alberta; **89.4** shutterstock (Basyn), New York, NY; **89.5** shutterstock (Phovoir), New York, NY; **89.6** shutterstock (Dima Sidelnikov), New York, NY; **89.7** shutterstock (Dmitry Kalinovsky), New York, NY; **89.8** shutterstock (Iakov Filimonov), New York, NY; **89.9** shutterstock (Dmitry Kalinovsky), New York, NY; **92.1** shutterstock (Daniel M Ernst), New York, NY; **96.1** shutterstock (Naeblys), New York, NY; **97.1** shutterstock (patjo), New York, NY; **97.2** shutterstock (Arndale), New York, NY; **97.3** shutterstock (byggarn.se), New York, NY; **97.4** shutterstock (iko), New York, NY; **97.5** Thinkstock (pavel_klimenko), München; **97.6** Thinkstock (wrangel), München; **98.1** shutterstock (Arab), New York, NY; **99.1** Alamy stock photo (RosalreneBetancourt 3), Abingdon, Oxon; **102.1** Thinkstock (Wavebreakmedia Ltd), München; **102.2** Thinkstock (amazingmikael), München; **102.3** Thinkstock (ajr_images), München; **102.4** Thinkstock (123ducu), München; **103.1** Alamy stock photo (Rob Walls), Abingdon, Oxon; **106.1** shutterstock (ChameleonsEye), New York, NY; **107.1** Thinkstock (Steve Mason), München; **107.2** Getty Images (Simon Watson/FoodPix), München; **108.1** iStockphoto (southerlycourse), Calgary, Alberta; **109.1** Fotolia.com (Jeanette Dietl), New York; **109.2** Thinkstock (AbleStock.com), München; **109.3** shutterstock (mimagephotography), New York, NY; **109.4** Thinkstock (Stockbyte), München; **109.5** Avenue Images GmbH (Photodisc), Hamburg; **112.1** shutterstock (YanLev), New York, NY; **112.2** Thinkstock (galitskaya), München; **113.1** Thinkstock (f00sion), München; **113.2** Thinkstock (toxawww), München; **113.3** shutterstock (ingehogenbijl), New York, NY; **115.1** Alamy stock photo (Jeffrey Zane), Abingdon, Oxon; **118.1** shutterstock (David Ryznar), New York, NY; **120.1** shutterstock (Li Wa), New York, NY; **120.2** Thinkstock (BarnabyChambers), München; **120.3** dreamstime.com (Sakuragirin), Brentwood, TN; **120.4** shutterstock (RUKSUTAKARN studio), New York, NY; **120.5** Fotolia.com (Jürgen Effner), New York; **120.6** Thinkstock (carolinepang), München; **121.1** Getty Images (Daniel Berehulak), München; **125.1** shutterstock (imtmphoto), New York, NY; **126.1** © 2007, Jill Townsend; **127.1** Banks, Lynne Reid, Stealing Stacey, Harper Collins, 2004; **132.1** Alamy stock photo (Richard Levine), Abingdon, Oxon; **133.1** Alamy stock photo (Pictorial Press Ltd), Abingdon, Oxon; **134.1** Getty Images (Universal Images Group), München; **135.1** Alamy stock photo (Jeff Gilbert), Abingdon, Oxon; **135.2** Alamy stock photo (Jeff Gilbert), Abingdon, Oxon; **136.1** Getty Images (The LIFE Images Collection), München; **137.1** shutterstock (Alessia Pierdomenico), New York, NY; **141.1** aus: PONS Schulwörterbuch Englisch, PONS GmbH, 2012. s.393; **141.2** from: Cambridge School Dictionary, Cambridge University Press, 2008; **145.1** Alamy stock photo (Richard Levine), Abingdon, Oxon; **145.2** Alamy stock photo (DAVID BARRETT), Abingdon, Oxon; **161.1** Fotolia.com (Photographee.eu), New York; **165.1** Thinkstock (Mike Watson Images), München

Sollte es in einem Einzelfall nicht gelungen sein, den korrekten Rechteinhaber ausfindig zu machen, so werden berechtigte Ansprüche selbstverständlich im Rahmen der üblichen Regelungen abgegolten.

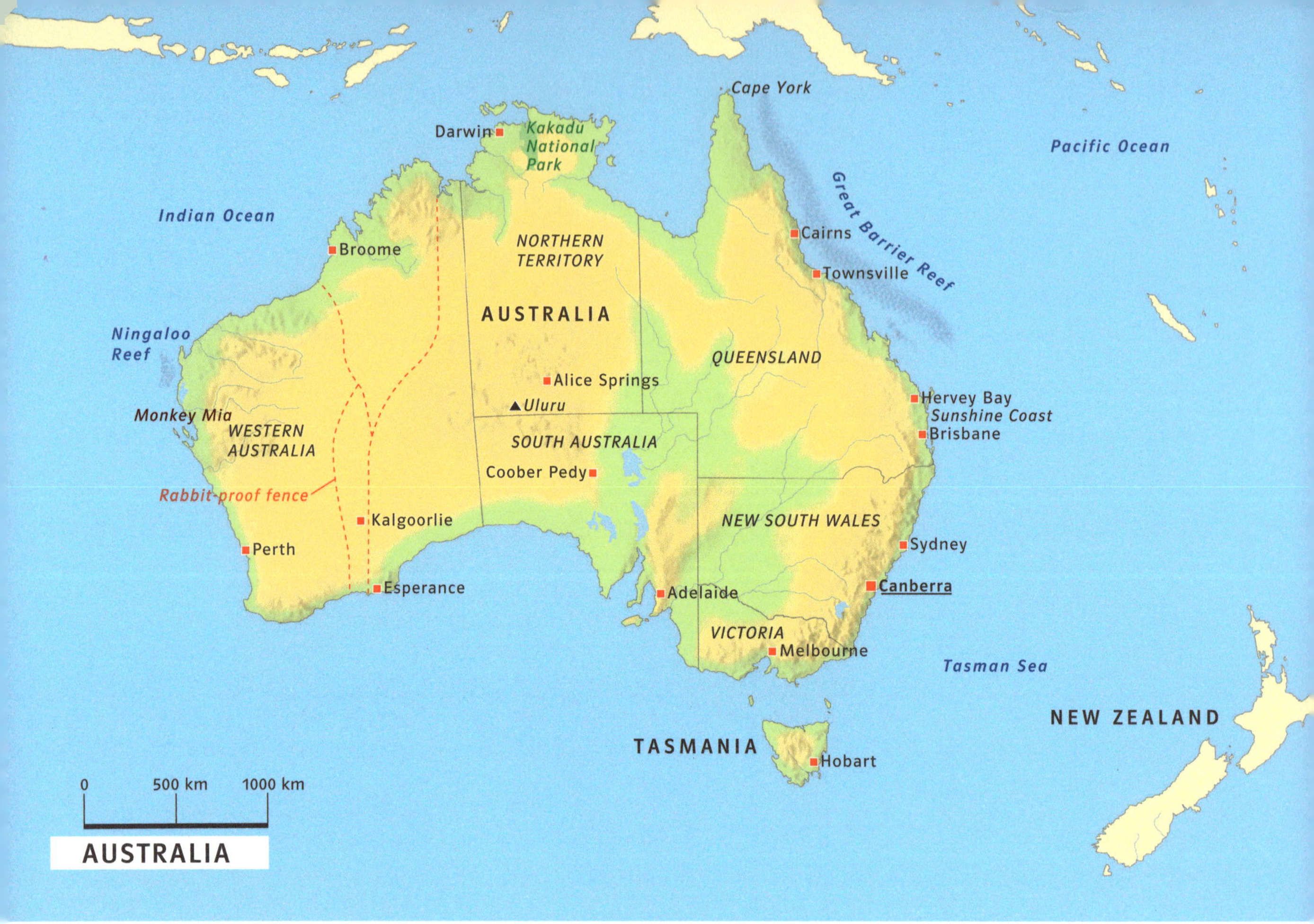

AUSTRALIA
0
500 km
1000 km
Cape York
Darwin
Kakadu National Park
Pacific Ocean
Great Barrier Reef
Indian Ocean
Broome
NORTHERN TERRITORY
Cairns
Townsville
AUSTRALIA
Ningaloo Reef
QUEENSLAND
Alice Springs
Uluru
Hervey Bay
Sunshine Coast
Brisbane
Monkey Mia
WESTERN AUSTRALIA
SOUTH AUSTRALIA
Coober Pedy
Rabbit-proof fence
Kalgoorlie
NEW SOUTH WALES
Perth
Sydney
Esperance
Adelaide
Canberra
VICTORIA
Melbourne
Tasman Sea
NEW ZEALAND
TASMANIA
Hobart

THE CARIBBEAN
U.S.A.
North Atlantic Ocean
THE BAHAMAS
BRITISH VIRGIN ISLANDS
Gulf of Mexico
CAICOS ISLANDS
TURKS ISLANDS
ANGUILLA
VIRGIN ISLANDS
SAINT MARTIN
Havana
DOMINICAN REPUBLIC
PUERTO RICO
BARBUDA
ANTIGUA
CUBA
SAINT KITTS AND NEVIS
GUADELOUPE
HAITI
Santo Domingo
DOMINICA
Port-au-Prince
MONTSERRAT
MARTINIQU
CAYMAN ISLANDS
SAINT LUCIA
MEXICO
Kingston
SAINT VINCENT AND THE GRENADINES
BARBAD
JAMAICA
GRENADA
TOBAGO
BELIZE
Caribbean Sea
ARUBA
CURACAO
TRINIDA
BONAIRE
HONDURAS
NICARAGUA
0
500 km
VENEZUELA
GUYA
COLOMBIA

REPUBLIC OF SOUTH AFRICA
NAMIBIA
BOTSWANA
ZIMBABWE
MOZAMBIQUE
Kruger National Park
Limpopo
LIMPOPO
Polokwane
Olifants
Kgalagadi Transfrontier Park
Mahikeng
Pretoria
MPUMALANGA
Nelspruit
NORTH WEST
GAUTENG
Johannesburg
Soweto
Springs
SWAZI-LAND
Hluhluwe-Imfolozi Park
Harts
Vaal
FREE STATE
Maloti-Drakensberg Park
KWAZULU-NATAL
Upington
Kimberley
Orange
Bloemfontein
Tugela
LESOTHO
Pietermaritzburg
Durban
NORTHERN CAPE
SOUTH AFRICA
Drakensberg
South Atlantic Ocean
Qunu
Indian Ocean
EASTERN CAPE
Bhisho
WESTERN CAPE
Table Mountain National Park
Cape Town
Cape of Good Hope
Port Elizabeth
0
500 km

HONG KONG
CHINA
Lai Chi Wo
Tai Po
Hong Kong Wetland Park
NEW TERRITORIES
Yuen Long
Tuen Mun
Tsuen Wan
Sha Tin
Sai Kung
Ten Thousand Buddhas Monastery
Golden Beach
Kwai Tsing
Sham Shui Po
Wong Tai Sin
KOWLOON
Hong Kong International Airport
Yau Tsim Mong
Kwun Tong
Victoria Harbour
Wan Chai
Victoria Peak
Happy Valley Racecourse
Lantau Island
South China Sea
Tian Tan Buddha
HONG KONG ISLAND
South Bay Beach
Cheung Island
Lamma Island
South China Sea
Po Toi Islands
0
5 km
10 km